NORMAN RUSH

MORTALS

Norman Rush was raised in Oakland, California, and graduated from Swarthmore College in 1956. He has been an antiquarian book dealer and a college instructor, and, with his wife, Elsa, he lived and worked in Africa from 1978 to 1983.

His stories, essays, and reviews have been published in *The New Yorker*, *The New York Times Book Review*, *The New York Review of Books*, *The Nation*, and other periodicals. He has been the recipient of numerous awards, including an NEA grant, a Guggenheim Fellowship, and a Rockefeller Foundation Fellowship. *Whites*, a collection of stories, was published in 1986 and nominated for the Pulitzer Prize. His first novel, *Mating*, was published in 1991 and was the recipient of the National Book Award. *Mortals* is his second novel.

INTERNATIONAL

"Broadens the scope of [Rush's] fiction while going deeper into the human dynamic of a country in the midst of profound upheaval. *Mortals* envelops the reader in a manner that modern fiction too rarely attempts . . . no one caught in its sweep will want the experience to end."

—*Chicago Sun-Times*

"Bitterly funny. Mr. Rush has a canny understanding for Africa, a profound appreciation for the fine points of romantic love, a muscular style of description, and an eye for character so frighteningly sharp that it argues against running across the man at parties." —*The Economist*

"The great joy in reading [Rush's] work is that it seems to proceed from an unshakable belief in the capacity of the novel to embrace everything: global politics, the nature of love, race relations, philosophy, religion, literature, the exact feeling of the dust in Botswana. . . . There is no denying its intellectual meatiness and its moments of intensity." —*Newsday*

"A novel as ambitious and spell-binding as his first. . . . Rush weaves an astonishing array of subjects into his story, from Freud, religion and politics to life, death and Africa. Rush is a master of his characters' minds. . . . Within [their] intense internal dialogues are thought-provoking, smart and often hilarious nuggets." —*The Baltimore Sun*

"The sheer energy and ambition of *Mortals* seems to mock its creator's earthbound status. . . . Reader[s] will be justly rewarded for persisting to the explosive climax that rips this novel's civilized veneer wide open."

—*The News & Observer* (Raleigh)

"Breathtakingly ambitious. By the book's end, Rush has given us masterful slices both of Africa's indelible beauty and of its ongoing chaos. Rush is a real seer, and he captivates us with his audacious fictional vision." —*Elle*

"A serious work that calls attention to the indissoluble link between the public and the private. . . . You'll find it hard not to be impressed with the scope of Rush's vision." —*The Miami Herald*

"[Rush] is economical with language, choosing the best words to distill ideas and express them in gems. . . . [He] has real affection for Botswana and its people. His rendering of the cadences of their speech is just right." —*St. Louis Post-Dispatch*

"A masterwork of literary art. . . . *Mortals* is a beautifully written, well-executed novel. It is written with passion, grace and flair. . . . Rush has a rare and beautiful gift of making readers feel true empathy for his characters. . . . A triumphant follow-up to Rush's *Mating*."
—*Fort Worth Star-Telegram*

"Full of situations that range from subtly humorous to near slapstick that reveal an unusually keen human insight." —*The Denver Post*

"*Mortals* is brilliant in its presentation of milieu, the heat, the squalor and the human misery of Botswana. The reader is immersed in an exotic culture and its political and social history rendered vivid by Rush's prose."
—*Milwaukee Journal Sentinel*

"Well worth the wait. . . . Rush's prose, wit and insight provide so many delights. . . . *Mortals* should solidify his reputation and win him new readers." —*The Oregonian*

"Wild and wonderful. . . . Rush inhabits the restless syncopative rhythms and associative bedlam of a male mind consumed by jealousy, disillusion and fading altruistic dreams. His observations are brutally accurate and funny." —*The Charlotte Observer*

"[An] absorbing and variegated novel . . . effortless and riddled with surprises. . . . For readers hankering after a novel of ideas, it doesn't get much better than this." —*The New York Observer*

"The ideas are a brilliant bonus. The writing itself is intensely readable: not dry but juicy. It is rare for a novel of consciousness to be also a novel of action, but it is one of the distinctions of this book to be both."
—*The San Diego Union-Tribune*

"Lucid, luminous, proudly literary prose. . . . Makes the erudition of Rushdie or Franzen seem show-off frippery by comparison."
—*The Village Voice*

MORTALS

MORTALS

A novel

NORMAN RUSH

VINTAGE INTERNATIONAL

Vintage Books • *A Division of Random House, Inc.* • *New York*

FIRST VINTAGE INTERNATIONAL EDITION, JULY 2004

Copyright © 2003 by Norman Rush

All rights reserved under International and Pan-American Copyright
Conventions. Published in the United States by Vintage Books,
a division of Random House, Inc., New York, and simultaneously in
Canada by Random House of Canada Limited, Toronto. Originally
published in hardcover in the United States by Alfred A. Knopf,
a division of Random House, Inc., New York, in 2003.

Vintage is a registered trademark and Vintage International and
colophon are trademarks of Random House, Inc.

Grateful acknowledgment is made to **Universal Music Corp. on
behalf of Volta Music Corp.** for permission to print an excerpt from
the song lyric "Town Without Pity," words and music by Dimitri
Tiomkin and Ned Washington. Copyright © by Universal Music Corp.
on behalf of Volta Music Corp. (ASCAP). International copyright
secured. All rights reserved. Reprinted by permission of Universal
Music Corp. on behalf of Volta Music Corp.

The Library of Congress has cataloged the Knopf edition as follows:
Rush, Norman.
Mortals: a novel / Norman Rush.—1st ed.
p.   cm.
1. Americans—Botswana—Fiction. 2. African American
physicians—Fiction. 3. Government investigators—Fiction.
4. Revolutionaries—Fiction. 5. Botswana—Fiction. 1. Title.
PS3568.U727M67 2003
813'.54—dc21   2002043289

Vintage ISBN: 0-679-73711-1

Book design by Anthea Lingeman

www.vintagebooks.com

Printed in the United States of America
10 9 8 7 6 5 4 3 2 1

*For my Muse and Critic, with
gratitude for the last ten
years of extraordinary forbearance,
creative impatience, unfailing love.
Elsa, you are unique.*

*And for Isis, Angus, Monica, and Jason,
beloved people.*

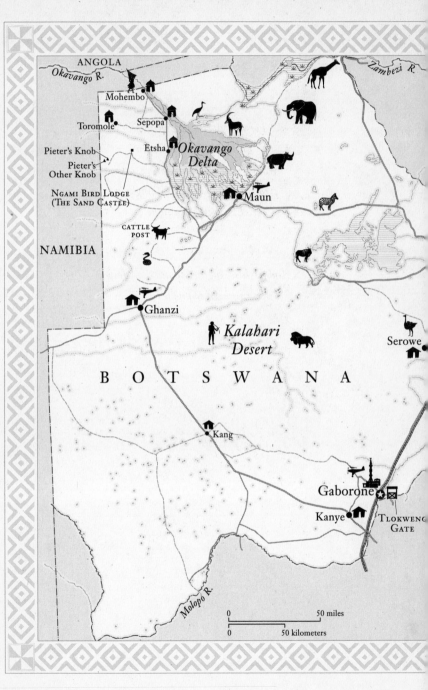

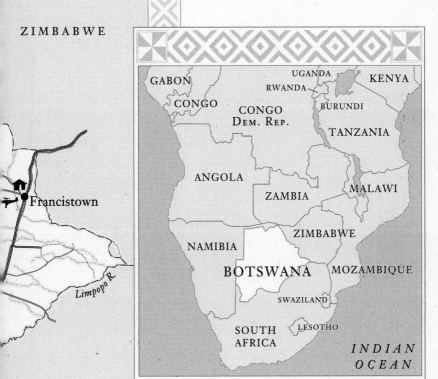

ZIMBABWE

Francistown

Limpopo R.

SOUTH
AFRICA

GABON
CONGO
CONGO
Dem. Rep.
UGANDA
RWANDA
BURUNDI
KENYA
TANZANIA
ANGOLA
ZAMBIA
MALAWI
ZIMBABWE
NAMIBIA
BOTSWANA
MOZAMBIQUE
SWAZILAND
LESOTHO
SOUTH
AFRICA
INDIAN
OCEAN

Contents

I. *Unrest*

I

Unrest

1. *Paradise*

At least whatever was wrong was recent, Ray kept telling himself, he realized. Because he'd just done it again, turning in to Kgari Close, seeing his house ahead of him, their house. Whatever was going on with Iris was different from what had gone on in earlier episodes, minor episodes coming under the heading of adjusting to Africa. This was worse because what was going on was so hard to read. He needed to keep in mind that knowing something was going wrong at an early point was always half the battle. And he knew how to stop things in their tracks. In fact that was his field, or one of them. Anyway, he was home. He loved this house.

He paused at his gate. All the houses on the close, in fact all the houses in the extension, were identical, but, for Africa, sumptuous. They were Type III houses built by the government for allocation to the upper civil service and significant expatriates like agency heads and chiefs of mission. The rooms were giant, as Iris had put it when they moved in. Throughout the extension the properties were walled and gated on the street side and separated internally from one another by wire-mesh perimeter fencing that had to be constantly monitored and kept in repair because there was a network of footpaths through the area that the Batswana insisted on using to get from Bontleng or the squatter settlements to their day jobs or for visits with friends or family living in the servants' quarters each Type III house came with. The quarters were cubicles set well apart from the main houses, which had possibly been a mistake because it made monitoring the flux of lodgers and visitors that much harder. If the quarters had been connected to the main houses there might be less thousand clowns activity in them, although you'd lose yet another piece of your own privacy. The perimeter fences were constantly developing holes so that the paths could keep functioning as they had before the extension was built, and it was a fact that their African neighbors were consistently more lax than the expatriates who lived there about keeping the wire fences fixed up.

The houses stood on generous plots and there was nothing wrong with a Type III house. They were single-story cinderblock oblongs faced with cement stucco. Their house was salt-white inside and out. Every third house in the extension was painted tan. The floors were poured concrete. He'd had to push Iris into the house the first time they inspected it because she thought the floors were wet, they were waxed and buffed to such an insane lustre. They had the best plot on Kgari Close, the largest, at the apex of the horseshoe the close made. They had six rooms.

He would admit that their moderne type furniture was on the ungainly and garish side. It was from South Africa. It seemed to be made for very large human beings. On the other hand it was provided free by the government of Botswana. Their bed was firm, and was vast. The corrugated iron roof, painted red to suggest terracotta tile, was a mistake, but only in the hottest part of the year, like now, when it converted the unshaded parts of the house into ovens, to which the answer was the airconditioners they had in their bedroom and living room, at least, at opposite ends of the house, except that unfortunately Iris saw herself as acquiring virtue by abstaining from using them exactly when the justification for using them was greatest. She always denied her attitude had anything to do with solidarity with Dimakatso and the other servants in the neighborhood out in their hot cubicles or with the un-airconditioned population in general, but he thought otherwise. She claimed it was because the airconditioners made too much noise for her. She was very sensitive to noise. Also she could be willful. For example, everything in the house could be locked up—regular closets, linen closets, cupboards, cabinets. The assumption was that you were going to be stolen from. The drill everywhere else was that the maid came to you to get the key when something had to be procured, and brought the key back to you afterward. But Iris kept everything unlocked even though their first maid had complained about it because she was worried that if anything went missing she'd be blamed. So nothing was locked, which was fine, she always did what she wanted. What was wrong now? He was tired of it.

Sometimes the yardman opened the gate, but usually it was the watchman, who came on duty at five. He overlapped the yardman's tour by half an hour or so, but the yardman could be anywhere, doing anything, including napping someplace. The watchman would normally be at his post under the thorn tree to the right of the gate, sitting on a camp stool and having a cup of Joko tea and eating the very decent leftovers Iris provided—a chop, chicken thighs, and the sweets without which no meal is complete, to a Motswana. On weekends it could happen that there wasn't much for lunch and he would think about the procession of chops and drumsticks that had gone out the kitchen door to Fikile that week, but he'd never complained about it. The watchman was coming. Ray liked Fikile, a short, energetic man in his forties. He wore the military jacket and service cap the Waygard Company supplied, but with them he wore heavy black woolen dress slacks too long for him and rolled up into tubes at his ankles. His ankles were bare. He was wearing shoes so cheap the leather of the vamp gathered up like the neck of a sack where the laces were drawn tight. They exchanged greetings and Fikile opened the gate. Ray walked into the yard. It was possible Fikile was illiterate. When he'd first come to work for them he'd always seemed to have reading matter with him, and then Ray had noticed that it was the same worn copy of *Dikgang* that they were seeing day after day. Then he had stopped bringing anything at all to read. Ray's theory was that having the newspaper with him had been for the purpose of making a good impression and that now that Fikile knew they liked him and were going to keep him he was excused from having to pretend he could read. His English was minimal. Naturally Iris wanted to do something, but she felt blocked because to ask him if in fact he could read or not, after he'd clearly gone out of his way to give the impression he could, might insult him. Ray suspected that behind her agitation over Fikile was a short story she'd broken her heart reading in which one of the wretched of the earth is tricked into thinking he can learn to read by staring at a mystical diagram and repeating a nonsense mantra he has paid some charlatan his last nickel for. And to hand Fikile some piece of reading matter of their own, in Setswana or English, would seem like a test. Iris seemed to want her fiction to be excruciating. But that was the way she was and he was sorry he'd asked, when she'd given up right away on something light he'd recommended, probably Tom Sharpe, Isn't it excruciating enough for you? He was always on the lookout for decent books for her, but being in Africa made it difficult and she made it difficult because she was cursed with good literary taste. She knew good writing from bad.

Here they had everything. He looked around. There were two discs of grayish struggling lawn flanking the flagstone path to the house where it diverged from the driveway leading to the garage. They were being kept alive by hand-watering. Someday the drought would be over and they could use the hosepipe again. Except for flowerbeds and the grass areas, the yard was bare red sand textured like a Holland rusk. The sand was raked every day in deliberate, sinuous patterns. He liked that. There were five palm trees spaced around the house, which he liked except when dead fronds dropped and banged on the roof at all hours. He loved his neighbors, and especially his immediate neighbors, for their lack of interest in him. One was the widow of the leader of an out-of-power Zambian political faction the Botswana government was partial to. Mrs. Timono was an actively furtive person. His other immediate neighbor, the Permanent Secretary of the Ministry of Education, was never at home. It was nice that no one had ever wondered, at least in his presence, why someone who was supposed to only be the head of the English Department at St. James College had been assigned housing in Kgari Close. He thought that was because the housing allocation process was known to be mysterious, and also simply because they'd been there so long. And he had been careful to let it be understood around that they were paying a serious premium for the house, which they could manage because Iris had received a small inheritance, lalala.

It was fun to put one of their uncomfortable metal lawn chairs in the center of one of the microlawns and sit there in the imperfect, lacy shade of the thorn trees. The trunks of the trees in the yard were properly lime-washed to protect them from termites, except for the palms, which had some natural resistance. There was a crate by the wall to stand on in the event something interesting seemed to be going on in the street. His wall was pink. He even liked the street itself. He liked the broad, clean, faintly convex roadway and the astringent odor given off by the gum trees planted along it. If he'd kept on teaching in the U.S. they might well have ended up in a university town someplace in the Southwest that looked pretty much like this part of Gaborone.

It always made him happy when the gate clicked shut behind him. Paradise was from the Persian for walled garden, probably the first fact anybody tackling Milton learns.

He thought, I ask them, What do you think the word *paradise* means? and they say various things. Their definitions of paradise are so modest: They reveal themselves: They begin to think about it: Odd that nobody in Gaborone knows what paradise means except me and my students and Iris. He lingered on the stoop. It was time to go in. If he waited Iris might stop whatever she was doing and come to let him in. If he waited the entire lower sky to the west would turn burnt orange. Ray liked working in the heat, being conscious of it. It was tonic for him, for some reason. Fikile was wondering why he wasn't going in, by now. You get a slight continuous feeling of virtue from working in the heat, on a level with wearing wristweights all day, he thought. He should go in. The best heat was now, in December. The west was solid orange and the peak of the sky was apple green. Woodsmoke drifting from cooking fires in Bontleng and Old Naledi would color the air for the next couple of hours, fading in and out, never overpowering, more a perfume, to him. Fikile would start toward him in a minute if he didn't go in. I would have been nothing in America, Ray thought. When he imagined what he might have been if they hadn't come to Africa it was painful. Not that Iris would credit any scenario in which his qualities went unused and unrewarded. She adhered to the great man theory of marriage. She loved him. Coming to Africa had been essential, but he had to be alone in knowing it and knowing why. That was the deal. It was unfair that something was going wrong with her just at the moment you might say all the moving parts in the machinery of his life were in order. He could walk to work. His health was fine, his weight was perfect. He thought, I love Africa, but not like the idiots who come over here and say Boy! Women with mountains of sticks on their heads. Look, an ostrich crossing the road!

Nothing is more useless than dwelling on grievances, he reminded himself, feeling himself about to twitch in that direction. He'd earned the right to some satisfaction. The easy part of his life had begun unannounced like a dream two years ago and he had a right to enjoy it. No one could know about it, obviously, but he was living in a state of triumph, and had been ever since Russia and all its works blew apart overnight. Before that he had been part of a war. What he was in now was more like a parade. Of course nobody knew who he was, except for Iris who had to know generally. She had no details. But when somebody wrote *The Decline and Fall of the Russian Empire and Everything Connected with It* he would be there between the lines. He couldn't generate the right metaphor for amazing 1989. He had an image of something like a metal claw sunk into half the planet suddenly disarticulating, but that was a weak image. Or it could be like this, he thought: You have a goliath of an enemy dressed in armor about to smite you who sits down suddenly and looks faint and when you open up his armor you find only his face is normal, the rest is sickly, mummified, and then he dies in front of you and it's all over.

This moment was what Iris was suddenly taking away.

The event was too huge for any image he had been able to come up with. It would take someone as great as Milton to come up with the appropriate image right off the bat. He felt he had no time to think, lately. Iris was full of mental homework for him to do that he didn't want to do, such as answering the question of why they had been so attracted to one another when they met—but it had to be *aside from* the purely physical reasons she knew he was going to overemphasize.

He stood in the foyer. No one was around. He heard the kitchen door close. That was Dimakatso leaving for the day.

He entered the chill bronze gloom of the living room, where the airconditioner was laboring for his benefit, obviously, since no one else was on hand and the room looked as though no one had made use of it that day. He walked over to the main double window. The louvers of the blinds were tilted downward, almost to the closed position. All the windows in the house were barred and tightly screened. He was fanatical about the screens. There was malaria nearby. He was the force behind both of them continuing to take chloroquine. Iris got worse headaches from the chloroquine than he did, so he understood why she resisted him.

There was still no one.

But I'm fine, he thought, trying not to relive a moment from the walk home that had made him feel fragile. Near the school was a rundown property whose occupants kept a goat. The goat had run up purposively to the fence as Ray came by and for an instant Ray had thought something monstrous was happening, because the goat's tongue seemed to be a foot long. He'd been frightened until he'd realized that it was only a goat eating a kneesock. Iris could be asleep. He would look for her, softly.

2. *Iris*

Ray moved silently through the house, coming to the shut door of Iris's workroom, her study. He knew everything about her study, every detail. He kept silent.

She was in there, at her worktable, doing something with papers, air-letters, probably. Three times recently he had come to the door in silence and been privileged to hear her reading aloud to herself from letters sent by her sister or, once, his brother. Privileged was the only word for the way he had felt. Obviously, reading aloud was a sign of loneliness. He couldn't deny that. She animated her correspondents when she read aloud, bringing them to her. She read with feeling, theatricality, even. The transom over the door was always in the open position. He wanted to hear her read aloud again. There was something rare about it.

Yesterday she had gotten sunburned. He could hear that she was inter-mittently picking up a sponge or cloth from a bowl of ice, wringing it out, and touching it to her face.

Storage dominated the small room. Metal filing cabinets came to chest height along three walls and were topped with a double tier of uniform cardboard cartons, each carton marked with a code number. The one break in the tiers of boxes was utilized to house a portable phonograph and behind it a tight rank of longplaying record albums. A postal scale stood on top of the block of albums. There was no decoration on the exposed white upper walls or anywhere in the room, and no rug or mat on the maroon linoleum tiles of the floor. A copy of the *International Herald Tribune* folded twice would be aligned with the upper right-hand corner of the table. Through the transom came a remnant scent of cleanser.

Her room was hot and dim. There was no table lamp. If Iris found something she wanted to read closely in a letter, she would slant the sheet to catch the dying light from outside. There was one double window, and the short side of her worktable was pushed to the wall directly underneath it. The wings of the window were normally cranked out to their maximum extension. She would be sitting with her left side to the screened and barred view of the servants' quarters fifty feet away. An arbor supporting a system of dead vines framed her view. On the tabletop, in addition to the newspaper, was a dust-hooded bulky typewriter set to one side and a tray of office necessities, like ballpoint pens, Wite-Out, type cleaner, and postage.

As he'd hoped she would, she began to read aloud.

"We are house-sitting in Sausalito for a public relations couple (People of the Fib) vacationing in Lappland. I should say 'estate-sitting.' It's going to be a long three weeks. The man I'm with, Joel, I chose for this because he was verbal looking. He really isn't verbal. People around here are being extremely social toward us. This is an area with many children deformed by utter wealth. In the next house we heard a child screaming because a swimming pool, which they have, isn't enough. He wants them to get a water bloom (fountainlike thing). He is on strike and won't go into the water. We heard his mother try to explain that water blooms are just trick things to make people satisfied when all they can have is (lowclass) aboveground pools, whereas they have this splendid in-ground pool. But he won't go in the water. Sausalito would be a good place for you to adjust to the fact, when you come back (and you are going to come back), that you now rather often see vanity in the faces of young children. I mean of the permanent, adult sort, not the fleeting kind any child gets when he or she figures out that he or she got the best Xmas present in his or her circle of friends that year. You see it more and more, and in children of both sexes. I feel I must prepare you. And it's not only in Marin County. By the way, isn't my handwriting more appropriate now? You complained that I was writing too bigly for airletters and sort of cheating you of information. But that is my natural handwriting and look how small I'm making it for you herewith.

"There are many hazards in this place of wealth. This morning Joel came out of the bathroom scowling and saying 'Ow, I just burned my ass on the towel warmer.' Joel is normally very silent, except when he hurts himself. I think I deserve someone more verbal than he.

"I myself live a very moral life, of my own sort. I try to live as though there's never anything good on television. That's why I get so much more done in my waking hours, which is a necessity because I'm self-employed. I am thinking of starting a new religion for the self-employed. It would be based on the never-anything-good-on-TV premise and would have as its main sin not returning telephone calls. I'm out of a job, incidentally, in a de facto way. I was working for a patter service, an outfit that mass-produces clever lines for politicians and celebrities to pretend they thought of themselves. I was doing pretty well with them and then I just turned noir and then went dry. I tried to produce things the rabid right could make use of. One was 'Homebodies are Somebodies.' The service thought I was being mocking. I think I got in a rut out of rage at the Roman Catholic Church. Everything I thought of was quasi-antireligious, which nobody is buying these days. Here's a discard: 'Aside from that, Mrs. Iscariot, did your husband enjoy supper?'

"Here's a little tip for when you return: NEVER ask professional people whose children are probably out of college a while what their children are doing, or even how they are doing. The chances are overwhelmingly high that their children are dysfunctional. And you can be sure that if a child is doing anything that suggests some degree of coping THIS WILL BE VOUCHSAFED TO YOU. Last night a proud father was bragging that his son was working as a sommelier. He was telling EVERYONE.

"That's all for now. My love to you. You belong in America. Rex."

She turned to an earlier letter.

"Nothing good is happening. My commode runneth over. We went to a thing of French chamber music, and how boring *was* it? So boring I decided to occupy myself by making up an imaginary program of the works of the widely unknown French composer M. Prépuce Joli. First on the program was his *Ratatata Cantata* (drum corps and Vienna Boys' Choir). Then a piano work the composer wrote in Italy, the *Polonaise Bolognaise*. Then his *Valse Gauche* (Waltz for the Left Foot). Then his majestic *Hymne Interminable*. And finally his rather depressing *Marche Inutile*. Then I fell asleep."

The reading stopped. She must have realized he was there.

3. Iris and Rex

Here I am," Ray said, and waited for the scrape of chair feet on the linoleum. Do not touch the door, he instructed himself. He wanted to know if she had locked it. Occasionally, these days, she did. There was a knob-controlled bolt lock on her side of the door that operated quietly, so that it was hard to hear the bolt being retracted. He stilled himself. This was her room of her own and the door could be locked if she wanted and that was fine. If something should happen to her in there when the door was locked, he could break in, so there was nothing to worry about. She was taking her time. She liked referring to her room as her den, lately. She needed a decent worklight on her table but it was clear she was going to stick to her claim that all she needed was the ceiling light, despite the fact that she was on record saying that she hated fluorescent light and that it was like gray dust. She was putting something away.

She was stubborn. She could call her cell anything she liked, den included, but the truth was it wasn't a room of her own in the full sense. She could only accept a room all for herself if it was actively in use for some other purpose as well. That was obviously why she was still finding things to box up and store in there. Which was unnecessary because there was plenty of space in the garage. It had been his idea for her to take one of the side rooms for herself, and now she used it all the time. He was going to put a circulating fan in there, and she could take it and put it in a box and seal it up and put a number on the box if she wanted to. But he was going to put a fan in there. He could do the same thing with a table lamp. He thought. No, it was bright dust she compared fluorescent light to. And the linoleum was ugly, it was the color of raw liver and had sun-welts in it. He could get her a reed mat at Botswanacraft. She was coming to the door.

He stood against the wall opposite her door, listening. There was no indication the door had been locked. It opened smoothly and she came out to embrace him.

It never changed for him, seeing her again after a day's separation, or even less. He felt a flowing, objectless gratitude so strong it weakened him. He wanted her touch. It was permanent with him. She put her hands on him and slipped one hand through the unbuttoned top of his shirt. She was wearing a plain white sundress and she was barefoot. The shape of her heavy hair against the light and the scent of it as he put his face into her hair were perfections, were absolute things. He was forty-eight. She was thirty-eight. A pleasure he had was catching flashes of surprise in people's expressions when she told her age, which she was always truthful about. He often had the satisfaction of seeing people look at him, obviously wondering what it was about him that they weren't seeing that made it reasonable for a woman of this quality to be with him, be his. He had always looked his exact age. And he also liked seeing them being given pause by someone at her level of physical beauty dealing with people so much more nicely than she should be, on their past experience of great beauties, which she was, which she was. These were instantaneous moments, but real. She was a democrat, a spiritual democrat. And then with women, and gay men too, sometimes, he would get the moment when they tried subtly to ascertain if they could possibly be right in their first impression that Iris was wearing hardly any makeup. There was a way they widened their eyes briefly and then focused again. Iris wore next to no makeup.

He wanted the touch of her breath on his throat. When they embraced after being separate that was what he wanted first.

"You are so beautiful," she said.

"So say we all," he said, being wry.

A line came to him, *I am the mirror you breathe on*. It wasn't quite right, though. If he wrote poetry what he would want would be a line that united holding a mirror up to the mouth and nose of a particular beloved to see if she was still alive *with* the mirror being the fixed register of her personal beauty. Could the line be *I am the mirror your breath is for*? He thought. No because it's slightly sinister. No because it's stupid. This was why genius would be so handy if you had it. Iris had no real appreciation of how beautiful she was. She was sealed off from that by her past, complications in her past, and he lacked the genius to strike through and say Look what you are! Look! and have her believe it.

Her hair was black and shining. She wore it centrally parted, with the wings caught together in a heavy shell clip low on the nape of her neck. He put his hands into her hair. The top of her head came to just under his eyes. Her immaculate part bisected an oval of highlights at her crown. Africa was too hot for hair this long, but she knew he loved it that way. She was almost a type. Euro-patrician would be the type, although her eyebrows, which were straight, like dashes, contradicted it. She wouldn't tweeze her eyebrows into arcs. People often presumed she was French. Her face was too graphic and lively for the type, also. And that was another thing he enjoyed witnessing, the slight shock registering when people met her for the first time and she was absolutely normal toward them and not fixed in the modes of underlying vanity or distance the culture had taught them would go with a presence like hers. He moved his hands to her back, under the broad straps of her sundress. Her nose was of the essence of the type. You could easily forget that it was a biological organ. Also it was euro-patrician that she flared her nostrils when she got incensed over something. She was getting too much sun. Her teeth were ideally white and almost childishly small. Her gray eyes were perfect, or their axis was, the tilt slightly upward from the root of her nose. The line *She makes the female face seem nude* was also not quite right and was also from the days when she'd inspired him briefly to wrench himself toward poetry, got part of what he felt and part of why he needed to protect her. Her underchin was taut. Age seemed to be touching her in only two spots—her mid-throat, in the form of a single fine line across it, and just under the corners of her mouth, in the form of incipient softness.

"Look how you dig me," she said.

"I think someone could see us here," he said.

"Not unless they put their face against the screen." But she closed the door to her room.

Her voice was another thing that went against her type, because it was too clear and strong or unregulated, sometimes. Her clowning went against it, too.

She pressed against him. He moved her away, saying "May I?" and pulling the yoke of her dress out so that he could look down at her small, plump breasts. They disagreed about her breasts, but she was wrong. She had never nursed. They had no children. Small breasts are best for the long haul. Even if it was nobody's fault that there were no children he felt guilty because not having them had left her perfect for him. Their sex had zeal in it. He didn't mean zeal, he meant something else. Their life together was erotic in a longitudinal way, he meant. The erotic was always there, not sporadically there in little segments set aside. At least that was the way it was for him, and unless it was an incredible act, it was that way for her too. But why should it be an act?

"Are you up to something?" she asked, and then fell against him, ending the episode.

Nobody knows who I am, he thought.

They were together in the kitchen. He was being companionable while she got the food onto the table. The lights were on in Dimakatso's quarters. Ray had a feeling the meal tonight might be vegetarian. They seemed to be drifting that way, which was ironic in a country with the healthiest, best-tasting grass-fed and cheapest beef in the entire world. Botswana beef had an odd taste. It was sweet.

The light in the kitchen was a trial for both of them. The room was lit by a fluorescent donut that belonged in an industrial museum. The house was all-electric. The fluorescent fixture emitted a fizzing sound from time to time that suggested it was about to malfunction. It would capture their attention and then the sound would quit and life would go on.

Iris said, "Everything spoils so fast in Africa, I hate it." She made a face as she unscrewed the lid of a mayonnaise jar she'd just taken out of the refrigerator.

"This needs to go directly to the Mayo Clinic," she said.

"Haha," Ray said, stating the laugh to show he was less than amused.

She looked at him for an explanation.

God damn me, he thought.

"What do you mean by that Haha?"

"Nothing."

"What, though?"

"Well I just wondered if you're trying to be funnier than usual for my benefit. I mean are you trying to be funnier?

"You don't have to, you know." God damn me, he thought.

"What are you talking about, Ray?"

"I don't know, I felt for a minute that maybe you were trying to mimic my brother. I mean he presents himself as such a wit. His letters to you are all about what a wit he is. What I'm saying is you don't need to be more amusing than you already naturally are. You can relax. You don't need to keep me amused." He thought, Anyone would hate this, I have *no* right to do this, But I had years of his wit to live with and that was enough.

She stared at him. Plainly he had hurt her in several ways.

"Oh boy. I'm sorry. I think this is what it is. I think I'm aggravated about Rex's sudden interest in writing to you all the time. His sudden desire to be your pen pal. You don't know him. You may think he's clever but there is, believe me, nothing there, he's useless, he . . ."

She broke in. "Well, you remember the potato salad I made last week that you praised to high heaven?"

He was in the pantry, searching for a new jar of mayonnaise.

"Can you hear me? That salad was made with baked potatoes instead of boiled potatoes."

Ray emerged from the pantry with the new jar of mayonnaise, which he handed to her.

"You mean now Rex is sending you recipes?"

"It isn't a recipe just to comment on a potato salad he had at a fancy buffet somewhere. He thought it was delicious so he asked the host what there was about it, that's all, and he passed that along, and you enjoyed it, I'm pointing out."

Dinner tonight would be deviled eggs, rice salad, Swiss chard, and slices of grilled daikon radish with some indecipherable toppings on them.

"I'm careful about the sun," she said.

If all was well he would normally pour his predinner Castle lager into a glass and drink it sitting in a chair, watching his wife cook, like James Joyce, sipping. He was restricting his alcohol intake. Tonight he drank from the can, standing up. She understood these things. She was no fool.

He was waiting for her in the living room. He was on the sofa, his feet up on their vast glass coffee table. Somebody had made an error in allocating this coffee table to them. Glass coffee tables like it were standard government issue for expatriate houses, but their table was larger than any he'd encountered anywhere, larger than the one in the ambassador's residence. The stupidest thing in this house was the pleated ivory Naugahyde room divider mounted in the archway between the living room and the dining room, which they kept belted to one side, permanently out of use.

"Are you ever coming in here?" he asked loudly toward the back of the house. She had left the kitchen for the bathroom and closed the bathroom door. There had been a time when he'd occasionally helped her shave her legs. But that had been on the impractical side because of what it inexorably resulted in. It was too provocative. It had turned him into a nuisance rather than a help. Her hair was true black. She covered the little bit of gray that was coming in with a rinse. She could be a fountain of gray if she wanted, as far as he was concerned. He considered his own hair to be midpoint intermediate between blond and gray, a noncolor, which was fine. Here she was.

She was bringing in a pitcher, their best green glass pitcher, of iced bush tea. She sat it down and hauled the armchair around to her side of the coffee table, opposite him. She wasn't going to be joining him on the hard, rouge-red sofa as she normally would. Her expression was less than open. It was too pleasant. He thought, Hell is that expression.

She sat down but immediately got up to correct the setting. She turned out the light in the dining room and adjusted the floor lamp at the end of the sofa to its dimmest setting. When they were relaxing in the evening they both liked there to be only one light source in the room, and a mild one. She sat opposite him, with some finality this time, put her feet up on the coffee table, and pushed the lap of her sundress down hard between her thighs as she settled.

"Would you mind if we talked about Rex?" she asked.

"God no, it's fine."

"You don't mean it."

"Oh God. Yes I do!"

"Really, what's all this God this and God that all of a sudden if it's so perfectly okay with you as a topic?"

"You don't understand. I want to talk about the man because I know you love him. You love him! His wit, his . . . whatever you love in the man. You love his letters. You know nothing about him except what he *prepares* for you. Concocts for you. Well, go ahead, Iris."

He could see her getting more composed by the second. She drew her feet off the coffee table. She sat up straighter.

"Look, I enjoy your brother. His letters."

"But you don't know the first thing about him. You have no framework for him. None."

"You two never got along, I know that."

"That isn't quite right. First we did and then we didn't, due to him."

"Could you say what happened?"

"This is the way the week ends for me. Hell. Too bad I don't drink scotch anymore."

"Well, you can, *as you know*. Go to the bottle store and get something and come back and let me watch you drink yourself to a point where nothing you say makes sense. Where I ask a question and you take an hour to answer it simply because you're contemplating what the best possible answer would be, naturally, and I deserve only the best, you're only being sagacious, you ———."

"Forget I said that. I'm sorry, Iris. Truly and no kidding."

"All right."

"Okay, when I say you don't know anything about Rex let me be concrete. Here's what his favorite reply to something you asked him to do was—Nokay. That gives you a hint. Nokay, and he would look at you I guess in order to see whether you thought he'd said yes or no. I guess that was a moment he enjoyed."

"That's so trivial, Ray."

"Maybe it is, but it's indicative. He was unremitting with stuff like that. You know the song with the line *The guy behind you won't leave you alone?* That's what it was like. Or here, relate to this. He became a master at pronouncing disgusting or insulting words so that they sounded so much like an innocent word you couldn't be sure whether you were being insulted or not. You had to concentrate when you didn't feel like it. At mealtime, he might say, Oh this is excrement!, smiling, his facial expression all full of appreciation, making excrement sound like excellent. He would make it seem as though it was the fact that he was chewing something that was responsible for your misunderstanding what he was saying. *Good evening, labia genital* was a line he got away with because he said it so fast when he was the toastmaster at his senior dinner. Heil there, he used to say to a gym coach he hated. Some of his little pals tried to copy him but, not being so expert, they got caught out. He was relentless. Anyone could be the target, he was no respecter of persons, just so he could keep his game going. You can smile but you didn't have to live with it. Our poor mother. Who was someone he loved, insofar as he loved anybody. But the poor woman. She liked to play the piano and sing for us in the evenings. He'd say Mom—he had this way of dragging the word out to make himself sound plaintive . . . Mom . . . can't you play Old Fucks at Home for us? He'd use a fake breathless rapid-fire delivery for camouflage. I'll think of more examples, now that you've got me started. And by the way he liked to make a big deal of my mother agreeing to play a couple of songs out of the *Golden Treasury of Old Favorites,* or whatever it was called, and he would excitedly go and inform my father about the treat we were all about to have, who of course had to pretend he loved it whenever she

would do this. It was not a great experience. The woman was self-taught.
So Rex would rush to wherever my father was, doing paperwork or reading his antiques magazines, and force him to come and listen. I say my
father, but I mean our father, obviously. The more I look back on it the
more harassed I can see my father was, in general. I've told you about his
antiques business. The fiasco *that* was."

Iris nodded.

"Oh, also for mealtimes . . . Is the soup dung yet? Or, This soup is
really swill, for swell, obviously. But sometimes Rex *wanted* to be understood. Say we were having franks and beans for dinner, and I noticed that
Rex was finding a lot of excuses to refer to what we were eating as frank
and beans, so I asked him. Oh that was just because he had observed that
my mother had only cut up one frankfurter for the whole dish, so the dish
should be called frank and beans. So he was just being precise and in the
process reminding all of us that the family was eating like the poor, yet
again. He projected innocence but he kept everybody off balance in an
unpleasant way. So, for him, everything was perfect. We *were* pretty frugal. The entrée we ate most when I was growing up was creamed tuna on
toast, which I loved, in fact."

"I could make that," Iris said. "But no doubt she put butter in the
cream sauce and that's why it tasted so good."

"Who knows? By the way, what *is* butter?"

She waited for him to resume.

He said, "Wait, I had something else about Rex that fits in here. Let
me think for a second.

"I know what it was. Tell me this wasn't diabolical. He goes to any kind
of performance, the gamut, from school assemblies to recitals, what have
you. What he loved to do and what you could count on him trying to do
was to start a half-assed standing ovation whenever he could. He would
stand up and begin clapping maniacally like someone overcome with the
dance or the accordion solo or the talk or whatever. And then he would
stare around in disappointment at the rest of the audience. And then he
would subside, looking crushed on behalf of the performer. Sometimes
he'd get a handful of other people to join him and the effect would be
even worse. The point was to show that the audience didn't really like the
performer all that much, except for Rex. I hated to sit next to him at anything. And I'd grab his knee to try to force him to stay when I thought he
was about to erupt. And of course if I left a bruise it'd be displayed later to
my father. And I would be in the spot he loved me to be in. How could

you explain using force against someone who had merely wanted to jump up in a moment of enthusiasm? He bruises very easily. You grab him with ordinary force and in fifteen minutes his skin looks like paisley.

"And Rex was always doing cartoons. One I remember showed a guy supposed to be me rushing downstairs his arms spread and shouting Dad's dead! And sitting there in the living room with his back to the stairway, reading, this character who's Rex, who says *I'll* say!"

Iris said, "But didn't you find any of this amusing, at all?"

Ray thought, This is a mistake: She thinks he's funny: One person can destroy a family: You can destroy a family through the exercise of your sovereign wit, she doesn't get it: I was his enemy, I was the traitor, I was in the Scouts, I was a traffic monitor . . .

"But all these things happened when you were still children. We're talking about a child, here."

"But not every child sets out to torment his family members to the brink of distraction. I didn't. There was something wrong with him. He was younger than I, but he sure wasn't following in my footsteps. In Rex you're dealing with a person with an absolutely gargantuan ability to resent things. Such as that I was named after our father. Rex thought there was something *unfair* about it."

"Oh, so were you Ray junior? I didn't know that."

"No, I wasn't. I'm not. I was Ray, my father was Raymond, simple as that. But my brother's sense of injustice was so exquisite he actually complained about the situation."

"It can be sort of strange with children and names. I knew a family there were four girls in and their names were Ruby, Pearl, Opal, and Doreen."

"Why do I think that sounds like something from Rex's cabinet of stupid marvels?"

"It isn't. It's mine. They lived in our neighborhood in Seattle."

"Maybe the parents couldn't think of another mainstream precious stone to name the fourth girl after."

"In case you're interested, your brother is house-sitting in Marin County. Talking about names reminded me of what he said about children's names around there. It seems the boys have lastname firstnames like Foster or Tuttle, like companies. The girls have romantic firstnames. He knows a little girl named Sunset and one named Autumn. He's house-sitting with a new boyfriend. You'd enjoy his letters. You *would*."

"Are you trying to convince me that I have no power to communicate with you *whatsoever*? Something critical is not coming across. I don't know what it is that I'm leaving out. When he was tiny but old enough to be in the bathtub by himself what he loved to do when his hair was lathered with shampoo was twist up his hair into two horns. In itself it's nothing. Like everything. *This* is nothing—he'd take a very fine crowquill pen and draw escaping pubic hair in bathing suit or underwear ads in my mother's women's magazines. Or axillary hair. But he would do it so faintly you might almost miss it. You notice the sexual angle here. He also drew fly vents on women's panties. His favorite comeback when he was mad at you was Oh eat hair! I know I'm all over the map. But that's because all this is pointing toward something that turned out to be ruinous for us, ruinous . . ."

She was pensive. "You mean something I know nothing about?"

"Right. Something I've never brought up, I guess partly because it has his trademark of making you seem stupid when you try to describe any event he precipitates. Everything reduces to Rex being an innocent surrounded by bullies and fools. But I promise I'll tell you about it sometime. I have to gear up for it."

It was evident to him that she wanted to hear about it now, but that because she loved him and could sense his upset she was going to let him postpone it. He had to postpone it. He needed to be at a lower emotional register before he began that story. Rex was fascinating her. It was revenge, more revenge on him. Of course all he was was friendly Rex keeping her cheered up in weird yet boring Botswana, as she would construe it. But the idea would be to disaffect her. Ray was absolutely certain about it. The point was to disaffect her in her African captivity.

Any second she was going to say he didn't have to tell the story now if he couldn't bear to. Why was she still so transparent? He remembered saying to her, at some point, You give everything away with your face and you need to learn to take a couple of beats before you judge something or commit yourself or confess you don't know something. Look around, he'd said. Realize that sometimes you know more than you think you do, he'd said, so don't be so immediate about confessing ignorance. He'd given examples of her being premature on matters he proved to her she knew something about many times. The line from her ear, down her neck, to the point where her shoulder was cut by the sundress strap, was an example of the bodily sublime, in this amber light. He hated the memorializing impulse, or rather what it meant that he was having it so often. He thought, Foreboding comes into your life in your forties, if you let it . . . comes into your thought like a stain, if you love your mate, especially: Abandon hope, all ye who enter a happy marriage . . . The foreboding getting stronger if you let it, like guys who take naked pictures of their wives, I understand it, poor bastards, Let me take a picture of your neck, your knee, your foot . . . She mocks me when I freeze in mid-act when she asks me something or says something, I freeze so I don't miss a syllable, I can't help it, "Close the refrigerator! You can listen to me and close the refrigerator at the same time," "Come in or go out!"

She was about to speak. He could preempt. "I have one more classic Rex example."

"But not the enormous one you were talking about?"

"No, but classic. Classic in the sense it shows how consummate he was as a breeder of disequilibrium. I'll make it short."

"You don't have to."

"I love you. The background to this is that my father had decided we should belong to a real church, the whole family should. This was after he was out of Ethical Culture for good, which is another obscure matter I wish I knew more about. Anyway, he wanted us to join a rather snooty Episcopal church in Piedmont. A Marxist interpretation of why he wanted us to join would be that membership would do him no harm when it came to his antiques business. He'd just opened the shop in Piedmont and it was near the church. And he was also interested in moving to a house over there. North Oakland, where we lived, was in the process of turning black. He wanted to sell our house. Rex hated going to church and he put up an argument, but my father was adamant. We had to get into the car and drive forty minutes to get over there, which added to the lack of enjoyment. I wasn't crazy about going but I didn't say that much. I was becoming a fatalist. We all had to go to church and that was it. Rex was eleven.

"Why are we using that pitcher of tea as something to look at? Let me get some glasses."

"No, I will." She did. They served themselves.

"So, one Sunday we went as usual and sat through everything . . . this was for services, not Sunday school . . . and got on line the way they expect you to after the service. You line up to shake hands with the priest.

"We got up to the priest and I noticed that my brother seemed to be wearing a large rustic homemade-looking wooden crucifix around his neck. That in itself was startling enough.

"But as he's standing in front of the priest he does something completely astonishing.

"He eats the crucifix.

"He eats it! Or rather he crams it into his mouth and starts chewing it up. What he'd done was take two big pretzel sticks and tie them together with string to make a crucifix, and then he'd threaded it on a string and put it on and covered it with his suit jacket until the right moment came.

"He just . . . ate the crucifix, with a staring expression on his face.

"It looked demonic, of course. Eating it insanely, with chunks and crumbs falling out of his mouth. I suppose people just thought Rex was a crazy person, but there was an electric pall cast over everyone. My father was stunned. There was terrible misery over it when we got home but Rex said he'd only done it because he thought everybody would think it was funny. He was full of apologies. Another one of his talents was that he could weep on cue.

"So he got exactly the outcome he wanted. My father was too ashamed to ever go back there. He knew that whatever he did he was going to be the father of the kid who ate the crucifix. Brilliant."

They sat in silence.

Iris asked, "Isn't it funny that I never met your brother? What does he look like? Like you?"

"Ask him for a snapshot. But no. He's bald, must be by now. Shorter than I am. He has a very small mouth. He had a trick he could do when he wanted to show that he was hearing something that was incredibly stupid. One of his subtle things. He could flatten his nose, sort of, and flare his nostrils out and make his upper lip puff out, shelve out. He knew it cracked me up. Also . . . well, he looked sort of feminine. His skin was very pale. These areas under his eyes got bluish when he was tired or sick. He resembled my mother's side of the family. Big extremities, big feet, big limp hands that look like paddles when they're lying in his lap. He had hips."

"So you're physical opposites."

"One other thing, because I think maybe it had some occult effect on the way he turned out. He had rather prominent, almost Dracula eye-teeth. I've wondered if maybe he was swimming in a sea of negative associations that people have for prominent incisors, thanks to the movies, and maybe he adapted to that. I don't know. It's a theory. He got them ground down before he went off to college. It should have been done sooner. It was never discussed. He was an awkward person. He looked awkward."

"So, pretty much, you're physical opposites."

I hope so, Ray thought. He felt that he didn't really know how he looked, though, or how he ranked rather. There was no question about his weight. He was lean. Iris kept telling him that he was handsome, that he was beautiful. But he was forty-eight. You have such great legs, give me your legs and take mine, she would still say. She thought her thighs were too soft. He couldn't convince her she was judging herself by some unreal standard. They had been married for seventeen years and statements made in the context of marriage about how the other looks were statements of a certain kind, except that in his case he was telling her the absolute truth. When he'd had to start wearing glasses she'd said he reminded her of the distinguished types they choose for display portraits in opticians' windows that show how glasses make no difference in the attractiveness of the truly handsome. You look like what you are, you look like a scholar, she'd said. He was used to the bush shorts and shortsleeved shirts and kneesocks he had to wear in Africa, but he didn't love wearing them. His arms were average. His legs were a far cry from the mighty instruments you could see walking up and down the mall. It had been a while since she'd said Your hair must be German because it's thick, blond, and obedient. Now he was going gray. No, what she had actually said was You look like what you are, a scholar and a fine person. Then she had tacked on that he was beautiful.

She said, "We can postpone talking about the main event until another time. I appreciate you, Ray. You're being very open. This has been your secret, really. I love you. I know you don't enjoy talking about these things. About Rex. I do appreciate you.

"I wish you could love your brother."

She had brought things to a close.

She pulled the lap of her skirt free and smoothed it out across her thighs. She began slowly inching the hem up, looking steadily at him.

"You seem to be a whore tonight," he said.

"Always," she said.

4. *Thank God This Isn't the Only Thing I Do*

Sometimes Ray started his patter for the occasional groups of overseas educators who visited St. James by saying Welcome to the only completely circular campus in the known world. It was true, so far as he knew, but he had noticed that lately the rector was showing a clear preference for not having the school described primarily in terms of the ways in which it was very unlike what the visitors were used to. And there were so many ways in which it was very unlike. But it truly was interesting that when the All Saints Trust had gotten permission to build whatever it liked in the broad, rock-ridden depression in the raw bush west of the capital, somebody had chosen to lay out the grounds in the shape of the ancient Greek world-serpent eating its tail, which happened to be his own private metaphor for the educational process when he was feeling down. But there was no one still around from the founding days in the sixties who could say why it had been done. His guess was that it had been an attempt to cohere symbolically with the universal preference for the circular in Tswana culture, as in the kraals and huts. He liked to point out the circularity of St. James because it was interesting, but the place was so extensive that its circularity was only noticeable from the air. The circle had been filled in solidly with distracting features—nethouses, rondavels, ovaldavels, completely rectilinear ablution blocks, sports fields, a chapel in the form of a rondavel with a bell tower stuck onto it, fig tree groves, the piggery . . . The most southerly baobab in Africa grew on the grounds.

The four people in the group waiting for him to begin were obviously impressed with his office. He had his own oversized rondavel entirely to himself. They liked the zebra skin on the wall behind him and the jennet kaross covering a good deal of the floor. His desk chair was thronelike. This group was from Cyprus, two men and two women. They were very courteous. They spoke English, but hesitatingly. He had a circulating fan grinding out a breeze for them. It was trained directly at them and they were grateful. They had glanced uneasily up at a white spider pod the size of a doorknob clinging to the thatch directly above one of them. They probably liked, without knowing why, the pleasant dissonance between the associations they had for the primal versus the refined aspects of his office—the primal thatch smelling subtly like bread and the primal skins and the spider pod versus the refined glass-fronted bookcases and the orderly array of books and periodicals they displayed. When they were gone he would knock the spider's nest down. The sad, comradely feeling he had for this group was real.

He began, "St. James College isn't a college . . . nor is Moeding College in Otse a college, nor is the other one . . . Moeng College, in Moeng, of course. A college." He heard himself sounding more British than usual. He'd just almost said And nor is. Sounding British happened to him at work if he didn't watch himself. Four senior staff members and the rector were Brits.

"We're a senior secondary school," he said, and went on to explain that they might be considered a somewhat elite school because not all secondaries awarded the Cambridge certificate as they did. Beginning by saying St. James wasn't a college always led to the temptation to tell about the Peace Corps volunteer teacher who'd taught for them for a year and then left after undergoing a breakdown and who in his terminal interview had said It looks like a bank but it isn't a bank, It looks like a post office but it isn't a post office, It looks like a restaurant but it isn't a restaurant. That had been his explication of why he had never adjusted to Botswana. The discrepancy between what he thought institutions were supposed to be and what they were in Africa had been too much for him, among other things about the country. There were aspects of St. James that would fit into a litany about things not being what they seem. St. James was denominational but the All Saints Trust that sponsored it wasn't a denomination. It was a peculiar institution. There were authentic religious involved in it, but a lot of the lay element in All Saints seemed to be ex–British military. The emissaries from the trust who came out to inspect every year all were. The trust was famously generous with bursaries in their schools in southern Africa, although he was picking up tremors and rumors that budget cuts were coming. Cuts would hurt. He would be all right. His position at St. James was good for as long as he wanted it. That had been arranged at a level far above the rector.

He handed out copies of the school brochure. There was a little conversation about the honors class he taught over at the university. They reported that Mr. Curwen the rector had told them how proud St. James was to have a scholar like him amidst their staff, a Miltonist! That was true. Curwen seemed genuinely glad he was there, culturally flattered, too, that an American seemed so interested in a poet he himself had been taught to revere but found unreadable. As the group left the office they could hardly miss the run of *Milton Studies* in which Ray's two articles and four research notes were buried. It was displayed at eye level in the bookcase just to the right of the door.

The group was rising. They had been seated around a conference table set endwise against the front of his desk. The men were in coats and ties and the women in skirts and sleeveless blouses. The women's forearms had left damp-prints in the finish of the table. He watched the damp-prints fade, annoyed because there was something he was forgetting to do. Curwen was outside, with an escort of Form Ten boys. One thing he had forgotten to mention was that the school was coeducational now, since a year ago. He heard Curwen's enthusiasm.

At the last minute he remembered to present the cyclostyled handouts giving the last examination results for the school. He went out into the heat to watch them go, Curwen gesticulating. Curwen had put his robes on despite the fact that there were only four in this group. The man was endearing. They were headed for a tour of the ablution block.

Ray thought, How can he keep doing it? . . . But we all do and we all do it the same way, by not thinking about it. About half of the last graduating class at the university had failed to get placements with the government, which represented a severe public shock no one had gotten over. Batswana used the Boer term for the government of the day or reigning power, Domkrag, which meant lifting-jack. Some of us are doing our best, he thought, but Domkrag is broken, Domkrag isn't working . . . But we do our best.

The other thing was to keep in mind what education was like not that far away, where the killing was still going on, Angola, students without limbs, from the land mines. He thought, Please raise your hands, Oh, sorry. He couldn't think about it.

Thank God this isn't the only thing I do, he thought.

5. *Crimes by This Family of Finch*

They were in bed together, naked under one sheet, sitting up and talking. It was late.

"I gather you want this to be about my brother again," Ray said.

She nodded, and he said, "Fine, but before I forget, let me give you another example of his, what shall I call it? his drive to be irritating. This is the kind of thing he was always doing. He was continually annoying his classmates by acting like a completely innocent literalist in the way he pronounced their names. Two examples: A girl named Margot became Margott. And someone named Lloyd he called Luh-loyd, pronouncing both l's. This is a small thing, but it's Rex."

"That sounds like someone who's bored."

"It was more than that. He got other people, other kids, to go along with it. That turns it into harassment. He had a claque. He created claques. Anyway."

"By the way he's starting up a new gay column. I think he said it's going to be in a free newspaper. But he still gets paid."

"His old columns weren't that funny."

"Yes they were. There were clever things in them."

"Such as?"

"Come on, nobody can remember exactly what it was that made them laugh. But there were things. Joke definitions. One of them was, Man is the only animal that prefers brand-name items."

"If that amuses you, okay. I think it's routine. It's patter."

"And maybe he'll get inspired and get more work with the patter service."

"I thought he decided he was too far left for them."

"You keep trying to say he's so left. Why? He mocks everything. He thinks there *is* no left. In his old columns he even had a department called *Life in the Afterleft*. You want to think he's so subversive. He makes fun of anyone. He makes fun of . . . that very famous . . . now I can't remember his name. But he was famous in the sixties and went to France in 1968 during the student revolution and appeared at the Sorbonne at the height of everything and got up on the stage and shouted *Le peuple au poivre!* Rex makes fun of everybody."

"He's left. I know him."

"You don't know him now."

"I know what he is. He's culturally left."

"I don't even know what that means. I don't think it means anything. You just let your animosity control you. I can't stand it. I can't stand it because I love you both."

"Good luck loving Rex."

"Please, Ray! All right. Let's be calm. Now. All right, tell me about this event he precipitated when you were children that was so titanic and let me just listen. Start where we stopped the other night."

"May I put on the airconditioning?"

"Sure, but then you'll have to shout."

"So obviously I won't put the airconditioning on. But if you don't mind I'll just rinse my face before I get into this."

Ray went into the bathroom. He cooled his face with a wet washcloth. He thought, This may be for the best . . . it might help . . . it may help us: It won't, I may cut my throat, which might help.

"I adore you," she said as he got back into bed.

"Thanks."

"I do, Ray. And you're gorgeous."

"I am? Hm. May I call you angel-tits, then?"

"Stop that. But listen to this, before you begin. This is wonderful. The other day when we were talking about why we're so attracted to each other . . ."

"Yes, the nonphysical reasons, if we could think of any. Yes indeed."

"Don't be so mocking. Anyway I realized something about you. This isn't exactly nonphysical but I bet it had something to do with how I felt. What I realized is that you look like the actor who played Woodrow Wilson in that biographical movie they made about his life and I realize I have just uttered a redundancy, so don't bother. But that was absolutely one of my favorite movies of all time. I saw it in high school and I thought it was wonderful. Woodrow Wilson, or the actor, rather, was extremely handsome in case you don't know. The same actor played Wilson young and then older. I'm comparing you to the younger Wilson. Can that movie be as good as I remember?"

"I never saw it, but this is horrible news, isn't it? You went for me because I reminded you of an authority figure you really loved? And I look like *Woodrow Wilson*? Didn't he look like a bank president or a leading Presbyterian, something like that? I believe he looked very boring. Also wasn't he a great failure, by any standard? War to end war and the League of Nations and all that? I'm not crazy about these associations, frankly."

"He was one of the four great presidents. He tried."

"Oh God and also in the end didn't he turn into a vegetable and his wife was discovered to be running everything? I *hate* these associations."

"Well, I can't help it. I think it was one of the first big Technicolor movies. That can't be right. I think it wasn't a recent movie when I saw it. We saw it for social studies. Well. Sorry I brought it up."

"I'm glad to know about this. And I have to report that I haven't thought of anything other than your supernal beauty that originally knocked me out about you. I'm still trying. Something will come."

"I don't want to hear about my beauty as an explanation for everything." She spoke seriously, but was half smiling.

"I know, I know. You forgot to say my *supposed* beauty, the way you usually do, by the way. Okay, no more."

"You know we have this difficulty," she said, still smiling.

"We do. I look like a movie star and you don't and never did. Okay. That's all on this subject. I'm sorry."

They sighed heavily in unison, and with the same impulse, they joined in pulling the sheet up to their shoulders.

Ray began again. "We were living in North Oakland and my father wanted to move the family to Piedmont so he could be nearer his store. Where we were was still very white middle class but the writing was on the wall. Blacks were well established on the east side of East Fourteenth Street by then and a certain amount of panic selling was under way in the better neighborhoods. Probably he was just being prudent in wanting to move, but there was a problem. My mother was tepid to lukewarm about moving but Rex was absolutely determined against it, so when she saw how upset the idea made Rex she turned against it in solidarity with him, still wishywashily, though. My position was that I was happy to move.

"Our house on Kingsland was really a peach. A building contractor had built it for himself, so it was only the best. It was a big mock Tudor, parquet hardwood floors upstairs and downstairs, hilltop site. The house was on a very sizable triangular lot surrounded by a retaining wall. This was late fifties. Rex was in junior high and I was in high school. The house sat up very high and you looked east at Skyline Drive and then the hills that hadn't been built on yet. There was a lot of open space in reach and a few vacant lots right in the neighborhood where kids could build forts and play nasty if they so chose."

"What about friends, did you both have friends around there?"

"Rex did. My social life was based around school by that time. But yes, in fact he had a particular friend, as it developed. His friend Michael. He did not want to leave Michael behind.

"So there we were. Now let me see if I can remember exactly how this got started . . .

"We each had our own room, did I mention that? We were opposite each other on the second floor. My room you could walk into anytime. Rex was totally secretive and kept his room locked. He started out only keeping it locked when he was in it, and that was accepted. And then he had to have the right to keep it locked when he wasn't in it and my mother would have to petition him to go in there for any reason. There was a battle royal before that was agreed to and he had to agree to let her look in from time to time, escorted by him, to see that he was keeping his room in order, before it was settled. But he got his way. Naturally I thought he was being ridiculous, but I was probably annoyed at the perquisites he was working out for himself that I was forbidden to have, just because of the way things had come about. I was hardly going to give him the satisfaction of seeing me copying his demands. I was the older one, after all.

"His secrecy annoyed me.

"I'm not sure of the exact order these next two items occurred in. First I should say that we were excessively frugal as a family, or we were supposed to be. My mother was the enforcer. Don't use too much soap when you do the dishes . . . return the milk carton to the refrigerator immediately after you pour your milk . . . and so on. We got screamed at if we left the milk on the counter for ten seconds or if we drank our milk before we put the carton back. Always do that first. Don't ruin things. Someone set a pot from the stove down on some new Formica and it left a semicircular scorch mark. She would have little seizures of agony every time she looked at it, for years. No one ever admitted doing it. In any case. Two things happened in some order or other. I was accused by my mother of using too much heavy duty aluminum foil when I wrapped leftovers up to store in the refrigerator. We were really kitchen slaves. I got good at it, or rather I got fast at it, so I could get out of there. She had just opened a new box of this foil and she discovered that some untoward amount of it was gone, so since I was the one who put things away most of the time I must be the guilty party. I said I was innocent, but no, I was slapdash, I rushed through things, I was guilty. I had to be. Now shortly after this, something strange was going on in Rex's room. I was hearing sounds of strange typing. Very slow typing, you know, hunt and peck. Late at night, this was. And the typing had a banging quality, tinny.

"I figured there had to be a connection between the typing and the missing foil. I decided to find out what Rex was up to, and, to make a long story short, I went up on the roof when he was away and hung over the edge so I could look in his window, albeit upside down, and see what there was to see. And this was what he was doing. We had this old Remington that he'd appropriated and he had set the thing to stencil mode and he was typing out some imperishable text, obviously that was the point, on some of the aluminum foil he'd pinched. I couldn't read it. But I did notice one other thing before my head filled up with blood, and that was a long, metal, screwtop canister photographers use, I guess about eighteen inches long. It was on his bed. Don't ask me how I knew, but I knew it went with the imperishable text and that he was making a time capsule.

"So I was in possession of an interesting piece of information. What did I do with it?

"In my defense, remember that I was ticked off over the missing aluminum foil business.

"I decided I had to know what the subject of his document was.

"I couldn't get into his room. Also I was bound by a certain protocol toward him that he had bullied the family into generating. I was never to touch him. Never ever to lay a hand on him for any reason. There had been some physical conflict between us, provoked by him, and of course I was in the wrong, being the older and bigger and wiser party, so we had all agreed I was never to touch him. Of course in a less well-regulated family I could have taken him by the throat and made him tell me what he was doing."

Iris said, "You mean you were so certain that what he was doing was injurious to you or so nefarious in some way that you had to find out what it was. You couldn't just let him go on with it, do whatever he was going to do with it, and forget about it. You couldn't."

"I don't know why I couldn't. I was convinced it was threatening."

"This is vintage you. You become immovable. You're still like that when you're convinced for no reason that you're right. The other night when I nudged you when you were snoring and . . ."

"I wasn't, though."

"May I finish? You *were*. You woke me up with it. I nudged you and you woke up furious and denied it and said . . . are you *still* denying this? I was under the impression you'd dropped this absurd . . . I can only call it a canard and I'm getting *furious* by the way all over again if this is still your position, that I had *dreamed* you were snoring? You meant it. You don't take it back, right?"

"Iris, you won't like to hear this but it is logically possible it happened that way. It *is* something that has happened before in human history, a person dreaming another person snored. Also the period when I was snoring is over with."

"Oh, good point."

"Look, you agree I ended that period of snoring."

"Well, until then, you had. But all right, you ridiculous person."

"I'm losing the thread. Okay. Lalala. Okay, so I had to find out what in hell this thing he was creating was.

"First I asked him. I wouldn't say I menaced him, but I caught him on the stairs and blocked his way down. I was going to make him tell me. He got enraged. I didn't tell him I'd actually peered into his room. I said I'd figured it out purely by the sounds coming from his room that he was typing something unusual and that he'd better tell me. Something for school, he said. I told him he was lying when he couldn't say what, exactly, his school project was. It got extremely tense.

"He was murderous but he was in a forked stick because I wasn't touching him and because he obviously didn't want my mother drawn into this, if he could avoid it. Then I pretended to lose interest. I acted disgusted and made as if to get out of there, leave him alone. He shot upstairs to his room then, clearly with the idea of securing his time capsule and keeping it out of my hands by any means necessary. He was clearly terrified I would get hold of it.

"I spun around and as soon as I heard him get his door unlocked I shot up there with the idea of forcing my way in after him and seeing what I could see before he started screaming for help. I was in the grip of the moment. I don't justify any of this. It was craziness.

"I did it. I pushed my way in just as he was practically falling across the typewriter to protect it and at the same time rolling this sheet of text down so that I couldn't read it. He began screaming immediately. But I saw the title, all in caps, on the handwritten draft he was working from, which was CRIMES BY THIS FAMILY OF FINCH, and then our address and the date.

"Instantaneously my mother was there. It was clear I had violated the rules and was in his room against his wishes, so that was all she needed to know. I was ordered to go and sit in my father's den until he got home. She wasn't interested in any explanations from me. She liked to hit, I was afraid of her. She'd caught me in his room and that was sufficient. It was so stupid of her."

"Why?"

"Because as soon as I was in Coventry he was free to bury his time capsule and cover his tracks. He did exactly what I would have done. At first, later, he claimed he'd thrown everything out, down a storm drain, destroyed it, when my father got around to questioning him. Hours later. Then, I don't know what it was, but he didn't stick to that position. Maybe it was just some instinct of defiance he couldn't control, but he said that in fact he'd buried the thing on the property, or hidden it on the property, rather. I think he implied he'd buried it. You understand that when my father came home and questioned me I told him everything.

"And Rex was astounding. He realized how upset everyone was about it, but he was like a prisoner of war refusing to supply anything but his name, rank, and serial number. He would only confirm what we already knew. He acknowledged the title of the thing he'd written, but he refused to say what he meant by it and he refused to reveal what the document said. My mother was pathetic. She was trying to get him to say that it was a story he'd written. And that was the only other substantive thing he would say . . . that, no, everything was true that he'd written. It was all true.

"I was pretty dumbfounded myself. I couldn't really imagine what this document was about. I thought maybe it was primarily calumnies against me, coming out of our terrible sibling situation. Or maybe it was a compilation of all Rex's grievances against everybody in the family. The situation was a Rorschach for everybody, I guess. Something about it drove my father particularly insane. I couldn't figure out, I still can't, if the original idea had been for Rex to privately express his paranoid feelings and then to bury them and then get rid of them that way, without intending any of it to come to the attention of anybody in the family . . . that is, perform a totally private therapeutic act in the form of a childish plot to get the satisfaction of somebody far in the future finding this account and thinking badly about the Finches, Rex excluded. I couldn't fathom it.

"It led to hell.

"I could feel it developing into hell that first evening. My father was in some way deeply wounded and maddened by this thing happening. My mother was frightened. I was horrified at what I'd wrought by bringing the whole thing to light in the first place. And Rex was becoming more obdurate by the minute. He had been given a role that was perfect for him. He was somehow able to play it as a free speech matter and take the position that what he had done was his private business. I had broken into his room. We were the ones who were acting insane, was Rex's message. I think he even seemed to get smaller, more compact. He was afraid of what kind of punishment he might get. But inside he was overjoyed, I know.

"My father kept shouting out new scenarios of what Rex was damn well going to do and what was going to happen to him if he didn't. He gave one deadline and then another deadline and so on. You have to look at it from his standpoint. Here he has an absolutely uncontrollable eleven- or twelve-year-old kid who has concocted some kind of slanderous document and secreted it someplace on the property. But he was also working himself up. There was something untoward about his intensity over this, and that got my mother and me more upset than we already were.

"And you have to keep in mind the family culture that made this so exquisite. Supposedly we were very against violence. We were liberals. My father was ex–Ethical Culture. No guns for toys, for us. That kind of thing. Don't hit back in school. Hitting was stupid—except for her, of course. Let the bullies demean themselves by hitting you. That reminded me of the only thing I could think of that might be in any way considered a crime of the Finches. There had been hysteria during the last year of the war when my father's draft category came up, and I had an inkling that he'd done something not quite right through a friend to keep from getting called up. This is the Second World War I'm talking about. But Rex was too young to know anything about that, if there was anything to know. On the other hand Rex was kind of a snoop. Maybe he knew something I had no clue about. He was definitely a sort of a snoop. And he was precocious. So there we were. It ended when Rex produced a coughing fit. He'd been crying, of course. He was asthmatic. It was a complete impasse, and we were all exhausted so we just stopped talking to one another and ate cornflakes for dinner. Except my father. He didn't eat."

Iris said, "You're sweating. But please don't blot yourself with the sheet. This story is very extreme. You're upset."

"I am. Let me get a towel. I'm perspiring. Put on the airconditioning for a few minutes. I'll be right back."

Iris attended to the airconditioner. Ray went again into the bathroom.

When they were back in bed, Ray said, "After all this time you still hold your palm over your shame when you walk around naked."

"Only sometimes."

"What governs when you do it versus when you don't?"

"Search me. But I think I know why I did it just now."

"Why?"

"I want to hear the rest of this story and I think I didn't want to distract you."

"But what about your breasts, which are twice as distracting?"

"Well, if I covered up everything it would have ended up calling even more attention to the, um, ensemble. I guess. Besides I don't know if my breasts are twice as distracting as my shame. My breasts are not what they were. On the other hand my whatnot is exactly what it was and it was always very good at distracting you. But I think the discussion we're having right now is unwise, I mean, on this subject matter."

"It distinctly is. But your breasts are perfect. And that's all I'll say."

"*Let's be wise*. We're talking."

"Right."

He waited. "Well, notice something about this situation Rex created. It was another manifestation of his genius in arranging events that are basically indescribable. Like eating the crucifix. Suppose my father had wanted to talk to a child specialist of some kind. Was he supposed to say that the problem he was having was that his son had written a criminal history of the family and buried it somewhere on the grounds? Impossible.

"So, dinner. We're all emotionally ravaged. My father had been savage, emotionally. Not something any of us had ever seen. We all drag ourselves to bed, ostensibly. But a little while later I hear something and I go to my window and someone with a flashlight is out there—my father, digging. No, the digging was later. That first night he'd had the inspiration that Rex had pushed this canister into one of the drains set into our retaining wall. There were about twenty of these and he was out there probing them with a broomstick. It wasn't a bad idea to check them. My father was out there for a long time. And no luck. It was the middle of the night.

"No, the digging was later. We had a big lot and only the parts close to the house were really landscaped. There was a patio on one side, the lawn and fish pond were on the other. But the bulk of the lot was given over to ground cover, ice plant and some other creeper that gives you purple flowers in the summer and attracts hordes of bees. The digging was sad because my father felt he could only do it at night, when he wouldn't be seen by the neighbors. He was afraid to do it during daylight. And people would have wondered. He had never done any part of the yard work. We did it, Rex and I, what there was. Lawn mowing.

"And the digging was going on, of course, because Rex was still absolutely defiant. Rex knew this was going on in the middle of the night. How could he be so cruel? This went on for . . . at least a week. Maybe two weeks. My father sits down opposite Rex at breakfast, stares at him, tells him in a steely voice that today is the day Rex is going to tell him where the tube is. Then he changed it to saying Rex was, that day, going to bring the tube to him, and then it was leave the tube in his den . . . Rex was mute. He was mute a lot during this period.

"Then it was the gamut of punishments you'd expect. Cutting off his allowance, no playing with Michael, stay in the house all weekend, like that. But Rex kept doing the things he always did to earn his allowance, like cleaning up in the kitchen. He was even extra sprightly about it. Then there were threats to send him away to boarding school, which were absolutely pointless because we all knew there was no money for it. The store in Piedmont was on a knife edge.

"The next stage of this was really bad. It was brutal. My father turned his attention to the house. The tube had to be in the house somewhere. It's a big house with lots of crawl spaces, a big attic, a big basement. He would come home from the store and change into work clothes and plunge into the business of rummaging around inside the walls upstairs, cursing, loud curses we could hear. He tore up Rex's room like it was a prison shakedown. Rex was shocked, but I thought he'd asked for it. My mother got very protective of Rex at this point, was on his side again, and to tell you the truth I think my father never forgave her for that. That was one of the aftereffects. There were plenty.

"Next up, a campaign of kindness, fatherly kindness. This was a process of erasure and it fooled nobody. There would be kindness and then there would be an appeal for Rex to please turn the thing over, slipped in. Then the kindness would continue. Rex went along with acting his prior self. I mean, he was still the same nasty, intricate person he'd been, but he was willing to be civil.

"Before it ended there was one return to total terror. My father shook Rex and yelled into his face like a madman. It went on for a long time.

"What triggered this last resort to brute terror was a feint my father tried that didn't work out. One evening he announced that he'd found the time capsule. Announced it triumphantly. He called it the crime capsule. He did his best to show that now all his worries were over. I think he also implied he hadn't read what was in it, whatever that was, and that he was going to destroy the whole thing unread. All this was a crude trick to get Rex to go out and check to see if this was true. Rex did something cruel, being Rex, like slipping out after dark and fooling around near one of the storm drains near the corner, which caused my father to pounce and embarrass himself, fishing around on all fours and finding nothing. Rex had seen through the trick. We all had. It was pitiful.

"So then there was an all-day armageddon of threatening. I think he might have hurt Rex if my mother and I hadn't been there. It took place all over the house. My mother and I stayed with them, wherever they went, so nothing would happen. I don't know if Rex was trying to provoke my father into some damaging act or not. Maybe the secret point of the whole exercise was to drive my father into violence, proving that he was a hypocrite or a brute. I don't know. He kept shaking Rex, hard. My mother intervened. Then it was just verbal for hours. My father had a very nasal voice when he was infuriated, pretty unattractive. And it was all fruitless.

"Then it was dropped. I guess I have to give my father credit for grasping that he had to accept defeat and let this go if we were going to continue as anything remotely resembling a happy family.

"But it was never the same. He took our house off the market. To be fair, I don't know if this was because of the time capsule. Rex got to continue his friendship with his beloved Michael, until Michael's parents interfered with that. Michael moved. We were somehow wrecked. I don't know. The store didn't work. He was conducting business for a long time from the house. The house filled up with antiques. It was like living in a warehouse and you had to explain to your friends. I think we all wanted to escape, after that."

"I have many questions," Iris said.

6. The Codukukwane Hotel

Ray wanted this to be quick. He had other things to do with what was left of his Saturday. This wasn't his normal sort of work, anyway. He was filling in. He didn't mind doing it but he wanted it over with quickly. It was a simple enough assignment. He was taking attendance, in essence.

He breathed on the front lenses of his binoculars, then wiped them clean with a tissue. He raised the binoculars and got a hard focus on the ridgeline of the low red hill above the donga where the Codukukwane Hotel dumped and occasionally burned its trash. His situation was perfect. His exit route back to the VW parked at the closest corner of the parking lot was a short straight line. He felt like reminding somebody that there were things he was very good at. This site was tricky. Here was a hotel stuck out all by itself in raw bush ten miles from Gaborone. The hotel proper, laid out flat against the road, was a thatched, one-story unpainted cement structure like a couple of boxcars set end to end. In its shadow, spaced irregularly around the back patio, were nine dank rondavels, or as the staff insisted on calling them, chalets. The site would be getting trickily active shortly.

His cover was perfect. The hotel was to his west. He was deep to the rear of it, behind a block of vacant utility sheds, backed by the main shed and nicely masked eastward by a bracket of clothesline loaded with freshly hung laundry, bed linen for the most part. I'm hidden, he thought. He liked being hidden, the moment, the act. He could admit it. Also he was well outside the fun zone developing around the patio and he should be long gone before the braai and the disco joy got too unrestrained. The hill he was studying was two hundred yards farther to his east. Parting the sheets anywhere gave him safe quick vantages of the rendezvous point his targets thought was so secluded, somewhere toward the end of the highest terrace on the hill, where it dipped and made a shallow pocket. The sun was where it should be, in their eyes instead of his. He loved Iris. She was on his mind too much. It was a problem. Being obsessed with someone you had been married to for seventeen years was probably a first. He needed her to recede a little, was all.

He scanned the red rock and parched brush below the hill ridge until he found the hollow brake of sickle bush he wanted. His group was there, assembling in the blaze of noon. He was supposed to confirm attendee identities, one in particular. But his eyes began to burn and interfere. He had an odd impulse. He knew this group was doomed to go nowhere. It was in the cards. And his stupid impulse was to let them know, so they could all do something else. They were known. Stupidly he wanted to tell them. He needed a pause, was all.

Ray paused. The thing to do was calm down and realize that the problem with his eyes was something local, from something local. He clenched his lids shut four times, slowly. There must be something in the vicinity he was missing. He could be reacting to something chemical in the laundry drying all around him, a residue, fumes. Otherwise it made no sense.

He got up. This was too much crouching. He moved to a different point in the line of sheets and crouched again. He was safe here for now. But drunks or guys who found the men's occupied could conceivably wander down into his bailiwick for relief, later. Or a dog could materialize because there was no goddamned control over dogs in Botswana or any part of Africa that he was aware of, none, the idea was in Africa's future.

He tried the binoculars again, but his eyes were still tearing. He put the glasses down, cocked his fists, and dug at his eyes with the backs of his wrists. Don't forget how good for you bananas are, Iris had said to him at breakfast. The bananas were for potassium, but why had she said it that way? Was there an unstated annex on the order of Remember about bananas when I'm not here to remind you, that is, when I leave you? Stop it, he said to himself.

He thought he smelled smoke. Smoke would be comforting. He inhaled hard. Smoke could be responsible for his eye situation. For braais, the Tswana sometimes used morula wood, which he would be willing to bet was loaded with resins, a greasewood almost. Also, they might have jazzed up the pit fire by slopping kerosene into it, speaking of fumes. He must be swimming in irritants. Just then the kind of music he hated most began to jolt and blare from the patio, right when he needed to concentrate, naturally.

His eyes were streaming. If he could dredge up the funny side of this, very fast, that might be brilliant. That was a thought. Something was making this happen. If sadness of some kind had anything to do with it he should try to get down to the hilarious side that everything supposedly has. Not that sadness did. There was another reason he should try this, something he could almost remember, something he remembered feeling uncomfortable about when Iris mentioned it, which should remind him. He almost had it. He had it, Iris reading a clipping to him proving that if you force yourself to smile your brainwaves change after the fact, proving you're happier no matter how rotten you felt when you started smiling, what *shit*, but true, apparently.

But what was something funny? It was like amateur theatricals, sticking his head out when he jerked these sheets back and forth. That was amusing. What else, lately? The goat eating the kneesock doesn't count, he thought. But the panic had been real, when he'd thought the goat had a gargantuan tongue, and when he'd tried to formulate what the panic was all about, the answer seemed to be that it related to some fear of his that the world wanted to be abnormal, or rather was abnormal.

To hell with it, he was going to go home.

7. *Doctor Morel*

Another thing he could take pride in was this. To find out if something of interest to him had turned up in Customs, all he had to do was drive out to the airport mid-lunchtime on Tuesdays and Fridays, roll past the arrival/departures hall, and notice if a whitewashed cobblestone in the ornamental collar encircling one of the thorn trees shading the scatter of tables near the curry and pap kiosk had been displaced inwise enough to reveal a black daub on the stone adjoining. All his contact had to do was come out a little early for his platter of bangers and mealie, disarrange the landscaping a matter of millimeters with a nudge of his foot, and nudge everything back to normalcy later on. All Ray had to do was park, go up to the prefab kiosk, and commiserate with the poor woman who was baking to death inside it while he bought an orange Fanta from her. Then he would wander along the cyclone fence to the back gate of the Customs warehouse, always being careful to have in his hand an envelope or folded sheet of paper to suggest that he had legitimate business in Customs, which he often did, in connection with shipments of schoolbooks or supplies for St. James. Clearing schoolbooks through Customs was a chore he had volunteered for on the second day of his employment at the school.

He was proud of all his systems. He had five signal or drop arrangements in play around the city at the moment, all of them simplicity itself, and foolproof so far. The airport was an ideal nexus because it was such an active setting, usually so crowded. A lot of people drove out to the airport for lunch. The airport management had yet to figure out that concessionaires are supposed to charge more for food sold at the airport, not less. The curry was extremely cheap.

Today the black mark was showing, so he drew into the parking lot, parked, and locked his Beetle, not forgetting to take along his paperwork dummy, a kraft envelope.

A new and bigger airport was going up on a site farther from town, near Mmadinare. He would have to adapt. He preferred small airports, or was it just that he was so used to this one? . . . its homely khaki main building with the black, white, and blue national colors painted in stripes across the front above the window . . . the presentation of various national flags over the main entrance unchanged and untended since the day the flags were raised. He wondered if anyone had ever complained about the sunbleached, bedraggled condition of the flags? Probably not, since all of them were getting equal disrespect. He liked the faint permanent insult of kerosene in the air. From the kiosk, he looked out at a nondescript escarpment wavering in the distance behind the heat waves rising from the runway.

He bought a pine nut soda and drank half of it leaning against the railings around the Independence Monument, a boulder set in a bed of white pebbles and bearing an enameled representation of the national logo, a medley of black and white hands seemingly pulling in opposite directions on a quoit. I belong here, Ray thought.

He went around to the back of the Customs complex and waited. Victor would see him.

His man was hardly the only asset in the airport. Ray was pretty sure the British had their own contact in Customs, as they did in the Air Botswana office. The Russians had tried to line up someone in the control tower. He wasn't quite sure how it was done, but the Americans, the Brits, and the Russians, at least, had regular and early access to the air passenger lists. Two other intelligence services had contacts in Immigration. The Chinese had assets in the maintenance staff. It can't be helped, he thought, airports are of interest . . . it looks like an airport but . . .

He felt cold for a moment. A good idea was not to let the image of a society invisibly occupied at certain key points by people who aren't what they purport to be get out of hand. And it was important not to forget the South Africans, who were in here somewhere.

His man, Victor Mfolwe, was an elder in the Zionist Christian Church and looked the part, in his gauntness, the gravity of his manner, and in his unvarying costume, an aged but immaculate black business suit with a Zed CC medal and swatch always pinned to the left lapel. All Ray's payments to Victor, in South African rands at Victor's request, were referred to by both of them as church donations. The Zed CC was an enigma.

The main body of the church was across the border in the Transvaal. It was well known that they had an accommodation with the South African government. But he had no reason to distrust Victor, who had been productive for him. He shook the gate to attract Victor's attention. He meant to find out more about the Zed CC when he had the time.

Victor arrived, inwardly on fire over something, his eyes alive.

Ray was let in fumblingly. Normally Victor was deft and quick.

Ray couldn't see any need to run, but they were going to, apparently. Victor never showed excitement, so this was puzzling.

The interior of the warehouse was divided into cagements that locked individually. The cage Victor had led them to was one of the larger ones. Again Victor was having difficulty addressing the combination lock. He stopped to dry his hands on the tails of the dustcoat he wore over his suit. The sides of the cage had been draped with blue tarpaulins and a worklight had been dropped over into the cage. They entered.

Victor closed them in, composed himself, and remembered that he had neglected to greet Ray.

"Dumela, rra," he said.

"Dumela."

"O tsogile jang?"

"Ke tsogile sentle, wena o tsogile jang?"

"Ke tsogile sentle."

Victor made a slight involuntary hunching movement revealing his relief that the ritual exchange of greetings had been accomplished.

There were ten shipping cartons, the maximum size, all marked as containing personal effects. They were here because although they had originated as seat freight, the last leg of their transportation had been via air, from Durban.

Well thank God for the South Africans, Ray thought, they make it so easy for us, they probe into everything. Every carton had been opened and contemptuously and halfheartedly resealed. Stickers had been applied stating that the examination of the cartons had been undertaken for reasons of security. The South Africans hadn't just sampled the shipment. For some reason they'd opened all ten boxes. That was interesting in itself. Why had they wanted to be so thorough? This kind of thing was so routine with the South Africans that the government of Botswana had given up protesting. It was time to get to work. What they were going to do was called, in the trade, canvassing.

"It is most bad, rra," Victor said, presumably so bad that he had to hold up his hand to block Ray's advance on the carton that had been pulled to the middle of the enclosure as the prime exhibit. The top flaps of the carton were standing upright.

Victor delicately extracted and gravely handed to Ray a framed art reproduction the size of a serving tray. The glass was webbed with fine cracks. Even before he was able to fully make it out, Ray knew he was being handed something wonderful, by which he meant promising in some unknown intuited way. Victor held the worklight up so that Ray could see what this was. Victor's hand was shaking.

He loved his men. His private name for his string of informants was his catena, his chain. He loved them. At that moment he loved them all, but he loved Victor for being transfigured in this way and for finding something that he was sure, for no good reason, was going to be more than interesting. He was grateful and he was having these moments of gratitude lately a little more frequently than he was comfortable with, but in this case it was justified. He had a sense.

Of course, catena was an indulgence prompted by his lack of opportunity to make use of his little Latin and less Greek. Victor wanted him to react. He had more to show. The carton appeared to be solidly filled with books and papers. Victor had already made a little selection.

The oil painting reproduced was of a surreal subject, a body on a beach, a reverse mermaid, a figure with human female legs and genitals and the head and body of a fish. There was a suggestion that this chimera was pregnant. This was a quality reproduction. This must be obscene, Ray thought. He felt it was. The figure was lying on the beach and there were breakers in the background. There was a title label on the frame, reading *Collective Invention*. This was a Magritte. He had never seen it before. He knew who Magritte was, but this painting was unfamiliar. Victor wanted him to be upset. He wasn't, but he showed distaste sufficient to release Victor to continue. The painting was a joke, of course. But it did point backward to a sensibility that was interesting and basically unpleasant. Why did the creature have to look pregnant? If the picture was meant to be hung in display, the Batswana would get a sort of bemused jolt out of it. There was something arrogant about it.

The heat in the warehouse was intense. There were no fans, nothing. Victor needs God if he's going to work in here, he thought. Ray was sweating heavily. He would have to stop at home for a fresh shirt.

"We must be more fast, rra," Victor said. "There are many many of this." Victor was handing him books. "And this."

Ray was looking at a thick trade paperback, *The Ghost Dance: Origins of Religion*, by Weston La Barre, self-evidently an attack on or deconstruction of religion from the standpoint of anthropology. The jacket comments confirmed that. There was a slip of paper inserted into the book. On it was an extract copied from the book's epigraph, a quotation from Lucretius. It read . . . *primum quod magnis doceo de rebus et artis religionum animum nodis exsolvere pergo deinde quod obscura de re tam lucida pango carmina* . . . Beneath it, in pencil, was somebody's translation, which read . . . I would teach of high matters and imaginings, and proceed to loose the mind from tight knots of religion. The translation could be improved on, Ray thought, but the point was clear.

There were ten copies of this item in the shipment, and the same number of another and more recent work by this same Weston La Barre, *Shadow of Childhood: Neoteny and the Biology of Religion*, this from a reputable publisher, the University of Oklahoma Press.

Victor handed him, gravely, a copy of Ambrose Bierce's *The Devil's Dictionary*.

Something was coalescing here. The shipment was for a Doctor Davis Morel, a medical doctor coming in as a working immigrant, according to the code entry Victor pointed out on his copy of the doctor's immigration paperwork. So they were not dealing with an accredited scholar or teacher of any kind. This was something else. Doctor Morel would be located on Tshekedi Crescent, in their neighborhood, or almost. He looked again at the code entry on the immigration carbon. Morel had been granted indefinite duration, a rare thing these days.

Somehow Victor had listed everything. There was a separate listing of all the books and pamphlets—many pamphlets—present in multiple copies. La Barre was at the head of the list, followed by *The Mythmaker: Paul and the Invention of Christianity*, by Hyam Maccoby, at nine copies, and then by *The Illusion of Immortality* by Corliss Lamont, at seven copies. Victor was no fool. One look at the titles of the pamphlets alone, which were from a miscellany of free-thought sources, would have been all it took to convince him that the shipment constituted an arsenal of irreligion and that Morel was the Antichrist if not the Great Beast himself. Some of the pamphlet titles struck Ray as fairly inflammatory . . . *Is God a Jew? The Church & the Nazis, Hinduism and Paranoia*. This was more than some crank's personal collection. Multiple copies meant that the point was propaganda. Victor had seen that straight off.

Victor was presenting him with sheet after sheet of inventory, one sheet at a time. That was to emphasize how very many sheets there were, of course, and it was unnecessary because Ray was aware that a huge amount of effort had gone into this. He was considering how much extra he should pay Victor for all this. He looked at Victor's typically Tswana handwriting. It was painstaking. The individually printed letters in their roundness and the way they were spaced recalled the school copybook style you were expected to outgrow. He loved Victor, he loved the man for his work. Probably Victor had never gone beyond Standard Four, like most Batswana, which might be an explanation for the pervasiveness of this unsophisticated penmanship among literate Batswana.

Ray could only skim the lists. Morel was a sexophile or sexologist of some kind. There were numerous books on the history of sexual customs. Victor had put stars next to these titles. There were books on the history of imprisonment, of punishments. There were histories of freemasonry. And this was very nice, a little collection of popular books unmasking the CIA, so *they* claimed. He was noting titles at random. Everything had a resonance he didn't like, such as *Bodies Under Siege: Self-mutilation in Culture and Psychiatry* by Armando R. Favazza, M.D. Ray's image of Morel was darkening. Ray wasn't altogether sure why Morel excited him as a prospect, but he was indisputably a person of interest. They would certainly see that at the agency. Ray refused to use the acronym, POI, when he was in discussions at the agency. Acronyms embarrassed him.

He would take the lists and go over them in detail later. His visits to Customs had to be kept brief. He had decided on sixty rands for Victor's payment. It was very generous. He had the bills ready.

Victor had checked the manifests on Morel's professional effects and discovered that there were two expensive photocopy machines in the shipment. They were state of the art machines, in Ray's judgment. He thanked Victor for everything, but there was more, something more Victor wanted him to see. Ray tried to be patient.

His feelings about the emerging character Morel appeared to be were complicated. He looked at this image from two angles. From one angle Morel seemed unexceptionable, a sort of educated proselytizing crank, flamboyant, who might even add a little texture to the intellectual life of the expatriate community, which could use it. Ray would hardly describe himself as religious in any acting-out sense, which wasn't what he meant. He meant he wasn't an observing religious type in any way. So he had no personal animus against what this Morel obviously had in mind to do. Ray felt, if he had to put it in a capsule way, that the Christian religion had worked out fairly well as the medium for a tolerable and variegated and improving set of societies. He had no profound thoughts on the subject. Maybe religion was going to evolve away ultimately and maybe not. Maybe decent societies could have been based on something else. He couldn't say. But as it was, Christianity had done about the best. Christianity gave us Milton, not to mention Bach and all the rest. And there was Botswana, which was a decent and placid country that was doing all right as it was. There was something goodhearted about Botswana. And it was a religious country, evangelized from top to bottom. It didn't need a Morel. By the numbers, Botswana was doing better than any other country in Africa. Christianity or the mindset bound up with it at least was helpful to the country, so far as he could judge. He'd never thought of himself as a limb of Christendom but of course in a way he was, and so be it. There was some potential for religious friction down the road. The Hindus wanted a temple. The Bahai were around. There were enough Muslims in town to support a mosque, and a mosque had been put up, and there was already some unhappiness with the volume the recorded muezzin calls were being played at. There had been a shortlived attempt, crushed by the government, by Domkrag, to insist that a live muezzin give the hourly calls, because of course that could bother nobody, human lung power being limited. But the Muslims had been able to prove that live muezzins were being phased out everywhere in Islam. So there were these recorded calls to prayer and the difficulty was that the Muslims were claiming that they were keeping the volume down when the experience of householders in the vicinity was that they weren't, in fact. He was lucky they didn't live in the vicinity. Iris would freak. The point was that Botswana was working, in a continent where almost nothing else was. It was developing a stratum of people who could communicate with you in your own vocabulary. Rex had been so precocious that he'd decided at eight or nine he didn't want to have pets because you couldn't converse with them, ergo they were a waste of time. Ray had wanted pets but he hadn't been willing to have them and be the only one responsible for pet chores. They had let Rex refuse to bear any responsibility. And the goddamned dogs they'd had early on loved Rex. So ultimately there had been no pets. What was his point? The heat was getting him.

"You are just dreaming, rra," Victor said.

"Sorry."

Victor was handling a framed eight by ten photograph. It was a professionally done portrait, head and shoulders. He was holding it up for Ray.

Davis Morel was black. Ray could see that Victor harbored some additional disapproval over that. Morel was black, though lighter skinned than an African, in the medium range. It had to be Morel because the subject was seated at a desk and there were medical reference books on a shelf behind him. If the photograph was recent, Morel was in his early forties. He was conventionally handsome and was giving a rather dry smile and overall a rather standardly forthright expression. Ray thought the expression was detectably self-consciously forthright, but maybe not. He was looking for slyness, without luck. Morel had an athletic bearing. He had a strong neck and wide shoulders. His hairline was very good, his hair close-cropped, not graying. He was an advertisement for his services, if nothing else. There was no jewelry on show. His suit was expensive. Sometimes Ray felt he could get deeper into a photograph if he looked aside from the main image slightly. He would say that, as faces go, Morel's seemed to be on the large side. He was square-faced and his grooming was perfect. His chin and his nose-tip each showed a distinct cleft. The flesh under his eyes was tight.

He returned the photograph to Victor, who resecured it in the bubblepack swathings it had come in.

Ray was a little unhappy and he knew why. He had been looking for something in the photograph that probably had to do with an old fantasy of his. At some point after getting into intelligence he had realized that something was lacking. His great enemy, some great personal enemy, was missing. He had no great antagonist. He knew this was literary and adolescent, and when it came to his mind, he had always laughed it away. But the truth was that the people he dealt with and processed and wrote up were in general not very smart or interesting and many of them were essentially just venal, which was unsatisfactory if you let it be. You could find it boring. The Russians and their creatures had been a blank system to him—and he noticed he was referring to them nowadays in the past tense, which was a sign of truth as to how things stood in the world. He had never had to work very hard to corrupt his targets, when that had been necessary, and it had been slightly bitter to learn that. The element of hard struggle was pretty intermittent in his work. Of course, he had chosen to work at a certain level in the game. He wasn't a thug. In fact he took pride in the certainty that he had never directly injured anyone in all his years in intelligence, not once, directly. And of course he had chosen to work in the borderlands of the struggle. He saw himself as a provider of truths that others would make use of, for good or ill, the morality of what they did with them being their problem and not his. It was where he was comfortable being, which was why this great enemy notion was so regressive and why he rejected it. It was essentially literary. But literature has power over us, he thought.

Ray wanted to look at the photograph again, but he was sweating, and it was late, so he decided against it. Victor had one last thing for Ray to see. He was rooting around in a different carton.

Morel looked disappointingly average, or did he mean above average? It was going to be interesting to find out why he had come to Botswana when everything about him suggested that he could get whatever he wanted out of life easily enough in Cambridge, Massachusetts, the venue he was departing from. He was smart, smart enough to get a medical degree of some kind, at least, he was black, he was presentable, a man for all races so to speak, and the way the apparatus of opportunity was configured right now in the United States meant that someone like this would have to take courses to learn how to miss the boat. Morel represented a commodity in short supply, unlike white male middle-aged academics in the humanities with degrees from nonstellar institutions, a category of commodity he knew something about. Morel appeared to be in his prime, moreover. American professionals coming to Africa to perform benefactions during sabbaticals or when they were past their prime made one kind of sense. But Morel had to be in his peak earning period. And he appeared to be coming to stay. And he was, according to the immigration paperwork, coming unsponsored, which meant that this was a personally driven and personally funded choice. And there was the question of choosing Botswana, which had its attractions but which was not picturesque, except up north. Something was off center. There was something here to pursue. The agency would see it his way.

Victor was gesturing at a jumble of shoes he'd pulled out for Ray's inspection.

Ray went over to look. They were all either high shoes or low boots. In every pair the inner heel, the inner right heel, had been built up significantly. There were many more shoes in the carton and they were all like these, Victor assured him.

Perfection is rare, Ray thought.

8. The List

He had a free period. It was three in the afternoon. The school was quiet. The phone rang. That was another thing that could go on the list. The call was going to be from Iris, who was calling him more often at work lately, which could mean she was feeling a need to keep better apprised of his movements, which was a new anxiety with her. And it had to be coupled with something else that was new . . . her requests that he let her know definitely if he was coming home for lunch or not.

He picked up the phone and said, "Here I am and I still love you." The caller gasped. It was definitely Iris.

"How did you know it would be me, you fool. Don't do that. I could have been anybody."

"I knew it was you."

"You couldn't have. My God. Please don't do that again. It's not like you. Don't be strange."

"I live on the edge," he said.

"No you don't. Please don't do it again."

"I may, I may not."

"Quit it, please."

"Okay. It's a deal."

"I don't want you to be strange." He thought that was interesting.

She said, lightly, "I just wanted to touch voices."

"I love you to say that. But tell me about lunch, your lunch date," he said.

She sighed, and then was silent.

He said, "I take it my recommendation wasn't great."

"Well, it was an example of why you could get lonely in Gaborone. We ate at the President, in the Grenadier Room no less. I dressed up. It was fine. Her name is Lorna, but she insisted I call her Lor, which felt awkward. I guess because she's married to an American I assumed she was too, but she isn't. Well, she is, she's a citizen, but she's Australian. Getting me to call her Lor and not Lorna seemed to be the main thing on her mind. They've been all over. She loves the embassy people. We had nothing to talk about, really.

"But, well she's nice and she's livelier than a lot of other embassy wives I could name. It was funny, she drank quite a bit of Cape Riesling during lunch, but the main effect it had on her was to stir up lots of umbrage about how much drinking there is in embassy circles. She managed to refer to the embassy staff as Alcoholics Unanimous a couple of times. She seems to think there's too much daytime drinking, particularly."

He thought, The fact is that I am talking to the most beautiful white woman in southern Africa, outside of the movies, and someone getting more beautiful, not less . . . these token signs of age make her beauty more acute, other women must hate her: How can she have friends? She needs friends, outside of me: Nothing can be done. The fact that he could give her pleasure, that life allowed him to, was immense to him. It was like gold.

"What?" he asked, he had missed something.

"I said, Lor and I are both insomniacs. Thank God, because that was basically our only subject. So we were talking and I tried to be entertaining by relating something you said the other night, don't worry, nothing embarrassing, but I thought it was a funny story. It was when I complained because you had just turned over, *like that*, flopped over and said goodnight when I was still my usual wide-awake self . . . It happens, it's no big problem, this is me. But this was early, even for you. You know how it is when I'm abandoned to myself . . . my own devices, at night.

"So then you remember I had an attack of pique and kind of yelled at you, 'I have no rights around here!' meaning, of course, that I have an unwritten marital right to sufficient notice before you go to sleep. And you said, when I said I have no rights, you said, 'You have the right to remain silent.' Well, it was funny. Still makes me laugh. But she didn't get it *at all* and I was drawn into one of those explanations, explications, that ends up making you sound like a complete idiot. Her interpretation was just that I was a tyrant and you were a policeman."

"That was pretty amusing of me. She didn't get the humor. Maybe because she's Australian, they don't have Miranda."

"It was a misfire," she said.

"Bad recommendation, I guess."

"It's not your fault. She's fine, really. But she's not going to be exactly a friend. I don't know what I mean, exactly . . . am I pathetic? I guess what I mean is she's not an answer."

"She's part of the problem, you're saying."

"I wouldn't go that far. She's okay."

"If she's not an answer, what is the question?"

"Ah," she said dryly and not happily.

"So what is the question, Iris?" He knew his tone was wrong. It was what she called his *bearing down* tone.

"Oh please don't get all relentless. *Please.*"

"I didn't mean to be. I'm sorry. I thought you were initiating something and clearly you weren't."

"On the *phone*? When you have to get back to work? I don't think I was."

"I'm sorry."

"Me too."

"Okay."

"Also she was wearing the most painful accessory in the history of jewelry. It was a choker made out of white plastic petals, pointed petals all awry and pointing in different directions. It was sticking into her throat, into the flesh. I couldn't take my eyes off it."

This is the way she retreats, he thought.

"It made a teeny clacking sound when she swallowed."

"I do apologize. If I'd known she was Australian I'd have mentioned it. It's another culture."

"Yes, it is. And I don't transcend cultures at all well. I'm not good at it."

Uh-oh, he thought.

"But Iris, you are good at it. You've done it here and in Zambia beautifully, and before that."

"No I haven't. You're confusing two things, Ray, one being that I don't complain and the other being your interpretation of that as how well I'm doing. Those are two different things."

"But you make African friends," he said, unnerved at how large these declarations were. Usually she was more incremental. *A bitter feast was steaming hot and a mouth must be found to eat it,* he thought. It was a quotation whose author he couldn't come up with. That was what he was facing, though. There was something unfair about quotations lasting longer than the names of their creators. He saw her recent declarations as thrusts or lunges, not tentative anymore. And this was going on over the phone and it was unfair, unless she was in a more extreme state than he'd guessed. Maybe she was. It was his brother's influence. She wanted liberation of some kind. It was Rex. Liberation was fine, he agreed with it, but all he knew was that at the heart of any kind of liberation worth anything there still had to be someone grabbing someone else and saying I'm yours, I love you beyond expression, something like that, embraces, berserk embraces, in his humble opinion. But maybe not, according to her, according to all this, according to his brother. It was unfair. He couldn't laugh at her anymore when she said something funny she hadn't intended to say. There was a recent example. She had complained that he was being parsimonious with some piece of gossip or information he had, and she had said something like It's like pulling hen's teeth getting anything out of you. So he had laughed, and although she'd realized immediately what she'd said, she still hadn't liked his laughing, even after he explained that he'd been mainly laughing appreciatively at how appositely the mixed metaphor worked. Well, he thought: Wife is unfair . . . as somebody said.

Now she was asking him what real African friends he thought she had in Botswana.

"Well, you have a lot of acquaintances . . ."

"But no close friends, Ray."

"Sure you do. You must. Maybe not right at this moment. One problem is that compatible people come and they go, if they're foreign service, say. It's standard. And you have African friends from Zambia you write to . . ."

She groaned.

"Let's stop talking," she said.

He shook his mechanical pencil to see if the lead reservoir was reasonably full. And he was not going to smoke. He hung up, then took the receiver off the hook.

Ray confronted his pad. There was a polished sheet of stainless steel exactly the size of the pad that he kept between the final sheet in the pad and the cardboard backing. He slid it out and inserted it under the top sheet as a preventive against leaving impressions on the next sheet down as he wrote. He tended to press hard when he wrote. Now he was ready. He decided to chance setting the receiver back in its cradle.

The phone rang. It was going to be Iris, and putting the phone back in use had been the right thing to do because this was going to be an apology and if she'd kept on getting a busy signal it would have led to frustration and the need for some kind of explanation later on. Also, knowing that she was trying to call him would have wrecked his concentration. He had had no choice.

He answered the phone.

"I'm sorry too," he said. He knew it was Iris.

It was. She sighed. "That's what I wanted to say, Ray. I hate myself."

"Don't hate yourself. We're both sorry. It's all right. I appreciate you."

"I know."

It was important that she hang up first. He waited.

She said, "Before I forget, there's one thing I found out that I wanted to tell you. Yesterday Fikile was looking up at one of our palm trees and smiling, so I asked him what he was looking at. He said it was rats. Apparently that place on the palm where the dead fronds hang down and form a kind of mass is where a certain kind of rat, tree rat, makes its home. He had seen one of them peeping out. He said we have quite a few. They're small, though."

"That's nice. Well. Is this something that needs to be attended to or do we just keep cohabiting with them?"

"No, that's not why I'm telling you. I don't think they bother anything. But I thought it was interesting because it might explain certain sounds we hear on the roof at times that we can't figure out. We thought they were caused by birds, but it seemed strange because it was nocturnal, remember?"

"I do."

"I was afraid I'd forget to mention it. I'll let you go now. I love you. One other thing is that I think my sister may be pregnant and not telling me directly, or that she plans to get pregnant. But I can tell you about that later."

He became alert. He wanted to know about this. Her sister was unmarried. The relationship between the sisters was strained and important to Iris.

"Wait, I want to hear this. You're not saying she's gotten married, are you?"

"No, not at all. This is all reading between the lines, really, but I think she's going to stay single and just do it. But see what this sounds like to you. This is from her last letter. I'd better summarize it instead of reading it. She eats lunch in a playground near her office every day and eavesdrops and reports things the children say that are cute enough but are not the wisdom of the ages in the mouths of babes she seems to think they are. This is only one example. She overheard some children arguing over whether there could be good monsters as well as bad ones. She drew some great significance from it. Now I can't find what I wanted to read you. But in every letter there's something about how profound children are if you only listen."

"When you answer, tell her that yes there are good monsters."

A silence fell.

"Well," she said.

"Well, but you do think she may be planning to reproduce? I find that reckless and also typical of her."

"Don't be so hard. Some child said It's noon o'clock, and she thought that was wonderful. And here's another thing she seems to think is beyond darling. She was visiting a friend of hers who has a two-year-old daughter, very delicate and sensitive and very resistant to going to bed. So four adults were sitting around and they decided to all yawn at the same time to show how tired they were and by implication how tired she should be. So they did it and the baby burst into tears because she knew it was so unnatural or manipulative or something. Ellen raves about the child. Oh, and, lest we forget, her friend is a single mother."

"I have to go. I have to sit revision," he said. He thought, Maybe I can cancel revision. He needed a list.

The International Postal Union was his enemy. It brought Rex and Ellen into her life, and his.

Curwen himself would take over Ray's revision group, as a favor. He loved Curwen for always trying to be like Christ, an idea of Christ, a cartoon but a completely benign cartoon. He even half envied Curwen whatever the restricting cultural history was that had led him into feeling that copying Christ was a fulfilling thing to do with his mortal life. The whole teaching staff exploited Curwen, the Marxists worst of all. Ray didn't like to do it, and he tried not to. Iris thought of Curwen as an ideal good guy on the basis of Ray's anecdotes. But Ray didn't, because there was a difference between good acts resulting from adherence to a model of some kind and some other way to be good, some more natural way, that for example women had. Women seemed not to need these models to kneel to and copy. It was true that Curwen got less appreciation than he deserved because you could predict his acts of goodness so infallibly. Curwen wanted to be loved, and Ray wanted to love him, but Ray knew that there was condescension in his attitude to Curwen that he couldn't do anything about and that wrecked it as a form of love. Life is unfair, Ray thought, unfair to Curwen.

He centered the writing block on his desk and adjusted the point length of his pencil lead. He wondered whether he should begin by generating categories first, as against putting down everything that came to him in no order, chaotically, which might be better because the project was making him feel chaotic.

He couldn't decide. This was difficult. It shouldn't be. He had done hundreds of profiles in his time, which was all this was. But of course very few profiles had been of women, almost none.

It came to Ray that he didn't like to think about women—the *subject* of women, he meant. He was surprised at himself. But of course the *subject* of women was not the same thing as *individual* women, which he thought about just as much as the next man, that is, all the time, off and on, depending on the mood or circumstances he was in, or what a particular woman might be up to. He wasn't counting involuntary trains of carnal imagery.

And of course, because something confusing was going on with Iris, she was on his mind constantly. So he did think about women, just not as a *subject*.

There were other things besides women he preferred not to think about. For example . . . death, say, and unidentified flying objects. But these were things you could decline to think about without feeling guilty. It was human not to want to think about death, about being mortal. And it made him irritable to think about unidentified flying objects because, as a phenomenon, it was in the hands of charlatans and clowns. He had seen something odd in the sky, once, so of course he was interested. The subject was completely surrounded by liars, unfortunately. And flying saucers were more and more irritating as a phenomenon in that they kept recurring, and the claims of what they were doing kept getting more elaborate. And of course *if* it was true that they existed, then the whole human enterprise obviously needed to be redirected toward finding out who was flying these damned things, especially since their occupants had supposedly taken up molesting hordes of people in their bedrooms at night and stealing fetuses and other absurdities. He wondered if there was some quality common to death, women, and UFOs that made him want to not think about them. He considered the question. They were all similar in a way, ontologically. They were all entities that nothing could be done about.

Was that it? Probably not, although in a cheap way it seemed to fit. He wanted not to be superficial. His life, or at least his life with Iris, depended on it. The problem was that he had thought until fairly recently that he had solved the woman question, so to speak, by getting happily married. And the conventional idea that he had been raised with was, roughly, that if everybody did what he did and got happily married there was no woman question, which now turned out to be an incorrect idea. He had been operating with simple, oversimple, ideas, obviously.

When Iris had said to him, hurting him, had said to him, Ask yourself sometime if you talk to yourself the same way you talk to me, and then tell me . . . that had been rough. It had been like being flayed without sufficient warning, or something. They had barely been able to discuss it later. The implication of the question was that he was talking down to her or shaping what he said to her in order to keep her pacified or in a cheerful frame of mind or something like that. Something good if painful had come out of it, he thought. He had concluded that it might be true that his manner of talking to her was less direct, or more processed or something, than he liked to admit. And he had stopped. Or he was trying, at least. The implication was that he was trying to control her.

Something else had come out of that moment. He wanted to sigh when he thought about it. He had noticed that the level of language he used on himself . . . was questionable, and limited, suggesting the influence of some force inside of himself acting to keep him . . . acting to keep him within certain borders. But that was a new subject . . .

The question of women as a subject came down to their *unhappiness*. And what was happening was that the general unhappiness of women was turning into a force and developing institutions and mandibles whereas before it had been a kind of background condition like the temperature, as he had thought, something that rose and fell within certain stable limits. He thought of his mother's unhappiness. Iris was not what he would call a feminist and yet, if he was anywhere near understanding what was going on with her, she was part of this great unhappiness. Just his luck. But then his luck had never been good, except for finding and marrying Iris, paradoxically, which had saved his life.

What was the general unhappiness of women about? He would have to concentrate . . . except that he wouldn't have to at all! The answer was in the category of answers you possess without knowing you do. He had the answer, he realized. Sometimes you carried the answer to an ultimate question around with you like something in a parcel, wrapped up.

Unwrapped, it was simple. It was like this. What they wanted, he gathered, feeling pleased with himself, was for their own personal rational deliberation to replace what? . . . to replace tradition and custom and instinct, what men called instinct, in arriving at the nine or ten major decisions life presents all of us with. That meant when to mate, of course, but not only when to mate, it meant whether to mate or not, and with which sex, even . . . what to be professionally and whether to have children. It was banal, but an insight can be banal and radical at the same time, apparently. It had a Freudian tinge to it too, as in Where id was, ego shall be. It was other familiar things. It was our friend the Enlightenment, still rolling merrily along, for instance.

He didn't know how he felt. It was immense, of course, because the only kind of societies the human race had ever been able to build were ones in which half the population was being very accommodating to the other half. Now it was going to be . . . Where id was, contracts and negotiations and taking forever to work things out are going to be. How was it going to work? Life was going to take longer. Everyone would have to adjust.

He felt better, strangely enough. He thought: God moves in a mysterious way, when he moves at all. It annoyed him that he was using one of his brother's bons mots, but it seemed to apply, a bit. The world ahead was going to be seriously different. He had a sense of it. He felt that if he kept his mind still he might sense even more of how it was going to be. It was going to be a world full of divorces, for one thing, and you could forget about people joining nunneries. That was about all he could think of. He had his limitations as a seer, obviously. But he was getting a presentiment of the magnitude of the change that was coming.

He felt, what? He felt uneasy. He felt melancholy, in fact.

He needed to get this over with.

Now to the list. He was dealing with fragments. He should assemble fragments.

One, she was more profane lately. She was saying Shit more than he remembered, and this was in the context of informing him that intramale sexual profanity could be intimidating to women in the vicinity. Probably there was no conflict there. But she was more profane lately. One, Shit, he wrote on the pad, at the top.

She was noticing things and making a point of mentioning them, and they were things that seemed to imply she was undergoing some deep revision of what she had assumed up to that point. It was on the order of going to the barber and getting your hair cut in a new way and looking into the mirror and discovering that, although you hadn't noticed up till then, you have a very small head. She had said I bet you don't know you have a tic of just almost imperceptibly hefting each forkful of food as you start to raise it to your mouth, as though you're weighing it, when you're feeling defensive about something. It had been a neutral observation, not meant to make him stop weighing his food. She included herself in these discoveries.

Three evaded him. He sat waiting for Three.

There was an exercise he sometimes did that was reassuring. He had put his head into a ten-year-old girl's bedroom back in the States, just glancing in, years ago. This had been during training. The point had been to memorize at least a dozen discrete items of decor. He still had every one. One, cat motif posters and knickknacks including a cat piggy bank. Two, painted decorated rocks. Three, Charlie Brown stickers on dresser drawers. Four, horse sculpture. Five, miniature watering can. Six, multicolor raffia-ring curtain covering doorless closet. Seven, music stand. Eight, pennants. Nine through Twelve, *Heidi*, *Stuart Little*, *Black Beauty*, a Laing Fairy Book. Thirteen, flocked riding helmet.

Three was about losing things. She was more absentminded recently, and she was losing things to the point that he had referred to their bedroom as the Lost and Found. There had to be a better Three.

Three could be Rex, instead, and everything connected with Rex. Or Three could just be the implication he was getting more and more often from Iris that he should find everything Rex wrote hilarious. He was loaded down mentally with quotations from his brother. He seemed to be cursed with total recall for everything Rex produced. What had there been along those lines lately? He remembered something from a sketch Rex was writing, about someone who's trying to be more decisive and aggressive and who writes a note to himself that reads *Consider starting to make an effort to try being at least a little less half-assed about things*. He wanted to forget Rex, not anatomize everything connected with him.

Four could be Iris's feeling that he, or they, he and Iris, were no longer as funny with each other as they had been. She'd said We used to say stupid things more than we do now. She had examples. One was when she said, after he'd been repetitious, You must be History because you just repeated yourself, and his instant comeback of You must be Power because you abhor a vacuum . . . cleaner, which had been an allusion to her lack of love for housecleaning, which by the way was a problem Africa had solved for her.

Then Five came to him. He didn't want this Five. Five was Iris saying to him apropos of nothing, saying, and looking steadily at him when she

said it, to separate it from everything else that had preceded it, saying I
know this sounds stupid but one thing I want in this life is to have nothing to do with . . . with cruelty. She had looked at him as though he was
supposed to make some kind of vow back to her. This was Five, and it was
Iris being suspicious of his work or her notion of his work. It was an
assault. He resented it. That was Five.

9. The Mobashi

Ray was enraged. This was reckless, and Victor had never been reckless before. This was sheer recklessness.

He was enraged as much at his own flux of panic as at the stupid act that had provoked it. There was an obvious flaw in the system he had developed for Victor. He had told Victor never to call him on the phone. So the flaw was that if something turned up that Ray needed to see urgently at some point between his scheduled visits, Victor was stuck with waiting. This had never happened before. Victor was obviously taking himself more and more seriously in his work for Ray. And then it had probably been a mistake to increase his remuneration so sharply the last time. No doubt Victor was seeing Morel as a treasure trove he had to plunder expeditiously before all of Morel's goods had moved through.

Ray went to the door of his office to reassure himself that he was locked in. The curtains were secure across both windows. He returned to his desk.

He turned on the tensor lamp and again sorted through the contents of the packet Victor had so goddamned recklessly gotten a courier to bring to him, paid a courier to bring to him, a mobashi. Probably that was the dumbest part of a dumb maneuver. The courier had been one of the ragged street children, the bobashi, one of them, a mobashi, than which or whom or whatever nothing could be more conspicuous standing next to the main gate into St. James as the students in their neat uniforms streamed past on their way to first period. And the packet itself had been absurd, an outer mailing envelope overlarge for what it had to contain, and a flat sweets box wrapped in two layers of kraft paper and that parcel tied with string and the knots sealed with crimson candle wax. And Ray's name was on it in pencil, presumably so it could be erased and the paper reused at some point. His name had been printed on the envelope and the inner parcel, both, in block letters.

He was calming down. Ray felt a kind of joy, handling the exhibits. Victor had been right to think that they meant something arresting about Davis Morel, although what they meant, exactly, it was difficult to say. They were at the very least suggestive of Ray's idea that Morel was planning to set himself up as a part-time Antichrist of some kind.

There were four exhibits. Three were printed cards. Victor had noted on each one that it was a sample taken from a quantity of the same card. There were several hundred of each kind. Ray was relieved that Victor hadn't gone on to make an exact count, which was the kind of thing he might well have done, for which Ray would have been obliged to praise him a lot.

The cards were four by six, on heavyish white stock, and professionally printed. Ray supposed that they were for handing out, primarily, although the typeface was large enough to permit display in the privacy of your own catacomb, say on your bedside table, or stuck into your shaving mirror. The cards bore free-thought slogans loosely speaking.

One read *The Creator, A Comedian Whose Audience Is Afraid to Laugh*, H. L. Mencken.

The next read WHAT YOU MUST LEARN ABOVE ALL ELSE IS WHY YOU SAY YES, *Der Jasager*, Bertolt Brecht.

The last one was, to Ray, weird. It read SYSTEMS UNEQUAL TO THEIR WASTES ARE EQUAL TO ONE ANOTHER. There was no attribution line. Ray felt that this was probably Morel's own creation.

The remaining exhibit was different. It was a listing. It was for display, but probably for personal display, for Morel's own personal display needs. The listing was, according to Victor's note, in careful—probably meaning calligraphic—handwriting. Victor hadn't, thank God, felt free to send the original, so he had recopied it in his own peculiar hand.

Piacocas, Punaxicas, Quibuquicas, Quimecas, Guapacas, Baurecas, Payconecas, Guarayos, Anaporecas, Bohococas, Tubacicas, Zibacas, Quimomecas, Yurucaricas, Cucicas, Tapacuracas, Paunacacas, Quitemocas, Napecas, Pizocas, Tanipicas, Xuberecas, Parisicas, Xamanucas, Tapuricas, Taos, Bazorocas, Pequicas, Parabacas, Otuques, Ecorabecas, Curacanecas, Batasicas, Meriponecas, Quidabonecas, Cupiecas, Ubisonecas, Zarabecas, Curiminacas,

Chamaros, Penoquicas, Boros, Mataucas, Otures, Veripones, Maramoricas, Morotocas, Caypotorades, Guaycurus.

This is a pure mystery, Ray thought. He read the list again. It related to nothing he could think of. It seemed vaguely Latin American, but that told him nothing. A job, he thought. He was pleased. He locked everything away in the top drawer of his desk. His top drawer locked frontally and also from the left via a special bolt arrangement activated through a side drawer. It was his own arrangement. The top drawer was lined with galvanized iron, which he had fitted himself.

The mobashi had asked for him by name. The boy, not more than ten years old or so, had been pathetic, with an injured hand in a filthy improvised dressing, a train of scabs along one leg, arms like laths.

It had been unwise but he had given the boy money, which had prolonged the exchange between them and exposed Ray to more attention than had been necessary. It was certain that Victor had already paid the boy.

Sending the boy had been an error and being prodigal with him had probably been an error. He had given him a five-pula note and the boy had been stunned. Ray hoped he wouldn't start hanging around.

But enough pity and terror for one day, he thought.

He wanted to know who was responsible for doing something for the bobashi. Someone had to be. It was terrible. There was something wonderful on poverty, in Herrick, but he couldn't remember the whole thing. There were better quotations Morel could have used. Come to me next time, he thought. What was English Literature for, if not to constitute a midden of thought-gems so acute, so beautiful, so apt . . . But you needed a guide to get the best ones. On every side of every issue there were gems. He thought, Take Herrick: Poverty the greatest pack: To mortal men, great loads allotted be, but of all packs, no pack like poverty. Marxists don't even know that it's there. He should look it up. That also would calm him down, his books, sometimes just touching his books.

10. *Facing Boyle*

Well here I am at the foot of the cross again, Ray thought as he entered the mall at its lower end, from the west. The phrase was a tic he was tired of but that was evidently going to be with him forever. He had once given directions to somebody re how to find the American embassy, describing it as being near the foot of the cross, which was to say that it was at the foot of the cross-shaped layout of large buildings enclosing the pedestrian mall that constituted Gaborone's semblance of a downtown civic center and embassy row all in one. The mall was in the form of the Latin cross but with the arms three-quarters of the way up the shaft shortened to stubs. The transection of the shaft and the arms constituted the main plaza.

Today he had to deal with Boyle.

He proceeded up the shaft of the cross, away from his destination, the American Library annex of the American embassy. He was early, and since he was agitated, he thought that keeping in motion was a good idea and that he would head on up to the plaza, look around, and be back for his appointment in plenty of time.

He knew something about crosses, now that he came to think of it. During training one of his exercises had been to study, for three minutes, the twenty main historical variants of the cross, and their names. He could probably still put most of the names and shapes together, if not all of them. Some were easy. Lorraine, Greek, Maltese, Tau. Anyway, here I go, he thought: The twenty are . . . Latin, Calvary, Patriarchal, Papal, Lorraine, Greek, Celtic, Maltese, St. Andrew's, Tau, Pommée, Botonée, Pattée . . . Avellan . . . Moline . . . Formée, Fourchée . . .

Crosslet, Quadrate . . . Jerusalem. He supposed he could still match shapes and names. They had been pretty amazed. I perform, he thought. Whether Boyle appreciated his performance was another matter.

He had twenty minutes.

Every meeting with Boyle felt urgent. They didn't know how to approach each other. Boyle liked to be called Chet, not by his whole first name, Chester. Ray couldn't make himself address Boyle as Chet. His whole being wanted to call Boyle Boyle, but since Boyle was his superior he couldn't. Boyle called him Finch, however, or occasionally Doctor Finch or Doctor. He had called him Doctor Finch only once. It had been hostile. Ray's solution to the problem of what to call Boyle was to call him Chief, just once at the onset of each meeting, and then to use You throughout the balance of their meeting. A meeting could be quite long.

Ray's mouth got dry just thinking about all this. Chief was a substitute for sir, which was impossible. He could manage Chief probably because Chief contained a slight hint of burlesque, very slight, in fact, almost nonexistent the way he said it, in fact probably nonexistent. Ray suspected that he was being called Finch because he was only contract and not staff.

Noon was approaching. The sun was intense and he slowed his pace as he passed through the bars of shade cast by the intermittent arcading. The crowds were as usual. Students from the nearby secondaries would be arriving any minute now, bound for the takeaways and the porridge and sweet reed vendors in the central plaza. The crowds were about twenty percent non-Tswana . . . whites, Indians, Chinese. The Batswana were on the slighter side, physically, which was a fact never mentioned.

Passing the Notwane Pharmacy, he was reminded of another coup coming out of his training period. This had been another flash memorizing exercise. They had given him two minutes to look into a medicine cabinet and study the contents, a typical medicine cabinet. And he had gotten all the prescription medications right, twenty of them, or fifteen, something he would still be able to do.

He hated Boyle, but not really. Boyle was new. Boyle was Boyle and not his predecessor, the beloved, to Ray, Marion Resnick, which was Boyle's fault. Besides, Ray had survived other substandard chiefs of station. Marion had been the kind of person other people spontaneously referred to as a lovely man, which was indicative. Where had Marion gone? It was a peculiarity of his vocation that it would be held against him if he inquired at all searchingly about it. But the fact was that he felt he

wanted to know where Marion was, now, in the world. He couldn't ask
Boyle, God knows. Marion was too young for retirement, so he was
undoubtedly still out in the field somewhere.

Ray had reached the paved part of the mall. Like the development
process itself writ small, the paving of the mall was a process of improvement that never seemed to get finished. Progress in extending the pavement from the plaza outward was slow and would halt for months at a
time while parts of the already paved section were redone. The cement
flagstones they were using tended to fracture. But worse was the problem
of soil subsidence, which, combined with subterranean ant and termite
activity, lent a funhouse aspect to walking on the flagstones as one or
another of them would sink or tilt underfoot. Something seemed to find
the grouting between the flags delicious, since it was always being sucked
down and replaced by little tumuli of red silt. The paving was like *The
Tower of Babel* by Brueghel, where half the edifice, the front and upper
half of it, is solid or under construction, and the bottom part of the edifice, toward the rear, is falling into ruin as fast as the top tiers are being
completed. The image of the Tower of Babel was fresh in his mind
because Morel had a framed reproduction of it in his effects, which Ray
had taken note of during his second canvass of Morel's things, out at
Customs.

To someone like Marion he could have pitched Morel's taste in art as,
in a certain way, a subject of interest. There was a theme. Another framed
reproduction was of a blown-up detail from Signorelli's *The End of the
World*, with Renaissance Italian men in the street staring up at the sky in
terror. What was that? There was no feeling that the individual pictures
had been chosen one at a time just because Morel liked them, the way he
or rather Iris chose their pictures, since that was her province. A true collection of art, the sign of its being a true personal collection, would be
that it was motley. Theirs was. Not that they had a collection. They had
an assemblage. Iris was very catholic in her taste. She liked Van Eyck. She
liked an American landscape painter named John Beerman and had nicely
framed a cover reproduction from a catalog of one of his shows, and she
tore out anything of his she found reproduced in *ARTnews*, to which she
subscribed. She liked Persian miniatures. They had some on postcards
from the Metropolitan and she currently had three of them taped up on
the wall above her side of the bed. Iris had stopped buying things for
their walls, now that he thought of it. But there was no reason it had to
mean anything. There was already a sufficiency of items to worry about.
For a while Iris had been interested in the reed baskets produced by the

Bushmen or rather Bushwomen in the north, and she had studied the meaning of the symbols in the designs, Tears of the Giraffe, Knees of the Tortoise, Urine Trail of the Bull, and so on woven into baskets. But she'd lost interest, synchronous with the Germans seizing commercial control of basketmaking and stamping all the art and individuality out of the baskets by making the basketweavers stick to the handful of templates the Germans knew would sell best. It was hard to stop thinking of the Germans in Botswana as West Germans. Reunification was still unbelievable to him. Already German external intelligence was getting more active in southern Africa, as befits a country getting back into the saddle as a major power. He knew who three of the main German agents in Botswana were. One claimed to be Dutch. German marketing was hoping to do to Botswana baskets what they had done to soapstone carving in Kenya. He thought, But that's the way the world wags, long may it wave. The Germans simplify the baskets and more sell and more money comes into the villages hence more mabele and more chibuku so three cheers. Some of my best friends are krauts, or they were, when I could still have friends.

If he let it, the mall could bring out a certain cultural feeling in him that was fairly standard, to the effect that the mall, the buildings, the technology involved, the infrastructure generally, the whole business was a gift from the white West and that what was being done with this gift was dubious. That was the image. Here was sanitation and technology and the buildings in which people were hanging around in order to get paychecks. All this had been provided to Africans who were only one generation away from herding cattle and chasing witches and going broke raising mealie on patches the size of tennis courts. The question of what was ultimately going to be done with all this by the Batswana was always just under the surface, and the question was kept hot by the steady fixation the Batswana seemed to have on beating back the white tide and getting expatriates down to reasonable numbers preparatory to, some fine day, getting them out en masse. Because as of now the white presence was going up, not down. In the meantime it led to a certain unpleasant amount of Schadenfreude among the representatives of the donor countries and the businesspeople in regard to the Batswana and their shortcomings as clerks and tellers and as functionaries in general. He thought, If the Batswana could understand that in our culture impatience is almost a virtue it might help, and it would help if there could be more jobs, any kind of jobs, almost, because unemployment kills and is humiliating and it won't stop, or we don't know how to make it stop—and the Tswana know we don't.

The mall hardly represented his idea of the West at its best, so to speak. The mall buildings were standard commercial modern, poured-concrete shoeboxes stood on end, with brick cladding or grooved or fluted or stippled or pebbled plaster facades, all or most of them about the same color as the sand they were built on. Only three or four of the buildings rose to the level of requiring elevators. The British High Commission did, at the head of the cross, and so did the President Hotel, dominating the whole left side of the plaza, looming. And there were three other buildings that did, actually. The mall buildings were less than magnificent. Now he was sounding like an asshole. And the buildings were not wearing well internally. Because people were expected to run up and down five or six flights of stairs routinely, and because doing that rapidly was some kind of fun for a lot of people, there were streams and blotches of handprints and hand grime on the walls of the stairwells at each landing, where people checked themselves on the downward race.

Nor was there anything magnificent about the street-level shops with their oceanic windows and their displays featuring pinspots, half-scrolled sheets of Mylar, and, in the clothing stores, the new faceless and raceless manikins. They were peculiar. Their heads were like grapes. It was the units of the South African chains that were pioneering them and they were now virtually universal. The heads on the manikins modeling women's clothes seemed to be slightly narrower than the heads on the manikins modeling menswear. Most of the manikins were beige. Some were gray. Some were clear Lucite.

All this could be hell for some and not others, he thought. It would be hell standing up all day in a bank and leafing endlessly through carbon copies of unalphabetized deposit slips. He was passing Barclays.

He felt sorry for the Chinese and Indian bazaars wedged between and fighting and losing against the chains. The bazaars had been there first. They had been all there was, with their bins and racks of merchandise shoved out into the right of way, their hellish repetitive reggae ambiences bulging out over the sidewalks as well, and with their supremely incoherent inventories. The one next to the American Library seemed to specialize, as best he could make out, in sandalwood room dividers, sporting goods, chutneys, and marital aids. Boyle hated Sirdar Varieties and Goods and wanted them out, away from the library, so Ray guessed that they were probably doomed. But Ray thought Sirdar Varieties and Goods added color. The owner's wife was a heavily scented matron who wore her hair swept back except for a fringe of oily fishhook curls across her forehead. Her husband was obese. He was bearded and when his fat cheeks bunched up in a smile it was like seeing cue balls rising out of a sack. Boyle liked or needed to project terribilità off and on. Ray thought that the habit of doing it might have gotten ingrained in Boyle in his last couple of posts, places where heavy events were more standard than here. Boyle had been in Guatemala and liked it, was the story. And he had been in Kinshasa. Boyle would sometimes allude to Kinshasa, but to Guatemala, never.

He had reached the central plaza, which was about as far as he had time to walk before turning back. In the plaza you were, to a degree, back in village Botswana. A few big cloud trees original to the place had been allowed to remain standing, and under them were tracts of reed mats each one occupied by a vendor presiding over mounds of pigeon peas or groundnuts or pots of fried mopane worms, which he had taken for pots of tiny pretzels the first time he'd seen them. There were vendors selling mealie porridge from washtubs, two vendors today, doing okay. The crowds were thickening. There were beggars around, more these days than before. Some informal system of regulation kept them confined to the forecourt of the main post office and the sinister alleys that pierced the mall rampart at intervals, connecting that mall to the parking strip that ran between the outer face of the mall buildings and the surrounding arterial roads. Beggars in Gaborone weren't aggressive. They didn't trail along after their targets or cluster around them the way beggars did in West Africa. They stayed put, looking piteous, which they were, holding out their cupped hands. They were orderly.

There was always something worth noting going on in the plaza, even if it was only something as minor as a new face in the team manning the Botswana Social Front's literature table. It made things easier that there was only one significant opposition party in the country to keep track of, and that they were so artless. There were two people running BoSo's table today and he knew who both of them were. The table was in a new location, a better location. Before, they had been by the walkway running past the Capitol Cinema, in the sun. Today they were in a shady alcove next to Botswanacraft. It would have to be seen how long the permission for that lasted.

He turned to go back. There was no time to climb the grand stairway that led from the plaza up to the second-floor terrace café of the President Hotel. It was loud but pleasant up there, under the awning.

It was an open balcony-terrace and you could survey the whole plaza.

In the old days someone from one branch or another of the South African security services had almost always been undercover there from noon through seven. You could set your watch by the Boers. How it would work now was going to be interesting. He liked the terrace, whose staircase had been useful to him for crisscross quick-turnover message drops more than once. For old times' sake he went up the broad steps as far as the first quarter turn and for luck touched the pediment of the newel lamp mounted just where you would put your hand for steadiness if you were hurrying. It was easy to slip something into or out of the slot under the base of the lamp particularly if you planned the crisscross for a moment when the stairs would be packed.

The Capitol Cinema opposite the President Hotel across the plaza was considered magnificent by most of the population. It was still the only movie palace in the entire country. The presidential family had a box permanently reserved for it. The theater was the size of a hangar and its facade glittered with bits of mica and broken glass. A problem was that the atmosphere and protocol established in the audiences who attended the kung fu movies that ran six days out of seven carried over when pictures like *Tess of the D'Urbervilles* or *Chariots of Fire* were being shown. Then the foregathered serious expat moviegoing public would be in a state of agony as, say, displays of sadness by white characters were being hugely jeered at. But the Capitol Cinema had its usefulnesses, too. The permanent uproar made it a good place to meet.

For a while the Libyans had used the popcorn seller to pass interesting items to certain people, including a handgun, which unfortunately had spilled out onto the floor along with the popcorn at the feet of a local constable when somehow the recipient of the gun was tripped up by person or persons unknown. He thought O Libya, Libya, give up. There were so many stories about the absurd Libyans that would never be told.

He had to get going.

He was nervous. Admittedly he was nervous. I have this feeling, Iris had said, I have this feeling of wanting to apologize to the world. Then there had been a baffling discussion that he had not been in need of.

He entered the American Library. There would be a wait. Lillian, the librarian, was occupied. The library was empty. He sat down at a reading table, on one of the tubular chairs whose Naugahyde seats were the precise color of Pepto-Bismol.

The discussion with Iris had gone weirdly. When she said she wanted to apologize to the world did world mean social world or natural world, the earth? She wasn't sure, but mainly she had meant the natural world, *maybe*. The feeling was with her a lot. Well, why did she think it was? Was it vocational, which was about all he could think of, in the sense that she wasn't doing anything significant with her inner potential? . . . but that would be the social world, wouldn't it? Well yes and no, but it was more the natural world because for example every tree that you saw was a representation of something in nature *doing its best*. There was something about the environment here, she'd said. It was so difficult for everyone, for everything. It was a very severe place. Then she had introduced a discussion about the term entelechy, discussion about doing your best by your entelechy. No tree is a failure, she had said, and neither were the saplings that don't make it, they're both just trees living out their programs, do you wish I were a tree, my dear? Everything was a bucket of fishhooks lately, that he had to get something from the bottom of.

How much Lillian knew about him was open to speculation. He was pretending to read, now, while he waited.

What he meant when he thought the words *Nobody knows who I am*, which he was doing a lot lately and which had a soothing effect on him, was that anyone who judged him as wanting in any one of the several capacities he was at work in would be judging in ignorance. That was the thing. No one who knew him knew everything he was doing. In order to judge him fairly it would be necessary to know what his whole array was, which no one did, so whatever judgments were being made of him he could take with equanimity.

He was an array. He was an ensemble. He was three things, on the surface. He was a scholar who was also a teacher. But he had another subtler task, which was to vindicate the art and genius of a supreme poet, the maligned and ignored and throneless John Milton. Ray saw himself as an agent for Milton. When Auden said that when Yeats died he *became*, he Yeats, *became* his admirers, he was talking about what Ray was for Milton, too. Milton had *become* the shrinking circle of his true admirers, and they had *become* Milton. Ray was an agent for Milton because he perceived something about Milton . . . there was a secret in Milton.

So.

And then of course he was a member of an intelligence agency, but a particular kind of member. He wasn't an officer, he was contract, which meant he could go or stay, which was a sort of freedom, a good thing. He was engaged in the overall business of bringing out into the light designs that for their own usually bad reasons certain people wanted kept hidden. He would defend his country as a decent package of forces. He had thought about this to the point of exhaustion. America represented a decent package of forces. Of course all governments were evil, or had a level of evil within them, but in the case of America wasn't it fair to say that being evil was forced on it by lesser and more corrupt other governments, would-be empires, fragments of old imperialisms, thug states, actual lunatic-run states like Libya, and so on? It was his feeling that now that it was over with Russia, America could relax into its natural shape, couldn't it? And when it came to working for the agency and judging the agency itself within the scheme of things, there was the consideration that working for the agency resembled working for a giant pharmaceutical more than anything else. Sometimes the pharmaceutical giant got it wrong. It put out the Dalkon Shield, say. But the overall effect of the pharmaceutical was to provide help against disease and suffering, wasn't it? So there it was. And of course he was a patriot. He exchanged his automobile magazine for a copy of the *Partisan Review*.

It was a good idea to review all this because there was not the slightest doubt he was going to be put through one of Iris's great inquests, in which the foundations of everything they had agreed to do together would be excavated. A point she'd needed to understand was that each of the kinds of work he did depended on the others. It was a conglomerate. He knew all the questions that were looming up: Why were they still in Botswana or anywhere in Africa, for that matter? Couldn't he teach in the U.S. so that she could pursue some kind of career, could be near her friends and her sister? What exactly was it he did for the agency beyond the little he had been willing to tell her, and didn't she have the right to know a few details, for example how much danger might he conceivably get into, and so on, like that. And he would have to swear again that he had never killed anyone.

So another great inquest was coming. He could feel it in his bones. These things were cyclical and got more harrowing each time, but undoubtedly the collapse of Russia, the astonishing collapse of all that power, was telling her it was the moment to dismiss what he did, did for the agency. He knew what she was thinking. She was thinking that the war was over, the game was over, so he could flap his wings and relocate

his talents, which she mistook for something they never were . . . probably his fault . . . but take his talents and liberate them in some venue she
would like much better. She was feeling that for the first time she had on
her side historical argument he would be forced to agree with.

In his work for the agency he was an *array*, too. Because he was more
than a collector. In the course of providing useful information he produced art. He was a writer. Back in McLean at the Biographic Registry,
they knew it. They called what he wrote Profiles, but he called what he
wrote Lives. He knew that his Lives had been used, at one time, as examples during agent training. Blessed Marion Resnick had said so. And he
knew it from others. And his Lives existed materially and would be kept
and someday might even be found, when the true history of the world
was written, but that wasn't important. No matter what kind of cretin
took over some station or other temporarily, his Lives would slide past
him and into the chute and into the archives and there would always or
someday be someone to see what they were. It was probably happening
occasionally now, as people referred to them for one utilitarian reason or
another. He had access to unique materials and had been given unique
latitude and he was turning his reports into something of clear literary
merit, something more important than their immediate function. Marion
had understood the art in what he produced because Marion was civilized. But enough on that. Except that Iris didn't appreciate what it meant
to him, the ways in which it was right for him as an artist. He had given
her Aubrey's *Brief Lives* to read, once, and she had never finished it. Basically, what he wrote went straight to posterity, is the way he liked to think
about it, without needing to be nastily reviewed in the *Washington Post*,
say, or the *New Republic*. And there was no being overlooked when the
prizes came out, no sweating over grant applications, no begging for the
attention of literary agents, no being remaindered . . . He sighed heavily,
drawing a look from Lillian.

Where was Boyle?

But an inquest was coming. Fortunately, she loved him. She always
returned to the subject of why he had gotten involved with the agency in
the first place, and he was always fairly frank about it. At the start, a lot of
it had probably been the being asked, solicited, by someone he respected,
a genuine scholar, someone for whom it was obvious there was no contradiction between the agency and everything that high, humane scholarship was supposed to mean. But ninety percent of it, he thought, was his
sheer aversion to mystery, and that went with his curiosity about how
things worked in the world, and he would definitely talk more to Iris

about that. Knowing how power worked was a form of power. It was
seductive. She loved him.

There was a lot to say on the subject. He had an earned right to object
to the mysterious. His childhood had been warped by mystery. Why his
own brother hated him so violently was a mystery. What had given Rex
the right, Rex who was younger, the right to always call him a baby,
repeatedly? There were other examples. His father had died mysteriously. He had driven their Hudson into a tree in Contra Costa County,
not far from the eastern end of the tunnel that goes through the Berkeley
Hills. The accident site had been an approach road to one of the parks in
that area, probably Tilden, so why his father had been going fast on it,
fast enough to somehow lose control and crash, was mysterious. It had
been foggy but not that foggy. And there had been a mystery guest in the
car, a young man, at least that was what the first guy on the scene had
reported. There had been a shaken-up young guy in the car, who left the
scene of the accident during the time it took for the motorist who found
the crash to hunt up the police. The theory was that the young guy must
have been a hitchhiker. He was never found. That had been it. His father
had been lavishly insured, as it developed, so that the family got to feel
guilty at being better off with him gone than they had been before, which
had been nice for them. And then his mother's almost instant remarriage,
or engagement, rather, and then remarriage, had been mysterious, marrying a mystery man who picked her up at her own husband's funeral, a
guy who had wandered into the wrong service, supposedly. His father's
service had been held in one of the massive funeral homes where there
would be four or five funerals going on at once, and Milo had taken a
wrong turn and ended up standing in the back at the wrong funeral and
being struck dumb by the widow's beauty. Milo had been younger than
his mother. And he knew the lawyer who was managing the insurance
claim, they'd found out much later, at a point when no one but Ray
thought that was interesting in any way at all. Then there had been the
long so-called engagement and then, bingo, the marriage. Milo had been
a surety agent, as he preferred to be referred to, rather than bail bondsman, which is what he was. In fact he had been the leading bail bondsman
in San Francisco, very successful, with franchises operating in Modesto,
Sacramento, and San Diego. There was money. His mother had adapted
completely to Milo, but *overnight* adapted to someone who carried a
snubnosed revolver and from the neck up looked more like the comic
strip character Mandrake the Magician than anything else, with his
slicked-back hair and pencil mustache. Where in hell had he come from,

really? After they got married they went on vacations incessantly. And mysteriously Milo had liked Rex, and hated *him*, a complete reversal of the existing sibling-preference situation, caused by nothing he could think of that he'd done, nothing. He'd continued being earnestly himself, so far as he could reconstruct. He still wondered if there are funeral gigolos, a type, certain types who go to funerals on the off chance they can get next to the widow. In any case, next it was Milo shot to death in his office by somebody who was never caught.

That was almost sensationally mysterious. And then it had turned out that Milo was also insured to the hilt. And then, mystery of mysteries, his mother, now ensconced with a certain amount of splendor in a deluxe retirement community in Corte Madera, had, after a lifetime of inaction, taken up golf, at which she had become stellar. She played in tournaments for senior women amateurs and won trophies regularly. Her face appeared on magazines! Her whole life, now, was golf. And she had been *actively mocking* about sports of all kinds, as far back as he could remember. He could still hear her distinctive, hacking laugh. Her attitude had even been influential with him, to tell the truth. He had never really cared about sports.

Possibly Iris could find it in herself to be understanding about his developing an interest in the *linings* of things at a tender age. Of course she already knew a lot of this.

So.

So there Ray was, if you could find him, in one or another of the communicating cabinets that he constituted or that constituted him. And he had even left out a part of the array of cabinets. He knew why he had left it out. First, it was hard to articulate, and anyway it was nobody's business. Secondly, it was a late part of the array. It was wrong to say it was new. But it had come to him in thunder recently and not, he hoped, just because Iris was getting labyrinthine and unhappy. This part of the array was himself as a perfect husband, to trivialize it, or as Compleat Husband preferably, except that Rex had contaminated even the most playful mental use of capitals for him. Thank you very much, he thought. But it was like this . . . in saving himself he had been saving Iris in the only way, an admittedly complex way, the only way he had been able to figure out.

It came to him then that probably one of the best things, or at least one of the simplest good things, you could do with your mortal life would be to pick out one absolutely first-rate deserving person and do everything you could conceive of in the world to make her happy, as best you might, and never be an adversary on small things, be more forthcoming than might be comfortable for you, hide anger and even justified irritation . . . always *wait* sexually . . . and think of Thomas Wyatt and *Patiens shall be my song*. It was right.

And the idea was to let this single flower bloom without notifying her of what was going on. Because it would be on the order of a present because it was only fair reciprocation for someone who enthralled you and who had incidentally saved you from your demons. Or the idea was to so charge her life with his appreciation that some morning she would sit up and say What the fuck is going on with us, I am so happy. The idea was to let this single flower bloom until it was something monstrous, like an item in a Max Ernst collage, something that fills the room and the occupant says *Oh, this is you, this is you, my beloved friend, my love, now I see*, something along those lines. He was going to float her in love and she would be like those paper flowers that open up. Water rising around her. She didn't know about him that he could get an erection just thinking in passing about her and that on one occasion he had had to claim he was having a hamstring problem, sitting facing Boyle was when it had happened, sitting facing Boyle and saying Ow and massaging his Achilles tendon so he could sit there until it was decent to get up. Boyle was divorced, or rather separated, since he was a Roman Catholic. He was in some null state with his wife, was the story. A lot of regular officers in the agency were divorced. A divorce would kill Ray. Maybe the evaporation of Russia would make this easier. He wasn't sure what he meant, unless it was that a certain pressure had gone out of that sector of his work. He couldn't believe it was over with the Russians, leaving only bullshit antagonists on the horizon, it looked like now. Maybe they could all relax some. And the joke of it was that Russia had gone up in mist not because of anything the agency had done, really. The agency had been amazed, startled. All this would probably never lead to a verbal event, where she says Good God, I seem to be floating in love. It would be enough if she just thought it, or something like it. No, he had been too average in his attitude and all that toward her in the past, and now he knew it and so would she, soon enough, although she would feel it before she truly knew it, but he was repeating himself. So this would be his new secret work. It would be like adding, say, potted blue hyacinths, one pot at a time, to a shelf or a ledge in the living room, one at a time, until the atmosphere was paradisiacal.

.   .   .

Lillian was looking at him with a kind of horrified expression. He must have been talking to himself. He needed to concentrate on Boyle, who was certainly taking his time.

When Boyle had taken over, all the procedures had changed. The flexibility had gone out of the relationships, his with Boyle, at least. He assumed it was the same for the others. All the irony went away, what there had been. Boyle's mission seemed to be that everyone needed to be reminded that all their activities were life and death, at some level. The cover at this embassy for the chief of station was consular officer. It always had been. And with Marion it had been perfectly okay to pop by upstairs on ostensible school business, say to discuss arrangements for student scholarships in the U.S. that the consular office had a lot to do with, pop in and talk about the real stuff, his assignments, how they were going. Marion had always let him read the Foreign Press Intelligence Summary cables that kept piling up. Now all that was dead. When he turned things in, Boyle never had much to say. Calls at the consular office had to be based on dire emergency only.

Now there was a whole new drill around seeing Boyle face to face. The embassy, a narrow three-story building, looked outward onto the parking lot flanking the mall. The American Library was built into the side of the embassy building and opened on one of the alleys that cut through from the parking lot to the concourse itself. The American Library had always been a physically separate entity. Somehow Boyle had arranged for the construction of a secret spiral staircase, housed in a tube stairwell, to connect his second-floor offices to the library's inmost conference room. In fact, the old conference room in the rear had been divided in half for the purpose of creating a new, secret meeting place for Boyle's use. Boyle's access to the room was by way of a secret panel rather than a conventional doorway. Ray had never seen Boyle enter or exit the back cubicle. He was always in place, set to go, when Ray was let in. There was a new keypad lock on the door to the main conference room, and two keypads for the lock on the inner door. Ray had the combination to the first door only. Lillian had to punch him through. He understood that the tube stairwell was a tight fit for Boyle, which wouldn't be surprising. Boyle tended to look flushed, often, when they met in back. In fact, he always did.

A few Batswana students had come in to read magazines. Ray wanted to get started with Boyle, but nothing was happening. Finally there was a signal. Lillian murmured something to Ray about picking up the photocopies he had come for. That was standard. He was glad to be leaving the reading room because a fine, gnawing, sourceless hum hung in the air, and something smelled powerfully of solvent. Lillian was thin, cold, and officious. She was a Motswana. She had studied library science in the United States. She had been posted to Dar es Salaam prior to coming home. She was about forty, he guessed. He always skipped offering her the traditional greetings, unless there were Batswana present, because he had gotten the distinct impression that she regarded the act as being condescending. Looking at her now, he wondered if Lillian was a genuine Motswana. She was very Nilotic, very elongated, with what the Batswana call "long eyes." She had arrived in the country simultaneously with Boyle.

Boyle looked like a composite. His body from neck to hips was pyramidal. There was a fat-distribution problem. His face tended to gauntness. He had once been much fatter, judging by the loose skin of his underjaw that hung like a keel fin from chin to throat. He would tug on this when he was annoyed with himself, Ray had noted. From a distance, Boyle's face had a healthy look, but the Celtic ruddiness in his cheeks, seen close-up, came from concentrated traceries of broken capillaries. He was in his early fifties. His rather golden hair was worn crewcut and was dense, like lawn. His eyebrows, too, were blond and dense, tousled, the right eyebrow interrupted by a vertical blank space, a scar, evidence of some encounter threatening to his eye, and a little intimidating, as all facial scars hinting at personal combat tended to be. His eyes were blue, a dull blue. Boyle was supposed to be a Knight of Malta, if that meant anything. Ray recognized for what it was Boyle's soft, heavily manipulative style of speech. Boyle would drift into speaking so softly at certain times that Ray would be forced into asking him to repeat something, which made Ray look bad instead of Boyle, of course. The point of speaking unduly softly was to keep the listener in a state of tense hyperattention and, in Boyle's case, to keep him subject to the startle effect produced by the occasional shout or loud groan of disgust.

Lillian had ushered him to the conference room. He looked away, up at the ceiling, while Lillian pressed the combinations in. That was the protocol. He entered the conference room and closed the door behind him. Ludicrously, a panel in the wall of the conference room slid open. He passed through, into the secret space.

Boyle was there. The room was more a cubicle than a room. The blond oval conference table was stupidly oversized, given the dimensions of the cubicle. Fluorescent panels overhead provided dull, even light. Ray took his seat, facing Boyle across the widest part of the table. Boyle's chair was thronelike. Ray had a folding chair. Weak airconditioning was at work. Boyle's thick hands were at rest on a folder in front of him.

Ray had fantasized about doing a Life of this man. He could do a classic. Boyle was a field of signs indicating that he probably thought of his physical emanations as very bad things. He used a cologne and an aftershave. The two scents were separable. He used breath pastilles once or twice during every meeting. His nails were groomed. His nostrils were hairless and scoured-looking.

Boyle nodded, but before Ray could say anything Boyle opened his folder and began writing something on a sheet of paper inside it.

Ray waited. Boyle was mostly faithful to the Western business dress mode, to suits and ties, which was possible for him because he existed in an unbroken regime of airconditioning. His BMW was airconditioned. Boyle dressed expensively. His only apparent concession to the climate of Africa was that he wore, on occasion, peculiar mesh shirts with stiff collars, still technically dress shirts, of a kind Ray had never seen on any other human being.

It was Ray's idea that another key to Boyle's presentation of self was a need he felt to project physical threat, to remind you that he was a True Man. True Men could hurt you, physically. True Men needed you to keep it in mind that they are caged panthers. But Boyle, at least since the onset of his weight or glandular problem, was not going to be credibly able to imply in any way that he might be able to spring at you if you offended him. But he was used to having the power to do that, so he had shifted the threat to things that he did with his face, his eyes, his voice. The idea was to prevent the rise of any notion that Boyle was, in fact, only a former True Man. This was reminding him of discussions with his mother on the subject of manhood, true manhood.

Boyle kept writing.

Ray observed that they had finally gotten around to carpeting the cubicle. The rug was the color of celery.

Ray reminded himself to be smart about how he put things to Boyle today. He might throw in a little jargon, for example. Boyle loved team talk and Ray avoided it. Marion Resnick had shared his ironical attitude toward it. If he wanted to cinch getting Boyle's okay for making Morel a person of interest, it might behoove Ray to throw some jargonese at him.

Boyle was writing and writing.

When it came to team language, there was a lot of it. How up to date he was was also a question. *Radish* meant a left group that the agency had created from the ground up. *Hull* was a more generic term and applied to groups under control, of whatever political complexion. Sources who gave you information for their own reasons and without accepting any kind of payment were called *chums*. In the old days the term for someone under control through the mechanism of blackmail was *orphan*. He hated this language. Then there were the noms de guerre certain agents were known by, certain agents who were specialists, dangerous people. There was the Seraph. There was the Cat in the Hat. Boyle ate and drank this pulp aspect of the agency, you could tell. *Skit* was the term for a major operation, something world-shaking, something where specialists took over. Skits were rare and had nothing to do, usually, with the contract arm, for which he thanked God. Skits were for line officers, specialists, and, a lot of the time, proxies from friendly other services. Skits were not his province. He had never seen one.

Ray couldn't believe what was happening. But he had to be steady and he needed to be pleasant while this was happening to him, because those were the rules and he had to be able to act if some notion of how to undo this should come to him. One thing Boyle did that Marion never had was to announce at the start of every meeting just how long you had. Boyle had given him twenty minutes and more than half of that was gone and there had to be enough time within the twenty minutes for Ray to get paid. It was payday.

Boyle was saying no to making Davis Morel a person of interest. He was being adamant. He seemed to be saying that it was no, even to making him a provisional person of interest, which was unheard of if the case being made was as strong as his was.

It was taking a chance, but Ray decided he had to put the proposition to Boyle again, from a slightly different angle. Whatever I thought was interesting, Marion thought was interesting, which let me in for moments like this, that eat shit.

Ray put it conditionally. "If I wrote him up it wouldn't have to be a full-dress thing. I can keep it crisp. And I could drop it if it turns out to look like what you say it is. It would be a probe, or a preprobe, you'd be authorizing."

Boyle shook his head.

What Ray couldn't believe, especially, was that Boyle the ultra, Boyle the Knight of Malta, was uninterested in what looked like it might be the start of a Pagan Liberation Front. Why was he uninterested in a fount of irreligion being set up? Maybe Ray had to broaden his picture of the stain that might spread from Morel if nobody stanched it and so on and so forth.

Ray went on. "Summing it up, it goes like this. You have this character and you know he has some kind of definite campaign in mind. We see the offprints he has ready to go. We see these handout cards. And the evidence is pretty good that he's planning to make tapes. He brought a shitload of blank cassette tapes with him. We know that. So that even the illiterates can get the message.

"Even if the only question we had about him was who in hell he thinks he is, it would be worth getting the answer. But anyway. There's also the list of peculiar names he had. Well, as I told you, I did figure out what that is. It's a list of South American tribes exterminated by the Christian soldiers of Spain, just in one part of South America. So the implication is pretty clear. Africa has tribes, Botswana has tribes, the white man cometh, you see the point. It's a litany of murdered tribes. It's not so hard to imagine where this kind of fragment might fit in, is it? By the way the list comes from a book called *Land Without Evil*, and the guy who wrote it was a Brit who was friendly with the KGB.

"So okay, and the operation he has in mind, from what little we know from this distance, the operation has the potential to get *all* the religious groups in the country upset, once they hear about it. The Muslims are already upset, for other reasons. And don't forget that this character is going to be identified as what he is, one of us, an American, which may be something we don't particularly need on our plate, this part-time Antichrist being one of us."

Ray was going on too long and he knew it, but he couldn't make himself stop. He had to put everything out. He hated the slings and arrows of staircase wisdom. Also it was getting to be so tough to get face to face with Boyle that he had to seize the moment. Boyle wasn't liking this, which wasn't fine. But he had to lay it all out.

Ray said, "Another piece of this, and I'm sure you know all about it, is that Doctor Morel has two patients in the cabinet. The Secretary for the Office of the President and the Minister of Local Government and Lands. You know, we're not the only people in Gaborone aware of this. Everybody knows it. You mention Morel's name and people tell you how he saved Montshwa, or rather how first he saved Fabius and then Montshwa. They were in the delegation that went to Boston. This is the story that's around. Fabius had some sort of leg problem and somebody sent him to Morel. And then Montshwa's back seized up and Fabius had liked Morel so much he brought Montshwa to him and the rest is history. They walk, they run, they dance . . ."

"*Lookit*," Boyle said, hard, which only showed Ray how long Boyle must have been out of contemporary U.S. culture. Lookit was a class-descriptor . . . lower class, and anyway it was long out of use. Even he knew that. Of course now Boyle was trying to be hard with him.

"Now lookit," Boyle said. "None of this *matters*, and . . ."

Ray interrupted. "Wait, I'm not saying this character is Rasputin or Stephen Ward. I don't think he is. But. But. Wait, I lost my train of thought. I think it was . . . he just gets here, he hardly gets here and he has friends in high places and people are noticing him and . . . sorry, I lost it."

"Lookit," Boyle said.

Again Ray stopped him. "Wait, before I forget this . . . I didn't mention this before and you might want to consider it.

"Okay, let's set aside all the friends in high places and think about this. I mentioned how one of the subjects our friend seems interested in agitating around is circumcision. I did mention it, didn't I? But what I didn't mention is bogwera.

"Bogwera is a ritual. See, at one time the Tswana circumcised their young men in these bogwera camps when they reached puberty. Well the tradition died down until very recently and now it's coming back, the same as traditional medicine is. It's part of a cultural revival. You can read notices announcing bogwera camps in *Dikgang*. They're big.

"Right, so someone coming out saying that circumcision is for idiots is not going to be popular. I mean, my guess is that the arguments that are going to be made against it are going to be that it's medically stupid, primarily. And there's one more point, just quickly, about circumcision, which is that most of the Tswana tribes, maybe all of them, used to do it, but the Zulus, and there are a lot of Zulus in the mix in this country, some of them doing quite well, and the Zulus don't do it, they think it's stupid. There's bad blood, historically, over the issue between the Xhosas, of which there are plenty here, especially around Mahalapye, and the Zulus. And this was because Shaka stopped circumcising his guys because it took them out of circulation just when they should be getting into shape for warmaking. The Xhosas actually see the Zulus as unclean because of it. It's serious. Down in the Republic it's part of the problem between the Zulus in Inkatha and the ANC, which is mostly Xhosa. Anyway, we have both groups intermingled up here. So potentially any kind of open campaigning on the issue is going to be inflammatory in a number of directions. You see my point."

Ray was parched. There was never ever anything to drink available in the room. He realized that the room had been made smaller by the newly installed soundproofing that Boyle had ordered. Ceiling and walls were now covered with porous sheathing, a good idea if Boyle was going to have free use of his shouting option. The room ate sound. That was why Ray was parched. It was voice-strain. He should always get a drink of water before he saw Boyle.

Boyle's long, slow sigh was meant to say that Ray was being taxing. That was fine. He had said everything he could. Ray gathered himself.

Boyle began. "Okay, let me just say it so you understand it. I don't give a fuck about this chiropractor. Wait till he sees it here. I know these guys who want to save the world, believe me I know them. This fucker will go home in six months when he sees it here. More like six weeks. This is some kind of prima donna who thinks he's too good to be a fucking chiropractor, so he decides he should be some stupid intellectual savior instead. I know him. Don't bother me with people like this shithead. This guy is black. He was living in Cambridge, for Christ's sake, so wait until he sees it here. Cape Town, someplace like that, he might end up in, not here. With these black characters it's a romantic black bourgeoisie thing about Africa and it takes about six weeks until they say uh-oh. Cambridge, Boston, places you can have a lot of fun. Believe me I know enough about this character to know he means *nothing* to us, and I mean nothing, zero, zero squared. These cards he's going to hand out. I wish I could be there and see the expression on the faces over at the takeaway. It's a joke. Believe me that this is a guy who likes to eat out. He was living on the best street in Cambridge. I know his story. He was up against all the local geniuses they have around Cambridge. So out here he's the biggest genius around. Fuck him. It's a safari, believe me. Over here in the bulrushes he's going to be Moses, a light to the nations, whatever. This is a man with his head up his own ass and finding it very interesting in there, very interesting, gee."

Boyle carried a menthol inhaler which he dug out now and applied to his nostrils.

Boyle went on. "Believe me, when he was in Cambridge what he was was a chiropractor. Now he comes over here and he's the light of the world. But tell me something. Why didn't the light of the world write a book instead? He never published a thing, so far as I know. Why not? Believe me when I say this guy is going to self-destruct. Besides I know twenty ways to get him out of here if he fucks around to any degree. I don't need to know a thing about this guy I don't already know. I . . ."

Ray couldn't help himself. He broke in again.

"Yeah, but you're leaving out Fabius and Montshwa. They swear by him. What about his protection? What about . . ."

Boyle said, "You know, words fail me with you. There is no protection I can't break. You don't know a thing about what I can do. I don't mean to beat up on your idea, but I don't think you understand a lot of things you should."

New times! Ray thought. Boyle was normally laconic, and laconic at a completely standard middle-class level of word choice. He was playing a rougher class. The profanity, or the profusion of it, was new times too. There was more of it than was necessary to make Boyle's point, which was that he was tough at the core, so watch out. And there was no way for Ray to miss the implications of Boyle's allusions to academics as pains in the ass and problems in general for the true heroes of the world—the hard men, the practical men, less overeducated men like Boyle himself.

"So then you don't want me to pursue this in any way."

"Shape or form. No."

"Even if I pick up something."

"No. Nope. Don't pick anything up. Don't. Don't touch him, don't think about him, don't have dreams about him. I'm sorry if you think he's fascinating. He isn't. Anyway there's somebody else I need you for, if I can ever get to it.

"Also, and this is a minor thing, but this is the way I want it, I don't want anything on paper necessarily, from you. Unless you want to come in here and write it here and hand it straight in. I guess that would be okay except that it ties up the room. I guess we could try it. The fact is what I would prefer, and I think we are going to get to this, is for you to come in when you have something and just tape it here. Put it on a tape, it's the fastest way. You can abbreviate. What I don't want is you working on profiles on paper outside this room, because you know and I know what can happen. Now. I understand it's not going to be as polished. It's not the same thing writing it in here out of your head or taping it. But I don't want you hit by a truck and there is all this interesting *material*, you know, in your backpack. I don't want that. The people here do not know how to drive. I love them but they cannot fucking drive. Maybe in fifty years. And I know how careful you are and how you keep all your notes safe when you write. I know all that. I know you have your burn box, I know you always use it. But I want to get away from paper."

Ray felt his face getting hot. It was possible he had brought this on himself by fighting to get Morel. That would mean it was a punishment that might be reversed at some point, if he what, if he what, if he could think of something to get it reversed, like what? Boyle was dropping back into his more middle-class presentation of self, showing collegiality now. Everything is a trap, Ray thought.

Boyle wouldn't stop. "I see your stuff and your stuff is beautiful, I grant you. And Marion told me all about it and how they love it at McLean. I looked at your file and it's beautiful. You know. So I don't say categorically don't write, but it has to be in *here*, and how you can fit that in I don't venture to say. You need to shorten up anyway, if you want to write. But the fact is that if I have it on tape I can do something else while I listen. You know. I have my problems with time the same as you do. Whatever I need to do I can do. I can replay if I need to. I can listen to you on the can and get two things done at once. You know. And. We might make an exception and you could tape either here or in back, sometimes, upstairs. I could fix it up as an exception. Part of it is that I have more stuff I have to read than I can handle. I'm buried in it. So as I say we're definitely going to tape only, fairly soon. It makes sense because you get more on tape faster and anyway we can go from tape to text through a machine if we need an extract."

I need to comprehend this, Ray thought. If he thinks he can make me quit with this shit I have news for him because patiens shall be my song: He may have been lying about Morel, why Morel is nothing to us, or he may not, why would he though? . . . I can't think in here.

From left to right on the table in front of Ray were an open pack of Rothman's brand cigarettes and a pale blue desk blotter in a leatherette holder, on which rested the file folder Boyle had brought. Boyle's thick hands rested overlapped on the folder, right hand on top, Boyle's absurd involved gold Knights of Malta ring, if that's what it was, gleaming on his middle finger. It was impossible not to be curious about what the ring meant, *but* it was also impossible to show you were curious because that meant you were someone unable to place such a ring, correctly identify its provenance, the device on it. So the task was not to fixate on it while it glinted away at you, big, big enough to have a secret compartment, like a Borgia ring. Boyle was waiting for him to assent, Boyle invariably had an open pack of cigarettes on display. It was there as a memento mori, in a way, and signified that time was fleeting and that Boyle couldn't wait to get upstairs and have a smoke. There was no smoking in the conference room. There were no ashtrays. You always knew you were keeping Boyle from having a smoke. You were intended to remember that, because it would keep you crisp and succinct.

Ray thought, I hate your fucking face, and said, "We can manage this. I um I appreciate . . . your time problems . . . your . . ." Then he didn't know what else to say. This is obedience, he thought.

"We're fine," Boyle said, just as Ray said, "No we're fine." Ray was embarrassed.

Boyle appreciated obedience, and was showing he did, Ray understood, by considerately opening the folder he was pushing toward him and swinging it around so that Ray could begin reading immediately. Boyle relapped his hands, this time with his ring hand underneath, his seal of power withdrawn, a sign of collegiality restored because Ray was being good. All of Boyle's inlays were gold, Ray had noted during one of the few times he had experienced Boyle laughing at something. He had no idea why that had come back to him.

Ray opened the folder, acutely aware that it behooved him to show there and then that he could absorb like a demon. He had to be in control. He had to kill his grievances for the time being, but truly kill them, including the recurrent feeling that life was just one goddamned unannounced test after another, which hurt because given the state of the world, he had a right to relax, they all did, the entire agency, not only himself.

The subject was a Motswana, Samuel Kerekang, forty, single, recently returned to the country after a protracted, successful, and, reading between the lines, heroic pursuit of a doctorate in civil engineering from the University of Edinburgh no less.

His hatred of Boyle was interfering. An itch between his shoulder blades began to gnaw. Another thing about the new improved inner sanctum he was trapped in with Boyle was that it was hotter than before, despite the fact that it was supposedly served by the same airconditioning system that cooled the rest of the installation. He was seeing himself as the assistant who gets into the slotted box the magician pushes swords through from every conceivable angle, and who has to defeat the tangle of swords through sheer contortionism.

Boyle was watching him read, watching him rather than turning to some little piece of makework as a courtesy, such as reading something himself. Maybe it was possible Boyle would change as time went on. He was not completely unadaptable. Somehow he had figured out that he should stop wearing the stupid bolo ties he had showed up in during the transition with Resnick. Maybe Resnick had said something. And he had stopped going around in the totally inappropriate guayaberas he had brought with him from Central America, flimsy things that let his mat of chest hair show like a dark shield, dark not blond or red blond like his hair, by the way. Without looking up to check, he knew that Boyle was studying him.

The room was oppressive, its windowlessness especially. He was seized with the desire to tell Boyle something he wouldn't want to hear, to wit, that everybody knew his secure room had a secret connection to the embassy upstairs. Somebody with the contractors had let it out. So Boyle had created a farce, like a set for a farce on a stage, French farce with doors opening and closing and people popping in and out. It struck Ray that this was a piece of true intelligence, a secret blown, true news.

Ray was finding Kerekang admirable, so far. His odyssey through various polytechnics in the U.K., the struggle for bursaries, and his final triumph at the University of Edinburgh, it was all admirable. The man was a prize, from the standpoint of the country, a jewel. This is pointless, he thought.

Softly, and as though in passing, Ray said, "At some point I may come back to Morel . . ." He waited for a murmur, a grunt, anything, from Boyle, but nothing came, only a penetrating silence. My life is important, Ray thought, appearances notwithstanding. He read harder. Boyle would give him nothing.

The feeling of confinement afflicting him came as a surprise, because, so far as he knew, he was especially resistant to that problem, judging by his occasional misadventures in tight places like crawl spaces and closets. Boyle would be amazed to know that Ray wanted to approve of him. It was a general rule of life that things went better if you liked whomever fate happened to give you as your boss. So now Boyle was launched on a program to make that permanently impossible.

He was dealing with a miscellany, not a coherent, unified profile. Even so, all he would normally need was one pass at a collection like this. But something there was that didn't want him to perform. He was retaining proper names, but not much more. He was going to have to reread, selectively and only a little, but it was still rereading, which Boyle would detect. This was a rag rug. He had to hurry. There was a stopwatch feature on Boyle's Rolex. This ragbag he had been handed was one more test, Ray thought.

Various British entities had been tracking Kerekang, MI5 and an office Ray had never heard of in the Overseas Development Ministry, but there were also some data from American sources. There was a skimpy contri-

bution from the American consulate in Edinburgh. The American interest had to be explained by Kerekang's two trips to the University of
Michigan at Lansing for special certificate study. The prose in the biodata piece was laughable, below the level usually found in the most routine profiling done by political-economic officers in American embassies.
Apparently the British were losing their grip on the English language as
fast as the colonials were. He was still failing to see what was wrong with
Kerekang. The transcripts showed good to very good academic performance. Naturally there were gaps in the transcripts for the periods when
Kerekang had been forced to pause and get work. And he had managed to
find work, off the books, piecework tailoring for dry cleaning establish-
ments. So there was another skill the man had. The fact that he had gotten work off the books was noted without comment. To Ray, it only
demonstrated tenacity and ingenuity. Kerekang had taken a six-week
course in barbering in one of the interstices in his odyssey, so presumably
he had picked up extra change cutting the hair of other students. There
were periods for which there seemed to be no documentation on
Kerekang whatever, but they hardly added up to the Lost Years of Jesus.
He didn't see anything sinister. And they could be artifacts of the reporting process, such as it was, easily.

"We want him," Boyle said.

Ray didn't reply. He needed Boyle to be quiet. He hated Boyle and he
didn't want Boyle to explain what he meant by wanting Kerekang. That
could mean several things. He was going to interpret it as meaning that
they wanted leverage, ultimately, on this poor, hardworking devil, who
had lived over a fishmonger's shop in Edinburgh for his last two years
there, which must have been fun. Somebody had gone around to check
out his lodgings. The top floors of the building were described as a war-
ren of tiny rooms let exclusively to foreign students. The author of the
report had taken the trouble to note that the owner of the building was a
Jew, a fact not necessarily revealed by the landlord's last name, which was
Brown.

Why was Kerekang not a pearl of great price? He wanted to tell Boyle
that Kerekang represented a truth about Botswana he was probably
unaware of, which was that some huge percentage of Batswana sent
abroad for advanced training returned to the country when their studies
were over. People wanted to come back. The Batswana liked Botswana.
They were patriots. And they seemed to like each other. This dry, peculiar country, who could love it? But they did, and they mostly came back

to be there. There was something in the social nexus, something there, comity, something, We stand outside it, Ray thought. Boyle has no idea he is outside anything . . . He thinks information gets him inside, I hate his fucking face, he knows nothing, he is destroying me: These people *do* like each other . . . Well, there are certain exceptions . . . They don't like the Bakalanga that much, and they think the Bushmen are a nuisance . . . There are always exceptions. Nothing is perfect, he thought.

Boyle was chewing another pastille. Ray could hear it cracking.

The material on Kerekang's Botswana background was between thin and pathetic, although it did contain the information that Kerekang was a graduate of St. James's, before Ray's time. Otherwise there was only paucity. In England Kerekang had been under mail cover. There were a few sample intercepts in the folder. A note advised that the samples were perfectly representative. The mail cover summary showed nothing out of the ordinary, with principal correspondents being family members in two locations, Chitumbe, far in the north above Maun, and Mahalapye, not so far from Gaborone, to the east. Kerekang's father, who was dead, had been from one of the senior lineages of the Tawana tribal group, a signifi-cant man, apparently. Kerekang's mother was still alive. She was part of the Xhosa enclave in Mahalapye. Clearly there had been a divorce or separation. His mother had raised him. The marriage between a Xhosa and a Tawana from different ends of the country was odd, but such things happened. His mother operated a small general dealership in Mahalapye now, but she had previously worked as a seamstress. There was an inter-esting story somewhere in Kerekang's parental background. He used his mother's surname. Again, everything looked innocuous to Ray. It was possible, he supposed, that Kerekang was illegitimate. But that counted for nothing here.

Boyle said, "You notice he graduated from your school."

"I see that."

"He wanted to work for the government. That got fucked. Now we hear he's up to something over at the university. We don't know what. We want to know. Get whatever you can. He's been seen over there."

Ray kept reading.

Boyle said, "What I gave you, that-there, isn't everything. More's coming."

"Then that might explain something," Ray said.

"What do you mean?"

"I mean there isn't much here against the man."

Boyle didn't like it.

"Don't worry about it. There's plenty in there. Lots. And as I say, there's more. Go ahead and finish. Everything you need is in that-there. Go ahead."

Ray knew he had gone a little far, forgetting just for a second that these were new times for him. But he hadn't really forgotten. It had been a test to see if what was happening to him was in fact happening, and it was. Insubordinate was the word Boyle was wanting to apply to Ray, to his slightest and mildest gestures at shaping what was going on here. Merely proposing that they focus on Morel was going to be insubordinate of him. This may be hell, he thought.

Kerekang's political history, looked at rationally, was barely even interesting. Where was his leftness? He had been briefly a member of a British Trotskyist youth organization that no longer existed. He had been expelled from it, which, depending on the reasons for the expulsion, could easily be a recommendation for him. There was no information about the expulsion, but the likelihood was that whoever prepared the report was operating with information provided from within the youth group, otherwise it would only have been noted that Kerekang had dropped out of the group. It would have been useful to have some indication of why Kerekang had been expelled, but Ray's guess was that it had something to do with a paper critical of the Trotskyist Unity Movement in South Africa that he had produced for a political science seminar but which had gotten into other hands where it had caused umbrage. There was no copy of this paper in the folder, stupidly. On the evidence, it looked to Ray as though Kerekang had been eighty-sixed as punishment for a certain mental independence. But it had all happened seven or eight years ago in any case, and there was nothing else anywhere to suggest a subsequent physical affiliation with any kind of political organization of the left. In fact, the records of his borrowings from two university libraries showed a clear drift away from politics and into the purely technical literature surrounding his discipline, mechanical engineering, with excursions into rural sociology, ecology, African ethnology. He was on the mailing list of the Schumacher Society. Someone had given him a gift subscription to *Living Marxism*, which was read by three-quarters of the British intelligentsia, but he had allowed the subscription to lapse. His only current subscriptions were to something called the *Herald of Permaculture* and to the *Arid Lands Newsletter*, with advice on how to squeeze blood out of stones in places like the Negev. He had a real interest, according to the register of library borrowings, in Victorian poetry. He loved Browning, apparently. He loved Tennyson. Boyle might not find that endearing, but Ray did. In fact the temperament that was declaring itself in these fragments was positive. It was attractive. There was nothing to show any connection with South African liberation apparatuses, no ANC or PAC connections at all, which was in its own way a little strange. He had put up a traveling member of the Black Consciousness Movement for a week or so, in Edinburgh, but this was someone who had been in exile in Botswana for years, a personal friend, apparently longtime. And there was absolutely no sign of any connection with what passed for the left in Botswana, the MELSians, the purists of the Marx-Engels-Lenin-Stalin Society, or BoSo, the vaguer and bigger but still essentially hapless Botswana Social Front. So there was nothing, really, although it had to be said that there were so many holes in the records that it was slightly hazardous to be as definite as he felt. Where was his sex life, for example? Whatever anyone had on that was missing. Unless there was nothing, and Kerekang was a complete ascetic, a celibate, which was a little hard to believe. Ray was nearly through.

There was one last item of recent date that Boyle undoubtedly thought bore heavily on Kerekang's supposed leftness. Mounted on a separate sheet was a photocopy strip, the product of one of the new microcopiers, copiers the size of a matchbox that were very popular with the Brits, who issued them to freelance intelligence scavengers called scouts. MI5 loved the microcopiers and loved scouts, a lot of whom were graduate students. The microcopiers had been developed for scholarly use, for copying bits of text from volumes too unwieldy for normal copying or from books in delicate condition. They were popular with scholars working in restricted archives, too, and were responsible for a fair amount of protected information making its way into the light of day. The note that accompanied the strip described it as a lift from the first page of an article this scout had seen Kerekang reading in the *International Review of Social History*, Volume Five, Number One, 1960. This was not the kind of thing that would turn up in Kerekang's checkout register, obviously, because it was something he had taken off an open shelf. Some pest tracking Kerekang had dashed over when Kerekang left his reading momentarily to go to the lavatory or out for a smoke. Not for a smoke. Kerekang was not a smoker. In any case, it had been a hurried take, diagonal, picking up only a part of the title and a swatch of text below it.

KARL MAR
AND THE REVO

I

German liberals of 1848 failed
hence incapable of managing the
come dogma. We tend to suspect
because it fits the "practical re
euvering safely among existing f
ideals and hope. In his recent a
Theodore S. Hamerow has shown th
liberals of 1848 failed not becau

It was a botch, actually. It annoyed Ray to find it there. It was more nothing, or it was nothing much, although, since it was dated to 1991, it was clear Boyle was going to take it as proof that Kerekang was a closet Bolshevik at heart. There was an additional note stating that Kerekang had been observed taking copious notes as he read this particular article. And that was everything, except for the photograph.

He had saved the photograph for last for a reason. Faces influence us unduly, was the problem.

"That's him," Boyle said.

Ray picked up the identification photograph. It was a passport photo, very clear, blown up to eight by ten. Letting a photograph speak to you was an art, of sorts. You had to let whatever was in it flow out to you in the first seconds you handled it. You could call the moment metaphysical. The point was to give in to the impulse to have the image utter something. Ray thought of it as a feminine mode of perception.

He studied the photo, not getting much. Being watched made it difficult.

Boyle muttered something Ray made himself ignore.

Ray received Kerekang as a person of force and intelligence.

He looked judicious and he looked intelligent. But judiciousness he should set aside as a possible artifact, a bleed-over from his knowledge that Kerekang was an engineer and thus presumably someone with a practical intelligence. Intelligence was there, in the eyes, somehow. How you could determine intelligence by looking at the naked meat of the eye was a deep part of the mystery of faces. Its presence seemed to have nothing to do with any relationship between the eyes and the rest of the face.

Boyle was murmuring and doing something.

Kerekang looked less than forty in the photograph. He had good, symmetrical features but was probably not particularly vain, since there were two or three white hairs at either end of his toothbrush mustache that he might easily have plucked. He had a good, unlined brow. The whites of his eyes were very clear, which could mean clean living. The bridge of his nose was higher than standard for a Motswana and it looked beveled or carved, the result of a repaired break, was Ray's guess. The cut of his eyes was interesting. There was a very slight epicanthic valencing visible. The lip-line of his mustache was a little ragged, which also told against vanity. His ears were small and almost flat to the skull, the lobes curved under toward the head. There were very faint initiation scars, like cat scratches, three on each side, fanning out from the ends of his eyes. He had a good, dense head of hair, recessed over the temples about standardly for his age. There was no vanity in the haircut, no shaping—it was just evenly cropped, top and sides. Kerekang was wearing a cheap tweed jacket and a dress shirt with long collar-points, one of which was a little scrolled. The shirt was an antique. The dark knit tie he was wearing was far from new. The knot was shiny. Kerekang's skin color, Ray decided, was what he thought of as medium black. It was funny how hit or miss the description of skin color still was, although possibly in some byway of physical anthropology some crank or other had proposed some scheme for descriptive standardization. Every paint company had different proprietary names for the identical colors, whereas you would think it would be in some general commercial interest for everybody to work from the same palette, but no.

Ray closed the file and was astounded that Boyle pulled it back instantly and swept it away to one side of the table. They were about to go on to something else, immediately.

They were not going to discuss it. If Ray wanted to demur he could fuck himself, was what Boyle was demonstrating.

Ray was breathless. He thought, You come here, you cocksucker, and you do this to me: You cock*sucker:* You don't know me: You do this like you're doing some minor thing, some *nothing,* but I will get you, I will fuck you, because this is you trying to kill me, you fuck, this is what I do in my life and you don't even know me: This is *stupid,* you stupid fuck.

Boyle was going to pay him now. He had taken out an envelope and was extracting rand and pula notes from it. Today was payday.

Boyle was laying out too much in one of the two piles he was making. The buy-money pile looked correct, the usual five hundred pula and two hundred rands, but unless he was getting more small-denomination bills this time, there was too much in the pay pile.

"You get a raise," Boyle said. He slipped a rubber band around the stack of buy money, but set another rubber band down next to the pay stack, so that Ray could count it and be delighted and band it up himself.

Boyle pushed two receipts over to Ray for him to sign, which Ray did without looking at them, pretending to be in the midst of thought. Boyle would never see him count his money.

"I got you a raise," Boyle said.

Ray took out his wallet and put the buy money into it.

"You're up a notch," Boyle said.

"I am?"

"You do a lot. You give us a lot. I don't like to be cheap."

"I try."

"Yeah. We appreciate it." Boyle's yeah was turning into the Boer yah you heard everywhere in Gaborone, unless Ray was wrong. He wanted to believe it. He banded his pay stack without counting it and set it in front of him. Boyle was showing nothing, no reaction to Ray's refusal to count the money. He was keeping his face dead.

Ray thought, It's genius to injure and reward, or demote and promote, in the same stroke . . . I am dealing with a genius.

Ray put the money into his wallet, uncounted.

He thought, This is adolescent.

What he was facing was the certainty that, under Boyle, the way it had been for him with the agency was completely over. He was a writer they were turning into a clerk. He was being mechanized. Now what they wanted from him was his notes, not his finished work, but not even his notes, really. They wanted what he knew and what he could find out, but in a checklist. Boyle was grotesque. Just now, waiting for Ray to say something appropriate, to succumb nicely, Boyle had found a piece of lint on his cuff and was scrutinizing it as though it were filth and in a second he would flick it away, in disgust. I *create*, Ray thought. Boyle wanted him to go now.

Ray sat there. It was essential not to beg.

He couldn't help it. He said, "I've never, never once, the whole time I've been working, never once lost control of any material, of my material. It just couldn't happen and it never has happened. I've never had a question on security from any quarter, not one. I have my drill down. And they know my stuff at Registry." This was begging.

"They'll miss me at Registry," Ray said.

Boyle said, "They'll get over it." He eased his chair back from the table. That was the signal for Ray to go.

He felt incapable of moving. He had to get home. But she can't know, he thought, she can't, this is killing me and she can't know: Also I can hear it, I can hear it when she says it's perfect. It's perfect, you *quit* . . . You quit, we leave, it's perfect, we go: But I can't. He wanted to tell her.

Ray got to his feet. By way of acknowledging the raise, since he had to do *something* adult, he patted his hip pocket.

The library proper was still unpopulated, so he sat down at a corner table, with his back to the room, and opened whatever magazine he had pulled off the rack as he passed it. It was *Car and Driver*.

What he was facing came in two parts. Part one was the vocational part, so to speak, which was bad enough. Part one said he was through doing any significant writing and that targets would be assigned to him like to a clerk. He would have nothing to say about who was of interest, nothing. As for the case of the great enigma Davis Morel constituted, he could forget it, the best enigma of his career, but he had to do nothing, find out nothing, and be quiet. That was the vocational part.

Part two was larger and, in a way, worse. No Quarter would be a name for it. It was a dark thing, if it was true. But it was going to be true because it would explain, among other things, assigning Boyle, someone like Boyle, as chief of station in Gaborone.

Part two was a premonition or presentiment. Ray thought, Part one is my clerkship, Part two is why I can't have Morel, but it goes beyond that and it explains why they do care about Kerekang and don't care about Morel. It says we don't get to relax, now that the Russians are down, it says Never Again! this is our Never Again campaign and it says we, the agency, but not only the agency, beyond it, above it, something is saying this is the task, whatever is left of the red menace you uproot, hit them while they're down, get them out of here, fuck them, never darken our door again. The moment of relaxing and enjoying the spectacle of this ancient enemy disintegrating practically unaided would never come. He felt he knew what had to be going on in the collective mind of the victorious West. This is what they think, he thought, we look at everything that went wrong in the world, since socialism became a serious proposition, as a gigantic bloody detour forced on capital and entrepreneurship and the reality principle and the parliamentary system by these red bastards, because without socialism getting hold of first one sovereign state and then a bloc of them, there would never have been, one, fascism, which was a reaction against socialism, fear of it, and, two, there would never

have been the long huge waste of resources the countries of the West had
had to bear once the socialist states turned into military monsters like us:
This is the way they see it, the sane forces of the world plunged into distraction for almost a hundred years, one distraction after another before
normal history could begin again . . . First we were stuck to fight fascism,
and that was close, and there never would have been any fascism without
the goddamned socialist states we had to deal with and fuck next, because
they were fucking with us from the start, that would be the history. Certain bastards had distracted the world with their system that didn't work
on its own anyway.

So Never Again made sense. He could see Boyle as a perfect vector of
this view of things. Boyle was almost a lens to him, through which he
could see this imperative articulating, swelling up. All Boyle wanted was a
new heaven and a new earth, someplace all clean and nice.

Where was it the Greeks had sown the earth with salt after killing
everybody there who annoyed them? It was like that. Pulling up root-
stocks, pouring boiling water down ant holes, grinding the earth clean,
cautery . . . This was what was going on. His head ached. He felt
unsteady. He had the hopeless idea of going back in and talking to Boyle
again, trying to. He might still be there. Boyle always stayed sitting until
Ray left the room. You mainly saw him sitting, like Roosevelt. There was
something wrong with one of his knees. *Of course* Boyle made sense being
in this part of the forest, *of course*. Because somebody had to do something
about the last real pocket of popular Marxism in the entire world, South
Africa, where the South African Communist Party was recruiting like
crazy and pulled plenty of strings in the ANC, which was going to gov-
ern, no question about it. *Of course* he had to be around here in case a
black majority communism got going in a country loaded with diamonds
and platinum and gold, in case Johannesburg turned into the Vatican of a
new race-communism. Of course Boyle would see it differently than
beloved Marion Resnick, who thought the South African Communist
Party would wither away once the struggle-elite in the African National
Congress turned its attention to getting rich. He didn't know why Boyle
hadn't been sent straight to the Republic of South Africa, although there
was plenty of work for him here. Botswana had been a main rear area for
the ANC and there were still plenty of live connections to the ANC on
the ground and under it. There were rumors of oil under the Kalahari.
And Botswana was stable, but how stable?

He needed to be with Iris. He had to tell her about Boyle, but there was no way he could. But he had to see her. He could go home. He could tell Curwen he was sick, tell Curwen something, Curwen loved him, for some reason. He'd have to tell Iris he was coming down with something. Maybe he could stand to return to St. James.

He left the library and went unseeingly out into the alleyway and then into the main concourse of the mall, where nothing had changed. He looked up at the sky. A string of clouds like bloated checkmarks was passing overhead, north to south. It was a short string, amounting to nothing, not part of a system. He thought, You feel hope when something dims the sun, you hope for clouds, for rain, because you become part of the thirst when the drought goes on as long as this one. His throat was dry, but water seemed irrelevant.

He had to get home.

He was not calm. He felt like marching, oddly enough.

He would go home, but Boyle would regret this. Because the fact was, he realized, that he was not going to obey. He would show Boyle what Morel was whether he liked it or not, and he would write his best Life, and it could be done. He had power—he had his powers.

He stood on the curb, waiting for the traffic on Queens Road to slacken. Normally he was patient enough with the unrelenting traffic that flowed in the streets surrounding the mall and accepted the necessity of being poised to dart through any plausible opening, since the etiquette of the drivers, especially of the government vehicles, was a little intermittent when it came to the pedestrian right of way. But today it was intolerable, the racket, the diesel fumes, the jammed minivans blasting reggae and socca. That people wanted to take the mufflers off their cars in order to let the true power of their engines be heard was something he could understand, but he could not understand why nothing was ever done about it by the police. It was hardly a violation that required deep subtlety to detect. And there were police in the area who did intervene occasionally in traffic incidents and snarls if they were severe enough. He had to get through. No break occurred.

He wanted to part the traffic with his hands, with a sweeping motion of his hands, irrationally. It was taking too long. Finally the flow of traffic did abate a little, but still he stood there. He then stepped off, and plunged through. What had finally made him move was a seizure of vivid, unasked-for images from his early life, images linked with succulence and moisture, himself standing in some garden after a rain and staring at nasturtiums with leaves as big as soup plates, and then once standing in an

East Coast snowscape, listening, after heavy wet snow had fallen, for the rare sound wet snow makes falling in clots into new soft snow beneath. He was parched but not thirsty.

Okay, it was definite. He was going to Kgari Close, and Iris. He could call Curwen to report in, or Iris could, although that would magnify things, which he didn't want. He disliked lying to Curwen.

Walking was helping. He was deciding something enormous as he walked and he knew that when he got to Iris it would be final.

He was in revolt. It was simple. How it would work was hard to say. *No one could know*, but he was. He would unmask Morel, one. It would help if when he got home he took off these shorts and this shirt and these socks. In Africa we're all in costume, look at us, he thought.

This felt right. It was strange. Things he had had to put up with in the past without understanding why felt better now, in retrospect, certain painful things. He could feel a sort of, what, concordance, taking place inside him. I am rising, he thought.

He had a faint ringing in his ears, he noticed, now that he was in the quieter streets near his house. And then that passed. He felt clear.

But when he got home and let himself in he found the house empty. There was no one on hand, anywhere. And there was no note evident saying where Iris was. No note meant he could assume she had been expecting him home at his usual ETA. He could hunt up Dimakatso and ask if she knew anything, of course. But he wouldn't. He was aware that Dimakatso had a tendency to decamp and attend to her own business whenever the coast was clear, which was just about what anybody in her situation would do, because the struggle for personal free time was a universal, besides which she was a hard worker when she worked. One part of why he didn't like the idea of bothering her in her quarters was that he had guilt feelings over how modest the accommodations provided her were, not that there was anything that could be done about it. The other part of his reluctance came from not wanting to advertise that he had no idea where his wife might be, the implications of which, the man-in-the-street implications of which, he had no interest in unleashing. Also Dimakatso had been clearing her throat obtrusively lately. She smoked dagga for her chronic upper respiratory complaints. Often when she came in after lunch her eyes would be like rubies or little taillights, and he didn't relish impinging on Dimakatso while she was at it, smoking away, in her cloud of unknowing.

He went through the pantry and into the garage. The VW was there, so Iris had walked wherever she'd gone. They were in walking distance of ninety percent of everything of interest, and she believed in walking, so she could be roughly anywhere.

The house felt dead without Iris, dead and clean and cold. There was a saucer with two cherry pits in it. The house felt like the *Mary Celeste*, except that Iris would be found. He remembered that he needed to call Curwen immediately.

He got through to the school and worked everything out smoothly but talking too fast. Mild food poisoning had been a good excuse. Curwen himself had had a touch of it recently.

He could use the time to his advantage. Unease about Iris was putting Boyle and all his works in perspective, a little.

It was conceivable that Iris was having another go at lunch with Lor. He had urged her to give it a third try. She needed friends. He took off his shirt and his shorts, his costume. He sat down on the living room sofa in his underwear, kneesocks, and shoes. Iris liked to tease him about his attachment to his classic undershirts because, as she pointed out correctly, they were bare under the armpits so that you sweated directly into your shirt but they covered up areas where you hardly sweated at all, and raised your body temperature to boot. He couldn't help it. He was used to them, and both his father and his stepfather had worn them. And he could get very decent classic undershirts easily, too, because they were still popular in South Africa with the time-lagged Boers. He couldn't sit there for more than a minute because Dimakatso was going to turn up at some point.

He proceeded to wash up. He put on a fresh shirt and bush shorts. It was seeming less likely to him that Iris had gone again to lunch with Lor. Their second lunch had been more of the same, the usual. Iris had repeated samples of the conversation to him, in Lor's voice: It's really so frightening nowadays in Joburg, especially Hillbrow, where we always stay . . . Because of the unemployed people everywhere living in alleys and on stoops and in every foyer, everywhere, running after you and forcing these unnecessary services on you, running along to open any door you approach, even automatic doors, standing there with their arm extended, ushering you into places of business they have nothing whatever to do with . . . Or if you parallel-park you're directed by people using big arm movements as though without them doing that you might crash into something despite the fact you have oceans of room . . . And the high-rises with laundry fluttering from every balcony . . . And all the squatters taking over and all the buildings to let or for sale . . . And the begging, so constant . . .

He went into the breezeway and contemplated his yard. For two days Rex's most recent letter, a jumbo with many closely written pages, had been left out, naked, on top of the credenza in the breezeway, out of its envelope, like bait or like the trap itself. He was ignoring it. It was right behind him.

Something moved along the shrubbery at the left-hand edge of his field of view. It was Fikile, early again. He was early today because on other days recently he had been late. Apparently he could offset his late arrivals by coming absurdly early on other days. Of course there was no need for watchguarding during the middle of the day. And there was doubly no need for it when he overlapped with the yardman, who came three days a week though not today. Ray suspected that Iris had said yes to this arrangement, it would be like her. If those oscillations kept on, Ray would say something.

Ray wasn't interested in any more exposure to his brother. He had made it explicit that he had no desire to follow every kink and dogleg in Rex's travesty of a career. The thick letter represented another unwanted task. He had too many tasks as it was. Iris presented him with more tasks than she knew. He was conscientious, and out of love and conscience he took as tasks many things, wishful things, things she might waft at him completely innocently. When she said Why is the French noun for war feminine and why is the French for vagina masculine, it wasn't as though he physically had to go and jerk somebody's hem at the Alliance Française or hunt around in his reference books, no. But he loved her and anything he could satisfy her on right off the bat became a kind of ghost task for him whether she meant it to be or not.

Ray hefted the letter, not looking at it.

These letters were getting longer because Iris was encouraging it, and encouraging it, it had to be, by being forthcoming about herself and her problems, a.k.a. their problems, their his-and-hers problems. He had no idea what she was writing to Rex, beyond what he could infer from what Rex wrote back. What she was writing to Rex was not something he was going to obsess on. He should remember that there were harmless models for what she was probably doing here. Rex was providing a gay ear. There was nothing dangerous about that. So many major women were linked to gay men as confidants that in a way Iris was only joining a procession. Iris was major. She didn't know it, but Ray did. Of course, in this case the bastard listening to her was his own queer brother, his enemy. Rex was spying on him through Iris. Revenge was going on.

Every ongoing relationship contains a quid pro quo somewhere, he thought: The task is identifying it. How intimate was Rex being in these letters? Very, Ray had gathered from hints dropped here and there by Iris. So.

He could scan, he could read excerpts, or he could read the whole thing. He picked up the letter and began to read it, leaning against the wall.

My Dear Iris:

We are still in Mexico, but in Oaxaca, in a weird hotel right on the zocalo. Our room has an actual balcony you can go out on to endure the musical performances blaring from the bandshell it overlooks, or purling up from the strolling mariachi groups who afflict the street-level cafés until late at night, or rising repetitively from the blind or otherwisely decrepit solo guitarists with their overlapping tiny repertoires.

Mexico is frightening. It's as frightening as Grace Jones and frightening in somewhat the same way she is. It's sort of beautiful but you get the feeling it wants to bite you. It's a nightmare that Joel is enjoying very much.

I'm up early and have come downstairs alone to have breakfast and write these lines to you in privacy. It's a glorious morning and as usual one part of God's creation is eating another part of it for breakfast. I hope to join in but I am growing faint. The service in Mexican restaurants is obsequious but slow. But to be absolutely fair the waiters in these arcade cafés have other things to do than bring you your food. For example they have to keep the doves off your table. Some can scare them away with a deft snap of a filthy towel they carry. Others have developed a peculiar screaming cry that seems to do the job, sometimes clearing several tables at once. Bending over your place setting to blow dove-molt off it is another task they have.

It is truly early. A detachment of the Mexican army marches into the zocalo every morning after waking you up at six-thirty with their reveille. Except that possibly you are already awake because

another nighttime activity that begins at just about the time when
the cafés finally close is the de-limbing, with chain saws, of the tule
trees that are planted throughout and around the zocalo. Pollution
is killing them. I don't know why the de-limbing is restricted to the
small hours, unless it's because the government thinks tourists
would be upset at the spectacle. But in my opinion tourists who
come to Mexico are very hardy indeed.

When I say Mexico is frightening what I mean is that almost every
aspect of Mexico that you confront contains something frightening,
like the bus driver who is all smiles and courtesy until you get to
your destination and he won't take your suitcase out of the storage
section in the bottom of the bus unless you give him a huge tip. I do
hope you know who Grace Jones is. It occurs to me you may not.
I'll send a picture. You go to the museum to see the antiquities and
these turn out to be mainly horrific representations in stone of
skulls and rattlesnakes. In the last earthquake, in Mexico City, an
innocuous building collapsed—I think it was the post office—and
what do you know, there was an operative torture chamber in it.

So now here we are in Oaxaca, where we can enjoy my kind of
travel. There are basically two kinds of travels, my kind, vegetative
travel, where you go someplace and vegetate and stay in your room
and sigh looking out at the palm fronds if need be, and the other
kind, activist travel, where people trudge out to every ruin, plant
themselves for a half second before every painting in the museum,
in short push their way into every nook and cranny of the Other in
order to suck out the genius in all the loci they can get to. So I
should be happy. But am I? No.

Do you know the Emily Dickinson poem that begins "A Day! Help!
Help! Another Day!"? That's almost me. I need you to help me with
Joel, or rather I need you to help me with certain impulses I am
developing toward him, impulses I disown but need help in curbing.
I suspect that what is happening is my own fault, in a way. Lately
Joel is finding himself irresistible. Somehow all my loving efforts to
build up his selfconfidence have born monstrous fruit. He has
begun to really love himself. He feels he is too good for anything.
Here is an outburst he had. He started to put on a shirt with his
monogram on it, a gift from his mother, but then stopped and tore

it off and threw it on the floor, saying I HATE MY INITIALS.
Suddenly he is too fine for them, or something. Later we were
getting on the bus for a day trip to Monte Alban and he was in a fine
mood, looking forward to it, we had a nice little lunch packed, and
he turned to me and said, "This is going to be neat. Now don't let
anything *I* do ruin our day."

Now he is preening himself and is on the verge of flirting with
other people. In fact he was flirting the other night, in a sidelong
way and over his shoulder, with a clot of tenured fauves from the
UC Berkeley Art & Musicology Departments.

As you know, and as Ray will have emphasized, I am not
prepossessing, physically. I could be described as pudgy. Also I am
being driven bald at an accelerated rate lately, through anxiety, I
believe, or possibly by something in the water in Mexico. I am not
saying I am repulsive. Let others say that. But on my best day I rise
to the average. Joel seemed always not to notice. So we got on
famously until I succeeded in convincing him that not only is he
attractive but he is *worth knowing* and worth treating nicely. The
problem that is emerging between us is teasing. I have a tendency to
want to tease, which I am basically in control of. But I began teasing
more as his rehab progressed, I think. I don't know why. Possibly I
am seeing him as a duckling getting ready to fly, and if he is going
to fly away it might be better for me if he does it now, before I get
further attached to him. So that would be one Surmise. Or the
impulse could be to tease him as a way of showing I still have some
kinds of power he doesn't. His attempts to tease back are pathetic.
Or the fact that I am footing the bill for everything could be
involved. One thing I do to make a little money now and then is to
sell one of the business names I've copyrighted. I have a list of these
names, in different categories, and I sold one, Bodysmith, to a gym
chain, and here we are, spending my fee together. We never discuss
money. We used to. He used to actually express gratitude now and
then. Or possibly I tease because teasing was the worst thing ever
done to me (ask your husband what I am talking about) and I have
some perverse drive to make Joel experience at least a dilute version
of what I went through. I don't even know what I mean by this. I am
trying to think of everything. I am drifting toward wanting to
humiliate Joel and I reject myself for it.

I see that my breakfast is here. On a plate with a dollop of refried beans and a piece of toast like a section of planking is a sunnyside up fried egg with a major bloodspot in it. The coffee is like ink. This may be a diet day for me. I have had many diet days in Mexico.

Joel makes me wonder who I am.

By the way, we must be Proud of our identities these days, we must be fierce, insulting, even, as we proclaim ourselves, flaunt our teeny individualities. A woman who teaches English at one of the junior colleges in Marin told me that a student requested she not be required to do a paper on a certain writer because he smoked. She explained that she felt strongly on the subject and would be much more comfortable expositing a nonsmoker. Believe me that this happened. This is not the sort of thing a normal mind could make up.

One thing that tempts me in re teasing is that Joel is truly a virginal mind. Teasing can be a form of instruction. And Joel is a dummy, in fact, but so beautiful that if it weren't for his accompanying stupidity he would be totally beyond my reach or grasp. I no longer say "A penny for your thoughts" to Joel. I hate being overcharged.

I want you to know that I don't blame Joel for his defects, by the way. He is the product of several tragedies larger than he is, so to say. He has no relationship whatever to the written word, for example, which is now common. All his referentia are audiovisual.

This is what I think is happening with American children in a very general way, and what I think happened to Joel. I think people are finding their own children boring. And this is due to two factors. Factor one is that by the time a child normally would be a developed persona, a real individual, he or she has become a kind of playback machine for various media tropes and loops: he or she has become what he or she beheld, that is, your child is old television, a rerun. Your child is things you have seen yourself and have outgrown. Then factor two comes into play, to wit, that when the parent looks at his boring child he knows that on television or video, even as he looks into the face of his child, there is bound to be something on that's more interesting than the child before him.

This is my Joel. His parents were bored by him. Add to this that they made their livings in media themselves and were, I would say, *themselves* boring. Even his beauty failed to interest them, I feel safe in saying. Both parents were goodlooking, so he was *expected* to be beautiful.

This is my television-as-the-root-of-all-evil general theory of American civilizational decline. You will observe that it explains a lot, including why children are out of control to the point of bringing guns to school and scribbling their initials all over the material landscape. By the way, I never wanted television in our house. Ask Ray. It was purely visceral with me. I didn't know why, but I hated the thought of it. Ray wanted it. So we got it.

I can pretty well re-create what happened finally between Joel and his parents. They didn't mind that he was gay, apparently, but they hated it that he was so childish. He tried to be a model, but something childish showed through in photographs and it didn't work out for him. I feel responsible for him. I'm not sure there are hordes of people who would want Joel once they got past his fleshly envelope, if you know what I mean. He has a little trouble with his fricatives, for example, not a real speech defect but kind of embarrassing and, I think, one of the reasons he got into the habit of not talking much. He has had the experience of being tossed away after something in him seemed not to live up to his exterior. Also, Joel is afraid of life, but in an adorable way. For example, every morning he makes me read the obituaries to see if anyone younger than he is has died. He doesn't want the names, just the ages, if there are any. And these days there often are. At this point I should mention a shining virtue of his. He is faithful. Fidelity is natural to him. Even if he flirts now and then, this is true of Joel. So, to continue. Joel gets an oversupply of attention for his exterior and I get a paucity of attention for mine. I have a rich interior and a poor (face it) sort of exterior. He has a rich exterior and internally he is a mixed bag, say. Nobody knows what I am because of what my exterior oh so wrongly suggests. So in a way we make a perfect object together.

I badly want you not to misperceive me over Joel. I sensed in your questions that you might be, thus I want to emphasize what I love

about him. He is the kind of man who can be loved. He is loyal. He
is still maturing. He is less precipitate in conversation than he was.
And he is beautiful. With him I have an experience of sublime
beauty beyond anything I ever thought I would have. His
innocence, when it isn't driving me insane, is probably good for me.
And I think I see more, now, of what he sees in me. It's my mind and
my wit that attract him, those things and my talent for striking
back. I get revenge. He has seen me in action, my fangs and talons
out. He sees me as an armed thing. He is, by nature, a disarmed
personality, which has been a disaster because his beauty has
attracted the unjust in greater numbers than the just.

Ray stopped reading, feeling coldness blossom inside himself. He
thought, This is for me, warnings for me, these letters are acts of war . . .
He is striking at me through her. Ray continued reading.

Also, there is a fact of gay life that comes into this that you may not
appreciate. I can have my beautiful man and enjoy him intensely as
long as I can and not worry about the things I would be worrying
about if we were planning to reproduce. There are gay men who
want to adopt and so on, a minority, and go for it, I say, if you want
that. But there is a certain freedom to enjoy beauty per se that
straights must lack, with their great mission of reproducing our
species, and so having to consider other qualities, such as brains, for
example.

Ray had to stop. He thought, I'm surrounded, this is demonic . . . The
idea is to suggest that Iris is my Joel, my ornament, my toy . . . We have
no children, et cetera, that's the subtext, that's it! The bastard!
    Now he had to finish the letter. He had to see what else there was that
was like this. His hands were shaking. He hadn't eaten. That had been a
mistake.

But getting back to what Joel sees in me, there's a little more to it.
Joel is developing what I would call stirrings of personal ambition, a
new thing. He sees me as a writer and a sort of facilitator. He has an
idea for a screenplay. In fact he has two ideas. In the first screenplay,
there is a pet uprising. Pets attack and kill their owners. And those
fortunate enough not to own pets are killed by wild animals who
sense their moment of opportunity and rush in out of the woods to

do the deed. Farm animals kill their owners also. Snakes leap up out of toilets, of course. That's the entire thing. He has made a few notes, mainly of clever ways that the smaller and more innocuous pets might dispatch their much larger human owners. I'm trying to be encouraging to him. By the way, there is no reprieve for humanity in this movie. The pets win. That's the first screenplay. The second screenplay is what he refers to as a screwball comedy. He doesn't really know what a screwball comedy is, but he thinks he is conceiving one. In the second screenplay a standard plot (he is vacillating between a western and a film noir) proceeds. The comic element in this western or film noir is as follows: everyday objects employed in the film, like guns or hammers or knives and forks, keep changing in size. In one scene a fork will be a tiny implement like a pickle fork and in the next it will be the size of a pitchfork. A character will, as Joel envisions it, charge around in shoes the size of coffins. Or he will attempt to charge around. Sometimes it will be impossible! The action will be totally impeded by this unreliability in the size of objects, but nobody will ever allude to it. Hence the comedy. And there will be no suggestion as to why this is happening. And that is the screwball comedy. He thinks we could collaborate beautifully on this. I do, in fact, think there is something funny in this idea. It's certainly high concept.

Just one of Joel's virtues, not so far mentioned, that I want to touch on. He is kindness itself. A great graphic artist named Posada is from here, a nineteenth-century artist. There is a little museum and gallery devoted to him. Posada was a genius who did upwards of fifteen thousand engravings and woodcuts. But of the original plates and blocks only about four hundred and fifty survive. The bulk of the graphic work was in periodicals that were destroyed or that moldered away years ago. There is no record. My Joel got tears in his eyes when he heard all this.

Why should I feel I want to humiliate this good, boyish man who seems to love me, almost? When you write me, give me any help you can, but also know that it has been helpful just to write this and know that you will be reading it.

My regards to Ray, who, I know, would like to see me humiliated in any way possible. This is something he has always wanted and

which was always as mysterious to me as my own feelings now
about Joel are. It could be genetic but I don't really believe that.
Ray hates me because I'm not a True Man. I think he has always felt
this way toward me. But if what he thinks is a True Man is a True
Man, then he isn't one either.

Ray paused, thinking Ah, the True Men. Their mother had been an
expert at discerning True Men, separating them from counterfeit True
Men in the flux of male celebrity. Gary Cooper had been a True Man, as
had Gene Tunney, General Douglas MacArthur, and, oddly, one singer,
Robert Goulet . . .

You may tell him I said this. I would love to hear any response he
gives you. A True Man would never be gay like me, he thinks. What
is a True Man? you ask. I'd say that at the heart of a True Man is a
sort of hunger to get as close as possible to the act of obliterating
some other True Man, either directly (war) or indirectly and
symbolically (nowadays via sports . . . action-adventure fantasy
products . . . killing animals as surrogates for killing other True
Men and using the tally to show everyone how high you rank as a
potential obliterator of actual men). You really have to distinguish
between the voluntary and the involuntary contents of the mind of
a True Man. True Men have to think about work and business, too,
in order to eat. Fortunately there is scope for a lot of transferred
aggression in economic life, especially at the entrepreneur level. So
men have to think a lot about work and making it and turning their
firms into killers of other competitor firms. Plenty of True Men are
gay, by the way. But I'm not one, and *neither* is *Ray*, mon semblable,
mon frère. Ask him. He was never in a war. He hates hunting. He
would rather not be outdoors with the True Men. He's not
interested in sports. There's a psychological thing called the Bem
scale. Tell him to take it and see where he registers. I dare him. But
I am willing to go on record as saying he will find some way never
to do this. I know him.

Ray stopped reading, not out of annoyance but because he was being
watched.

11. *They Played Games*

Ray always knew when he was being watched. He was being watched now. It was a faculty he had and not a product of his connection with the agency.

He saw who was watching him. It was Dimakatso. She was standing just within the extreme right edge of his field of view, just visible outside the frame of the breezeway window overlooking the front yard. She had come around that side of the house. She was in and out of sight, but mostly out. He had seen her without moving his head or looking up. He continued ostensibly reading. He had caught her without any movement, he was sure, that would have let her know he was aware of her. Now only her little paunch was showing. He wanted to know why she was behaving so furtively. He couldn't remember her being furtive in any of her outdoor activities before. She was the opposite. There were times when you had to look away, in fact, like when she pulled up her skirts and rinsed her legs at the standpipe or when she was rubbing the soles of her feet against a piece of log she had, to get rid of calluses.

Something was going on.

He moved closer to the breezeway window. His view comprehended the drive forking from the gate and most of the gate. An overgrown rubber bush half obscured the gate. He was sure Dimakatso had gone back around the house and was now out there somewhere to his left.

He moved even closer to the breezeway window, pretending to be reading with more absorption than before, moving only to get better light.

He wanted to know why nothing, nothing, ever, was straightforward for him in the last year, say. Blame it on a guy named God, he thought.

He thought, Okay! Because there she was, standing, waiting for something. He had caught her edging out from behind the garage. She was poised to go to the gate. She had already made one false start and drawn back, looking in his direction. He kept his head down, which was hard because he was looking into brightness without being able to shade his eyes.

It was clear what this was. He could, of course, go out and see what she had to say. But there was no question about what this was. She was waiting to intercept Iris coming back from wherever she'd been, to warn her about what, though?

It looked like the universal conspiracy of women, stanza nine billion, on the face of it. She was out there to signal to Iris that he was on the scene, contrary to what she expected at this time of day.

He hated it.

The question was whether she would try to signal from the wings or actually run out to give the message. It would be the second. There was something urgent about this business.

Too much is enough, he thought, I have too much to deal with, I have Boyle, I have no more writing, I have my orders, my POI is *not* Morel, no, it's whoever the most virtuous character in *Pilgrim's Progress* is, Kerekang is his equivalent, my POI is, if you can believe that.

Dimakatso made another false start.

He thought, Then on top of that include the bastard my brother that no one has ever been able to do anything about: I have to do something, though, from Africa no less, but what?

Dimakatso was in motion, rigidly *sauntering* up to the gate. As a piece of acting, it was pathetic. Iris had to be coming.

He went out onto the patio, still holding the letter, trying to look idly okay.

Dimakatso met Iris at the gate. He had been right. The point had been to alert her, and it could be completely innocent, the reason being a considerate desire that her mistress not be taken off guard. Iris liked the incredibly sour Dimakatso. Or the reason could be sinister, for want of a better word, except that the word had never applied to anything Iris did and couldn't. Iris saw him.

Iris struck a pose of comic surprise, hands up to shoulder level, palms out. Dimakatso sidled briskly off, looking at the ground. He heard the kitchen door bang.

He loved his wife, shimmering there all in white. She was dressed up, he would say, that is, dressed up for her, dressed up a little more than usual for going downtown. She was wearing a long white rough linen skirt he particularly liked her in, a longsleeved white silk blouse with shoulder tabs they both thought were funny, her best sandals, but with stockings, which was unusual, and one of her conical Lesotho sun hats, one of the extreme ones with a sort of raffia sphere sitting on the peak. They were ungainly objects and she had to keep this one on her head with cords run through a slip bead and cinched under her chin. The cords left faint, transient grooves in the flesh of her jaw that he liked to press away. Generally, she was well covered up for the sun, as she was supposed to be, except that she wasn't wearing her sunglasses, which he ought to upbraid her about at some point. A line of brass buttons closed her skirt along one leg. He wanted to unbutton her and tell her everything, which was impossible. Now would be a good time for one of the imaginary crude pickup lines she used to laugh at, whatever they were, like Gee I bet you look tremendous naked, or Let's go take each other's pants off.

She came up to him, looking concerned. They were going to talk first about him, about why he was there, at home, and that would leave the delicate question of whether or not she was going to volunteer anything about where she'd been. Or would it be up to him to ask? Questions of her whereabouts had never been an issue, but now that he thought of it, her whereabouts were a gray area, something like opening mail addressed to her before she got to it. Neither of them ever opened letters addressed to the other, although either could read any mail opened and left around. Of course they were both aware he belonged to an organization that gave him access to diabolical machines that could flush out and print whatever was inside an envelope and never leave a sign.

"Is anything wrong?" she asked.

He said that he had felt lightheaded after leaving one of his meetings at the embassy, so he'd come home instead of going back to St. James, and that once he had gotten home there had been an episode of diarrhea, that he was feeling better, now, but Curwen had told him to take the rest of the day off. It was almost identical to what he'd told Curwen. Her breathing was a little rapid, he felt, even allowing for exertion, for hurrying.

She looked somber. She undid the chin cord tie and took her hat off. There were the marks in her jaw flesh. She was wearing her hair straight back, unparted, held by a white bandeau he didn't think he'd ever seen.

He said, "I feel okay, now. It was quick. Whatever it was."

"Are you sure? You look a little green. God, I wish I'd been here. I was out walking. Why wasn't I here? Did you think of calling me to come for you?"

"No, I just hoofed it. I'm fine, Iris, fine, nothing to worry about."

She touched his forehead with the back of her hand. She was lying.

At least it was possible she was. The way she had tried to slide across what she'd been doing and over onto an adjoining subject was bad. And she was wearing stockings, she would never wear stockings to take a walk. Now *this*, he thought.

"Come inside," she said.

If it was a lie, he was entering a new world here, a cold place. He hated this place. He shivered, and she noticed it.

"You aren't well. Look at you shivering."

He knew he was putting her through something, but there was no way he could avoid it. What he was putting her through was the generic fear of falling ill in Africa, where small things turned fatal because the medical system was what it was, so full of gaps, and because if you started shaking it could as easily be malaria or sleeping sickness as some kind of minor electrolyte imbalance.

He was, now, actually beginning to feel unwell, obviously in sympathy with the story he had told. You could call it a talent, he thought. But of course he hadn't eaten since breakfast, so that was part of it. Undoubtedly stress was pouring buckets of acid into his stomach. Her lie was the worst thing, it was the worst. He had been okay until she lied, physically okay.

There was no proof she had lied. But he wanted to know since when was she taking walks in the middle of the day, for example? If they walked, they walked in the cool of the evening. If she was out in the midday sun wearing stockings it stood to reason it wasn't for exercise or for the breeze. There was no breeze. She wasn't carrying anything, which would fit with walking for its own sake. She had her waist pack on, twisted around to the back, the way she preferred to wear it despite the fact that it was less secure than wearing it on the side. But she wouldn't wear it on the side because she didn't want to bulk out the line her hips made. She was entirely deluded about her hips. She was womanly, was all. She was so obstinate, in ways. My hips fill the universe, she liked to murmur as she was getting undressed. And then he would reassure her. It was a routine.

Still carrying Rex's letter, he followed her into the house. She had noticed the letter in his hand but, obviously, had decided not to mention it at this juncture. He thought that must be because she didn't want to go down any byways right now. She was thinking. He could tell. She needed time to think her way into her lie. If it was a lie. She needed him not to engage with her for a while. I know you so well, he thought. She would try to stow him away while she thought. That would be next.

"You need to get off your feet," she said. "And let me get you some cold tea. Also your pulse, I want to take your pulse. We're sure this is something you ate, right? That would be the best thing for it to be . . ." Now she was looking pale herself. Before she had been flushed, in fact. It was happening. He was frightening her.

"Excuse me a second," he said, and stepped into the bathroom. He ran water for a moment, then stood immobile while the water ran. He did it not to deepen his act but to get more time to think, himself. He was in turmoil. Lying is murder, he thought, she is killing me, she has a lover.

Iris insisted that he lie down in the darkened bedroom, which he did. She began naming the teas he could have.

"Give me anything. Give me orange pekoe, then. Or Earl Grey. And tepid is fine. I don't need it to be freezing."

She was in favor of an herb tea.

"You gave me a choice and I chose. Orange pekoe is what I want."

"All right, all right." She signaled to Dimakatso, who was in the door-way, waiting for instructions.

"Are you angry at me?" Iris asked him.

"No, no I'm just not feeling that great."

"Did you get something at one of the takeaways? King's?"

"A drumstick, in effect. I had some chicken peri-peri at King's before my meeting. I didn't finish it. It tasted all right."

"Usually the takeaways are safe. They overcook everything so drastically."

"I know."

He declined a warm compress.

She sat next to him on the bed and took his hand. Tea came. He drank some, then lay back, closing his eyes, trying to drive the word *whore*, which was unfair, out of his thought-stream.

She got up carefully. "Stay here," she said, leaving.

He wanted to sleep, not that it was conceivable. *Dreaming of dreamless sleep* was somebody's line and not bad. An interval of blankness might help him. He had to get through this. Nothing was going to be right until she admitted she'd lied. She had gone someplace she didn't want him to know about and then she had lied about it.

He didn't know how he was going to be able to sound normal when he talked to her until this was cleared up. She had seemed guilty, or evasive, at least, out on the stoop.

So, had all her unhappiness and discontent lately come to a point in sex with someone else? Or had the sex not happened yet, which would be something, anyway. It could be in the preliminary stages, in the flirtation stage.

But why would she do it if there was nothing the matter with their own sex life?

The last time, she had asked him, Do you want to know what it feels like to a woman when . . . What it feels like when you come really hard? And she just had. And he had said of course he wanted to know. And she had said, Well, part of what it feels like is like this, that you're just a drop of oil on a white tablecloth, just a tiny, still drop of oil, and then in a flash you're expanding outward in every direction, evenly, turning into a stain, a little drop expanding into a bright stain that covers the universe, the process of that, the expanding . . . that's part of it . . .

Anyone in his right mind would take that as a compliment from his wife.

Of course, she was unusual. She had an appetite for sex that was probably unusual. She liked it about herself. She was humorous on the subject. When he had said, and this was a compliment or at least an appreciation, when he had said Don't you think you let yourself be felt up more than the average woman does without complaining? she had answered I have no idea how much the average woman complains.

What was he supposed to do? What?

He was accommodating, also, in his opinion. They did what she wanted. They played games. They had fun. There were so many examples. What was her problem? There were so many examples, even recently. The last game, how had it started? He couldn't remember, but there had been a discussion of what it would be like to have sex with someone who was in the hospital. Now he remembered. It had come up because someone they knew had done it. They had speculated about the mechanics of it and she had gotten mildly aroused and what with one thing and another she had asked him if he could imagine himself making love to her when he was in the hospital, when of course there was no lock on the door to his room. And he had described himself doing it to her when she came to visit him in the hospital during this imaginary convalescence. And then to amuse her he had gone into the bathroom and wound gauze rather obscenely around his naked torso and then come back to her, and it had amused her, and she had gotten into the spirit of the game, though afterward she had teased him for the gauze, for being so literal.

One last thought and then he would stop thinking along these lines, but the fact was that at thirty-eight the conventional wisdom was that she was at her peak, or just getting there, and she had always been sexually lively. And then the last thought was that, of course, the point of some of the games was for one partner or the other to be somebody else, so maybe games led to an appetite for a real somebody else, which would constitute an argument against too many games.

Where had she been? Who was there *for* her in walking distance? But since anything could be a lie, it was possible she had been picked up anywhere and dropped off down at the corner. Or she could have walked one way and been driven back afterward and dropped off. Or was it conceivable the whole thing was to trick him into thinking she had done something she hadn't, make him jealous so that she could dissolve the whole thing by proving that she'd been someplace innocent? But that was ridiculous because she'd had no idea he would come home early and find her gone.

He heard the shower. Iris was in the shower.

That's nice, he thought. Normally she showers in the morning, so why is she showering now? Morning or evening, always, unless she was rinsing the evidence off, if there was evidence.

There was no point in pretending to sleep. He was too agitated. He had to be doing something.

Perfect, he could read some more Rex, as much as he could stand, anyway. He skipped onward from where he'd stopped, by a few pages.

> At the market in Mérida there was a madman Joel found
> fascinating. This was an emaciated indio who sat on a straw mat for
> long periods holding up a hand mirror at various distances from his
> face, sometimes holding it close up and sometimes at arm's length.
> Then at intervals he would go into an apparent state of rage and
> violently shake the mirror to get his image out of it, presumably. He
> shakes it so hard you think he is going to get hurt. The moment is
> frighteningly violent. And that's the climax of his act, after which he
> starts another bout of staring. Now Joel is finding an increasing
> number of things to complain about, like the absence here in
> Oaxaca of anything as picturesque as the madman in Mérida. And

about the absence of something which is, so far as I can tell, totally
unobtainable in Mexico, which I tend to take as a sign that he wants
us to go home to dingalingdom quite soon. He needs Toll House
cookies.

Well, time to cease, for now. I've been at this so long, Joel will be
fuming.

Later. Definitely, we are coming to the end of things here. Now
Joel is tired of the processions, which formerly were his chief
delight. Many, many processions empty into the zocalo, either at
the Cathedral next to us or at the Gobernación across from us,
behind the bandhouse or pergola or whatever it is. I myself like the
processions.

From your balcony you look down one of the streets that end here
and you see, for example, what looks like a column of giant lollipops
approaching. But it turns out to be women, matrons, wearing
taffeta party dresses and sporting sunburst headdresses and keening
something. Political processions go straight to the Gobernación
and graffitize the walls of it (while the army & police look on
benignly) and then as soon as the processions disperse, a special
team comes out of the Gobernación with paint rollers and paints
over everything. They use extremely fast-drying paint. They have
to, because there are sometimes two political manifestations in one
day. The peasant demonstration yesterday afternoon, someone
explained to me, was because gunmen secretly connected to the
government were killing them, of all things. The banner they were
carrying was a sort of naive art masterpiece, huge, and featuring a
rosette of red fists around some monogram or other. Joel likes the
religious processions better, or did until one night when a very
short procession arrived consisting of a flatbed truck with a hideous
effigy of a saint on it attended by little girls dressed as angels and
mechanically making their hands do falling leaf motions to, I guess,
show adoration. Joel rushed down to see and arrived just as
someone in the truck began tossing cherry bombs down among the
feet of the few watchers. Now Joel doesn't like religious processions
at all. Now, in fact, to this man who was formerly nonstoply
snapping his fingers and grooving generally, to this man Mexico is
"too noisy."

Well, dear friend, that will be all until next time. I don't have
them with me, so I can't comment properly on the limericks
you wrote.

What limericks?, Ray wanted to know: *Which* limericks?

Ray and Iris had collaborated on limericks. But that had been long
ago. He put the letter down.

The droning of the shower continued, which he didn't like. Iris was
always economical about showering because the geyser that heated the
water ran on electricity and electricity was expensive. This was the longest
shower she had ever taken, it seemed to him. Thanks, he thought.

He couldn't deal with more venom, more Rex, and he couldn't keep
lying there doing nothing. He had to deal with Morel, was the main thing
he had to do, but he couldn't think about it, not now while he was being
lied to.

He had to occupy himself with something practical.

Valentine's Day was coming and he had his traditional poem to do. He
did one every Valentine's Day. He would force everything out of his consciousness except that. He could work on his poem and make it sing.

He didn't have much, so far.

> *Does Julio love a sunlamp?*
> *Does Tarzan love a Vine?*
> *Does dumda love a dumda?*
> *Are you my Valentine?*

The title was going to be It Goes Without Saying. If he could think of
something that implied the sentiment without stating it, he'd use that
instead. Or it could be untitled.

Everything is so delicate, he thought. There were cases where wives
fucked outside the hearth just once or twice and then regretted it so
much they became even more doting than they'd been before. These
were in literature. So one route would be to remain passive, just agree to
be deceived for some period and then see. This is fantasy, he thought, I
am injured, literature is not life.

> *Did Nero love a fiddle?*
> *Does Yeats not love a Trine?*
> *Does dumda love a dumda?*
> *Are you my Valentine?*

He thought, *But why am I doing this if I think she's betrayed me? . . .* because she may not have, except that I smelled fear on her . . . that's the thing, unfortunately.

The shower went on. The length of this shower was important.

Or I could make it the best valentine I ever wrote, he thought, shame her and remind her. There had been a decline in complexity, a decline in the amount of effort he put into the project, over the years. And there had been a drift to the more humorous and away from the grandiose, as he now considered them, the grandiose efforts of the early days of their marriage, his efforts at real poetry. Although it wasn't all his fault that he'd stopped attempting a certain kind of valentine. She had complained about some of the early ones. That wasn't true. She hadn't complained but she had noted that they seemed to contain a despairing tone not exactly appropriate to the occasion. One of his lines, *The last light slips from the highest peaks,* had led to a discussion he had come away from depressed, he remembered, or deflated. Also, now she was writing limericks herself, apparently. What could he do?

The shower-sound stopped. A dense silence replaced it.

There were other things in their past . . . like the game of Baseless Admonitions, where one of them would shout completely arbitrary or inappropriate injunctions and warnings and accusations at the other, like *You love only gold!* or *Be true to your school!* or . . . what others? *This means war!* Christ, there had been dozens of these canards and where were they now? *You mate with any beast!* had been another one, thank you very much. Why had the game dropped away? This was an interesting question, and so was the question of who had been the first one to stop initiating these exchanges.

Last year's valentine had been the shortest.

> *Rude Time won't go away*
> *But neither will my love for you,*
> *So that's okay.*

But she had claimed she liked it, loved it, and now this . . .

Iris came tentatively into the room, wearing a bathrobe now, a towel around her neck. It meant nothing, necessarily, that her eyes seemed red.

"You're awake," she said.

"Well, the shower . . ."

"I'm sorry."

He reassured her that he was better.

She came to him, took his hand, and looked imploringly, he thought, down at him. Something was coming. He pulled himself up against the headboard. She had something clutched in one hand, a card, white, a note? It was going to be relevant. What was it?

She sighed, looked away from him, then reached over and pushed Rex's letter out of the way, as though she wanted the zone around him empty of any distraction. She tried to begin, twice. It was clear she didn't know how to begin with whatever was coming and about to kill him, no doubt. She patted his hand, which was the worst sign possible. He was numb.

"Your voice sounds so hollow in these rooms . . . because of the high ceilings," she said. He shrugged.

She was circling. She couldn't bear it, either, which was something. He thought, Does Gallo love his wine?

She mastered herself, swallowing. "Anyway," she said.

"Anyway . . . Did you know that my father once told me he wouldn't read Conrad because Conrad was a Jew, something he concluded from the jacket portrait on *The Portable Conrad* I'd given him for a present. It was frightening. I was stunned. I'd never known he was an anti-Semite. But you repress things. I'd forgotten about it. It was out of the blue."

Ray was listening. It was clear that this was deeply fraught for her. She seemed to be in a state of upheaval. Life is insane, he thought.

"You can probably tell I've been talking about this kind of thing, Ray, and . . .

"And anyway, *I've been seeing someone . . .*" She rushed it out, squeezing Ray's hand and moving closer to him.

He couldn't speak, at first. He could groan.

"Oh God," he said finally.

"Wait, but what's wrong. I haven't . . ."

"What's *wrong*? You said you're *seeing* someone, I mean this is the way the world ends . . ."

She broke in with "Oh please can we discuss this without literary quotations coming into it, *please please please*. No I'm sorry.

"No, I'm seeing a *doctor*, a very fine, well, therapist, but he's also a doctor of medicine, which I know is important. Oh my darling, no. A doctor, which is where I was today when you came in, and of course I hadn't told you and I didn't want to tell you. But. *But*. Ray, *I have been unhappy*. Oh but God you're an idiot!" She stopped to compose herself a little.

"I've been three times. It's very helpful, Ray. He's just around the corner. It's been really important for me, really good. Amazingly good. And I didn't tell you because you have enough on your plate and I thought I could go a few times and, well, feel better, and I could avoid bringing you into it because you know the way you are. You hover and worry and you hover and you worry about me if I . . . Well, you know. You want me to be happy *so much*. And that's what I want, for your sake, really. Mine too, though.

"And I didn't even go originally because I was unhappy, really. This is true. I went because I thought my urine looked too dark. Which I mentioned to you and you thought I was being absurd I guess. You said it was chloroquine, but we've been taking chloroquine for years and I never noticed that effect. But you didn't look, you just insisted that we all fluctuate or whatever you said. So.

"My urine is fine, by the way.

"But anyway he's, well, quite holistic I suppose is the term, and he asked about whatever else might be bothering me. He could hardly not see it.

"And, well . . . So I go to him now. I was going to tell you. It's just that you surprised me today and I wasn't ready to.

"So that was stupid.

"Also he'd told me to tell you."

What she'd been clutching was an appointment card. She handed it to Ray.

"This is the man," she said. "You'd approve of him."

The card read Davis Morel, M.D., 16 Tshekedi Crescent, Gaborone, Eclectic Medicine. Her next appointment was for the following Tuesday, at noon.

Ray reached for her and, trembling, embraced her fiercely.

She relaxed.

12. *He Knew Astonishing Things*

Two days had passed.

Tonight dessert was half a papaya each, perfectly ripe papaya that deserved to be savored bite by bite, he knew. He had tried to eat companionably, at her desultory rate, God knew he had, but there were things to do. She seemed to have forgotten that they were going out for a walk this evening.

Surely now she was finished. The scraped papaya skin was a flimsy thing, like a silk scarf and like the platonic idea of the color orange. Idly she held it up to the light to get the pure orange effect the skin yielded when she did that. She was sensitive to color. She was an aesthete, a genuine one. She stopped to notice aesthetic events there was really no time for, fleeting conjunctures and juxtapositions of things. Later you were glad you had bothered.

He got up. They could go out in a minute.

One thing did bother him about her seizures of meticulousness, and that was that there was another explanation for them, and that explanation was boredom. Elongating simple tasks like eating half a papaya into protracted, meticulously executed exercises. Peeling carrots and destringing celery earlier, she had arranged the carrot peels and celery strings into the letter I on the counter as they talked. When she was starting to sauté something for supper, she had drizzled some symbol or other, maybe her initials, with oil, in the pan before it got hot. He thought, This could be boredom, and boredom kills, and what can I do?

She was in back, getting ready to go out. Their toilet flushed thunderously, which was its way.

He thought, Remember you overinterpret. A case in point was his recent alarm over a band of cursive doodling in ballpoint pen on the kraft-paper jacket of their address book. At first glance he had taken the band of doodling for something like a border decoration in Islamic or Greek art. Iris was always doodling. He had never paid attention to her productions, which in a small way was funny because doodles were something he had been trained to be interested in. And he was certainly well aware of the lengths the agency had gone to in the past, and presumably was going to even now, to retrieve doodled-on materials from certain persons of interest in certain settings, which he hadn't thought ridiculous when he'd heard about them. The idea was that someone who doodled was leaking signs and hints. I'm not boring, he thought: Except that a lot of me is like the storage areas in a good museum.

But the decoration, the arabesque, on the phonebook jacket, which she had taken the trouble to continue across the spine and around across the back, in her very neat way, had frightened him because, if you looked closely at it, it seemed to be saying No over and over. In fact he would take a look at it again, while she got ready to go out sometime before cockcrow.

He went into the living room and, locating the address book, got a surprise. The cover was gone. The book was its chipped, cheap black plastic self again. He looked around to see if possibly the cover had simply fallen off. But there was no sign of it. The cover had been discarded.

Iris had said that that was a design she had been doodling since before she remembered, and she could see why he thought it looked like No's, except look how many of the o's look like lowercase e's. She had reassured him . . . Said it was nothing.

Handling the phonebook, he noticed that of all the doodling on the former jacket, only the Nonononono had left an impression on the plastic cover. She had been bearing down.

Asking where he was as she approached, Iris came to a halt in the living room doorway and stood there waiting for a little appreciation. She was ready to stroll. In honor of the occasion, she had gotten herself up a bit. She had a bright look he slightly distrusted. She was made up and wearing earrings. She had put on a longsleeved chiffon overblouse, despite the heat, because she was attractive to mosquitoes, unlike him. The blouse was a shade of orange just a degree lighter than the illuminated papaya skin.

"You look like a movie star," he said.

"That was the point."

Fixing herself up was for him, only for him. There wasn't much chance that they would run into somebody they knew when they went out. He wanted her to be happy.

"You're too beautiful for this joint," he said, not knowing exactly what he was implying. It was a line out of the ash heap of dead movies lining the bottom of his mind, of course, her mind too. Probably it was also an apology of some kind.

She beckoned him to come along.

One difference between them was that he had seen more movies in his life than she had, especially in his young life. So he had more referents. He thought, One of us is closer to death than the other and we really have no idea which of us it is.

Abruptly, he was overjoyed to be going out to walk with her. Abruptly, he loved the idea. The prospect filled him with emotion and reminded him of the answer a famous philosopher whose name he had forgotten had given when he was asked for an example of an absolute or unalloyed good, and he had said Having coffee with my wife.

That was what it had been like, in the old days, going out walking. Going out walking now was a reminder that things were no longer the same. They were trying to recapture something. She knew it too. Up until two years ago they had been fairly constant about going out to walk, so how far back were the old days anyway? He fought to hold on to his feelings of pleasure and anticipation. The fact that he was suddenly seeing this as being in the same category as pathetically renewing your marriage vows was beside the point. She was ready to be festive. He could be, too.

Fikile ushered them out into the roadway and stood in the street so that he could watch proprietarily until they turned the corner. They both liked the weight of the night, these hot winter evenings. There was a red nail paring of a moon. Nights in Africa were easier than days, because you weren't fending off the sun every minute you were outside.

He could tell she was enjoying things by a certain softness that was coming into her movements, and by her breathing, too. He wanted deeply to talk about anything except his brother or her sister. He especially wanted to stay off the topic of Ellen because the woman appeared to be seriously considering single motherhood, which would be a gigantic mistake, but one that was apparently becoming as popular in the United States as it was in Botswana. At least in Botswana there was a purpose to it other than reckless self-indulgence. The point in Botswana was for a woman to produce a child prior to marrying, as an ad for her fertility, once she had reached the age of twenty or so and hadn't been chosen yet. Apparently Ellen was being influenced by having met a darling child. Iris had read him some of the child's bons mots, and they had been cute enough. But was Ellen under the impression she could pop out a stellar child just because she thought she deserved one? We contain monsters. The most darling child can flower into a monster. Rex was an example. He couldn't make this point. He would also rather not talk about the future. Anything else was fine.

Petty crime was up, but mainly in the form of housebreaking. He was alert, though. No one seemed to be walking tonight but the two of them.

"We like to do this," Iris said, as they settled into their steady-state stride.

He smiled. No reply was required, because the line was resurrected from their past, specifically from the prattlings of a precocious child, speaking of precocious children, they'd known. They both knew what it meant. It was a parajuvenile way of mocking what they were doing, in a gentle way.

This was the stride they liked for strolling, aerobic but not so fast that they would slight any interesting detail in the passing parade, although in truth there was less to see now, as the formerly common wire frontage fencing was replaced with solid walls like theirs. It was more like going strolling in upper-class neighborhoods in Mexico, that is, more a tour of blank walls and gates with the tops of trees as the main points of interest. The standard wall was getting higher, too. Also, it was embarrassing to be seen overtly exercising. Sauntering was fine with the Batswana, but jogging was a thing for ridicule. The Batswana would pass comments when joggers went by. And the Batswana thought heel-and-toe walking was a hilarious form of lunacy. The one heel-and-toe walker in the extension was the deputy chief of mission at AID, and he was secretly famous for it all over the country. He was a paradigm of lunacy. Walking together was nice, but there was a practical cause for letting it lapse as they had. There had been something artificial about their constitutionals, except for the company. They both walked a great deal during the course of the day.

"We like to do this," she said again.

The subject matter of her sister was en route, and this unconscious reaching back to a precocious child in their own background was the signpost. It looked as though he wasn't going to escape. Mainly he hated it because it led back, by implication, to their own childlessness.

"We like to do this," he said.

"My doctor. Weren't we just talking about him before?"

"Not that I recall. Unless I missed something. Maybe you were having a mental dialogue of some kind."

"Maybe I was. I do that." She seemed blithe enough, saying so. Depart this subject, he said to himself.

"So then, I take it another one of his specialties is South Africa, I mean, he is an eclectic, after all."

It was dark, but he could make out the familiar quizzical but good-natured look she was giving him that was meant to ask *What* is your problem? So far they were dealing lightly and fairly openly with his skeptical, as she read it, attitudes toward Doctor Morel.

Ray had no problem. If he had a problem it was the oversupply of experts on South Africa that just being in the region seemed to stimulate, the superabundance of people who thought they knew everything, but knew, in actual fact, nothing . . . people just off the plane who had talked to one alcoholic exile in the airport bar and thought they knew the shape of the future.

Iris said, "He knows a lot about everything. He's a polymath. Like you. Very much like you."

Ray said nothing.

"He's very attuned to words," Iris said.

Ray waited. They walked in silence for a few minutes.

She said, "He's attuned to what we're really saying when we talk and why we select the particular words we do."

"Who would this be?" Ray asked, knowing who she meant.

She smiled, tightening their arm link, drawing his arm snugly into the side of her breast.

It was quiet for a Friday evening. Very florid stereo music pulsing in a couple of the houses didn't necessarily mean that any social festivity was going on, because the preferred way to listen to stereo music was at high volume, not only among the Batswana but among the younger expatriate audiophiles as well. It was universal, or becoming universal. Bringing a torch might have been a good idea. The streetlights were set at wide intervals, not all of them were functioning, and those that were delivered a weak icy blue light muffled, especially in this season, by swarming insects. Luckily they were past the peak of the termite mating season, when the melee around any available light had to be seen to be believed. He couldn't think of a metaphor to describe the dense, shimmering, heaving fluxes the termites created as they swarmed in midair. Getting used to Africa was getting used to termites. He remembered eating dinner with Iris in a hotel in Serowe during the worst of a particularly ferocious mating season. An attempt had been made to keep the insects out of the dining room. There were screens at the windows being pummeled, was the word for it, pummeled by the insects trying to get in. And then as people went in and out, no matter how quickly they tried to manipulate the screen door, clouds of termites had come surging in to join their mates in the swarm dance already going on around the ceiling lights. He and Iris had hunched over their plates to keep the falling, shed wings from getting into their food, their plates of goat stew and samp. The floor had been treacherous with their slippery, silvery wings, which formed a cover something like the artificial snow no longer on the market that people mound up around the bases of their Christmas trees. The Serowe trip must have been a considerable time ago because he remembered it seeming exotic to them, not nightmarish, the way it would now.

The increase in the guard dog population made walking out at night less tranquil. Many of the houses, maybe most of them, now had guard dogs and warning plaques on their front gates saying Tsaba Ntsa! Beware of the dog! Iris was trying to make herself heard above the howls of the dog they were currently irritating. She was saying something about South Africa.

"It's interesting, isn't it, how the South Africans cleverly got away with using the term *unrest*, as in *unrest area*—for a township that was actually going up in flames. All during apartheid an unrest area was a place that was actually in active revolt. There were lists of unrest areas in the paper."

This nitpicking about the term unrest annoyed him, no doubt mainly because it was the sort of aperçu he was used to having her pick up from him. "There still are unrest areas," Ray murmured blankly, caught in himself, in a grievance he could normally keep down. He was running through the panoply of ignorant experts he had to deal with on a regular basis, while he projected his deep interest in what they had to say, which was his lot. Usually he was fine with his lot. But there was a rub, if he let himself feel it. One of the tensions he was supposed to live with unflinchingly was knowing more than he could show, just in general. His lot was to play the intelligent but naive guy always ready to receive the wonderful opinionettes and insights and whathaveyou blowing in from the permanent passing parade of blowhards and parvenu commentators on everything. That was his role and gosiame, he accepted it. That was how it worked. That was *what* worked. While in point of fact he knew astonishing things, he knew genuine secrets. He *possessed* astonishing information. It was his. Just off the top of his head, there was the way, for example, the South African Defence Force had been selling field radios, hoppers, they were called, to every army south of the Sahara, that contained a secret feature that let the South Africans listen in to everything that got transmitted by every army in every action or maneuver undertaken over the last twenty years, radios sold specifically because they were guaranteed secure with their waveband-hopping capacity, which was why they were called hoppers. Every army was an open book to them and it would be interesting to see just how quickly the ANC would decide to let everybody in on this naughty little truth when they got control of the SADF, which would be soon.

He got sympathy over this recurrent experience now and then, but always when he needed it, from Iris. She knew what he was, who he was, and when he overdid his dumb act, she let him know it. He knew how much she would love it if he just once jumped out of his role and wiped up the floor with a member of the cretinate, just once.

"What?" he asked.

"Nothing," she said.

They had come to the point at which they often turned to go back home, at a crossroads, and outside a house Iris liked to consider mysterious. The property the house sat in was walled and gated, but the solid wooden gates were often left ajar, revealing a front drive flanked on one side by a tall, heeling hedge. The main house was small and gave only intermittent evidence of occupation. It was his lot to share in her puzzlement and speculation about the house, but in fact he knew all about it. This was a safe house paid for by the Libyans but used on a courtesy basis by an assortment of freelance thugs who did odd jobs for Zimbabwe and a couple of other countries. The house was wired. The groundsman was in the pay of the agency and provided service on the surveillance systems. There was an old story around regarding a body buried on the premises, which he doubted was true.

They had decided, without discussion, to prolong their stroll. They crossed the main road and turned north toward the embassy compounds.

They were being too silent. He didn't know what to do. A thing Iris was afraid of, she had told him a number of times, was becoming part of one of the married couples you see in restaurants, saying nothing to each other the whole time they ate their dinners. The last time they had eaten out, at the Carat, he had pointed out to her that that particular fear was a good example of fearing a thing that had never shown the least sign of happening with them. They always had plenty to say. Although it was true he sort of mobilized himself when they went out to eat. In fact he would probably like to collapse into dull silence more than he was able to, in restaurants.

"Wait," Iris said, and he thought he could detect a trace of relief in her voice at finding a topic.

"Wait, I bet I can tell you something amusing you don't know about one of our neighbors. You don't know everything. Want to bet?"

It was utterly clear to him. Right now the main effort of his life had to be to become again what he had been to her before, although before exactly *what* was still a question. But everything else on his plate had to be secondary. And that was what he had to do, and would do with all he had, so they could have their life again. And anything that stood in the way of that would be leveled. He felt clear.

She said, "A certain dispute? Heard anything about a certain dispute in a house one street up from us?"

"I'm glad I didn't bet," he said.

"A dispute between Hedda and what's his name at DVS? I'm surprised if you don't know about this, in certain circles it's a famous incident. Among women, for example, if women are a circle. Are we?"

"Hedda and Maret," he said. "Maret is the head of the Dutch Volunteer Service, he's the director. Yes, Maret . . . so?"

"Maret, Maret, *Maret.* I know you disapprove of me when I forget names. *Maret,* yes. Anyway, Maret went to a DVS conference in Nairobi without Hedda. I think the Nordic volunteer services are rather strict about that, leaving the wives out of it on the theory evidently that the conferences shouldn't be fun. They try to hold them in cheap hotels, too. But there was a mix-up about bookings and the conference was transferred to a very nice place on the Indian Ocean, Bamburi Beach Hotel, a very euro spot just above Mombasa, euro in that there is topless swimming going on and that sort of thing. I think there has been rather a plethora of conferences lately to which she has not been invited. So that's the background. And while he's away she gets a call from him informing her of his good luck about the change of venue to Bamburi Beach. He raves about the cuisine. They are having parrot fish for lunch that day. Apparently this is a true departure from the rough venues, the rundown convents out in the bush and so on, that he's used to. So anyway while he was away she decided to do some renovating. She painted the breakfast nook or something. And Maret was always grumbling about the living room furniture, which dated back to the sixties and had probably been comfortable at one time but was becoming shall we say very ratty, so Hedda wanted to do something about that. It was regular overstuffed South African bourgeois seating. For some reason DVS doesn't get staff furnishings from the government. They have to go out and buy it. But Hedda was in a bind because there was no money in the budget that year for amenities like decent furniture. But she got an idea. She decided to replace the living room suite with furniture made in a workshop that DVS sponsors, the one out in Mmadinare. I guess she was tired of the old furniture, too. She had to throw madras prints over the sofa and stuffed chairs, had to keep straightening them out incessantly and they still looked like hell, so she was tired of that. You know the furniture workshop they have in Mmadinare, where they teach people to make benches and refectory tables and other furniture, all out of wood? It's very severe, very Lutheran. The sofas are more like pews than sofas but they do have these pads you can tie to them with straps, you know the place, right?"

"I know it," Ray said.

"So visualize this. This is the furniture the DVS is proposing the rest of Botswana should sit on, and Hedda could get it for nothing, virtually, and she would be supporting the project and advertising it at the same time.

"So for his homecoming she threw out all the old furniture and installed the workshop products.

"Which produced a veritable explosion. Maret was furious because the new furniture was excruciating, in fact, and because, unbeknownst to her, he had been deeply attached to one of the armchairs, despite his constant complaints. How was she supposed to know, for God's sake?

"And do you know this about the Dutch, this custom of working their fury off by driving a stake into the ground? Apparently it's a folk thing. If you're enraged you sharpen a hefty stick or pole or something and you take a mallet and drive it into the ground. So he was reported as doing that, by the next-door maids. The DVS people don't have maids, so we have to rely on next door!

"But unfortunately he remained furious and his ongoing response is this . . . to go out and sit in their Beetle every night, evening I mean, to read *Dikgang* and drink his preprandial Amstel. And Hedda stands in the doorway, fuming, until she has to get his dinner, I guess. His ritual was to read the paper and sip lager in his armchair, but now he stalks out and sits in the front seat of the Volks. He claims it's their only comfortable seating now. And of course he's stuck. He can't get rid of the furniture without it being a critique of his own project. Also they get evaluated by their own volunteers, staff gets evaluated, on how close to the level of the people they're managing to live. So I suppose their incredibly uncomfortable furniture could be good for them in that way."

" 'Like diamonds, we are cut with our own dust,' " Ray said.

"Webster. I love that." She was pleased with herself.

She said, "It's very Dutch, his reaction, somehow. I think of them as very rigid. Actually, I don't know for a fact that driving a stake into the ground is a peasant thing. It might be from some school of therapy or other.

"So there you have it. They're in a feud that every woman in the extension knows about, plus one male, you yourself."

"I'm grateful," Ray said. "He'll get over it, though. But I didn't know about it and I do find it interesting."

"My pleasure," she said.

"This is far enough," Ray said, and she nodded.

They turned to go back. He could sense that there was something she wanted to broach and probably would, before they got home, something not comfortable. Walks had a way of inducing things to come to the surface, repressed things. He had no theory as to why that was so, but wondered if it had something to do with sheer locomotion itself, the conjuncture of expelling something weighty or unpleasant and simultaneously leaving it behind physically. He thought, You escape your words as you go, in a certain way. He was close to bringing up Morel, the eclectic. Ask *nothing* about Morel, he said to himself, sternly.

They both spoke at once.

"Your doctor," he began, as she said, "My sister."

"Sorry, what about her?" he asked.

"No. Go ahead. What about my doctor?"

"No, you first. It's nothing."

"No, you."

"No *you*, because . . . because ladies first."

"No, you first, because the fact is you're *obsessing* on him. There. So. We should get this out."

God I am stupid, he thought. His theory of why walks induced secrets to exfoliate had left out the most obvious explanation for why the situation would apply to him, at least. It was the fact of surveillance. Outdoors was safe, or safer.

"So go ahead," she said.

"No I'm just being stupid. You go."

"No, because, Ray, you are *obsessed* with this man." Her voice was rising.

"I am *not*. You go."

"You are. You show it in so many ways, including your pauses. Your pauses when you wait for me to amplify something I might say about seeing him that you think should be more exhaustive. If his name comes up you turn into a kind of crouched thing, a crouched *listening beast*, listening for what everything I say might *mean*, beyond the simple thing I said itself, you know what I mean, like you are going to *crush* every word I speak and then *treat* the dust. You turn into a *beast* of attention. I don't know if you think I'm in love with him or what, if it's something as stupid as that. You know this man is helping me. Maybe that's what you can't stand. No, I take that back. But this man is helping me, it's helpful, to talk to him. And you don't even know you're doing it. You even breathe differently, softer, so you can hear better, I guess, I don't know, I don't really know. This is my experience. I'm sorry, but you're reading me. Scanning me. It feels like suction when you do this. It's the worst thing, I love you . . ." She had broken their arm link.

He said, "I wonder if we could *pipe down.* And I wonder if rather than going nuts on me in public you could talk about your sister. *Please.*" Ellen is the lesser evil, he thought.

She was silent for a long interval. He was doing everything wrong. She gave a sigh bordering on a groan. Her sighs kill me, he thought.

"Okay, I give up," she said. "Maybe what I said is all I have to say, all I need to say, about my doctor. Maybe you heard something you needed to hear. But we need to talk about Ellen anyway, so okay."

She relinked with him. She is saving my life, he thought.

The mouth of Kgari Close was in view. She asked, "Do you mind if we keep walking up and down before we go into the close, during this?"

"No, that's fine." *During this* definitely meant there was something to undergo.

"Ray, I'm worried about Ellen. No surprise to you. But she's pregnant, definitely pregnant. And we have to think about my going back for her delivery. I know you don't like it. Groan all you want. I may have to. I can see myself there for two weeks, or at most for a month, that would be the worst case. You have to get used to this, love. Don't have an attack."

"*Why* is she pregnant?"

"It's very overdetermined. You know most of it. She's thirty-five. She's tried harder to find somebody to marry and go the usual route than anyone I know. But she had no luck.

"She has no luck in general, just in general. Listen to this. And this is an example of trying everything, which she *has*. Listen to this, she joined a trail club. This is all by way of prologue to why she got pregnant, because you really have to understand. She joined a trail club thinking that might be a good way to meet someone maybe a little older than the men she usually went with, a little older but still in good shape, maybe someone divorced. Ray, she deserves credit. She has no great love of the great out-of-doors, but she joined up and was enjoying it okay despite the fact that there seemed to be no one, no men anyway, who were plausible for her. I guess they were mainly quite a *bit* older. So she decided to stay with it in hopes there might be some turnover. But she got along with the older people, who were nice, including one woman about sixty-five she liked. Ellen has had more unnerving experiences than she deserves. This was a woman who owned her own business, a normal person. Also I suppose Ellen was thinking that even if these people were older they might have younger friends and all of that. She might be invited to dinner. Poor Ellen. So she stuck it out. Then on one outing they climbed a mountain and arrived at the beautiful view they had come for. And when they got there, at the top, her friend led Ellen off to one side and pointed into the distance and said, 'All that over there is hell.' She was pointing at some distant valley where there was an industrial chimney, and she apparently believed that that was where hell was located, biblical hell. And then that was it. The woman resumed being herself."

"Maybe it *was* hell. Maybe the woman was right. But no, if you couldn't hear the screams of the damned, it wasn't."

"Maybe it was out of earshot."

"Well it's definitely here someplace. I think it moves around, though."

"Anyway, that was all. My sister questioned the woman gingerly, or shouldn't that be gingerlily, just enough to confirm that this was actually what the woman believed. Yep, she was just being informative. It was just something she thought Ellen might want to make a note of."

Ray said, "There are certain interesting syndromes in which people are completely normal in their belief structures except for one narrow little niche, where they believe something odd. If you believe that a member of your family has been replaced by an exact double, you have Capgrass syndrome. People who have it are normal in every other way. I forget what they call it when you think you have somebody else's internal organs."

"This isn't really funny," Iris said. "Well, it is, but it's part of a very sad picture. She's tried everything. She advertised in the *New York Review of Books.*"

"I know. You wrote the ad."

"I edited it. She wrote it. Ai! Something bit me. If you keep your arms moving it seems to help.

"I forget why she didn't marry the advertising guy she was living with. The one after the shirt model. I know what happened there. A certain percentage of guys she goes with decide they're gay, which has to be tough. But she lived with the advertising guy for quite a while, it seems like."

"He was a drunk, she stuck with him for too long. He was tremendously goodlooking, like she is, she attracts people physically on her level.

And very goodlooking men are a dubious proposition most of the time. That's what she attracts."

"She didn't have your luck."

"Why bother? You know you're a handsome dog."

"So you say. Except that the other day you said I look like Woodrow Wilson."

"Please let me finish about my sister and then we have to go in. I mean, I love this feeling of parting the night as you go, but another something just got me on the neck."

"We like to do this," he said.

"We like to do this."

Then they were silent again. Cars passed by, not many, two sedans and a bakkie.

He said, finally, "Anyway you don't need all this propaganda, which is what it is, for abandoning me when your sister gives birth. Okay if you want to shatter our *Guinness Book of Records* record for people not being separated, married couples, okay, then go. I'm only kidding. It's okay if you go, of course. You don't need me to say that anyway, you know it. Except that these things have a way of dragging on. Don't they?" He thought, Every arrow being fired on the planet is curving up and over and into my heart, Boyle, her sister's needs, my brother's what, his bile . . . but what was it she said the other day about some woman?. . . ah yes, she said I feel sorry for anyone so self-pitying. He thought, her pity covers the earth, like Sherwin-Williams paint. It might not be necessary for her to go, something might happen, God forbid, how vile am I, how stupid. He didn't want her to go, and if she went it would mean she was blind to what was going on with him, which of course was the condition he was trying to keep going, never to be pitiful to her. She was saying something he was missing.

". . . definitively pregnant and the way it happened is not what you think, not what you assume. Not coldblooded, in other words. Not asking an old male friend and not going to a sperm bank.

"What she did is go from a high-achieving hopeless alcoholic to an underachieving very bright but hapless . . ."

"May I just guess, very goodlooking also, just by chance?"

"Yes, very nicelooking . . ."

"Not goodlooking, nicelooking in this case . . ."

"Well goodlooking if you will. A hapless man and a very bright man, but goodlooking. That seems to be a constant. Anyway, Frank is very bright, a very good writer, no a very good *mind*. He's fortyish. He works in a bookstore. He's a very good writer, but he has an imprimatur problem, as Ellen put it. He's published a few things in small-circulation magazines, but the main thing he's been working on is an encyclopedic thing about American intellectual life that everyone who's seen it says is brilliant and radical but needs to be revised, as in seriously cut. And he agrees with them. But when he starts to revise he also sees things he needs to add, new developments in the culture that just make his thesis even stronger. Also he's what used to be called an independent scholar. At one time they were respected things to be. But he has no academic affiliation whatever. He has a B.A. in modern European history from prehistoric times, but that's all."

Ray thought, This could be me . . . this poor fuck could be me . . . the reverse, I mean.

"Frank is also shy. She met him in the bookstore he works in when she was hunting for something in the children's section. He was very knowledgeable, and they got to talking, and that's how it started. It became a platonic friendship, strictly, in which she got interested in taking him under her wing and getting him marketed, or rather first she wanted to get him to break off from his magnum opus at least for a while and write some pieces that could get published and generate some interest in him as an intellectual persona. He was going to waste, she thought. And there was still time. Obviously she was transposing *herself* going to waste, into *his* situation, something like that."

"So you're telling me this wasn't love. And of course the question you want to ask is why this investment if love wasn't involved. Why not put this time into those things she was doing you told me about. Going to meetings of the War Resisters League? Esperanto? Amnesty International?"

"Well, that's a good question, but nobody is just one thing. She never went to Esperanto, she just asked my opinion about it and I told her. Try to be fair."

"Go ahead."

"Well, she read through his immense manuscript. It was erudite and complicated and utterly brilliant. But it was hopelessly complex. It had numbered paragraphs and instead of notes it had sections in a minute typeface that represented expansions of the main argument. And she objected to that and he said it was a terrific way to condense things and he had gotten it from a book by Nikolai Bukharin, not that he was a communist, he Frank. It was just that this was the way things had to be done. So this is a hapless person, hapless in every way. Here's another example. He went down to Washington to use the Library of Congress and borrowed a friend's apartment to stay in while the friend was out of the country. Now Frank is someone who's very distressed about the homeless. On the way to the Library of Congress he passes a blind homeless person begging and Frank reaches into the pocket and drags up all the change he has in it and dumps it in the guy's cup, then goes a block and realizes that he put the apartment key—he only had the one key—into the beggar's cup along with the change. What should he do? He sidles back to the blind man and hovers there and sees that his key is right there in the cup. So he tells this man what he's done, nicely, but gets no reaction because this poor fellow is deaf as well as blind. So he decides to reach in and subtly pluck out his key. Unfortunately for him the beggar wasn't mute because he screamed out that he was being robbed and he screamed and screamed. A crowd of other homeless people—he described it as a lynch mob—gathered. There were no police in sight and he was being converged on by frightening people and he had his hand in this man's cup. So, there are no police, and he's being converged on by something he described as the Elizabethan underworld, giants, dwarfs, ragged people waving crutches and so on, so he runs away. He ran off. Now, and here's the most pitiful part, he realized he has no means of getting in touch with his absent host, knows no one in the building, he can't find the super. So he spends the next two nights sleeping in his car. Or three nights. I don't know."

Ray grunted. By being minimal he hoped he was encouraging Iris to get through this story. He wondered if what she was doing was trying to fill the air with narrative to occupy the space that questions about Doctor Morel would rush into once she stopped, since she knew they were coming.

But he remembered a car trip he'd taken with a cousin going through a cruel divorce, whom he'd asked, just by way of conversation, what he'd been reading lately, which had produced an almost line-by-line retelling of *The Autobiography of Lincoln Steffens*, a late literary discovery his cousin had made, a lost classic, and so on. The object had been not to talk about the main ingredient in his collapsing life. It had gone on for two hours.

They had come into Kgari Close.

"So she found this man touching. And you do understand that up to the point I'm describing, they weren't lovers. I think he had tried, clumsily, to start something intimate. I'm not clear when that happened.

"She loved his mind, not his body. She had a program for him. She had a campaign. She was serious about getting him into print. For example she had him get business cards printed so that he wouldn't always be scribbling his name, address, and phone number in matchbooks, and this plays a part in what happened, by the way, as you'll see. She was maternal toward him. That's her word. What she had done was this. He was a brilliant conversationalist and she decided she would freeze, that is tape, without his knowledge, one of his arpeggios and then confront him with it and tell him to write it down, turn it into an essay, I guess.

"Well, astonishingly this worked. He had a product. It was an essay comparing certain people, one a Japanese who killed and cooked and ate his girlfriend but got a light sentence and moved to France, where he became a popular celebrity, another someone named Howard Stern who is, I gather, a disgusting radio personality, and the third a famous reactionary named Joseph de Maistre. She said it was absolutely brilliant.

"She got to work and a party was planned where Frank was going to be placed in the path of the editor of the book section of a big paper, this would be a place it would be worth being noticed in. She considered Frank a natural reviewer.

"The plan was just for Frank to engage in his usual conversationalism with the book section guy, but of course Frank is shy, she knows this. So she talked to Frank beforehand and extracted from what he was saying the best, funniest topics, four or five of them. And she drilled him on how to bring them up. She coached him. Now remember how shy this man is.

"She told me what the topics were but the only one I remember now was that in England somebody had just developed a process for putting advertising on eggs, and he had a riff on this. They were cultural topics, striking things.

"It's too horrible. Keep in mind how shy Frank is. So the party transpires and Frank does as he's told and brings up his topics one-two-three, and makes an impression, clearly, to the point where the editor asks him if he might want to consider doing something for them, to which Frank says yes and hands him his card. He thought. In fact, and without Ellen's knowledge, he had prepared a pony for himself, not only listing the topics he was supposed to take up but giving the little stage directions Ellen had thought up. He had written this pony on a card. He'd been afraid of forgetting something, losing one of the topics. And when he thought he was giving his business card to the editor, of course he was giving him this embarrassing aide-mémoire. He discovers this after the party is over and Ellen is congratulating him.

"Well, you can imagine. He was beyond deflated. He was suicidal. He was certain he was never going to hear from the book section editor again. And he didn't. So what was her role? Well, what with one thing and another, she slept with him, sort of right on the spot.

"It was to cheer him up and convince him he hadn't done anything so cataclysmic as he thought. She was claiming this guy was just going to be puzzled, not think anything about it. I guess also she was feeling responsible for sponsoring this thing that had turned into such a humiliating event. Also, as they talked, they were consuming nightcaps, from nervousness. Neither of them had been able to imbibe during the party out of anxiety. We know the way that is. So she ended up screwing him and without a condom, and don't say what you're going to say."

"I wasn't going to say anything. I'm just astonished at her."

"Well, don't be. In the first place she knew his life inside out and he had been celibate for five years. She was properly hysterical about it the next day, though, she made him get an AIDS test as soon as he left work so she could kill him if it was positive. And then, strangely enough, he was offended to the quick. This was a breach of trust. He had told her his whole life in detail. He had never been so disappointed. He got the test, but that was it for them. The test was fine, but they were over. So then when she missed her period she felt that events were making her mind up for her and she should become a single mother. The father has no idea. I don't know if she'll tell him or not. Neither does she. She was leaving Chicago in any case because she had enrolled to take Montessori training in Florida, in their main training center. You know about that. She's out of advertising forever and she's going to be a Montessori person. She thinks she's going to be a teacher, but she'll end up administering because she's so talented. But let her start as a teacher . . . So that's where we are now.

"Now. My mother is useless for this kind of thing, like being around for the delivery. And she disapproves of single motherhood. And she hasn't offered. And Ellen needs to know someone is going to come. And that's me."

They walked in silence up to their gate. Fikile was nowhere around, so they let themselves in. They had just entered the house when the phone began to ring. He had never acclimated to the standard ring pattern in Africa, the two peremptory short burrs and a long interval.

Iris started toward the phone but stopped herself when she sensed Ray wanted to take it. He did.

It was one of his notification calls, with the information he needed coded into the wrong number or wrong resident name the caller would claim to be trying to reach. Iris had a good sense of when one of these calls was coming through. It was odd. She would hesitate. She would look at him as if she knew in advance what kind of call it was, not always, but often enough to be odd.

A voice he knew said, "Dumela, rra. Is this number 5412, 5412?"

"Dumela. Sorry, rra. No. Tsamaya sentle."

It was good news. His man had successfully removed and unloaded the tackhead microcam Ray had taken the risk of having installed in Samuel Kerekang's bedroom in his dismal lodgings in Bontleng. He would have the footage tomorrow, ready for reviewing. It wasn't a good idea, but he could get hold of the footage now . . .

"Finally you look happy," Iris said. "But are we through with my sister for tonight?" She didn't like his wrong-number calls. She was showing it more than usual tonight. He did his best to keep them to a minimum. But there was only so much he could do about it.

"I don't know, are we?"

"We are if everything is clear about my trip back. Because I definitely am . . ."

"We have no argument, my babe. You'll go. Of course."

"You're not enthusiastic. I wish you were. I need you to be."

He could see she meant it. She was distressed about something he'd just done, or about the call. She turned away rather abruptly and left him, heading toward her study. He assumed she wanted more enthusiasm about their separation. He started to follow her but decided against it and waited. He didn't know what to do. He wanted to see the footage. He was tempted, but it wouldn't be right. It would wreck the night. There was a chance, a minute chance, that this might give him something that would satisfy Boyle that Kerekang was nothing to them. And that might untie his hands for the question of Morel.

Iris was back, bearing a clutch of photographs, papers, and index cards.

"May I just show you a few things from Ellen to win your heart, Ray? I'm after your heart. I need you to want me to be with my sister. This is the last thing I'll bother you with on the subject, I promise."

He couldn't go out, which was what he wanted to do, and he didn't want to go through the pictures, the miscellany she was bringing to him, because he was tired and because it was supernumerary, and because in effect he had already agreed she could go to the States, that she should go. She had won, and this was a way of gilding the lily of his defeat, it felt like to him.

He said, "Suppose we do this at breakfast instead? I'm tired. I'm flagging. I'll get us up in time to go through your things. We won't have to rush. That's a promise."

She seemed to Ray to be flattered that he was so unhappy at the prospect of being left alone in Africa. She acceded graciously to the postponement, but then she was always gracious.

Later when he couldn't sleep, he decided that breakfast would be the wrong time too. She had a pile of things to get through and he was agitated about the Kerekang tape, which he could handily secure and review before noon, thus getting it off his back. Then at lunch he could be himself. So now it had to be lunch.

13. A Personal Ritual

Ray felt triumphal over what the footage had given him. But it was subtle and he had to formulate the meaning of the captured images, the ritual, so that Boyle would grasp it. What they had was Kerekang performing a personal ritual. What he had would be the capstone of a Profile, a Life, if he were still writing them. That day could come again. At moments like this it was a curse not to be able to discuss something like how to present this to Boyle, how to phrase it with Iris. She was subtle.

Lunch was a leftover pork chop with applesauce, brown rice, and fresh peas. Iris had laughed at him when he had shown himself dutifully prepared to eat with a fork the roast garlic puree served to him in a ramekin. It was a garnish, not a dish in itself. He knew that. They had had it before. He had forgotten.

Iris said, "I think what happened is that Ellen fell in love with this darling child of her next-door neighbors in the condo. She's very precocious. An only child. Ellen's downfall was baby-sitting for this child, Catherine."

Iris dealt out three Polaroid photographs of Catherine.

"Completely adorable," Ray said.

"She is. Everyone is always suggesting she should be taken to a modeling agency, hideously enough.

"So in any case Ellen decided that Catherine was indeed adorable, and not only physically. Ellen began writing down her little bons mots. At first she just included them strewn throughout her letters and then later she began printing them sort of calligraphically on these index cards, which I now have a small archive of. The child is barely four."

Ray pulled the stack of cards toward him. Was sampling enough? Probably not.

"Are these in chronological order?" he asked.

"I don't think I've kept them in order, actually. They're from when Catherine was two or three. Some Ellen wrote up after the fact, from stories Catherine's mother and father told. The order doesn't matter."

Ray browsed. Some cards recorded brief anecdotes. Others seemed to record examples of a precocious ability to classify things.

Catherine was given an Etch A Sketch for her third birthday. She produced two jagged parallel lines right off the bat and said "I have drawn a crevasse."

Of course you cannot drink bathwater, it is not a beverage.

Catherine's parents note Catherine's fixated gaze at a passing wheelchair, the first she'd ever seen, in which was seated a visibly spastic child about her own age. As the wheelchair drew abreast of them, Catherine said, "Interesting chair!" Then she said, "I feel sorry for ghosts. If I ever saw one, I wouldn't be afraid. I would try to comfort it."

Iris said, "They're not complicated. And you don't have to memorize them, either. And you don't have to read all of them. Give them to me and I'll try to pull out the best ones."

He returned about half of the pack to her, but continued his own browsing.

It was friendlier to read them aloud.

"I like this.

"Catherine went to the zoo. She said of the elephants, 'They have no knuckles.' Later, when her parents said to Catherine that it was time to go to bed, Catherine said, 'Unfortunately, I don't want to.' "

Iris said, "Listen to this. These.

"Her mother wanted Catherine to wear her Birkenstock sandals but Catherine preferred to wear her sneakers. She pointed to the sandals and said, 'I won't be *nimble* in those.' "

Iris was looking dreamy to him. This exercise was depressing her, he could tell. It was involuntary. He was sorry.

She said, "This is the last one. I guess it's very recent. It's a poem Catherine wrote.

> *"Two people were walking down the road*
> *They saw two insects down below*
> *One was a flea*
> *And one was a bee*
> *And the flea was wearing clothes."*

Iris was very inward now. Mechanically, she squared up the packet of cards.

He tried to be brisk. "Well you can see what happened here. Of course you have to go to be with her. It's fine with me, Iris, it really is."

Iris said, "I should mention two other things about this. She thinks the mother is much too cavalier about this child. For example, the parents make no effort to get these gems written down. You know how precious these things are when your child gets older. I mean, we can imagine it. So she began writing these bits and pieces down and then, as a gesture, gave them to the child's mother, who was, I gather, put off by it, basically. I guess she felt criticized. So Ellen sees her own qualities as a mother going to waste, and the rest is history. The other thing is that she thinks the father is evil because, when they were having terrible trouble with Catherine over her bedtime, he proposed the idea of having her hypnotized and giving her a posthypnotic suggestion that it was time to go to sleep. They'd snap their fingers and she'd go off. I'm sure it was completely in jest, but Ellen can't stand him now. So there you have another thing that might incline her to leave the father out of it. There's much more of Catherine in the letters."

Sadness will kill you, he thought. He got up. He had to find time to rehearse what he was going to say to Boyle. He thought, It could go like this, we have three weeks of taping at Kerekang's place, we covered two rooms, bedroom and kitchen, the only two places he could use for meetings, and we did both sampling mode and straight coverage of six through twelve every night . . . now this was all during the time you were convinced he was having meetings there twice a week, at least . . . we know from our other sources when he got home each day, all during this time, and there are no meetings going on . . . But what *is* going on? . . . He has one thing that he does before bed without fail every night, which is what? . . . He goes up to his bookshelf and touches his books and then he turns the light off and goes to bed early, and what books does he go up and touch? . . . Not *Das Kapital*, nothing by Trotsky, no, he goes up and touches his *Complete Poetical Works of Tennyson*, Cambridge Edition, and his little Everyman *Palgrave* . . . He sleeps in his underwear . . . There is nothing for us here.

"What if I like it better there when I go back?" Iris asked softly.

He was startled.

"You won't, my girl," he said, and thought, She can't.

He walked around the table to stand near her. He put his hands on her shoulders. *Down*, misery! he thought.

14. *You're a Better Man Than I Am, Kerekang, So Bravo, That's All*

"Why was this so sudden and urgent?" Iris wanted to know.

She and Ray were walking, at a good pace, to the embassy residence. They were hurrying because the invitation had come late and without much warning.

"You are verging on running, Ray. And it's too hot to run. And it's Sunday, it feels odd to be sprinting down the road on Sunday.

"And why is this a command performance anyway? Why is the ambassador suddenly back from Wankie after just leaving to go there, and why all these reminders about dressing appropriately for a memorial service? They emphasized it when they called the second time on the radiophone. Was that meant for me? Do I go around like a gypsy? What is all this pressure about? I know how to dress for a memorial service. I'm not an idiot."

Ray said, "All I can tell you is this," thinking in passing that here was a good title going to waste. A lot of good titles were going to waste . . .

"Will you *complete your thought*, please," she said.

"All I know is that this is an emergency event and what the premise for it is. Walk faster. What I know is that the embassy has a problem. You know about Dwight Wemberg's wife being killed last week, the accident. You didn't know Dwight. He's an older man and he was just coming to the end of his AID contract at the agricultural college when his wife was killed. They lived in Sebele, on the grounds of the college, and they never came into town much. Go faster. They stayed out in Sebele and were apparently pretty happy there. They got along with the locals. I should say that *he* wasn't around Gabs that much, but Alice was. She was a volunteer with a church group that works with the bobashi, I think. She was rather a saintly person, one gathers."

"I know who she was."

"Part of the problem is the way she died. She was stopped well over on the shoulder on the Lobatse Road and she got out of her car and a CTO truck swerved over to avoid something and killed her, smashed her to death while she was locking the car door. And then the Ministry of Transport mishandled it. The driver was taken into custody and let go without being tested for alcohol. And then there was the statement saying it's always better to get out on the side away from traffic, which is implicitly blaming her, of course. There were many stories about what the CTO driver was prudently trying to swerve away from.

"So anyway, Dwight was out in the bush, way out, at a project the college has in Hukuntsi. Melon cultivation. He was out of reach, out of touch for three days, doing his job. The rest you know. He comes back hysterical and discovers that they've buried her. There were no bad motives involved. I know she was very messed up. But somebody wasn't thinking ahead and didn't inquire into the law here, which says you have forty-eight hours to get a body out of the country, forty-eight hours only, after which the body has to be interred. Which leads to the rub. Which is that once the body is buried you can't get it exhumed unless you go through an impossible bureaucratic procedure that can take you years. He wants to take his wife's body home. The government won't make an exception. He's griefstricken and enraged at the same time and he's made a number of scenes at various government offices, trying to get them to let him have the body, Alice's body. He's insulted certain senior people directly to their respective faces, which you cannot do. So it's a tremendous mess and to top it off his contract is up and he's going to be out of a job. He has his passport and his visa is good for another year. The embassy wants him to go home and let them handle the exhumation application for him but he doesn't trust them. He's off the deep end. He doesn't trust the embassy and he's right. He may not know something else that's relevant, which is that right now our relationship with the Ministry of Health, which controls the exhumation, is shall we say negative, for other reasons altogether. But that's another story. Or maybe Dwight does know something about this, now that I think of it."

"How terrible this is. And he's not young."

"So, anyway, the event. It's not exactly a memorial service. I think they're calling it a remembrance. I knew they were going to do something, but they hadn't decided anything the last I heard. This event is a psychological operation to convince Dwight to go home. You hear them talking about closure. It's supposed to produce closure and get him the hell on the plane."

"I wonder if I should've worn black. I don't think so. I think this is fine." She was wearing a dark blue sleeveless dress with a full pleated skirt. She had tried and rejected several sun hats as not right. Over her shoulders she wore a white lace shawl, rather sprung in places. She had a number of tortoiseshell clips in her hair.

"Everything black I have is in the party category. I think this is all right." She had very little interest in clothes, which he loved in her. He was wearing one of the few safari kits he owned that had full-length pants, a rust-colored outfit he hated.

She was wearing half-heels, which she was unused to. They were now almost jogging. Somehow her sunglasses hopped off her face and he was able to catch them as they fell.

"Are we a team?" he asked her.

"We are," she said. "A track team."

They had reached the residence compound. They could slow up. There was a backup of stragglers ahead of them at the gate.

Iris said, "I put too much sunblock on. My face is slippery. These things happen when I'm pressed. I never want to be rushed like this again. I turn into a fool."

"You never do," he said.

They got seats in the next to last row of chairs protected from the sun by the canopy erected over the ceremonial area on the side lawn.

"This is an outpouring," Ray whispered to Iris. "The idea was to get everyone so that Dwight can see how seriously his situation is being taken. They have shaken the sack. There's a buffet after." Even the seats behind them that were exposed to the sun were filling up.

Ray sat back. He liked the moment. There was nothing for him to do until this was over, in fact nothing he could do while they were there, waiting for the event to begin and end. Probably he would have liked being a commuter, if he liked this.

He counted the crowd. He estimated two hundred and ten, so far. There were tricks to crowd-counting. He would say that the attendance was about fifty-fifty black and white, which was excellent. The overflow crowd of standees was irregularly distributed among the gum trees and silver oaks lining the compound wall, wherever there was a chance of shade.

Last-minute improvisations were under way. The podium needed to be moved forward so that the speakers would be in shade as well as the listeners, so the first two rows were being emptied, chairs were being taken away, and a complex process of negotiated reseating had begun. They themselves were not going to be affected, so it was interesting to watch the negotiations. He could see Maeve, the ambassador's wife, showing distress about the lawn, which was not robust in the best of times and which was taking a beating today. Iris had taken to referring to the lawns in their neighborhood as brownswards.

Almost all of the final arrivals were Batswana. Almost all the people who had gotten seats in the shade were white and almost all the standees were black. That hardly looked good. There were no more than nine or ten Batswana in the seated crowd, not enough.

He turned around to see if it was really as bad as he thought. It was. The news photographs of the event would be strange, showing black people standing back in flowerbeds, the glass shards set into the top of the wall behind them glittering in the sun. The grounds here were in worse shape than his. The empty swimming pool was carpeted with dead oak leaves. There should be a photographer, or at least someone on staff detailed to take pictures for Dwight, as part of the operation, something for poor Dwight to take away with him. I should have been an ambassador, he thought.

The ambassador hadn't appeared among them yet. Ray thought, You become an ambassador and you think *Great*, and then they send you to a place like this, a desert . . .

They waited. Iris took his hand. He closed his eyes. I envy no one, he thought.

"My hips are out of control," Iris murmured.

"I certainly hope so," he said lewdly. He knew what it was. She was noticing someone whose hips were too big. Lately she would ask him if she resembled overweight women her age that they passed in the street, asking if her upper arms were as far gone, if her waist was as thick.

He looked to see who it was she was comparing herself to. She was fixing on the DCM's secretary in the row ahead.

"Not even close," he whispered to Iris. "You're a ridiculous woman."

"You see nothing, you know nothing, and you lie," Iris said.

"If you say so." He closed his eyes again. But I see everything, he thought, I am a camera . . . The worst image for a life has to be the one bad poets love the most, a candle, burning for what? giving off light for *what?* . . . There is no image for life. *Life is a sexually transmitted disease*, according to my brother. That aphorism had made Rex a bit well known, briefly. People used it. It would get into anthologies of bright sayings.

Iris nudged him. "Open your eyes. It doesn't look good to seize this opportunity for a nap."

Programs were being distributed. One reached them.

"There's going to be music," Iris said.

"Oh yes. Of sorts. They were trying to get hold of a woman in Mole-polole who plays the zither, a Peace Corps volunteer. And there's a choir group from the Anglicans. They probably have something on tape, too. The big speakers are hooked up over there."

"What about the refreshments. I'm starving."

"You go from being stuffed to being starving so rapidly it's pathologi-cal, do you know that?"

"I know."

"I believe the collation is going to be fairly deluxe this time, not just samoosas being waved about by fleet-footed servers. Samoosas yes, but piled up in platters in one place so you can get at them. Many many sal-ads. Chicken salad."

He opened the photocopied program and flinched.

"What?"

"The notables, the Batswana. They shouldn't have put this in print. Two of them won't come, no matter what they said. The Health permsec will *not* come. Not a chance. Matsila may or may not, or he may come so late it amounts to the same thing. They hate us at Health. This thing should have started by now. I can tell you exactly what's going on inside the residence. The ambassador is arguing with somebody about whether to start now or wait until everybody they have on the program is on the premises. I could write the script. But Segoko won't come. If he does, I will kiss your introitus numerous times."

"Are you *insane?*"

"You obsess me."

"Clearly."

"Nobody can hear me. Besides, nobody around here knows what introitus means. You can ask them."

She crossed her eyes at him. She should have let him rest. During the reception part of this, there would be work to do. Everybody was here. Boyle was, radically misdressed in a white linen suit and wearing a red

bow tie and, apparently, a leather baseball cap, and holding a handkerchief folded into a pad in one hand, at the ready to tamp away any offend-
ing fluids he might produce. The menthol cigarettes Boyle favored came
from some outlaw manufacturer in India, probably the last source in the
world for these lethal products.

Iris was saying something. She was asking him so softly that he could
barely hear her why, by the way, was kissing a certain area of hers a
penalty of some kind.

"I'll explain later," he said. They were both playing. But actually she
had a point. He had to think about it.

This event had to be about to begin. The amount of life you wasted in
waiting for things to get under way was enormous. In one of his letters to
Iris, Rex had written on the subject of starter tabs on toilet rolls, an inno-
vation in the States. *Now* they invent these things, referencing his lost
hours picking at toilet rolls to get them started.

What had been in his mind was to impose on himself a penalty that
was *in fact* a pleasure, in saying Kiss your introitus. But of course the fact
was that she would know very well that he had been doing rather less of
that than when they were younger. Although she was as forthcoming in
that way as ever, she liked it. He was forty-eight. She was thirty-eight. He
wished he had never mentioned it. She would come back to it. But there
were other sexual, what? festivities of theirs that had dropped away, like
her purposely giving him erections in potentially embarrassing public
circumstances. She could do it in a second without touching him any
time she wanted, still. I came out of the shower and we were late for
breakfast, he thought, remembering . . . It was at her friends' place in
Carmel and they were waiting for breakfast and she got me hot the way
she does, whore that she is, and then I said Now how am I going to go out
there? and she said Backwards? She liked to be called a whore during sex.
You have the heart of a whore, he would say.

She was waving at someone behind them. It was the man, undoubtedly.

"Is that your doctor?" he asked.

"Yes, it is," she said, her voice betraying something, some extra lightness. He wasn't going to swivel around to look at the man. She wanted
him to.

Their huge ambassador was at the podium, giving his usual broad ini-
tiatory smile but then quickly thinking better of it. He was six foot five
and enjoyed his toweringness in this country of small men enough to add
to it by routinely wearing cowboy boots with significant heels. He was a
man who had been reckless about his exposure to the sun all his life and

was now paying for it. He looked dappled. His jaw and cheeks were marked with the sites of excised basal skin cell carcinomas. It was a continuing thing. The last tranche of cancers had been removed by a South African surgeon, who, out of some misplaced aesthetic impulse, had scoured out the sites in the shape of perfect circles. Ned Van Ness had spent too much time in the sun first as a developer and builder and then as a yachtsman, and now he was out in the sun too much here. His big bald pate bore spots of another kind, liver spots, probably. Van Ness had to be missing Galveston, where he was said to be the maximum leader of the city elite, and where you could go yachting. His face was pear-shaped, with full, soft jowls.

Because of his age, Van Ness couldn't be blamed for being reckless about sun exposure, since the bad news about photodamage had only started getting around in the last five years or so. Ray himself had always been, by instinct, sun-averse. But he had been the only one in his family. His impression was that Rex still went regularly to tanning salons. The explanation there was that having a nice tan would give him his only good feature, physically, so he blocked out the bad news about ultraviolet. His brother was not attractive. He deserved credit for persisting with things as he had, coming on to people, looking for boyfriends despite everything. But why, now, Van Ness couldn't seem to adapt to the African sun was puzzling. He wouldn't wear hats. The consequence of it all was that his head looked increasingly like a decorated thing.

The microphone gave a keening sound. The ambassador made a prayerful gesture, his head bent briefly, then resumed his manic smile of welcome. He couldn't help himself. He was an odd man. He was an awkward man. Ray liked the ambassador because he sensed that the man was having fun. He was a political appointee, here for the status that having been an ambassador gave you for the rest of your life. He would go back to his former life still odd. There was something carefree about him, and it showed in his odd, abrupt, ringing, undiplomatic laugh. Ray had seen Batswana flinch at that overwhelming laugh. He was certain that Van Ness found Africa funny. And the ambassador was transactionally odd in other ways. He was a perfectly amiable character, but when he reacted to something said to him there was often a lag in his response that could be unnerving. He tended to consider you with a long stare, while he thought, and when he responded it was normally sensible or reassuring or whatever was required in the situation. But in the meantime you had been unnerved. Ray liked the idea of patently odd men holding positions of power. He was interested in trying to scope out what it was in them that allowed them to escape the marginalizing juggernauts that crush the standard odd man, the average odd man. At some point in his past Van Ness had worked with a professional to rid himself of his Texas accent. This struck Ray as a strange thing to have done, since presumably his cronies in Galveston all spoke traditionally. Yet he'd bothered. The result was a neutral, actually foreign-sounding style of speech. His wife Maeve still had her accent. They had been married since high school. So when they were together there was always an unspoken question hovering, which was If you're both from Galveston why does one of you sound like you learned English in central Europe? Whatever the prescription was for the lenses in Van Ness's glasses, it had the effect of magnifying his eyes, which you couldn't help but notice when he was staring at you.

There was another balk. The ambassador was waiting now as his wife tenderly escorted Dwight Wemberg to the seat reserved for him in the front row. Ray had a proviso to his inclination to like the odd in positions of power. They had to be odd but decent. Boyle was fairly odd, but he was not a decent person. Maeve Van Ness was the reverse of odd. She was a hive of industry. She never rested. She was a rather hunched woman with a hard, intelligent face and stiff, bright blond hair. She had her hands full with Wemberg, who seemed distraught and recalcitrant.

The ambassador repeated his prayerful gesture, then startled the gathering with one of his laughs, a blasting, baffled laugh prompted by Maeve dumbfoundedly standing and sitting and standing again as Dwight Wemberg got rigidly up and left his seat to make his way around to the rear of the seated crowd and over to a place among the standees at the wall. Most of the expatriates sat frozen, watching Wemberg talking to himself, saying something over and over.

This is somebody's fault, Ray thought. The embassy nurse began sidling along through the crowd at the wall in order to be nearer Wemberg. Iris dug her elbow into Ray's side to make him turn back around.

It was going exactly as Ray had known it would, excruciatingly. The eulogies had been wooden albeit fulsome. The thing was lifeless. Everyone was reading from prepared texts. The order of presentation was a shambles. No one had come from Health. The choir of five young women provided by the Anglicans was being overworked in attempts to buy time for speakers or guests not yet on hand. Their repertory was small. They had sung "Ke Bona," twice. Ray wondered what the model was for the slow, strained, nasal style that Batswana female choirs uniformly employed. Nothing was going well. The podium would stand unoccupied for disconcertingly long moments while, obviously, the ambassador was inside the residence imprecating, trying to get people to make something come out right. Twice Ray detected raised voices coming from the residence when the ambassador was away from the ceremony. Then there had been some sideplay around the discovery that the two Portosans hired for the occasion had been delivered in a locked condition and that the man with the power to unlock them was missing. Food had been brought out prematurely and then taken back, but not before a presence of hornets had been achieved. Worst of all were the cooking odors washing out toward them. What must have happened was that the crowd to be fed was larger than anyone had anticipated and so extra frozen samoosas had been scared up and these were now being deep-fat-fried. The light had gone dull. A high, milky haze was overspreading the sky.

"What's happening?" Iris asked. A murmur was passing through the assembly.

Ray didn't know.

There would be a substitute speaker, Doctor Kerekang, representing the gleaners, a project very close to Alice Wemberg's heart, as the ambassador put it.

Ray started to explain more about the gleaners to Iris, not getting much beyond the basic facts—that they were destitutes who lived at and, actually, on the municipal rubbish tip, and that most of them were solitary homeless children but that there were women and a few whole families among them, too.

Kerekang incarnate was the medium-tall, spare, serious man Ray had expected him to be, but there was more to him. There was something immediate about him. And he had something else . . . aplomb. That would be the word for it. He was at the podium, still collecting himself after self-evidently being hustled over to perform without notice, but he was already taking control of the restive audience. Ray wondered if women would find Kerekang attractive. He thought probably yes. Kerekang's hair was fuller than in his photograph, fuller but not to the point of bushiness, and it was grayer. His hairline was deeper at the temples, also. But there was something confident about his hairstyle, or actorly.

Ray realized that he was full of expectation, for no obvious reason. He thought, There is very little magnificence in life, at least in my life, by which I mean external magnificence such as being there when the greatest actor in the English-speaking world gives his greatest Hamlet or when Nijinsky stays so long at the top of one of his leaps that people in the audience gasp . . . Or being present for the Gettysburg Address, although the story is that Lincoln got almost no applause. When he thought of himself as being ready for something magnificent, he didn't know exactly what he meant, because 1989 and 1990 had been magnificent, the Berlin Wall coming down, all of that had been magnificent, but in a generic way, and then, of course, he hadn't been present, he had been in Africa. And Mandela's release and everything following that, up to CODESA, all of that had been wonderful, and he had been closer, physically, to those events, but still he hadn't been in the Republic, he'd been in Botswana, onlooking from there, from where he was, from where he still was. And of course he had Iris, had Iris and her love, but that was in a different category. It was a given. It was lifelong. It wasn't climactic, he guessed he meant. The truth was that he didn't know what he meant. But he knew that wherever he was, Boyle was unhappy right now. Boyle was away from his seat.

Kerekang lifted his hand, half in greeting and half as a signal that he should be given full attention. When he had that, he beckoned softly and then urgently in the direction of the gate. The hush he had created deepened. Eight ragged children, bobashi, their eyes downcast, filed in. Three of them were shirtless. Kerekang directed them to stand together to his right, a little back. Ray didn't know what Kerekang was doing but he suspected it was brilliant. There was a phrase in Setswana that meant waking people up to the truth of a situation and it translated, if he remembered correctly, as Throwing salt in their eyes. He had invited poverty to come to the feast. Good, Ray thought. White or black, everyone present had more or less escaped poverty, except for the bobashi, and poverty was alive in Botswana, getting stronger, this was good! It had been come-as-you-are for the bobashi. There had plainly been no time for them to be gotten into proper dress, what would be considered proper dress for this, if indeed that could even have been done.

"Who *is* he?" Iris whispered. "Do you know?"

"Not really," he answered.

She wanted to know why the children's heads were shaved.

"Lice," he said. There were two girls in the group. They were wearing headscarves, but their heads, too, had been shaved. The children looked clean enough. And they were thin, but not emaciated, not the worst off. There was a feeding scheme for the gleaners that was doing something, at least.

Ray looked in Wemberg's direction. Someone had put a chair under him and he appeared to be asleep. The embassy nurse was shielding him from the sun with a placemat.

Kerekang introduced himself and identified the children by name. In terms of type, where did Kerekang fall? Ray let himself free-associate about Kerekang. He could be the reliable uncle in a family, doing some sober job, the one to go to for school fees, emergencies, unmarried, too wounded in an affair of the heart to try again, someone like that, or he could be the one decent teacher in a boys' school, unflamboyant, meek, a coward even, the one who turns heroic when the Germans occupy and the gym coach is revealed as a shit and a collaborator. What would we do without literature? Ray asked himself, feeling a little dumb.

Ray could see that Kerekang was unhappy with the microphone. He didn't like being mediated by it, that was Ray's guess. Certain men, or people, rather, had a sort of presence that made itself felt almost in a vibratory way. What Kerekang had, Ray had seen the counterfeit of a thousand times. People said that D. H. Lawrence had been that way. He was getting ahead of himself here, of course. He was trying to remember the description of Gandhi giving *darshan*, if that was the word, in something by Vincent Sheean that had made a gigantic impression on him when he was young and stupid. In the scene he remembered there had been a silent gathering and Gandhi had just been there, sitting or standing, raying out something that people felt in their bodies, their nervous systems, their fillings, maybe. Or it could be called glamour, not in the modern sense, but in the sense in which Malory used it. You're still stupid, he thought.

Kerekang bent the microphone, on its stalk, away from him and out of play. His eyes were moist. In fact, as he began speaking, two tear tracks showed on his cheeks. But his voice, an enviable, strong, low baritone, was unaffected. Immediately Ray wondered if Kerekang had voice training in his past. It sounded like it, training either for singing or the stage. There was nothing in his dossier to suggest it. They were always arresting, small men with voices larger and richer than they were supposed to have. Not that Kerekang was small. For a Motswana, he was on the tall side. But he was shorter than Ray. A small man is any man smaller than you, Ray thought.

He looked at Iris. She was transfixed, he would say. She sought out Ray's hand and squeezed it.

When Kerekang's eulogy was over, Ray felt vindication. He had been right. It would be too strong to say he'd been rapt, but what he'd felt had been close to it. He could tell it had been the same with Iris.

"Amazing," he said to her. She was still dabbing at her eyes with sodden wads of tissue.

It had been artful, and not only in transmitting feeling. Kerekang had also covered the waterfront in terms of essential information. Ray had learned certain things he hadn't known. Apparently Alice Wemberg had worked faithfully on her own in a vegetable gardening project for the gleaners, *the* vegetable gardening project, rather. She had been a principal. *This fountain brings up both bitter and sweet* was from Jonson and could be about the West bringing wealth and poverty at the same time, wealth for the swift, and so on. And she had given significant time to this even up to, as he had put it, annoying her husband. Who was another very very good man. So he had learned today that Kerekang was also significantly connected to the gleaners, not just casually.

The assemblage as a whole had responded about as he had. Not that they had been able to get everything, for example, Kerekang's bravery in bringing up Dwight's rebellion within the Agency for International Development over the hybrid maize seeds the agency was pushing. He could imagine the AID people saying that this was not what they needed to have shoved down their throats at a memorial service. Dwight had changed his mind about the hybrid maize seed. The hybrid seeds had to be bought new each season and couldn't be saved over. But some people, in desperation, following custom, had saved them and then done what they always had when they were desperate, eaten them instead of saving them, and then, because the hybrid seeds were treated with mercury, had died, poisoned. It still happened, in bad years. So when Dwight had understood this, he had turned against the hybrids, which was not what AID had sent him to Africa to do, which meant that AID had its own separate reasons for wanting to wave goodbye to him. Kerekang had praised Dwight and Alice equally, as examples of whites who had come to Africa to be of genuine assistance, in contradistinction to many other whites who came to Africa and, in the guise of helping, took more than they ever gave. They were not to be classified with the white ants. That had gotten Ray's attention. *The White Ants* was a pamphlet in which the agency was interested, very. It was an inflammatory parable comparing whites in Africa to termites, but the truth was that literarily it had a certain grace and force, which was not an observation Ray could share with Boyle. *The White Ants* seemed to be everywhere.

And all this had been packed around a splendid thing, a virtuoso reading, not a reading, a rendition, because the performance had been from memory, of a poem by Tennyson, a fairly long one, "The Golden Year." Tennyson was not a poet Ray considered interesting, but during the rendition he'd kept thinking *Bravo*. Somehow Kerekang had penetrated Tennyson and found something splendid there. And although the Tennyson had been just one ingredient in the eulogy, it had been the heart of it, for Ray. It was what had rapt him away. He was sorry to say that this didn't happen to him much anymore. It could still happen with Milton, if he got rolling, reading late, alone, on an empty stomach, oddly enough. Or if he was tired. Then it could happen. It had happened the first time he'd touched Milton. It was the whole point of literature, or one of them, anyway. *Absent awhile from my designs* was a line from somewhere that described that feeling of being extricated from yourself in a flash, in a liquid way, without struggle. Movies lacked the power to do it for him, certainly never movies on tape. He felt in his breast pocket for a handkerchief and in the process switched off the microcassette recorder he carried there. Kerekang was on tape, if he wanted to hear this again. The quality would be poor, probably, due to distance, although this was a new machine and the damned things were getting more miraculous all the time. Gerard Manley Hopkins had been a revelation, a jolt, the first time through. But Hopkins was too rich, unlike Milton, who was just rich enough, just bejeweled enough. Knowing how to distribute his effects was a great secret Milton had, one of many.

"What was that thing he read?" Iris asked. Ray wanted to keep thinking about it, not talk about it.

"Tennyson," he answered, " 'The Golden Year,' " letting her see that he didn't want to talk.

She didn't see it. "Get me some Tennyson, then. That was wonderful."

"You won't like it," he said.

"Well, what if I do? I think I might."

"I don't think you will. What we just heard was exceptional because of the performance part of it."

"I liked Milton and you were certain I wouldn't."

"Well, I was selective. Also I don't think you liked Milton a lot, did you?"

"I did. I loved *Areopagitica*."

"That isn't poetry, of course."

"It's Milton."

"Okay! I'll get Tennyson for you, I will, I will."

"If I wasn't up to Milton, I wonder if there was anybody around qualified to remedy that pathetic situation."

"You mean I should have been your tutor."

"Who better?"

"I don't know. Maybe you're right. We could try again, I guess."

"Please don't overwhelm me with your enthusiasm."

He didn't want to get into the vexed question of her literary education
and what, exactly, his responsibilities in this area were. The ideal
observer would say that since he taught Milton at work, he had a right
not to have to teach it again when he got home. Or was it that, in not
bringing Milton to Iris, he was trying to protect himself from a declaration from Iris that Milton was . . . less than she expected?

Also, he didn't like the way one thing led to another when the subject
came up of what she should be reading. For example, since he claimed to
love the novel, why didn't he read more of them, and why, when he did
read them, did it seem he read so few novels by women? Did his interest
end with Jane Austen? The problem was that they had a fundamental difference over reading, revolving around the proposition, her proposition,
implicit, that whatever you read should be discussed and dissected with
your mate, which created a certain pressure to read works of a certain
caliber and to read with a certain mindfulness you might be in the mood
to escape from. Right now he didn't want to think about it.

The gravamen, roughly, of the poem Kerekang had recited was that
those who strove for the coming of universal justice should never be
downhearted, because, as Ray was reconstructing the sentiment, in the
act of virtuous struggle you are somehow partaking of the Golden Year
even though it hasn't temporally arrived yet. He would have to listen to it
again, or read it, but that was about right. It sounded lame in summary,
yet it had been thrilling, especially during Kerekang's complete, heroic
embrace of the Welsh accent in which the heroic member of the hiking
group expressed his defiant positiveness about the future. Sections of the
poem were still with him.

> *When wealth no more shall rest in mounded heaps,*
> *But smit with freer light shall slowly melt*
> *In many streams to fatten lower lands,*
> *And light shall spread,*
> *and man be liker man*
> *Thro' all the season of the golden year . . .*

And then the windup, in the voice of the old, indomitable do-gooding Welshman in rebuttal to the pessimism of the younger men in the party about the possibility, ever, of justice, general justice, being achieved.

> *What stuff is this!*
> *Old writers push'd the happy season back,*
> *The more fools they, we forward: dreamers both . . .*

Then something he'd lost, then something ending with

> *That unto him who works, and feels he works,*
> *This same grand year is ever at the doors . . .*

Ah yes, and just before that, Leonard, the old man, has broken his walking staff in fury at the younger man's pessimism . . . and then came the conclusion to the whole thing with that blast in the slate quarry, for emphasis, how great! . . . *Now* tell me literature is dead . . . Look around! . . . The true voice of feeling, exhilarating! . . . Okay it was Victorian, but in the best way . . . Splendid man, and I rest my case, and Boyle must have seen it, he had to see it, how could he *not* see it? Victorian, but fine stuff . . . the best kind of Victorian, here by time machine . . . You're a better man than I am, Kerekang . . . So bravo, that's all.

And then, crowning the already perfect climax, Kerekang had turned to his tatterdemalions and, like a maestro, summoned from them a great shout of, of what, of defiance, the shout standing for the quarry blast, Ray supposed. The poem had described it and the children had embodied it. And the shout had expressed farewell, too, as the children had raised their right arms in a mass salute aimed at Wemberg, the fascist salute actually, although that was obviously a completely accidental resemblance not affecting the impact of the thing. He thought, Anyway the fact is that there are a limited number of physical gestures available for the expression of the emotion of solidarity, which is why dance, thanks to the limitations of the silent, lumbering body as a means of articulating anything, constitutes the lowest rung on the ladder of art, in his humble opinion, dance with its grabbing motions to signify desire and its pushing motions to signify aversion and its grabbing then pushing then grabbing again to show ambivalence, for crying out loud. Iris missed the ballet. He didn't. The cry of the children had been the perfect opposite of the pinched, supplicating noise of the Anglican girls' choir.

And then there had come the terrible, perfect conclusion, the answering cry of sorrow and ruin their act had torn from Wemberg, at the end.

Iris was gone. She had been affected too. He shouldn't have been annoyed with her over Milton. He was too selfish. If God were a reader he would have brought the shade of Tennyson back for this moment. But it was time to find Iris.

He hesitated. He would find Iris shortly. But he wanted to say something personal to Wemberg, not that he had any particular history with him, but the impulse was there. What he wanted to say came down to something like *We're all dying, don't worry*, an impossibility, but something. It wasn't just a cliché about universal mortality he wanted to impart. What he wanted to do was acknowledge that something he feared himself, dying in Africa and leaving a mate to figure everything out, had somehow cruelly happened to this unfortunate man, in spades. It was the fear of being left alone in Africa, where nobody loved you. Iris was afraid of it too. And she was going to leave him in Africa so she could visit her sister, not the same thing but it had a certain relationship to the real thing. She was definitely going. She had her ticket. He was divided. He also wanted to say something to Kerekang, pat those children, register something, which was not a good idea because he knew better than to give Boyle any opening to think of him as aligned with Kerekang. The crowd bulged toward the buffet.

Wemberg seemed to be gone. Ray couldn't find him.

More late arrivers were appearing. It appeared that the embassy had lost control of the gate long enough for this to happen. The strong cooking smells that had afflicted the end of the ceremony had come from frantic lastminute deep-fat frying of extra samoosas, as he had conjectured.

Someone had compiled a tape loop of various largo movements from the classical symphonic repertoire. Between repeats of the loop the *Moldau* played. The sound coming through the public-address system was too loud, but no one was paying attention. It was the kind of thing Iris would take care of, but where was she?

When he found Iris letting herself out of one of the Portosans set up in the back drive her eyes were red.

This was bad. "What is it?"

"Nothing. Come look at this. Someone urinated on the wall of the Portosan while I was in there, can you believe it? I guess the same guy who tried so hard to get the door open while I was in there. I was terrified. He went around to the back and peed on the Portosan. I heard every drop."

"That's disgusting. But that's not why you're upset."

"Nothing is *organized* here. They should have the toilets gendered, but they just set them up and it's a free-for-all."

"I know. But what's wrong? Do we need to leave?"

"This will go *away* if you stop asking me about it. Can you do that?"

She was never like this.

She relented. "I guess it's nothing. I was very moved and then . . . then just stupidly started thinking about, this is so stupid, my own death. But not even that. My own funeral service or memorial or whatever I get when I die, what that would be like."

He guided her to a more private spot beside the garage.

She was continuing. "And what I was thinking was what a joke it's going to be. I have done *nothing*. There will be absolutely nothing to say. Nothing.

"But of course people will say things. They have no choice. But it will be lies and it will be nothing like what that man just did, that wonderful thing we just saw for Alice Wemberg. No one will feel that way and why should they, for God's sake?

"Everything will be lies except for what you have to say.

"This is pointless. I can't be doing this. It's idiotic."

"My darling girl, everyone has something like this at memorial services."

Something was making it worse for her. She was distraught. She was weeping and not trying to contain it, now.

She said, "And look at you. Half of everything you do is secret . . ."

He shook her lightly, alarmed. He pointed back in the direction of the Portosans, to remind her that she had to quiet down, that there might be listeners.

"I know. But what would I say about you? I only know half of your life. Even I don't know about your other involvements, your what, your other accomplishments, Ray. I'm sorry . . ."

"Maybe we should go home."

"*No.*" She was vehement. He reached out to hold her, but she stood away from him. She fought to compose herself.

"We don't have to stay beyond this," he said.

She was adamant. "No, I want you to meet my doctor, meet Davis, like a normal human being, like my normal husband."

He groaned. "Is this the best moment, Iris? My God."

"I'm fine," she said. She was recovering. It was okay if she looked like she had been crying here. The rapidity with which women could recompose themselves was something.

"You know *nothing* about him, Ray."

"I'm happy to meet him," he made himself say. Look bright, he thought.

She said, "I want you to be normal when you meet him. Don't be formal. Don't be frozen, the way you can."

"I hear and obey," he said, not as lightly as he'd meant to.

They found Morel standing under a silver oak, his back against its spindly trunk, batting now and then at the parched dead leaves that occasionally drifted down past him. Feet spread apart, he was truculently posed, Ray thought. Morel folded his arms across his chest as Ray and Iris came up. He was undergoing a harangue, but managing to radiate goodnatured skepticism for the benefit of the small miscellaneous crowd loosely gathered around him.

Morel was jaunty, which for some reason surprised Ray. And he was definitely in the handsome dog category, alas. His safari suit, which was black, with a shortsleeved jacket-shirt, was custom-tailored and clearly expensive. His arms-folded pose nicely presented his cultivated biceps and the ponderous wristwatch he wore. The man looked solid as a horse. He had the kind of overdone upper body development paraplegics determined to overcome their disabilities have, and undoubtedly the motive for it was to compensate for his short-leg condition, undetectable as that was, thanks to the genius of his bootmaker. Ray knew charm when he saw it. But charm goes with vanity, he thought. Vanity was there. The cut of Morel's attire was toward formfitting. Wrists as thick as those could only come from hours of boringly squeezing grip-builders, a pair of which Iris had given him several years ago, Ray now remembered, and which he had never used.

"Say hello," Iris muttered to Ray.

He was going to.

He disliked Morel, genuinely, which came as a relief since up to now his attitude toward him had been based on assumptions. Morel was lighter-skinned than he had appeared to be in his ID photograph. Plenty of Batswana would interact with him as a lakhoa. He would have something to work against. American blacks could be the most disappointed people you came across in Africa. I hate arrogance, Ray thought, and

inward arrogance like his I hate the worst. Ray judged himself to be mar-
ginally taller than Morel, although it was hard to see why he bothered to
care about it since he knew that in fact Morel's height was a function of his
orthopedic footwear. He felt stupid for caring about it, but he couldn't
help it. And only one of Morel's shoes was built up anyway. He put his
hand out. He kept his gaze up, not to show any interest in something he
was supposed to know nothing about, Morel's invisible disability.

Iris said hello, tentatively.

Morel's hair was close-cropped and dense. In general he was as represented by his photograph, if just that much softer at the edges that a couple of years of passing time would guarantee. Ray thought, Age operates
in one of two modes, it either withers you, or it puffs you out . . . I am
withering.

Morel shook Ray's hand with average force and smiled at him and Iris.
There had been nothing to notice in the moment of acknowledgment, which had been casual and quick because Morel was busy being
upbraided in Setswana and English by someone Ray knew about, a character, the head of the Star and Arm of David group, one of the thousand
offshoots of the Zionist Christian Church.

Unless he was a superb actor, Morel had had no particular reaction to
seeing Ray for the first time. It looked as though Ray could relax a little.
Of course he had been impossibly positioned to pick up anything in Iris's
expression that might have been there when Morel greeted them,
because she had been almost behind Ray as they approached, hanging
back, which was unlike her.

The harangue stopped as a young woman, someone associated with
the moruti's group, arrived presenting a plate of food gathered from the
buffet. Morel declined, saying he was fasting. Probably this was an eva-
sion. The food was as usual—leaden-looking samoosas, fried chicken . . .
drumsticks only. There were small paper cups of oily bean salad, but no
forks, so that eating the beans involved a maneuver more like drinking.
Only Morel and the moruti were offered anything. The young woman
attended her moruti, wiping his hands for him with a paper towel when
he was through. He asked her to find him some tea and she went off to do
that.

Ray moved forward, intending to say something more to Morel, but
the moruti subtly blocked him. He was a heavy man, all in black, in his
late fifties, Ray judged. On a ribbon around his neck hung a medallion of
some kind, which he kissed brusquely before resuming with Morel.

"Should we go?" Iris whispered.

Ray was definite that they shouldn't.

The moruti was proceeding in Setswana. The harangue part one had been mostly in English with short deviations into Setswana, or so Ray had gathered as he'd approached the group. Morel was listening, with his head down, respectfully, and then, startling Ray, he replied to the moruti in *Setswana*. Woodenly, maybe, but in Setswana. This was new information. It changed the profile. Even Boyle would surely see that.

Not learning Setswana was something Ray held against himself. His original rationalization, because that was what it was, for not learning any particular African language had been that there was no telling where in the continent he might be posted next. He had known it was a rationalization but he had never been able to make himself go beyond learning the basic necessities in the local language anywhere, and in a certain way it had been useful, because host-country nationals would say things to one another in frankness in front of him in their own languages and feel comfortable doing that, and sometimes he had had the option of taping them and securing material somebody else could translate, useful material, often enough. He was normally set up to tape at the drop of a hat. He was today. So over time the original rationalization had gotten stronger. Also, foreign languages had always been difficult for him, a subject outside his best aptitudes. Working in foreign languages, for him, had been like working underwater. He was thinking of his struggle with Latin, which he had been forced to master out of fealty to great Milton, fealty and love. And had been unnatural and difficult for him and he had discovered in himself a mental tendency to forget what he'd learned, like the body expelling a foreign object. And that had led to a defect in his embrace, his total embrace, of the body of Milton, as compared to that of the show-off Latinists in the field, the others. Certain things were not in him, and he had paid for it. Some of his resistance to learning other languages could be attributed to chauvinism about English, some hard relic of his upbringing. Undoubtedly there were other relics as bad or worse he had never had the time to fix. Iris would know. She might have a list. There were seven hundred thousand words available in the English language and in the next closest, German, only four hundred thousand. Someone had written a very funny poem saying that German was originally the language that gargoyles spoke. And as for French, he couldn't wait for it to become a dead language, since no nation, a nation of peacocks, had ever deserved it more. It was coming, they knew it and were hysterical about it, but adieu, adieu. But still he should have learned Setswana.

And if he wasn't going to go ahead and learn Setswana, it was certainly stupid of him, and also indefensible, to have pretended to Boyle that he was fluent in it. How base was it to make himself into a liar to Boyle, and how pointless was it to do it over something that didn't actually matter to his work, to his productivity, and also how stupid was it to try to impress Boyle by claiming a skill Boyle wouldn't have the sense to value?

Comma Lesole was there in the crowd around Morel. Comma had recently been promoted to chief of maintenance at St. James and Ray couldn't remember if he had congratulated him or not. Guiding Iris, he moved next to Comma Lesole and touched his shoulder.

"Dumela, rra," Ray said to him. "Can you say what this is going on about?"

"Dumela, rra, when he can stop I shall say it to you." But he wanted to be able to listen closely for the moment.

"Very good. But the moruti is . . . ? His name is what?"

"He is their bishop, rra. He is called Bishop Tsatsilebe and you must call him your grace every time."

He didn't think Iris had ever met Comma. She was going to be curious about the name. Ray wouldn't be able to help her because he had never asked Comma why that particular name, his registered Christian name and not a nickname, had been given to him. Odd names were commonplace in Tswana town culture. Questioning people about them was gauche and stamped you as a greenhorn. You just could not overreact to the recurrent necessity to address someone you worked with as Toboggan or Judas or Substitute.

The bishop's tone was angry. Morel was listening, but saying less and less. He was having trouble knowing when it was appropriate for him to respond. The bishop left large intervals between the points he was making, presumably to allow them to register, but the intervals were just that. A sequence of pronouncements was in progress and the bishop was making it plain that Morel's attempts to respond to each point were premature and unwelcome. Ray didn't need to know Setswana to recognize that a good deal of the bishop's presentation involved emphatic repetition of the same statements.

There was a pause as the bishop was handed his tea, extended by consultations with several of his followers as to whether an umbrella should be held above his head. A woman who was probably his wife pushed a tam-o'-shanter into his hands, which he tossed angrily away. He declined the umbrella. A follower retrieved the tam-o'-shanter.

Morel had a trait which, in Ray's experience, was common among important or self-important people. This was a reflex tendency to be aware at all times of who in the immediate area of the important person might be more important to talk to than present company. It was a scanning reflex. Morel was doing it now.

Ray decided to bother Comma Lesole again.

Still reluctant, Comma Lesole said, "I cannot tell you all what-what he has said, rra. This chap." He indicated Morel. He said, "He has said many things, many things. Well well, it was not good. Ehe."

Ray liked the standard local pronunciation of "said," making it rhyme with "aid," as "says" was pronounced to rhyme with "gaze." It elevated what was being reported, somehow. Maybe it had a biblical ring. The American "sed" sounded vulgar and inferior to him, if he thought about it.

It occurred to Ray that possibly he was being unfair to Morel, who really was trapped. The scanning Morel was doing might not be the one Ray hated, the one that made every conversation with the self-important party provisional and interruptible. After all, Morel was under pressure and all his scanning might be driven by simple fear that somebody like the ambassador might happen by and notice that Morel was agitating a valued guest. That might be. We shall see, Ray thought.

Iris crowded closer to him, clutching his arm. This scene wasn't what she'd had in mind.

Comma said, "You see, I don't know him well. In fact, I don't know him. But this lakhoa is saying such as how we must say bogwadi is no more true amongst us."

The word meant nothing to Ray, but he noted that Comma was indeed seeing Morel as a lakhoa.

"Can you tell me what that means?"

Arduously, Ray wrested out of Comma's reticence a semblance of an account of the exchange between Morel and the bishop up to that moment. There was widespread belief among the Batswana that widows were a source of certain diseases. AIDS was one of these diseases. AIDS was something that the Batswana had known of for many years. The bishop had given this information to Morel for him to understand, so he would not be misled. The Tswana name for AIDS was bogwadi. The idea was that widows, resuming sexual relations after the long period of abstention that followed the death of their husbands, would release toxins stored up in their vaginas. These toxins caused diseases. That was why it was so urgent not to be the first man to sleep with a widow after the death of her husband. This the bishop had said many times. But the doctor had said it was not true, at first. But then the doctor had said only that he had

not heard of this cause, after the bishop began mocking him. That was
the point they had come to.

This was new to Ray. Comma confirmed to him what he suspected,
which was that bogwadi was considered curable by the sangomas. So here
was another nightmare that somebody at the agency and at the embassy
would have to incorporate. He would pass it on.

AIDS was murdering Africa. He hated to think about it. Ten percent
of the population in Botswana was seropositive. The percentage was
higher in the towns. So here was another obfuscation to deal with. The
agency was already exerting itself against another popular belief, which
was that AIDS was a piece of white biological warfare against Africans,
which somehow was associated with the belief that AIDS was a trick to
make Africans use condoms and reduce their population growth. And
there was yet another belief that only makhoa could contract AIDS, that
the Batswana themselves were immune. It was a mess. The picture of
AIDS in Botswana was incoherent and the disease was galloping. A small
campaign had begun. Posters were up here and there, saying DON'T SUR-
MISE! CONDOMISE! The posters were frequently torn down or defaced.
The agency was interested in knowing who was doing that.

Comma said, "In fact this man is apologizing very much. You can see."
Comma seemed greatly relieved. Ray understood it. Here, Morel was
seen as a white man. Batswana arguing with Batswana was one thing.
Batswana openly arguing with whites was another. There was something
distinctly unusual about it. The past was still alive. Antagonism expressed
obliquely was closer to the norm than confrontation, and antagonism
denied or concealed in evasions and the lie direct *was* the norm, although
that was putting it harshly.

Apparently it was over. Morel was doing a certain amount of bowing
and scraping. The bishop was collecting his people. Ray would be able to
do a supplementary on Morel with just what he had so far. Morel was
injudicious . . . insensitive to the prerogatives of people with status or
blind to the self-evident status certain people possessed . . . and then
there were the implications of his command of Setswana.

Now he could say something to Morel, interact more adequately with
him from Iris's standpoint, as he'd promised he would.

Ray was cordial. Morel was cordial in the way professionals are cordial,
Ray thought. To a member of the free professions everyone is a potential
client, and they present themselves within certain limits.

"Excitement," Ray said.

"All my fault. How are you?" Morel asked.

"You tell me, Doctor," was Ray's answer. All smiled.

To Iris, Morel said, "Hello my dear," rapidly and lightly, avuncular. Ray didn't like it. It was provocative. It was Morel formally asserting a role toward Iris that *surely* Ray couldn't be expected to take seriously. Ray told himself not to bridle.

Iris was herself in the few words she spoke to Morel next. There was nothing guarded that Ray could see. They seemed to be coming to a standstill too soon for Ray. He wanted the exchange to continue a little longer.

Ray said, "That man was a bishop, in case you didn't know."

"A bishop?"

"In one of the Zed CC splinter churches."

Morel had a good but not great voice, tending toward tenor. Stress was probably driving his pitch higher. His speech was accentless, purified. The man could be a radio announcer.

"He got upset with me. He even . . . I think this happened . . . not sure. I think I was referred to as the Antichrist. I think. Not directly but to some of his people."

Comma Lesole came forward to verify what Morel had said. "In fact, he says you are, very much."

"This is more than I deserve," Morel said, shaping his tone for Iris and Ray.

The ambassador's wife was suddenly striding toward them, making scooping motions to urge them toward the buffet, to Ray's disappointment. He wanted more time with Morel. There was more to see in him. And what he wanted to see was the hardest thing there was to see and be sure about. He wanted to see, to know, if Morel was a settled man. It was his own term. A settled man meant something different than a True Man. A settled man was . . . a *sound* man. Applying the category to Morel was difficult for him. He wanted to know how he, himself, would fare if comparisons were ever to be made between them in that category. And beyond that, he wanted to know what kind of man Morel would be for Iris, to Iris, if the unthinkable happened. A settled man could still be an enemy.

They were moving toward the buffet. He could mention the Antichrist matter, if he did a supplement, except that he had his doubts about whether it had really been said. He felt it was likelier that Morel had said that the bishop's notion about bogwadi amounted to a calumny against innocent women and that it was un-Christian to falsely condemn them and that the bishop's reply to Morel had been misconstrued by Comma. Although he could be wrong. African Christians tended to be fairly promiscuous with allegations that their critics were Satans and Judases and so on.

He hoped he'd done what Iris wanted. He certainly hadn't been able to bring himself to any sort of expression of gratitude for all that Morel had done or was doing for her, whatever that might be.

It's a battlefield, Ray thought. Today, so far, he was winning. Surveying the scene, he felt a familiar passion flow into him, not a passion exactly but a passionate appreciation for the riches the scene held for him. It was more than just a carnival of egos to him. He knew more. He brought more knowledge of the secret histories the star egos were impaled on, usually, and the brighter the star, the more he tended to know. He liked the feeling. He couldn't help liking it. *Weigher of souls* was what he said to himself when he felt he was liking this feeling too much. There was the rub. He tried to mock himself when he needed it, and there were times when he did need it, because he had to be his own critic. He had a master but no colleagues. He was alone in his work. Nobody knew the extent of this. He couldn't have friends. He had no friends.

They had joined a queue. Morel had left, saying he'd be back shortly.

"Just eat the tomato salad," Iris said.

"They have some kind of frikadellen that looks good," Ray answered.

She looked pleadingly at him.

"Ray, you have no idea what's in them."

"I'm sure they're fine, but if you say so."

She worried about him. Iris was his one great friend, his sufficing friend, his pivot and anchor, all of that. She was perfect. But there was a lot he couldn't tell her. Aside from Iris, it was fair to say that he had only enemies, or adversaries. Even his little helpers in the game were adversaries in the sense that they were there to produce as little as they could and still get paid, and he was there to induce them to produce more than they wanted for what they got. And those associations were fundamentally mercenary in any case. When it came to his family, he had only critics and adversaries. Rex was his enemy. His mother was neither friend nor enemy. He wasn't present enough in her consciousness for her to have an attitude toward him. She had stronger feelings about the game of golf. In his opinions on Milton, in his publications, he was alone. He had no seconders. He belonged to no particular school of interpretation. Sometimes his views were objected to, briefly, and set to one side. He could deal with it. That was the world. He would like to get a closer look at Samuel Kerekang. He liked him. He felt a dim bond with him through the man's evident love of English literature. Kerekang would inspire friendship, Ray thought. When he thought of the world as a spectacle of enemies, he tried to be resigned about it, telling himself that the lives of most men could be shown to resemble his. How unusual was it for men not to have close friends of the same sex except in the context of athletics, of team life? But even that didn't scan. Team life was riven with rivalry, especially at the professional level. He had had a few friendly superiors in his career, the greatest of them being Marion Resnick of blessed memory. But of course that's what Marion had been, his superior. That said it all. They had been business friends. And of course real social friendship outside of the agency had been structurally ruled out for him. The feeling of affinity that had overwhelmed him the first time he encountered Milton had been a form of friendly feeling, he supposed, but different, naturally, because Milton was dead and was alive to him only in lines of text. But he loved Milton and had recognized, with some surprise, an element of *personal* sympathy or pity in his feeling, part of a sense that in some way he could help Milton, help him to be better apprehended and loved. This was nonsense, but he wondered how other English specialists chose their men, chose their people, wondered if there was something like what he had just recognized, if choices were made on the flaws, certain flaws in the achievements of the artist, certain appealing flaws that you might help with. That he had been feeling sorry at some level for the sublime Milton was good for a laugh. The idea of friendship with the dead, in itself, was also good for a laugh.

They were falling back in the queue as Iris let people slip ahead. She was under the impression she was holding a place for her doctor.

"He's not coming back for this," Ray said.

"He said he was."

"He also said he was fasting."

"But then he got on line."

"No, he let himself be put on line by Maeve, out of courtesy. That's all. He's not coming back."

She looked distressed. "I thought he'd changed his mind about eating," she said.

"Is he a vegetarian?" Ray asked.

"He favors it."

"But is he?"

"Pretty much."

"Does he have an explanation for the rise in age at death as populations consume more meat?"

"You want the frikadellen."

"I'm hungry. I'm seeing white. I'm having bizarre ideation."

"Eat whatever you want, you poor thing."

"Remember when you said Don't come to me when you fall over?
During one of our first shall we say discussions about meat?"

"You remember my formulations when they're simple, don't you?
They stay with you. Anything simpleminded."

"That wasn't simpleminded. I knew what you meant. You meant when
I fell over with a heart attack."

"The cute me. That's what you like. That's all right."

Don't come to me when you fall over dead, however she'd put it, had
seemed amusing when she'd said it. His talent for making things worse
was making itself felt.

The queue stalled.

"Wait, I need to tell my doctor something. I think I see him in the
house. I'll be back."

That was fine.

The line had stalled because the frikadellen had run out.

He thought, Liberation is what she wants . . . I have it . . . What is it?

Wemberg, it appeared, was missing. The man the present event had
been created for was gone. He had evaded his handlers, which was surprising because he had seemed so inert. That must have been an act. This was
looking to everyone like an escape. People were reminding one another
that the Wembergs had more friends among the Batswana than anyone.

The substrate of confusion under today's enterprise was starting to
show. There was awkwardness everywhere. The ambassador had managed to pack together a little delegation of local clergy, including the
bishop Morel had offended, with the idea that they would offer a group
condolence to the bereaved. Now Wemberg was nowhere. The ambassador was striving to keep the group of clergy entertained while somebody located Wemberg.

Ray didn't mind scenes of great confusion, things falling apart, just so
long as he bore no responsibility.

In a minute the ambassador would have to release the group he
had drawn together. He was deflecting his embarrassment into blasts
of staring affability directed almost randomly. His height made him so
conspicuous.

Ray had loaded his plate with tomato salad, nothing else.

Iris beckoned to him across the lawn. She was part of a constellation consisting of herself, Morel, and Kerekang that was drifting, each star remaining at a fixed distance from the others, across the lawn, in the direction of a horseshoe pitch in the lee of the main house and receiving some shade from it. This was the group he wanted, excellent! Iris was carrying two plates of tomato salad, one of them probably intended for him. He raised his own plate to show her that he was already eating an abundance of damn tomatoes.

Signs of disorganization continued to multiply. It was deadly bright and hot, and people had packed themselves into the seats under the canopy to eat. One man was standing and eating at the podium. A presentation of flowers, gladioli, had just arrived late and were being set up. A low hiss emanated from the public-address system speakers. Staff people who should have been in evidence were not. Obviously many of them had been hurled into the search for Dwight Wemberg.

Following Iris, Morel, and Kerekang toward the shade were the gleaner children, in a body, moving carefully and attending to the full plates they were carrying. Ray watched them settle in the horseshoe pitch, at Kerekang's feet. Morel and Kerekang, now lounging against the wall of the main residence, were in mid-conversation. He was going to go over there. Iris was kneeling among the children. The children shifted, moving even nearer to Kerekang. It was vaguely like a scene from the Gospels.

Ray was set up to tape. His wife was beautiful but he wished she were standing. She could be careless about people interested in looking down her front. She had one top with sagging, too generous armholes that he wished she would eliminate from her wardrobe. She was careless.

Going by the gestures in play, Kerekang was engaged in a verbal attack on Morel. This was not Morel's day. Ray couldn't imagine what the issue might be. He had to hear this. He tried to call up anything he knew of Tennyson's beyond what everyone knew from *Locksley Hall*. Nothing was coming.

Halfway there, he was invisibly deflected. Boyle crossed in front of him and gave a double cough that meant Ray should follow him, mark where he was headed, and then find a discreet way to get there and meet with him. Boyle had studiously not looked at him as he was crossing his path, which was usual. Anyone who had intelligence business with Boyle was to avoid public contact with him on pain of being considered something between an absolute idiot and a walking threat to the continued existence of the Central Intelligence Agency as an institution. Ray wondered if anyone had figured out that a good way to winkle out who was doing Boyle's work would be to make a list of the people who were always feverishly scuttling out of Boyle's neighborhood at gatherings like this one.

Ray was furious. He should be with the constellation. Boyle was using a cane today so maybe there was hope somewhere. I curse you, he thought. If Boyle was descending toward immobility there was hope, unless because he was so invaluable he would be kept on even if all he could do was sit in a chair and concoct actions. The agency loved Boyle.

Normally he would feel pity for anyone moving along with such evident difficulty as Boyle. He wished Boyle would fall. That way this mission he had been summoned to the same way a dog is summoned by his master's whistle would abort, presumably, and he could go where he should be. Boyle was heading for the Portosans.

He had to hurry. He signaled vaguely to Iris, not sure she was getting what he was trying to convey. He handed his plate of tomatoes to the wife of the embassy's communication officer, who was there making herself useful but who seemed nonplussed at his act.

Boyle led him past the Portosans and around to the back of the residence garage. There was a door in the rear wall and Boyle would have a key. He had keys to everything. He gave Boyle time to let himself in and light up his Santos Dumont. He would be ready for Ray when he could address him from the center of a cloud of smoke. This was going to have to do with Wemberg.

Ray entered the garage. Boyle, in his flowing white linen suit perfect for the temperature but wrong for the memorial service, was there, glimmering and smoking.

It was about Wemberg. It was urgent, supposedly. Boyle handed him a notecard with five license plate numbers scrawled on it. He had nobody else to send on this errand, which was to go three blocks away to a parking area and ascertain which cars with the license plates indicated were *not* there. Ray could tell that Boyle saw the Wemberg situation as not much above the level of a nuisance, but that since he had been brought into it he was certainly going to clear up the mystery before it got worse.

There was no time to talk because people would be leaving. It had been established that Wemberg was not back at his flat or at any of the other likely locations. Somebody, some group sympathetic to Wemberg's complaints against the government and the embassy, had given him sanctuary, was Boyle's guess. The idea was to move fast. If this was an ad hoc thing, the faster they moved the sooner they would find Wemberg and get him on a plane. The ambassador wanted Wemberg on a plane tomorrow, or at least no later than the next day.

I have no interest in this, Ray thought: Let me alone before I miss everything. He had to get back to Iris and Morel. Mine enemy gleams, he thought. He was sounding rather high-romantic to himself and wondered what that was about.

Just as Ray was about to go, Boyle stopped him. He wanted to be certain Ray could read the scrawled license plate numbers, so he took out his penlight and held the beam on the card while Ray read the numbers aloud for him. Ray had been able to make out the letters and numbers perfectly, using available light. It was all a waste of precious time and it was typical of Boyle. Boyle was insane.

Securing the license plate information had taken less time than Ray had anticipated, but locating Boyle once he was back with the information had become nightmarish because stupidly they hadn't fixed on a rendezvous point in advance. So he had had to find Boyle, who was busy machinating someplace, without showing to anyone the slightest interest in where the man might be. He had found him after a tedious period of wandering through the dissolving event. Finally a crisscross pass had been arranged by the usual winks and nods. When it was done he was tired of life.

Poor Iris. Her lot had been to wait and watch patiently while he came and went, circulated, self-evidently doing nothing. She had known roughly what was going on. She had waited, abandoned, sitting in the horseshoe pitch on an upturned wastebasket, feigning interest in a fashion magazine, which had probably been for his benefit. There was no subject she hated more than fashion. Morel had gone. Kerekang and his urchins had gone.

He collected her.

"I am dying," she said. "You abandon me." They were walking home, although dragging themselves home would be closer to it.

She went on. "You abandon me. You aren't supposed to."

"I know," he said.

"I should be used to it. I guess it hasn't happened for a while because it hit me this time with a sort of shock, like the old days when it happened all the time. Which led to an understanding, you may recall. You would not let this happen to me unless it was an absolute emergency."

"Which this was. Well, it classified as an emergency."

"I won't ask you what it was. You know I was out there in suspended animation for a whole hour. I considered holding the magazine upside down as a distress signal, would you have noticed? I won't ask you what the emergency was because I know you can't tell me."

He considered violating the house rules. She would appreciate it if he did. And this situation was something she had undoubtedly put together for herself already.

He said, "I'll tell you what it was. But please tell me you won't ever do anything like that magazine trick. People notice things. Say you won't."

"I never have, I wouldn't, but I wanted to. I wanted to hold the thing upside down, and wave it in the air every time you passed."

"Good Lord."

"Don't worry."

"Anyway, you noticed how Dwight was nowhere to be seen. Well, they have him set up for a flight home tomorrow at noon. He was supposed to go back to get his bags, which Maeve had packed for him, and then come back and stay the night at the DCM's.

"He's a missing person. And he didn't just wander off somewhere.

"The theory is that he prevailed on somebody to hide him out so he can continue his campaign. He kept saying he wouldn't leave Africa without Alice's body, and he meant it, apparently.

"So now we don't know where he is. He has a wide circle of friends, Batswana friends, and so did Alice. They need to find him right away, so I had to go and check some license plates. They know he left in a car. I had to check on which cars had been parked in a certain place and no longer were, if you see what I mean. I had no choice. There was nobody else to do it. Everybody else was tasked up."

She was listening closely. She looked at him with an expression distinctly combining gratitude and surprise.

"Thank you," she said. "I mean it."

He thought, If she thinks this is the thin end of the wedge, she's wrong . . .

"And all the wandering around mysteriously, what was that?"

"It was part of the deal."

"I know, but it seemed so strange and protracted . . ."

"It wasn't very strange."

After a silence, she said, "I know who you report to, by the way."

This didn't surprise Ray very much. He shrugged.

"And I'm sorry for you. I knew before today, so don't worry that it's anything you did this afternoon. Anyway it's the new consular officer and I pity you, I do."

"Are you saying that because it's always the consular officer? Because it isn't always the consular officer."

"No, everybody knows. He's awful. All the people I know, know. I just look interested. I play dumb, don't worry. Also if your previous boss was that very nice Marion Resnick, I'm sorry for you. What a contrast. You can confirm my guess by pulling your earlobe if you want to."

"I can't say anything about this."

"But you do understand that everybody knows."

"Maybe they only think they know."

"Oh I don't think so. But that's all right."

She stopped, spun against him, and locked her arms around him in a hard embrace, there on the street. Immediately he felt calmer.

He noticed that he was hungry. He hadn't eaten anything since breakfast.

On impulse, he said, "Should we go someplace for coffee?"

She said, "I like the idea, but it's Sunday. One of the hotels would be about it. I don't want to get caught in the braai at the Sun, but we could go to the coffee shop. Everything else is closed, the regular places."

The hotel they were nearest to was the Sun, but she didn't love going there. She disliked it because the tone of the place was corrupted by the casino, the types it attracted. The Sun was off his normal beat, for obvious reasons. He was a schoolteacher. But when he had a plausible reason to go there, he went. He liked it for the same reasons that Iris didn't. It was a sink of vice, so you saw temptation winning or losing, loss of composure, certain extremes.

They decided it would be a good idea. He was touched that she was agreeable to going. They changed their route.

She was splendid, fundamentally. They were going to the Sun for his sake. There were plenty of reasons she would usually prefer to avoid the Sun, the gauntlet of prostitutes you had to run in order to get in the door being one of them, but that was usually only a nighttime problem. There were the beggars who assumed that everybody leaving the Sun had broken the bank. There were the Boers who had come up for black sex where nobody they knew would see them. But it was the hawkers, the lace sellers, who upset her the most. There was a vendor encampment extending along the road paralleling the Sun's frontage. The lace sellers dominated the encampment and completely controlled the choice area directly across from the entrance gate. Their lace goods were displayed along fences or on makeshift racks, or carried out into the traffic by the hawkers, hardlooking matrons, and unfurled for pedestrians and slower-moving cars. For occasional shelter from the sun the hawkers would repair to lean-tos crafted from sticks, cardboard, and burlap sacking. The encampment was a hell of dust, shouting, and carbon monoxide pumped out by the idling engines of vehicles pulled up on the shoulder of the road for the purpose of browsing. The ratio of sales to stopped cars was pitifully low.

Iris had a history with these people. She had tried to help them. The bedspreads and tablecloths and mantillas and runners being sold were items that united incredible craftsmanship with appallingly cheap materials. That was the problem. The shawl Iris was wearing constituted a case in point. She was forever fiddling with it, gluing up broken threads, tightening it up in one way or another. Iris had spoken to several of the lacemakers about the mismatch, and they had seemed to understand. As he remembered it, she had gone so far as to locate a source for better linen thread for them, and they had seemed interested. What was the point of constructing these intricate and potentially beautiful objects out of what amounted to packing twine? But there had been no outcome.

It occurred to him that Iris had spoken to the wrong people. There was a hidden government among the hawkers. There always is, he thought. He could delve. There was a top woman, who occupied the prime spot in the encampment and whose lace stand was shaded by golf umbrellas, new ones. She was probably the one to speak to, not that it would do any good. He could find out, if Iris wanted to pursue it. She liked to correct things. She thought the world was more pliable than it is. Every time she saw the cordon of prostitutes around the entrance to the Sun, her mind ran in the direction of what could be done for them. She had a general impulse toward social helpfulness that somehow never resulted in organized action, like working with the gleaners the way Alice Wemberg had, actually getting out of the house and going to the site of the iniquity. He knew what she would say about that. She would say, if they were ever able to discuss it honestly, that he discouraged it, in part because it would raise their profile, which was always to be avoided, and in part because . . . he needed her so inordinately. For example, he always wanted to know where she was and that wherever she was it was a reasonable place to be, a safe place. Because the fact was that without her the world would be unintelligible to him. That much was true.

"Did I miss anything?" he asked her.

"Oh, only a fascinating dispute between the man who spoke so beautifully, Mister Kerekang, and a man who's still not your favorite person, I gather."

"Tell me."

"Well I didn't get all of it, remember. Possibly because I had to stop and concentrate on particular things I knew you'd find interesting, like the reasons Davis gave for wanting to be in Africa . . ."

He felt taut. It appeared that what she had was Morel's mission statement, or what he was interested in having people think was his mission statement. He was taut because the underlying burning question of what exactly was going on with her over at Morel's was with him constantly, like indigestion. That question would be coming up and into the light sometime soon, if not tonight. It would happen before she left for the States, that was certain. It could be tonight, depending on what she had to say about Morel in the next segment. Going to the Sun rather than going home was a way of postponing the conversation, for him if not for her. Was she cooperating with his struggle to postpone the Morel question, the full-dress moment? She seemed blithe enough. He was the one with the problem. He was the one with the full plate. They had to be at home when he picked the moment to thrash the thing out, or was it thresh the thing out? For an instant both words seemed equally correct in the phrase, a sign that he was getting old, proof positive.

"Let's see," she said. "Let's see how I do with my memory palace."

"Your memory palace."

"You know what that is?"

"I think I do," he said. Of course he knew. "You mean where you visualize a building you know every detail of by heart and then use different features of it to pigeonhole pieces of information so you can recover them by association."

"Davis suggested the idea to me. It's a simple concept. I must've heard of it in the past but just never paid attention to it or never thought it was relevant to me. He mentioned it when I was complaining about my short-term memory."

"You think your short-term memory is worse lately, but it isn't. You've always had an erratic memory."

"Well, I beg to differ. But it doesn't matter. It was bothering me, so I included it in my long menu of objections to myself and my body. And Davis made this suggestion, which I've been employing for a few weeks and which, well, which I think helps. I could be wrong. Do you notice any improvement?"

"Maybe so. I don't know. You're variable." There was nothing wrong with using memory palaces if you needed to. This device had been covered during training. But he never used it. His memory worked without tricks. When he absorbed a scene or a sequence it was an effortless process. It was a form of becoming the scene, surrendering to it. He was unusual, when it came to memory, it was a gift. In the agency he was regarded as a prodigy, or once had been. He was pleased if using memory palaces was genuinely going to work for her. They would see.

He wondered what template she used for her memory palace. It would be one of the houses she'd lived in when she was growing up, undoubtedly. That was what he'd used when he'd tried the technique out. He was curious to know.

"I'm curious," he said. "I'm curious to know what edifice you're using for your memory palace. I don't mean to be intruding." He realized that he wanted it to be the house they were living in.

"Oh nononono. There's nothing secret about this. Please. Actually I have two I use. One as you might expect is our house, going in the front door, to the right and then to the left, room by room, and I can start with the driveway, the yard, to expand it. That's one memory palace. But I have another one for less complicated sequences."

He broke in. "Ensembles," he said. She might as well know the technical term.

"Thank you, ensembles, then. So for less complicated ensembles I have another one that works very well, even better. I use it all the time. It's dynamite."

Ray was used to acting as her spare brain, her spare memory. He remembered the titles of books she'd read, and their authors, for example. She had relied on him, deferred to him, when a question of authorship came up, or the question of the title of a movie she could remember the basic plot of, and not much else. He might know who wrote the background music, not that anyone ever plumbed him for that. Amazing things from the tail end of movie credits would stick with him. Directors, he always knew. His remembering one thing or another for her had never been the occasion of any sort of fireworks or notice. It was just that he remembered the passing world better than she did, in more detail than she did, and so what?

He asked, "So what is the other template you use?"

"Hm," was all she said.

"Oh come on."

"I'm having second thoughts, I think."

"Now I'm interested. Come on."

"Hm," she said again. She was being coy.

He said, "To my coy mistress, please tell me."

"Okay," she said. "I use *you*."

"In what sense?"

"*You*. I use your body. You naked."

"Good God."

"If I dress you up, say, and put things in different pockets and so on, it doesn't have the same power."

Eros, he thought . . . Oh my.

She said, "I tack different items to different body parts."

"My naked body."

"Yes."

"And this was your own idea, not something the good doctor suggested."

"No, my very own."

"Using my body as a sort of bulletin board. I guess I'm flattered. And so where on my body would you tack say the most important thing in an ensemble that you wanted to remember?"

"Try and guess. Where would I put the seminal item?"

"Shame on you. Ahem. Well. You were going to give me your doctor's mission statement."

"Don't call it that again, if you don't mind.

"It wasn't something he was eager to talk about. It wasn't an announcement. And how would you like it if someone was being so bold as to ask you why you were in Africa, you yourself, why? You wouldn't like it. You'd be taken aback. But of course it's a legitimate question to ask any non-African who's hanging around in Africa. It's just that it doesn't normally *get* asked, people are too polite. The answer to the question of why people turn up in Africa is never simple. Look at us. But he was asked, so he answered."

"Don't be defensive."

"I'm not. And one other thing, just refer to him as Doctor Morel or just Morel if you can't stand to call him Davis. You've met him now. He introduced himself to you as Davis. I don't particularly want to hear good doctor or your doctor anymore. So call him Morel, which is probably what he is to you. Call him that. Calling him Morel has a slight touch of hostility to it, which you have toward him, so be up front. It's fine with me."

"Done," he said.

"*Pointless* hostility I might add."

Say nothing, he thought.

"So. What he said. There are three gifts, donations was his actual term, three donations the white world has given Africa, three poisoned gifts that have wrecked or distorted Africa's own course of development, however that might have come out if Africa had just been left alone a little longer. These are perduring, his word, donations, things persisting long after the physical occupation of Africa ended, persisting long after independence.

"The three donations are, one, plantation agriculture . . . two, the nation-state . . . and three, the Christian religion.

"There was a parenthesis on slavery, the Atlantic slave trade, which would normally be included among the main poisoned gifts. He leaves it out because, even though it stimulated local slave-trading into something much more monstrous than it already was, it's over with. And there were even worse sponsors, like the Muslims. The Arabs, that is.

"This he sort of rushed through. He sees himself in some ways, at least, as a beneficiary of white or Western civilization, an African beneficiary to boot. And he feels an obligation to do something about what the West has done to Africa."

Ray contained himself.

"And he thinks Africa is dying.

"Obviously nothing can be done about the nation-state system.

"And nothing can be done about plantation agriculture. And here there was a little exchange with Kerekang, who wanted to know if Davis was including extractive industries, like mining and timbering, in the category of things that nothing can be done about, to which the answer was yes. I would say also that Samuel Kerekang was reserving his position on whether or not something could be done about agriculture, if somehow or other export agriculture couldn't be supplanted by something else, but he agreed that it was a titanic problem.

"But something can be done about Christianity, which Davis thinks has had the worst effects of the three. So the major thing he is pledged to do . . . in addition to his medical work . . . is to lift the yoke of Christianity from the neck of Africa, help to. I don't exactly see who he's going to be helping, since nobody else is doing it that I know of. But that was his formulation.

"Also, I know from things he's said at other times, not today, that he probably should have included the standard Western urban diet as another one of the poisoned gifts, and also one of the things he wants to do something about, in a lesser way. But I know what he thinks of the town diet the Batswana are adopting, the Simba chips and the orange Fanta, the grease and sugar way of life, the reduced food palette . . ."

Ray said, "It's funny to think of bush diet as a palette. People desperately scrabbling through the landscape for tubers and insects . . ."

"Yes, but you know what he means. In the bush the diet has hundreds of vegetable items that disappear in the town diet. You don't disagree with this. People move to town and in old age they become obese, they gain mass, instead of getting leaner, which is healthier, and which is the norm in the countryside."

"But he didn't bring that up today, you said."

"Right, he didn't. Anyway, he laid some stress on his deciding to come to Africa and do this work particularly because he's black, which brought a smile to Kerekang's face because Davis is pretty light. His mother was white. I think he saw it wasn't going down especially well, so he dropped it. But he has a perfect right to mention it. His background is Caribbean and everybody who's black in the Caribbean was once a slave, even if his family somehow did very well in Montserrat and then when they came to the United States.

"His father was black. It's an interesting family. His father taught at Harvard Divinity School for many years. Davis refers to him as a Protestant divine. His father also owned the company that produces the prewritten sermons Protestant ministers use when they don't have time to write their own. It was enormously lucrative, I understand.

"I knew you'd find this interesting. His mother was an actual Boston Brahmin. Davis was close to her, but not to his father."

"I wonder why not."

"I don't know, but this brings me close to the end of what I know about Davis. He trained for the ministry but not for very long. He switched to medicine."

"Thus overthrowing his father."

"I suppose. And then in medical school he fell in love with a Nigerian exchange student and married her and that didn't work out . . ."

"What went wrong?"

"There was a divorce."

"But over what?"

"His wife betrayed him, which almost killed him. There was a bitter divorce. There were no children, thank God. So then he finished medical school and went through a process of disillusion with conventional medicine, and he developed his own ideas of what goes on in healing . . ."

"Eclectic medicine."

"Right. And that's the story up to the present. He had his practice and he met these people from Botswana, government people, and he decided to come here."

Ray said, "He tells you everything."

"No he doesn't. He tells me what I get out of him. You know how I am."

"Well pardon me if I find this unusual. He could resist your curiosity if he wanted to, great force that it is. I would think. He could draw lines, right? He's the doctor, you're the patient." Contain yourself, he thought.

"Well one thing he thinks is wrong is the conventional doctor-patient relationship."

Great, Ray thought. "But tell me, was his wife unfaithful with a white guy or a black guy, what race, just out of curiosity. Just to fill the picture out."

After a silence, she said, "That's really all I know."

"No it isn't," he said flatly, surprising himself.

"That tone. You are so certain sometimes."

He said, "You don't have to answer the question. That's your prerogative. But don't deny I'm right, that you do know."

"You are uncanny. And you are *oppressive*. You are . . . And I don't lie to you, and you know that. You rely on it. You exploit it. You want me to tell you something you know I'd rather not, and you take unfair advantage of me to get your way."

"I don't deny it," he said.

They proceeded in silence. Why was this something she wanted to withhold?

"I don't really know this for a fact," she said. "I didn't hear it from him. It's from someone else, so when I said I'd told you all I know, that was actually true. This is a different quality of . . . of information. It's gossip. I think his wife left him for a woman. And what her race might be I have no idea."

Now he knew what her impulse had been. She had been trying to protect Morel's image. It was humiliating to lose your wife to a woman. She hadn't wanted him to know. He didn't like it. Why should she be protecting Morel's image? What was it to her?

"God," he said. "No wonder he wants to overthrow Western civilization."

"Don't trivialize. Nobody said he wants to overthrow Western civilization. Anyway, what's the connection?"

"Well. I can't think of much, offhand, that would more completely unhorse me and make me want to pull down everything within reach. I guess I'm speaking for myself, but I'd sure want to do something about my fate. I can get with that. Western civilization is our fate. So. Ergo. Look, you have at least two betrayals going on at once. You're betrayed as a person, and your gender is being betrayed . . . and then add to the picture that your wife is Nigerian, you're being betrayed by an African. That makes it worse, somehow. So you think that something cosmic has to be wrong with the world that's doing this to you. So . . ."

"Listen, do you want to hear what else I have to report about the day's events? Because there is a bit more. Or do you want to keep on psychologizing, something I thought you hated, by the way."

He couldn't quite let it go. "I do want to hear, but don't tell me psychologizing isn't in order now and then. If something like this happened to me, I . . . well . . . I might very well decide to do something . . . amazing . . . instead of slitting my wrists right away."

She sighed hugely.

"I'm sorry I told you."

"Iris, don't be. It's interesting. In a way it's no crazier or more Promethean or whathaveyou than any other kind of missionary activity over here. It's just a new annex on a familiar edifice, isn't it? But it is interesting."

"I don't know how much of this is just talk, Ray. It's his medical work that's really important. I think."

"Okay, so what else was said? And who was the audience?"

"Those children, myself, your friend the engineer, Kerekang. Toward the end there were other people coming over who wanted to exchange pleasantries with Davis. He has a following. Patients and people who've heard about him."

"Now this is after his mission statement?"

"You're getting the wrong picture. This wasn't something he declaimed, some grandiose statement he was just waiting to unveil. You could tell he knew it was going to sound grandiose. And it was said more or less man to man, to your friend. I happened to be there. He wasn't being portentous in any way. Okay, I would even say there was some irony in the way he said it, although at that point I was pretty much in an eavesdropping position. My point is that it wasn't something being declared for the benefit of one and all, and certainly not for my benefit. What I think happened is that your friend . . ."

"Stop calling him my friend. I don't know this man Kerekang."

"Well, but you seem to like him. So do I . . ."

"And I don't keep referring to him as *your* friend, do I?"

"No, but you obviously like him. So did Davis. He's very appealing. You approve of him."

"Well let's call him Kerekang, for simplicity. I call your doctor by his last name and you and I call Kerekang by his last name. Or for even greater simplicity we could both refer to your doctor by his last name. No? Jesus, what *is* this? Everything is getting in the way."

"I know, and it's not coming from me. Anyway.

"Anyway, they went back and forth about Christianity for a while. I think Davis was trying to feel Kerekang out on the subject, find out where he stood. They were sizing each other up. It was fun to watch.

"I'm now, for this discussion, in a different memory palace, by the way.

"Kerekang seemed to be taking the position that even though Christianity wasn't exactly true, Africans had some things to be grateful to certain Christians for. And he mentioned how Livingstone and Moffat had run guns to the Batswana so they could repel the Boers. And in a more general way he was saying that he didn't see that it was so terrible for people to have in their minds a model of someone unfailingly kind, acting kindly. And then the discussion got a little miscellaneous on his part and he alluded to the role Christians had played in getting cab horses treated decently in London in the nineteenth century and also to the part they played in stopping the gladiatorial games, although I had the sense that Davis had some alternate explanation for that that he couldn't quite lay his hands on, or didn't, anyway. And then Kerekang went on to the work of Christians in ending the slave trade, although he did say that Christians had participated in it and profited from it from the beginning. And Kerekang also admitted that Christians in Europe had basically forced the Jews into being slave traders during the Middle Ages by making it one of the few trades Jews were allowed to engage in.

"So then Davis wanted him not to rely on single instances, but to look at the larger effects of the doctrine in Africa, and not to look at this or that good act by white Christians here and there in Africa. He wanted him to focus on what Christianity had done to Africans, to the African minds it had penetrated and was still penetrating. Wait a minute."

She closed her eyes.

"Okay, then Davis gave as an example what Christianity had done to homosexuality in Africa, making the point that universally there was no stigma attached to being homosexual within the traditional cultures, but that Christianity had brought persecution of homosexuality with it, introduced it where it hadn't been. Kerekang took this for a good point."

The flagpoles of the Gaborone Sun were coming into view.

"Then, and this was very sotto voce between them, they talked about abortion and how all the churches were united against legalization, which is true. And then they came to AIDS.

"Davis is passionate about it. He hears things through the medical grapevine that other people don't know. In the morgues in Zimbabwe they are stacking the AIDS corpses three to a tray, for example. The Catholics are against condoms and the Protestant churches are barely in favor of them and the independent African churches are bastions of insane folklore remedies for AIDS, which is galloping unbelievably. He thinks seropositivity is almost twenty percent here.

"Then Kerekang tried to take a sort of evolutionary position. This was that people would progress from animism and local gods to monotheism, the monotheisms, and then to Deism and finally out into post-religion. We would all someday be like Sweden, where nobody believed anything having to do with religion anymore. He's visited Sweden. But Davis was absolute against that view, saying that it's the liberal denominations that are declining into unimportance and the fundamentalist branches of religion that are gaining strength. And he wanted Kerekang to admit that this was especially true in Africa, which Kerekang did admit. Davis said Kerekang was a religious Menshevik, thinking that religion was going to turn into secularism the way the Mensheviks thought capitalism was going to evolve itself into socialism. For some reason this was a big hit with Kerekang. He has a wonderful laugh. How am I doing as a rapporteur?"

"You're astonishing me."

She was very pleased. He loved this flushed, sturdy creature. All this was for him, all this effort.

She said, "*Then* . . . what? . . . I think a reprise of the question of white Christians doing good things, which Kerekang couldn't quite escape from, ending up in this exchange . . . Kerekang saying Some people come to Africa to help us very much. Davis saying So did I. Kerekang saying They came to build things up. Davis saying Like me. Kerekang saying They came to create things. Davis saying Yes and the things they came to build are falling on the heads of Africans all around us.

"And then I believe this is the end of it. And I learned something I didn't know. Davis pointed out that Kerekang, who's a Xhosa, should appreciate that Christianity was behind the destruction of his people. In this way. In 1856 a prophetess ordered them to slaughter their entire national herd, half a million cattle, as a sacrifice, which they did and which impoverished them, it ruined them, it's so horrible. The prophetess . . ."

"Nongqawuse."

"You see, you know everything."

"Not quite, babe."

"But that's really impressive."

"No it isn't. It's one of the main events in the history of the region. The Xhosas who settled here in Botswana came north after the cattle massacre. There's a big settlement near Mahalapye, which is where Kerekang comes from, if my guess is correct."

"Well in any case she was a Christian convert who had decided that all the cattle had to be killed because they had been reared by people who practiced witchcraft, as the Xhosas had for generations, which meant that the cattle were defiled because the Christian god hated witchcraft. They were in a period of stress at the time. I don't know if it was drought or what. They were continually under pressure from the Zulus. So the prophetess promised that their tribulations would be over once they'd killed off all the cattle. He made the point, Davis did, that most people think of this act of destruction as something arising from primitive tribal craziness. But this was not a thing the pre-Christian tribes had ever done. It was Christianity that did it to them. Did you know that?"

He hadn't. He hadn't known that Nongqawuse was a Christian convert. "I may have known that, once. Maybe not. No, I don't think I did. No, I didn't."

"Any last comments on my report?"

"Impeccable, my dear girl. Impeccable, Iris."

They had reached the ring road. They turned up it. A quarter of a mile ahead of them on the far side of the road and occupying a site at the top of a long, slow rise was the Sun.

"So that was all. Davis gave Kerekang a card and invited him to a lecture he's planning to give. And then as a last afterthought he grabbed Kerekang before he could leave and made the point that it wasn't only Christianity he was concerned about, it was all religions, all religious belief, in case that hadn't been emphasized enough. And I believe Kerekang invited Davis to come have a look at the gleaner camp. And now I want something cold to drink."

He was full of gratitude toward her.

A realization he had suppressed came back to him. He had almost done something unforgivable. It had almost happened. During her recital, he had unthinkingly reached toward his shirt pocket to activate his microrecorder. But he had caught himself. He would never tape her. The temptation to do it then was understandable. The impulse was an artifact of the intensity of his focus on his enemy, Boyle, his preposterous enemy. Someone forgive me, he thought. Priest could be his code name for Morel, if Boyle could be made to see reason.

They were in sight of the hawker strip. Their approach galvanized the hawkers, who began heaving themselves up from the ground or struggling out from their cardboard and burlap hutments. The hawkers would mob them in a minute.

A heavy, owl-faced woman with a withered leg, the hawker closest to them, was toiling painfully toward them, determined to be the first to present her goods.

"That woman is crippled," Iris said. "Oh God."

They had to buy something. It was distressing. Hawkers from farther up the line were racing at them, overtaking the crippled woman. He suspected that word had been passed along that Iris was wearing one of their products, which made her a serious prospect. The crippled woman was in desperate haste. As her competitors came past her, she began unfurling her goods, pitching them out toward Iris and Ray, trailing them through the dust as she forged forward.

"Buy the biggest piece she has," Ray said. "Buy the bedspread." It was unlike him, but he was hot with gratitude toward Iris. He was usually careful with money.

"You know how they overcharge for these," she said.

"Get the bedspread. The tablecloth." It was blocked gratitude speaking. Of course they overcharged, for what they gave you. But he also knew that she'd get more pleasure buying this dubious object than she would buying something for herself that she really wanted.

"You're great," she said.

"Not yet," he said.

15. *I Would Like to Reassure*
You About My Penis

She was going to think he was perverse, getting into a hot bath on a hot night after a hot day . . . but sometimes there was a need. A scalding bath like this was for moments when everything hurts, from the soul outward, from the folds of your soul to the soles of your feet, and what the burning lake did was unify miscellaneous pains into a single physical one, briefly, which then turned into pleasure as the water temperature became bearable, something like that. Everything hurts, he thought, and there he was. But he could see the future. Iris would drift in, take note, say nothing, and convey everything by body language, as in rolling the eyes.

She would roll her eyes. And with some justification. From her viewpoint, there he would be, a Dagwood in his bathtub, but in darkest Africa. She would react, because what he was doing was odd and because if she wanted to talk more, which she did, she would be physically uncomfortable there, she would think he was deliberately creating a milieu uncongenial to conversation, which he would be hard pressed to deny, although it wasn't true. And what was the name of the actress who had been trapped into playing Blondie film after film by her physical appropriateness for the part, a good actress but never able to escape that one role? Singleton had been her name, Penny. And there had been others in her situation, including the poor fuck who'd fallen into playing Superman forever, on television and not even in the movies, and who'd finally shot himself to death, sick of it. And then in fact hadn't something similar happened to the actor who'd played Zorro? He thought so. Money made them do it. I do nothing for money, at least, he thought. Sometimes he wondered if his affection for the Zorro movies had any connection with his attraction to the dual life he had ended up leading and enjoying, for the most part. He had loved Zorro. Or he had loved the Janus metaphor underneath Zorro and the others, the introvert who had an armed and dangerous alter ego who could hurt you but wouldn't kill you, he would just tie you up and expose you to ridicule. He thought, We can never get down to the slurry of narratives we took in through our pores when we were growing up, and that sits in us, sloshing around in our foundations. Iris was coming in. She was nearby. He could sense it. And someday someone would come up with a process like psychoanalysis but devoted to ripping up the rotten subflooring of cultural junk in our depths, getting it up so it could be hawked up and spat out, genre, clichés, ads, commercials, formulas of all kinds, all of it. Women don't spit, he thought. Men hawk and spit. Iris claimed not to know how to hawk. She suffered from postnasal drip from time to time seriously enough that he had tried to teach her how to clear out the back of her sinuses, just to help with keeping ahead of the flow, but she couldn't do it. The process repelled her. He considered his legs, his lower self, in the faintly tawny water. If you like them lean, come to me, he thought. Iris was getting wider through the hips, fractionally, but it was happening. The water was perfect. Sweat crawled down his scalp. The concentration of chlorine in their tap water varied from day to day, and sometimes the odor could be distractingly strong, but tonight it was minimal, vaguely medicinal, like the ozone tinge produced by the electric coil in the geyser mounted high on the wall where it would crush his feet if it ever came down when he was in the tub. Every expatriate male he knew had talked about the damned menacing geysers and they all did what he did, which was to tug compulsively on the brackets that held the massive things in place whenever he was in the room. *Africa*, danger everywhere, he thought, mocking himself.

"Aren't you suffering in there?" Iris asked from the hall.

"In a good way," he answered. "I like it."

"It can't be good for you."

But she didn't pursue it when he didn't reply. He heard her withdraw . . . toward the bedroom, he thought.

If she wanted to join him in the tub room, there was a problem. There was no place for her to sit, except the uncomfortable rim of the tub. There was nothing in this cubicle but the tub and the washbasin. The toilet sat in its own cubicle, if a cubicle could be taller in the vertical dimension. If she was determined to come in and chat she could drag in the hamper from the toilet room, or bring in a chair, though she had never done that. He ran fresh hot water into the tub.

He thought, All hail the monster bathtub, the one true good thing the British left in Africa: Oversized because the imperial classes were so large in stature they hated to be hunched up when it came to bath time and time to relish their conquests that day.

Iris was back. He turned to look at her in the doorway. She was down to her bra and panties now, fanning herself. She still wanted to talk. *We have talked our extinction to death* was the one line he remembered from the whole corpus of Robert Lowell. He thought, Nobody talks about Lowell these days. The fading of great reputations was a hazard for people doing English . . . He was lucky with Milton. She wanted to talk about Morel and so did he, as much as you could want something to happen that you simultaneously dreaded, for no good reason.

"How long might you be in there?" she asked.

"I don't know. This is a treatment, I." She was going to be surprised at that. The use of I as a nickname for her, or a diminutive, one or the other, had fallen away years ago. It had been his earliest nickname for her. She'd never liked it much, actually.

"Treatment for what?" she asked.

"For what ails me."

"You're going to dissolve."

"That would be okay," he said, reaching for a tone that would suggest to her that he was midway in a process of some importance to him that he wanted to continue with, but that wouldn't sound unfriendly. They were going to talk. Of course she was already paying someone else to talk to her, if he wanted to be childish about it. He was certain she was well into some sort of talk therapy with Morel. He thought, Every man whose wife goes out to get help of this sort from a male, another male, feels something like this. He knew he was being a cartoon, but it made a difference that the therapist was male, whether it should or not. It was a stupid fact, but a fact. She was getting therapy, but therapy for what? What was the subject matter? His guess was that a certain proportion of what he was paying for was what could be called general conversation or general thoughts on how difficult life was, that kind of thing, and why couldn't she get that at home? But no, she wanted to warm her hams at the fire of another intellect, Morel's intellect and not his . . . This is a good place to have unworthy thoughts, he thought.

Silently Iris entered the bathroom, carrying a camp stool. She had put on a dark green silk kimono, his favorite out of the four or five kimonos she owned. These costume changes were about something. She was very deliberate in the way she opened and lowered the camp stool, setting it down at the foot of the tub. By being so delicate about it she was giving him space to object, he supposed. It was comical.

He arranged his washcloth over his genitals, for no reason. Apparently this was going to begin.

But instead of seating herself, Iris went to the basin, posted herself there, and proceeded with brushing her teeth. After a moment she said something that sounded to him like "I can't stand the world." Then she left the room, still brushing.

She was one of those people who have a need to walk around while they brush their teeth, in whom the act of brushing sets up a tension over the basic nullity and boringness of the procedure that they have to release by strolling while they do it, holding one hand cupped under the chin as they go. People in that category were always assiduous brushers. More nominal brushers like himself could stay in one place until they finished.

She passed by the doorway and said something unintelligible, completely unintelligible this time. She was under the delusion that she could say whatever she wanted while she was brushing her teeth and that it would be comprehensible to him because of the care with which she enunciated. It was his fault, because during their life together, since he had usually been able to divine what she was trying to say, he had never revealed his true feeling about it, which was that it was annoying and uncouth, like talking with your mouth full of food. So he had led her to believe she was being normal. He was unable to translate what she had just said.

At the basin again, she concluded by brushing her tongue.

"I couldn't make out what you said, your last thing," he said, when she was done.

"Just as well." She extended her tongue and studied it in the mirror.

It would be hostile to add more hot water to his bath at this point. He asked her to sit down if she wanted to.

His offer went unacknowledged. She said, "I do everything I'm supposed to . . ." The tone of grievance was there. He waited.

"I read somewhere that it's good hygiene to brush the back of your tongue when you do your teeth, so I do *that*. I sterilize my toothbrush, same reason. Nobody we know does that. The same with our diet. Whatever, if you're supposed to do it, I do it."

"I don't exactly follow you," he said, but in fact he had an idea where this was going. What was unstated was the conclusion her declarations implied, something along the lines of "I do all this and what does it get me?" she meant, get her in general. She was all over the place with her declarations of dissatisfaction, which was what this amounted to. Not that she would put her dissatisfaction as nakedly as he had.

She sighed, turned, and said musingly, "Do you know that I don't know if your penis is particularly large or not?"

It *is*, by God, he thought, outraged. But what was *this*? It was pure provocation.

She said, "You claim it is, but how do I know, really? I'm almost a virgin, I mean I was almost a virgin when I met you."

He was agitated. He had to keep himself under control. The tone had to be light. This was new. He could say "Gulp he said," but that was witless. Anxiety was doing this to her. She was flailing. She was being random.

She left the room, which was not possible.

"Iris, come and sit down," he called after her.

"It's so hot in there."

"Please, though. Please."

"The heat is too much."

"It's cooling down," he called. He wasn't going to give his treatment up. He needed it. "Please," he said. "I would like to reassure you about my penis. I think that's important."

"I have to come and sit in that steambath? All right, I will."

He listened intently. She was doing something.

She came in naked, and sat on the camp stool. "I hope you don't mind," she said.

He thought, on the contrary. But somehow it was completely apposite that the discussion they were going to have would be conducted with both of them stark naked. She was comfortable naked. Maybe that should worry him. Her breasts were small and full. She had never nursed, of course, but her nipples were on the tan or darker side, away from pink, which he assumed went with her coloring. And she had larger areolas than you would expect for someone who had never nursed, he thought. He was glad she was sitting down. The body of a naked woman standing in front of you could be a face looking at you, the breasts, the navel, the pudendum. He needed to be serious. She was intelligent about her nudity. She rationed it. She kept it a treat. She always wore something to bed. That was strategy, it was smart, and he loved her for it. But this just now was nudity for political reasons. It was coercive, to show what she had to put up with in order to come to grips with him. Sometimes after a bath his cleanness would provoke her into immediately sucking him off.

She said, "You know that was just kidding, about your penis. Just to get your attention."

"I know," he said. And he did know.

"I'm sorry."

"Don't be. There *is* the fact of your limited exposure, due to marrying me when you were a child bride. That's real."

"Well, and I also never saw my father naked. And of course I had no brothers, and then I was in girls' schools. Men have endless opportunities to check the full range of breasts and everything else in the movies, and magazines, and nudes in paintings. There's no parity. And of course in pornography the men they select would represent an extreme. So. And nude paintings are mostly females . . . and of course if it's a male, it's a flaccid male . . ."

"Men are shy," he said.

"I was just stirring things up."

"No, forget it," he said. He knew he was fine. He was better than fine. He had observed enough to know that. The men in his family happened to be well endowed. He had seen his father's penis. And when his brother reached puberty, it became clear he was going to be in the money too. She could write Rex and ask him, if she wanted to, they were so close. Or he could get a medical book and let her look him up, measure him and look him up. There was a sexy idea.

Now they were going to talk about Morel. Somehow the die was cast. He felt it. She felt it.

But she got up, yet again, and said, "I have to do something about the light if I'm going to stay here. I'll get a couple of candles, if that's all right."

He nodded vigorously. She left the room and he added a little more hot water to the bath. The geyser rumbled the way it did when a new demand was placed on it. Crush me, he commanded it.

She was sensitive to lighting. She hated the overhead light in this room. He was sorry for her. He wanted to help. She had a way of making things worse. Now the idea that he was going to hear something much worse than he'd expected was growing. She was in love with Morel. Or she was falling in love with Morel. Or they'd done it and now she was sorry. Never, he thought. He was being extreme. Or they'd done it and she wasn't sorry. It had been wonderful and now she didn't know what to do. He would have to help her. That was going to be his role. All her pre-ambling was making things worse.

She brought in two tall candles in a candelabrum, a wobbly craft object from Uganda. She tried different floor placements for the candelabrum, finally settling on a spot to his right, near the wall. She turned out the ceiling light.

They sighed together. "This is mysterious," he said. The new lighting tended to make the scene more extreme. She was mainly a shape to him. Half her face was in shadow. Her hair looked wild, as though it were swelling outward as he looked at her. She had taken her bandeau off. The Medusa effect he was seeing had to be an optical illusion or a consequence of the steamy atmosphere.

He asked, "What are those paper flowers that expand from nothing into complex blooms when you put them in water called?"

She was blank. "Paper flowers was what we called them. I don't think I ever knew any other name for them, like expando flowers or something like that. Paper flowers."

He said, "But of course there are all kinds of paper flowers."

"I know."

The wavering light the candles produced was fundamentally unhelpful.

Go first, he thought, but too late because she was saying in a constricted voice that they had to talk about Davis now, it was the right time.

Resentment drove him to say, hotly just under his breath, "Son of a bitch." She didn't hear it. She was continuing. This was not something she was enjoying, at least.

"Ray . . . I want to go two or three times a week to Davis, go on a regular basis instead of off and on the way I do now. I have really decided. That's one thing. So it's going to cost something we need to budget for."

He made an ill-considered dismissive gesture, to show that the money was nothing, ill-considered since his arms were underwater and the gesture splashed water out of the tub, alarming her instead of the reverse.

He apologized.

She said, "The more I go the sooner it's over. I don't plan to be going to him forever. So that's one thing. I love you. And now the other thing is that I need it to be agreed that I don't tell you anything about what we discuss, our sessions. This is standard in therapy, but it's going to be hard for you, for us, because it's so unlike the way our life together has always been. And I know you'll be curious, but I want you to promise you'll just leave these sessions as terra incognita. I know you. I know the way you try to get things out of me. You do it almost automatically, you can't help it. So I need you to promise that you won't. I want a pledge. That you'll try."

"Is this pledge something your doctor proposed?"

She didn't want to answer.

"Why?" she asked him.

"I'd just be curious to know who it emanated from, him or you?"

"Both."

"Okay, that's fine, but you give me pause in a certain way. And we should discuss this now, I guess. Because what I see is, okay, you're going into therapy, psychotherapy, and the money is not an issue, you understand, that's all fine. But here's a consideration. I'd like to understand how this . . . process . . . this process can be useful to you if you have to observe certain limits in what you can tell him about your life. That is, our life, your life with me." He thought of Boyle's chamber.

He continued. "He would consider me a spy."

"You *are* a spy," she said.

"Well," he said. Despite the heat of the bath, he felt a sensation of cold in his chest, like a lozenge the size of a bar of soap.

"I apologize for raising this, but I can't help it. Is this correct? . . . that a whole constituent of your life and the problems it causes will be left out. We're agreed on that? I mean, I know we are, but I seem to be asking for reassurance . . ."

She was silent. He needed to be able to see her face better. The abominable lighting was against him.

Finally she said, "I don't see that as a problem."

"Okay, you mean you accept these limitations . . . And you don't think that leaving all that out will, well, moot the process you're . . . paying for?"

She was slow to answer. He thought, In the States the agency has its own roster of cued-in shrinks for this kind of thing. Talk about sinecures.

"I accept," she said.

"Then it's fine."

Maybe I shouldn't do this, he thought, saying, "Maybe I shouldn't ask you what I'm about to ask you. But it will just be this once. I would just like to know in a general way *why* you're going to him, need to go to him."

"How can you stand this?" she murmured, meaning the ambience, the heat, and not that she was relenting or showing sympathy toward him.

She was trembling slightly. "You know why. At least you know why I went to him initially."

They went through it. She had thought her urine looked too dark. Ray had been dismissive. She had gone to Davis Morel and Ray had turned out to be right, but Davis had discovered something else. He had looked at her and seen something and had questioned her.

Ray sat up straight in the tub. This was new.

He held his breath while she talked, so he could hear everything. Because Davis had listened to her and gone beyond the original complaint that had brought her to him he had discovered that she was suffering from hypoadrenia, which was not something Ray should worry about and which was essentially being taken care of. Davis had questioned her about her energy level, about which she had complained listlessly and endlessly at home. Because Davis had listened to her he had found something that Ray with his congenital optimism had never acknowledged. She was telling him more about hypoadrenia than he needed to hear. What it was was obvious. Her energy had been low. She'd been having adrenal insufficiency due, most probably, to the universal cause, stress . . . although stress included not just emotional but physical, chemical, and thermal varieties. He had tested her for the Ragland effect and it had been positive. Now she was taking glandular supplements and heavy B complex and malic acid and magnesium and she was enormously improved. The whole thing had been fixed so rapidly that she hadn't bothered to mention it to him. The extra supplements she was taking fitted in with the regular vitamin pills they took. So that had been the physical side of why she began with Morel.

He could read between the lines. His attempts to buck her up and tell her to rest had been a mistake, a form of letting her down. She didn't have to say so directly. It had been a mistake to judge her by his own condition, which was that his energy level went up and down too. His policy was to ignore his fatigue. He thought, I could be Bartleby in ten minutes, little does she know . . . I could stop, freeze . . . I could permanently relax . . . terminal relaxation, retire physically, stop exerting. But he couldn't retire. They hadn't figured that out yet, but it was coming up. Candles are perfect for this. He thought, I am guttering . . . at fifty she'll be fine but at sixty I won't unless I relax. It was time to think about retirement. It was almost too late, in fact, so it was definitely time. He needed a new way to get significantly ahead.

He said, "What you're telling me . . . this is good. It's great. And you do seem fine. Of course you always did, but, this is wonderful. Kiss me when you get a moment. I love you. I'm grateful to this man, truly."

"He really does go beyond," she said. "You may not want to hear this but it illustrates something."

She hesitated, then said, "He really studies you. Okay, he smells you, studies that aspect. He feels your hair. He smells your breath, something no doctor I ever heard of does. He looks at the whites of your eyes . . ."

"Okay, okay, I get it. I'm not crazy about it. It's a little theatrical for me, but what do I know? So. So does it involve any touching along the way? Just curious."

"Oh please. He feels your trapezius muscles for a second. But listen to this. The way he deduced I might have hypoadrenia was by looking at my hands. People who are the most likely to experience adrenal problems have certain physical characteristics, such as being long-waisted like me, and miscarriages, a history of miscarriages. But a main indication is that the index finger is more rounded than the others and longer than the ring finger. Which again is me. Realize that this is not an extended process. It's brisk. There are people around, in and out all the time. Also, if I may say this, the fact is that regular doctors *do not* look at you. They look at your history while they're talking to you. There is *nothing intimate* about this examination he does. It's the same for men, I'm sure. That's it. I wanted you to know about this from me before you hear about it from someone else, because it's different, what he does, and it's going to be talked about, God knows. That's really it."

He thought, I am burning with love, what can I do? . . . She loves him, I think.

The fact was, he loved talking to her, the sheer talking, whatever the subject was. It didn't matter that they were at odds and that she was extracting his heart from his chest like an Aztec. Her voice was a gift to him when it was aimed his way. "I am leaving you!" she could be saying and he would still want to hear it.

"So in effect this is a onetime thing he does, not something that gets repeated time after time, as I understand you."

"Of course not."

"So *that* part of this is in the past."

"Absolutely."

"I love you."

She loved him too. He said, "So that covers the physical part, I guess. So now we come, briefly as we can, to, to, anything you can tell me about these sessions . . ." No way could he say what he wanted to say, which was What is wrong with me that this is happening, for God's sake, and what was the *Hauptsache*, the main thing, a German term that came to him from his Introductory German, for God's sake. Maybe we are lost, he thought. He continued his thought, ". . . I won't ever ask you again, but anything you can say about why you are going and what I should assume you're talking about *in the most general way*, I would appreciate, Iris, and I beg you to God to forgive me for asking you this. But anything you

can tell me about what is going on here, tell me, and I apologize. But tell
me . . ."

"It's conversation."

"But what should I assume? Conversation about what? About your disappointments in life?"

"It's conversation. It's partly about philosophy. He gives me things to
read as part of it. From time to time. Homework."

"That's interesting. Are those things I could know about, your syllabus, the things he recommends."

"I don't know. I can tell you what I'd prefer."

"Not to. Not to tell me."

"Right. And if you see me reading something, since I'm not going to
put brown paper jackets on everything, just let me proceed with it without any commentary being elicited."

"That's fine. I don't know a lot of what you read normally, anyway. You
go into your sanctum."

"I'll tell you what I'm doing, what I want." She got up and stood away
from the tub, her arms folded. She wanted him to understand the seriousness of what she was about to say, although the stance she was taking,
with her legs slightly apart, meant that the bottom of her pubic fringe was
backlit. It was the main feature in the silhouette she was presenting to
him. He didn't need to be reminded that they were a couple of animals,
however civilized they were in a situation like this. He turned his gaze
away, up toward the geyser, again willing it to fall and crush him.

There was a substantial pause while she calmed herself with a breathing exercise he'd seen her perform a couple of times lately, a new thing.

"This is what I want. What I want for myself is like that line in the
Bible, 'Let your yes be yes and your no be no.' I want my life to be like
that, this is yes, this is no. *Yes* I am your friend. No I'm not your enemy. I
want clarity. You remember when everybody was talking about that religious fanatic who's dragging a cross around the world, when he showed
up in South Africa? He's been at it for years. This is supposedly his mission. But in the photograph in the paper, it was obvious there was a
twelve-inch wheel attached to the foot of the cross, meaning he isn't
really dragging his cross around the world, he's rolling it, which a person
might think was still pretty admirable . . . but it isn't the same thing.
Nobody referred to the presence of the wheel. I want clarity. And I want
to feel really good, not just physically. This is turning into a collage, isn't
it? And I want us to get to a new level, which I don't have a definition of.
But I want us to be at a new level. And I want to stop *chopping ashes* . . ."

She was so animated. "Chopping ashes?"

"Kgabatlela melora. It's what the Batswana say about someone who's doing something really pointless. I guess our closest equivalent would be 'pounding sand,' but that doesn't really capture it in the same way."

"Everything you want is what I want, Iris."

"I know. I believe that." She returned to her seat at the foot of the tub.

He said, "Could you, though, give me just an indication of the kinds of things he's giving you to read?"

She sighed at him.

"Literature," she said. "You are so *relentless*."

"Okay, that's fine. I love you."

"But I'll tell you something he wanted me to read that I absolutely gave up on. It was Thoreau's *Journal*, Volume Six, and I said no after I'd read fifty pages because I'd *gotten the point*. Davis thinks it's the greatest literary work of art of the whole period, I don't know, since Shakespeare. I got the point, which is that Thoreau is really paying attention to the world, in detail, seeing everything there is. I said to him that there was no *development*. Maybe he thinks I'm shallow, I don't know. He was nice about it. And please don't give me your opinion of Thoreau or get into that whole thing you have on English Literature versus American Literature."

"I won't. Okay."

"Also, out of fairness I ought to tell you that some of what he's giving me is writing of his own. Chapters, drafts, for something he's writing, a book of essays called *Idol Meat*."

"*What?* Meat? Idle?"

"It's i-d-o-l meat, Ray."

He felt like a fool. And the title hurt him. He liked it. He thought of his own unwritten books, with pain, his book plans, all embryonic. He had ideas. There was no time.

She said, "Idol meat is . . . "

He interrupted her, saying, "I *know* what it is."

He hadn't meant to say it the way he had. "Idol meat is the leftovers, isn't it? The burnt offerings made by the pagans and the Jews, cooked animals, meat, that Christians weren't supposed to partake of if it came their way. Taboo meat."

"Right."

"Are you making suggestions as you read?"

"If something strikes me. But don't get the idea I'm editing him or anything remotely resembling that."

"He appreciates your contributions, though."

"He seems to."

"I'm not surprised."

He wondered if they had come to the end of the discussion. Apparently not, because she was still sitting there, unhappily. There was more, then.

She said, "One of the areas I'm trying to improve in is telling the truth, not being as politic as I have."

"So you have something more you want to tell me."

"Yes. God help me, though."

"Say it. Say it."

"I know you know about this, Ray. There were certain schools of Greek philosophy where doing this was part of achieving virtue or enlightenment. It was called *parrhesia*. It means *saying everything*."

"The Stoics," he said.

"No, the Cynics, the Cynics. *Parrhesia*."

"The Cynics, not the Stoics, are you sure?"

"*Parrhesia*, the Cynics. I'm completely sure. The Cynics are very misunderstood. In fact the Stoics are a dilution of the Cynics. Well, in my humble opinion they are."

"Obviously I have to go back and look at my Phil One notes."

"No you don't. That's not what I want."

The truth was that he remembered not that much about the ancient Greeks. He hadn't found them interesting, partly because what they seemed to find most interesting was pederasty. How great had they been? They had given their empire away by stupidly fighting among themselves and then their superbly civilized upper classes had invited the Romans to take over when the plebs made the slightest trouble. As he recalled, Stoicism was about numbness, being numb, their great object. What else was it that she was going to say? He had references, he could look up the Stoics. He could deal with this. He was not a child.

"I never took philosophy in college," she said. "Did you know that?"

"Philosophy is a joke," he said, hotly, trying to think of what his actual position was. She was making him suffer, without intending it. She could *not* come to the point, obviously because it was going to be too painful for him. What else could explain this? What was it?

He knew what he wanted it not to be. He did *not* want it to be about their failure to reproduce, again. That was settled. It had to be a settled thing. A solid scab had formed over the issue. And of course it was exactly the kind of issue that was going to turn up once she began free-associating through the universe of her disappointments. Why they had no children was complicated. There had been delay and bad luck involved. They hadn't started trying early enough. They had been living in Africa. Getting it definitively established that she was infertile had taken years more. They had stuck with different regimens for too long before that, before facing the truth. He didn't think he had been halfhearted about having children, despite certain reservations he might have had. Inwardly he knew that he would not have enjoyed being his own parent, being a parent to the child he had been. He had never been captivated by the idea of reproducing himself. But he had wanted it very much, for Iris. He had, despite the fact that children exposed you to hellmouth, which was the opening up of the mouth of hell right in front of you, without warning, through no fault of your own. It was the mad gunman shooting you at lunch and it was the cab jumping the curb and crushing you. It was AIDS and it was the grandmother, the daughter, the granddaughter tumbling through the air, blown out of the airplane by a bomb, the three generations falling and seeing one another fall, down, down, onto the Argolid mountains. With children you created more thin places in the world for hellmouth to break through. Morel was hellmouth for him. Hellmouth was having the bad luck to be born in Angola anytime after 1960. And hellmouth was Bertrand Russell coming home from a bicycle ride and announcing to his wife that he had decided he didn't really love her, like that. That was hellmouth, too. When it had come to adoption, he wasn't opposed to it. It had been Iris who dropped it. She had been so determined that it be his flesh, his child. Now at forty-eight he was at the limits of eligibility, if he hadn't already crossed them, unless they went for a half-grown child, which was not what she had wanted. Now her sister was fanning the flames. And Iris was going to be with her, in the middle of it, while an actual infant was produced, to feel and hold. Was there going to be some state of the art nostrum Morel would give Iris?

She began to speak and he saw that he had been wrong. It was something else and it was worse.

She seemed to be saying that she felt he ought to know that she felt a certain attraction to Morel. She was talking about it because it was important for her to tell the truth about things, for her own sake and for his. Ray was numb. He went over what she had said so far. First of all, she was going to go to Morel *despite*, as Ray understood it, this attraction she felt. Nothing had happened between them and nothing was going to happen. She had determined in her mind and heart that nothing *was* going to happen with Morel and nothing was going to happen with their marriage. But, as he understood it, she didn't want to go to Morel under false colors, false pretenses. He, Ray, was the only one who knew this attraction existed. Morel had no idea. There had been no flirting, no exchange of vibrations, none, and there would be none. All this had come out in a rush, involving a divagation about men feeling attraction for the women they worked among all the time, and wives knowing, seeing it at parties and in other transactions and having it denied to their faces. Her plan, he gathered, was to proceed smartly through her course of therapy and get what she needed to out of it and then remove herself still unstained, better, happier, a happier self, for him, for Ray. The thing was that *telling* him was killing him. It was good she was going away for a while, or was it? He didn't know. *This is the spit on which we turn. Time is the fire in which we burn*, was a fragment of his attempted poetry, from the deep past. This moment would pass. He knew something about the therapy relationship that she didn't. One thing he knew that Iris didn't was that a woman named Daddario whose first name would come to him in a minute had done a doctoral dissertation showing that thirty percent of women who sought counseling wound up having some form of sexual contact with their therapists, from kissing and petting to sexual intercourse. Linda was Daddario's first name. It was odd that he remembered that.

"Ray, don't tell me you haven't been in situations where you felt attracted to someone. And don't say yea or nay if you don't want to. I know you have. I've seen it. Married women are used to that."

"But I don't," he said. "I don't look, I don't flirt. I don't."

"I didn't say you flirt. But you look. But *that's not what I want to talk about.*"

She was getting distraught. He wondered if it could be as simple as telling her not to go, telling her to forget it, saying he wouldn't pay for it, taking the choice away from her . . . as if he could do such a thing. Then the idea would be for her to go to someone else. Except that there was no one else. They were in Botswana. It was a total fluke that someone with Morel's credentials had bobbed up in Gaborone, available for her. The idea that what she wanted was for him to command her to desist was a fantasy. Alas, he thought. There was no one else for her. There was the Italian head of the mental hospital in Lobatse whose English was a national joke.

Something nice was happening. She was joining him in the tub. He hadn't proposed it. "Take me in your legs," she said.

. . .

It was still about Morel, on the subject of religion. Ray hadn't been listening. He had to listen.

"But this is what he says. How he says it. That . . . *That*, separate from any problems the particular narrative your denomination has decided to believe in might have, might have regarding ordinary reality, the virgin birth or whatever, there's the problem of how *it* articulates with the rest of what's in this sort of narrative heap, the Bible, which is somehow both internally contradictory and *holy*. To the naked eye the Old Testament disagrees with the New Testament, very much. So the Bible is put in your little hands and the fact that it doesn't add up is supposed to be beside the point. So in church you're undergoing modeling in overlooking contradiction, being trained to push contradictions out of your consciousness just like the respectable adults who run the church do. They seem to thrive on it. But you slowly turn into a dunce, of sorts. You could call this the original sin of religion, is the way he puts it. You become a Christian by ignoring contradictions, not only between the magic-contra-reality elements in your own denominational story but between it and the other weird flowers in the folly garden you got it from."

He thought, She has no idea how obvious the novelties in her vocabulary are, like contra and folly garden and narrative, the way she just used it.

"I think he's right about this. Ray, I was such a serious child. I was so good. I wish I could remember more about my wretched time in Sunday school. I was so good while all this was leaching into me. I wanted my parents to love me, obviously, which is why I went along, obviously. The thing is that I think I liked Sunday school, being a dunce, and even looked forward to going. I don't know. I think I was even sort of thrilled when I had confirmation. We were Episcopalians then."

"So you were a believer for how long?"

"Well, a believer . . . I don't know. I went to church, I was in a club called Chi Rho. What I mean is I don't know how *actively* I believed. I try to recapture it and I can't."

"So you were an Episcopalian and what happened? Because when I met you there was no sign or real residue of that, at least so far as I can remember." His cheek was against her temple. He was speaking against her skull. They were bone to bone, almost. If only his love could travel into her mind physically, by pure resonance in some way, straight in, so she would feel it and know it. Her hair was perfect. Her body was heaven to him, the pastures of heaven, perfection.

"It was funny because I think once I was confirmed and had gotten into adolescence it was as though my parents lost interest, almost as though they had done their job by exposing me to Jesus. And I suppose they thought it had taken, I was inoculated to be good, and so that was that and they could go back to not going to church once that seemed to have taken place satisfactorily. It was like what they do to cattle here, for ticks, run them through a spray, or like orthodontia. My parents stopped going, my father first. Then my mother. And then I kept going to church, and then just to Chi Rho, and then I stopped going to that. There was never much discussion around it."

"Did your family say grace?"

"We did for a while at Thanksgiving and Christmas dinner. I remember it as feeling awkward."

He pressed his cheek harder against her. Her breath was empty, neutral, which meant ideal. He was cupping her breasts lightly, protectively, was what he was aiming for. Getting erotic was wrong for this juncture. He asked if her family had tithed.

"Tithed? No of course not. I don't know. I don't think Episcopalians tithe. I think Jews do, and Mormons. They did put money in the collection plate, but secretly from me. It was always already in an envelope, so I have no idea how much they gave. Parents are odd. They were odd. They never got in line to shake the minister's hand on the steps after services. They slid around, somehow, nodding. Of all the events the church gave, we only went to the massive ones, where the crowds were. Don't get an erection, I beg you. We're not doing anything tonight. Don't get an erection and make me feel guilty."

"I'm trying," he said.

"Well *succeed*."

Touching her between the legs at times like this was something they liked to call getting away with murder. He was never absolutely sure when she was going to permit it, when they were in casual mode, which was a good thing, no doubt. Take nothing for granted was what it said.

"Even after my religion went away I kept putting Episcopalian on the line that asks for your religion on application forms, like a robot. Then I began putting Protestant. And then I started leaving it blank and to my astonishment discovered that nobody cared if I did. What I really wanted to write was None of your business. But I never did. I'm sure the reason we were Episcopalians was because St. Michael's was the church closest to us in our neighborhood, walking distance.

"So there went my religion . . ."

"Your shackles turned to dew," he said.

She was struck. She swallowed. He felt it. She sat up a little.

"That's a beautiful line, what is it?"

There was a problem. The line happened to be his own. Let your shackles fade like dew, or as the dew, he couldn't remember which, came from his delusional period as a would-be poet. What he did not need just now was admiration for his aesthetic ejecta, leading to questions about what else he should be doing with his great talents rather than working for the agency.

She sat up fully. He kissed the nape of her neck.

"What is that from?"

All he remembered about his poem at this point was the struggle to get it right, which he had lost because he hadn't found the right image for shackles turning to dew and then subsequently rising away like mist, dew in the morning sun, something like that. Fade was wrong.

"I don't know what it's from. I don't know. I'll try to think . . ."

"I have to know," she said. "Can you track it down for me? I'm asking you to."

"Tasking me. I'll try." *May your shackles turn to dew*, had been the original line . . .

"I'm going to remind you," she said.

Then he understood. It was for Morel, for his use, for his armamentarium, he knew it as clearly as he knew anything. She loved it as an image of liberation and she wanted to bring it as a gift to her mentor, which was what he was becoming, not that she would ever admit that that was why she wanted it.

She said, "Because I would love to pass it on to Davis. For his writing. He's constantly writing."

She sank down again, to her former position, drawing his hands back to her breasts. Everything is a wound, he thought. He didn't know what to do. Everything with her was Morel, not that she could help it. He was afraid. He wanted to know if behind all this declared attraction something worse was moving its slow thighs, something like individual vacations, something middle-class decadent like open marriage, whatever that was. He was afraid of conceptualizing what he was afraid of. Something was coming. He thought, She's wounding me, I could die . . . She doesn't know. His heart was beating rapidly. She should be able to notice that, unless she was dismissing it as sex, which she didn't want, tonight. Was it because Morel was black? Was Morel using that? Would this be happening if Morel were white? Injustice to blacks had been a preoccupation of Iris's. Of course suppose the Africans had had the Renaissance first and then gone off to conquer the world, how different would it have been? Every race is as bad as its power permits it to be was his opinion.

"You're hurting my breasts," Iris said.

"God I'm so sorry. It was unconscious." He took his hands off her, but again she caught them and pressed them to her breasts.

Something was coming that he didn't want to hear and it was coming at the worst moment, because in a way everything was perfect. The color of her skin in the color of the bathwater was perfect. The water in the tub was the exact shade of something . . . Jasmine tea was what it was. He thought he knew the particular cup of tea, even, and the restaurant they'd been in when it had been served, years ago, before Africa. The scent from the citronella candle burning in the hallway was contributing to the moment . . . the scent was enough like perfume for her, enough not like perfume, closer to an astringent, for him. Physically nothing was hurting. It was excruciating.

He had to know what was coming. It was, and it didn't matter why it was coming, it didn't matter why it was coming, whether it was the issue of their childlessness aggravated again via her sister cleverly devising to get pregnant by an absolute fool, or if it was the first cold wind of menopause beginning to blow, or if it was boredom with him versus the black glamour of the black bastard he had the power to destroy utterly, if he was careful. She prefers a jackass who says contra instead of versus, as if that made any kind of difference: she wants to mate with a larger vocabulary, he thought. But larger vocabulary wasn't what he meant. He meant gaudier vocabulary, flashier.

Do it, he said to himself. "What do you want?" he asked, his tone strange to his ears, realizing as he spoke that this was clumsy and would only baffle her.

That was the effect. "What do you mean?" she asked. He had succeeded in baffling her.

"Iris, I don't know what you want, if you want us to have an arrangement . . . something like an arrangement . . ." He could barely hear himself.

She sat up and torqued herself violently around in order to look hard into his eyes. She seemed amazed. It seemed genuine.

She had covered her breasts with her hands, reflexively, as though she had suddenly found herself in the presence of a stranger. She was staring at him, shaking her head minutely.

Anyone would want her. She was interesting. Yesterday she had raised the question of why there was a single term in English for affirmative head movements but that for the negative you were forced to use three words? He had no idea why there was no one-word antonym of nod. Her questions came from nowhere, you were never prepared. She was good company. There were her peculiar dreams, her amusing dreams, many of them lately, he realized, about getting rich. A few mornings ago she had said to him, "I dreamed I got rich on a doohickey I invented that would let you put your hair up in a bun shaped according to your religion, cross, crescent, star of David, a little Buddha . . ."

"You poor thing," she said. "I am *in pain* if you thought I was thinking of anything like that. *Please*. Oh my poor *thing*."

He thought, She wants Morel, despite all this she does, she won't do it with him, but this is where we are . . . she prefers him . . . I'm more interesting . . . I am, not that she can see it, but I am.

Still regarding him steadily, she said, "We love each other."

He flinched. He felt weak. It was too much.

"I mean us, *us*," she said, clearly alarmed. She touched his face.

"Give me a minute," he said.

The pose she was holding was impossible. She turned and resumed her previous position, but bracing her heels on the tub above the tap, she drove herself more forcefully against him than before, which he took as a declaration combining love and punishment for idiocy.

He began, mechanically, to soap himself. "You just nearly killed me," he said.

"You're an idiot," she said. She made a spiral pattern in the lather on his right kneecap.

She sighed heavily. A pause followed. "But don't you think it's interesting, an interesting thing to realize, that our wonderful huge white civilization is all a big misunderstanding? I mean, Jesus was not a Christian, at all. And that's only part of it. I know I'm going on and I'm sorry. Hate him if you have to, but I learn interesting things from this man you hate. It's like your first year of college, before it turns into a drag. But there is something so staggering about it, first the Church stealing Jesus from the Jews, claiming him, and then libeling and killing the people who *gave* them Jesus. Fantastic. You have Judaism and you have Christianity and Islam, these two heresies, coming out of it, and you have these heretics trying their best to kill the people that produced them! There is something astonishing about the magnitude of the lying going on. What you have is this image of a huge upside-down pyramid which is the denominations, all the denominations, and churches, and the mosques, and

they're all balanced on a point, and the point the whole pyramid is standing on is . . . is lies! Certain untruths . . . and nobody telling . . . Jesus was
never anything but a devout Jew, you know, he was never a Christian at
all. And the Jews didn't kill him. It was the Romans.

"So it isn't just There is no God with Davis. It's about lies. But I promise you I am not going to keep talking about him. I'm sorry. Also I don't
want to be restricted for no reason. But don't worry."

Essentially it was over, this episode, he supposed. She had a bingo. She
had everything she wanted. She had carte blanche to see Morel, and to
what? flirt with him was what it came down to, with her husband's
approval, although calling it flirting was probably unfair. It would be fun
for her. He wondered how she would like it if he proposed a deal like that
for himself, except that he was forgetting it was her opinion that men as a
class already had a de facto right or privilege to flirt and worse without
anyone taking notice of it let alone assessing damages. Love is a strain, he
thought. Now was probably not the best time to establish exactly how
many sessions per week she was going to have with Morel. But he had to
know that.

"What do you think brought him to Africa?"

"Well, Africa is the one part of the world where you're getting four
new Christians for every two you're losing in the rest of the world. He
has the figures. Don't sound so grave."

"I'm not grave, I'm pensive."

"Why should the subject of religion make you so pensive? We aren't
religious, I thought.

"Do we believe in God, for example?

"Was that a shrug I felt?"

He was tempted to be perverse, which would be a mistake.

"Well, yes and no."

"What do you mean?"

"Indirectly."

"What?"

"Well, you might say I believe in someone who obviously did. Milton."
This is stupid, he thought. "Without his religion there would've been no
Paradise Lost, no . . . none of it."

"You think it's impossible that he might have written something else
great, as an unbeliever?"

"No, nothing like what he did write, of that . . . stature. And he
couldn't anyway because in his time any declaration of unbelief got you
locked up. Where *Paradise Lost* is, there would be nothing, believe me."

"I believe you and I love you. You don't know how much more we love you than you love us, in general."

"You mean, how much more women love their men than men love their women, how ridiculous. How unsupported can you get."

"How many women know their husband's Social Security number versus how many men know their wife's? Venture a guess."

"Fifty-fifty."

"Wrong. About seventy percent of women know their husband's. The figure for men is thirty percent."

She would never know how tired he was of her facts and figures, courtesy of the good doctor. Now they were doing something interesting together, he and Iris. They were collaborating on a fiction. The fiction was that what had eventuated between them had been a very small thing and that all was well. It was remarkable about how few collaborations in making fiction worked out at all, Ford and Conrad excepted, and the two women who wrote novels about Irish country life. What she wanted from him was childish, on the face of it. She wanted, as he understood it, to see Morel and have fantasies about him and not have to feel guilty about it. That was on the face of it. But there was more going on. The more was a new Mode of Being, or, better, a New Mode of Relating, and his brother was right that there was a larger place for capitals in writing and expression generally than the times were permitting.

She said, "I didn't mean to get into that and I'm sorry. It's marginal. I want to say just two main things. I'm going to see him *and* nothing is going to happen. I love you and you're my husband. But I'm going to go to him and when he's helped me I'm going to stop. Helped me, to my satisfaction. But I just don't want you sensing something you don't like, suspecting something untrue, and my being forced to deny it over and over."

He was going to say something he shouldn't. "You'd tell me first if something was . . . was starting? You know what I mean. Not that this should be any kind of condition for your going to him, but you would, you would tell me?" He felt like a fool. She was silent.

He said, "I feel vacant. This is making me feel vacant."

"I'm very sorry if it is. It shouldn't." He was hearing a tough tone that was new toughness.

I am nowhere, he thought.

She was brisk. "Nothing is going to happen. I am swearing this to you. I swear it." She pressed her palm to her sternum, like a diva, but in all seriousness.

Nonsense was pushing its way into his mind. They began to begin to be gone, he thought, three times, making himself stop when he felt the phrase entrenching itself. He needed to steady himself. He had to keep in mind that she was going to be away in the States, which would postpone everything as well as giving him time to strike back at Morel.

She said, "I really want you to understand how helpful he's been to me. In the smallest ways.

"For example. He taught me to spit, how to hock up mucus, rather. Everybody knows how to spit. But how to hock up mucus from the back of my throat, when my sinuses are going crazy."

"Hawk, I think you mean."

"No, it's hock. He says hock. I think hawk must be a corruption of hock. Because it's hock. He showed me in the OED."

"Ah, lucky guy. He has the OED? Are we talking about the real Oxford English Dictionary, not the microscopic edition you read with a magnifier?"

It was the real OED. Ray could tell she was feeling sorry for him. She wanted him to have his own OED, the real one. He hated the microtext edition. He loved the OED. But it was a tool he could use at the university library if he needed to. And he rarely needed to these days. And the real OED was too massive a possession for people as mobile as they had to be prepared to be. He could afford an OED. That wasn't the problem.

No doubt he had only himself to blame for this moment arriving. Although what he could have done differently at any point in his earthly life so far was a question he would love to thrash out with someone as sapient as the great all-seeing eye she was paying through the nose to visit, although in fact the fees were pretty low. On the other hand was it possible he should construe her confession of attraction slightly differently, as in its being a way of stopping herself, preempting herself by alerting herself and him too, something done as an act of love? Of course that was slightly too self-congratulatory to be true, probably. She was in a malaise, was what this was about. They both were. Maybe this was simple, florid feminism of some kind. Brute feminism, and with no way he could go into it, but was it something like an attempt to undo something she disliked that was a fixture of regular life, such as the truth that men feel more threatened when their mates show interest in another male than women do when men partake in the more or less general reflexive sizing up of the world of women? some impulse like that, such as wanting to make everyone suffer equally? But he had never much gone beyond the golden mean in noticing other women . . . Although when he had, she had been quick enough to object, in fact. What was he supposed to do? In his work it was important to blend in. His work was in the male world. Was he supposed to walk around at gatherings like a parson? The sexes are different, he thought. Seeing someone you're interested in naked for the first time would be an example of how it was different for women and men. For men it was the act of getting inside the mystery, the secret that clothing hides, the package, the getting to see, and then if what you see is splendid, then so much the better. But his guess was that with women it was different and revolved around the fact that a particular man *wanted* passionately for them to take their clothes off. Urgently. That was what they loved. What they loved was men wanting them to the point of begging them to strip *now*. Of course what they saw when the importuner himself took his clothes off had to fall within a certain range, physical qualities did go into it, had to go into it, but with a woman a short leg would be nothing if the male had counterbalancing stuff, like power . . . or intellect. Women who talked about buns and dick size were to an extent faking and going along with the male model, which might truly be triggered by bigness in the shoulders and so on, but it was essentially like claiming they liked to watch football on TV as much as their mates did. Where am I? he thought. He had no idea.

She said, "Anyway, he has been concretely useful with problems I had. Or have. I told you about the hypoadrenia. Another thing, and something you may not know about, is how routine it is for me to get mild cystitis after we have sex. Not every time, I don't mean that. But it's a thing to deal with and he had a suggestion which I haven't really had a chance to discuss with you . . . but now I will. I just lived with it because it wasn't much and it went away. But. Anyway, he thinks if you were careful to wash yourself with mild soap just prior, just before . . . it could be that. It's variable. It may be that when I don't have the reaction it's because you were by happenstance very clean at that time, just out of the shower. And this is not to say you're not a clean person, Ray. It's just that there may be certain salts on the body, something like that. And also I didn't want to mention it because it goes against spontaneity. I don't know, maybe there's a scintilla of urine or something I'm sensitive to."

"My God," he said. "I will certainly . . . hear and obey. Good God. Who knew?"

He was enraged at Morel.

"You're not offended, Ray?"

"No, I'm delighted," he said, but very fast. He should be feeling guilt, obviously, but why was he hearing about this only now? I am apparently foul, he thought.

"It's just an example of something practical, another example."

"No, live and learn. So what kind of soap should I use. How mild is mild. I want to get it right."

"Oatmeal soap. I have some for you."

"Oatmeal soap it is, then."

"It fades pretty fast if I drink a lot of water, so I'm not trying to say it was the end of the world."

"Say no more. We can do without it." He thought, Crush him: Find a way.

"God I love you," she said. In a minute she was going to offer to wash him with this correct soap, he thought. He was picking up slight shifts toward softness. She might not even be aware she was tending that way. It would be instinctual to wrap something as bitter as she was handing him in sweet sex, coat it. She was idly touching her breasts.

She said, "About cleanliness, this is interesting, since so much in religion is about ritual purity, getting clean, being clean before God . . ."

So I am foul, apparently, he thought.

"I'm trying to reproduce what Davis says on this. Yes, it's why ritual purity is so universal in religions, which is because the father, the generic father, won't handle the child or baby if it's soiled, nasty. God is a stand-in for the father figure. By the way do you know that the Peace Corps had to let their messenger go because he refused to carry stool samples from the Peace Corps nurse to the laboratory?"

"I hadn't heard."

"Men here will not handle feces. Women have to collect the cow dung they use to plaster the floors with in their huts, in the countryside. Of course the men are completely willing to walk up and down on it.

"Once you look at it, almost everything people do in religion fits one way or another with the attempt to recapture a moment when there was an all-powerful protector-lawgiver figure in our lives, and we go through motions in this regressed state that deep down we believe are the kind that ought to attract the corrective attention of this all-powerful person. This comes from neoteny, the long period of dependency human infants have. When we get into a crisis, we want to regress into the power of a fatherlike entity, a patrimorph is what Davis calls it. Then we recapture the endorphins we got from being taken care of or attended to, historically. It's a theory. It's partly from Freud except that Davis doesn't think this collapsing back is sick, a pathology, the way Freud did. He thinks it's normal, and even, in a way, healthy. But it's also a joke, and silly. Everything really fits with this. Confession. All the kinds of self-mortification, to make yourself more like a deserving injured or perfect child, all that. All the born-again symbology. Purity and obedience. Making yourself either pathetic or into the simulacrum of a deserving child covers just about everything from fasting and rending your garments to all the thousands of mortifications of the flesh, to being celibate, meaning you're making yourself into a simulated presexual being, like a baby."

She was intoxicated with this stuff. He needed to be respectful, or not disrespectful. Of course there were any number of retorts to such a simple-minded view of religion, there must be. "And then, and this is the last thing I'm going to mention, his theory is that the contradictory and absurd notions we embrace when we're religious amount to a variation of the same thing. When we embrace the absurd we are doing something the equivalent of mutilating our common sense, as a sort of goodwill offering. The most ridiculous varieties of religion, the fundamentalist ones, seem to be thriving right now. Davis thinks that things are happening, societal things, that are making people regress."

This too shall pass, he thought. He grunted.

He guessed it was a good sign that she was adding fresh hot water to the stew they were in. She wanted to be with him. That was real.

He needed to remember that there had been previous enthusiasms of hers to deal with, for example when she'd decided that Ken Russell movies were supreme examples of something or other and she'd made him sit through *The Devils* twice, at the Capitol Cinema.

This was different.

He gripped her shoulders and began kneading her trapezius muscles with his thumbs, which brought back Richard Chamberlain as Tchaikovsky doing the same thing for his new wife and then, when his wife says Yes to the question You'll stay with me forever, won't you? converting the massage into an attempt to strangle her, until he comes to his senses not a moment too soon. Iris and he had laughed afterward and had replayed the scene for laughs themselves how many times?

She said, "Never forget how truly grateful I am to you. I never want you to think I'm not."

He didn't much like the tone of what she was saying, since it had faretheewell written all over it whether she was aware of it or not.

"Here's an example why. I feel like a parasite on your knowledge sometimes, which doesn't mean I'm not grateful. But as an example. Your knowledge of Greek. In Crete. Remember?"

She had no idea how marginal his command of Greek was, at least at this stage, after years of disuse.

"You have no idea what I'm talking about, is that possible?"

"No, say more."

"This goes back to our Crete vacation in '83, the incident . . . When we went to see the pornographic movies in Heraklion?"

He concentrated. He did remember generally, and elements of the evening came back to him, but only in step with her retelling. He remembered the torso of the event, so to speak. They had gone, purely on impulse, as a lark, to see what a pornographic movie would be like in Greece, in Crete. Pornography had been legalized fairly recently, they had gathered. They had walked in on the last tenth of a movie about a licentious Orthodox priest, which the audience was watching in total, fixated silence. Apparently it was a genre. He remembered the priest hanging himself at the end. And then he remembered clearly the suddenly different, rowdy, raucous response to the second feature, a piece of French pornography. The premise of the French film, beautifully photographed, as he recalled, had been odd. It was about a superbly beautiful matron, possibly a widow, who would only allow her lovers and suitors to perform cunnilingus on her. All of them were willing to do it, but they also, naturally, wanted to have follow-up regular intercourse. But all she would permit was the other, and there was no reciprocation from her, oddly enough for a pornographic movie. She rejects all the penises aimed her way. That was his recollection. He was remembering more. The woman was not a widow. Her husband was a society dentist who relieved his frustrations via other female characters who had more reasonable attitudes toward the penis. The dentist was getting it from the other sluts but not from his maddeningly spectacular creamy blond wife. He remembered thinking it was a slightly off-center premise for a pornographic movie. But the main thing she was reminding him had happened was that there had been a claque of young guys in the audience shouting out, at each instance of cunnilingus, *Mathe*, Vassilios! *Mathe*, Vassilios! Now he remembered that. And each bout of yelling had been followed by roars of laughter. And he remembered translating what they were saying, for Iris, when she asked. That he remembered. And the next thing he could remember was being back at the Cretan Sun and having memorable sex with Iris, in their freezing room.

"And you don't remember my begging you to wait a second and wanting to wait around in the lobby?"

"No. But I remember it was freezing."

"And you don't remember being with me in the lobby, unwillingly, but waiting there with me, anything about that?"

"No."

"And you don't remember when finally after everybody else had left, after they were turning out the lights, dragging himself out was a poor physically fucked-up person, one leg dragging, this pitiful man with very white skin, an obvious sort of outcast, dragging himself out past us?"

"No, what I remember is the next act, same night."

"Which was?"

"Well, back at the Cretan Sun. Making love there. Our room overlooked the market and we were right above the spice vendors."

"And you don't remember we exchanged looks when we saw this poor devil, this physically unfortunate man, or neighborhood idiot, or whatever he was? And we were sure he was Vassilios?"

What he remembered was hating the Cretan Sun, the cheapest hotel they had ever stayed in, the poster of Delphi above the bed with the line *Il y a des poux dans cette chambre* penciled neatly along the bottom margin, the miserable shower that gave two minutes of warm water.

"And you don't remember we exchanged glances . . . And by the way, when you tell people about our adventures in Crete I would appreciate it if you'd leave out the note on the poster about lice being in our room."

He was obviously blocking out what should have been cognized as the main event, apparently, of that night. Sex was the reason. Somehow getting aroused, which he had, at the movies, had arced over to the sexual event, events, back at the Cretan Sun, and obliterated the interim for him. It had been that night at the Cretan Sun when he had come up with the affectionate term nethers for her pudenda, which had come from Netherlands, and which he still used from time to time.

He said, "We didn't discuss this at the time, that night?" She shook her head.

"And we didn't discuss it the next day, either, did we? That is, we never got into a *discourse* about it."

"No, we were too stunned, I thought."

"I remember *noticing* an oddlooking guy. But that's all."

He thought, Here it is, a thing that has never been an issue: But here it is courtesy of the female mind for which there is nothing dead that can't be made to live again. He had failed to recognize the situation at the theater as the burning emblem of man's inhumanity to man it obviously was for her. Then it hadn't come up the next day due to their *katastrofi*, when she stepped into a hole in the pavement and cracked her ankle and then the nightmare come true of trying to get medical help in Crete had begun. He remembered every detail of that. He loved her, that was why.

But here it was again, the past that lives forever, in detail, with women, like the women in Joyce, "The Dead," ruining everything. Then at the museum in Heraklion they had been unable to see the murals because the galleries were closed due to a recent *katastrofi*. And then there had been the *katastrofi* of the side trip to Anoja in the White Mountains where the insane monster winds had blown his pitiful, hobbling wife flat into the sides of buildings and walls time after time.

She pushed herself to a standing position and got slowly out of the tub, distractedly, not punitively abandoning him, apparently. She was through. She was keeping her back to him, which could be just accidental.

He got out of the tub and dried himself off very thoroughly. He followed her damp footmarks into the bedroom. Once there, he malingered, dragging out finding the right pajamas and selecting a bathrobe from his oversupply. He had four, all gifts from Iris and all too expensive and all more appropriate for some rich parasite than for him. Why she kept buying him bathrobes that lacked pockets was a mystery. He settled on a black silk robe he thought he looked pretty good in. He combed his hair. Iris was in bed. Still naked, looking at a copy of the *International Herald Tribune* he knew was at least a week old.

It was so clear and so dumb, what was happening. He was being cast as the incarnation of Secrecy. It was inevitable because he worked for the agency and the agency was what, Secrecy Itself. And at the same time she was casting Morel as the dry light of the mind that goes everywhere, anywhere, as Truth with the bit between its teeth, the maypole of Truth she was traipsing around like a berserk Isadora Duncan, flinging her arms around like a jerk, naked, flutes and ribbons all over. That was the scene he was trapped in.

But at least his costume was perfect. He was uncomfortably warm, a natural consequence of dressing himself in a daze, putting pajamas on without reference to what season it was. Black matched his mood. It was his fault that she kept giving him pocketless robes. The first robe she'd given him had been pocketless and he'd praised it. The absence of pockets had seemed to him like a fairly central objection, especially considering the effort she'd gone to, delegating her sister, transatlantic phone consultations. And it had been when they were starting out, when she was insecure about buying things for him. So now all he needed was a cocktail shaker and a Santos Dumont in a cigarette holder and it would be clear he had wandered in from an adjoining farce, a Noël Coward farce. In fact they were both costumed perfectly for the scene, layers and blackness for him, and for her . . . nudity, symbolizing fearless disclosure.

Now she was sitting on the edge of the bed, her back three-quarters to him, examining the sole of her foot. The great aesthetic absolute, he thought.

She caught him looking too raptly at her. "Why are you looking at me that way?" she asked.

"I'm not looking at you, I'm beholding you."

"Well this is the wrong moment for it. By the way, I think you have mild priapism."

"That's the best kind."

"Well don't," she said, smiling a little.

She was going to sum up. He could tell. She held her mouth in a certain way.

She said, "First, nothing is going to happen to us. Second, I'm going to go and be with Ellen and I'll be back in six weeks and everything will be okay, I promise."

"When did we say *six weeks*?" he asked, not calmly enough.

"Well six weeks at the outside."

Do *not* resist, he thought, saying, "Well six weeks then, although . . . it wracks and harrows me." He was surprised at himself. Somehow he had decided to be slightly poetic just then. It was insane. She was looking at him with a certain heightened interest, he thought, although it might be concern and not interest. There were still moments in his life when he felt capable of poetry. When the impulse was there he was normally afraid of it, for the simple reason that he wasn't a poet. The Irish, or some of them, felt free to burst out with it. But even in the case of the Irish talking gorgeously he knew they were working from a fixed menu of tropes and images and not engaging in individual invention. What was he doing? He wanted to send her away with an absolute knowledge of how lovely she was to him, was all. But this had been like a deacon suddenly breaking into a juggling routine. You can't just wrench yourself into some new and cuter state, he thought. He was embarrassed. They were both going to ignore it. He thanked God.

"I don't think we should have sex tonight," she said.

He couldn't agree more. Having sex would dishonor their differences.

"I couldn't agree more," he said. His tone dissatisfied him and he added, "I mean that. I seriously do. And if you would slip into something less comfortable it would be a help."

She was amused. He went to the closet and got out his favorite robe of hers, a blue and white yakuta they had bought in Paris. He draped it over her shoulders and she got properly into it in a rather piecemeal if not exactly teasing manner, he thought. He was a little surprised to realize that the blue elements in the pattern were winged seeds, on the order of locust seeds, and not the Horus eyes they had been in his mental picture of the garment for years. Lately he was looking too closely at everything around her. It was fear. It felt valedictory.

How could he tell that they weren't, even now, through yet? It was in the eyes. What else there could be was beyond him. He was probably safe in assuming that they were down to odds and ends, that she'd started with the more offensive items and was working down, the way he would have. There was no guarantee about that, though. Now he was scaring himself.

He said, "Look, the best thing now would be if you would just tell me everything that's still on your mind, if anything is, because . . . because here we are." In hell, he thought.

"I don't think there's anything special," she said. She was undecided, he could tell. Was she trying to gauge what he could take at one sitting?

"This is truly minor," she said.

But it wasn't. She could barely bring it out, which could mean that it was about what, their sex life, as in too much or too little . . .

"I think I want to take a break from reading novels . . . by men. I don't know why. I just feel like it. Don't be so stunned. You know how grateful I am to you for your help and effort getting me good books. I've depended on your recommendations and they've been wonderful. Maybe it's that I want to take a break from novels per se in general."

Injustice never sleeps, he thought. Finding decent and reasonably current reading for her in Africa had been a major task, a career. Help and effort was right, especially effort. It took work to develop literate social contacts, who inevitably got reassigned. Taste among the embassy people ran at the level of James Michener. The paperback leftovers that turned up in the jumble sales departing embassy officers gave were an embarrassment to the United States. The American Library had no budget and what it had it spent on Young Adult titles.

"Look, my function has been to cultivate my contacts to get you things that are current and good and that you wouldn't be able to get very easily on your own. Or things that you asked for specifically. You know what the public library is like. I doubt I've been biasing my selections toward male authors. Have I? I get you every Iris Murdoch as it falls crashing from the press. I think the last novel I got you was by A. N. Wilson, a man, unfortunately, but you liked it a lot, I thought. I think you wanted more by him. I got you every Barbara Pym there is, somehow."

"I love A. N. Wilson. But I think I don't want to be worrying about the problems of male narrators anymore. I do not want to be worrying about the problems of men, sad as they may be. It's similar to not wanting to read novels about the drug life or other kinds of self-destructiveness. I've read them. And I don't care how sensitive they are, I don't want to read about drunks."

"Hey, fine," he said. He could tell it was distressing her to do this. She was in the grip of something.

"You don't think it's fine."

"I do. I guess maybe you've had enough of the Male Gaze, as they call it. I can understand that."

"I have no idea what the Male Gaze you're talking about is. I don't know if . . ."

He interrupted. "It's not complicated. It's feminist. It's a concept that says, sees, that in the arts, especially the movies but also books, everything, even by women, gets expressed in the male viewpoint, in what interests the male psyche."

"That seems too simple. It may be the novel per se . . ."

But he knew what it was. He thought, So much for my syllabus: Her new one is from a darker hand.

She said, "I think all it may be is this. I think I've gotten too automatic when it comes to novels. I think I have a dependence. I get panicky when I don't have a good one on hand. You know. Maybe it's novels by anybody. Don't stand over me like that. Come sit here." She patted his place in the bed.

He took her hand. Why was it he was absolutely sure there was something more? There had to be, because her breathing was still tight.

"Ray, I love you and I want to be completely fair with you.

"About Davis, maybe you already know this. It's a problem with you. I don't know what you know.

"But I think I do need to mention this last thing. About him. I gather from things he says that a main reason he left the U.S. and came here is because of objections he has to the CIA. As a citizen.

"It seems like everything I'm saying to you tonight is causing you pain, and I am so sorry, but I can't help it. He thinks the agency does terrible things and operates with impunity. Or *has* done them. It's historical, but of course it would have to be historical because whatever the agency is doing now is secret. I sound stupid. You see what I'm saying."

Beware, he thought. He spoke evenly. "Please. He knows nothing."

"You're probably right. It's mainly the agency in Central America he objects to."

Ray said, "He thinks he knows something he doesn't."

"Well. Guatemala and Nicaragua, specifically, if that's any comfort."

"I don't need any comfort."

"I know. It's the contras, most of all, and the fact nobody cares that sixty thousand Nicaraguans died, paid for by us, and nobody was punished. He makes a case. It's my fault for bringing it up, or causing it to be brought up, rather. I was naturally curious about why he came here and wants citizenship. He plans to be here forever, if he can, can you believe that? I got off the subject immediately when I saw what he was saying, believe me, Ray. I just listen and nod when the subject comes up, which is rare anyway. This is not something that's going to get any kind of response from me. You know you can trust me about it. You do know that. I'm sorry it came up."

"What he thinks he knows hardly matters, Iris. You know me and you know whether I would ever do anything dishonorable." He felt false. He had said this before. Of course Nicaragua had been wrong and brutal and no way would he have been part of it. But this was Africa.

She said, "Don't hate me."

It was odd. Twice in the past when he was undertaking critical operations that had turned out to be mortally dangerous for him he had gotten a distinctive feeling in his hands and here it was again.

"What's wrong?" He didn't know what she meant.

"You're wringing your hands," she said. He stopped.

She was not the villain here. Nothing was her fault. He had to keep her from regretting doing this.

She said, "I never want to hurt you, Ray, my good love. I'm just so sorry if any of this has. Please don't worry. And about my reading, I think I'm in a phase. Reading novels is . . . I feel like . . . it's like *waiting*, a form of waiting."

"I understand everything," he said.

"I don't know what we're *doing*, Ray, that's all. I don't know what we're doing but I want to *stop*."

When had she been this unhappy? He couldn't remember a time.

They embraced, trembling equally.

16. Milton, We Are Surrounded

Iris was sleeping in. He would be alone at breakfast, which was for the best. He was never precisely himself early in the morning, but today he was particularly off, still raggedly adjusting to last night's announcements. He felt frail.

The thin orange drapes on the yardside window had been closed against the sun. He disliked the hell-flush they imparted to the atmosphere of the room, but not enough to do anything about it. He looked into the kitchen before taking his seat. Dimakatso was at the stove, muttering. He knew he should run through the formal greetings, but he decided to let himself skip it. She seemed to have her hands full. This was not a standard compilation she was working on. Obviously, Iris had left instructions for her to prepare something more elaborate than the usual. It was a gesture.

He realized that a funny thing had been going on recently, involving the issue of the *International Herald Tribune* that Iris had been reading or pretending to read last night. She had been subtly flourishing the damned thing in front of him for a few days. It was here, on the table opposite him, where Iris would normally be sitting, folded to the width of one column and doubled under in order to expose some particular article. He knew his wife. There was something in the paper that he needed to know about that was likely to displease or depress him. She preferred not to be seen as bringing it directly to his attention for fear of seeming to endorse it or to be taken as wielding it against him, especially in these tense days. And clearly she had been gathering that since he hadn't mentioned whatever this was, he hadn't seen it, which was right. She had her ways. All this was the fruit of her tenderness.

Dimakatso was at his shoulder, carrying the tray with his breakfast on it. She stood there while his meal cooled. He knew what she wanted. He got to his feet.

He said "Dumela, mma. O tsogile?"

"Dumela, rra. Ke tsogile sentle. Wena o tsogile?"

"Ke tsogile sentle."

"Gosiame."

"Gosiame." He could sit down. The Batswana were so exacting about etiquette. Maybe it was admirable. It was better than the reverse, which Iris was going to not enjoy in the land of the free soon enough.

His breakfast was royal. There was streaky bacon, the only cut in that part of the world at all like normal American bacon, two strips of it cooked as crisp as it could ever be gotten to be. There was an egg over easy, and two heated buns. He had switched from sunnyside up to over easy earlier during their time in Botswana as a way of lessening the starkness of the daily encounter with the unnatural amber color of the yolks of the local eggs. There was a ramekin of chopped parsley he was expected to strew on his eggs. That was Iris's idea. She admitted it was notional. She'd awakened from a dream with the absolute conviction that eating parsley at every meal would guarantee extreme longevity. They had laughed over it together. But parsley was making suspiciously frequent appearances as a garnish. There was a tumbler of pear nectar, not chilled. There was a lump of leftover potato rissole. There was brewed coffee.

He ate for a while, then reached for the paper. He was meant to read a review of a new book on Milton. Christopher Lehmann-Haupt was the reviewer and the author was a woman, Marianne Wormser, whose work he remembered seeing and dismissing years ago. Now apparently she had produced the book that would change forever the way Milton should be read. He steeled himself. The word magisterial would no doubt show up. So, Milton was the laureate of obedience, generic obedience. He had to get through this rapidly, because it was going to be painful in every way possible. At the heart of Western culture was this unfortunate epic of obedience deified, disobedience condemned. Milton was the subjugator of women in his own family, which no one disagreed with, although some allowance for the demands of a disabled genius frantic to complete his masterpieces might have been granted. Reading on, he thought: The old refrain: Milton says, "Service to God is perfect freedom," and since God is male, need we say more . . . Women hate Milton because of Eve, the portrait of Eve, which they misunderstand, especially where her first thought on biting the apple is that she might someday be Adam's equal and her second is that she might be his actual superior. What they fail to see in Milton would fill a book . . . Ah here it is, of course . . . Women are to blame for both sin and death, because a female, Sin, was born from Satan's brain in the thought of rebelling against God, and seductive Sin was raped by Satan, and she gave birth to Death, so women are to blame for both Sin and Death . . . Ah she thinks Death is also a daughter, a female? . . . This has to be wrong . . . It's absurd, a reading so tortured. Could Wormser be right that Death was female? He would have to check. It was something he should know like the back of his hand. How could he not love Iris, who was trying to arm him against his colleagues in case he had missed this? But he had no colleagues. Their minds were elsewhere. Little did she know.

He read more. Wormser restating the obvious . . . It was Satan's rebellion against God's appointing his Son as his vice-regent that had started the whole human ball of doom rolling. That was the premise, of course. He thought, Regurgito Ergo Sum, we have heard it before, goodbye. Next it will be the angel Raphael lecturing Adam and Eve against speculative thought . . . and here it is! The book had won prizes. The pillars of Milton studies were being shaken. *Paradise Lost* was reduced to symbolic recantation for Milton's participation in regicide and republicanism plus fear and hatred and vilification of the female. Christian civilization was a galley ship, poor blind Milton was beating the drum for the galley slaves. Calumny never sleeps, he thought.

It was intolerable and it was wrong and, worst of all, it was shallow. Where had Marianne Wormser been publishing? What he would give to have time to rebut this shit! It was important that Iris not accept this cartoon as having anything to be said for it. He had to find time for that before she left. He had to. He could see where she thought Lehmann-Haupt had placed him in yet another category of error.

He thought, There are two Miltons, they only see one . . . Empson saw them both . . . The true man, the suffering man, is *both* rebellion and obedience, the ecstasy of apostasy and the hell of inevitable compliance . . . We are all of us Milton, rebelling and complying and rebelling and complying until we die exhausted.

I saw this thing, he wrote across the top of the review.

He got up. Milton, we are surrounded, he thought. Sometime he wanted to write a short story beginning with the sentence *Day fell*.

17. *So, My Boy, Now You Have Him*

He was in awe over Marion doing this for him, with some awe left over for himself, his temerity in reaching out to Marion and asking for this help, his own ingenuity in setting up everything on the technical side of this secure connection. It was going to happen.

If he was tense, it was understandable. He was in a vacant house, crouched over the phone he was going to use, trying not to worry about the phone accoutrements he had put together. There was a certain amount of jury-rigging involved. It was twilight, which meant it was still morning where Resnick would be calling from, Washington or thereabouts. In a minute he would hear the voice of a civilized man.

He was sure he was safe. He was in an empty house for rent, in Broadhurst, which was a quiet district. He was showing no light. He was in the pantry off the kitchen and he could close himself in if there was some difficulty with the volume control on his descrambler unit, which was the only possible weak point in the work of art his technical setup constituted, in truth. Where he was positioned, he was out of sight. In the unlikely event of anyone noticing him in the house, he was a prospective renter sent there by an estate agent. He had some paperwork to justify his presence. He had the house key with the estate agent's tag on it. All the utilities were on, but he had a torch in case the electricity went out, which could always happen. Explaining why a long extension had been spliced into the house-phone cord would be a little tricky in the event anyone made note of it. He would claim ignorance, be puzzled himself. Splicing in the extension had been the only way he could get the phone into the pantry where he needed to be. By the time anyone could get physically into the house he would have all his accoutrements and tools out of sight, packed away in his knapsack. He heard a crackle in the descrambler.

He could get mournful at the drop of a hat, thinking about Marion's downfall, but he knew very little about why it had happened. He had been an imbiber, which in the agency was part of the culture, a little like the use of chewing tobacco in professional baseball. People were cautioned or sent off to dry out, and their careers continued. Marion. Marion was a red wine maven, a Bordeaux maven. He called his glass of wine *red joy*. Why had Marion fallen? Marion was *in* the agency, whereas he was *of* the agency, which was perfect because it meant he had nothing to fear from the wars of the ins and the outs back in Langley, the fights between the Brahmin liberals and the papist ultras like Casey, which he didn't care about. And now he was hearing about a Mormon beachhead in Clandestine Services. Marion had run the station well, as far as Ray knew. And how could anyone hate a man who was a Scrabble master and a collector of ancient Roman brothel tokens, *sprintriae*, they were called. But someone had hated him and now he was spending his mortal life running a Magic Marker through sensitive passages in documents going out under FOIA. He was a clerk.

The descrambler was emitting definite crepitations. He rested his hand on it, a small model in black plastic about the size of a cigar box, to feel if it was warm. It was. These machines were astonishing. Anyone cutting into a transmission would get pure static. The smell of ammonia in the pantry was fairly strong. People are the same everywhere, he thought. The pantry shelves had been scrubbed, all except the top one, which Ray had checked out by standing on the first shelf.

It was too bad that when the call came it wouldn't be Marion's natural voice. The descrambler had a way of flattening out tones and, depending on the setting, stretching out the delivery. He would cope. Also he would cope with the fact that this had to be a one-way transmission, Resnick to Finch. His role would be to signal that receiving was in progress by pressing a confirm key at intervals. It was remotely possible that Marion would employ a voice mask as an extreme added precaution. He hoped not. Ray was ready. The handset was clipped into place and he was holding down the hook switch. He was unsure how Aesopian Marion was going to feel he needed to be. It was normal prudence to avoid using the proper names of key parties in these communications, but he might go further. The phone rang. He released the hook switch. A sound like a weak moan came from the descrambler speaker. It was Marion.

Marion began. *It was too loud.*

Ray had to do something. It was much too loud. He stripped off his shirt, wildly, and bunched it against the speaker. It was still too loud. You can never relax, he thought. He needed something like a towel or blanket, which he didn't have. The house was unfurnished. Desperately he thought of getting out of his bush shorts and adding them to the mufflage the shirt was providing inadequately.

The sound wasn't blaring, but it would be audible outside the house at this level. He couldn't bear the idea of terminating the call.

God save me, he thought, and struck the volume knob with the butt of his flashlight. It worked. Something did. It brought the volume down.

"Hello my darling," Marion said, startling Ray. It was possible he was drinking. If he was it was a measure of the risk he had been asked to assume and Ray could forgive it, forgive everything.

"Hello my boy, are you there? Can you hear?" Ray tapped the confirm key. Marion's voice was metallic but it was recognizable as his. There was no voice mask.

Methodically, Marion went through the basic biodata, part of which Ray already had. Marion was reading from notes. It was good to get exact dates.

In sum, the subject's paternal family was of very haute black bourgeoisie origins, upper civil service, in Antigua. Then it had been Baltimore and then Cambridge, where the subject's father had become a fixture at Harvard Divinity School, Professor of Christian Morals. There was more that Ray already knew. Subject's mother, now deceased, was white, a birthright Quaker. There would be more about her. There were no siblings. And so on.

As an only child, and only son, much had been expected of the subject, despite the disability he was born with, monobrevipodia, one leg shorter than the other. The subject's mother had brought money, more money, into the family. Now the prep school list was complete.

"Mine eyes dazzle. She died young," Marion said, quoting John Webster for no reason apparent to Ray, until he realized it must refer to the early death of Morel's mother.

"Our subject was always a holy terror to his poor parents. He was precocious. He was enrolled in the divinity school for six months but quit and somehow slid over into the medical school, where he developed shall we say an outspoken attitude to the imperfections of orthodox medicine.

"The man is trouble. He left divinity school announcing that he was going to convert to Judaism because it was clear to him how dastardly Christianity had been to the Jews. He was threatening to do it out of solidarity, you understand me, not belief, because he had become, better yet, an atheist.

"There was some violence between father and son.

"Circumcision came into it. There were fights with his father when he said it would be easy to become a voluntary Jew, since he was already circumcised.

"He was something. I can give you his IQ, by the way . . . 170."

Ray didn't believe it. He would stake his life on it that this was a fluke or wrong. It was unnecessary information! But of course Marion had no notion of how Ray was involved with Morel or why he should be tender in anything he reported.

"Now we have some events florid enough for anyone, God knows. The subject's mother dies after refusing to eat. It could be true. The subject's mother left senior over his entrenched womanizing. Then senior remarries . . . wait I forgot to say junior had married a Nigerian woman. She was living with the subject but in senior's very nice house. She divorces our subject and marries senior. How long before the divorce something had been going on is unknown.

"Junior gets his medical degree anyway.

"You would be amazed at the way this was handled at Harvard. There was a fistfight in Widener between father and son that never happened. There were other incidents.

"By the way when subject's mother left the hearth, she became an administrator at a Quaker conference center, Powell House, far from Massachusetts. This was much earlier.

"They're slick, at Harvard. The factors managed everything. Tap and show you can hear me, my boy." Ray did.

"Our subject graduates, does his residency in internal medicine.

"So then our man becomes a public nuisance in Cambridge. He opens a practice in Cambridge, and over in Malden a storefront not for his practice but for, let me look at something, his organization, the Giordano Bruno Society. He founded it. They hold meetings attacking religion.

"He is the published author of two books, here they are, *dEaTHICS*, with the title done in clever typography, small d and small a and the rest caps, you get the point. And the other *Theolatry, Mankind's Curse*. Both of these are published by Diagoras Press, Diagoras being the first atheist on record, as I know you know. He is, by the way, the founder of Diagoras Press and its only author.

"Someway he finds time to get qualified in chiropractic, certain varieties of massage, and medical hypnosis.

"His practice develops. He has a female following, largely female, which is not so surprising since this is unorthodox medicine. Does he miss his ex-wife, now his stepmother? Doesn't look like it. He has girlfriends, several, from his patient population.

"You know how fucked I am here, by the way. I won't go into it. I'm almost through with this. I'm almost out. Not a decade too soon. Please you've got to hit the confirm key every once in a while. You know how to do this. They hate me. You know how this works, hit the thing. Good. Thank you.

"I shouldn't be doing this. I don't care. They'll never find out.

"I am the fox."

You are and so am I, Ray thought.

"Harvard, speaking of Harvard, did you know that the people who invented the idea of giving points for alumni parents were the factors at Harvard, so they could cut down on the number of Jews they would have to admit?

"I've got to tell you something annoying I hate. My wife joined Al-Anon, you know what that is. Just to put pressure on me I don't need. She thinks I'm an alcoholic. The whole world runs on somebody being able to have a drink once in a while.

"Let me tell you something. My mind is wandering.

"One thing I can let you know. At a certain place of work, you can forget Jews. Believe me and prosit, you will never see us at the top here again, not until they drive Israel into the sea. Then maybe."

This was about the Pollard case and its ramifications. Marion should leave this alone. He willed him to get back on the subject, so to speak.

"This is what I did for you. I talked to two of his girlfriends . . ."

Ray was amazed. No doubt Marion had contacted them by phone on the pretense of doing a full field investigation for some nonexistent government job for Morel, which was the way it was done and which was highly illegal. Marion was surrounding the news with silence so that Ray would appreciate the significance of it. He did. He was not in a position to do anything in return for Marion, which Marion knew. This was more than he deserved. Ray hit the confirm key.

"So what I got was that the man is a gentleman. They had nothing but good things to say. Both of them were academics and they both volunteered that their relationships had come to an end because they were relocating, essentially. Both had married other people. They seemed to miss him. They were both ex-patients and they both seemed to think he had fixed up whatever it was they went to him for in the first place. I couldn't get off the phone with one of them. She wanted to talk about the man. So."

Ray pressed the confirm key. A pause began that worried Ray. It went on. It was impossible not to wonder if something had gone wrong. He reviewed Marion's delivery to date. Marion had been careful.

People had no idea how careful you had to be these days if you wanted not to be picked up. In a way he found it hard to believe himself, how amazing the seining operation being run from New Zealand, Echelon Dictionary, was, in what it could do, which was to process the entire spectrum of nonencrypted communications of every sort . . . phone, radio, fax, electronic . . . worldwide. He wasn't supposed to know about Dictionary, but Marion had told him about it, mainly to make fun of it. Marion thought seining was stupid. It cost billions. What it did was capture and scan any and all digitized communications for key words, like Arafat or bomb or Mandela, store the ones of interest, use them to trace down the senders. But all you needed to do to defeat Dictionary was to camouflage your referents, use a little circumlocution, as Marion was doing adequately so far. Dictionary was run by the National Security Agency but the Central Intelligence Agency was a partaker, in a big way. There was a race angle to Dictionary that Marion hated. It wasn't just all the noncommunist White Guys International, oh no. It was Anglo-Saxon—the U.S., Britain, Australia, New Zealand. It occurred to him that Marion's bad luck in the agency might have something to do with indiscretions in other quarters about Dictionary. Marion had felt strongly about it, he knew that. The pause was continuing. It was distressing. Of course Dictionary was monstrous. He thought of Gerard Manley Hopkins and *Christ compared to the air we breathe*. Make it The State compared to the air we breathe, he thought. Marion was back.

"Let's see. I ought to mention his radio program, half anti-God and half against aspartame. It gives you brain damage if you take it with MSG, if you're a rat. It was alternative radio. Got nowhere. He stabs at things, now this now that. Trying to find a nerve, I guess. He organized some picket lines against circumcision at Harvard General. Nobody got arrested. He's clean up and down. Not even a traffic violation.

"You can see the picture emerging. He's out for trouble. He wants to be a Jew, *doloris causa*, and put his father out of business.

"So at the same time he's evolving as a professional irritant he's making a mint with his practice.

"I think the man is a devil. There are people around you could call devils. Divils, the Irish call them." Rex is a devil, Ray thought.

"I think the point was to make himself a spectacle in Cambridge, under his father's nose. That was the original thing, I believe.

"Then. Father dead, stroke, in 1989. Religious ceremony at the funeral, of course, subject will not attend. Who knows if it played a part that his ex was the grieving widow.

"Not only would he not attend, but he mourned his father outside on the sidewalk by giving out copies of a pamphlet, *Was Christ a Nut?* during the funeral service. I have one. Should you want it.

"But it gets even worse. The papers covered it. Somehow it had been arranged for the flyers to, well, fly down on the mourners inside the church, courtesy one of the subject's followers, no doubt. I forgot to mention that senior died on vacation in the Caribbean, on a beach, and that a certain columnist wondered if the stroke was sun-induced or son-induced, s-o-n. The papers have it that the widow came out and spat in the subject's face, and she did, but she missed.

"Man, he was being notorious! What fun! But it was getting to be more than that. The widow, by the way, is with . . . a major international financial institution. She's an economist. She's no longer in the Cambridge area."

Ray realized that Marion had started to identify Morel's ex-wife's workplace as the World Bank, something Ray already knew, but had stopped out of prudence.

"Senior I should add was a majestic figure, patrician, fine head, fine voice, very tall, both legs the same length.

"So with senior gone, and senior's wife relocating, he continues his practice. And I have to say that as a healer, people swear by him. They still do. He had to limit his clientele, because the way he proceeds is to talk to you in extenso about your probably defective view of life compared to his. You get a reading list and a pamphlet casting doubt on the existence of God along with your foot rub and recipe cards. He calls it eclectic medicine. You have to deal with his notion that God-belief is toxic, something it's better not to swallow, credulism is his term, I believe. All he asks is that you contemplate his proposition, not that you accept it as a condition of treatment. He was especially good with musculoskeletal problems. Headaches too. I'm trying to see if I missed anything . . . Yes, he went to Taiwan for six months to get a certificate in Chinese herbs."

Marion's theory was that Morel, with his father and ex-wife off the scene, had suffered a certain deceleration. There were only two notable events in the period between senior's death and the subject's great encounter with a particular African gentleman and subsequent decision to leave Cambridge for Africa forever. One event had been a shortlived lawsuit against the Catholic Church for consumer fraud or false advertising. The subject had encouraged a young woman whose psychological reaction to an exorcism performed by a priest, an employee of the diocese, had been severe, to hold the church liable. It was very convoluted. The church sponsored various spots on television, which the subject had attempted to construe as advertising for a package of doctrines of which many were manifestly false, such as the assertion that demons existed. That had gone nowhere. The only other event was obscure. He had irritated a certain group *not of interest* to the extent that they broke the windows of the subject's storefront. But this was a group *not . . . of . . . interest*. There was a pause.

Ray was puzzled. Marion was letting him think. Ray saw it. The emphasis on *not of interest* had been meant to signify the presence of an acronym, NOI, Nation of Islam. He hit the confirm key twice, hoping that Marion would understand he was signaling that he got the message.

Marion began recounting, with extreme circumspection, the coming together of Davis Morel and the chronic bad back of the Minister of Local Government and Lands of the Government of Botswana, Petrus Tshenelo. There had been an investment promotion exercise at Harvard starring Tshenelo, the scheduled main speaker and presenter at the event. Ray knew a lot about Tshenelo. He was a power in Domkrag. He was bright. His back had gone out on the eve of the seminar, immobilizing him. Regular medicine had failed to help him. Then it had been exit-orthodox-medicine-pursued-by-a-bear, and enter Doctor Morel, recommended by a porter who had been restored to paid servitude by him. Tshenelo had been magically restored. Marion added a stray detail about Morel's fees. Apparently you paid only if you felt he had helped you. You could pay above a reasonable minimum if you chose to and could afford it and many of the overprivileged did.

"Thus the famous bond begins, which you know more about than I do, since you have it in front of you. Suddenly, Africa interests our man greatly. In six months it was bon voyage and over to you.

"That's about all I have, my boy. But I want to say something. You get these guys pretty rarely. He goes to extremes. He does that. But don't look only at that. What I want to say is . . . the man is real. You know the Quakers during the war who wouldn't cooperate with selective service? They called themselves absolutists. He's like that . . ."

Marion had injured him. Ray hated the idea that Marion was implying a distinction between the two of them, Ray and Marion, what they

were, and Morel, of the kind that he seemed to be implying. I know what
I am, he thought.

"As a historical type he reminds me of Tommaso Campanella,
although he probably won't spend twenty-seven years in prison, although
that might be what would make him happiest, you never know with these
guys. Anyway, he was a relentless, amazing man."

It was time to hang up. Using the word prison had been a departure
from the level of prudence established from the beginning. He didn't like
it. Marion was liable to very . . . what, very flowing presentations.

"The key to the man is his mother, poor woman. I would say. She died
of what the Romans called *inedia*. She ate less and less and then stopped
eating altogether. For a long time, she concealed what she was up to and
kept working at this place I mentioned. She was an extremist, in her way.
She came from a famous antislavery family, abolitionist, people always on
the right side of the issue when the Quakers were temporizing, some of
them. It seems she conceived a horror of the world, or something. Imagine that. Her friend says she died of her disillusionment. She never asked
for custody. She was in bad shape after the breakup. I saw the medical
records. She was very petite, a very fine person. Very active person in the
civil rights movement before she married and for a while after. His aunt
had possession of his mother's ashes and he went to some trouble to get a
portion of them to take along to Africa.

"So, my boy, now you have him. Leaving us was no gesture. He has
nothing here, no property, not a dime in the bank. He sold all his stocks.
He's not a tourist."

That seemed to be all.

"Goodnight, my boy. Be good."

"I will," Ray said. He turned swiftly to the task of packing up.

He hadn't thanked his friend. What was wrong with him, not to have
clicked?

"Goodnight. Thank you," he said to the device now cooling in his
hands.

18. The Piggery Had Its Uses

It had taken a certain amount of art to get Ponatsego Mazumo properly disposed toward the mission Ray had for him. Money alone might have done it, of course, but that would have changed the relationship between them forever, and Pony was a fixture at the school and someone he had to work smoothly with for as far into the night as he could see. How much Pony believed of the rationale for Ray's proposed operation was beside the point. What was important was that they both have an unsordid rationale they could coexist in respectably with one another. *Rationale* was a subheading in the *Acquiring Assets* segment of the agency training program he'd gone through. He'd done well in *Rationale*, but then he'd done well in most subjects, not excluding *Flaps and Seals*, which was boring.

Pony was in a considering state, still, gazing up into the thatch. It was nearly dusk. They were seated across from one another at the conference table in Ray's office. Pony was pursing and unpursing his lips. Ray had the feeling Pony was enjoying being there and might be prolonging things just for that reason. Not very many of Ray's colleagues had been invited to visit Ray's office. There was almost a deal. But Pony was obviously savoring the ambience. No place smelled better than Ray's office. It was furniture polish, books, thatch, the pipe tobacco in the humidor whose lid he left cocked for a few minutes from time to time to remind him of the pleasures of the vice he had overcome.

The deal would come. Cash hunger was overwhelming in this part of the world, or rather cattle hunger was, which was what the cash was for. The Scandinavians wanted there to be a cooperative movement in the worst way . . . hypermarkets, sorghum mills, garages. In theory it was a good idea, an excellent way to get prices down for the marginal farmers who were at the mercy of the transplanted Boer businessmen. But the movement was perpetually collapsing because petty cash was always disappearing and these were not undertakings that could run without a petty cash system. So the Danes and the Swedes were endlessly topping up the co-op cashboxes and finding themselves reluctantly having to bring charges against various pillars of the community, the big cattlemen who had joined the cooperatives precisely because there was sure to be loose money around, cash, the pula they could use to sustain their herds during the drought. Cattle ownership equaled manhood. It went deep. People would rather let their cattle die during drought times than sell them while they still could to the abattoir. It was subtle. Selling the cattle diminished the numbers in a way that letting the buggers die naturally did not, somehow. It was important to be known in perpetuity as *having been* the owner of a herd of maximum size. This was the famous insoluble offtake problem they kept complaining about over at AID. Pony's cattle post was at Pandamatenga, north of Francistown, far from Gaborone. Ray didn't know how many beasts Pony had. It was impermissible in the culture to ask that question, but Batswana seemed always to know that about each other, somehow. It was occult. Apparently anything could be a fundamental object of desire to somebody . . . yams, pigs, beadwork, extra wives, real estate, gold, shoes.

Pony was twenty-five. He was slim, very dark-skinned, with good presence and good English. He was a definite blade. He was unhappy working for the bursar as a clerk, or as he described it, as a scribe. He dressed above his means. The cream-colored safari kit he was wearing today was pricier than anything Ray owned. It was tightly cut, according to the mode. The breast pocket of Pony's shirt jacket bore a monogram so lavishly worked that it stood up off the cloth like a brooch. Pony was guarded, like most Bakalanga. He was a defiant Kalanga, keeping the nail of the little finger of his right hand long, out two inches or so, and filed to a point, for use as a nosepick, was the story. Ray had never really seen it employed in that way. The Kalanga had a right to be guarded, since they not unreasonably saw themselves as a minority tribe not popular with the majority Bangwaketse and their allies, as scapegoats-in-waiting should something go seriously wrong in Botswana, especially something wrong in Botswana's intermittently tense relations with Zimbabwe, where the other three-quarters of the Bakalanga lived uneasily in a condition of similar underappreciation by the Shona and the Ndebele who ran the show there. In Botswana, the Kalanga were denied the use of their language in the schools, which rankled. They were a nation, in fact, or a micronation.

For some time, he and Pony had been what he would call attuned to one another. They had gotten into conversation in the school library and Pony had remarked that Kyle Innis, the head of the maths department, was violently of the opinion that the collapse of Russia had been the result of a conspiracy among the capitalist powers to destroy the great homeland of socialism before the Russians had a chance to integrate computers into the running of the collective system, which had been all that was lacking to make the planned economy fully competitive with capitalism. This conspiracy had involved the Poles and the Pope. What was interesting to Ray was that Innis's Marxism had always been, up until then, totally crypto. It had been the debacle of the Soviet system that had brought it out, obviously. Ray thought there were probably others like Innis, keeping quiet and waiting for Mother Russia to ripen into true socialism someday soon and then getting the message, Drinks, gentlemen! and the pub was closing for good. Pony had asked Innis if by socialism he meant communism, which had made Innis glare at him before answering *Of course*.

Ray decided that they should go for a stroll, to wrap this up. Pony was agreeable.

Outside, Ray steered them in a direction that would take them away from the frequented parts of the campus and toward a feature of the place that could always be expected to be clear of humanity of any kind, the piggery. The stench of the facility, which was being incompetently managed, guaranteed privacy. They kept hiring and losing people who claimed to be competent as pigherds, or whatever the correct job title was. The wire-fence enclosure containing the two remaining pigs, sows, was in need of replacement, although in their present state of lethargy, the pigs hardly seemed to need containment at all. The piggery had its uses, and Ray had voted against closing it, the last of the school's small-stock projects, siding with Curwen, who had a sentimental ruralist streak stemming no doubt from his jolly childhood on the great estate in Northumbria his family owned. The piggery was raggedly shielded by a horseshoe planting of dry gray elephant grass reaching to a height of seven or eight feet. As they approached the site, Ray noted that Pony put his hands in his pockets to raise his pants cuffs well clear of the pismire, which was what it was, extending far outward from the pen, which had been moved around the area in the past.

There were two parts to the deal with Pony. One had to do with a bad investment he'd made in a haulier. Pony had advanced money to a friend for the purchase of a used Bedford. The truck and the friend had slipped south across the very porous border with South Africa near Ramotswa. Pony had information that the truck had been licensed and registered for business in Mafeking instead. In exchange for Pony's help with his project, his operation, Ray would cover Pony's four-hundred-pula loss, as a grant, in addition to arranging, through unspecified friends at the American embassy, for Pony to receive exact information on his absconded friend's whereabouts, so that a face-to-face meeting could occur, something Pony desperately wanted.

For Ray's part, he decided to tell Pony he was asking for help because certain people at St. James's were concerned that, through Rra Innis or others, there might be formed at the school a cell of students sympathizing with the very unclear and possibly dangerous ideas of one Samuel Kerekang, who had recently founded a cyclostyled journal, *Kepu/The Mattock*, copies of which had been spotted circulating among the upper forms. There had been, as Pony knew, a confidential struggle, long-standing, to keep another, older, political group, the Marx-Engels-Lenin-Stalin Society, out of St. James's, if only to prevent the students from attaching themselves through hot feelings and idealism to an idea whose time had come and gone and in the process being stamped with an association that could dog them forever, when, as many of them would, they applied for government posts. The school had been successful to date in the struggle against MELS. An aspect of this problem involved the Bakalanga students in particular. As Pony well knew, they faced enough difficulty in working themselves upward in government without taking on anything else that might come to constitute a drawback. Pony understood clearly. That had been an important touch.

That was the larger design. His object being to secure Pony without nakedly making him a pure asset, this design had seemed best. There was a light breeze coming from the west. They maneuvered to keep themselves upwind of the pen.

The school needed to know much more about this person Kerekang, but he was very secretive in the way he was forwarding his program. He was closely vetting the people he invited to his little meetings here and there. It would be unwise for Pony to go directly into these meetings, even if it could be arranged. The school was anxious to learn all it could, even if only to determine that this man's materials were innocent. But indirection was needed. The idea was that Pony should be brought together with Kerekang by seeming accident, in another venue he was lately being seen in, lecture meetings being given by an American against God and religion. Kerekang was active in these meetings. Ray wanted Pony to become an attender and to secretly tape the colloquies and presentations, especially those where Kerekang made some points. Even if Kerekang was not present, Pony should tape these proceedings, just to supply background. They needed a full picture. They needed to know what the relationship between these men was. In any case, Pony would form a connection to Kerekang, enough of a connection so that the school could determine what he was about. And when he became known to Kerekang, Pony would consult with Ray and they would see what should come next. If there was more to do, Pony would be compensated for his time. But it might all be done with very quickly. There was nothing complicated about the taping process. The recording unit was a Sony M5 the size of a deck of cards, something Pony had seen Ray use in preparing students for declamations and recitations, except that this model happened to be voice-activated.

There was one last element to the deal still outstanding. It had to be finessed. They were inside the elephant grass hedge, effectively hidden. The sows were asleep. Ray hoped they were asleep. The wind had relented.

Pony wanted to sign something, by which he meant he wanted something signed, a letter in his file saying that he had attended these meetings in behalf of the school and not because he was drawn to them for any other reason. He wanted to sign something, or rather he wanted to put his signature chop on something. Many educated Batswana signed documents and letters with complex ideograms only distantly related to the letters composing their names. Pony's chop was the most extravagant Ray had ever encountered, a vast scrawl executed in a flash and always, strangely enough, identical, document to document. Pony had a need for that act. It would have to be circumvented, for obvious reasons. The operation had to be traceless. The operation he was constructing served his own needs perfectly. He would be able to mollify Boyle with the appearance of circumspect action against Kerekang. And he would have the beginnings of what he needed for his private campaign against Morel. Boyle would surely see the supposed logic of all this. He would frame it differently for him, of course, but Boyle would have to go for it because he wanted Kerekang so much. Ray would get Morel, and sooner rather than later. He wanted his essence. He wanted Morel's essence on a stick, proof of what he was. Pony was referring to the authorizing document he wanted from Ray as a charter.

Pony said, "So you can see, rra, why I must have this charter."

Ray answered, "Of course, rra, just as I would in your place. But consider that, as to material in the files at school, really how safe is anything from prying eyes . . . you see?"

"Rra, I take your point." Pony thought for a moment. "So then I might take this for my personal holding, someway like that?"

"No, because no matter how safely you think you have hidden a thing, strange things can happen." Ray was improvising. This had to go away. He was thinking of fantasy solutions like drawing up a document in vanishing ink. He would have to come up with a stall.

He was being reflective. While he reflected, he extracted a packet of pula from his hip pocket and slid half the packet into an envelope. He was going to offer two hundred pula, half of the amount agreed on, as a down payment or rather surety, as they would call it here.

Ray said, "May we do this? Once you attend for a time or so and bring me some material, we can sit down and see if you still want some kind of charter. You may not. There may be nothing to any of this. In the meantime I can think of what's best, whether I should hold some document for you in my files, or what. And meantime let me give you surety, now, for half what we agreed on."

He had surprised Pony. The breeze was up again. They danced to a new position on the other side of the pen.

Ray said, "Of course, I can find someone else if you say no. I think I can."

"No, rra, that will be just all right," Pony said. He waited for Ray to press the money on him.

They left, hurrying. Pony was ashamed. Ray loved him for it.

19. *Two Pieces of Intelligence*

Ray had two pieces of intelligence for Boyle, one that Boyle would want but that Ray was not going to give him, and one that Boyle ought to want but wouldn't and that Ray was going to try to force on him. Both pieces of information had come to Ray via sheer luck, with the assistance in one case of another force he distrusted, intuition. And both pieces of information had left him shaken. He had something critical on Kerekang, an extension and confirmation of what he had already concluded, but new.

It was doubtless the suggestion of guidedness in human affairs that luck and intuition stood for that he hated. There was no design, no occult design. Odd conjunctions not even rising to the status of coincidence also annoyed him, like the odd fact that the previous chief of station had been a collector of ancient Roman whorehouse tokens and the present one was secretly notorious within the agency for his practice of founding high-end whorehouses as part of his collection regime wherever he was posted.

What Boyle would not get out of him was that he knew where Dwight Wemberg was. He couldn't believe the way he had come to know this fact. Something had told him to go over to the university library to see if he could find the complete original copy of the *International Review of Social History*, Volume One, Number Six, from which the palm-copier sample reading that was in his file had been taken and used to impugn Kerekang, who had made the mistake of abandoning his reading long enough to go and empty his bladder. At the side of Ray's mind had been the shadow of an intention to see, at the same time, if he could look up any of Marianne Wormser's early papers on Milton, to reassure himself that he had been right that she was unpromising. So he had gone there, following his whim or whatever it should be called. He had never gotten to Wormser.

Boyle had agreed to see him, in the consular office, this time. Ray was in one of the holding cubicles, in a box, essentially, in a tan wood-veneer-over-chipboard box, sitting in an Eames chair, with the fine hum of the fluorescent lighting for entertainment. When Boyle was ready for him a buzzer on the door would sound and a red light set in the wall would begin flashing, a light concealing a CCTV minicam and an audio ear. The miking of these cubicles had always struck Ray as pointless. The surveillance in the cubicles was being imposed on people who had already passed through two metal detectors, so what could anyone possibly be expected to detect?

For the record he was there on school business, carrying his permanently pending file of names to be proposed for Phelps-Stokes fellowships. It was time to redo the file. Some of the candidates on it were dead. That file and the exhibit he had especially prepared for Boyle on the Kerekang matter were contained in the red rope portfolio on his lap, and he noticed, now, that his palms were sweating enough to leave marks on the portfolio. He dried his hands in his pockets, irritated at himself, because the sweat marks were just the kind of small thing Boyle might pick up on. The fact was that Kerekang was not a communist, not a socialist, not a follower of Karl Marx. He was a follower, if that was the word, of someone else altogether, Karl Marlo, a thinker of a different kidney completely. Ray had the proof in his hands.

My life is taking forever, he thought. At the university library he had found bound volumes of the *International Review of Social History* in the stacks, but only from 1980 onward. The card catalog entry was partly illegible, but seemed to say that the earlier years of the journal were in one of the storage areas. He knew the library and was known there. He had made his way to the box rooms, as the storage rooms were called. In the first one he entered, he'd found what he'd come for. The box room was in chaos, with slopes of vandalized, hurt, and deaccessioned books reaching from the overburdened worktable surfaces to the edges of the room. He had had to walk on books to get to the wall shelving, where, displayed at eye level, he found the back issues, unbound, of the *International Review of Social History*. The lot was tagged as scheduled for microfilming, but the order was dated May 1981. Nothing was happening with these periodicals, he'd decided. He'd slipped the number he wanted into the waistband of his bush shorts, under his shirt.

At that point, he had found Wemberg's hiding place. A smell, a faint rankness, had arrested his attention. On three sides, the space between the top of the main worktable and the floor had been walled with stacked books, the walling partially masked by the drifts and dumps of spilled books lying against it. On the fourth side, the space was closed with a sheet of cardboard, which he shifted to the side. He'd had to strike matches to see inside the cave. He had cursed the Lion matches for the flimsy, sputtering, unreliable product they were. Inside the cave he had found a pallet, a sakkie containing soiled clothing, a water bottle, and a framed photograph of Alice Wemberg. On impulse he'd taken all the bills he had in his wallet, about fifty pula, and tucked them under the frame of the photograph, obscuring Alice Wemberg's face so that Wemberg, in his distraction, wouldn't miss seeing the money. Then Ray had left. Thinking now about Wemberg was upsetting him, again. There was nothing he could do for the man without too much danger to himself. He felt for Wemberg. He identified with him, another poor bastard going mad over a beloved woman. With Iris away, he was feeling more of a bond with Wemberg than before. He was worried that leaving the money had been stupid, that it might startle and unnerve Wemberg and lead him to abandon his hideout, which was a sensible hideout, well located because that end of the library building faced rough, blank bushveld, so that Wemberg would be able to duck in and out without being observed, especially at night. He had to turn his thoughts away from this. There was nothing he could do.

Boyle was taking his time, per usual. Ray took out his exhibit and shuffled through it. If he did say so himself, it was conclusive against the idea that Kerekang was any kind of socialist or revolutionary. The whole misreading had begun with the sloppy job of copying the article's title, slashing across it to yield

Karl Mar
Socialism
Revolution of 1848

when the correct full title was "Karl Marlo, Guild Socialism, and the Revolution of 1848." In Marxian terms, Karl Marlo had been a reactionary. He had been a defender of the guilds. He had been an opponent of industrialism. He had wanted the extension of the guild system, with its masters and apprentices and its slow, merit-based upward mobility and employment stability.

The whole thing was interesting. And Marlo had hated the liberals, who were for the industrial system, more than anything, which ought to recommend him to the liberal-hating Boyle, except that the historical context was so wildly different. What Kerekang wanted in Botswana was something like what Marlo had wanted. He had been influenced by Marlo and by an American named Borsodi. He wanted households to raise their own food and have fruit trees and raise small stock and sell any surplus on the open market. What was so terrible about that? There was a cosmic joke going on here. The reason Marlo had hated liberals was because they wanted to open everything up to the market, which he knew would mean doom for the guilds, and he had been right. Kerekang was an individualist, rightly judged. He wanted every family to be allocated an equal plot and house and access to water and he had schemes for raising a variety of agricultural products and taking the surplus for sale, which would sustain the family. You would have a base and you couldn't be turned out into the street, like the homeless, but you could do wage work on the side, to the degree you chose. It was yeoman democracy, more than anything. It was Jeffersonian. It was innocent.

Ray had photocopied the entire twenty-page article. And he had made a separate presentation sheet consisting of excerpts, highlighted, because he knew Boyle would never read the original piece. Ray was doing this out of principle. It would be against his best interest if Boyle paid attention, because of the scheme he had going with Pony. But if Boyle decided to forget Kerekang, Ray would send Pony for a couple of visits to Morel without authorization. Ray would have what he wanted, Morel au naturel, talking the talk.

Of course there was an unusable aspect of Marlo that might endear him to Boyle if he ever looked into it. The great expanded guild system Marlo had proposed was for everybody but Jews. It wasn't that Marlo had been anti-Semitic, but he had been a man of his time. Boyle had no excuse for his own attitudes and he had no idea how much Ray knew about them thanks to the beloved Marion Resnick. Boyle was Jew-fixated. He blamed the Jew Kissinger for leading Nixon to break the wall around China, which had led them to go capitalist enough to become an enormous economic as well as military threat. The idea was that they should have been left alone to doldrum along with their inefficient communist system. Boyle was an ultra. Ray thought, If you're politically insane, things will leak out no matter who you are: and Marion can't be blamed for talking about Boyle. Boyle hated the African National Congress not because blacks were going to come to power through it but because Jews, some of the greatest stars of the ANC, were, and of course communism was the invention of a Jew and Jews had been prominent in getting it going in Russia, and Lenin was a Jew, or half-Jew . . . That was Boyle. He had to live with him.

The waiting he was being put through was deliberate. He decided to read through his exhibit, sampling it.

"If the guilds were to play an important part in Germany's future they would have to stand for more than simply the selfish demands of their class . . . the road back was closed; the future demanded more than nostalgia; it would not accept mere selfishness . . . the guildsmen were aware of the need for a more general appeal and a wider vision; that they were was largely due to the efforts of one Karl Marlo—the social theorist of the German guild movement during the years of revolution."

Learn something new every day was Resnick's line. Socrates, when he was about to drink the hemlock, made everybody in the room shut up so he could hear the end of a song, new to him, being sung in the street. Ray knew the name of the singer, if he could remember it . . . Stesichorus.

"Marlo was not a guildsman; he was a chemistry teacher in a trade school in Kassel, Kurhessen." He had been a technician, like Kerekang.

"Marlo's native province was a land of small villages surrounded by carefully cultivated fields and inhabited by peasants and the master tailors, smiths, bakers, carpenters, and shoemakers of the guilds, who, with their journeymen and apprentices, formed a comprehensive guild system as yet undisturbed by free enterprise and still protected by ancient monopolies and a determined insistence on prerogatives and precedent. It was here that Marlo carried on his social research and here that he found an 'organization of labor' whose principles he hoped to see embodied in an economic order which would protect Germany from the ravages of the Industrial Revolution."

And here was Marlo himself speaking despairingly. "Nothing remains for even the most intelligent to do, but to surrender his social independence and put himself in the service of the capital-rich entrepreneurs, and leave to them the greater part of the fruit of his labor." Ray could see clearly why Marlo appealed to Kerekang.

Here was the core of it. "Industrial and agricultural enterprises would be limited to a certain number of workers, and each merchandising firm would be given a monopoly over a part of the national market . . . Those who amass more capital than is needed for their enterprise will be able to lend it to those who lack the money but not the competence to exploit their share of the national market. The state must keep interest rates low, and must also assure to each citizen 'a sphere of activity' equivalent to his abilities. Would not, Marlo asked, such a state be able to ward off the wild struggle for markets and capital, the destructive competition, and the dangerous concentration of wealth and power in the hands of a few which have transformed modern societies into vast arenas in which occur chaotic struggles for survival? . . . Every citizen will be expected to contribute to health, old age, and life insurance programs . . ."

It sounded to Ray like Sweden in the fifties. And the outcome for Marlo was that his advanced ideas had enraged the liberal revolutionaries who wanted to break the guilds, and the socialists who wanted to vest ownership of everything in the state, and he had been tried for treason when the reactionaries came back to power after the crushing of the revolution.

Ray thought, Outcomes are funny: Imagine that somehow Marlo and this renovated guild system had won out in Germany, what might have been next? Well, for one thing, no German Marxism burgeoning up enough to drive the ruling classes crazy and no ruling classes putting Lenin on a train to Russia and no Russian Revolution and no Stalin and no Red Army carrying fire and blood and doom to what was left of the crazy old regime, thank you very much: We outsmart ourselves! . . . How can I possibly get this across? We destroy moderates at our own peril, something like that: He won't get it, he's Boyle.

When it came to Kerekang's political life in Britain, reading it correctly took only the smallest amount of sophistication and goodwill. Kerekang had never taken out physical membership in anything. He had been sampling this and that in the nonparty left, over there. He was a pilgrim. There was no evidence of anything more. Yes, at the very beginning of his time in the U.K. he had fellow-traveled with a couple of Trotskyist sectlets or groupustules, Boyle's tweaking of the standard derogatory term for miniature left groups, groupuscules, but Kerekang had clearly found them wanting. He had rejected them and gone elsewhere, which ought to count in his favor. He had been a sympathizer with something called the Commonwealth Party, now defunct, a precursor to the Green Party. The man was a seeker, and where he had come out was, if looked at without jaundice, innocuous. But Boyle was Boyle. He remained Boyle. What was wrong with him? What was wrong with the world?

It occurred to Ray that a prime reason people want power is so they can say no, have that pleasure, exercise the power to prohibit. It was how some people made the world simpler, people who hated the confusion of the world. It was primitive.

The buzzer sounded, the red light flashed, he rose up wearily.

20. *He Didn't Like What He Was Suspecting*

With Iris gone Ray could eat anything he wanted, and he had planned a transgressive meal for himself for tonight, which, now that he was sitting down to it, he didn't have much appetite for. He had to get past Boyle's *No*, Boyle's brevity with him on top of it, Boyle's expression when he had examined Ray's case for making Morel a POI and his attempt to show what effort it was taking to keep disbelief from turning into a horse laugh.

He had a fine clod of fried steak before him, with baked potato and salad, flageolets dressed with oil and vinegar, a salad by British standards only. It was a thick steak, silverside. Cliffs of beef, he thought. The garnish of sautéed garlic and onions was less thoroughly caramelized than he liked. Iris would have done them perfectly. As a cook, his weakness was impatience. He was doing his own cooking. Dimakatso had offered to take over, but she was a rotten cook and he would have had to praise everything.

He was on his second Ringnes beer. The brand was just lately available in Gaborone and it was wonderful, and strong, which was why he liked it, of course.

He missed Iris cruelly. She would call tonight. He was hoping for a call less consumed by the detail of what was going on with Ellen and her new baby girl than the previous calls had been.

He should be happier right now. He was set up to read and eat, a combination he liked, a pleasure in itself that a happily married man generally experienced only when he was eating away from home. He had two *Times Literary Supplement*s still in their glassine sleeves. He didn't mind eating in the kitchen, despite the too-bright overhead light, because everything he might have forgotten to put on the table was close at hand.

The phone was on the table. It rang and he picked up the receiver. It was her voice. He wanted her back home. He wanted to kiss her mouth, feel her open it under his kiss. He pushed his plate aside.

"Oh God I can hear you," he said, which was not how he had meant to begin. Somewhere he had a list of things he wanted to mention. It must be at work. There were key things on the list. The point was to attract, to attract, for want of a better word. One item was that they had fennel now, at the Chinese greengrocer's in White City. But that was the least interesting item on the list.

She thought he was referring to the phone connection, obviously.

"I can hear you too," she said, twice.

He wanted to do something, talk French to her, something, attract her, remind her of how much he loved her but without just saying it over and over.

"I love you," he said.

"I do too," she said. He knew what she meant. It was fine. He didn't know what he wanted. He wanted something stronger.

She was proceeding with the news about the baby, still unnamed, fully recovered from the mild case of jaundice she'd suffered from when she was born. Iris was keeping Ellen as calm as possible. The baby was at home with them now. It was good that she had come. Did he have any suggestions for a name for a girl, keeping in mind that it had to go well with Gunther.

"Not right now," he said, realizing that he wanted urgently to escape the subject. The last time he'd been engaged in baby-naming exercises was during one of Iris's false pregnancies, long ago.

"But please help us, Ray. Think about it. You have good suggestions. Anything with a little literary feeling to it would be welcome to Ellen. She's getting the most absurd suggestions from her friends here. I hate them. That's another subject. I'll tell you later. Just rebarbative is what I'd call the whole bunch of them. But there seems to be a trend going to find a name that's got trashy associations like Lulu or Lola or Ruby. I don't understand it. Or she'll be enthusiastic over a name that's just plain weird, like Merle. Of course there was Merle Oberon . . . But the worst is that she keeps muttering that if black people can make up any sort of name they want for their children, then why can't she? Who knows what she might come up with. Ladeeda or Ladido or something."

"I think the father should have some say in it, Iris."

"The father. No."

"I don't understand that."

"Ray, he knows about the baby, she told him, he just doesn't know she's been born yet."

"Shouldn't somebody inform him, Iris?"

"Of course! But this is the way Ellen wants it. He's in another state. He got married. I don't know how this is going to work out, but she wants me to help with an insane letter she wants him to sign. He's getting his mail at a post office box. It's all a mess. He works in a bookstore. He has nothing. He's in terror of his wife finding out. He always calls, when he calls, from a pay phone. And he always whispers. I don't know what I'm supposed to do. I might call your brother . . ."

"Now why in hell would you do that?"

"For *advice*."

"What in the name of hell does he know about legal . . . the legal realm?"

"There's no reason to be upset. He might know someone I could talk to. He knows amazing people. Did you read the sort of joke guidebook for returning to the States he sent me? I was going to show it to you. It turned out to be useful, really. He seems to know people in high places, gay people. The number of people you would never think of being gay that he can identify is pretty staggering. He reminds me of that diabetic woman at the embassy who named all the secret diabetics she knew about in Washington. Your brother can be very helpful."

"Call him, then."

"I did, once. But not to talk about this. Just to say hello."

"How is he?"

"I think he's all right. I couldn't tell. He's so funny. He has a new motto for the CIA. Do you want to know what it is?"

He was silent. If he kept silent long enough it might remind her that there was a rule. He hadn't been able to tell her about Dictionary Echelon but he thought he impressed a general rule of caution about certain references.

She sighed. "I know what I did, Ray. I'm sorry. But don't you want to know?"

"Okay, what is it?"

"Peek and ye shall find."

"Very amusing."

"Anyway these names she likes are, this is a guess, from movies we haven't seen, with cheap women as heroines. Arva is another one she likes, and Thelma. My sister is excitable right now. I think it's stress and postpartum and I think she'll be better. My mother can't come. She's in a wheelchair with gout. Also she's so out of it. She's not leaving Michigan. Since she heard there's no father on the scene or even in the wings, she really has nothing to say to Ellen. I am overwhelmed here. It would be heaven if you could be with us, but you can't, I know that. If I didn't give you the tourist reentry thing your brother wrote, go and look on the second shelf of my nightstand. It's brilliant . . .

"Ray, I want to talk to you forever. Can we?"

"You know we can."

"But you didn't ask for this expense with Ellen."

"It's all right." He was attracting her, which wasn't the right word, still. He was getting something going . . .

"Ray, how are you, are you eating decently?"

He said, "I don't have much appetite," to his surprise, because it wasn't true.

"No appetite?" she said. "Why is that? Then go eat out . . ."

He had committed a mistake. She felt criticized.

"You don't want Dimakatso to cook, so okay. She is perfectly adequate. I don't want this on me. I don't want to hear about how only one person can feed and nurture you the right way. I'm sorry. I'll tell you what to do if you have no appetite. Don't eat. Don't eat for *one day*. I bet your appetite might come back. Do you have any idea of the insanity I am dealing with here, a tiny infant child, my sister, her friends, do you have the slightest idea? Wait, I'm sorry. I'm sorry. Oh God. I'm marginal. Oh Ray my darling. It's stress. Pay no attention."

It was his fault. He had been tempted to go for sympathy by the stupid Ringnes. That was enough Ringnes. The pleasant feeling of having a little extra space in the top of the skull was declaring itself nicely. It was excellent beer, Norwegian. He liked Norwegians. Swedes he could take or leave.

"Please forgive me," she said.

"Come on. Nothing to forgive."

"I have so much to tell you, Ray."

"Tell, then."

"I think it's good my sister had this baby. I know it's a mess with the father, but still. They love Ellen at the Montessori Institute. The job part of her life looks solid. She likes doing publicity. They pay pretty munificently. They think she's brilliant.

"She needed this child. She was volunteering to baby-sit for all her married friends and she was falling in love with their children. They could do no wrong. She would baby-sit for a twenty-one-month-old holy terror who would go through the apartment dismantling it. But after each depredation, like tearing the knobs off the stereo, he would toddle over to her holding out the thing he had torn off as a gift, giving this darling smile. Or he would go into the bathroom and grab a container of shampoo and come out and give it to you as another gift but leaving a trail of spilled shampoo all through your living room. Of course Ellen doesn't keep the caps screwed on. But anyway the child would be picked up and she would slowly discern her apartment was in ruins. She had been in a dream. I met one of the children who pushed her over the edge, a darling little girl, just a toddler. When she came over to be baby-sat she brought along a whole menagerie of stuffed animals. Going to sleep meant collecting them into a heap and lying down on top of them. She had fantastic names for them. When I asked her about her animals she said, 'I use them as friends.' Ellen wrote the names down so she could refer to them correctly on the phone. They had a phone relationship. Look at this. I'm at her desk now and here's a card with the names of the animals. Here they are . . . Snartz, Gwinty, Pobeel, Woot, Fard and Dardena. Don't you love Dardena? How is St. James College?"

He knew what he wanted from this conversation. He wanted to attract her and he wanted some evidence that he was succeeding. He wanted to hear that she was keeping her personal footing in all the upheaval around having a baby, particularly as the proposition might apply to her. He wanted her to miss Botswana, if that was possible. He wanted to hear what it felt like to be back in the States, if she liked it there. It was probably fortuitous that she had gone to Florida, which, if he was any judge, she was going to find boring and extreme, culturally. That was what he hoped. He had to say something about school. There was nothing attractive going on. The pigs were dead.

"School is fine. No big changes."

"I think she'll be a good mother. My fingers are crossed. Do you know what cradle cap is?"

"Some type of bonnet for a child? No idea."

"No it's a scalp condition. It's like a crust. It's unattractive. Newborns get it. You're supposed to leave it alone, not be scrubbing it or oiling it every minute. Ellen can't leave it alone.

"She just has to calm down about this baby. I think she will. Her breasts are immense. She was never large-busted, Ray. She was like me . . ."

So far, her attitude to the new baby wasn't alarming. It was unromantic.

"What is going to happen to this child? I suppose it's a good thing it's a girl. They say they're easier. This child is not a good sleeper."

There was one other item he needed from this conversation. He needed to know if there was any chance that she had been in contact with Morel, any sign suggesting it.

"Well, anyway. America. I have to say Davis was right about one thing, unless it's just this particular neck of the woods. I think it's all over. He was right about credulism reigning and spreading. That means religiosity . . ."

"I figured," Ray said.

"Credulism," she said. She seemed to love the word. "The country is in a religious frenzy of some kind. Everybody has Jesus bumperstickers saying one thing or another. Anybody who thinks religion is going the way of the goatee is in for a shock. I don't know how happy Ellen is going to be, living around here. The local people have a feeling against single mothers, I gather, that she's run into, because the day she put a sticker on her bumper saying God Is a Single Parent someone twisted her windshield wipers so that they had to be replaced. She sees a connection, but who knows. Also the kind of religion that's around is kind of gruesome. One sticker has the image of a hand with a nail through it and the text says His Pain Your Gain. On Monday if you go someplace for fast food the cashier just automatically reaches out for your church bulletin so they can give you your ten percent off. Is anything happening at the embassy?"

"Not a thing."

"Have they found Dwight Wemberg?"

"No." That was a true statement.

"I think about him. I wish you could find him."

"What would I do if I did?"

"Well, help him. Put him up. I don't know."

"Concretely, though . . ."

"Find out what he needed you to do. Intervene for him."

"Well, it's a fantasy."

"It's so pitiful, love coming to an end that way, the way it does. This separation from you is so painful, Ray, because it brings up . . . you know what I mean. It's like a rehearsal." She was insanely truthful.

He was in pain. He said, "You mean the final separation. I know, I know. Look, don't talk about it. I want you back here, my good girl, my love . . ." An odd sound came out of him.

"Stop, I'm crying," she said. "Wait a minute till I find some Kleenices . . . I know I had some, a new packet."

The love of a woman with a funny mind is the definition of paradise, he thought. The word Kleenices was, of course, plural for Kleenex. It was an old item between them, but he hadn't heard it for a while.

"Here we are," she said. "I knew I had some. I put them in my purse, unbeknownst to me. This is what I want. If I die first, this is what I want you to do. Take my ashes and put them in an urn on the coffee table and then every now and then lift the lid and shout the latest down into it, whatever is going on."

"Then you do the same."

"Don't say it. I can't stand it if you die first. It's worse if you die than if I do."

"Please don't say that and please let's not have this conversation when you're there where I can't hold you." Save you, was what he meant.

"I'm wretched without you," she said, her voice very low.

His breathing was easier, distinctly.

She was irreplaceable. That was the problem. She was uniquely funny. Now his mind was flooding with moments and episodes that proved it. They had stayed overnight at the Tshwaragano Hotel in Serowe where the management was bell-mad and rang a ship's bell for every meal, including breakfast at seven. And they had dragged in dead tired at three in the morning and gotten to bed and then for no reason someone had begun banging the bell at five-thirty, waking them, and he had asked why in hell they were doing that and she had said, "They're practicing." And when he had noticed in the paper that Belfast and Beirut had become sister cities, she had said, "What do they do, exchange rubble?" He remembered being with her in a diner when they were dating, before he'd had any notion about how funny she was, and when she was being offered a second cup of coffee by the waitress she'd said, "Oh no thanks, if I drink that I'll be up all day," making the woman laugh. And when he'd wondered aloud what the correct name for a male ballet dancer was, she had said *ballerino*. And then when he'd mentioned that physicist who had concluded that the universe was made up of just three kinds of matter, she'd said, "Yes, I know, ether, phlogiston, and ectoplasm." She liked to deny that she ever farted. And when he'd been passing by the bathroom when she was in the tub and he'd heard something suspicious and said, "Did you fart?" she'd said, "Certainly not. I was just submerging my head to belch." And when he'd once remarked, "Wasn't that a particularly virtuous lunch we had," she'd said, "It was more than just virtuous, it was actually unpleasant." And then she'd said one morning, "If I make us stop drinking coffee and only make tea, will you start hating me?" and he had said no and then she had said, "Well then, if I keep making us coffee and forget about tea, will you *stop* hating me?" That one was slightly ineffable. They had an idiom together. That was it. She was the author of it. He was never funny. Except that she had laughed when he described her chest as the Globe Theatre, a literary nothing, his pinnacle. He had to escape this.

He said, "Before I forget, we can get fennel now. They have fennel at Notwane Gardens."

"I lost you. We can get what?"

He raised his voice. "Fennel. Fennel." This was not what he wanted, to be shouting fennel to his darling girl. And she was a girl. He was forty-eight.

"Well, eat some," she said.

His hunger was coming back.

"Are you eating okay, not too much meat and potatoes without end? And you're keeping up with the garlic capsules. If you don't take anything else, take those. Let me see if I can put Ellen on for just a sec. I think she's still asleep. Let me check. She sleeps more than the baby."

He waited.

She returned. She said, "Still out. Which gives me a chance to tell you something else I don't want her to hear. Her friends around here. They're mostly arts and crafts, and some who consider themselves artists. There's a little antiques store and art gallery enclave where they all love her. She buys so much crap, is why, crap of theirs. I won't ever complain about the embassynians again, I promise. We went to a couple of openings and at one of them I got into an argument in a flash with a woman who got a certain disappointed expression on her face when we were introduced and she understood that I was using my husband's last name. This was a big disappointment to her since I was Ellen's sister, Ellen being a paragon of freeness, being unmarried and having this baby and all. This woman's given last name was Johnson, paternal last name. So I merely observed that she was choosing to privilege, that's a very popular term with them, privilege, the name of a male, her biological father, over the name of her presumably beloved chosen husband, accident over choice. And of course her dumb name also incorporated somebody being the son of some ancient John. It was hardly as though she had dumped all her nomenclature in favor of something completely invented, like Dora Violin Moonleaf or something. By the way, all the people in this milieu have the most blinding white teeth. Everyone over a certain income is getting bonding and capping like crazy. Even my sister bleaches her teeth at night, every night. Even in the hospital. So that was round one. Round two was an artist whose work was on display under gigantic *lenses*. In the catalog she was described as a micromuralist, which does *not* mean that she was a very-small-in-stature muralist. I pray God Ellen can't hear this. No this was a person, you will not believe this, who inscribed little primitive scenes on pebbles and in a couple of instances on actual *lima beans*, dried limas. And I couldn't help but wonder out loud why anyone would say mural in connection with these little . . . *scratchments* on pebbles. I wanted to know what they had in common with murals, with big, broadly executed, jammed, huge wall pictures. Now if the artist had carved a tiny figure with its back to us at the bottom edge of these scratchments, as though the figure were looking at the image, there might have been a case. I didn't make a big scene. I just asked one or two people, but it got around. They make you want to act philistine.

"I'm going on like this not because it's interesting but because I can't let you go. You'll be gone when I stop telling you things. So I'm telling you everything I can think of."

"I love it," he said.

"I love you, Ray, meboy. Oh do I. I miss you. How's your penis? How's your trusty penis?"

"My rusty penis? That it is."

"You heard me."

"I think this is phone sex."

"I know. We'd better stop. It isn't fair to Ellen. What if she heard? Okay, so what else can I tell you. Well. Thinking. Even around here there are homeless. And another thing you see is people laying out displays of belongings, clothing and personal items, on the sidewalk. It has to be done quick, before the cops come. And this is not a poor neighborhood, either.

"And I have to tell you that Davis was right about something else in this country. It's not his idea but it's true. He gave me an article about the exteriorization of the self. It's pretty self-explanatory. You see it everywhere. People advertise what they are, young people especially, by signage, essentially. People advertise what they are, their affiliations. They wear tee shirts with messages instead of plain, like we wore. They wear violent personal ornaments and tattoos. The idea is that when people dressed more or less all the same, within the same middle-class spectrum, you demonstrated who you were in the things you revealed when you talked to people, what you read, what you knew. Now nobody knows anything different than the next guy. It's all music and media boilerplate on the inside. So therefore why not get wondrously overmuscled or put metal studs in your eyelids? This I've seen. This article calls it a panic over differentiation. And it's true. Well.

"I love you I love you. And speaking of Davis, Ray, could you do me a favor and call him?"

Now this. Ray had been about to take a surreptitious bite of steak. He put his fork down.

"Call him?"

"Yes, would you?"

"Call him and say what?"

"I'm about to tell you. Call him and say I don't think I'm going to get much homework done on this trip."

"What kind of homework are you talking about?"

"Well, a journal I was supposed to keep. And also a book I'm supposed to read when I have a free moment, *Homo Hierarchicus*, by an anthropologist. It's something you might be interested in, but it has absolutely nothing to do with me. It's about the caste system in India."

"Couldn't you send him a card? I'm sure he'd love to hear from you, not me. Or you could call him."

"A card takes too long and I don't want him to think I'm doing something I'm not doing. And I feel awkward calling. I don't think this rises to the importance of a phone call, and I don't want to spend the money for that when you can just give him a ring. This is already costing a fortune, this trip. I don't like to think about it."

"I will, then. Tomorrow."

"Ray, it's only partly that I have no time, to tell you the truth. When I start writing in my journal it turns into reams of hysterical stuff I already know and don't want to think about, mainly regarding my mother and also Ellen, who has a sneaky side to her personality. And I write about you. I write things about you you wouldn't mind reading. But I just don't want to be doing this now. My job is to keep my act together. I have to cope. But I said I would do this stuff and now I'm not going to."

She was in anxiety. Why was Morel back in this conversation, he wanted to know. It was bitter. It was bitter.

He didn't want to talk anymore. She disliked the silence he was making. He could sense it.

She said, "What about the CODESA talks, Ray? Where the ANC walked out? Is this very bad news?"

He was a little startled. He said, "No it's only going to be temporary. Don't worry about it." But he felt it was odd that she had brought it up. It just happened recently. She wasn't getting the *New York Times*, there in

Florida. It was big news in Botswana and the Republic, of course, but it was odd that she had heard about it, or was it? Of course she was always nervous about the chance that things would go badly in South Africa and that danger and disruption would come back across the border to Botswana. He didn't like what he was suspecting, which was that she had in fact just been in touch with Morel and that everything she had said in that connection had been a deception, which would explain asking him to do something that was, in the circumstances, going to be unpleasant for him, calling a man she knew he had negative feelings about, contriving to show, by that, how minor a presence Morel was for both of them, how unthreatening Ray ought to find him, to desensitize, to desensitize. His thoughts were racing. He hated this.

"Where did you hear about it, Iris? Are they covering it on TV?"

"No, not really. In the paper."

"The local paper there?"

"It must've been. Ray I didn't ask about Dimakatso. You know to give her my love. But how is she doing?"

It was possible it had been in the paper, but he didn't believe it. And now she was showing regret, showing she wanted to get off the subject and he didn't like that. He could be wrong. He could be. He wanted to be wrong.

He had made himself too unhappy to continue.

"I haven't eaten," he said.

"Well for goodness' sake go and eat. I'll talk to you tomorrow or the next day."

"Right, and my love to everybody. I love you. Get a name for that baby. I'll talk to Ellen, one of these calls, tell her."

"I love you," she said.

He said, "And so, goodnight."

21. *The Apostles of Reason*

Pony had overproduced, at first. Ray hadn't been prepared for it and had even run low on replacement cassettes at one point. And then there had been a change. A trajectory was developing in Pony's attitude that was making Ray uncomfortable and wary. The issue of a chartering letter, which had come up twice, sharply, after Pony had begun this work, was now gone, dropped. And information on the whereabouts of Pony's debtor, the absconded haulier, very preliminary information at that, had been received perfunctorily. Pony had gone from tense volubility, from presenting Ray with full lists of attendees so that all the voices on the tapes could be identified, to a new mode of dreaminess and diffidence. And when it came to identifying participants Pony had gotten vaguer and vaguer, claiming forgetfulness, claiming not to have been introduced to half the group attending. Nor was Pony pressing for supplementary payments, Ray realized. He had the money for him. Something was up.

But then something was always up. Even if Pony was planning to exit the assignment, that would be manageable, because he had been so copious to date that Ray was dealing with more material than he'd had time to get decently through, much less decently assess. Critical information had come out of the tapes. Morel was creating two groups, a public group called the Apostles of Reason, and an inner, esoteric group, cadres, whose name Ray had yet to discover. Morel was recruiting cadres, which was why the tape he was going to listen to tonight, for the second time, was worth better attention than he'd been able to give it. It represented a sort of catechism session of a young fellow from Mahalapye, an assistant pharmacist, Themba Kise, someone being groomed to go out and beat the drum for irreligion in the northeast part of the country, a sort of franchise being given to him. Apparently the way it worked was that the most promising contacts, the ones considered eligible for the inner circle of proselytizers, would come and stay with Morel for a residential immersion lasting a week or so, ending in catechism.

Dark of night galvanized him. It was very late. He was at ease on the sofa, his bare feet up on the vast plain of glass that was their coffee table. The living room blinds were tightly drawn. The odor of charred garlic was heavy in the air, heavy and sweet. That evening he had cooked his third steak dinner of the week. He could get frozen fish tomorrow, hake. The best parts of his thesis had been written in the middle of the night, before he'd met Iris. Now that she was away he was being reminded how much he liked to work at night. Maybe he was regressing in a general way. He had a craving for creamed chipped beef, a dish he hadn't had since high school, a specialty, if you could call it that, of his mother's. At night your enemies are asleep, he thought. Working for the agency did provide him with more occasions for solitary late night work than the usual job would. He shouldn't complain. But marriage and teaching can't help but nail us to the light of day, he thought. He was happy tonight, he supposed. He put the earphones on.

He had to bear down on this tape, not let his mind drift. It was important. His periphery was reasonably clear. Iris was all right. It was obviously a piece of luck that her landfall in America had been Florida, which was turning out to be more floridly, so to speak, part of the Bible Belt than either of them had realized. She had reported hearing a young girl's call to a religious radio talk program. The child had been anxious to know if it was allowed to sleep late in heaven. Ellen had settled on a name for her daughter, Mame. He didn't care. It had been between Mame and Mitzi. It was good that Wemberg had shifted his hiding place out of the university library and to someplace unknown. That had been a relief to Ray. There was a story around that Wemberg was sleeping rough in the maize fields in Sebele.

He was ready to begin. Hearing this taped session the first time had brought home to him how little interest he had in changing anyone's mind on any subject, any important subject. He thought about that a little more. He had been part of a war all his adult life, but he had never felt impelled to try to change the views of any of his opponents, ever. He had tried to trip them up, dismay them, undo them, but the idea of attempting to convert any one of them to his own views was embarrassing to him. So Morel, who was making a passionate vocation out of changing the minds of other adults, was what, a horse of another color altogether.

Part of the prologue was missing. They were a little way into the catechism. Morel's voice was without much color. He was tense. His voice was high. He was working to keep himself at the right level for his listeners. He was conforming his speech pattern to what he thought was appropriate for his English-as-a-second-language Batswana audience, speaking more slowly and formally. We all do the same thing, he thought.

"So, then, what do we say to the question, Who was this man Jesus? We accept that he was real, unlike Moses, he was real, and he walked the earth of ancient Palestine.

"A Jew. Always a Jew. Up to the end, a Jew. And is there anything about his name that might be mentioned?"

"I forgot. His name in truth was Jeshua, which is saying in Hebrew that Yahweh is soon to come back. Yahweh the God of the Jews."

"So go on with more. How else do we know he was still a Jew?"

"Rra, because he wore the boxes on his body . . ."

"Yes, those are called phylacteries. It's good to use the correct name if you can remember. And what are phylacteries?"

"Rra, they are foolish small boxes with Jewish writing on little scraps."

"But remember, Themba, we try never to mock . . . as we go. We *describe* . . . And what else shows that this Jesus was a Jew?"

"He said go to the temple many times if you have done something wrong, and give taxes . . ."

"Let me interrupt, rra. The tax, which he agreed all Jews should pay, was one thing. It supported the temple, maintained it. But he also said that Jews should be dutiful and pay the fees for atonement for particular sins. You might purchase a dove to sacrifice, to make up for some wrong you may have done. And of course it would have to be a dove that was perfect, which we are coming to."

"Ehe, and he wore earlocks, although we are not sure. Yet we think so."

"These earlocks, they are called . . . ?"

"I forget what."

"Just a minor thing. Peyot. They are called peyot."

"Peyot, ehe. And fringes to his sleeves."

"Good. And they are called . . . ?"

"Tzitzit." But he had hesitated over the last syllable.

"Themba, if you are unsure as to pronouncing a word, a foreign word, it's best not to try, because there may be someone who will catch you on it to destroy your greater message. But tzitzit is correct. Now, and what is it that is recorded that Jesus said, that shows him to be a faithful Jew?"

"What he said? As when he taught in synagogues? Synagogue is not the same as temple, it is smaller, but we know he went because it is set down as to his being in synagogue on a Sabbath, at which time a man presented him his withered hand to heal. As well we know he himself paid the temple tax because of a coin found in a fish caught by Peter that was the right amount for both of them. But as to what he said at those times, I am not sure."

"No, I wasn't asking about what he may have said inside the synagogue or temple, no. What is it reported he said generally about the Law of Moses?"

"Ehe, he says he is among them to fulfill the law and that no one must change it by a jot."

"Tittle or jot, is the whole phrase. And do you remember he says, 'I was sent to the lost sheep of the house of Israel, and *to them alone.*' Which is Matthew 15:24. And this is one chapter and verse you will need to remember. The same statement is in Mark. In Mark. Now you remember I said that when you quote scripture you can start just by being sure you have the chapter right, so you might say only Matthew 15. But then as you speak more often, the verse number will come to be fixed in your mind. But there are some statements you will want to have by both chapter and verse. This is one of them, because it shows that even when the followers, later followers of Jesus, were trying to make it seem that his message was for the gentiles across the world, they were forced to admit, because it was so well known even then, that he was speaking purely and solely to the Jews. And do we have some other proofs of this, in his own words?"

"Ehe."

"So . . . well how else do we know that his message was meant solely for his fellow Jews?"

"It is because when it comes up to gentiles they are mere dogs or swine, as he calls them. And when he sends his disciples off to carry his message about, he says Oh do not go, please, among the gentiles, and never among the Samaritans. And this is strange because the Samaritans were believers in Moses and his books but not some other books and scriptures. But he said to shun even these people."

"Good. Great, Themba."

"And once when a Roman soldier asks to have his servant healed and

Jesus does so, we believe now that the servant was in fact a Jew. Except for a Syrian woman he called a dog, all the healing and casting out demons were done for Jews, only."

"Good. Now, so he was a Jew, and what else would we say about him?"

"As to his . . . his lepele . . . ?"

There was a moment of laughter, and someone said "Ncucu," and there was more laughter.

Finally, Morel understood. "Ah lepele—his penis, you mean. Oh you mean his circumcision. Yes, that he was circumcised on the eighth day after his birth. That can be mentioned. No, I was asking a different question. When I said he was a Jew, but what else would we say to describe him . . . Do you see where I'm going?"

"Nyah, rra."

"He was a special kind of Jew . . . ?"

"Ah. Oh. Ah because he says emunah is everything we must do?"

"Nonono. Yes, in a way, but that comes later. No. He is a *mad* Jew, setsenwa, a mad person. We would say he is *delusional*, a doctor would say. And we have to be very careful when we say this. But why would we have the right to say it?"

There was no answer given.

When he was tired of waiting for it, Morel said, "All right, just think about it for a minute. I'll come back to it. I want to stress something for us. We establish that Jesus was wholly a Jew who is stolen and refashioned by the Christians after his death. But it has to be shown that not only Jesus was stolen from the Jews but everything else, every piece of furniture in the new church. What did the Christians steal from the Jews? Oh . . . well . . . angels, devils and demons, the Devil himself—who was in the Jewish belief a character named Mastema who was a, a, forensic officer, a kind of inspector general sent out by God to see how well individual believers were holding up under temptation . . . Of course, those who failed the test would be condemned to eternal damnation, but it was nothing personal with Mastema. He was an employee of God, a civil servant.

"What else did the Christians steal from the people they then decided to torment for two thousand years? How about monotheism, or rather, as we talked about, henotheism, which says, okay, there may be more than one God but you only worship the best one. In this case, Yahweh. What else did the Christians steal from the Jews? Well, heaven . . . hell . . . eternal torment . . . virgin birth—except that in the Jewish scriptures the most God did was make barren and over-the-hill women able to conceive miraculously by their very own flesh-and-blood husbands . . . but it's close, I think . . . The Christians improved the idea by making an actual virgin give birth. What else? Baptism, copying the conversion-baptism of the Jews. The Eucharist came from the Passover meal, probably. The resurrection of the body, women as a source of pollution, and sex as a source of pollution. The end of the world and the replacement of all human institutions by a supernatural regime of endless perfection. The Incarnation, the Ascension, the Holy Spirit, except that it was called Sophia by the Jews. The Trinity also comes from the Jews, but it would take too long to explain that right now. The Book of Life. The only thing the Christians contributed to Christianity was priestly celibacy—or so it was thought, until the Dead Sea Scrolls came to light and it turned out that they had some celibate priests, too. Faith healing, also.

"So you can see that Christianity, so called, is nothing but a heresy of Judaism, a Jewish heresy whose most striking peculiarity is that it commands its followers to *hate the Jews*! Hate its authors, its *inventors*! . . ."

There was something off about Morel's intervention. It was like a striptease stuck into an opera . . .

He thought he knew what it was. It was Morel showing off, in all likelihood showing off for Kerekang, trying to keep his attention if the catechism was proving to be a little slow for him.

Here was Morel again. "Before we go back to our question, very important to remember about the beliefs of Jesus is that his brother James, who succeeded Jesus as the head of the group, which was called the Jerusalem Church, was also completely a Jew, always present at the temple in Jerusalem, observant in all ways, he had knees so callused from kneeling and praying that they were compared to the knees of a camel. Yes, James seemed to believe that his brother might return when the messianic age came. But the outcome he expected was the same as what Jesus expected, and that was that the Jews would be the teachers of the world. Under Yahweh. And what they would be teaching was *their religion*, of course. Judaism. Okay . . . So. Themba . . ."

"Ehe. We are saying now why can we call this man mad?"

"Good. Right."

"It is because of the kingdom, what he was saying as to the Kingdom of God coming definitely very fast, at any time."

"That's right. You can say it like this. Jesus was convinced that in his lifetime he would see God come downstairs and establish a physical kingdom upon the earth. It would be a Jewish kingdom, brought about exclusively by the devotional activity of Jews. All the tribes of Israel would be reassembled and the twelve apostles of Jesus would sit in judgment on them. You remember that the name we gave to his belief that the Kingdom of God was coming almost at once was *imminentism*? And it, imminentism, is in fact supposed to be the main belief, the basic belief, of Christians, if they understand their own scriptures—and not only of the evangelicals, who are *galloping* in their numbers in many places in the world, a mighty horde, really.

"And it is entirely mad to think that at any minute a giant fatherly presence is going to bring history to an end and set up his kingdom. Jesus was mad."

"So these evangelical men who say they are born again are becoming born again as Jews, rra. It makes me laugh that they don't know this," Themba said.

"Right, and how do we know that this mad belief in the imminent end was held by Jesus? . . . aside from the clues given in his statements and acts, which are turned around and softened by certain people today who say there will be no Second Coming, no physical kingdom, because in their view Jesus was catering for a spiritual change only . . . We call them *immanentists*, not the same word, the ones who say that the Kingdom of Heaven was already present in the world in Jesus' time and forever, and that it consisted of human beings acting charitably toward one another, and nothing more supernatural than that."

"Em, ah, rra, we say Jesus is mad and expects the end of the world because of what he says and because his teacher John the Baptist tells that this is to come, and Jesus becomes John's follower. Yes, and as well, Jesus' closest followers, Paul and James, say this is to come, the end of the world, ordered by God, is to come—although they disagreed on other items. And next in time to follow Jesus came Mark and Matthew and Luke. And in all they wrote is the belief that the end of time is coming soon, as Jesus said."

"Perfect!"

"Ke itumela, rra."

"Now, under this kingdom . . . no, first, what was the name for all the other people of the world?"

"The nations. The goyin."

"No, goy*im*, with m at the end."

"Sorry."

"It's nothing. And what did Jesus say would become of these goyim, the nations, when God came down?"

"They will bend their knees to Yahweh. For some very long time, up to a thousand years whilst being judged. And some people from among the goyim nations would be fine as to entering heaven when there is heaven. You see, there is not yet heaven, at that time, though there is hell. Some must be pushed into hell, even from amongst the Jews."

"Who is likely to be cast into hell?"

"Rra, it is confusing to me, very much. Some we can say with ease will be pushed, such as those who offended Jesus in time past. And if once you have eaten meat with blood, you will be pushed, we can be sure. But as to the gentiles, *most* of them will find themselves in hell. I can study more as to these rules, rra. These rules of Noah by which some gentiles could pass through into heaven after all the judgment is finished."

"No, you are right to be confused, because in the Bible the text is confused. And it is confused because the original question had to do with Jews, first and foremost. And very little thought was given to the gentiles.

"Now, what else can we say about this age, the age when Yahweh has created his kingdom on earth, the messianic age?"

"Em, well . . . still yet we do not see Yahweh ruling, I believe. The Christians began to say that in this time it would be Jesus ruling over the world for God. They were the followers of Paul.

"But as we saw when you spoke, it was a Son of Man who would rule, riding on clouds. We cannot say if Jesus was saying *he* was this Son of Man. Very likely he thought, yes, I am that man, because he was saying often to the apostles that he would sit on the right hand of his father, God. So, but perhaps that Son of Man can be Elijah. We cannot say, only that he rides about on clouds at times. But I must study these laws of Noah because to Batswana if you say Rra, Jesus says if you have eaten blood, Jesus of old, in his true doctrine before he was stolen by the Christians, if you taste blood you are going to the pit of hell, well, my word, *all* Batswana have tasted blood, as in puddings of blood, and other ways at the cattle post, expressly when they are ill. So you can see it will raise their eyes on this matter. They will listen."

"Themba, we have to be very careful with this. I would leave it alone."

"No, because you see up to this day at the butchery where they say they are halal, 'we are halal,' they say, 'and our meat is drained, you must eat this or you will be condemned someway' . . . it is from these same words of Noah and it is a curse on the Batswana . . . These Muslims say your meat is not clean, rra, except as you eat what is halal."

"No, but this would be the wrong way to approach it. At the Muslim butcheries . . . No. Maybe at some future time, Themba. But your point is correct. But just not *now*."

"Ehe, rra."

"So we are in the messianic age and they have finished judging. God's judges have. Then what?"

"Em, ah, oh yes, you must have a new kind of body to last forever and ever. The dead are all raised, I believe, and they, well, I believe they would be most in need. They would be rotten, rra. Ai! E bodile . . ."

"No, no," Morel said, to one or two people who were laughing.

"So, but rra, you must have a new body of spirit or electric or whatso-haveyou because it must be such as to let you fly and repose in the blue sky. Em, and as to the dead gentiles, nothing is said, if they are brought up, the saved ones, for new bodies or no, so it is confusing."

Morel made a reproving sound. Themba was playing to the crowd, which was not wanted. Ray knew what Morel, that asshole, was after—when you destroy some poor bugger's belief system, become a technician, neutral, like a doctor bringing sad news but not being involved yourself, Ray thought. You had to have the demeanor of a funeral director.

"And then, in heaven, what happens? The Jewish heaven."

"At all times you are not to work."

"What else?"

"At all times you must not play after young ladies. At all times you must wear a crown and sit upon a throne. It is one man, one throne . . ."

Morel was making Themba wait. This last little thrust had earned him a touch of the silent treatment. No levity allowed, Ray thought. Morel was strict.

"And when the Jewish Sabbath comes, Themba, how should we understand it?"

"Ehe, for one day you are to live as it will be in heaven, with no work to do, no amusements . . ."

"Themba, let me read from our great scholar, Vermes, you have this, page 125 . . . On the Sabbath 'abstinence from all work of the occupations of the children of men, and a total devotion to worship by means of offering incense, gifts and sacrifice in the sanctuary, symbolize and mystically achieve God's reign on earth.' "

"Ehe, and you must sit and receive from God his shining forth."

"See if you remember what we call that, or rather the Jews did."

"I forget what."

"Shekinah. Radiance of God."

"Ehe, and, em, whilst you receive this shekinah you must in no way look straightaway at God. Even if you are in your new body, it can kill you to see his face."

"Such is the Kingdom of Heaven, Themba. Not much moving around unless there is some scheme to shift thrones so that all can have a chance to sit near God."

There was a ripple of amusement among the hearers. Morel is not playing by his own rules, Ray thought.

Themba said, "I think the Batswana can never be Jews, if there shall be no cows in heaven."

Someone in the audience said "Ke dunetse," meaning he agreed.

"So this heaven you describe is the great, final end that the Jew Jesus was urging all his people to work and die for, we see. And we are talking only about what we can tell were the beliefs of Jesus himself, in the time *before* Paul, and *before* the four Gospels were written—beginning about how many years after the death of Jesus, would you say?"

"We say Mark is written down about the year seventy, rra. Paul was writing earlier but still it was fifteen years after Jesus was killed, but Paul tells nothing of the life of Jesus and he tells only some few words of the beliefs of Jesus, which is strange."

"Right! This is the important thing to emphasize. Great feats of scholarship have taken place in the last thirty or forty years, so we can now extract and separate, this is the point, the *original* ideas and beliefs and instructions of the Jew Jesus, take them out of the books of the Gospels of Mark and Matthew and Luke, where we find other beliefs and interpretations alongside them, coming from Paul for the most part, added to and plastered across them, obscuring them. And Themba, all of you . . . it is from these encrustations and superadditions and plasterings that Paul and his followers turned a dead Jew into a God for the gentiles, a new God, at the same time twisting, Paul was *twisting* the sacred writings of the Jews to make them say that they prophesied the coming of a divine Savior for the *Gentiles* . . . for everyone. And that way lies Christianity, invented by Paul.

"But we are not coming to that, yet. No. People do not like to hear any of this, really. So we must first make clear to them that we are talking about the original and pure beliefs of the Jew Jesus. And the first thing you must make clear is the answer to the question of how Jesus came to believe that the world was to come to an end at the hands of Yahweh. He thought he knew what had to be done to *make* Yahweh bring an end to the world as it was and create his kingdom. And other Jews of Palestine were *also* seeking ways to make God descend. But they were saying there were other ways to make him come, three ways. You remember the three ways?"

"Ehe, rra. Em, in Palestine the Romans were oppressing the Israelites very much. And the Jews were saying it must cease. This must cease. And they had from their scriptures stories telling of God coming to their aid, as when they came to the promised land and found it stuffed fat with enemies and vipers, and God helped them to kill their enemies . . ."

Morel said, "Yes, you remember we said that such a God might be called a serial killer, in fact. But this is among ourselves. When we discuss this, we say only that he killed many opponents of the Jews."

Themba said, "In Palestine in past times, some victories would come when Yahweh would strengthen the captains of the Jews but would cause the walls and towers of their enemies to fall down. Or he would send angels to aid in the killing. So in their belief they ask how can we make Yahweh come to us once again.

"The Romans were their enemies. So they were saying, if we take up arms against the Romans, Yahweh will come down to help us. But the priests of the temple were saying they must not bother the Romans. These priests were in the pay of the Romans, of course, much as like the Zed CC saying we must not bother the Boers."

Morel was quick. "Well, but rra, it would be best not to make overmuch of that. We have many Zed CC followers in this country and they would be, well, aggravated if they saw us criticizing their brothers in South Africa when they themselves are blameless, you see. So it would be very much the best not to make such a comparison."

"They are tiresome," Themba said.

"I know, but they must not see us attacking them. This is what we must do, remember. We try to enlighten about beliefs, but we must let the holders of those beliefs see for themselves what our criticism means about their churches, you see? Do you see what I mean? And as to taking one denomination and saying you are particularly in error . . . *no*." Morel was being very deliberate.

Themba said, "Still, it is true. They are tiresome. They will listen to you less than anyone else, and when you finish they say if you only will drink salt water you will change and see God. This is what they stated to me, rra."

"Proceed, Themba."

Themba said, "The worst were the daggermen."

"Who were called . . . by what other names?"

"Sicarii."

"Yes, and they were called Zealots, also. And they, the daggermen, would assassinate not only Romans but Jews as well . . . Jews who were helping the Romans . . ."

Themba said, "And those men were for war against the Romans and they would say that when the Jews made an uprising, at that time God would come down as with Joshua and give them the victory over the Romans."

"And what ways were some other Jews proposing for bringing divine intervention?"

"Ehe . . . at the Dead Sea lived some Jews in caves. Essenes they were named."

"Well, no, rra . . . They lived in camps, and in regular buildings as well. Their writings were found in caves where they had been hidden, found only in recent years, you remember."

"Yes, rra. And these Essenes were quite fools, who said if only they might become as clean as angels, God could come. The Zealots believed war would bring God, the Essenes believed cleanliness would bring God. Every rule of cleanliness these men would observe many times over, as to washing and putting women to the side. And in their thoughts they would be pure. As well they would be training as an army at the ready, to join with the angel-army God was sure to send when at last they have become clean enough. And so the Romans would be thrown down. So this way was through cleanliness . . ."

"Okay, good. But I don't think we want to call any particular groups we discuss *fools*, do we?"

"But rra, they are long dead. There are none to offend."

"Just the same, Themba. It's best to avoid those words."

"Yes, for fear they will give offense at times. My word, I would not do it. But here we are free, isn't it?"

"Within these walls, yes. But we must train ourselves here to be always prudent. So. Now. So far we have violence and purity. What other means did Jewish believers propose to bring God to intervene on earth?"

Themba said, "So we come up to the followers of John the Baptist, who is stating God will come only if many Jews repent of past sins."

"And, if you remember, there was a name for this repentance."

"It is . . ."

"You may consult your study cards. And Themba, as I recommended to you, the best place to keep your study cards is in your Bible, as bookmarks, your Bible, which you will be consulting in any case. And that way you avoid having to search your pockets for them. And then as you search out things in the Bible you pass your eyes over this material and are helped to retain it."

"Ke itumetse, rra. I will do that. And when you repent it is called teshuvah. Teshuvah is saying sorry. And Jesus was for a time following John the Baptist. And it is teshuvah when you are pushed into the water and washed, when you are baptized. But in fact, there was no coming down of God from all these teshuvahs of John the Baptist, and time was passing by. And so Jesus turned away from John. He was impatient. And then the king put John the Baptist to death, so as to teshuvah, it was the end."

"And then what did Jesus do?"

"Jesus said if you cannot summon God down by means of war— although these daggermen were still raising up from time to time, if you cannot summon God by washing and bathing, and if you cannot summon God by repenting all past sins you have made and going into the water for a sign, then perhaps, he said, the Jews can summon God down by emunah."

"Okay, good, and does Jesus continue with baptizing?"

"No, we do not see that. Only in one place in the Bible does it say so, but we think that is wrong."

"And how would you explain what emunah is and what it meant among the Jews of that time? I know you have this in large letters on your study cards. It is *important*. In fact you may feel free to read off the definition anytime until you have it in your memory," Morel said.

"Ehe, rra. Emunah is complete trusting faith, complete trusting faith, as children have it. It is becoming as a child in every way. It is to never question but only always believe. You take no thought for yourself, and in that way you show your trust in God to care for you. I remember very well what is in this book of Vermes. Emunah demands the total commitment of the soul to God. You must do away with all things in yourself that would make God hate you, were you a child, bothering him. You must wish him to be left in peace even when his eye falls on you. You do not pester him with oaths in his name, because when you take the name of God in an oath you are forcing him to become a party in some little disputes you have with your neighbors. So as well, you must avoid ill-doing because all people stand as your brothers under God, and God the father is best pleased when there is no fighting in his home. He hears *everything*, the God of Jesus, so we can see why these oaths pelting him like rain must be displeasing, very much. And when it comes to stories told by Jesus, we see that so many of them are about God, and are saying he is above everything a father who is greatly pleased, most pleased, when one of his lost sheep or sons who has been erring is returning home. And these he loves much more than those who have stayed in the fold and been obedient toward him for the most part. But that is the nature of a father, Jesus is saying to us . . ."

Morel said, "Well, but stop there because we are going to go through the proverbs and parables later, to see how they show this craze for childish devotion, for emunah, every one of them. Maybe that will be after we eat something."

There was a sound of chair feet scraping and then of boot heels knocking on the hard floor as Morel commenced pacing back and forth in front of his audience. Morel was partial to cowboy boots. The refreshments to come included maize porridge and chicken stew. Morel wanted refreshments served at all Apostles of Reason occasions, he told the new cadres. He explained that they were a draw. They should be served not sooner than three-quarters of the way through an event.

"Emunah is what, above all, we must understand and make others, the ones trammeled and trapped and stumbling in the nets of Christianity, understand, because it is the whole heart and soul of the message of the Jew Jesus. *Everything* that he taught is secondary to emunah, including every rule and regulation of his religion. All the six hundred and fifteen rules and regulations of the Torah, which Jesus continues to accept with all his heart and being, are made subordinate to the one goal of building up emunah, and emunah is what? Is being as a *child*, becoming childlike, in absolute faith, unquestioning faith. We all remember that the chief commandment of the Torah, the one held by Jesus to be a summary of all the other commandments, the commandment that you must love God with all your mind, heart, and soul, is no more than a formulation of emunah, and the commandment that stands second to this, that you must love your neighbor as yourself, is aimed to stop all strife displeasing to a father, as Themba has just said. So with Jesus, emunah is all, namely that the trust, the emunah, of a child is the conditio sine qua non for access to the kingdom.

"Think about what this means. All of you. Think. It means that being like a *child*, a boy instead of a man, is the most basic condition you must meet for salvation!"

Feeling had come into Morel's voice, true urgent feeling. His register was lower.

"So but can we not *see* what we *have* in these beliefs of Jesus the Jew, in this early branch of Judaism, which we must never forget his religion was, and remains forever, since he never changed it?

"When we tell Christians that the closer they are to the original Jesus the more they should consider themselves Jews, they jump, they want to scream, because they have been poisoned by the hatred of the Jews spoken in the Gospels. The new sect of Christian Jews defamed their rivals, the other Jews, and put their lies in the mouth of Jesus the Jew.

"No, it drives Christians crazy to be told that if they truly love Jesus, they're Jews. So we have to be wise as serpents and gentle as doves when we blast them with this news."

Morel was continuing. "This is what I wanted to say. We have to see that what we have before us in the religion of Jesus is as clear a crystallization or distillation of what is going on in *all* religions, one way or another, as we could pray for. That is, the falling back into the status of a child before some figure or idea identifiable as a version of the all-powerful lawgiving father, a patrimorph, as I proposed we call it, a patrimorph, a thing in the shape of a father.

"Go back to your notes and see that I called religion *organized regression*, and the falling back is to that time when we were coming to consciousness of the world during our helpless infancy and childhood, a period longer for us than for any other animal. This period is called *neoteny*, the scientific name for it is neoteny. I hate these names but we need them, *patrimorph* and *neoteny* . . . And this falling back into a time when our father was a god to us strikes us when we are in pain and suffering, with nowhere to turn, as can happen. As *does* happen.

"And then we fall back and become a thing like a child, a *pedomorph*, just to give the last of these technical names, a thing like a child, and we feel, again and again, with the help of the costumed liars of whatever church, we feel safer, happier, secure in the shadow of our father. And then they do what they like with us, of course. We fall back and we feel *rejuvenated*, notice the word. We are a species cursed with the shadows of fathers, and false fathers. This weakness is the abyss that is always at our heels, that we drag about with us, that follows us, dogs us. The abyss is sweet. There is real comfort there. We are made so that we wish to pitch ourselves into it. That act releases sweet chemicals that infuse us, our brains. The abyss. It is the common sand every church is built on, all churches and temples are built upon.

"Our task is to become fatherless . . . khutsana."

Morel stopped for something, a glass of water, probably.

"Emunah is *the whole of it*, in the message of Jesus the Jew. We must make this clear to, to . . ."

A new voice broke in. "To the multitudes."

This was Kerekang's first intervention. There was more to come. Kerekang's tone was wry, but carefully wry.

Morel continued. "Yes, the multitudes. Oh yes. Emunah . . . Please notice that every act that is being urged by Jesus is meant to amplify, in a believing population, the proportion of it, the part of it, that resembles a mass of distressed and neglected but trusting children. When he tells his followers not to take any thought for the morrow, for example, not to think ahead about where the next meal is coming from, he is recreating in that attitude the situation of a child unable to get its own food and depending on the goodwill of the family under the control of the sovereign father. We'll see this over and over, clearly shown, when we come to examine, when Themba comes to examine, the parables and proverbs attributed to Jesus. But the overall picture here is unmistakable—Jesus is engaged in an experiment in collective emunah with the Jews of Palestine, conjuring or coaxing them into the shape of an enormous *baby* in order to bring God downstairs to tend it and change the world forever in the bargain.

"What was moving in the mind of Jesus to lead him to this we can only guess. But it seems likely that what he sought through mass emunah was to undo the sin of Adam, whose *dis*obedience plunged humanity into death and misery and labor and pain in childbirth for women and on and on, undo it by turning disobedience into its opposite, perfect obedience, spectacular compliance with the will and whims of Yahweh.

"Emunah! We must make ourselves call things by their right names, comrades. If you were asked to come into a church so that you might join others in groveling, would you go in? No, but if they call it worship, you go.

"Now once we can see that the whole work of Jesus was this campaign to pump up eruptions of emunah, we can then see that it must follow that, correctly considered, there is *no moral instruction* to be gotten from his message, from his original message. Jesus tells those who would truly follow him that their duties to him, their duties to emulate him, are greater than, for example, their most sacred duties to their parents, such as burying them speedily when they die.

"What we see out of all this is that every act you must do is *instrumental. No good act is done for its own sake, because it is good. None. Not one.* Every act is done to flatter and arouse the imaginary father to descend to earth! No, more exactly, every act is an attempt to *shame* God into taking action. Jesus *knows* God's jealous and murderous and capricious side, his murderous vanity even when it comes to his closest servants. He punishes his beloved agent Moses with death over some *insanely* minor shortcoming, depriving him of the privilege of entering the promised land with the people he has led through the wilderness for forty years. Jesus knows all about God. And he knows perfectly well also that God's acts of benefit are for the most part generic, as in letting the sun shine for all and sundry, while his enmity is specific, personal in a way, and often petty, as when he condemns to death some perfectly nice Jewish children for the sin of teasing Elijah about being bald, as we discussed. He has them eaten up by a bear! He is a jealous God. He says so himself. Jesus knows. He knows God sent the serpent.

"No, this emunah . . . ah we are so pathetic . . . no one more than Jesus himself. So here is the task he has given to himself . . .

"On the one hand it is to trick God into acting by calling up *surges* of unsustainable piety. And on the other hand it is to trick the people into feats of piety by misrepresenting God as an angel of goodness and loving kindness. The sleight of hand Jesus performs is everywhere. Look closely! He deceives even himself as he goes on about love and forbearance, devising to trick God downstairs through acts of organized innocence, get him to come downstairs and *crush the shit out of the enemies of the Jews*. Through the weakness and need of his people God will be induced to crush not only the Roman oppressors but *also the bad Jews who doubted the message of Jesus*.

"He is secretive, this Jesus. He is Prometheus, in what he attempts.

"His evasions are stupendous. He calls men to imitate God, the famous Imitatio Dei we spoke about. The sheep in the churches nod and think this is fine, this must be ethics. But look closely. Jesus says be like God in performing feats of giving and forbearance and *ask nothing in return*, expect no compensation. But this is not like God at all. God *requires*. God will forgive your debts only if you forgive the debts of others. There is nothing unconditional here. God is famous, *notorious*, for laying down conditions—ask Lot's wife. God is continually setting out conditions, a chief one being, and you can find it in his dealings with Abraham and Job, *never question my motives*. What does 'Judge not, lest ye be judged' mean? It means imitate God *only* in those ways that do not intrude on God's power to judge and punish. Leave the punishing to Daddy God. It would be arrogant not to, because God *likes to punish*, consign people to hell or misfortune for their shortcomings. Making judgments is the province of adults, and if God is to like us enough to come downstairs, we must remain as children. 'God loves a terrified face,' it says in the Psalms.

"This is a God who loves deals, covenants, all of that. No, the famous Imitatio Dei is a confidence trick, another one, to flatter God that you are acting as he, in his sunnier moments, may, at times.

"This is a *complete story*, let us never forget, from beginning to end it's all there.

"The story of Jesus the Jew is the story of an experiment in mystical mass psychology that *fails*. It *fails*. It is a complete story whose end features the disciples of Jesus denying him, and running away, and he himself, the poor man, asking Yahweh why he has forsaken him, why he has not come downstairs, alas, alas. Eloi, Eloi, lama sabachthani? are the hardest words to hear. The author of the experiment is being tortured to death and he says My God, my God, why hast thou forsaken me? And then he dies. That's it.

"I am sure it went, with poor Jesus, after his time with poor John the Baptist, *what more can we do*, we Jews? Well, we can be children, we can be worms, we can be spat on, hit, we can double the length of the errands the Romans require us to run, we can be *pathetic* . . .

"Well, I have to stop because . . . I have to stop . . .

"But let me not stop until I point out how perfectly and how completely this embarrassing experiment represents the falling back into childishness we find at the heart of every religion. I won't go into it right now, but there are three ways to get salvation if you're a Hindu, and one of the ways is through bakhti, which is identical with the emunah of Jesus the Jew. Do you understand that this falling back is *universal*, in religions? Take fasting. You approach God with your stomach rumbling, how could a father not help? Celibacy. What a good idea. Make yourself presexual, just like a baby. Shave your head, like the Buddhist nuns and monks. Be as bald as a baby. In both Matthew and Mark, remember, we are given to understand that in the resurrected state we take neither husband nor wife, but live sexless, like angels. Rending garments is a good idea! . . . an ill-clad child will move God's heart. Shrink yourself up when you approach God, make yourself as small as a child, lower your head, your eyes, fall on your knees. Speak in tongues! Nice idea. God might think you're babbling like a baby. Adorable idea. And be sure not to approach any venue God might inhabit if you are less than perfectly clean. A soiled child does not delight a father. Slaughter your best cows, put the first best part of the harvest right there on the altar, and be sure to be mournful, be bereft, as you do this, because what God needs is not the soul of another cow or the perfume of a sheaf of wheat you just cut . . . no, it's the *misery* that parting with these goods makes you feel. And remember, only the *best* for our maker, only unblemished doves, only the best. God savors your misery, not the smell of roasting kine. God has everything already. By definition. And *burnt offerings,* by the way, is yet one more piece of priestly trickery, because *nicely roasted* would be more like it, and because the priests got fine dining out of the offerings until there was a fuss about it and more got distributed outside the temple, but that's another story.

"Jesus was an innovator. The emunah rising up to God through the conduit of the temple during regular sacrificial ceremonies was not enough, obviously. Now keep firmly in your mind the difference between John the Baptist's teshuvah, repentance, which *accompanied* the act of sacrifice, and Jesus's emunah, childish love and awe. Teshuvah was not enough. Teshuvah was saying you were sorry and wouldn't do it again if you could help it. But emunah is consciousness of weakness, including weaknesses leading to sin, *while you are going on about things,* even repeating bad acts like collecting taxes for the Romans and occasionally overindulging, going on, but at least feeling rotten and low about it.

"Jesus makes a new package. He proposes to take the satisfaction God got from the regular observers of Torah, their routine piety, and add to that the *emunah* of the sinners and the screwed, trapped in their situations for one reason or another, and create a blaze of feeling that would surely rouse God to action, especially when he added to the mix his own personal performance of absolute trust . . . which he was clearly contriving to happen . . . in the form of placing himself in peril of death.

"I need to stop. And so, well, the point has been made. I keep thinking of things to add. Make yourself as miserable as a child in distress, preferably a male child. Restrictions on the presence of women at groveling services used to be practically universal. You can search the scriptures until you go blind and never encounter the phrase *daughter* of God once. By the way, if you're a Hindu, a gift you can bring to the goddess Devi is sleepiness. Certain rituals you attend in a sleep-deprived state because of course what could stir the attention of a patrimorph or matrimorph for that matter more than the sight of a sleepy baby? So. Make yourself miserable, gash yourself, mortify yourself, lick up crumbs of the host off the floor like the Jansenists, sleep on a plank, wear a hair shirt. Poor babies!

"About women, though . . . You know, look around, so far we have no women with us in this work. But that will change. There is . . . I have a woman I think is ready. Or soon will be. I think so. Gosiame, we can eat now."

Ray wanted to hit the tape player. He turned the machine off, his hands shaking. *What* woman? he thought.

What woman was Morel talking about? Who was she? Had this gotten past him the first time he'd listened to the tape? What woman was he talking about?

He got up and began pacing around the house. The possibility that Morel was referring to Iris was outrageous, making Iris a priestess of reason or whatever they called it, irreligion?

He decided it had to be a Motswana woman, but who?

That wasn't it. He knew it wasn't. He wanted to demolish something.

He went into the bathroom and sorted through the painkillers until he found the ones with codeine, which he took three of. That was the best thing about Africa, the paracetamol and the other preparations loaded with codeine you could get over the counter.

He pushed his shorts down and sat on the toilet to urinate. His legs were weak. He had never urinated sitting down except as an adjunct act, in his whole life, he believed.

He was remote from Morel's arguments, completely. He wondered what that meant. Morel was passionate about his theories, his discoveries, obviously and to say the least.

But he himself had gone through these questions a long time ago and reached conclusions and moved on to other things. That was what he wanted to think. But he suspected that the truth of it was that he hadn't considered the questions Morel was raising. How much truth there was in one side versus the other was presumably important. There was his hatred of Morel and that was real. But the rest of it was not real to him. It was taking place behind thick glass.

Some complex process he was no longer interested in had disposed him to be where he was and doing what he was doing and, on the whole, feeling okay about it. If he wanted to, he could feel slightly bemused at finding himself cast as some sort of defender of the faith, surrounded by passionate questioners eagerly biting away at the pillars of regular life. The idea of going down, down into the foundations of life and X-raying the historical accidents that had led to a world not completely satisfactory was unreasonable to him. It made him tired.

His attention was on the foreground, where it had to be. It was where he lived. Anyway it was a luxury to be able to devote yourself like Morel to hermeneutic orgies, not bad as a term for what Morel was doing. Resnick would appreciate the phrase, but nobody else.

The fact was that he had his own life to save, his and Iris's. That was it. That was it. That was all there was.

. . .

He had come almost to the part he wanted to hear again, urgently, the rebellion. It was simple to follow. There were only two voices, Kerekang first and Morel second and then in unbroken alternation like that to the end. What was nice about it, apart from the drama, was that it had been unexpected. We love the unexpected, he thought. There was no question his own aversion to boredom was abnormally high and that this aversion explained a lot of the attraction that working for the agency held for him. Justifying working for the agency was turning into a compulsion, lately, and he resented it. Still, it was true that boredom kills. When he looked around at what others did for a living he felt like a Martian.

He wanted to be sharp for this. The pills were making him vibrate. They were Iris's pills. He was used to having to make a case for taking them. It was a comic ritual. She knew he only proposed taking them so he could get sympathy for a particularly bad headache. He could perfectly well take them without saying anything. It was a ritual. We need rituals, he thought. Morel was blind.

He was fast-forwarding and rewinding, searching for the exact beginning of Kerekang's eruption, which followed Morel's rather sneering deconstruction of the Sermon on the Mount. Apparently there was nothing to be said for it at all, and the bulk of it was retroactive ventriloquism from parties unknown, followers of Paul. He had to admit he had learned something in the interesting-if-true category, to the effect that the true reason the Lord's Prayer had been commended to believers was for its brevity. The idea was not to go on with the long, rambling, free-form prayers characteristic of traditional Jewish worship and also of the pagans. And the deeper idea, in line with the rest of Morel's analysis of the original religion of Jesus as a scheme to trick and flatter God, was to avoid irritating him with lengthy petitions in consideration of the fact that he already knew what everybody wanted, being omniscient. So it was about brevity. But there was something peculiar about Morel's approach to spreading irreligion in Botswana. He could use some advice. Ray had an opinion about Morel's standpoint. Morel was being pretty cavalier about actually existing Christianity, the living varieties of the beliefs that people today were bothering to adhere to. It was as if, after proving to his own satisfaction that the original ideas of Jesus constituted a fantasy form of Jewish fundamentalism, that that was enough, should be enough for anybody. The subsequent misappropriations and misconstruings of these original ideas, which turned into Christianity in all its branches, seemed not to be of interest to him. Where were the Trinity and sacerdotal celibacy, what have you, auricular confession, full or partial immersion? It was these misappropriations and misunderstandings and the denominations built around them that were now front and center, on any sensible view of the matter. Yet Morel seemed to be ignoring the beliefs of live, walking-around Christians, in all their particularities. Although maybe that would come later, in other presentations. Here was Kerekang, with his fine voice, his inflections showing his long exposure to British English.

"Rra, yah, you see, I did not wish to speak. But I feel I must, if I may. If my brother Themba says go, and if you won't mind it, rra."

"Of course. For sure. This is what we like."

"And does my brother Themba say I may go, as well?"

"Themba says fine."

"So then, rra . . . all you have said may be very true, I think, as to the thoughts of Jesus. I can believe you are right."

"Well, thanks, my brother. I appreciate that. Of course the general idea of what religion is I take from Freud . . . 'God is an exalted father, nothing more.' So I am in his shadow, and unfortunately he didn't know how much stronger his interpretation would have been if he had fully appreciated neoteny, this period of helplessness we experience in infancy. And Freud went off the track in many silly ways, it has to be said. But when I apply this basic truth, God as an exalted father, to the history of Christianity, I get a certain result."

"But, rra, continuing as to Jesus, and what has come of his life, and even admitting how greatly he was mistaken in some of his hopes . . . Rra, this I know will not be pleasing to you, but you must hear it, because you shall hear it from others . . . And I am not happy to say these things, you understand.

"But let us say he believed untruths. Some untruths. And from these untruths some people, misled, built up some tales that have come to us, from time past.

"From time past we have a tale that there was a man sent by God.

"And this tale says that this man said, as to the poor, that they are beautiful in God's eyes.

"And from this, if you wish, you can think, Ai! . . . then as *God* is loving them, it is perhaps best if we can love them too, if all could do so . . ."

"Hold it! Wait." This was Morel, agitated. "Wait, yes, but we are talking about a myth, a myth . . . tlhamane. . ."

"Oh surely so, rra. A tale told by fairies. Ditlhamane, many myths, we are talking about."

"Well just so we keep that in mind."

"Ehe, righto! And this man says you must not be ashamed if you are sick or you are too shy, because God is a friend to you above the rich.

"And you the rich, for shame, you cannot pass through the eye of a needle so easily as can the poor.

"So we can see that God is saying the rich must feel shame, which is what we would wish in this country today. With us, the rich have no shame. They can just sweep out the poor, brush them away, if they please to.

"And this man from God says we must not fall into fighting and we must love our neighbors.

"And so forth, rra, and so forth. This man says to be merciful, and says you are most blessed if you seek after justice.

"You can see how I am differing, rra."

"Yes, go on."

"And so this same man, you can find him at table with the poor . . ."

"Wait wait wait. Okay, just to be accurate, it's not specifically the poor he seeks out to have meals with. No, it was with tax collectors, who were in fact agents of the Roman state, whose hospitality he accepted. There is no evidence in scripture that he ever sought out the poor to eat with! He fixed them up with loaves and fishes, miracle meals, when they came out to hear him and dinnertime came. A small point. I don't mean to interrupt. I want you to object. We are going to get a lot of objection."

"So but let me go on, rra. Right, he was eating with sinners at the table. Right. So the people can say this man is pushing no one to the side if they will only listen to his message. And you have said this man was making an experiment in mass psychology, and that it failed. But how can you say it failed, rra, with so many Christians abounding? The experiment produced the kindly ditlhamane, did it not?

"And in these ditlhamane, which, okay, say we know them to be untrue, we have been told Jesus is going forth and healing without charge, healing the sick like a nyanga. But he asks nothing for this service.

"Go to the dingaka in Broadhurst and Bontleng and see if you must pay them. It is the way it is. You yourself, if I may dare to say this, you do not give your injections without charge . . ."

Morel was aggrieved. "Ah but I do. I do. So much of my practice here is charitable, my brother. In fact you know this."

"For the most part, is what I am saying. Look, man, I am your friend. I am not criticizing. It is the way it must be done. If you go to hospital, in many cases you must take your own food. And you as a doctor must replenish when your stocks of medication are low, and you must pay out sums for that. Gosiame.

"And so in the ditlhamane, this man Jesus says that he knows the heart of God and God wishes the Batswana to live in peace and be kind to enemies, which if I may say, our great Botswana Defence Force, they are very Christian when it comes to the Boers pushing over into our country and killing and killing. But I am just joking about it. They are turning the other cheek. Nah, I am joking.

"Nah, I think I am saying that in these tales you see this man Jesus never to be surcharging for any act of his—although it is true you can take him to dinner at times!

"So . . . this man says there is a God who is watching you and wants you to be kind, be pleasant all round, stay from the courts and judges, give with your left hand and right to the beggars and if someone asks can you lend me something you should agree. In fact, you must forget that you have made such a loan. You must give him your coat, in fact.

"And when you marry, remain with your wife.

"So, right. So these stories are saying to behave in these ways and if you fail you are going to burn up in hell.

"And so we see this man . . . but I forgot about the children. He says to bless them. Which is very good for Batswana to be told. Because we are working these children all day, making them fetch like dogs and sending them off to watch cattle, whatever we wish.

"Ehe, and I forgot as well about adultery. This is also good advice for the Batswana, else these sex games in the schools will go on and on with more young girls falling pregnant as they do now every year in every school. It is true here in the capital and it is worse in Mahalapye. So there is not just one tribe to blame. And the fathers of these babies, who are they? Teachers, often enough, or men who just come creeping . . .

"So if we could do one tenth of what Jesus is saying, Botswana would be a very much better country. And . . ."

"Okay I think your point is made, Keregang. And I would like to answer it, if I may." Morel was being curt.

"I must finish, rra. Because I know these are thoughts that many are having amongst those who are here tonight and who love you, as I do, as you know.

"And yes, he says, Jesus, if you give to charity, do so privately not making a show, which, I point out, is how you do it, so you must be a Christian of some kind. No, I am fooling. But at these fêtes and benefit doings it is very different, with great displays as to who is most generous. But I was fooling, rra. You are no Christian.

"So. And don't lay up gold. Take the log from your eye. Beware false prophets. So that is the man, ecce homo, as they put it. That is the man in the tale.

"And so the story comes to its end . . . And what is its end?

"Domkrag hates him and puts him on a cross to die in pain. Rome is Domkrag.

"So Domkrag kills this man who is the friend of the poor people.

"Sha!"

Ray knew what Kerekang was doing. Sha was a strong expression, meaning shame, and it was accompanied by a sharp wagging of the right hand.

"Sha! But . . . But he rises from the cross, this man, and is not dead, he is seen rising up, walking about, you can see his wounds, you can put your hand in his right side to test if this is the man. So he rises to be with God . . . and what does he leave the Batswana?

"I can tell you that many of them will say this man is still hereabout, like a mist, or the wind. And he has left his words of what you must do and it is this . . . it is this, rra . . .

"That you must try to please God by good action and kindness. In the church they will help you to be like God's son.

"So, and now are some people arriving who say all this is mere lies, and very mistaken.

"But I am saying to you, wait, sir. Sir, wait.

"Because if you will admit they are making a hell in Botswana for the poor, the ones without cattle or with cattle but no borehole, if you wish to admit this, why shall you cast off these stories that can help us to gather up these poor, these selahtliwa, these outcasts, and make them an army against this hell? Hell is amongst us tonight, nearby to this house, in Old Naledi and Bontleng, and in the bush we can walk into hell, straight into it, like that. Where I stay is hell, in Bontleng. I want to extinguish this hell, my friend. I shall do it. I tell you so tonight.

"Now soon I will be finished . . . Rra . . . Rra, these tales are with us already, here. They are in the minds of the people and they are as stones, hard things, and you are facing a battle to unearth them. You can see it when the people flood in *rivers* to the stadium to pray to God and Christ Jesus for rain. You may wish to look aside from this. You may say they are wasting their time, to do so. But I say you will be wasting your time if you oppose it, and wasting more, it may be. Because rra, even as I tell you the tales about Jesus, I feel in my heart that if such a man could join us, we could carry the day.

"Because. Because if we are to clear this hell that we have made with the help of the makhoa, all the people must come with us. We must have every man! We must have men of every kind, from those who are wise, very wise, like yourself, because you do oppose this hell, down to the fools if need be. *Every* man! We must have the women, too. And we must have these people as they are, believing these tales or not.

"Rra, I say these tales of Jesus can help us. Think of Germany, the Peasant Wars, and the destruction of the princes. And you can go to Aiyetoro, in Nigeria, and see many people living and working as one, with no one rich, and they are all Christian, there, at Aiyetoro.

"Rra, this is what I must say . . . I have said it . . .

"What I say is, let everyone come who will, to join hands to cast hell from us. I will take every Christian, I will take all good people. But I will take bad people, devils, too, if I can find them and I can tell them a story to make them stay alongside me. My friend, you are casting down a sword before you go to battle.

"And am I sorry to be saying these things to you. I have learned many things here, coming to these teas and evenings of yours, and I have got from you reading I shall keep by me always, and I shall think of you. I have books enough and lists of books enough to keep my eyes open until I die. E. P. Sanders, Mr. Vermes. Robert Ingersoll, great thinker. I like him. And this fine book *The Ghost Dance* that shows the foolishness of man so truly you must choose whether to weep or laugh. I am reading it now.

"Rra, for a long time I have wished to say this to you, that I thank you. You have fed me. So I am saying all this now because I will be going away at some time, I think soon. Yes. But I want to say something to clear my heart. It is a small thing.

"I know what you say about the Roman church very well and it is true. But I held myself from saying what I think, at times. So, rra . . . I think it is very good to have saints. I like it. Perhaps not those saints they recommend. But to raise up some one or two people or more, singled out to be praised for a good life, for honor, is a thing I like. I think we should have saints of our own kind, when the world is more what it should be. I cannot bring my heart against this church, as you would say I must. And as well I think we must see this church as very clever, not only for saints but for saying they can take so many homosexualists and have them work to build the church and since they have no heirs their work will benefit the church alone. And this is a point, that the church is not saying see how in the Bible it says you are evil, get away from this place, oh my no. No, it says abide here, and do not express yourself toward boys, and all will be well. And they have benefited greatly from homosexualism, a thing their scriptures tell them to hate and abjure.

"So this is what I wish to say to you. I know your heart, my brother.

"Your heart is for a world far better than this one, of course. We are brothers. Your heart is for a world where every mind is set free. And your heart is for what minds set free at last might do together, with all these . . . these chains and curbs and dodges struck away. You see in your heart a world made by minds standing straight up at all times, where in past times most were stooping or trammeled down. You see a beautiful place, differing in all ways to this place.

"Ehe, yes, perhaps such can be . . . *when we have done away with all this that you see*, begging of children, this suffering whilst the rich are opening their hands the wider to clutch more and more of this country. Soon they will have all the cattle, and the villages will be roofless places, and then sand and dust. And there will be even more of the poor than at present pushing in from those villages to fill up Old Naledi until it is a solid ring of suffering around us. And . . . *sha!* Yes, it is a shame, what you see about you here, but in Sehitwa, in Shorobe, you can see worse. Come with me once to Shorobe. Well, I have said everything."

The silence that followed was difficult, Ray could tell. It would have to be.

When Morel spoke, his voice was cold and loud, but there was a fine tremor in it at first.

"You are wrong, Kerekang."

There was another silence, until Morel began again. "Kerekang, listen to me please.

"You remember when we began to discuss these things for the first time and I told you that faith was a terrible poison and you laughed because you thought I was making too much of it because in your experience it was a weak thing. You had been living in the U.K. where the established church is indeed in a rather etiolated condition. You found it hard to see the church as a live part of anything that people were deciding to do or not to do. This is what you compared it to. You told me that when you first ate in a good restaurant in England, the first couple of times, I believe, you said that when the proprietor came to the table to ask how you'd liked the meal, you'd been truthful, praised a couple of things but criticized others. And you'd seen a certain reaction among

your friends and in the proprietor, of shock. And from that you had realized that obviously the custom was quickly to praise everything that had
been served, whether you had liked it or not. And you proposed to me
that religion was like that. Religion was like the protocol of saying everything was delicious, with the proprietor knowing it was unlikely or
untrue and your companions knowing it was untrue . . . because they had
complained during the meal . . . and you yourself knowing it was untrue.
Nobody really believes, you said. Most people say they are Church of
England, if you press them, you said, but nobody believes. The priests,
many of them, certainly don't, you said, and the priests know that nobody
sitting in front of them believes. But people keep going at Easter and
Christmas and saying they are C of E the rest of the time. Oh, and I
think you also compared it to makeup on women, am I right? They all do
it, you look at them, women, wearing makeup, and you incorporate it
into your assessment of them without being aware you're doing it, even
though the woman knows and you know that you aren't seeing the truth
and she isn't showing you the truth. So you proceed anyway. It's minor,
you said, and doesn't hurt.

"And then what else did you say? I'm trying to recall. Oh yes, that the
church was a useful thing if only for the fact that, just by stopping in
irregularly, you would have a chance at getting a few people to turn up for
your funeral who otherwise wouldn't have, which was, you said, a comforting prospect.

"So, okay. England misled you. I showed you that in the world at large
faith was expanding, credulism was expanding, and that the particular
types of religious belief that were expanding the fastest were the purest,
most primitive, the dumbest ones. And this is true in England now too,
though it's early days yet for the Muslims and others.

"And then we went country by country over a map of the world, my
brother Kerekang. And I demonstrated to you that where the older sects
and denominations that had in one way or another made certain accommodations to scientific reality were declining, these fiercer, simpler
strains of faith were coming back. And we counted the actual theocracies
existing in the world and you were surprised, weren't you? And I gave you
the statistics on beliefs in the United States of America, and you found
them hard to believe.

"And then you hardly seemed pleased about the situation in Africa,
where the rate of conversion is the highest in the world and going up all
the time and more than making up for the denominational declines in
Europe, and where two beasts, the Christian beast and the Muslim beast,

are fighting to see which can eat the most Africans before dark. Because the darkness is coming. Is coming.

"And I explained how faith is a toxin, a peculiar and dangerous toxin because even in dilution it waits in the blood to blaze back into madness under the right conditions of fear and trembling. In its most virulent forms, it prevents the host from knowing that it is going to die, to die *forever*, that the host is a dying animal, that we are merely mortals, and that death is our common fate, the fact of life that should make brothers and sisters of us all. And I tried to show you how even in dilution religion addles and undoes our ability to see death, how even in dilution it sweetens death, allows it to be denied, allows the deaths of others to be made casual."

Morel paused. "Our task is to do everything, in a way. Too bad, but we may just have to do everything. Too bad for us, but unless we bring free minds to the work of renewing the world, keeping our minds fixed on death and the disguises death puts on, we will raise up a new hell, like Russia where they closed the churches and made the state their god. We must say no gods. None.

"And be sure to remember that the great architects of injustice in Russia were products of centuries of Christian processing, beginning with the seminarian Joseph Stalin. Hitler always considered himself a good Catholic, despite the superficial pagan paraphernalia he held up in front of the German people for a while, and the good soldiers who did his filthy work were as Christian as you could ask for.

"And before you or anyone begins about the mission schools and hospitals . . . and they are worthy, okay, and you may want to say, well, these people are good, they are saving our lives, how can you argue? Which would mean that we should be quiet on this subject. But I am telling you to see the matter *whole*.

"Here is a picture. You conquer a country and give the vanquished a clinic. Look around Africa and see if this seems familiar to you. No, conquer a country and then give it a clinic, and oh, also some *mission schools*, and some Christian bookstores to pump out cheap Bibles to change the children of the land into Christians. The conquerors in this continent and in South America and in my own country came pushing their crosses ahead of them.

"Look, go deep inside yourself, Kerekang. We have been tainted at the deepest levels, deep in the foundations of our minds. Say a man lives his life without regard to faith, as he thinks. But he hasn't gone deep enough, because to his surprise, when he falters, lo, here it comes, a deathbed conversion. I could keep us here all night with the history of deathbed conversions, amazing ones. A great poet writes *Loss of faith is growth* and the next thing you know he's beckoning the priests to his deathbed. We are penetrated with it. It works invisibly and insensibly to direct our accommodation with the world's evils. God help us!

"Belief is like this . . . It falls into three types and I ask you to tell me which kind of faith is more dangerous than the other.

"We begin with any society saturated with belief. I'm talking generically. What types of believers do you have? First, the devout, who believe everything up and down and in and out. They make us despair. In Kenya the devout bring death to the sick because the word *condom* shall not be spoken aloud, on the radio, anywhere. The same in Zimbabwe, with the fine Roman Catholic prime minister nodding yes in the corner. So let that stand as an example for us of a contribution by the devout.

"So then, the next type, the hypocrite, who believes only in himself but who pretends to believe in scripture and uses the blindness of genuine believers to satisfy his own desires. No need to say much about them and the harm they do.

"Ah but then we come to, what shall we call them, the half-believers, like the bulk of the British, the ones who say let the little ones believe that their classmate who jumped off London Bridge is in heaven and happy. Or like the half-believers who say it won't hurt to have children mumble the Lord's Prayer every day in school, if they do it under their breath. Which brings us to the half-believer at his most dangerous, the character who begins to feel inwardly that his beliefs are untrue but who cannot *bear* that feeling and who sets out to perform feats of loyalty to convince *himself* that he must in fact believe, like killing a doctor who gives women abortions. As their belief weakens they become terrors of the earth, mesmerizing themselves with acts that plunge them into peril, that spread ruin everywhere. They convince themselves through their transgressions that they must, in fact, be believers.

"In America the beautiful, in the mountain West, you have armed madness of just this type. They are under the odd impression that Jews . . . the ancient enemies of God, according to lying Christian scripture . . . control the federal government. Therefore government officers are limbs of Satan and therefore appropriate targets. We have already had one president of the country rambling on about the Second Coming. All these types, through the normal workings of the democratic system, are percolating up into positions of power, more and more of them.

"Listen to me, all of you! Do you love Africa? Then let me ask all of you why Africa must be the greatest nursery of fools in the entire world. They are all here, all the churches, and you say we should allow it, no matata you say. Africans fought honorably against the Christian mental slavers, and for a hundred years the external churches were wringing their hands in disappointment at how little progress they were making. But they were relentless, and now they are back in force, with their radio nonsense, their cassettes, technology taken from the science they tried for so long to strangle. Turn on the radio and turn the dial and see how hard it is to find a spot where the moruti are not droning and droning and . . ."

"Baruti. Baruti." Someone was correcting Morel. He had used the singular for preacher when what he wanted was the plural.

"Baruti, I meant. Thank you. Always correct me."

After a pause, he began again. He was losing control over the pleading note in his voice. Ray didn't like to hear it, for some reason.

"Rra, Kerekang my man, listen to me. I think I'm failing you. I don't want to. I need to give you the essence, again. I think. Themba, I apologize for taking the floor like this, really. But I have to give you the essence . . .

"The essence is . . . is *not* just the misdirection of human effort, huge huge misdirection of human effort, you get with religion. That's a *consequence* of it, and you understand that. It's everywhere. It's going to the stadium to pray for rain instead of putting the unemployed to work digging the system of underground cisterns that would make this country droughtproof, virtually—according to the author of the scheme who is sitting right here and who cannot for the life of him get a hearing from government, you yourself, my man."

Ray knew about that. Kerekang had tried to interest the government in some grandiose self-help project copying the ancient Persian system of linked water-harvesting underground reservoirs, qanats—Ray even remembered what they were called, to his own surprise. Kerekang had presented the scheme as something that could be scaled up or down as much as anyone pleased. He wanted these qanats dug, and he wanted every roof and threshing floor in the country reconstructed for rain capture. No question he was right about the labor for it being there, floating around unused. That Ray conceded. Unused labor power was something that drove Kerekang into frenzies. He wanted to take a megaphone and organize the idle into corvées, immediately. He had been ridiculed over it, in the government paper, caricatured in just that way. The campaign against him had been merciless. Domkrag was seeing Kerekang as an irritant, someone whose objections to social conditions meant more than the rare criticisms coming from the official opposition or the Botswana Social Front, with its discredited cadres of hacks and scoundrels and windbags.

"The essence is . . . it isn't just misdirection, as I said . . ." Morel was struggling. He was grasping at the hope that a perfect formulation or statement of the case would salvage everything. There was desperation in his effort. He was trying to pull up and consult some inner checklist of talking points. Where had his smoothness gone? Sad business, Ray thought.

"And the essence is not . . . repetition. Repetition is an outcome. It's a form of misdirection, like others. Every religion known to man prescribes repetition from birth to death . . . chants, mantras, hit your head on the floor seven times a day, fill up your life with repetitive acts and go into a state, same thing over and over, go to mass, burn up your mortal life with repetition. My God! Take one book, one set of texts, and read it *over* and *over* and *over*. Play with your beads over and over. Come to church, stand up sit down stand up, Lord's Prayer, same prayer over and over ad infinitum. Say the Shema say Hail Marys. Somebody, not God, sent the Enlightenment, which is what I worship. No, this is the thing, that even if you manage to tear yourself free from religious belief, you come away with an appetite for repetition that may mystify you. It was taught to you, ingrained in you without your permission . . . Well, I won't get into that.

"But to get to the *essence*, and forgive me, Themba, again . . . It, it's difficult because it's so penetrating, like a gas. We see the carnival and we flatter ourselves that we're not part of it, but in our depths, we are. *Pervasion* is the word I want. It's like, like the poison fumes coming up through the floors of the site and service houses in Old Naledi. Exactly like that."

Ray pressed the pause button. He was vague on this, but it had something to do with a disturbance, recently, in Old Naledi, in the squatter upgrade project. He remembered. The practice of dumping a drum of DDT into the soil under the floor plates of the new rondavels going up, to discourage termites from coming into the structure, had gotten widespread. Kerekang had tried to bring the Ministry of Health into it. The cement floors were porous, despite what people believed, and the fumes came through, especially when it was damp, in the rainy season, and with the fumes came birth defects, cancer, the lot. The DDT was being purchased from suppliers with connections to one of the ministries.

Kerekang and his gleaners, his scout troop, or whatever they were, had stopped and damaged a truck making a delivery of DDT.

"My friend, my friends, listen to me. The essence of it is a voice, a residuum, a voice of thunder in some and in others a whisper, saying, inwardly, This you may think and This you may not think. And this will come, this comes, to feel natural to you. Think of it as a universal affliction manifesting at the strong end as murder, and mania, and at the low end as a peculiar enfeeblement, like an undiagnosed anemia. Man, we need something better to work with, wouldn't you say?

"You can't strike a match on a crumbling wall. You can't lift a cheesecake with an iron hook.

"In a way the differences between religions don't matter, because they are all debilitating in the same fundamental way.

"Not that the differences are uninteresting. Say you're a little girl growing up in India. You're going to grow up incorporating into your consciousness the realization that male gods are benevolent and female gods do evil, *unless* they are wives or consorts of male gods. Disease, possession, the hot season, pollution . . . blame the feminine. Put that in your psyche and suck on it for the rest of your life. A gas is seeping through the floor beneath our feet and we breathe it day and night. Self-direction blocked everywhere. Ah, and our common tragedy, our inevitable death, pay no attention, you will be reincarnated, you will become a being of light, you will sit on a crown, I mean throne, sorry. Of course here we concentrate on the Christian faith for obvious reasons. But it's the same infantilizing gas everywhere, in different concentrations, the same universal fucking silliness . . .

"Kerekang my friend, you want to change the world, so you must understand all this when you go among your Christian friends.

"And by the way, what is this *going away* we're hearing about from you? We don't want to hear it. Where will you go where you can do more than here, with us? Man. Man! Have I not spoken strongly enough? Kerekang, faith is the carrier of obedience, and obedience, ultimately, kills. Look. For Christianity it goes like this. I'll be concise. I'll be concise.

"One, Jesus fails to get enough emunah out of the Jews to make God act, and he dies trying, under the mistaken impression that he is in such a close relationship with Abba that his hideous suffering would do it, and it doesn't. *Fini*.

"Two, his followers, bless them, convince themselves he never died, really, and one particular character among them, Paul, decides that emunah is only part of it, but that now what is needed is the added element of identification, mystical identification, with the ascended, supposedly, Jesus, who is actually about to return, Paul says!—and the point of life is to be among the elect Jesus is *not going to punish*. A shift. A distinct shift.

"He gets the gentiles in on it. And in Paul's formulation what you need to do is avoid politics, forget about the Romans and slavery, just concentrate on unifying emotionally with this icon of perfect obedience, Jesus. I mean, come on!

"But then that fails too, no god descending.

"So, phase three. The church, Paul's boys, picks itself up off the floor and stretches out the horizons and says yes, God is still coming, but the important thing is to not get into hell in the meantime by various kinds of disobedience. And then error mates with error and the progeny of error tear one another apart and here we are. Stupid cruelty, death, and terror. Just one example. Then I'll stop. But. *Just look at this*.

"Communism, socialism, what have you, based on mistaken interpretations of a few lying lines in Acts of the Apostles about a common purse and so on, the common purse being in fact a mere expedient for driven people who knew, *knew*, the end of the world was coming and Jesus coming back and so forth, very interim, but expanded absurdly into a model for national economics, somehow. And *that* gets conflated into *socialism*, which frightens the horses of the conservative branch of Christianity into a killing rage embodied in the good Catholic, Adolf Hitler, who no one ever bothered to excommunicate, by the way. I won't go on.

"Except to say this. This is the position. If I can just get this right.

"I have imagined a destination. A world purged of the *fictitious*. A place fully lit for the first time. I visit this place.

"I visit it in my mind, a place where the rude fact that *we are all dying animals* has transfigured every part of life, where the great lie of life eternal has been dethroned and every form of division between human beings *based on* that lie is a memory and nothing more. I have seen a world where the shadow of the imaginary father is lifted. It was only a shadow, but it weighed like lead.

"Don't leave this, my man! Stay with us. Abide with me, *I have no faith*, my man, my brother."

I get it, a paradise of reason, Ray thought. Was Morel insane? Was he serious? Did he have any *idea* of the strength of the forces against him? Did he not know what man was, churches or no churches? A cartoon of Morel's paradise came to Ray, in which the citizens of this paradise dressed uniformly in tweed jackets with elbow patches and pipes walked around stroking their chins . . . taking taxis where the dashboard shrines featured *The Thinker* instead of the jiggling Jesuses so common in Mexico but also now in New York, too . . . signs saying Irony Saves.

"I have no faith, but I believe in the pledge given by brother to brother, which I thought you gave to me. Well. So I thought.

"I'm running out of ways to say this, my friend . . ."

A light commotion could be heard, nothing unfriendly about it.

Kerekang began to speak. The tape ended. That was all Ray had.

22. A Homecoming

He was going to be late and it was because he had been overpreparing the event, stupidly, admittedly, overgrooming himself for the moment of homecoming with the result that she was going to be standing there annoyed or worse, and exhausted from the flight.

He hurried, sucking his mint pastille, unhappy. He disliked his appearance more when she was away, deprived of the tinted mirror she was for him. Of course, he never slept as well when she was absent, and that showed.

Ray disliked the overextended new big airport and disliked in particular the absurd, oversized terminal rearing up in front of him. The runways were endless and represented so much overcapacity that Zimbabwe thought there was a military rationale underlying the facility. The Botswana Defence Force had been called in to bomb or shell certain small koppies in the surrounding plain where baboon colonies had been established since the dawn of time, according to the animal rights people who had ineffectually protested. Even as things were, the baboons had come back, to a degree, frightening or delighting airport passengers, depending on who you talked to.

The way he felt was that the grandiose airport misrepresented the country. Botswana was a modest place. And the terminal was ugly, to boot, a tall vast Corobrick building with a serpentine, pushed-out facade and a peculiar fluted-concrete roof whose turned-up eaves gave a pointlessly oriental touch to the whole. There was enough parking for an army. This airport was for the thin stratum of winners, and for expatriates and tourists and official busybodies from Washington and London. It had nothing to do with the hewers of wood and whatever the rest of the quotation was that described the overwhelming mass of the Batswana stuck out in the swamps and velds, the drawers of water, although that hardly applied because of the drought. The site was perpetually underpopulated, except when the large tour flights came in, but the whole operation was geared to run on the fiction that it was a hive of industry, with long arrays of booths and stands offering elephant-foot wastebaskets and Bushman hunting kits and packets of groundnuts and other necessities. The arcades were melancholy. Most of the stands had portcullises that were dropped during closing hours, but it was not uncommon to see dispirited stand-clerks napping inside these cages in the middle of the day, portcullises down, because there was no business. Ray liked the humble, antique airport where Victor worked. It was devoted to cargo and military exclusively.

He was inside, on the concourse. The terminal was underlit. Someone had chosen dark pink flooring, so a dark pink gloom was generated. There were tall ventilation slots in the upper walls, housing in each slot a single vertical louver permanently fixed, apparently, in the open position, which accounted for the permanently gritty condition of the floor and the endless swabbing activity the blowing sand necessitated. It made no sense that there was no mechanism to close the slots in the event of storms. But then it equally made no sense that in half the toilet stalls the door bolts were mounted well above or below the receptor slots.

Where was she?

He saw her, his darling. There she was, leaning against the wall just outside the mouth of the arrivals tunnel, her swollen carry-ons at her feet. There she was, but how was she? She was beautiful and he was seeing that again, her graphic face. She waved and he waved. He hurried toward her. They never checked baggage when they flew. Africa had traumatized them permanently in that department.

His jewel was back, his what, his pivot, his unwobbling pivot, his wife. The question was, had she come back clearer about things and more like the way she'd been at the beginning, and happier to be with him? Her sister had been an ordeal. She would be glad to be clear of that.

The house she was returning to was clean to a fault, the yard policed, food in the refrigerator, no tasks waiting for her, only his needs, lucky woman.

Was she thinner? She was wearing something new to him, elf pants, he was tempted to call them, very tight green leggings, he guessed they were, so tight they made her legs seem flocked rather than clad. That was fine, but not for Botswana, which she undoubtedly understood. She was

wearing a white tee shirt, sneakers, and her travel tunic, a pretext of a garment composed entirely of pockets of different capacities, not a jacket
but an undeclared third carry-on. The pockets were jammed. When he
put his arms around her it would be like embracing a sack of rubble. She
was wearing her hair pulled back. If there was something distant or vexed
in her expression, it didn't matter. It could be because he was late. And
God willing he would obliterate it with his love.

He reached her and caught her in his arms. Her breath was perfect. He
said, "Thank God to see you," demonstrating his confusion. She didn't
take notice of it.

"Oh Ray," was what she said, followed by nothing, not that she was so
glad to be back, not that this was where she belonged, nothing like anything from his maximum dreams. He loved her. He had wanted something unalloyed and stronger.

"How late am I?" he asked into her neck. He couldn't let go of her.

"A while. It's all right." His embrace was harder than hers. *Clasp me,
delicatest machine*, he thought, which was Wallace Stevens and which was
what she was.

He held her. He thought, There may not be such a thing as a perfect
human being, but there is such a thing as the bell curve and there is such
a thing as a woman who fits into the thin part that covers only the very
best.

He stepped back and bent down to gather up her carry-ons.

She said, "I have to tell you something."

Still bent over, he froze, seized by the certainty that something omi-
nous was about to be said that he needed to hear every nuance in.

"Don't *do* that," she said, truly irritated.

He knew what it was. It was that tic he had, which was to stop whatever
he was doing in order to hear perfectly what she was saying, if for some
reason or other he thought it might be something potentially significant.
He might stand there not closing the refrigerator door while she completed a sentence. Between them there was a phrase for his tic, which was
Caught in the Headlights of Your Love, which wasn't quite right literarily because it was his own love, love and fear, that drove him to want to
suck the marrow out of some particular statement, or else.

He straightened.

"I'm sorry," she said. "But you know how it drives me crazy when you
do that."

His tendency to fear what was coming in certain situations with her grew out of what, in him? It grew out of the fear that something she was saying was the precursor to I am going, goodbye, You are nothing. He thought, Cocteau called it *the storm coming from the depths of time* or something close, which can be anything from personal death to You are really nothing, my dear.

"I'm sorry," they both said.

He asked what it was she had been about to say.

"I'm suffering. There's something I haven't told you, Ray."

I knew it, he thought, in agony.

"You are determined to kill me. Go ahead and tell me."

"I wrote Ellen a check, for a lot. At the last minute. At the airport."

"Oh *in the name of God*, Iris! So *what*? You terrified me there."

"For a lot, though, Ray. Three thousand dollars."

"That's perfectly okay."

"We can still stop the check."

"We don't need to. It's fine, it's fine. Come on."

"I felt guilty about leaving her. It was an impulse. I need to discuss it with Davis. I don't like that I did it so impulsively, Ellen is almost in and out of reality, almost to that point. So I wrote the check."

He squatted, got the carry-on straps over his shoulders, and stood up, with difficulty.

As he turned to lead the way out, he saw or thought he saw what he wanted least of all at this moment to see . . . Morel, dodging out of sight into the Tiro ya Diatla fabrics stand. Rage filled him.

I could be wrong, he thought. It ought to be easy with someone who had a short leg, because his gait would betray him, normally. But Morel's gait was perfect. He had trained himself to hide his condition and done that admirably.

"What is it?" Iris asked. Clearly she had seen nothing. And it had been brazen. Clearly Morel had been hiding in among the skirts at Tiro ya Diatla and scanning the arrivals scene. Ray had to get Iris out of there. He felt like telling her what her limping swain really was. He was a *paranoid*. He had a universal diagnosis for the world's ill, which if it wasn't paranoid was close to it. In his humble opinion her glorious boyfriend was a *panacean*, so to say, not that he would ever really be her boyfriend, so help him God. Of course something was wrong with the world, clearly. But what was wrong was hardly just one thing, like the existence of national languages with the cure being Esperanto. And what's wrong isn't that the workers don't rule, either, he thought. And who was the one who said it was all due to people not having orgasms, a German? Reich, another panacean, he thought. It was possible he had coined the term, right there.

A porter drifted toward them, but he waved him off.

"Why don't we get a porter?"

"No this is faster. The porters make you wait while they go for their carts."

"But we have time."

"No, I want to get home."

He was making for an exit door at the extreme north end of the terminal.

"Where are we going?" she asked.

"Over there."

My life is taking forever, he thought.

"Where are you *parked*, Ray? Why are we going over there?"

He had no answer.

"Why are you running?" she asked.

How she had managed these monstrously heavy bags was something he wanted to know. She was strong. Or he was getting old.

There was no kiss, he thought, with pain. It was true that the recommended protocol for expatriates in Botswana was decorum in public. The Batswana were supposed to find kissing objectionable. The injunction was in the embassy orientation pamphlet. Even the Westernized younger Batswana who took up kissing would, he had been told, rub their forearms across their lips before they went at it.

"Why are we here?" she asked. She meant Why had they emerged into an overflow parking area not in use, with barrier booms down at its entry and exit points? Their Volkswagen was in the main lot. They had doubled the distance they had to travel to reach it by coming out where they had.

He was making a show of scanning intently around.

He said, "I thought I saw Moyo come out here. I need to talk to him about St. James. You have to catch him when you can. He has no phone. Well if he was here, he's gone." It was the best he could do.

"Africa," Iris said. "I need my sun hat."

"Take mine," Ray said.

"Yes, and kill you. You'll get a stroke as it is. We should have gotten a porter."

He toiled on. She would warn him about his knee, shortly.

"Why don't you rest for a minute, Ray?"

"Because we need to get home." And because Morel could be anywhere, he thought. He had wanted to get her away because an encounter with Morel would have wrecked the homecoming. Now he was wrecking it himself. There had been no pleasantries from her about how good it was to see his face, nothing. He had done everything he could think of at home, including buying a new pair of shoes for Fikile.

"*Please* let me take one of those, Ray."

"There's the car. I'm fine."

"I worry about your knee."

"I know, but it's fine and that was years ago. What have you got in this big one, anyway?"

"Something I have to tell you about. There's a huge manuscript."

"What manuscript?"

"I'll explain it later. It's your brother's."

"Oh God let this cup pass from me. Don't tell me this. What am I supposed to do with it?"

"Read it."

"But what is it, a memoir, something embarrassing about his miserable life?" A bitter triviality from the stupid past thrust itself on him. For a long period, growing up, Rex had gone out of his way to claim that his favorite thing to eat was mashed beef-stew sandwich, saying this on those occasions when children were expected to answer with spaghetti or hamburger or chocolate cake. Their mother had been proud of her boeuf bourguignon. And rightly so, as everybody seemed to say these days. And at one point Rex had childishly mashed his beef and carrots and pearl onions into a spread and clapped it between two slices of bread. He had given Ray a bite. Ray had found it delicious. But when Ray had tried to make the same sandwich for himself, his mother had turned on him and he had been prohibited from doing such a thing. It had been fine for Rex because he was, and apparently continued to be for years, a baby. Rex had been able to make sandwiches out of his boeuf bourguignon for as long as he chose to. And he had chosen to for years, rolling his eyes and smacking his lips and even elaborating the process, to taunt Ray, dropping capers into the mixture, or olives.

And now he had written a book. Ray wanted to write a book. Ray had a book to write. But now he had his brother's book. He didn't want it. He didn't want it. He had Morel to crush. He had no time.

"I have talked so much to Rex," Iris said.

"So describe this manuscript." My problem is that I was raised by idiots, first two idiots and then just one, so of course I grew up to be an idiot, he thought.

"I don't know how to. I don't know what it is, exactly. It says *faits divers* in large letters on the title page but that's crossed out. It's fragments. I've read here and there. It's very fragmentary. I'll explain what I can, which is not much. He sent it to me to bring to you because he wanted to be sure it didn't get lost. It's called *Bright Cities Darken*."

"Poetry?" Poetry wouldn't be a problem, because any poetry by a family member, private poetry, secret, was ninety percent of the time going to turn out to be pathetic.

"Oh no, prose, definitely."

I was raised by idiots, he thought. He wanted the last line of *Moby-Dick* and couldn't get it, something about I alone have escaped.

He said, "I was raised by idiots."

"Oh I know," Iris said. "You can see that in Rex's book."

They had reached the car. He was exhausted, but he managed to load up and get them all set to go with celerity. His knee hurt.

First she had wanted to go into her den, her study, and sit there in the baking silence for a few minutes with the door closed. The mail, sorted out on a huge platter by him, she had ignored.

Afternoon was dying.

They had laughed at the alp her travel tunic made, dropped on the floor.

He waited.

She was lying full length on the sofa in the living room and he was preparing to rub her feet, at her request. He had aimed two electric fans toward her, one at her head, the other at her midsection. Nothing had been said about the house, the way it looked. He was back with the Nivea cream.

He sat down. Her naked feet were in his lap.

He said, "Do you want to pull off those elf pants, me to pull them off?"

"You want sex," she said.

"Of course, but this is a separate matter because those things look hot. They look uncomfortable."

"Stirrup pants is what they call them. You may remove them."

"I am not sort of crushingly out for sex, my dear."

"Oh mais non."

"Well I'm not."

"Sure you are."

"Well I am and I'm not, you know how it is."

Her perfect legs were out, there, perfect things, gleaming.

"You can have it if you want it," she said.

"I know."

"It won't be full-dress. I'm so tired. But you know me. I'm happy if you need to."

"Non, merci."

"You have a right."

"No I don't. There is no such thing."

"Please," she said. "Please. Be real."

She began rubbing her eyes with her knuckles, producing a sound, a creaking sound he hated to hear. It was too organic.

"Ray, I can accommodate you anytime."

"No I think I'll wait instead of taking advantage of a lagged-out wreck of a darling and guaranteeing that when I die I'll go directly to hell."

He sat at the end of the sofa and took her feet into his lap.

She had her forearm over her eyes. It was possible she was concealing tears, trying to.

She asked, "Did you masturbate?"

He hated this. It was mere liberationism. She knew who he was, for better or worse. He was someone used to there being more of the unsaid in love-talk, love-communications. I'm almost fifty, he thought. Of course this might be an attempt at seduction, getting him onto the slippery slope and then getting sex over with so she would feel better because she had taken care of an obligation.

"No," he said, lightly, as lightly as he could. This subject was sediment stirred up, he was certain, by the weekend Antichrist, Morel, whose doom was coming. He would arrange it. He thought, He thinks I'm Bottom . . . I'm Tamburlaine . . . He'll see.

He rubbed Nivea cream into the soles of her feet.

She was persisting. "Really not?"

He moved back so that her feet were decently remote from his genitals.

"No. It was part of waiting for you to come back, Iris," Ray said. It was perverse, what she was doing.

"Did you have wet dreams?" she asked.

"Iris. Yes, I had wet dreams. Since you ask." Suddenly, he was enraged. She was pushing him around.

"I masturbated," she said, which was more cheap fucking damned liberationism, offensive, offensive.

"You did?" he said, but lightly, calmly, falsely, to his ears. He wanted to ask her if she had thought of him, if he had been involved in her imagery, if imagery had been involved in the act, which would be a tremendous mistake on his part.

"Did you think of me?" he asked, thinking that if she hesitated before saying yes, it would mean hell, of a sort, was here. She had not even glanced at the mail. Where was she?

"No," she answered, not hesitating, which was a plus, a great plus. He loved her for her truthfulness.

Now the worst thing he could do next would be to ask further along this line rather than being superior to it. She could save him from ignominy by volunteering something, images from the movies, something innocuous he could live with. This was not like her. Why was she doing this if she loved him? She thinks she wants truth, he thought. Truth for him, when he saw her at the airport, would have meant some act like pressing his hands along her physical outline in the world, hard, like an idiot, a scene.

Tears were leaking out from underneath her forearms. She was trying to disperse and spread them around with arm movements so he wouldn't notice.

Here we are, he thought. The tears could be over anything, anything, her sister, secret adventures, anything.

Her panties were red lace, ones he liked but not his greatest favorites, the one or two high-cuts she was willing to wear only for sex.

"Stop staring at my mons."

"I'm not, or not exclusively, anyway. I'm staring at your whole pleasant body."

"Peasant body?"

"Pleasant." He enunciated.

"Sorry, my ears are still clogged from flying." She tried to work up a yawn, but failed.

Now she had both arms crossed over her eyes. Her tears increased. At least she seemed not to be actively crying. Her rib cage movements were slight. She wasn't heaving out the tears, it was more like leakage, an overflow. He decided to let her weeping run its course, to say nothing until he was solicited. It was always possible he was going to hear that these were tears of relief. He kept kneading the soles of her feet, feeling like weeping himself. What was it about individual vigorous pubic hairs poking here and there through the lace at her crotch that he liked to see, loved, in fact? It was festive, was why.

She said, "Tell me everything."

"I think I kept you pretty up to date on the phone. Let's see. Around here, not much. We're still waiting for the Boka Report. There's been plenty of funny business in the Housing Authority and it's possible the vice president will be hurt. There's a new press law, very objectionable. Somebody in admin at the embassy posted a complaint about the Batswana leaving rubbish behind when they eat in the building. The word pigs was used. Barrage of apologies.

"South Africa is looking okay. You know de Klerk got sixty-seven percent in the white people's referendum. The oil embargo is off, not that it was ever really on.

"What else . . . I would say it's going okay except for Natal. The killing won't stop in Natal. And you know that Winnie and Nelson are separating."

"I heard that. She seems to be awful. But it's sad."

"She had lots of boyfriends, apparently."

"Well, but *Ray*. He was in prison for years. What do you want from people?"

"I know."

"Why even *mention* that, when it was about that insane football club she ran and that boy they killed?"

He said, "I had a dream last night. I dreamed there was an ad in the paper for see-through spandex shorts or something. I was going to buy some for you."

"You don't need to convince me you're concupiscent. My offer is on the table. Don't worry."

"I'm not worried. Let's see. The drought, bad here but patchier than in Zimbabwe. The maize crop is bust.

"Nothing definite on Dwight Wemberg, although there are theories that he's gone to ground up north. And by the way, I'm getting the distinct impression that I'm supposed to bring him in. Me. He's *my* responsibility. I may have to go up to Maun. There's no logic to it. Whenever there's a fugitive around here the conventional wisdom is that he's hiding up in the swamps. Like the mass murderer. Lord Lucan. They thought he was in the Okavango."

"No, the Tuli Block."

"Same thing. The imbroglio at St. James you know about, except the latest. There was the Too Much of Cabbage rebellion and then there was property damage, then the school was shut down. And where it is now is that the parents want somebody to give the miscreants a big punishment event, with the miscreants getting lashes. All hands refer to the students as miscreants, by the way, myself included.

"So, you know Curwen. He won't hear of any lashing business. There's a standoff and I don't know how long we'll be closed. The House of Chiefs, big surprise, has come out against Curwen.

"You met Pony, the young guy who worked in the bursar's office. Curwen was grooming him for bursar, although I guess he had never gotten around to hinting to Pony that that offer was coming, being a Brit. Anyway Pony has disappeared.

"Which we think has to do with something else. The government finally drove our friend Samuel Kerekang into the wilderness, literally. He was creating incidents over everything, it's true. He came out with the claim, probably true, that the country is already about ten percent seropositive for HIV, which nobody wanted to hear. He couldn't get work anywhere. And, um, there were a number of mishaps connected with his paper *The Mattock*, copies disappearing on the way to the distributor, and then a fire wrecked his printery. And then somehow the Anglican women's guild got very interested in taking control of his gleaners group. And now they've done it. Suddenly they had all kinds of money.

"So Kerekang decided to pull back to Galilee, if you know what I mean. He has a family claim to land in one of the villages way the hell up on the Cunene River, almost into the Caprivi Strip. And he's organizing some sort of commune up there, turning the northeast into his version of Yenan, is what the government thinks. Now that he's out of town they're even more hysterical than before. Domkrag want something done! *The Mattock*, or rather *Kepu*, because it's three-quarters in Setswana now, is circulating again. He puts a lot of poetry in it, by the way.

"What nobody likes is that a number of kids from the university dropped out and followed him. Some of them are sons and daughters of big men in Domkrag. Sons, I should say. Only two young women are among the missing, versus seven guys."

The flow of tears had stopped.

She said, "Don't press so hard on the top of my foot, there's no flesh there and you'll bruise me. In fact, thank you, but you can stop now. I am so sorry about everything, Ray.

"My sister. My *sister*. Ray, I encouraged her to have this baby. I don't know if I was identifying or what. I thought it would be fine. People are doing it all over. I am coming back to you a crock of woe, just what you need. I kept trying to find a metaphor on the plane for how I am and that was what I came up with. Woe is you. I mean woe is what you get. From me. I am responsible for my sister. I mean . . . I don't know what I mean. I mean beyond the thousands I gave her, I have to do more. Thank God for the way you are. You are my God, you know, which is the problem, Davis would say, but he would be so wrong. We have gods. I don't know. My sister. I am responsible. Now she has Margo."

"Who's Margo?"

"Oh, you don't know. Margo is her baby. Ellen went back twice to change the name at the registry place, making scenes. She kept changing her mind. Nothing I could say. I shouldn't have left. She gets me hysterical. She is completely provocative.

"Here's an example. I don't know if I told you about this or not. The first time she nursed in public somebody made a face or passed a remark, which was lighting a fuse if only they had known. Now she just throws out her breast for nursing anywhere in Tallahassee she happens to be, the more public the better, the more dubious the location the better.

"She is totally miscast in Tallahassee, by which I mean *totally* out of place. Except with her associates at the Montessori place, of course, she's in a frenzy. She goes around *raging*. She wants to make citizens' arrests! She should be with my mother. But my mother is out of the question. She keeps going on about illegitimacy. They could never get along. She has no room. Ellen drives me to the edge. I was on the verge of taking the postman aside and pleading with him to tear up her copy of *The Progressive* when it comes. Of course, I didn't. But she reads their classifieds and orders the latest inflammatory bumperstickers, which they seem to specialize in. She has one she hasn't put on her car yet because she can't find it. Guess why. I hid it. *WWJD—Who Wants Jelly Donuts?* I have to think of what I can do."

"Do what, though?" Ray said, thinking *There is no physic for the world's ill, it will burn in a fever forever.*

"I have to walk around for a minute," she said, getting up abruptly.

He watched her. Doing something for her sister was going to mean bringing her here, he knew it, and it was impossible.

Iris walked in a circle, leaving oily footprints on his clean floor.

Abruptly she lay down again and returned her feet to him.

She said, "I don't know what to do. That child cannot just vanish into state care. Say something."

"Such as what?"

"Maybe she could come here. Not forever but for a while. We have the space, Ray. I could give up my den." She liked to call her room of her own her den.

"Well, I mean, the idea is pretty staggering, Iris. I, um. What. We, I think, um, we need to monitor the situation first, don't we?"

"If we could just calm her down, Ray. I know Davis could help her."

He felt suffocated for a moment. It passed.

He resumed rubbing her feet.

"Be gentle," she said. He didn't feel like being gentle. He felt like ripping her feet off and cutting his cock off and starting life over as a eunuch someplace where there were no phones.

"I'll have to think about this," he said. Think about opening a madhouse, he thought.

"Okay, good. Bend my toes back. And hold them back forever. And if you can remember from the reflexology book the spot you push for constipation, work on it. If you remember, from when you were doing reflexology before we decided it was ridiculous."

"I do remember," he said. He thought he did. He pressed his thumbs into the balls of her feet.

"That isn't it."

"Right," he said. He began a random sequence of pressures, assuming that he would strike the spot at some point. The sole of the foot is not Asia, he thought. Maybe this would help.

"I don't think we loved our siblings enough," she said.

"Oh right. That's inane, Iris."

"No I'm serious."

"You mean we should have stayed in America and loved them, just loved them a lot, and none of this would have happened?"

"All I know is that my sister is lost."

"A lost cause."

She sighed in a conclusive way and he was encouraged to think she had come to the end of the topic, for now.

She sat up sharply. "Oh boy," she said.

"What?"

"You can stop now."

He released her feet and began grinding his hands dry in a bath towel. She went off toward the bathroom, thanking him over her shoulder, in advance.

. . .

They had eaten. She had liked the collation he'd gotten up, especially the crab salad. They were at the kitchen table. Three candles provided their light, their only light. They were sipping chilled fresh guava juice. They were closer. Tonight he would give her a *wrenching* orgasm, if at all possible.

"We have to discuss your brother," she said, not eagerly.

"How is he?"

"It's hard to tell on the phone. We spoke a lot. He's like you. It's hard to tell how he is. We spoke a lot about the book and the arrangements and whether he could, well, impose on you to read it."

"Well and how's his roommate?"

"I'll come to that in a minute."

"Come to it."

"I shall. I have to say, though . . ."

"What?"

"Don't be . . . your usual way on this."

"My brother has never been anything to me but a source of pain and embarrassment, to start with a given."

"Okay, so you're hostile. But I learned something talking to him you never bothered to mention. Our name isn't really Finch, or yours isn't, so mine isn't."

"What are you talking about?" he asked, spacing his words for emphasis.

"Well, in passing it came out, when we were talking, that your family changed its name from Fisch, F-i-s-c-h, to Finch, which is fine, if they wanted to do it, but it does raise the question of why you never mentioned it."

"It just never arose. It's ancient history. *Look.* Look, it was during the First World War, for God's sake, and there was a lot of feeling against Germans, so my grandfather decided to change the family name."

"Germans?"

"Yes of course."

"Well I thought Fisch was a Jewish name."

"No it was because we were *German*, Iris. And then when the Lindbergh baby was kidnapped there was a Fisch involved in that, so my grandfather had to consider it a doubly good idea."

"Your brother obviously thinks it's a Jewish name. He says you're Jewish, or half or some part."

"Well, a perfect example of my brother's nonsense. Look, and may I add that by the time Hitler came along, they were very glad to be Finch, I would guess, with what Hitler did for being German."

"You're saying the family was never Jewish?"

"Never, so far as I know. Fisch is a common German name. It can be Jewish, of course. But we weren't. The family is from Stuttgart."

"Your brother is so convinced."

"My mother has whatever papers there are, if you want, you can follow it up. But Rex says things just for effect, you know, Iris."

"It would be interesting if you were Jewish, Rex."

"Look, if it's interesting to you, then get in touch with my mother. If there are any papers, she has them, so get in touch with *her*. Take up genealogy. You might enjoy it."

He said, "I'm sorry. I am not testy about this, in fact. I'm just not interested in it. If you want to pursue it, fine with me."

"You *are* testy, so forget it."

"No I'm not. It's just that life, now with the assistance of my dear brother, is presenting me with more tasks than I can currently shake a stick at. This is Rex getting attention, Iris. You know the line 'Family I hate you'?"

"Yes, Ezra Pound."

"You mean I've quoted it to you before?"

"Yes, and we discussed it. I don't admire Ezra Pound. And I don't admire the sentiment. I know things about your brother that are pitiful."

"I have a feeling you're going to share, as they say."

She looked pityingly at him, and said, "I intend to. There are certain things you have to do . . ."

A sudden impulse to break secrecy startled him. He fiercely wanted to tell her something he had learned about Boyle that he shouldn't tell her. Probably it was to get sympathy. There were heavy movements going on behind the scenery. There was some very unusual conferencing taking place. Things were abnormal, or getting to be. The agency was going to do something instead of sitting there collecting data forever. He could tell. He didn't like it. He was about to break secrecy, in a minor way only, really. He wanted to.

He said, "I want to tell you something funny about Boyle, Iris." She looked amazed. They were both so practiced at circumlocution when it came to his work with the agency that what he was saying felt major to her, obviously.

He went ahead. I am not thinking, he thought.

"This is Boyle for you.

"There are certain times when the chief of station may have to call all his actors together into one conference, to get at something, to fix something, to stop something from happening that it's urgent to stop.

"These are called action inquests or operation inquests, if they're taking place after the fact, or called just, well, plenaries, if they're for preemptive emergencies." There was no need for him to offer technical terms. But he felt like it.

"By his actors, I mean the whole range of operatives, from contract agents like me to staff members, officers, to various special short-term contract parties, informants, occasionally. Now of course the key thing, a key thing, is to preserve internal ignorance about who is working for the agency. The actors are supposed to know who their boss is, no more than that.

"Now in a very large station there are sophisticated ways of planning things and maintaining general anonymity, using high tech. You can convene and deliberate and get what you want and nobody finds out who the next guy is. But in smaller stations, it's a lot more difficult. As you can imagine.

"So Boyle had a situation come up in Central America. Namely Guatemala. He was new in the post. The technology was out of commission for some reason. And this need arose. So Boyle improvised. He found a venue and called a plenary and got his thirty or forty actors in one room, with every one of them wearing a paper bag over his or her head, with eyeholes and mouth holes cut into them, and Boyle presiding and shouting out to them to press the mouth holes tight across their faces so that words were not muffled up in these bags. And there were numbers on the foreheads of the bags, so he could keep track of who was contributing."

Ray was laughing. So was Iris.

"That is hilarious! And Ray, thank you for telling me! And I mean that. And it shows me something I didn't know about the business you're in. It was interesting!"

She had a grateful look, soft, he thought.

"This goes no further, of course."

She nodded, offering a friendly, comic-mournful expression he realized he craved from her. That was better.

She took his hands across the table. "Your brother's book, Ray."

"I'm listening."

"First, he's been working on this for years. It's huge. I'm going to do my best to describe it. The title for the whole thing is either *Strange News* or *Bright Cities Darken* . . ."

"*Clarae urbes*. He stole that from Horace."

"What?"

"The phrase. Also *Strange News* is Elizabethan. Yes, it's Thomas Nashe. The title has been used."

"Please don't just pour out scorn and objections before I even get two words out on this subject. Please. You don't know how important this is."

She went on. "It's in four sections, Sentences, Paragraphs, Incidents, Plots, and each section contains a thousand items, that is, a thousand sentences, a thousand . . ."

"I get it."

"And each item or exemplar, as he calls them, is on a separate page, so you can tell how many reams of paper you were hauling around."

"No wonder my knee hurts. That's a joke. May I ask a question?"

"Sure."

"A *sentence* on a single page, a paragraph . . . ? Can you explain what that's about?"

"Well, as I understand it, it's so you absorb, in a complete way, the particular item on the page, really take it in. He described the book in various ways, but mostly he described it as an anatomy. And he was explicit that I should tell you that it was *not*, was *not* just *faits divers*, you would know what that means. I can tell you what he told me it means . . ."

"I know what it means."

"Every individual element is numbered, but the numbers don't mean anything. What I understood him to say was that they were just numbers. He also described the book as a machine and also as a game, or was it that there's a game buried in it? Can't remember."

"It's a machine to destroy my spare time, what little I have. Machine is right."

"It's so hard to remember everything he said. Oh, one was that you shouldn't start reading this with the idea that it's some kind of Commonplace Book. It isn't. Nothing is from other books. It's all real, from letters, overheard items, his observations, stupid things said in the media. There are very few names. There are initials, mostly, where they're needed. He said you would recognize some of the people and incidents. Don't groan like that. Some of the items are from his childhood. He said he's been working on it all his life, but not knowing it until he got into his twenties.

"Sigh all you want. This is important. I'm even leaving things out."

Her eyes were moist. He needed to control his feelings about Rex. Questions like who in hell Rex expected to be readers for such a piece of massive self-indulgence could wait.

"Give me a second to think, Ray. Oh, another way he put it. This book is about literary significance, that's the subject, was the way he put it. He even thought of calling it Significance. Now this is me speaking, but what I gathered is that he thinks if you read through this you'll find here, scattered around, what narrative literature does in an extensive way, but in very emblematic or condensed form . . ."

"Ah, so you would never need to read another novel again, something like that? Because if you did you'd see . . . well . . . after Rex it would all be déjà vu. Is that what he meant, would you say?"

"Ray . . ."

"He is putting an end to literature, rendering it nugatory, shall we say. No small thing to do. It must be something like this. The most original novel or story that ever was or will be is in *fact* a mixture of tropes and images and connectives and trajectories that my brother has captured and pinned down in his book for your pleasure! A wonder, in short."

"Well, Ray, you'll have to decide if that's a fair summary. It's certainly a hostile one."

"And have you read his book?"

"God no. I've read very little, just here and there."

"And how do you like it?"

"Some of it is hilarious, I think. Some of it is just more or less mysterious, but you get glimmerings of . . . something. Some is brilliant, though, which is the case whether your anticipatory sarcasm is justified or not. A lot I just didn't have time to really get, to concentrate on. But I'm not the one to judge it, you are, I can't judge it as a whole."

"So this is just about stories, narrative literature. Not poetry."

"Correct. Oh no. Poetry, I have to tell you this, he is very dismissive about. He claims he doesn't care about it. He thinks it's *lesser*. I tried to remember his exact words because I was pretty sure you were going to ask me. Here's how he put it. Poetry is about the poet . . . in a way that stories are not about the storyteller. Structurally narcissistic, he called poetry. He isn't out to vivisect poetry, so you can relax."

"You have no idea how abysmal his notion of poetry is, how sophomoric." He wanted that sentiment to reach me, Ray thought.

Then he said, "He is . . . I was going to say an idiot. For example, does he think *Paradise Lost* is about Milton the man? But pardon me if I point out that this is classic Rex. He hands me a literary task and what? demeans my specialty. Incredible. My life is incredible."

"No, Ray, it's my fault. You know how I am. This is awful. I was groping around with him trying to get a clear grasp on what I was supposed to convey to you about what this was. And he wasn't always clear. Which is another thing, oh God, another thing . . . So I was the one who brought up poetry. This was not something he was volunteering for you to be sure you knew. I am trying to do everybody justice. I was the one who said does this have anything to do with poetry. I got it *out* of him. It is *important* that you believe me about this, Ray."

"You know that I haven't spoken to him for years, Iris. He knows that. We are not reconciled in any way."

"You have to be, though. I'll explain it."

"I'm perfectly happy this way."

"You won't be. You'll see. So. I'm not competent to tell you more about how the different ingredients, I guess you would call them, elements, relate, in the book. I think in the Sentences, he takes care of metaphor, as I recall, maybe similes, maybe aphorisms. Also you have your choice of how you want to read this collection. You can go randomly, like reading the *I Ching*, if you want . . ."

"Like a pillow book. Like the hugest most monumental pillow book ever."

"I think I've told you everything I can, Ray."

"And I am expected to do what, once I read this thing? Use my contacts in this hub of international publishing, Gaborone? I have nothing to offer in that department, I hope he knows. I have no connections in publishing. I never had any. There's no one I could recommend this to who has. That is the fact. If he imagines I have literary friends in power, he is mistaken."

"I'll tell you what he wants from you, if you let me."

"Tell."

"He wants you to read it and judge it. He wants a trained literary intelligence to read it and judge it. And I don't mean sample it and judge it, I mean *read* it and judge it . . ."

Thousands of pages, he thought. He realized unhappily that he was incorporating into his consciousness Morel's theory of religion as a conspiracy against free time and applying it a little differently, free time being mortal time, limited, limited, applying it to other, what, entities, like family I hate you, families as blind machines using up their progeny with demands on their time, whatever was left of their lives, the progenies' lives, the time before the toad arrives, death the toad. But I have no children, he thought. He knew through Pony that on the wall in Morel's meeting room was a papier-mâché Mexican carnival mask with a toad or lizard occluding the smiling face.

"Ray, he wants to know if this is a brilliant thing, major, or if it's a failure and a mistake. He doesn't know, Ray."

"What about the possibility he's done something in between, something pretty good, say?"

"I don't think you're going to think it's mediocre."

Ray said, "I'll do this. I'll do my best."

"Ray, look straight at me when you say that."

He did. "I'll do my best."

"Because I want you to say this as your*self*."

"Don't follow."

"There is a difference between *being* yourself and *playing* yourself, which is something we all do. You do it when you're tired and want to get through something that's difficult in some way. Men do it more, I think. I don't think I do it much at all anymore, since I started going to Davis. But the paradox here is that since I started going to Davis you're doing it more. But please don't do it now."

"I am now not doing it, to the best of my knowledge."

She didn't like that answer, clearly. All this for my brother, he thought. It was baffling that Rex was making an appeal to the bond between them that Rex himself had sought all his life to deny and destroy.

Ray's experience of brotherhood was hardly what anyone thought. Brotherhood, or brothership, a better word for it, had been something he had gotten from being in the agency, even if, except for his friendship with blessed Marion, it had been more abstract than not, an appreciation of membership in a male alliance, it was like, he imagined, being with the Allied armies during World War II, despite pattern bombing and the betrayal of the White Russians. He had a live brother, no thank you very much, who had made brotherhood odious, gone out of his way to do that. He wondered if the attraction the agency had always had for him would have been there if his experience of brotherhood with Rex had been normal. He felt pathetic for a moment, which enraged him.

"Ray, I know I'm putting you in a hard place. You can tell I want you to think this thing is wonderful . . ."

"A masterpiece, if at all possible."

"Of course. That would be my dream."

"But of course I can't promise to like it."

"No, and if it turns out you don't, I'm going to ask you to agree to something in advance. Will you?"

"Will I what?"

"Will you agree that if you don't like it you are going to negotiate with me what you are going to say?"

"You mean the *wording*?"

"More than that, really."

"You mean you want veto power, or what? I am having difficulty with this."

"What I want is your agreement to negotiate with me as to what gets said to Rex, but that I get to decide, when it comes down to it."

"This is like nothing I ever heard of, my weird woman."

"Now you're hearing of it."

"I mean, am I cognizing here that I'm supposed to let my judgment about this thing come out as a lie, at your hands, is that it? If this is not a masterpiece?"

"Yes, but before I answer that . . . well I just did answer it, but what I meant to say is that there are certain things you need to know."

She was about to weep again, he could tell, it was coming. He wanted to be kissing her face and fucking her, but this had to be gone through, which was a shame because he was floating on a wave of heat toward her, real heat, the kind that dissolves everything into hot perfect form, perfection renewed. Everything dissolved into the fevered onset, in that state of heat, milk glands being palpated were transformed into different items, different, celestial items separate from any function. It was a realm and he could be in it, like that, if she would finish with this, with his brother, sometime this century.

"Don't be upset, Iris. Okay, it's a deal. Reminds me of when somebody asks you for a reference and you say You write it I'll sign it, but . . ."

"Then thank God," she said.

What was this? She was almost vibrating. Part of it might be jetlag, but what was he missing?

"Two, then, Ray, you also have to promise to do this with speed. You have to address it right away. Can you do that?"

"Wait a minute. How can I promise that? You're talking about thousands of pages of . . ."

"Yes, but some pages have only the one sentence, so . . . At least can you say that you'll try? I'll make it easy for you. I won't bother you. I . . ."

"I want you to bother me. That's the point."

"Please agree to this."

It was too much. He was being bullied. But she was almost vibrating. He nodded.

She was wringing her hands, not something he could remember seeing her do, ever.

"The importance of this . . . You know, how he sent this to me."

"He knew I was leaving by a certain date and he wanted me to carry it personally to you and he hadn't even finished photocopying. One thing I have to do first is take care of that, maybe at St. James. Of course I assume he has the original drafts these pages came from, in some form or other. But it needs to be photocopied straight through. I won't ask you to do that . . ."

"Oh thanks."

"So what he did was send this to me by courier. And I don't mean by a courier service. It was a friend of his."

"He paid a friend of his to *bear* this to you?"

"No that's another remarkable thing about this. He didn't pay him. This guy paid his own plane fare, Armand. This is just someone who loves your brother. He has a kind of group, or following, Rex."

"Some sort of homosexual what, um, would you call it, homosexual what would you say, civil rights group?"

"Oh they're gay, but that's not what defines them. They're friends of his. They love him. Can you imagine . . ."

"Not really."

"You know what I mean. It's remarkable. I can't imagine people doing that for me."

"Please calm yourself, babe. It's okay. My babe. Please."

"I'm almost fine," she said. "Just one more thing I need you to do. Ah wait. I have to go to the bathroom again, oh thank you . . . *Please* retain what it is you did to my feet. I am so relieved. I just need you to read two things of Rex's. In his handwriting. Just these two things I need you to read and I think you'll . . . you'll see what I see. You'll see it. I'll get them." She left the room rapidly.

He waited. Family I hate you, he thought. He was dreading something, with Rex. He thought he knew what it was, but why she hadn't been more direct about it, if he was right, was more than he could figure out just then. His brother had some weird charm, or charisma, even. It was an ancient mystery. Now Iris was in his thrall, if that was the right word. Somehow Rex had always possessed what could only be called glamour, he supposed, as peculiar as that was.

The problem with Iris conducting him into this prolonged new waltz with his brother was that it was energizing and resurrecting memories and incidents he had successfully and happily forgotten. Pick a scab, any scab, he wanted to say to her sometime when she was stirring up the sediments of his past. The idea that it was helpful to go back and relive the most annoying passages of your life was one of the dumbest notions ever to acquire a following. He had read something by or referring to a therapist who specialized in treating Holocaust survivors who had come to the conclusion, after years of the opposite approach, that the survivors who had done the best job of repressing their hideous experiences were the best off, the happiest, the most successful, and that the practice of re-living was ruinous for a lot of the relivers, ruinous. But who knows? he thought. Of course Morel would be all for reanimating injustices, dead things, like Frankenstein, no doubt.

He had to have her. He had to be careful. He had to be gradual. He could do prolonged kissing all over her body, in some pattern he would think of, and postpone touching her puss and going in until she said uncle, please, enough. Of course that was fine as a plan but less fine as a campaign on the ground because it got him too fucking hot too soon, her too. It was possible he could surprise her with how long the kissing would go on. She would be expecting something else. It had to be fine between them, that way. It had to, with Morel hovering, it had to.

Rex was clever. He granted that. And he would like to forget it if he could. It had been his luck to have as his brother a sacred monster. The designation had never occurred to him before, but it was apt, and it was a little comforting.

Here was Iris. She handed him two airletters dated well before her trip, with certain sections checkmarked. Then she turned and went to her luggage and began rooting through it for something, another piece of writing, which she found and brought to him, murmuring that he should take his time while she took care of a couple of things. She fiddled with the papers, arranging them in the order she wanted them read, before leaving the room. She was agitated.

He took up his task, thinking Love your enemies. She seemed to have it askew, poor dodo. She seemed to love *his* enemies, his brother. She was indiscriminate. She loved the world, and insofar as he could love it at all, it was via her in some way. He should tell her that, or, rather, never tell her that. She would resent it. In her place he would hate it. It would make her responsible for him just at the moment she was what, experimenting with her feelings or whatever she was doing. It would be fatal to interfere with that. He had to keep her, keep her or what, die, was his situation.

Iris reentered. She presented him with a magnifying glass, a surprise. She left again, hurrying.

He hadn't known she owned a magnifying glass. He did appreciate having the use of it, not because there was anything wrong with his eye-sight, but because his brother's small but perfectly formed handwriting could be a trial for anyone. Rex's excruciated hand was on the border between the eccentric and the insane, in his opinion. Good eyesight ran in his family. He needed to be attentive to reading in a good light more now than previously, was all. He would begin in a minute.

He had to get going. He would like to know what, exactly, she was doing, as he began. He held his breath to help him listen in her direction, for any clues. He thought she was on the phone. He wasn't sure.

Item one before him was a segment of Rex's tips for long-absent returning natives, a joke genre created specifically for Iris's benefit that of course relied on the canard that Iris was hearing nothing about movements and events in American cultural life from her husband, not to mention that she was herself an assiduous reader of everything from the *International Herald Tribune* to *The New Yorker*. Rex obviously wanted him to be a what, a stumbling block, an incubator of ignorance.

Here was his brother:

I want you not to be amazed by a startling development taking place within the African-American, formerly Afro-American or black, community. What we have is a significant element in the community, a vanguard element, executing something called the Islamic Turn, and dragging a good part of the masses along in that direction. It is serious. You will be greeted from time to time in Arabic. These leaders have brilliantly found a way to align the justified complaints of their people with the interests and image of the main certified declared enemy of the United States of America, the radical Muslim powers. This of course is an eerie replay of the situation in the thirties, forties, and fifties when the vanguard of that time, notably Paul Robeson and W. E. B. DuBois, cleverly sought to align their followers with the then main enemy, the USSR and its cat's paw the Communist Party of the United States. So how excellent is it for black/white relations to have leading African American intellectuals sucking the hem of the main new enemy, now that the former main foe has collapsed in a heap, switching their adulation to the political descendants of the champion slave-trading powers of all time? Yes, the Muslim slave trade went on for thirteen centuries versus two for us, involved a higher overall total of slaves taken, by about a million (thirteen against our twelve), *and*, *nota bene* please, featured the *castration* of black male slaves. *Nota bene* that there IS NO BLACK DIASPORA IN THE MUSLIM COUNTRIES for precisely that reason. Also *nota bene* that the only places in the world where chattel slavery persists like a fossil are, guess what, Muslim countries, Mauritania and Sudan. O my coevals! (You can

ask my brother what this comes from.) O tempora, O morons! Oh
and by the way, with this brilliant feat of identification (Louis
Farrakhan, the head of the Nation of Islam, is a pal and associate of
Muammar el-Qadaffi) these guys are giving the back of their hands
to their former best and most effective friends and costrugglers the
Jews, friends with power and influence and money and conscience.
In addition, not only does the Islamic Turn cut the black
community off from bien pensant Jews and their resources, but
down the line it also threatens relations with the bedrock of African
American community strength, the bedrock black Christian
churches, in the following way—it is stone doctrine in Islam that
Christ was a fake, a kind of hologram, on the cross. You can read it
in the Koran in so many words, Christ was a phantom, of sorts. Of
course this has yet to strike the consciousness of the black church,
but it will, as the pastors rouse themselves to figure out why Islam is
the fastest-growing religion in the United States, leaving them in its
dust. Oh by the way, above I should have added that the Nation of
Islam has gone specifically out of its way to defame the Jews as
being leading slave traders in the 18th and 19th centuries, a
calumny, of course. And also of course, what they forget is that the
Islamic Arabs of Palestine in the thirties and forties were fans of and
collaborators with the *then* main enemy, the Nazis, through the
Grand Mufti of Jerusalem. Also, just as they line up next to the new
main enemy, these guys are shouting out the main demand they
have agreed on, reparations for slavery they would like the present
white person majority to vote to give them, good luck, given their
public relations status. Oh and naturally nothing is going to be
asked from their pals the Muslims, who are still in the slave trade
business in Mauritania and Sudan. O everybody! But such is this
mod'n contemporary world of today in which we live in, to echo
Paul McCartney, my dear.

Ray thought, Rex sees himself as Mencken, the gay Mencken, and also
as the gay Tocqueville, apparently . . . and what he doesn't realize is that
what he's doing is exactly the same thing the trend analysts that Marion
made fun of think they're doing . . . This is thin stuff: I could do it.

This was Iris's next assignment:

You need to appreciate certain important deformations that are
becoming prominent in Americanese. What is manifesting in our

language is a strange hatred of consonants, especially the letters
t and n. M is shouldering n aside, but m should not rest. It too is
doomed. I realized I had to lay this out for you before your arrival
when, the other day, I heard a word used that completely eluded me
but that was perfectly intelligible to the people it was being
addressed to. The word was plampaernheut. What was being said
was, of course, Planned Parenthood.

Anyway, here's a compilation that will show you what's
happening, pretty much—

> imput
> turmpike
> temminutes (ten minutes)
> avertising
> love one (loved one)
> produck
> aministration
> aventure
> owrage, owlook (outrage, outlook, the t
> swallowed)
> he braw me home (he brought me home)
> gramparens
> exackly
> carboar (cardboard)
> Febuary
> tempature
> goverment (the t survives in this one so far)
> ornjuice
> estatic

Ray detected a carelessness or coarsening of his brother's handwriting
in this specimen.

The next selection seemed to be about the same vintage as the one
before it, at least in terms of the peculiarities in Rex's handwriting. But
there was something else about it worth noting. It seemed oddly or badly
organized, for Rex.

You could call these some useful current tropes you are sure to
run into. I am providing them to you partly for desensitization
purposes, so that you won't be disoriented when you hear
them used so repeatedly as you will, and partly for you to use,

yourself, should you wish to pass for an uptodate denizen anytime you like.

Herewith the candidate tropes and prefab expressions social interactions are increasingly made up of.

—The premier thing to say if you should injure someone whilst you are regrettably in a rage is *Let the healing begin.*

—Say of any scene of natural disaster that it is *just like a movie* and if people have been hurt *just like a war movie.*

—If there is a huge government scandal but you happen to be favorably disposed toward the party in power and responsible for the mess, say *There's enough blame to go around for everyone.*

—Remember that however miserably you have wasted or screwed up your life, you should say *I'm a survivor,* meaning that you are truly proud of uh, well, not being dead. And if you have had a *grossly* misspent life, be prepared to tell anyone critiquing you that it has been all for the best because you are about to embark on a career as a motivation counselor.

—If a close friend or someone in your family is killed by a malefactor but the malefactor is caught, say *Good, but nothing can bring him/her back.*

There was more, which Ray was going to skip because it would be similarly annoying. He would read a little more of this rant and then go on to the last assignment.

—*Be there for you* is a phrase that will quickly make you as sick as it has me, because it means nothing. It is everywhere. It is a phrase that *purports.* What it promises is that the promiser will lounge lovingly in the vicinity of the person who is in terrible trouble but without undertaking anything as concrete as lending money or driving him to the clinic from time to time. On television recently the phrase was used by a woman who has the largest collection of teddy bears in the state of Oregon. She was asked why she collected the teddy bears so madly, and yes the answer was that it was because they were always there for her. Yes, this phrase says, I will always be there watching the mess you've gotten into but not really assisting you, just sadly smiling. You will discover that if you get into deep trouble the people who said they would be there for you really did mean in fact only and nothing more than that they would hang around as spectators to your decline and fall. There is no love.

Ray thought, Man how he hates America! There were apparently no redeeming features! What had America done to deserve his hatred, other than destroy the gay-hating Nazis and the Russians who until recent years had thrown gays into prison? And hadn't it been the great god of Russian literature Gorky who'd said homosexuality was a product of fascism? Rex hated America, but how could he explain a guy running for the presidency and pledging to legalize homosexuals in the military? Of course Bush was going to crush him, but still.

He didn't want to read more. He wanted Iris to prance into the room naked. She might.

This last item he was supposed to read was startling. It wasn't clear what it was. Was it a dedication?

Partly it was. It was a series of statements printed in turquoise ink, waveringly, drunkenly lettered, on a sheet of vellum. There was no heading.

> I present this to the great friend of my life, Iris, my great friend, this assemblage of truths and secrets to peruse.
>
> O my coevals! The secrets of a people are revealed in individual asides. Our lies reveal the deepest truths about us.

Please, Ray thought. This man was supposed to be the nemesis of the cliché.

> In jests we show our deepest sorrow. All the secrets I possess are here, somewhere. You must juxtapose. Wake up and smell the offal!

The thing was signed ungracefully, atypically, which reminded him of something odd in his own history. His signature had been rather stiff and careful up to the time of their father's death. And then he had begun signing his name more loosely and in fact in a form very much like their father's. He hadn't thought much about it.

Well, he was surprised. Unless this was a draft of something better, he was very surprised. But it seemed not to be a draft. It seemed to be a demonstration of Rex's gnomic and aphoristic aspirations going mad on the page. They were feeble.

Ray felt he was on the point of being dragged into collaborating with someone seeking the lowest form of literary immortality as established and pioneered by the annoying James Joyce, who thought it would be

such a good idea to create puzzle palaces for thousands of specialists to
wander around in forever, using his genius to fabricate and drop clues
and conundrums, or conundra, that would turn the body of his work
into an everlasting object of academic interest and industry. That had
been Joyce's crap idea of immortality, endless lines of clerks, really, *clerks*
fondling his clues and getting tenure out of doing it, hives of clerks working to reconstruct the so playful so antic so smart mind of James Joyce.
There was enough natural mystery to go around and enough social mystery as well, and mystery was his enemy. Of course *Dubliners* was great,
and *Portrait* was, unless the concluding sentence was a trick and joke
intended to let you know you had identified with a protagonist who was
in fact an intellectual peacock and a fool, but his great work had been
prior to all the puzzlemaking, for which fuck him.

He sat there.

Iris was in the doorway, naked, virtually, with a gauzy green stole
around her neck and hanging down over her breasts and leaving her
beautiful lower self exposed, to his joy. But she looked unhappy.

"What do you think?" she asked.

"What do you mean?"

"What I mean is, don't you see the decline I see?"

"Yes, his penmanship, unless he was just in a hurry to throw together
this preface or whatever it is."

"But Ray, not only in his handwriting. There's a loss of clarity."

"You could be right."

"I am and you know I am."

She was back at the luggage again, bent over delightfully to him and
then squatting, searching for something, more evidence. She had it. She
presented him with a snapshot, a Polaroid, of Rex. It was dated February
1990 and it didn't tell him anything. It was his fat brother, unsmiling,
wearing a beret.

"This doesn't add anything," he said. He studied the photograph.

"There's something pitiful, Ray."

"I don't know. He doesn't like his teeth. He always had to be begged to
smile when anyone was trying to take pictures."

Ray was having a definite event. It was inward but it was also visual and
felt like an image coming forward through his head and through his eyes
and out vaguely, out into the air between his eyes and the photo of Rex. It
was the image of a minor character from his boyhood, Crawford, a contractor their father had hired to build an addition to their house and who
had become a recurrent presence with them over the years, when some-

thing needed to be done or redone. His father had made him redo a flooring project. Was Crawford his first name or his second name? Ray couldn't remember. Rex looked like the dark, heavy Crawford, the heavy but preening Crawford. This could be a picture of Crawford. Ray had always been uncomfortable around Crawford, for no reason that he could remember, for no reason that he would have been able to name at the time. Crawford had never been a handsome dog, and in his forties, whatever charm he'd had was gone, or almost, although he strutted around like a peacock. He had gone around with the collar of his windbreaker permanently turned up, a sure sign of vanity in that period of time. Ray felt peculiar and light. His brother was a cuckoo, or cuckoo's egg. He was sure of it. He couldn't tell this to Iris. He had no proof at all.

"You're pale," Iris said.

He didn't answer. Someday he would talk to Iris about this, but not now. He couldn't. She would think he was trying to slide around and away from what he knew she was going to come out with now, her conclusion. It was remarkable. He wondered if he had known this about Rex but without letting himself know it, a kind of thing that could happen. It was true. It was absolutely the case. He must have known, without knowing what he knew. He felt so peculiar.

"You're pale," Iris said again.

"No I'm not," he said.

"You are. You think what I think. I think your brother is ill, Ray. That's what's happening."

"HIV, you think."

"It's the first thing you think of."

"Well, in the Polaroid he's still pretty heavy . . ."

"No he's much heavier in some earlier ones I have, much."

"Well."

"It can affect the nervous system. I think that must be the explanation. I mean, God help him. I think it is the explanation."

"Well, we don't really know, do we?" This was terrible, all of it. She could be right. Or she could be wrong.

"Something is required," she said.

He knew it.

23. The Denoons

Ray and Iris were there early. Ray doubted that much of a crowd would turn up for the celebrated couple, the Denoons. Tricks had been played, not by the agency so far as he knew, but by others, the government. There had been last-minute cancellations of the venue and even, briefly, a false venue and date carried on Radio Botswana. It wasn't impossible that the agency had been involved. These two would be certifiable radicals in Boyle's view. All Ray knew was that he hadn't heard anything. And while he was thinking about the matter, he decided to make an inward pledge never to engage in petty obstruction campaigns in the future, in his onward life. He knew how to evade getting involved in certain categories of business, as things stood, and he would just add another category to the list. That's that, he thought.

He was very eager to have a look at Denoon and his wife in the flesh. They had an interesting history, not only in Botswana. And of course Iris knew something about them, enough to make her adore them. They were social heroes, both of them.

Iris was very fixed up. He wondered if she expected Morel to attend. There was nothing he could do.

The venue was a classroom normally used for nurse training, one of two modules in a flimsy annex to the administrative block at the Princess Marina Hospital. They were in a long, narrow, windowless room with pea-green walls. There were seats, student desk-armchairs, for sixty. As was standard for government space, the room was scrupulously clean, the floors were gleaming, the blackboards scrubbed, a scent of lemon soap was in the air. On the wall above the blackboard were two framed portraits, the obligatory photograph of the current president, Masire, and beside it, to the right of it, interestingly enough, an unofficial portrait, obviously cut out of a magazine, of the deceased founder of the country, its first president, Sir Seretse Khama. Masire's photo was hanging crookedly, but not Khama's. It could mean something. When Masire's likeness had appeared on the currency there had been a short-lived movement to turn in the new bills for the older ones bearing Khama's likeness. He himself had overheard a woman on line ahead of him at Barclays explaining to the teller that she preferred the old pula because the new pula carried the picture of a jackal and she would not be happy to have such pictures in her purse. It had had to do with tribal feeling, Masire not being a Mongwato. It was a typically Tswana sort of protest, in its mildness. It was what he was used to. Now everything was changing around him, for the worse, for the worse, and he was to blame, he was to blame, not for all of it, for some of it, he was. Woe, he thought. He controlled himself.

The room was lit by a train of large hanging lamps containing very dim lightbulbs, inverted milkglass pyramids serving incidentally as receptacles for the remains of dead insects. The pyramids were open at the top and each one held a black load taking up, he estimated, about a fifth of the lamp interior. It was remarkable. The character of the light delivered was affected. It was remarkable, like everything.

They had their choice of seats. There were a few attendees, women, Indian and Batswana, in the back rows. Iris wanted to sit at the front so she could see everything, which was fine because the room would fill, if it filled, from the back forward, and they would have some time to talk freely. He had something to tell her that he was trying not to think about.

They took seats in the second row directly in front of the lectern. A small table and a chair had been set to the left of the lectern, and a chrome steel utility cart had been pushed up against it on the right. The cart bore a display of bouquets obviously recycled from the hospital wards. The centerpiece was a protea in a pot, drooping in a gold foil calyx. A gooseneck microphone was mounted on the lectern, needlessly, considering the dimensions of the room.

"These chairs always make me want to write," he said. He made writing motions.

"Then we should get you one."

He left it there. He was going to decline to pick up the invitation to reopen the question of the glorious, or at least better than this, life he was going to lead someday post-agency. She wanted him to go back to poetry, be what he had tried and failed definitively to be. That was what she seemed to want. She had all his ancient efforts somewhere in her files and boxes, her archives. She wanted a vocation for him that she liked better. He understood it. He wouldn't mind living a life closer to what she might consider ideal. For the Denoons it had worked out rather oddly and bitterly, it had to be said, although they were living a life that by Iris's standards had at least started out ideally. They were full-time against injustice wherever they could find it, and they had been lucky enough to find supporters who were living less than ideal lives and who were delighted to pay them for their efforts. So Nelson Denoon had founded a city of women in the heart of the Kalahari, where women ran the show and were ennobled and so on and where *they* inherited, as against the standard Tswana pattern, and all he had to say was bully for all concerned. Who wouldn't love to found an actual city, given the opportunity and the resources, running according to one's own notions and preferences? What human luck to be able to do that, found the most celebrated development project of the 1980s, place it in the hands of the beneficiaries, derive a splendid mate out of it, and go hand in hand off to some new venue of injustice, trailing clouds of glory, go to India, as they had done, India, constituting a buffet of injustices for them, a perfect place to go, castes, bonded labor, purdah or other woman's problems, all of that. Iris adored them because they were wearing out their souls in the service of man. And she wanted to wear out *her* soul in the service of man, if it could be arranged, before it was too late, and she wanted him to do the same, if only obliquely, by for example writing poetry, an *improving* thing to do, something she could accept. He was being unfair.

He said, "You didn't bring your book for him to sign." She owned a copy of Denoon's *Development as the Death of Villages*.

"That's not why I'm here," she said.

"I know."

"I have her book, too."

"I know."

"I'd be embarrassed."

"I understand that."

Iris wondered aloud why the meeting was being held in such an inadequate setting and he told her that the Denoons were in bad odor with goromente for reasons not entirely clear to him. The government had put certain obstacles in their path. For example, they had been given a stingy, five-day-only visa. She wanted to know why. She was under the impression that the women's colony he had established was a success, something the government was proud of.

"Well, yes, a success, but it's a success as a German plantation. That's what it's turned into, in effect. It's true that a sort of female elite runs it for the Germans, but it's not the same place it was. Grapple plant grows wild in the Kalahari and the Germans were buying all they could get to put in some aphrodisiac concoction. The biggest health food chain in Europe got involved. There was a boom. And then a collapse in all the growing areas except the one around Tsau. It's a tuber and you have to leave half of it in the ground if you want it to regenerate, which is the way Denoon had taught the women at Tsau to proceed. The other foragers had just ripped the whole thing out of the ground. Anyway, so the Germans moved in on Tsau, gave them contracts . . . and paid plenty because devil's claw, which is the other thing they call it, had gotten so scarce. Now it's like gold. So Tsau is a little like a company town on the order of Hershey, Pennsylvania. The women are doing quite well. Some of them are married to Germans who've settled there. There's a long waiting list to get in, and the female-line inheritance deal Denoon got the government to allow is a big draw, but it hasn't spread anywhere else and it's breaking down informally at Tsau. It's very gentrified, compared to what it was. And the Denoons are unhappy with the way things have turned out and they are letting everyone know how they feel. So they won't be making a visit to Tsau on this trip."

She said, "Hm. That's sad. But why is the government being so unfriendly to them?"

"Well, goromente is perfectly happy with the way Tsau is going. So that's one thing. But it's not mainly that. I think it's because of what happened in India. Botswana wants to keep the Indian community here happy. They're well off and they have a lot of influence. And the Denoons made trouble in India. They're persona non grata there. They got kicked out of Poona. So—"

"Yes, and kicked out when he was still convalescing. After what happened. And he's still convalescing. I think it's a scandal." She looked at him. "You're a cornucopia of information on almost any subject I raise, Ray. That's lucky for me. I'm serious."

"I try, my dear girl." He lowered his voice to say that the file on the Denoons was huge.

"I hope more people come, Ray."

"We'll see. But anyway, I don't know a lot about what happened in India. Essentially, he was invited out of Tsau because it was time for the women it had been meant for all along to take over. So she, Karen, came back from the States and took him by the hand and married him and when he told her he wanted to go to India she said fine, they would find something useful to do there. And so they did. You know what I know. They got into the movement against dowry murder. They plunged into it. She learned Hindi . . ."

She said, "I wonder why she took his name, though. For a feminist, and one so prominent, it seems slightly strange. Do you have any idea why?"

"Oddly enough, I do. Her true maiden name wasn't the one she grew up with, Karen Ann Hoyt. That was the name her mother gave her, but it was an invention chosen because her mother thought it sounded classy, better than Dooley in any case. You may think it's amazing I know all this, and it is, it is. Karen Ann hated her name, and that was because her mother, a simple person, at some point confessed to her that she had chosen Hoyt because it sounded like 'hoity-toity.' And the name Karen Ann had been copied from some local subdeb in the area who was always in the local news."

"What's a subdeb?"

"Subdebutante. I guess that term is out of use now. So she had reason to hate all her names. Her birth certificate reads Baby Girl Dooley. She dropped the Ann part of her name when she married Denoon. So now we have Karen Denoon and your question is answered."

"I understand the feeling of wanting to change your name. I don't love my name. And I know what you're going to say, Ray, so don't bother. Also, thank you for telling me interesting things."

"What I was going to say was that I love your name. And I do."

"So then is what happened in India that he was setting a trap, setting up to video an attempted wife-burning and planning to jump in and stop it after he had his footage, and the plan went wrong?"

"It went way wrong. The wife got out okay but the fire got out of control, there was a conflagration, and for a while they thought Denoon was caught in it and incinerated. But, as God wills, he survived. Somehow he curled up in a niche. They have it on tape, Denoon emerging from the ashes like a phoenix. They may show it tonight, although I don't see any monitor . . . well, maybe one is coming. But he came out of it with damaged lungs. He can't speak above a whisper. Even then, he talks in bursts and not for extended periods, they say. But they're still campaigning. She hauls him around with her. He's pretty much an invalid, apparently. It's done wonders for the movement. You could see him as a burnt offering that worked."

"Oh, dear. Thank God he didn't get burns, externally I mean."

Denoon gets into trouble, Ray thought. Before hooking up with the dowry murder people, Denoon had made efforts to get into the campaign against indentured labor in Madras. He had been unwelcome. The campaign had been totally in the hands of orthodox Marxist groups and his heterodox leftism had been found more than annoying. He had been beaten up, at one point, in a confrontation, but whether it had been a confrontation with the authorities or with organizers of the campaign, Ray couldn't remember. Martyrdom was a proof of virtue, of course. Clearly it was for Iris. He wondered if unconsciously that was what she wanted for him, if she would secretly prefer him to be hurling himself against the brick wall of the world, like Denoon or like her doctor, instead of being the what, the fierce champion of the inevitable she undoubtedly saw him as. But that was life. He was her lot. Or he was her lot for as long as she would accept it, which was the problem rising in the sky over them, a new orb. Morel would have a theory of Nelson Denoon, no doubt seeing him as reflexively aping the Christ myth, blindly mimicking the martyr archetype that's buried alive and twitching in the soul of every member of the West, the Christian West. But in fact Denoon's feints at martyrdom could just as easily constitute a creative way of dealing with depression, say, when the only other option for dealing with it was to pay somebody to paw through the leaves of the book of your soul, some cretin who thought your problem was that you never got over your mother and who meted out wisdom in commercial units of time when in fact you were bleeding all over the place and the protocol was to stop when the timer went ding, no thank you. Iris was squeezing his hand.

"We haven't really suffered," Iris said.

"Speak for yourself," he answered, trying for lightness.

He was suffering because he had to go away from her. He had just gotten the order. It was the worst timing. She was barely home from the States. He was being ordered into the field, urgently. He would tell her tonight. He couldn't stand the prospect. But there was real trouble in the north and in a complex way he could be considered partly to blame for it, which he couldn't tell her about, not yet, although someday he would have to, if he still had her. His connection to the trouble in the north was an impossible subject for contemplation. It was de facto. He had to avoid that aspect of this misery. He hated going into the field not because he was possibly a little old for it and not just because he felt he had been around long enough to earn enough consideration to keep him from being sent, no. No the fact was that he worked well in cities. He was built for cities. He had learned all his moves in cities, towns, cities and large towns. In the bush he would be improvising. He would be raw. His Setswana was weaker than Boyle realized. Much weaker. But resentment was his enemy. He had to go, imminently. And it could be for a month or more, depending. Iris was looking around the room for someone. He knew who. But he didn't know why a country would choose the protea for its national flower, as the South Africans had. It looked peculiar, like a giant artichoke, not really attractive. The room was filling up.

A show of organization at last, he thought. A few supporters, Batswana men and women of college age, none of them known to him, had appeared with the necessary paraphernalia of movements, packets of literature, a banner, collection baskets, bottled water for the speaker.

"Here they are," Iris said. She was tense.

"Don't stare," she said. But she was the one staring.

It was dramatic. The Denoons made their way up the side of the room, Denoon moving haltingly, assisted by his wife. Just behind them came a woman maneuvering an oxygen tank on a wheeled stand, and behind her a man pushing a wheelchair. The crowd was still. The wheelchair was parked in a corner in reserve. The oxygen tank was placed just behind the table on the left of the lectern, and the breathing tube and mask the tank was equipped with were laid on the tabletop for easy access. Stiffly, Denoon seated himself. Karen wanted him closer to the lectern and proceeded to drag the seated man in his chair, to a point that allowed her to reach down and take his hand. She was clearly physically powerful. She arranged herself at the lectern but broke off to provide Denoon with a pad of folded tissues. She touched the corner of her mouth, obviously to indicate to him that he needed to touch away something objectionable in the corner of his own mouth.

They're a success already, visually, Ray thought. Together they communicated valiancy, if there was such a word, that and an impression of worthiness and splendid weariness, aided of course by what the viewer knew about them, but still. Denoon was a gaunt but improved version of the persona Ray was familiar with from the photographic records. Adversity and weight loss had rescued the strong, hard face he had been meant to live behind. He would be in his late fifties. He was leonine, with long, almost completely white wavy hair pulled back loosely and finished in a neat pigtail, not elaborate, but it showed that somebody loved him, no question about it. The effect of the pigtail wasn't feminine. His gaze was piercing. Iris was enthralled, Ray could tell. As to defects, the linings of his nostrils were inflamed and he had an inordinately large Adam's apple, although whether women considered that unattractive, Ray was unsure. Probably not, Ray thought. Denoon was unsmiling, but then why wouldn't he be? Denoon seemed costumed, rather than dressed, to Ray. He was clad in a white dhoti over a black tee shirt and stovepipe black jeans. He was wearing sandals with white gym socks. Did he represent a subtle orchestration of pallors and darknesses, with his bloodless cheeks and his black eyebrows, and all the rest of the chiaroscuro? If it was chiaroscuro. It was always hard to know what was deliberate and he had to be fair. They had glamour, this pair. They really did.

Karen Denoon was in her early forties. She was square-shouldered, moderately tall, very attractive, he thought, but fighting it. He had seen the phenomenon in other particularly goodlooking women in leadership positions with cause organizations. The olive drab tunic she was wearing was useful in obscuring what was obviously a good figure. She was a sturdy specimen, athletic. He liked her. Her fine, bold face was innocent of any makeup he could detect. He liked her type. She wore her very abundant auburn hair drawn severely back into a tight bun at the nape of her neck, and she was ignoring the gray streaking showing up in her hair that, if she chose to, could be wiped out with a touch of color, but no. And of course she was without adornment, jewelry of any kind, and was wearing a man's ponderous wristwatch, a diver's watch in fact. There was something fiery about her he liked, and he liked her sexually. It was natural to wonder what her love life must be with Denoon, considering the shape he was in. Ray was having more sex thoughts about the passing parade of women than usual. It was since Morel, he was sure of it.

They were past the preliminaries, which had been uncomfortable. Denoon had mouthed some sort of greeting to the crowd. Karen had opened her presentation with a few minutes in Setswana, a piety, given that the attendance was overwhelmingly English-speaking. The crowd was less than a third Batswana, he estimated, and that third was a young, mostly female, educated-looking group. Indians made up the bulk of the audience, men and women about equal among them, an older group overall. And the remainder were Anglo-Canadians and Americans from different development organizations predominating, again men and women about equally represented.

Iris was transfixed. She wanted his hand, again.

Karen Denoon was a practiced speaker. She was not employing the microphone. Her voice was clear and light, with a singing quality show-

ing in it now that the summary matter was done with. And he was learning something tonight. Dowry murder was getting worse in India, not
better. He had assumed otherwise. The most recent figures were triple
the figures for 1980. It had been his impression that India was sliding
toward reason and light. He had read something in the *International Herald Tribune* suggesting that managing the wandering cow population had
gotten more humane there. Ray thought that a problem with causes, and
public meetings on their behalf, was that if you were reasonably au
courant you already knew about the evil being protested and already
agreed that it was wrong and what you were doomed to was normally a
presentation of the facts so simplified for ease of understanding that it
was boring. He particularly didn't like attending cause events relating to
Botswana. They tended to stir up all his subterranean foreboding about
where the country was going, plenty of foreign exchange in the bank but
poverty not improving that much, squatters like a thickening noose
around the capital, and the virus spreading relentlessly. Living as an out-
sider in these painful parts of the world was an art. But tonight he was
learning something. Karen Denoon had provided a vivid picture of
dowry crime, which, as he understood it, involved a woman marrying on
the basis of a promise of money payments to the groom's family in cases
where the whole sum couldn't be paid up front, which was increasingly
the case since dowry payments were spreading downward into the poorer
castes where people were less able to come up with the wherewithal than
were the richer castes they were trying to emulate. That was the problem.
At first when payments were not forthcoming women had been harassed
to pressure their families, and then it had gone to torture, and then it had
gone to murder, which left the groom free to make off with the amount
paid to date and to marry again. The most common form of murder was
burning, stage-managed kitchen accidents, and a criminal cottage industry had sprung up, murder specialists for hire, that the Denoons had gotten into trouble for exposing. There were thousands of murders annually,
thousands. There had been two thousand two hundred in 1988 and five
thousand in 1990 and these were only the ones actually proved to be
murders. Thousands more had gone unpunished, mischaracterized as
accidents or suicides. It was estimated that only five percent of the total of
murders were ever identified as such. The room had filled up. There
were standees. Unfriendly murmurs were coming from somewhere.

A voice cried out, "You are of Lal Nishan. You are communist. Lal
Nishan is red flag. That is its meaning . . ."

Denoon was shaking his head. He seemed to want to get to his feet.

"You are completely wrong," Karen said.

The objector was Mrs. Mukerji, a leading person in Hindu charitable organizations in Gaborone.

"My dear, we have passed laws against this as from 1961, if you don't know," Mrs. Mukerji said.

"I do indeed. The 1961 law is ineffective. And let me tell you that we have nothing to do with Lal Nishan. That is a lie. But please wait if you wish to attack me."

"But we see you are providing us copies of *Manushi*, just as Lal Nishan does at home. We know you."

"Can you just wait for the question period? *Manushi* is a journal for all women. It has no affiliation with Lal Nishan or with any other party in India. You should know this. And Lal Nishan is in Maharashtra. We are our own organization. Our base is Poona. Or was in Poona, since we have been expelled by your country. Look at our banner. We are called Shree Shakti, which means woman's power or power of woman. We are a member of the All India Woman's Conference, our group is. I think it is rude to remain standing but you must please yourself . . .

"Yes, this terrible thing is spreading, despite the laws. And these lives that are being taken are the lives of women fully grown and developed. I know that some of you in this room stand with the churches here against allowing women to choose abortion if they must, if they feel they must. But here we are speaking of women, human beings with all the thoughts and feelings of human beings. Not fetuses, women, and we need the churches, and you, to stand with them."

Mistake, Ray thought. The Indians were very conservative on this, and so were a fair proportion of educated Batswana women.

"So here is what is happening. The upper castes, where dowry reigns, are now the model for the lower ones, where in the past, bride-price the opposite of dowry, was paid. The groom would pay moneys to the family of the bride, as is done here in Botswana with lobola payments. And never was there a question, then, of killing the groom, the husband, if there were difficulties with the payments or if retroactively someone decided the payment was not sufficient or needed implementing, sorry, I mean supplementing, adding to, I meant to say. No, if an Indian man was in default in some way he was never in physical danger, then, because even if the bride's father was upset, the object of his rage was a man, or a man's family . . ."

Mrs. Mukerji said, "You are just saying Oh this way in Botswana, it is more advanced. You are making trouble here. You are no one. We live very well together here and yet you have come praising one way over against another. You are criticizing."

Ray had an excuse to turn around and have a good look at the crowd. There was no sign of Morel, which was something.

Karen said, "No. I am here to speak to you about a matter in India. But, all right, in this question of marriage payments, where have you heard of men dying over it? No, if there is a problem with payments that come from the man, or the man's family, something is worked out, isn't it? There is a council, a cup of tea, a clan meeting, the men consider, something is worked out . . ."

But her remarks drew objection, actual ululations, in fact, from a new quarter, from a group of young Batswana women.

"Lobola, nyah! It must not be!"

Iris was distressed. So was Karen Denoon.

Karen said, "No, my sisters. I am not here to praise lobola. What I have said about it is only that defaulting grooms are not murdered in Botswana as many defaulting brides are in India . . ."

"Lobola, nyah!"

"And of course surely in the future world of women there will be no need for lobola, no need for impediments to the choices women make as to whom they shall marry . . ."

"I must speak, my sister." This woman's last name was Nteta, he couldn't think of her first name, and she was a traditionalist. She was married to a chief.

"Yes, please."

"I am happy to call you my sister but I must say on this . . . about lobola. Because with lobola you can see what kind of man is coming after your daughter, if he is sound or what-what. Because if you say no to lobola, your child can just go wherever about and say Oh this chap is fine but in fact he is a sham, a stick, a fine face with nothing behind. And there is nothing behind and he goes off and she is left with his children. We see this in every town . . ."

Ululating and hissing rose in intensity.

"Now you are putting sister against sister, as you see," Mrs. Mukerji said, triumphally.

Denoon said something to Karen, who beckoned for a display easel to be brought up, which happened. A packet of photographic blowups was placed on the easel tray. The top photo, in color, showed a burned body in cruel detail. The room quieted.

"Ah me," she said. It was heartfelt. She was fatigued.

"I'm not here to set sister against sister. We can disagree among our-selves on anything, and why should we not? I am here to say we have to look around us and when we see things *drifting toward evil,* drifting and drifting . . . we have to do something. What are we if we refuse?"

A lull followed. She could proceed. It went on. He had to look away from the exhibits, the worst ones. Iris was squeezing his hand to numb-ness. Karen Denoon was more than competent as a presenter. In passing she let it be known that this was not the presentation as it was usually given, because certain items of audiovisual equipment, including an over-head projector of theirs, had gone missing. Still, she managed to build a cathedral of pain for the audience, pain and shame. When it was over the crowd was pretty uniformly where she wanted it to be, he thought.

The Denoons were on their way to Zimbabwe the next day, and because her husband was in need of rest they would only take questions informally, and say hello to old friends, as they prepared to depart, at the front of the room. Ray wanted to stay put while the event dissolved. There were a few people present that he knew he should probably greet, but he wasn't going to. The air in the room was thick, until someone opened a door to the outside and began fanning it back and forth. Ray knew Iris was seeing something in the Denoons, something not helpful to him. The Denoons were living a grueling life. After Zimbabwe, they were going to Kenya. If the Indian communities in East Africa were as organized against them on the dowry murder issue as the Gaborone com-munity was, they were headed for trouble. They were doing good things, but he hoped Iris could at least see there was stress involved, and a certain lack of glamour. He wished them well.

Iris wanted to join the modest throng around the Denoons. He would wait, in his seat, but he urged her to get going before the Denoons disap-peared. His problem, his assignment, revived, hard, as she left, beating in him like a second heart. It was the worst time for him to be away from her that anyone could devise, with Morel machinating, her feelings for Morel, her sister showing only the slightest signs of better coping . . . but at least they were at a point of rest with Rex, rest or standstill. It was impossible to know how long it would last. For the moment, there was nothing he or Iris could think of to do. They had called Rex three times, inconclusively. In their first two calls they had run up against an unhelp-ful Joel claiming that Rex was away and unreachable and promising that a callback would come when Rex returned. They had waited and there had been no return call and then they had tried again and gotten Rex and found him evasive, insisting that he was fine, his delivery breathless and

oddly deliberate. Rex had declined to speak directly with Ray. Iris had
attributed Rex's unforthcomingness to discomfort over Ray's presence in
the vicinity of the call. And it had all concluded with Rex announcing that
he preferred communicating by mail and that he would write soon. At the
very end he had betrayed some agitation in asking if his manuscript had
been put in Ray's hands. When he had been told yes, the call had abruptly
ended. In the body of the call, Rex had backed up Joel's earlier story that
he had been away, but without any details given, and he had added that he
would be traveling again in the near future. Iris had seen Rex's performance as more extreme than Ray had. She and Rex shared at least a little
history of private phone calls, so she did have a basis for comparison. In
any case, they were nowhere, they'd been pushed back. Iris had poised
the receiver to enable Ray to overhear a good deal of what Rex was saying, which had been a painful experience. They were connected beings,
he and Rex, and there was a baffled residue of what, abused affection, that
the call had stirred up. His brother had, after all, made him laugh, growing up, when he wasn't contriving to enrage him. That was it. They were
being held off. There was a reason and Ray thought it was as simple as
Rex wanting to preserve secrecy about his condition, if their darkest fears
were right, and they were going to be.

Iris had managed to say something to each of the Denoons. It had
been fleeting and she would be disappointed. The Denoons were in
motion, Nelson via wheelchair now. The speed with which the couple
felt they had to leave was adding to the telescoped, unclear tone of the
ending. Their flight to Zimbabwe was a very early one, and Nelson was
clearly tired. Karen Denoon loved her husband. She kissed the top of his
head a couple of times as she drove him forward, into the night, toward
the next battle. Ray closed his eyes briefly.

A young man obscurely familiar to Ray emerged from the crush
around the Denoons. Who was he? He was a distinctive character, tall for
a Motswana, willowy, with regular, handsome features and a discordant,
aggressively meek, hunched presentation of self. Who was this character?
He was wearing a vaguely sacerdotal metallic-looking black band-collar
shirt with not one but two Shree Shakti buttons pinned to it, front and
center. Who was he? He had a collection basket and he was the one
who had gotten Iris's donation. He was jittering around, hurrying, why?
He was in signaling contact with two associates. He was wearing tight-
fitting designer jeans with the price tags still fluttering, which Ray had
heard was a current fashion trick obviously intended to show that the garment being worn was brand new. There was a market for stolen price

tags. It was something that was going on. The collection team was gone, suddenly. It would come to him who they were. Iris returned to him, withdrawn.

The room was still emptying when the lights were snapped off, which prompted an outcry. The lights came on again for a moment. The room cleared instantly.

Outside, the scattered lighting in the adjacent grounds was also going off prematurely. This was harassment. Matches were struck. Ray always carried a custom penlight, agency issue, with an astonishing beam. He got it into use. Iris asked for it. She was concerned for the Denoons. She wandered around with the penlight looking for them and then gave up. A group collected around his penlight and Iris led the way to the car park, where, shortly, someone had the presence of mind to get headlight beams aimed back along the route from the administrative block. Everything was in order. They could make for home.

He had it, the name of the character with the collection basket. He knew who he was. Admittedly it was inferential. But he knew he was right. The character was a thief, he was the thieving Paul Ojang, and Iris had given her donation to him. Good God, he thought. This Ojang was an asset of Boyle's, someone he had bragged about, a prize catch in Boyle's recruitment exercises among the more dubious elements of society, to be euphemistic. Ojang had, as a boy, done yard work for expatriates in Gaborone, and then moved on to church robberies, one or two of them pretty spectacular, and he was the ringleader of a band of pickpockets, shoplifters, and housebreakers, but one of his specialties was tapping public solicitation events, any occasion where cash was being publicly collected. He was a pest, a parasite. He had been caught infiltrating Rag Day activities, sending his underlings out costumed to blend in with the University of Botswana students in their academic robes running around the streets and rattling canisters of coins in the faces of the public as they collected for charity. And Ojang was suspected of working diversion schemes at open-air political rallies in various places, rallies run by the opposition party and not the governing party, it went without saying. And Boyle had used Ojang in instances where an investigative entry needed to be camouflaged as a routine house job. Ray wondered how this rather impressive-looking fellow had come to this vile calling. He had never met Ojang, who was out of Ray's bailiwick, but he was sure he had his man. Boyle was so proud of Ojang. Ray had heard him lovingly described. Yes, and Ojang had a cover name . . . Curate. Remarkable, Ray thought.

They continued in silence all the way home. At their gate, he stopped and pulled her against him. He had to bring his news out before they went inside. He felt that urgently, he didn't know why. He had been clumsy, pulling her to him. She was alarmed. He was clumsy.

So he rushed it out, all of it, the emergency, his lack of choice about going, and that he would be gone for three weeks, which she should be able to deal with, and that he was sorry about not having been able to give decent notice but that she had to realize he was in the same boat. He heard himself say both that the emergency was deadly serious and that it was essentially bullshit, not to be worried about. Too much of his own fear and dismay was coming through. Because he was clumsy.

She was saying nothing. He couldn't read her. Clumsily, because he was miserable and she was saying nothing, he brought up something entirely different.

"Love, how much did you contribute this evening, out of curiosity?"

"All I had on me, a hundred pula. I know it's a lot."

"No, that's fine."

"I felt . . . I don't know. These are people I admire. And I doubt I'll ever see them again."

"It's fine, it's fine."

"Now you have to go away."

"It's nothing. It's a situation. I'm sorry."

"God but I hate it. You know how I feel. I couldn't tag along with you, of course."

"Not possible. It's not that kind of thing."

"Yes and that's what's so frightening. I don't know what it is, what you have to do, how dangerous it is, if it is . . ."

"Forget that one. It's . . . I'll be reporting."

"This comes exactly when we don't need it. You're saying three weeks."

"About. It could be under and it could be a little over."

"It's too long."

"I know. But don't think you have to worry. I can't tell you anything about what's going on but the phrase opéra bouffe is a phrase orbiting around my mind right now."

"Nothing is resolved about my sister. And we need to resolve it, we have to."

"I know that."

"You *cannot conceive* how I hate this, Ray. Oh and yes, of course, I'll have some sort of drill to go through when people ask, some lying lying thing about where you are. You'll give me the script."

"Sorry."

"Something has to change," she said, her tone grievous.

"I know," he said.

"I mean, it *really* has to change."

"I agree," he said.

"You do? Truly, do you?"

"Yes," he said, as hard as he could. She wanted everything to be different and she was probably right and that was what was needed, or something close to it. He was planless. He was planless. She wanted him out of the agency. He understood it. But was that going to be the necessary and also a sufficient condition for going on together?

"I want to believe this."

"Do believe it."

"Okay then, but you're going. So what should I do? I have to think. I have to do something . . ."

She hated being alone, generically. He knew that and was sorry.

"I know what," she said.

Good, she had thought of something. Why was he afraid?

"You know what I could do? This just occurs to me. I could do an intensive with Davis. I could use your absence for that."

"Do an intensive. What is an intensive?" He thought he knew.

"It's a residential period you spend with Davis. It's the equivalent of the immersion method in language learning. You get everything . . . diet, body work, counseling, healthy cooking, and you detoxify . . ."

She said more, promotionally. It was difficult to listen. He was barely hearing her. He was hearing as through a wall, poorly, which was a funny line of hers from better days. What he did understand clearly was that intensives were sleepaway propositions. And that Morel offered intensives so infrequently that this had to be looked at as a rare opportunity. And that indeed she did need to detoxify, everybody did, she did even though he was right that she was in basic good health. She was overselling, but that was natural. She wanted to do it. She was nervous, presenting this as just another good idea. He could tell.

"So you sleep over the whole time." He hadn't intended to make her say so again, but there it was, he had.

"Well that's part of it, the immersion. I know I could walk home every night, we live so close by. It's possible I could arrange it with him . . ."

"Nonono. No need, my girl. It's the mystique. It's a concept. I understand it. Things work a certain way." Let her go, he thought. She wanted this. There was feeling behind it. Palpable. Whether she had wanted to do it before it had unexpectedly become possible for her to do, he didn't know, but she wanted it now. Show trust or die, he said to himself, sternly. He looked up at the African sky. She wanted to do it and he could taste it. She was his light in this world, his one light. She gave out something no one else did. The stars over southern Africa were thick and florid, a feast of stars they were neglecting to enjoy. *What ees the stars?* he thought, the line spoken by the old fart in the O'Casey play the Brits had put on, the line they had reused comically ever since. What ees the stars? The constellations were different, over Africa. It was the laggard pace of progress that made the stars in their African majesty available, and the two of them were being oblivious, she as much as he. Attention must be paid, he thought.

"You go when?" she asked.

"Day after tomorrow."

So she would do something and he would do something. He had to show trust in her, be absolute in that. So she would do something and he would do something and what he would do might not be the terror of the earth but it would be *something*. She would see.

"On we go," he said.

In the Cup

24. *Kerekang the Incendiary*

Ray had been feeling like an idiot more or less continuously for the last six days. They were long past the easy part of the excursion, the reasonably civilized stopovers in Kanye, then Kang, then Ghanzi. They were well north now, deep into the sandveld, the tarred road two days behind them. There were aspects of this journey that he ought to be enjoying, like the spectacular emptiness of the land, the sheer extremity of the desolation, the occasional glimpses of exotic wildlife, ostriches mainly, so far. But unfortunately he was an idiot. He should enjoy having a driver, enjoy being essentially a passenger, enjoy having a driver he liked. Keletso was a taciturn man but pleasant, a scrupulous driver healthily fixated on the absolute primacy of keeping the Land Cruiser moving through a terrain no sane human would want to break down in. The Land Cruiser was their cottage, their fortress. Keletso was decent company, just communicative enough, and a demon about keeping all the fluids essential to life and locomotion topped up. Ray was minutely studying Keletso's moves and routines to be certain he could take over on his own if he had to, depending on how things uncoiled, not a prospect he relished. Keletso was nothing like an idiot. They were on a lumpy stretch of gravel road, passing through a sea of high dead yellow grass. Since Ghanzi, the land had been interminably flat. Trees here were so occasional that the rare specimens possessed, for Ray, an exclamatory quality. That there were trees present at all was surprising, the poor crabbed things, thorn trees exclusively, with brittle-looking black-green crowns. It was hot, but this wasn't the worst time for travel in the western Kalahari. Winter was ending. It was mid-September. The night frosts were over with.

He had to stop feeling like an idiot. It was serious. So he would *one last time* go back through the steps on the path that had led him to this non-sense. It had gone like this. *One*. One, he had sent Pony to tape Morel. Two, Pony had abandoned the assignment almost immediately after he had attached himself, become a follower, or so it had seemed, of Samuel Kerekang during Kerekang's brief period of participation in Morel's educational soirees or whatever it was they should be called. Ray had received exactly two tapes and then nothing. Pony's conversion, to dignify it with the term, had been unanticipated. In fact it had been unanticipatable. So right there any responsibility Ray might be adjudged to have . . . thinned, truly, to the breaking point. Except for his having commissioned Pony in the first place, of course. Sending in a live asset had been rational, granted that he had been in an irrational state himself over Morel. He had been in a frenzy to find out all he could about him, because of what was happening with Iris. When he thought of her, here where he was, he couldn't stand it. It was like hearing a supreme piece of music for the first time, as a child . . . he couldn't have been more than four or five . . . and he even knew which piece it was, *Pavane for a Dead Princess*, listening to that for the first time and trying to draw the melody in more richly, get more of it into his ears, willing it to come through his skin, even, his mother staring at him from the record player. Ray had never reported anything to Boyle about the tapes he'd received from Pony. He had told Boyle only that he was still searching for a suitable asset for use in connection with Kerekang, for which he thanked God. He had been able to be astonished over developments, with Boyle, and get away with it. So. Pony had become an apparent convert to Kerekang's silly homestead populism.

Then what? He couldn't bear to think about Iris. He had to not lose the thread.

So then Kerekang had decamped, pulled up stakes, gone to the wilderness, gone to the people, gone north, taking a dozen or so followers with him, young people from the university, Pony included. Kerekang had left Gaborone because he was being blocked and messed with by the government, denied employment, messed with in a number of ways Ray could imagine. But that hadn't been Ray's doing. He had liked Kerekang, and had tried to protect him, argue for him, as much as he could, anyway. It was possible Boyle had concluded that he was being stalled by Ray and that Boyle had gone around him to give a little extra push to the government's anti-Kerekang tricks and games.

So *three*, then, was Kerekang turning his face away from the capital and retreating to a piece of land allocated under some tribal arrangement to one of his followers, the deal being to establish a cooperative of some kind and use it as a base, that is, build strength in the countryside and work back to the towns instead of vice versa. Kerekang had been laying the foundations of the colony for over a year, unbeknownst to anybody in government, apparently.

Keletso touched Ray's wristwatch. It was three-thirty, which meant they were going to pull over for tea. Wherever they were, Keletso took the civil service tea breaks he was entitled to at ten-thirty in the morning and three-thirty in the afternoon, without fail.

As communes go, Ichokela had been standard, not only in its structure but in the brevity of its heyday, that is, a couple of months of florescence and then disaster. There was some comfort for Ray in the idea that Kerekang had been preparing the commune for a while, popping in and out to check on the progress of things, because that meant he hadn't been suddenly driven to creating it as a desperate recourse by anything the agency might have been part of. That was probably an idiotic thought. But then he was a complete idiot. Ichokela had been the standard commune mixture, meaning simple living, early to bed, turning over your capital when you joined, a common purse and honor-system access to it. The day had been divided in three parts, one-third for collective labor like construction or gardening or farmwork, one-third for study and relaxation, and one-third for extension work, pestering the local peasantry with good ideas. From all he could gather, it had been a straightforward sort of experiment, lacking any demeaning psychological nastinesses like self-criticism sessions. They had published a bilingual paper, *Kepu/The Mattock*. He had copies.

Kerekang's commune had been more a training center than anything else. It wasn't clear how long participants were supposed to stay there, but it was clear that Ichokela wasn't meant to be a permanent residence for any of them. Things had been thought through. There had been a mechanism for getting at least part of your capital back if you decided to quit the movement. Kerekang had been expected to be in and out, employing Ichokela as a base, a site for demonstrating his courtyard horticulture concept and promoting a miniature sorghum mill run by pedal power, one of various inventions of his. The commune had been established on Tawana land near Toromole, a tiny village between Etsha and Sepopa out in the savanna west of the Okavango swamp, about seventy-five kilometers south of the Caprivi Strip. What else was there? One point of interest, for him anyway, was the role poetry played in Kerekang's agitprop exertions. *The Mattock* was busy with snippets of Victorian social poetry, doggerel most of it, bilingually presented, and when the reading circles Kerekang was hectoring the locals to join met in the kgotlas, a centerpiece of the proceedings had been poetry-shouting performances by a commune troupe, the Songsters, Dimoopedi. Kerekang's general taste in nomenclature was on the poetic side, too. The name of the commune, the full name, Ichokela Bokhutlon, translated as Endure to the End. Isa, the verb meaning to make happen, was what Kerekang had decided to call his movement. It meant something about Ray that never in his life had he felt a twinge of attraction to the idea of submerging himself in the romance of any sort of communal existence. No doubt it was his rigidity that was behind that, his lack of imagination, some defect. He was an idiot, after all. Keletso was slowing. They were about to stop. There were many stops, with Keletso, many for setting the hubs for four-wheel drive, which was the drill whenever the road ahead even hinted at difficulty, many stops for tire-pressure checks, for piss breaks, and for meals, which were separate from the tea breaks. Twice Keletso had stopped in order to suck grass seeds out of the radiator grille with a drinking straw, a preventive against the engine overheating and seizing up. Keletso could be anywhere between thirty-five and forty-five. Ray felt inferior to this spare, angular, steady man whose personal hygiene practices put him to shame, his scrupulous toothbrushing in particular.

He had misread Pony, deeply. On that he stood convicted. And four, step four, had been Pony discovering that he was not made for the simple life, if he ever had been, and deciding to finance his future after his departure from Endure to the End by an act of embezzlement. He had taken not only the petty cash but another large sum lying around that had been destined for purchases of agricultural equipment and building materials, a loan. Kerekang had torn up the vicinity looking for Pony, without luck, because Pony had taken the money for the all-consuming central purpose of life in Botswana, cattle acquisition, and split to the opposite side of the country and in fact beyond, to his own cattle post at Pandamatenga, half of which overlapped into Zimbabwe, where he was unreachable. Pony was in fact Ndebele. He had misrepresented himself at St. James's. A crash audit of the bursar's office was in progress. The crime had crystallized Kerekang's hatred of the national passion for cattle. He saw the drive to convert money into flesh in the form of cattle as violently deformative and out of control in Botswana, a position he had belabored in all his publications but with special intensity in his latest pamphlet, *The White Ants*, which Ray, after realizing Kerekang was its author, had read closely. If you had money, in Botswana, you turned it into cattle and cattle would multiply your money biologically, through sheer reproduction, and you could just watch it happen and watch your prestige grow at the same time. It was the herder mentality so utterly opposed to the townsman's idea that you took money and put it out at interest or bought a machine to make products to sell. Of course the townsman ideology was in need of correction too, according to Kerekang, but it was not flatly insane, socially and otherwise, like cattlemania, where the decision to sink everything into beasts ran crashing against the facts of recurrent drought, disease, and the ecological unsuitability of most of the land area of Botswana for cattle raising.

So Kerekang had briefly turned Ichokela into a posse to hunt Pony down, and that had failed and the commune had failed. Earlier, Kerekang struck out at the passion for cattle through attacks on two ranches near Toromole, fenced ranches with titles widely considered bogus, owned by big men, absentees.

It was conceivable that Kerekang had meant his actions to be symbolic or at worst cautionary, gesticulations against the continuing spread of illegal commercial ranches in his area, where they had been late to arrive. His raids had involved some property destruction, but nothing major, and no injury to anyone. But a fire had been lit. There was tinder everywhere. It had been the wrong act at the right time. Mimic attacks, arson attacks, had occurred, radiating outward from Toromole. Three boreholes had been dynamited.

The ground was layered with the receptive aggrieved, in fact. Bushmen being paid for their labor with salt and tobacco, smallholders finding traditionally common waterpoints being closed to them, incorporated into the commercial spreads.

They had stopped, in full sun as usual, up on the shoulder of the road, tilting moderately. Next Keletso would get out his parasol.

The fifth step had been Boyle going into a raging panic at the first reports of disturbances in the northeast and immediately taking Toromole as Kerekang's Yenan and the springing of arson attacks as the beginning of an unstoppable jacquerie, expecting to see the safari camps in flames next, whites driven out, Armageddon, the governing party overthrown and Botswana propelled into an Anschluss with South Africa by radical forces, a South Africa by then in the hands of the African National Congress, itself in the hands of the South African Communist Party, and seeing Mugabe in Zimbabwe joining the new union, and presto, a new race-based world communism emerging with its Vatican in Johannnes-burg and gold, diamonds, and palladium piling up in its treasury—and all of it getting started on Boyle's watch, the end of the world on his watch.

Step five had led instantly to step six, this excursion.

Ray had been sent out because Boyle had needed above all to be seen as acting, machinating, furiously taking steps. He wondered how many other contract officers, stringers, assets of all types and kinds, had been hurled into notional missions like the one he was on. Step six was this, the present, himself in the lap of nowhere, bearing a false identity as a school sites assessor, which was an invented job description that would presum-ably justify his poking around anywhere in the bush. His letter of autho-rization, jointly signed by the Ministries of Education and of Local Government and Lands, commanded all district council and school staff to accord him "all support in his endeavors to examine all about every place as to school building and placing of schools at some time."

Getting him launched had been a miracle of speedy improvisation . . . the requisitioning and equipping of the Land Cruiser, arranging tempo-rary duty for Keletso, concocting the stupid code terminology he was supposed to use when he reported back through the radiophone links he was expected to locate and get access to through a district council or police facilities. And his task was, well, *merely* to find out what was behind everything, really behind everything, and right away. He felt leaden. He felt like a projectile aimed at nothing. And Boyle had insisted on issuing him a stupid damned Smith & Wesson .38 caliber revolver and two boxes of bullets, no matter what he'd said. Nothing had been thought through, but here he was. It didn't matter. Kerekang was doomed . . . he had per-formed in the flesh the act that the local wretched of the earth had until then only allowed themselves to imagine. That was the way things came apart. Kindness was on the cross, where they were going. And the heavi-est and stupidest injunction he was carrying was, *whatever he did*, to help this eruption disappear without becoming public knowledge, no less.

There were some historical models for making that happen, making insurgencies disappear silently and tracelessly, that he knew of. Guerrero in the seventies was a case in point, and there had been two lesser cases in Nigeria. So far nothing was showing in the press or on Radio Botswana about the unrest in the northeast. The feat to be accomplished was stop-ping the trouble and erasing the news about it at the same time.

Certain measures were already being taken. The army and the police were being deployed very delicately, if at all. In fact they were probably being pulled back all through the Nokaneng-Mohembo corridor, where he and Keletso were bound, because soldiers talked. So did police. Something subtler might be on order, obscure forces, if it got bad. These would be identified as "bandits," and they would strike and it would be hellmouth and they would be gone in the morning and it would all end in mystery and confusion and forgetting. Cupping, it was called.

The bandits would be mercenaries from Namibia. It was something the authorities knew very well how to arrange, in extreme circumstances. The authorities, the hired security people, were brilliant. He felt like a fool, but of course he did because he was an idiot. He was still an idiot. He had never in his career been anywhere near a cupping exercise. Cupping had nothing to do with him. Tonight the moon would arise and drag into erect states millions of penises worldwide, but that was idiotic because it was simply the shadow line coming over mankind night after night that did it, darkness, not the moon itself, unless it was the stars, but *what ees the stars?* The stars burn, he thought. The Bushmen thought the stars were the campfires of the dead.

They always had to stop in the open because Keletso was afraid of the trees, such as they were. For shade, Keletso had sawed the handle off a large parasol and jammed a long metal rod, sharpened at both ends, into the hollow shank. The resulting item, stabbed into the sand, was impossibly top-heavy when the canopy was opened up and had to be firmly held on to by someone to keep it from keeling over. But it served. They took turns keeping it upright. The parasol fabric was bright pink. They took their refreshment while they sat on camp stools. Keletso was in charge. Tea was sun tea. Every morning Keletso sealed up four Joko tea bags in a jar of water, which he then secured under the ropes binding the load in the truckbed, on top, where it would be exposed to the sun. A square of canvas, with a hole at its center for the umbrella support, was always laid down to sit on. The formality of it was bemusing. It was domestic. He had no attitude about it. It was fine. The trees were objects of fear because the soil in their shade was often infested with populations of a large, flat, violently aggressive tick. Tampans, they were called, and when any warmblooded animal trod the soil under the trees the vibrations would alert the tampans and then the effluvium of the beast would electrify them and they would shoot up out of the ground and fasten themselves on the hapless intruder, sucking viciously. Their modus operandi was to extract as much blood as they could from the animal before it could shuffle back into the sun, where the temperature was inimical to the ticks and they would have to drop off and stagger back to their cool underground burrows. Typically they attacked in volleys, in the hundreds at a time. They could leap. Supposedly they could get so much blood in their first volley that the animal would faint. It was possible. This was Africa. He thought, O Africa, beware the sun, beware the shade . . . Be careful.

In any case, that was the whole story. He was through with himself. He was definitely through with himself. The thing now was to proceed, do no harm, and get back home in one piece to face the bitter music playing there, sinfonia domestica playing just for him. It was urgent to proceed *without thinking about Iris.* He could do it. He ought to be able to treat this business as a vacation, given that people came from all over the world, paying thousands of dollars to be up in this wilderness, although the thousands were paid for vacations well to his right, in the Okavango swamp, the delta, the only succulent part of Botswana, not for this dryness stretching without relief all the way to the Atlantic. Ahead of him was a beheaded river, which is what the delta truly was, and to his left, if you went far enough, was the Skeleton Coast, with its decor of shipwrecks. It was possible to make out the swamp, if you used binoculars and got on top of the Land Cruiser's cab, as a green line to the east. That was where the giraffes et cetera were.

He was through with himself, and with the fantasy conviction that if he could just find Kerekang and reintroduce himself and speak man to man he could talk him out of what he was doing, on some basis or other, on past acquaintance and their love of poetry and on an extensive apology about Pony, his part in that, something like Stanley and Livingstone. That kind of fantasy could go away now. Life is what? he thought. In all his years in Africa Livingstone had converted exactly one African to Christianity, one.

But he was through with himself. It was pointless to envy people like Keletso their simpler existences and pointless to go to the ultimate question of whether the world would be better off, net, once the main effort of your life had been added up, and especially pointless in his case because the main effort of his life had been to collaborate with others in preventing certain events from transpiring, so that his work product consisted of a null set, a sequence of zeros, unevents, very difficult to judge to say the least. His life was like the medals the agency gave its heroes and put into a vault and told nobody outside the agency about. Of course the true main effort of his adult life was and always had been to have Iris's love, which sounded selfish put in that way, selfishly concentrating on his well-being, in essence, and not hers. But this subject was outside the realm of things he could deal with now, in the desert. And then there was poetry, Milton, where he had done *something* . . . a little something. But that was enough about him. He was through.

But speaking of poetry, he was having the odd feeling that poetry was trying to reassure him, poetry acting as a kind of fraternal entity. *I came na here to view your works in hopes to be more wise/But being that I'm gang to hell it shall be na surprise*, Burns of course, had come to him while he was scanning a particularly bleak piece of the territory. And then riding along in depression, the lines *Zeno's arrow in my heart/I float in the plunging years*, author unknown, had lightened his misery. Very little Milton was showing up, which was strange given the surroundings. Of course he could summon Milton up anytime he needed him. Even poetic fragments of his own invention were declaring themselves, like *The Stars Also Burn*, a title, obviously, appropriate for a certain type of middlebrow crap novel. *The drop that wrestles in the sea/Forgets her own locality* was from Emily Dickinson, a poet he hadn't read attentively enough, since clearly she had something to say to him. There was a lot of Dickinson manifesting. Of course her main subject matter was death, so the less said about that the better. Death was bad, but not as bad as someone else licking your wife's cunt. *Stop*, he thought. That was the kind of thing lines of poetry were leaping up to quench. Poetry, his past reading, was turning out to be a god for him. The conceit forcing itself on him was that poetry was an autonomous friendly composite, interested in capturing his predicament favorably to him, a thing like an Arcimboldo portrait, but alive and not composed of different kinds of fruit but made out of friendly sentiments and aperçus jostling for his attention, like puppies in a basket playing and jumping up eagerly. The urge to declaim accompanied particular surges of poetry, especially in moments when he was off by himself. Urinating, he had found himself saying loudly *I know that I shall meet my fate/Somewhere among the clouds above/Those that I fight I do not hate/Those that I guard I do not love*. It had felt like a retort to what, to the Kalahari, to the heat. Keletso had probably noticed something, but he would assume it was religious. Keletso said things under his breath from time to time, often it was the Lord's Prayer. For reading matter, Keletso had brought a Bible, that was all, and in fact it was the Olive Pell Bible, a version created for the use of girls in finishing schools and stripped of all the sex and violence. He had bought it at a jumble sale, for its compactness, and he kept it on his person at all times.

Ray was perforce becoming an authority on the left side of Keletso's face, but not on much else about the man. Keletso's ears were heavily wrought, the upper rims so thick they made the ear tips bend faintly downward. He needed to not exaggerate this tireless man's qualities to a religious level. Not only was he tireless but he had the ability to fall asleep within seconds of lying down in unlikely positions, the unlikeliest, an ability no doubt attributable to the soporific effects of a spotless conscience. But of course that was an assumption. What he could say was that he was developing cracks in the corners of his mouth and Keletso wasn't. It was stress, was all. Now it was time to get out and have tea. There were four minuscule bananas left, from the supply they had picked up back in Ghanzi. He wanted Keletso to have them all. He wasn't hungry.

He stood next to their vehicle, actively appreciating it, patting it, honoring an impulse that kept renewing itself. It was supplicatory, partly. They needed good luck with their machine, their steed, their ship of the desert. The Japanese Land Cruiser was displacing the British Land Rover everywhere in Africa. It was a rout. The Land Cruiser was a superior machine, an oversized pickup truck with a shortened but still adequate open bed and a tall, roomy four-door cab that elevated its occupants high above the road, a crucial advantage in negotiating dangerous terrain. Land Rovers were earth-colored, uniformly. Their Land Cruiser was electric blue, very jolly. The back seat in the cab was narrower than the front seat, but it was still wide enough for sleeping on. They had been reduced to sleeping in the Land Cruiser a couple of times, and there would be more of that. They had agreed to take turns on the back seat. The ingenious Keletso had come up with a way to shroud the propped-open doors of the cab with mosquito netting, which allowed the sleeper to lie full length from time to time, feet extended out into the darkness. But generally they kept the doors closed, out of general fear, even though the received wisdom was that all animals shied away from motor vehicles. He needed to have the door open more frequently than Keletso. They had mosquito screens that fit into the space left by half-open windows and they used them faithfully at night, vigorous ventilating being the necessity it was for lives being lived at such close quarters. Keletso never needed to get up at night. Ray was discovering that his occasional needs in that direction had entirely evaporated, no doubt in response to the fear of being eaten alive and the like.

They should be all right. They had everything they could conceivably need, it seemed to him. In fact, there was too much. Keletso knew where everything was in the swollen load in back, under the tarps that covered it. Ray was developing his own mental map, against the day he sent Keletso home. They had water in a hundred-gallon drum, and paraffin, petrol, and motor oil in smaller drums. They had extra tires, an extra battery, various other automotive spares he needed to catalog for himself one more time, a mechanic's tool kit, a foot pump, a winch, flares, mats for getting out of sand traps. They had hatchets, axes and extra ax handles, machetes, shovels, trenching spades, torches, lanterns. Bolted to the rear base of the cab was the general tool chest. It had a false bottom, beneath which his revolver and ammunition were kept, along with packets of rands and pula, about a thousand dollars' worth in each currency. The false bottom was a chore to free and raise. It had to be pried out in a particular way. There had been a plan to devise access to the secret space through a slot behind the backrest in the rear seat, but there had been no time to get that done. They were hugely overequipped for camping. They had a tent, bolts of mosquito netting, multiple drop cloths, folding camp furniture, sleeping bags and blankets, both. They had metal cookware, a reflector oven and a Coleman stove, miscellaneous grills, enough plates and tableware for a festivity. They had a washtub and smaller basins, laundry powder, a steel mirror, a full crate of toilet paper. They had a portable shower unit, a black rubber bladder to be filled with water and fixed to something high up and out in the sun. The instructions that came with it advised that before releasing the sun-heated water the potential bather should lather up and be prepared to speedily rinse off. Like the reflector oven, the shower unit remained unused. The idea of standing naked in the Kalahari was something neither he nor Keletso was ready to embrace, at least not yet. The massive food locker contained, in addition to sensible goods like canned food and dry cereals, a silly array of condiments. There were three kinds of chutney. There was an aluminum cooler which would be useless unless they stumbled over an iceberg in the Kalahari. They had four down pillows. There were three air mattresses and a patching kit that went with them. They had both mosquito coils and citronella candles. They had spools of nylon rope, soft wire, and twine. The first aid chest was the size of a camp trunk and they had it just inside the tailgate where they could get at it instantly. Its contents were frighteningly comprehensive. Their personal gear, in two large duffel bags for Ray, a single suitcase for Keletso, was stowed on the floor in the back seat. There was a sewing basket. Everything was new. The tarps had a powerful, fresh, resinous odor. America, you are rich, he thought.

They were inching north. They were tacking. They were tacking deeper toward the west than toward the east. They were vamping. They were finding veterinary roads, old trek routes, taking anything leading off the main north-south road and following it until they decided not to follow it anymore. Then they would camp. Or they might return to the main road, where at least they had the comfort of seeing, although at rarer intervals the farther north they got, passing trucks with people in them. Now Ray was fighting the lunatic conviction that he would know the moment when his betrayal definitely occurred, that there would be a sign, that he would feel something. It was possible that this was a useful lunatic conviction, because there had been no sign so far, which meant that nothing had happened. It meant she was resisting and he could be happy. What the sign would be, he had no idea.

He had had about enough for today. Keletso hated to drive at night, so it made sense to turn around now while they had a chance of making it back to Route 14 in daylight. They would have to sleep in the vehicle again, unless the attraction of some halfway normal accommodation in Sehithlwa, the next settlement up Route 14, would be enough to motivate him to drive at night, against all his better judgment. Ray realized he had no idea what he meant by halfway normal accommodation. Sehithlwa was a Baherero village. One thing that that meant was that everybody went to bed early. No one would be up when they got there. So it was likeliest that they would get back to Route 14 and just pull off and eat and sleep. Of course the sign that Iris had betrayed him was likelier to come at night than during the day, which meant it might come in the form of a dream, a nightmare. More betrayals took place at night, of course, that was obvious. He didn't think he'd had any particularly striking dreams since leaving Gaborone. That was good.

Whatever Keletso thought of Ray's site-assessment performances, he was keeping it to himself. He was a good soldier. Ray was putting less and less effort into his performances, his imposture. He would signal for a stop, descend, make sure his pants cuffs were jammed solidly into his boot tops, spray his lower self with insect repellent, pull the brim of his hat down all around, and set off with his binoculars and clipboard for some spot in the range of one hundred yards from the vehicle. They were within the baobab zone now and he had been selecting locations near particular specimens to carry out his site-assessment charades on. The species had come to fascinate him. They looked untenable, massive gray columns tapering upward and splitting and finishing at the apex in a frenzy of spindly limbs and branches bearing derisory foliage. He hadn't yet observed anything resembling a grove of baobabs. They seemed to thrive in isolation, although perdure would be a better term for what they did. Birds seemed to avoid them for nesting purposes, if his limited familiarity with the tree could support such a conclusion. The hard, smooth bark of the baobab invited stroking. They inspired affection, of a certain sort. Whatever they were, they were perfect.

Ray signaled Keletso to stop. He saw a baobab he liked. He and Keletso had evolved a considerable repertoire of hand signals that saved them a lot of surplus talk. In lower gears, the engine made enough noise to render conversation effortful. And he and Keletso shared a preference for silent travel anyway. Ray amplified his hand signal to indicate that Keletso should turn the vehicle around for the return leg, while Ray was doing his assessing. Turning could require some art, depending on road conditions. They had been proceeding in what was in essence a broad, shallow ditch, sticking to the ruts, spoors as they were called, pressed into the soft sand by whoever had preceded them. There was a lay-by, or something like one, just ahead, where a turn could be managed. They had been wrong in choosing the road they had, misled by the fact that the first few kilometers had been freshly groomed, in the usual way, by a government truck dragging a monster bouquet of thornbushes along the surface. So it had seemed promising. But the grooming task had been abandoned. The thornbush bouquet had been jettisoned and pushed up on the shoulder. The government truck curved off straight into the veld, possibly in pursuit of opportunities to do some poaching. Keletso had detected duikers moving through this neighborhood, in the distance, twice.

Ray leaned against the baobab and watched Keletso delicately maneuvering the Land Cruiser for the return journey. How long these monumental vegetables lived was something he should be able to find out. They looked ancient. He wouldn't mind being buried under one of them, being drawn up molecule by molecule into the ridiculousness and permanence they represented, if they were, in fact, longlived, like sequoias. He loved these goddamned things. They were like monuments, but slightly gesticulating monuments, when the breeze rattled their silly branches. He wasn't being mordant. Everybody had to be buried someplace. He assumed he was going to be cremated when he died, but ashes had to go someplace too, and under a baobab would be fine with him. Molecules weren't the smallest particles, though, nor were, what, electrons. All he could think of were monads, which came from Leibnitz and philosophy and not physics. He thought, Au fond we are monads, with gonads. He moved around to the far side of the baobab, where he was out of Keletso's sight line.

The realization that you, yourself, are going to die, in fact, declares itself in funny ways, he thought. He could give a new example. Iris, in assembling the mountain of reading matter she wanted him to have, had included three months' worth of unread *Times Literary Supplements*. And as he was reading through them, in the desert, he had noticed that his reflexive impulse to tear out and save advertisements for books he might want to read at some point was gone. A year or so back he had given up clipping titles from the Books Received listings of the *TLS*, which he could see had been precursory to this. Something was letting him know that there was enough on his forward reading list to occupy him for the rest of this life. In fact, there had been a longer progression. He had been serious about bibliography, cutting out ads neatly and gluing them to index cards color-coded for urgency. Then he had devolved to tearing ads out. And so on down. And now he had enough in his stuffed folders, enough. He had been serious. He had thought of literature and Milton in particular as subjects he would conquer like Shackleton or whoever it was had gotten to the Pole first, but not Shackleton, Peary or Amundsen, who? Definitely not Shackleton, he thought, shivering. He was getting old. He thought, In my time machine I would probably, before I went to Milton's deathbed, go to Shackleton and the other one, Scott, and say Don't go, leave the wastelands of the world and stay home . . . Grow old and perish at home in the arms of your wife . . . Goodbye and good luck.

It was time to write on his site-assessment form. It was something he had to do, had to be seen doing. He had put down a few scribbles already, during his approach to the baobab, for Keletso's benefit. But, out of Keletso's view, he would do something new. It had started as a joke but it had turned into something a little interesting. Instead of jotting down fake notes and observations, he had tried relaxing and closing his eyes and going blank and letting himself write in a dissociated state, or as much of one as he could attain. It was automatic writing, a weak variant. It was something to do. So far mostly he had gotten poetic flotsam, weird doggerel, grandiose self-instruction, pure nonsense, and sequences written so illegibly it was impossible to tell what was meant. He slid down to a squatting position and set the clipboard on the sand in front of him. Another nice thing about baobabs was that tampan ticks avoided them, the shade cast by the baobabs being so negligible. He got his Bic out. He tried. He had waited too long to get started. This wouldn't work if he felt pressed. But he tried. He hummed to distract himself. He wrote a little. He hummed more vigorously, the *Ode to Joy*, always his first choice when he needed a tune to block something out, distract him. He was trying. It was no good. He couldn't let go. He looked at what he'd written.

o hell o hell you look so well I'd like to touch
your Annabel
o brother snake I am awake
Ah me and my I like to die he hit my eye go home
ye fly
Thy alabaster cities gleam from
she to shining she

This was his worst effort. Thy should be thine. The glints from the dim past were boring. As a child he had thought someone saying *He hit my fist with his eye* was funny. He had known what he was writing as he was writing. The Bic was wrong. With the Bic he had to bear down too much. A pencil required less pressure and the results had been better, although still stupid. He got up to go.

Lately his appetite was problematic. His clothes were fitting more loosely. Keletso didn't like it and was being maternal. Keletso wanted him to eat what he had just been handed. He wasn't sure what it was. It was a mass. He probed it and concluded that it was a concoction of two kinds of dried fruit, apricot and pear, boiled soft. He was supposed to eat it with some of the warm box milk. He couldn't.

Keletso was eating his own portion demonstratively. Ray was touched. It was possible that he could eat some, a little. They sat in the solid heat.

It was definite that government presence in the region was withdrawing, ceasing to be, where it had existed at all, in widely separated nodes, hamlets strung along the main north-south route. They were finding government offices closed, with no explanations for the closures posted. Government vehicle traffic was down to almost nothing. They were still seeing the occasional Wildlife officer. The last one they had seen had told them that the two fishing camps between Sepopa and the Caprivi Strip, on the western edge of the Okavango, had been closed, mysteriously.

Keletso was waving a shaker of cinnamon at him. He accepted it. Keletso wanted him to sprinkle cinnamon on his compote.

It was Ray's turn to hold the umbrella support, but Keletso was refusing to relinquish it to him and at the same time making head motions indicating that it was more important for Ray to concentrate on eating. So he ate.

Keletso said, "Rra, someway you must phone up your wife, isn't it?"

Ah, Ray thought. This was bold of Keletso. He was picking up that their radiophone contacts with Gaborone had stopped, just about. Clearly it worried him. They had gone four days without being able to find a link. Keletso was beginning to appreciate the strangeness of the zone they were in. So far Keletso hadn't asked for any messages to be passed along when they had managed to make calls. He mailed something once. He was a bachelor.

Ray said, "You're not married, yourself, rra, you told me."

"Not as yet."

"So, still, do you have any need to send word to anyone, when we phone next? Do you, rra?"

"Yah, well, no."

"I apologize for not asking."

"It is fine because in any case we must be returning back soon."

Ray nodded vaguely. Keletso wanted to be reassured that this was going to end soon. Ray couldn't help him. He didn't know when it would end. He was waiting for a sign. But it was definitely time to get back, from any standpoint. He had had a nocturnal emission, for one thing. He thought, No it's nomads with gonads, what we are.

Keletso said, "Rra, I must find a wife yet. I am searching even now." He swept his hand around broadly.

The man was in his forties and seeking his true love. Ray hoped he found her soon and that no one would take her away once he had. Constant Pain would be a good title for something.

"Because, rra, you can see, else we cannot be at ease. So I must seek. She can be hereabout. It is no matata if she can be from the bush and be pleasing to me, I can take her. You see, a wife is like some rose flower. And as well the Bible commands us to marry. So we must search about."

Ray made a show of looking around, and they laughed together.

"Have you some children, then?" Keletso asked.

"No, none. We were unable to."

"Ah, shame."

"Yes."

"Rra, if you can pray, God can aid you. Even as you are older than some fathers. If you pray you can go back and see your wife and she can say, Ehe I have fallen pregnant whilst you were off."

"That would be truly amazing."

"It can only be if you pray."

"I understand you."

"I can tell you from the Bible that many an old man, monna mogolo, is made to be a father, by God, nonetheless."

"Yes," Ray said. He had eaten everything.

Nothing prepares you for life as a human, Ray thought, and when

Keletso looked questioningly at him he knew he had uttered his thought-gem aloud, which was not good and was a thing that was happening too much in the last day or so. He was declaring his vacuity. With his thought-gems he was like the drunk at the last embassy party who had taken him aside to say, portentously, Life is sincere.

"Sorry," Ray said.

He needed to watch it. He was shooting his mind off. Yesterday it had been necessary to attempt an explanation for exclaiming *It's Edward Young, for Christ's sake*. In his head he had been unaccountably attributing the line *O my coevals* to Milton and it had been a relief to suddenly have it right again. At times Keletso was seeming a touch afraid of him. He couldn't have that.

The day was the mixture as before, cruelly bright and hot. Earlier Keletso had pointed out two or three rogue thunderheads off to the northeast, but now the sky was unembellished. They were six hours west of Nokaneng, and that was as far west as he wanted to be. Dust, blowing, was an increasing problem, away from the delta. It would look better if they could return eastward without retracing their route, to enable him to stare at fresh territory in accordance with his supposed mission, so he had decided that they should leave the track they had been following and transit six kilometers of open bush with the aim of reaching a grade four veterinary road indicated on their sector map. So far the map had been reasonably reliable. The area to be crossed was hardpan, very level, treeless for the most part. They should be fine. So far, aside from having to circumnavigate a single long low dune, they were proceeding uneventfully.

Ray tried to doze, succeeding fitfully for a while until a change in the light registered through the blankness he was cultivating. The air was gray and seething. They had entered a phenomenon, a storm of flies, not just a cloud of them following the vehicle but a dense swarm extending out indefinitely on all sides. It was appalling, which was the right word, since it was a pall of flies, in fact. Iris liked the Exaltation of Larks game and was good at it. A pall of funeral directors would be a candidate for the game and so would a pox of whores or rash of whores or rash of dermatologists, but what constructs that she had come up with could he remember? He remembered some of his, a skeleton crew of coroners, a surplus of misers, a dearth of nonentities, but he didn't want his, he wanted hers. He wanted *her*. She was fun, his wife.

Keletso was being stalwart but it was clear he was unnerved. He was sweating and murmuring. The explanation for the flies had to be something arising from rainfall, sudden heavy rainfall. The locality they were in had received a drenching. They had passed abruptly from furnace to steambath conditions. The windows were fogging. One of Keletso's thunderheads had obviously delivered, and the sudden moisture had either drawn or hatched, if that was possible, this abomination. He had never read about it, but there had to be a connection.

There seemed to be two kinds of flies involved in the spectacle, big clumsy ones interested in banging against the vehicle, and smaller and faster glittering ones not. To the right was a long object on the ground not immediately recognizable as the carcass it must be because it was clad in a seamless, glinting, writhing coat of flies. This would not be the place to die.

He was sorry for Iris. He had gotten her when she was young. In retrospect, that was a problem. Her premarital sexual experience had been so paltry it was unfair. It was pathetic. He was what there was of her sexual universe, with, as he recalled, two ancient exceptions, both unsatisfactory. How her condition could be what, undone, reversed, at this stage of the game without terrible pain he had no idea, but she had a right and he recognized it and he loved her. He needed to keep in mind her mother, how dreamily repressive her benighted mother had been when it came to sex. After all, Iris had been thirteen years old before she realized it was permissible to actively wash her genitals as opposed to gazing up at the ceiling and whistling something merry while soapy water passively traversed them in the shower. She had made the discovery during a summertime visit to the country place of one of her girlfriends whom she had observed routinely giving herself a good scrub between the legs, case closed. It was licit. But when he said she had a right he meant that she did and she didn't at the same time, because there was a preexisting deal of course, their marriage, all his love, their love, years of it, her vows and his, of course. All he knew was that he had to keep her. And if he could possibly construe Morel as someone for her to be into and out of, and then back to him and into his arms wiser and with a better sample of the real world of unsleeping penises and a notch on her garter belt that would make her feel better, then . . . then good luck with construing, since it looked like he was going to be unable to expel her doctor from his personal universe by the main scenario he had come up with. He thought, Help me, but it would say something if she came back to me post facto, not that I can bear to think about it. He was full of pain again. If it would help her after the fact, he could concoct a lie about fucking someone he hadn't, but that would require conviction, details, be impossible. Don't ask me to, he thought. He couldn't. Keletso was mumbling that it had been a mistake to leave a gazetted road. Ray was in no position to disagree. He would try not to propose doing it in the future. Keletso had turned the windscreen wipers on, the flies were so thick.

Were events like this extraordinary to the local population or were they the equivalent of leaf storms in September in Massachusetts? It felt to him like a what, a genuine abomination, Miltonic, an epiphany or revelation about some underlying corruption pressing up, the earth rotting from the heart outward and breaking the surface and the flies pouncing, summoned from everywhere, some conceit like that, some nonsense like that. It was getting darker, amazingly. Iris had to be free. He thought, If only you could pluck certain thoughts out of your head like thorns, via machine, if there could be a device for that like the blackhead extractors that used to be advertised in comic books, bastard things. He had owned one and it had produced little bloody wounds and scabs on his face, essentially. Why had he persisted with it for so long, refusing to credit that the thing was worthless and having to explain his face downstairs in the morning, his purchase?

He thought he was detecting a scorched smell in the air. It reminded him of something from his past, and he knew what it was. The dead past is forever, he thought. But he knew what it was, it connected to his brother's asthma, when he had been delegated to watch a pot boil containing water and chopped-up grapefruit rinds stewing to make a home remedy for Rex, a thick liquor. His family had loved home remedies as opposed to quick going to the doctor and paying something, no, the thing was to go endlessly with home remedies and time would pass and all would be well for free. And he had gone off to read while he was waiting, one of the Fu Manchu books, and he had gotten engrossed in it and the elixir had boiled down to a foul gum and then scorched, sending a stench into the bedroom, where his mother sat incessantly stroking his brother's forehead while he coughed histrionically, giving her a fit. It's amazing what stays with you from childhood, not to mention what doesn't, he thought. Recently he had been embarrassed to have to admit to Iris that he had forgotten what his first words were, or word. He must have known at one point. But with age the fabric of the mind started to develop blank spots here and there, like cigarette burns, as it had been described to him once upon a time. His mother might remember what his first word had been, or she might not.

It was unbelievably dark.

Ray thought, She is my light, my nightlight, my pilot light, and she is out, going out, out and about.

Keletso was looking at him. Obviously he had done it again.

"Nothing," Ray said.

Sudden commotion from the front seat brought Ray sharply awake. The flies were behind them. It was sunrise, still dim, and Keletso seemed to be half out of the cab flailing one leg violently against the side of the vehicle, *why?* And he was cursing, which was unheard of, another shock. Ray bent across into the front in order to help, to do something, and grasped that Keletso was fighting a snake. In terror he climbed over the seat and lunged for the storage pocket on the right front door where there should be a machete, unless they had moved it. They had. Then it would have to be in among the miscellany of infrequently used tools and oddments under the seat. He found it. They had never used the thing and it was still tight in its canvas sheath but he had it and freed it and flourished it as he got out of the vehicle on the passenger side shouting, *"Here I am."*

He ran around to Keletso, who was spread-eagled, gripping the top of the open door with one hand and the edge of the cab roof with the other and kicking out so violently that his undershorts were slipping off. A dark green snake about as long as a boy's arm was somehow fastened to the heel of Keletso's right boot, the heel proper if he was seeing correctly, below the foot, and he was wagging the snake in the air like a pennant and groaning terrifyingly with the effort. *I brought this man here*, he thought, guilt rearing in him.

Ray was shouting at the snake, intending to be helpful and obviously failing, since Keletso, seeing him in his shorts and barefoot, was raging at him to get back into the vehicle and to stop dancing, which was what he was doing no doubt looked like. He couldn't help it. He was trying to find an opening to use the machete. He had to do something. Keletso was worried about other snakes. He had a point. Ray was being as careful as he could. What did Keletso want? What should he do?

With a cry of triumph, Keletso brought the snake down hard against the doorframe sill, where he managed to pin it with both boots. Instantly Ray was beside him with the machete, ready to strike but finding it impossible with Keletso so much in the way. Ray forced himself to seize the still-lashing tail of the snake with his left hand, stretching it down against the chassis. Crouching, he gained the scope for a clean maximum blow. Keletso's legs were vibrating. His undershorts had fallen to his ankles. The snake's skin was dry. The beast was powerful. Ray hacked at the snake with all his strength and it came apart. Bright, sweet-smelling blood spat into his face from the wound. He had gotten a third of the snake, it looked like. He had no idea what the top part of the snake could still do, the head. Now he knew why Keletso always slept with his boots on and why that was such an excellent idea.

Keletso had gotten his shoulder under the top rim of the doorframe and, braced so, was able to exert decisive force downward. Blood gouted up between his boots. It was okay.

Keletso leapt free of the vehicle. He dragged his boot along the ground and the battered ruin of a snake came away from it at last. Ray was still holding his third of the snake in his hand. It seemed to twitch, and he dropped it.

They were fine. His right hand was numb but that was nothing. Ray looked around. They had passed the night in what was a beauty spot, for the Kalahari . . . a low, level, sandy spot near a stand of magnificent, mature cloud trees. The sun was up. In the early morning you could love the sun and not hate it.

Keletso was winded. He gestured vehemently at Ray's bare feet. It was past time to dress for the day. He realized that, but he wanted to examine the snake and identify it if he could before Keletso buried the carcass, as he was evidently preparing to do.

Ray returned to the vehicle and dressed hurriedly. It occurred to him that it would be interesting to save the head and take it in for identification at the university.

For some reason Keletso had chopped the snake up further, into six pieces or so. And he had scraped a shallow trench in the sand. The snake's head was already in the trench, at one end. The wide flat head and the black underjaw meant that it was an adder of some kind. The head was damaged but would still make a curio, once it was dried. But Keletso was laying out the chunks of snake in the trench in a semblance of their original order. Clearly he was following some Tswana protocol or other. Ray wanted the head but felt unable to take it or ask for it. Something he disliked was keeping him from acting. He knew what it was and he disowned it. It was a feeling that he might not be going back. He disowned it. He disowned it.

Keletso kicked sand into the trench, burying the carcass as far as the head. He paused. He composed himself. He spoke hotly under his breath in Setswana. He took something out of his shirt pocket. Ray was baffled.

Keletso squatted, snatched up the head of the snake, and with a nail file
dug out the snake's eyes and flicked them aside, away from the trench.
His hands were trembling. He thrust the mutilated head back into the
trench and shot to his feet. Still imprecating, if that was what he was
doing, Keletso gestured for Ray to participate as the trench was finally
filled in.

Ray assumed he had just witnessed something customary, some ritual-
ization of snake-hatred related to the practice of cutting down and burning any tree a snake had been caught in, which had struck him as extreme
when he'd been told about it, considering the importance of trees for
shade and shelter in arid Botswana. Noga meant snake, he remembered.
The cry Noga! would bring villagers running with torches and hoes and
axes. Or so he had been told.

Cleaning themselves up, and then later eating breakfast, they seemed
to have nothing to say to one another.

En route again, Keletso asked Ray to go through the snakes section
of the Safety Book, his name for a skimpy, anodyne pamphlet on safety
in the wild issued by one of the safari camps. Ray didn't know offhand
where the pamphlet was. At one point Keletso had strung a rawhide
thong through it and worn it around his neck. Keletso thought it must be
in the glove box and it was. Plainly Keletso was laboring against the
apprehension that he had fallen short in his duties to take care.

"Can you find some advices, rra, as to snakes coming for shelter
beneath trucks at night?"

The booklet had a faintly rank smell. Ray began scanning it, but he
was distracted. He was full of dark feeling. Maybe I should have committed suicide and gotten out of the way when I was in the mood, he
thought. In early adolescence he had briefly been suicidal. There had
been a philosophical dimension to it. But paradoxically the outrages of
his brother and the rivalry and injustice that went with it had dragged
him back toward life, life the necessary condition for revenge. He
wouldn't mind telling Iris about this someday, but he wondered what she
would think of it if he did. Life was odd. He believed it was his indignation at the outrageous favoritism of his mother toward Rex that had relit
his will to live. The drive to penetrate that impenetrable behavior had
given him a vocation, or the seed of one. The agency, whatever else it was,
was the nemesis of mystery, plots, secrets, the hidden. I hate a mystery, he
thought. That was the story, in any case. Suicide was best for the young.
Once dependents appeared on the scene it was impossible.

He was unhappy to be thinking about his temptation to not exist, that period of his life. It hadn't come into his consciousness for years. The Kalahari was bringing it back because the Kalahari was saying something to him. It was saying to die, actually. He was being notional and he knew it. But in the first stillness of dawn, especially, there was an infinitely faint ambient whine or hum detectible. He had to hold his breath to hear it. A similar thing was alleged to happen in the Arctic. In the Kalahari he assumed insect song or activity to be the thing behind the whine, but that could hardly be the case in the Arctic. It didn't matter. No, what the desert was saying was that you would die if you got out of your iron bubble of food and water and first aid. Nobody could live in such a terrain except the Bushmen and they died at what ages, early, worn out by the effort to exist. Everyone said they were happy in that place, liked it.

Keletso was impatient. Ray began browsing in earnest. The message of the pamphlet was not to worry. Wild dogs were pack hunters, were mostly nocturnal and not interested in humans unless *excited*, whatever that meant. And wild dogs were getting scarcer in the Kalahari in any case. He presumed that it was the dogs that had to be excited in order to be dangerous, and not their human prey.

"Rra, we must not excite the wild dogs," he said to Keletso.

Leopards were nocturnal but rarely did they attack man. The implication seemed to be that any predator that was nocturnal could be forgotten about because at night the traveler would be sensibly sealed up in a vehicle or a tent *with a floor lining*. Also, leopards were in decline and were scarce, very scarce, in the dry parts of the Kalahari, which seemed to Ray to be all of it, that he had seen. And Cape buffalo were placid animals not interested in humans. But it was advisable not to be caught in the path of a stampede, and the same was true for all of the larger ungulates. Ray agreed completely.

Lions, again, were nocturnal hunters, but best of all they were *very lethargic* during daylight hours. Although if you stepped in amongst them while they were at rest the chances were that you would be eaten.

"Have you found about snakes as yet?" Keletso asked.

"Nearly there."

Here was yet another reiteration of the warning against ever taking food into your tent. Even normally man-aversive animals like caracals would claw their way in if they smelled food. Chacma baboons were distinctly no problem unless teased. He came to the snakes section.

Only six types of snake were depicted, in a set of crude sketches. None of the drawings resembled the creature they had killed. Two of the sketches were identical, an obvious error.

He was up to a sentence he loved. *It should be remembered that only half the snakes natural to Botswana are poisonous.* And more good news was that one of the commonest snakes, the shaapsteker, even if it struck you would only leave you with a severe headache, so weak was its venom. There were no cautions given about checking under vehicles in the morning. Keletso seemed relieved. They had done everything they should have. They had avoided overhanging branches and they always made a sort of fuss and racket wherever they walked. They had the three antivenins listed, hypodermics, everything.

Keletso seemed morose. He wanted Keletso to cheer up, but he couldn't think of how to make that happen. Death-thoughts were poisoning the atmosphere. *Death where is thy stingalingaling* was from something Irish, but what? What he really wanted was to tell Keletso how unhappy he was. But of course he couldn't do that. Soon enough he was going to have to send Keletso back to safety. It was almost time to do that. And until then he would need Keletso to think all was well with him. Otherwise he would resist. So he had to cheer up, himself.

He wanted to be light. He said, "When I get back to the States and somebody asks me what the main thing I learned in Africa was, it's going to be never to take food into your tent, not under any circumstances."

"Ehe," Keletso answered, blankly, unresponsively. He hadn't thought it was amusing, it was clear to see.

It was like a marriage, in some ways, with Keletso. Because in marriage when one partner was radiating dejection and discontent it turned life into a waiting period, a null time. There were times in a marriage when for one reason or another it was impossible to just wait for the mood to dissolve on its own. Action had to be taken. They were in a perilous place and action had to be taken. The problem was to know what would work. One route that was blocked with Keletso was humor. What did the Batswana find funny? What?

He was at a loss. He did know they thought it was funny to say of a man married to a harridan that he ate his overcoat. That gave Ray nothing. And he had been told that they thought it was funny to say that the penis was always landing up in trouble because it had only one eye. That was all he'd been able to glean. American jokes eluded the Batswana, was his distinct experience. It was conceivable that a whole people would find nothing funny in the jokes of their what, their oppressors, their colonial masters, their laughing masters, among whom he would be included, of course. It was possible there was nothing universal about humor.

Being read to was something Iris loved. It was almost magical, the effect it could have on her spirits. Undoubtedly what was happening when she was being read to was that she was regressing to experiences in her childhood that had been consistently pleasant. It was excellent to have pleasant tracts of childhood to regress to. He must have some. Of course he did.

They were proceeding slowly over level ground, so reading something aloud to Keletso wouldn't be impossible. He pulled his sack of reading matter out of the back and sat with it on his lap, planless until the uneasy thought came to him that it was past time to dispose posthaste of all his Kerekang briefing materials. They were a liability, a potential threat to his imposture, should he and Keletso have to endure some hostile scrutiny, which could happen. He couldn't believe that he had let it go for so long. Now he was anxious. He had to jettison this material as soon as he could manage it, and in some way not too peculiar and alarming to Keletso. They were getting closer to the epicenter of the trouble. It would be natural to slide the material into a cooking campfire. But they had been using the Coleman stove for cooking. Ray didn't want to leave the material intact out in the desert. He knew there was a solution and that he was magnifying the problem out of anxiety. Ray had dispensed with campfires in the interest of maintaining general low visibility. He liked campfires.

"The kippers are finished," Keletso said, gloomily.

Keletso loved kippers. They were a delicacy to him. Sometimes he would eat them twice a day. They were low on pilchards, too. The tinned fish was running out. He's collecting grievances, Ray thought. That was a process that could get out of control and that he needed to interrupt.

There were three issues of Kerekang's *Kepu/The Mattock* in his net bag. He extracted them. They were crude things, cyclostyled. He should just crush them up and bury them off in the bush when they made the next rest stop. An odd feeling of resistance came over him at the thought. He didn't want to do it.

He strongly didn't want to do it. He was surprised. He felt incapable of doing it. What was it, though? And then he knew. *Kepu* contained the only poetry in the iron bubble. Iris had forgotten to be sure his Modern Library Milton was in his reading midden. There had been the *TLS* back issues. But he had gotten rid of the *TLS*es as he'd finished them, not that he usually read the contemporary poetry they contained, but with the *TLS*es in the vehicle there had been poetry of some sort within reach.

Kepu was full of poetry. Kerekang was mad for it. His taste was for nineteenth-century English poetry in general, but he restricted himself to social protest verse in *Kepu*, with a heavy reliance on William Morris. Every selection was presented bilingually. When had the man had time to do all this translation work? What Kerekang felt about poetry, Ray thought he understood. It was a bond between them. I am an adolescent, he thought. He didn't want to be in a situation where he couldn't lay his hand on poetry. He realized that he always assumed poetry would be in his vicinity, somewhere, in the normal course of life. And now he had no choice but to destroy his copies of *Kepu*. You are being a child, he thought. He couldn't remember who it was who'd said that poetry was as essential to civilization as hot water. With poetry it could be one poem one couplet one line, even, and you were immortal forever. For just one poem it would be Chidiock Tichborne, to name just one. It could come down to that, one little line of letters saving your name forever. People would want to know what you looked like, forever. That was what his brother was straining to do, generate just one sentence, one paragraph, one glorious thing. He wasn't close. He would fail. He said to Keletso, "Rra, do you like poetry at all?"

"Ehe, the most when it is from the Bible."

Ray looked for something to read aloud to Keletso. He paged through Volume One, Number Three, of *Kepu*. There was a William Morris verse.

He would read it to himself first.

A Death Song

What cometh here from west to east awending?
And who are these, the marchers stern and slow?
We bear the message that the rich are sending
Aback to those who bade them wake and know.
Not one, not one, nor thousands must they slay,
But one and all if they would dusk the day.

There was more of the same. This was not the ticket for cheering Keletso up. It was grim. It was hard to believe this was the same William Morris he associated with big improvements in wallpaper design.

He found something that looked lighter, by a poet unknown to him, Robert Brough. A note described Brough as a famous republican who had died of drink at the age of thirty. Kerekang was teetotal, Ray remembered.

"Would you like me to read you a poem?"

"Ehe, to pass the time."

"I have the poem in Setswana and English. Dintsha le dilebodi le diPeba le dikatse. I'll try it in Setswana."

"It is to do with animals, then, rra?"

"Yes. Well, listen. Here I go."

But after two stanzas in attempted Setswana, Ray concluded it was no-go. Keletso was laughing, and there was nothing that amusing in the verses he'd read to him, so it was his performance that was funny.

He began again, in English.

"The title is *The Terriers and the Rats and the Mice and the Cats: A Fable*. And this was written in England long ago, written against the king and the nobility that supported the king, at that time. And you'll see, the dogs, the terriers he talks about, stand for the ruling system, Domkrag, with the king at the top. And under the dogs are the cats. The dogs are ruling the cats and the rats are ruling the mice. Anyway . . ."

> *"Once on a time—no matter how,*
> *(By force of teeth, or mere 'Bow-wow,'*
> *   Let studious minds determine)—*
> *The Terriers upon Rat-land, seiz'd,*
> *Its natives hunted, worried, teas'd,*
> *In short—exactly what they pleas'd*
> *   Did, with the whisker'd vermin."*

He was going to have to skip. Looking ahead, Ray saw the piece was endless, all the verses showing that the mice were on the verge of revolt. He continued reading.

At last he was at the end. The revolt had been frustrated.

> " *'We beckon out the biggest rat,*
> *And ask him, with a friendly pat,*
> *To join our side the merrier—*
> *We teach him how to bark: with shears,*
> *We dock his tail, and trim his ears,*
> *Give him some bones, to calm his fears,*
> *And tell him he's a Terrier.' "*

Keletso seemed unsure of what to say. Ray had read the piece, the bulk of it, partly in the spirit of experiment. He was curious about what a Motswana would make of this antique republican agitprop.

An awkward silence began.

"Rra, who are these cats and uprisen mice? What nation is that?"

"Well, it's no particular country, it's an imaginary country, a country made up so the poet can tell a story about how the terriers, who are the kings, the nobility, the big men, rule the rats in Britain. The cats are the ones in another country who are inquiring, to learn how they can dominate the mice in *their* country the way the terriers dominate the rats. But in any case now this poem is being reprinted and translated for the Batswana of today."

Keletso was silent.

Ray said, "So, rra, if you were applying this fable, fable is what it is, to Botswana at this moment today, what would it mean?"

Keletso, giving Ray a sidelong glance, said, "Rra, what is your opinion?"

"Well, could we say that in Botswana the terriers are the big men and the chiefs and, well, Domkrag?"

"Ehe, you mean as when they can pinch away leaders from BoSo to make it weak? As we had in Gaborone when BoSo elected their man mayor, and then he switched across to Domkrag, like a flash . . ."

"Yes, right. That kind of thing."

"Nyah, rra."

"You say no?"

"Your eyes are too small, rra."

"I don't know what you mean."

"Because if you would say who are the big dogs today in Botswana, it is the makhoa. Sorry."

"White people, the white man, Europeans, you mean . . ."

"Ehe. When you put the question, I say the makhoa."

"So we are the dogs, still, you feel?"

"Such is what you can take from this poem, rra."

"And it is what you take from it?"

"Rra, it is."

"You say it without hesitation."

This was the wrong tack to take, and Ray knew it. But he couldn't help himself.

He said, "So, is your view, then, that despite independence . . . and you've been independent since 1966, isn't it? . . . that still the white man is . . . is *maneuvering* at the top?"

"He is, yes. You cannot always see him."

"Ah well," Ray said.

"Yah."

"So it is, then."

I'm hurt, stupidly enough, he thought.

Twice during the afternoon they had noticed lines of black smoke, like scratches, rising from distant fires far to the north. No discussion had come out of it. This was the wrong time of year for the veld fires the Bushmen employed to drive game into traps, if they were even still doing that. The Bushmen were operating under restrictions. He had no idea what they were still allowed to do. Their hunting was controlled. That had to be a joke, though. How could anything in the Kalahari be administered, that was the question. He didn't know. He did know he should always say Basarwa and not Bushmen. And he did know that they were facing extinction. He knew that. Did they?

He wasn't looking forward to turning in tonight. His pillow and to a lesser extent his sleeping bag had a consommé smell, rank. He had beaten his pillow and his pillowcase against a tree trunk. He had flicked after-shave on the pillowcase. The odor was in the pillow itself. Drifting off, he had to smell himself, as he fell . . . there was no escape.

They were nowhere, still. And they would sleep in another section of nowhere, beside the road, again. They were inching. There had been rain in the area. The road was viscous in spots and Keletso was being exquisite with his driving, as he should be doing. There was a movie with Yves Montand driving a load of dynamite over roads like this that had nothing to do with their situation that he could think of. Ah yes, *atopia* is where we are, he thought. *Black cotton soil* was the name for the treacherous sort of surface that showed up in places along the spoors after heavy rainfall. The guidebooks warned about it. He was studying Keletso's technique. He had to get it down.

The silence of the desert was entering them. It was hard to talk, to converse, harder all the time. The stupid silence was conquering them. The desert was ruled by stupid life, except for the quick-witted Basarwa, geniuses of staying alive through their thirties, dancing away from death from the time they could toddle. All the things that could kill you in the desert were stupider than you, or they were automatic. Inanimate, he meant.

A couple of days back they had stopped at a Basarwa encampment set

up at a crossroads. The inhabitants had come out of their huts and into
the road to make them halt. There had been no more than five or so huts,
dome-shaped, plastic sakkies mixed in with the leaves and sticks they used
in constructing their shelters. The people had been dressed, half-dressed,
many of them, in assemblages of rags and skins. It had been a beggar
settlement, essentially, not a functioning hunting and gathering community. Old women lived there, mainly, with only a few younger women and
three or four children in evidence. The community was an organism
devoted to begging. The Basarwa had formed a cordon with the children
directly in front of the vehicle. They had begged for salt and sugar and
tobacco and tee shirts. They knew the word, tee shirt. He had given them
a tee shirt and he had given them a box of salt and they had accepted two
containers of cooking oil, Royl, disappointedly, he'd thought. There had
been no tobacco to give them. They had refused canned goods. That was
a mystery, unless it was something as elementary as their not owning a
can opener, which hadn't occurred to him at the time. Their poverty had
been as bad as anything he'd seen, worse than anything in Old Naledi.
He hadn't given them the right things. Keletso had been eager to push
on. He hadn't had time to be creative with what they had on board that
they could afford to give away. Keletso had been ashamed of those people. That had been it, he knew. If there had been more time, they could
have done better by them. If it happened again when he was by himself he
would do better. Not that he could ever find that place again on his own,
but he might come across others. And he would do better next time.

He wanted to sing something. That was odd. He felt like singing. He
didn't know what it was he wanted to sing, but he definitely did want to.
After he released Keletso he'd be able to sing all day. *The Desert Song* was
a musical. He had seen the movie version. It had nothing to do with any
of this.

Covertly Ray felt his sides through his shirt. He was losing weight,
judging by the prominence of his ribs. Iris was funny. She had once said
to him lewdly that she liked him to be thin because it made his penis look
big. That was the sort of thing she was likely to come up with. She was
unlike other women. She was.

It was night again. Ray had his fire. He had complained that he felt cold
and Keletso had collected firewood for him, going to some trouble to
search out a particular kind of wood that produced what he'd called *sour
smoke*, a smoke that flying insects disliked. The fire had smoked copiously

at first but now it was fine. The smoke had been something to endure. The wood was obviously saturated with resins, like greasewood, that made it flare and spit. He had forgotten what it was called. He should probably find out, for the future. Although knowing the name would be pointless if he was by himself. So forget that, he thought.

Keletso could be insistent. Once he realized that Ray had meant it about sitting out in the open for a while after dark tonight, he had crafted the ridiculous thing Ray was ensconced in. Keletso had taken the tea-break umbrella and taped and pinned drapings of mosquito netting to it. To make steadying the staff easier, Keletso had driven it pretty deeply into the sand, which imposed a certain degree of hunching on Ray as he sat on his camp stool. But he appreciated the thought and the effort and it was doing its job.

Keletso was in the vehicle doing what? He was monitoring Ray from time to time, Ray supposed. There had been a delicate discussion between them. From now on at night they would urinate in jars rather than leaving the vehicle for relief. It was the shadow of the snake event over them. Keletso was even more fixated on danger than before. He had walked around the perimeter of their encampment sprinkling petrol like holy water because the larger predators were understood to hate the odor. Ray was going to write a letter of commendation for the dear fellow that would knock his socks off.

Finally he had done it, burned all the incriminating papers, his Kerekang material, leaf by leaf, taking his time. That was it, adieu, up in smoke, they were gone, all the testimonials to simple living, to the glorious sunrise at Toromole, all the early to rise, garden work, study, out to talk to the grateful locals, all those stories, all the bean recipes, the other vegetariana, all the raised-bed gardening advice, all the paeans to loving one another and cooperation. All of it was gone, and also gone were the telex flimsies and the memoranda and savingrams from the various arms of government crying havoc, and good riddance to them.

At every meal at Toromole someone had read poetry, he gathered. He felt he understood Kerekang to the marrow. He was a victim of poetry. All the poetry-reading and the public chanting of poetry at the poor devils he was trying to convert showed it. He wanted life to be Tennyson for everybody, or some other highminded worthy. He was stuck in the nineteenth century. I could help him, he thought. He knew what the idea was, in the heart of his mind, he knew. First, it was to shed attachments, burn them away via poetry, and this would be for the privileged, the jeunesse dorée he was attracting as cadres, that would be step one. But then the larger step was to live at the level of poetry, everybody. Kerekang had felt himself rise, in poetry, to a certain stratum of what? benevolent feeling, universal benevolence, what? . . . what? To where it is beautiful . . . not ugly, and where poverty is is ugly, clearly ugly, was that it? Here is where you can live, he was saying, Kerekang. Every poem is a cry, Ray thought. And of course that was the paradox. It was a cry of agony or pleasure, joy, but mostly agony fixed up in one way or another, his friend wanted to utter, his friend Kerekang, intellectual friend. Milton is all agony, he thought. He wanted something he couldn't have, a cucumber and tomato sandwich on whole wheat toast, with aioli in a little tub on the side. So the poetry was gone but it had been doggerel, really, underdoggerel, to coin a term. Rex would like that. And Marxism could be underdogma, why not? His brother was on his mind because only a mystery paperback sans cover lay between him and the thick block of pages from Rex's *Strange News*.

That was it also for Kerekang's unfortunate manifesto, *The White Ants*. The copy he had burned had belonged to Boyle, and Boyle's hysterical underlinings and annotations had been as alarming as they had been amusing. Only the first six pages, out of twenty, had been marked up, demonstrating the depth of his address to the piece. He had misunderstood everything, taking the manifesto as directed against whites in Africa, expatriates, when in fact *White Ants* was simply the translation of the Setswana word for termites, and the termites in question weren't expatriates but the national gentry, the large cattle owners. Briefly Ray had entertained the idea that the pamphlet was a forgery coming out of South African intelligence and intended to stir up divisions between certain constituencies of the Botswana Social Front, which had been maneuvering to accommodate bits and pieces of the aristocracies of the minor tribes, large cattle owners all of them. But then he had decided it was genuine. It was heated. It was poetic. It was Kerekang. And it was what had earned him the title Kerekang Setime, Kerekang the Torch Thrower. The Boers made trouble all over the region, for their own reasons. They hated the Botswana Social Front because it was friendly to the exiles of the Pan Africanist Congress, which they hated more than they hated the African National Congress. *The White Ants* was Kerekang denouncing in an almost biblical style the folly of embodying human labor in herds of cattle which periodic drought and disease could be counted on to lay waste to. The termites were the gentry. That was his obsession.

He parted the netting and put his head out into the night. He gazed up at the stars. He loved the conceit, conceit being the wrong word, the Bushmen had for the stars . . . campfires of the dead. He couldn't get it out of his head. The Milky Way was like a broad stripe of paste. He had been somewhere outdoors with Iris at night and she had said in some connection, "I don't need to stare up into the firmament in order to be convinced of my own insignificance." Probably she had been reacting to some dumb musing of his own. My girl, he thought. Saying anything with girl in it, when it came to her, had mostly fallen out of their household discourse in the last few years. But she was his girl, his beloved girl. He would be able to shout it out if he felt like it, after he released Keletso. He felt like shouting it out. He felt like shouting it at Morel.

The fire was on its last legs. While there was still some illumination coming from it, he should grasp the nettle of the mystery paperback. He had to know what he had to look forward to, or not, whatever the case was. He thought, Hell is just another word for nothing left to read. Rex would like that. Or it could be Hell is just another word for nothing good to read.

The book was *Madame Bovary*.

He felt dead immediately. Or he felt killed, struck, killed by a blow to the face. Why had she done this? Why this book?

In a state of developing shock, he examined the paperback. It was the 1943 Pocket Book Eleanor Marx Aveling translation. The translator had been a suicide, Marx's daughter, one of his daughters. Where was his Modern Library Milton? Why had Iris left that out and why had she put this, *this*, this bomb in his net bag?

Iris was not cruel. She lacked the capacity for it. So why this book, now, lying in wait for him?

He had to digest his shock. He got out of his umbrella-tent and laid it carefully aside so that he could reenter it when he had gotten the Coleman lantern going. He needed light. He needed more light. He had to understand this or die.

He was ready. The lantern was going. He was back in the umbrella-tent. He had put a pillow on the seat of the camp stool. It was necessary to keep the shank of the umbrella clamped between his knees and he had to hold the paperback at a difficult angle to catch the lantern light. He was not comfortable. His back had begun to hurt already. But he had a water bottle. He would be fine.

He thought he knew how she could have innocently put *Bovary* in with his other reading matter. It could be there because she was scrupulous about keeping her eye out at jumble sales for cheap copies of classics that he had admitted to her he hadn't for one reason or another gotten around to finishing earlier in his reading life. She had found a *Vanity Fair*, for him, for example, and either *Bleak House* or *Dombey and Son*. She loved him. She wanted him not to have lacunae, was what was behind it. And he had, he knew, mentioned that he had started *Madame Bovary* and not finished it. It must have been in the early years of their marriage. He hadn't said why he hadn't finished the book. He wasn't sure she'd asked. But he knew why. Partly it was because the idea of a wife committing adultery was upsetting to him. But he hadn't liked the book for other reasons. He had concluded that the main character was an idiot, and that what the book looked like was a beautifully written sequence of repetitions to show how stupid she, and any woman like her, had to be, any woman captured by romantic sentiments. He remembered thinking how smug the book was. He was sure that Bovary was from ovary, not that he could prove it. The book was against women. A woman had given Flaubert syphilis, thus his attitude. The men were fools, too. He had gotten as far as the liaison with Rodolphe and given up.

He began paging along, reacquainting himself with what he had read, the part he remembered. The school business was still vivid to him. Charles Bovary's first marriage, that too he had clear. His eye snagged on the last paragraph on page 36.

> Before marriage she thought herself in love; but the happiness that
> should have followed this love not having come, she must, she
> thought, have been mistaken. And Emma tried to find out what one
> meant exactly in life by the words *felicity*, *passion*, *rapture*, that had
> seemed to her so beautiful in books.

His heart was beating too hard. The struggle was going to be to find out if Iris was speaking to him through this book, and if so, if so, if so, then what she was saying, exactly?

He was going to have to speed-read the rest of this thing, because he had to understand. He had to verify that the story was what he had assumed or picked up through his reading it was.

Emma had been put in a convent where she read contraband romantic novels and poetry. Then she had married a clod who became a successful country doctor doing his best and she had hardly been able to wait to betray him, first platonically, so to speak, with a young clerk, as he recalled. She was always waiting for something to happen. She has a child by her husband but sends it off to a wet nurse. She had hated the child for being female. She had gone to live in a provincial town, Yonville, inhabited exclusively by fools and jackasses. Over and over human stupidity was presented against landscapes of terrific natural beauty.

Ah, page 116, "What exasperated her was that Charles did not seem to notice her anguish." And there was no sex in the fucking thing, no described sex. He wasn't up to Rodolphe yet. Léon, the first guy, had been a tease. Was it possible Iris was saying she was at the Léon stage and she needed to be stopped before Rodolphe? That was probably insane. He didn't know. He was up to Rodolphe. Rodolphe was introduced as a cad. Could Iris be saying Morel was a cad, using Rodolphe, making a cry? He would hold the thought. He had reached the point at which he'd stopped years ago, he was pretty sure. He mustn't seize on details prematurely. He had to conclude on the basis of themes, or something. He had to finish reading this thing, at once.

By page 196 she was well into it with Rodolphe.

> Everything in Charles irritated her now; his face, his dress, what he did not say, his whole person, his existence, in fine. She repented of her past virtue as a crime, and what still remained of it crumbled away beneath the furious blows of her pride. She revelled in all the evil ironies of triumphant adultery. The memory of her lover came back to her with dazzling attractions; she threw her whole soul into it, borne away toward this image with a fresh enthusiasm; and Charles seemed to her as much removed from her life, as absent forever, as impossible and annihilated, as if he had been about to die and were passing under her eyes.

He was reading furiously.

Rodolphe ditches her. Every line in his farewell letter is a lie.

Madame goes into a collapse. Rodolphe is gone but Léon is back and this time it's not platonic.

Emma was bankrupting her husband and trying to borrow money from Léon . . . and then there was this, page 316 . . .

> "Morel is to come back to-night; he will not refuse me, I hope" (this was one of his friends, the son of a very rich merchant) . . .

Morel. Morel! . . . but it could mean nothing.

Back to Rodolphe. She is desperate for money and can't get any.

Then death. She takes poison out of remorse at what she had been, a fool. Her daughter ends up in child labor. She leaves a ruin.

He had no idea what to think. His mind was all over the place. There were no checkmarks or underlinings or *nota bene*s anywhere in the volume, no page corners turned down. What was the signal, the message? Was he Bovary, a fool distinguished by the fact he believed every lie she told? Was he on page 363?

> Besides, Charles was not of those who go to the bottom of things;
> he shrank from the proofs, and his vague jealousy was lost in the
> immensity of his woe.

In the scene prompting that characterization Charles has construed an explicit love letter from Rodolphe to his wife as probably suggesting a platonic relationship only.

Was *Madame Bovary* a communication to him, was the question. He had to assume it was, since even if she'd put it in his pack by accident initially *something* would have gone off in her mind to say stop, halt, this will cause Ray to freak, what was I thinking?

So there it was. She was neither stupid nor cruel. So there it was. How he took *Madame Bovary* was critical. What kind of book was it? You could take it as a Christian homily if you wanted to, a tract saying marriage is an ordeal but violating your stupid vows is even worse. But that was farfetched. He had learned something by suffering through this book, which was that the *TLS* could be wrong. He remembered reading someone very authoritative writing in it that there was only one major novel, a thing called *The Golovlyov Family*, a nineteenth-century Russian novel Ray hadn't read, in which every character presented, without exception, was loathsome. Surely *Madame Bovary* belonged in that category, if you didn't count the poor child. Every adult in the book was vile.

He had to know if he was supposed to see himself in Charles Bovary. Every detail seemed to answer in the affirmative. For example, what did it mean that her husband botched an operation on some poor devil with a clubfoot, making it worse, making him lose his leg? Poor Charles does it out of hubris stoked by delusions about what he was competent to do. So was the analogy the agency, the agency's interventions, the agency's hubris, and his part in what she might think the agency was up to? He was feeling paranoid. He was hoping this was paranoia. He had to get up and move around. His back was killing him.

He walked in a circle around the dying fire. He was still enclosed in the quasi-tent, carrying it with him like a fool of some kind. He needed to list the options he had for interpreting what she had done to him, putting *Madame Bovary* in his hands. But fire interrupted him, a bloom of flame declaring itself around him, dragging the breath out of his lungs. The netting had gone up. He had dragged it across an ember. He pitched the burning mass away. He was all right. He was trembling. His hair had gotten singed in back, was all. He had made a spectacle. Keletso was coming to him.

Nothing in Africa is fireproof, he thought.

It was morning and somewhere in their cargo was a magnifying mirror. He needed it.

He found it in among the first aid paraphernalia. His reflected image was not gratifying. He was less presentable than was good and less presentable than he'd expected. He had a mild burn on the back of his right hand that looked worse than it was because the Vaseline he'd smeared on it seemed to highlight it. He touched it and it hardly hurt. If he ruffled his hair he could still produce a shower of black specks, bits of charred hair. A good shampooing would take care of that. He would never understand why people insisted on saying they had circles under their eyes, dark circles, when what they had were semicircles. No one had circles under their eyes. The lashes of his right eye were mostly gone. He asked himself if it might be a good idea to trim off the lashes of his left eye in the interest of symmetry and the answer was no, it was an extreme idea and in addition his hands were too unsteady. That would pass, like everything. He could keep the idea under advisement.

On waking he had found himself in possession of the conviction that yes, providing *Madame Bovary* had been deliberate, but that the point of doing it had been precisely to show him that she was fundamentally innocent, so innocent that she felt free to include the inflammatory thing in his reading because, *precisely* because, *it meant nothing* and was there only because it was something he had in fact said he hadn't finished reading. So it had been a deliberate declaration of innocence. But that conviction had proved to be delicate. He had lost it. He had lost his grip on it during breakfast. He had held it too hard. He had crushed it.

But he had gotten rid of the *Bovary* enigma anyway, another way. He had gotten rid of it the way Johnson refuted Bishop Berkeley, in that spirit, at least. He had been creative and burned the thing, pushing it into the embers of the breakfast fire. He resented mystery and he had dissolved that one by destroying the occasion of it, the object, the evidence. He knew himself. Know thyself, he said to himself, for reinforcement. If he had hung on to *Bovary* he would have returned to it for obsessive research. So he had saved himself. And already it was easier to stay longer with the idea that the whole thing had been a mistake, a bêtise on her part, something she had done automatically in the rush of throwing his personal supplies together for him. He had to focus on how much she wanted him not to limit his leisure reading to crap, even the better sort of crap, vintage Penguin mysteries, Dorothy Sayers and Simenon, and how much she wanted him to use that for filling holes in his lacunae, which was an incorrect construction, a bêtise, like saying someone has a loophole up his sleeve, but not exactly like it. Iris had made up the loophole phrase, being funny. He was losing a funny woman.

He was looking gaunt, there was no question about that. But a good bath would help and a careful shave would help and the end of the world would help.

Keletso had taken a chance. And then Ray had taken a chance. And it had been because they were both a little desperate for fresh fruit.

They had noted a solitary homestead just off the road, very tidy-looking, two rondavels inside a low mud wall painted in a red and black checkerboard pattern, and Keletso had decided it looked abandoned and that therefore there was no reason not to stop and go in and knock down a couple of pawpaws growing on a tree next to the main rondavel, the one with the trimmed thatch, the male rondavel, as they were called. Rondavels with untrimmed thatch, sometimes called weeping thatch for no reason Ray could think of, were considered female. They had passed other abandoned compounds along the way, more than a few when you added them up, especially in the last week.

How Keletso had been able to tell the compound was abandoned rather than merely vacant while its occupants went about their business elsewhere out in the bush had been unclear to him. And Keletso's conviction about it had been called into question by the celerity with which he had vaulted the wall and hauled himself up the tree and cut the fruit down and then gotten the hell out of there. And then there had been his not wanting to cut the fruit open until they were almost a kilometer, by Ray's reckoning, from the compound.

Keletso had come back with two papayas, large ones, brownish and withered-looking. When they had stopped and rather feverishly cut them open, Keletso had rejected one of them as dubious but declared the other one, which looked identical to the one rejected in every way, fine to eat. The flesh of the supposedly fine pawpaw had been dark and hard and, in Ray's opinion, soapy to the taste, but to be companionable he had eaten some, a small amount, while Keletso had eaten a lot, chewing heroically, and was now sick, vomiting, behind the vehicle.

But he himself was fine. In fact he was in an elevated state, he might say. Burning *Madame Bovary* had helped him deeply, somehow. They were in a broad, dry valley. They were suffering with the universal dustiness, but he wasn't minding it. At some point in antiquity a river had run through this desert. It was impossible to imagine what that must have been like, not that he was trying very hard, because he was feeling elsewhere, he was feeling *above* things. He could enjoy small things like the rare moments of coolness when a cloud passed over. And also there were golden knobs of something, horse droppings, in the road, that looked aesthetic, at that moment.

He put his head out of the vehicle and asked, loudly, if he could get something for Keletso.

"Nyah, rra," Keletso answered, with some difficulty. He wasn't through retching.

Ray wanted to be cremated when he died. Definitely.

It had been the best idea, burning *Madame Bovary*. And he had another idea, a fine idea, and he was going to carry it out before anyone could object. He needed to hurry.

His passport was in the glove box. He extracted it and looked at it. He liked the color, navy blue. And he was proud of its thickness. Extra pages had been incorporated into it because he had used up the available space for visa stamps.

He got out of the vehicle, taking his passport with him. He walked up the road, toward a bobbing cloud of gnats. They would have to drive through it later.

He knew what Iris wanted. She wanted a different man. He could be a different man. When he returned he could be a different man.

Nothing could happen to him if he had his passport with him. That was factual. Nothing could touch him once whoever came to oppress him, as people liked to say, saw his passport. The iron wings of the United States were over him, gently beating, wherever he went, so long as he had his passport to wave in the face of anyone who knew what was good for them. There was a skit going on. They were seeing evidence of fire again, lines of smoke, four of them at one time, once. The omens were that trouble was coming to meet him face to face. His passport made him a prince.

Keletso was part of his armor, too. And Keletso was going to have to go back. He set the passport on the ground, open, spine up, and with his cigarette lighter set the interior pages on fire.

He was proud of himself for a stupid reason. He had never memorized his passport number, a ten-digit thing. He didn't know what his number was. But he had resisted the temptation to take a look at it before burning his document. He could pick things up in a flash. He was trained to do that. He would have remembered it and he would have been able to recite it if need be and that could have been a loophole, a loophole up his sleeve, conceivably. But he had resisted.

The pages were burning satisfactorily but not the cover, which was a plastic sort of fabric. He tried harder to get the cover to burn, picking it up and holding the lighter flame steadily at one corner. The cover began to curl and blacken and finally it began to melt. He was burning his fingers a little. He was succeeding. It was unrecognizable. Half of it was viscous. He mashed whatever was left of his passport into the sand.

Keletso surprised him. He stood up and faced him. Keletso looked ghastly and he would want to know what was going on. He hadn't thought ahead.

"Rra, are you all right?" he asked Keletso.

"Ehe, rra, but I am empty and you must drive."

"Of course."

"Only until such time as I am recovered. I can have tea, I think. But what is this fire?"

"This fire is . . . a fire I just made."

"Ehe, but why? What is it about?"

"Ah well, while I was waiting I saw these gnats and I thought while I was waiting I would go and smoke them out, smoke them away."

"Nyah, that is just foolish, rra."

"Yes, because you see they are still there. But it was just, what shall I call it, passing time till you came back."

Keletso shook his head. He looked searchingly at Ray. He wanted to say something, clearly, but was thinking it over.

"I feel great," Ray said.

"Nyah, it is not right. But come out of this sun. I must wash my teeth."

Ray got back into the Land Cruiser. A blister was rising on the pad of his thumb.

He was going to feel elated, he knew it. He had done it. There was no color of protection in his remaining documents, his driver's license, his letters of reference and authorization. Without a passport to accompany them, they would automatically be suspect. They would prove nothing.

He expected to feel fine soon, very soon.

25. Cries and Chants for Sale

Keletso was asleep, which was good because he disapproved of Ray reading himself to sleep with the aid of a flashlight, because it was wasteful of batteries. He had never said anything directly, but Ray could tell how Keletso felt. There were plenty of batteries left anyway, and if not there should be batteries available in Nokaneng in whatever travesty of a general store they would find there. They would make it to Nokaneng easily tomorrow. Alternatively it was possible that the light from Ray's reading activities made it hard for Keletso to fall asleep, not that there was the least evidence of that. Africans seemed very adapted to total darkness. In the villages you could find them sitting around having discussions in total darkness. Maybe their eyes were better. His eyes were still good. He was going to be forty-nine and his eyes were still good, knock wood. But there was no wood to knock. Forty-nine is not fifty, he thought. His eyes were better than Iris's. She owned reading glasses but she was, he would say, a little furtive about using them, like someone in politics. Her eyes were beautiful things. When they got to Nokaneng he would begin to machinate to send Keletso home, out of this, out of the fire. He had to.

Tonight he had the back seat. For reading it was workable, but it was shallower and not as comfortable as the front seat. He had learned on this excursion that he could fall asleep in a propped-up position and stay asleep for as long as a couple of hours before cramping made him change his position. Also he had learned how inextricably connected, for him, reading and falling asleep had become. It was alarming. It had crept up on him and established itself and he had never noticed it because in his life, his normal life, there was always a surplus of reading matter. And now his ability to fall asleep for the immediate future reposed on his brother's what, his bits and pieces, his ejecta, his literary essence supposedly, his literary effrontery, his posturings. It didn't matter. He had sworn he would read through his brother's corpus, this ragbag pretending to be a florilegium, whatever it was. He could be fair, but he knew what he was going to find, to wit, the debris of Rex's ambition to be the gay Mencken, one, or two, the gay La Rochefoucauld, or both.

He could begin anywhere. He could skip around from flotsam to jetsam. He had before him pages and pages of isolate phrases, sentences, paragraphs, each entry numbered, the numerals in ink, in differing hands, it looked like. There was plenty of white space. He had a twinge briefly relating to the fear that unless he rationed his reading, this collection wasn't going to last him all that long. He was in a ridiculous position. The numbering of the different entries was not consecutive, which you would think meant that ultimately they would have to be reorganized consecutively, but according to what Rex had told Iris, no, the numbers were what, decorative. Iris had irritated him by referring to his brother's slumgullion as a poem, some postmodern equivalent of the classic epic poems, some conceit like that which it would be no trouble to disprove. *Strange News* was something, but it was not going to be Milton.

STRANGE NEWS, or BRIGHT CITIES DARKEN

He began with the face page.

*12. Cries and Chants for Sale, with Indications of Their
Possible Purchasers, in Some Cases*

> Arm the Homeless!
> > What do we want?
> > We don't know!
> > When do we want it?
> > *Now!*   (for the younger set)

> All Together Now: Every Man for Himself!   (Libertarians)

> Power to the Feeble!   (Left)

> Reason's Greetings!   (atheists, holiday card)

There was a note in the margin, in pencil, in his brother's microscopic penmanship, which gave him a stab. *Def.: the Homeless—Roofless Cosmopolitans*, Rex had written.

Ray saw that he was going to have to endure Rex's penchant for antic capitalization.

8. Types

Fair-haired boy: a gonnabe

118. Proof of God's Love

Proof God loves us is that he makes us deaf to the vile, wracking snores we emit that so torment those who choose to sleep beside us.

That was odd, a synchronicity, given the sleeping situation he was stuck with. Synchronicity was boring. Keletso had an intermittent tendency to light snoring, to which Ray felt he had adapted pretty well, without complaining. He could sink directly back into sleep most of the time. It was part of life in the Kalahari. But what is life? he asked himself, taking a sheet of typescript at random from deeper in the stack of pages. I don't like this, he thought, seeing what he had come up with. *Strange News* was turning into the *I Ching* on him. He resented it.

359. Life Is . . .

Life is a sentence of corporeal punishment. Or, Life is corporeal punishment. Life, passages of Sturm interrupted by sequences of Drang. From puberty to senility life is continuous foreplay interrupted with declining frequency by actual sex.

So what he had before him was Rex's desperate attempts to achieve wit, and then what, then use it as a hammer to smash the stale cake of custom plus the frozen lake within and all of that, all of that wrongness, Wrongness. But Rex was not the soul of wit. Twice he had gotten his column suspended because his bons mots had given offense to women, in one case when he'd referred to them as *the leaky darlings*, which alluded tastelessly to the fact that they menstruate and are sentimental and prone to weeping, and then in another case when he'd called them the Cleft Sex. He was reckless. Rex had been writing for gay publications, and Ray could see that he'd been attempting to carry off a sort of parody of old-hat gay attitudes toward women, but he'd misjudged his readers and the power the new literalism had over them. In the same spirit he had defined men as the Apposite Sex, but he hadn't gotten in hot water over that. Probably people had just found it baffling and gone quickly past.

I am not your editor, Ray wanted to say. But that was going to be the plot. He was designated to boil this froth down into a bouillon cube of near greatness, even if there was only enough for a chapbook of the best thrusts and gems, to be given away, distributed somehow to some population he had no idea how to identify or reach. But he had to, because Rex wasn't well. There was strange news coming, bad news, and there was nothing he could do about it. This was what he could do. This was his fate, part of it. It was hard to credit.

An unwelcome sound came from the front seat, followed by a few low-spoken unintelligible words of, conceivably, apology. Barely audible mutterings could be called mutterances, why not? Suppose I had turned my mind to producing glittering nothings like Rex's, what would I have? he thought.

He plucked out another sheet at random and there was more synchronicity for him, annoyingly. Entry 308 was death-related. Or more precisely, it was life-residue-related. He ought to stop the random selection business for a while. He was toying with some imaginary thing. It wasn't good.

308. In Memoriam: A Report

I have to speak at her memorial service and what kills me is I can't mention the one thing about her that was genuinely remarkable. I went with her for about six months in the seventies and after that I didn't see her for years, so it's not that I know that much about her. But I'm a celebrity so they want me, so I don't mind. I understand it. But what I've never told anybody and what was really the only interesting thing I know about her is this. She had a weird talent. You're lying down with her watching television and you have one of those moments when your color set goes black and white for no reason. This was before cable so you have no one to call up about it. You fiddle with the set every way you can but nothing corrects it. You even twiddle the little hidden knobs on the back. But this is what she would do. We discovered it by accident. The first time it was more an expression of exasperation than anything else. But this is what she could do. She could spread her legs and buck her pelvis hard at the thing. She would pull up her nightgown and do it, and by the way she had no panties on. But when she gives a couple of hard bumps or grinds, whichever, the color comes back. She did this at least four times. There must have been a rational explanation but we never figured out what it was. Somehow maybe it was some delicate condition in the wiring in her building. But just pounding on the wall behind the set did nothing. We laughed hysterically. I don't know what I'm going to say about her unless I make something up.

There you have nothing, he thought. He went back to working consecutively through the manuscript and immediately couldn't believe his luck. There was an inclusion, something from Iris stuck in with his brother's flotsam, something with her writing on it. This was Iris. This was the kind of thing she did.

It was a Xerox of a Peace Corps document headed INTERRACIAL EXPERIENCE ASSESSMENT FORM. Across the top of it Iris had written *Do you know what you have to go through in order to get into the Peace Corps and get sent to an African country? Somebody at the embassy got hold of this and is passing it around. I love you, Ray. Iris.*

You used to, he thought.

Interracial Experience Assessment Form—Page One

1. Recall your first significant interaction with a Black person. Describe the situation and your feelings at the time.

   Answer: My first significant interaction with a Black person was when I was five and ran away from home with a friend my age and we went to the dock area, the harbor area, and a Negro dockworker gave us some of his lunch and called the police. My feelings were as follows. I felt relieved yet betrayed.

2. What was the strongest fear you developed as a child about interactions with Black persons? Estimate how strong that fear is today.

   Answer: You might fall in love with a Negro and have children that would have a miserable life because neither race would accept them.
   That fear is much less strong since we began doing all the questionnaires and games, by far.

At the bottom she had written *Sorry I only have page one. Love again, Iris.* He touched her name in both the places she had signed it.

Sleep was being coy. A lot of what he had to read he was finding vaguely agitating. To convert *Strange News* into a pillow book he was going to have to separate out and consolidate the longer paragraphic entries, which tended to consist of various micronarratives, subanecdotal most of them, illustrating some hilarious defect or other in the mental landscapes of everyone in the world except the author-observer. It took narrative to put Ray to sleep. Narrative was the syrup. It wasn't the sheer dynamics of reading that did it. Poems, even, needed some narrative weight to work. The Conversation entries were dubious, from the narrative standpoint, judging by what he was finding in them so far.

19. Conversation

Two guys had been drinking together.

The slightly older of the two said, "My friend, I will confess something to you. My old friend, I find my children boring."

"Me too."

"So if we find our children boring, who is to blame, is it the peer culture, is it—"

"Nononono. I wasn't saying *my* children are boring. I was agreeing with you about *your* children."

"I see," the older guy said.

Ray thought, Here is the problem: This is not a joke: It's on the verge of being a joke but it doesn't arrive. Rex had something, but he wanted to be more, to be brilliant. There was a roster of the brilliant and there was a roster of the nonbrilliant and there was one for the formerly considered brilliant. Every serious writer considered any appellation other than brilliant an insult. If the word appeared, glittering, somewhere in a review, then any objections the review contained surrounding the word were nullified. They turned to mist. *A brilliant failure* was just fine. He was prepared to salute anything brilliant he found in *Strange News*. He meant it. He would be happy about it. This was Rex's attempt at a monument and he was willing to help, more willing than he had been. His feelings were changing. How serious the core of *Strange News* was remained a question, but that was all right. He pitied serious writers. The best that ninety-nine percent of them could hope for was a glancing appearance in a survey course at lengthening intervals. Even Milton was dropping to survey status more and more, even at the graduate level. It was true. And the next step down would be the collateral reading in a survey course, the books only the strivers got around to. I was a striver, a Striver, he thought. And then it would be down to a footnote in a title in the collateral list. And then what, some academic trivia game. And then nothing. It was possible for a writer's creation to be of academic interest *solely* for whatever influences could be seen in it of prior writers, more brilliant writers. That was life, the literary life.

114. Untitled

> X decided to stay home and pass the time by
> counting his feet.

> Shall we watch TV?
> X said, "That's what it's for."

> X said, "I really think people watch television
> because there's too much to read."

> Where are you going?
> "Out this door," X said.

It was clear that a penstroke had converted an original J to X. J would be Rex's Joel, these were echoes of Joel.

Not all were cases of camouflage, only some.

His brother was sick. He could be dying. He could be dead. Ray couldn't bear it. He would work with the fact that *Strange News* was a mélange, workroom scraps, with lame political shots and shafts that would get dated. Rex's trust in a campaign of bons mots against the world's evil was touching. He believed more in the power of the word than Ray did. Rex had no idea how solid the machine in the basement was. He was an innocent. Literature is humanity talking to itself, Ray thought. Rex thought it was more. Ridicule changed nothing. If its targets even noticed it, all it did was madden them. Ray had the beginnings of a fair collection of narrative-like entries to use for soporific purposes.

There were little lists of enemies in different spheres of the arts that were going to be difficult for Ray to edit because so many of the names were unfamiliar to him. He had to be careful. Some categories could be combined, he supposed, like the *Wisdom of the Mob* and the *Wisdom of the People* entries. The Mob wasn't the Mafia. The Overheards could remain, or most of them could.

408. Overheard I

At a party one time I asked who a familiar-looking ancient guy was. He could hardly stand up. X couldn't remember his name but said he was a Yale Younger Poet.

X said The best way to keep a secret is not to tell it to anyone.
    This is true. A woman I know went to a psychotherapist and was upset when the diagnosis she got was that basically she was too greedy.

I feel so good after a high-fat meal I could run around the block and beat the shit out of somebody, unfortunately.

Man and wife were buying sundries in a job-lot discount emporium. The woman filled her basket and took it to the counter to pay for her choices. Her husband, who was handling tools in the hardware section, suddenly ran up and added a hammer to her purchases. "We have a hammer," she said. "So, I'm getting another one. It's cheap." "Why would we need two hammers?" "*I'm getting this.* We need it in case two people have to hammer at the same time."

Hey how about *air burial* for pilots and stewardesses and plane passengers who die in flight.

It was more fun than eating on the roof.

My penis is sensitive lately.
    Well I should hope.

His problem is he can't tell his anus from the Mammoth Cave or some other tourist attraction like that.

Ray realized that he was encountering very little gay matter in *Strange News*. Has it been sanitized? he wondered. Because it would be logical to have something so central represented, if this was Rex's true monument. Anything he could learn on the subject from Rex would be fine with him. But maybe there was nothing to learn and it was what it was and that was it. Something else was hanging over his efforts. He might as well acknowledge it. It was possible he was searching for something directed openly to him, some statement or apology or he didn't know what, something.

All he could do was doctor this chowder he had been given. A certain amount of shuffling was required. For example All Power to the Country Clubs! should go into the Cries and Chants for Sale section, and maybe Put Paid to Poverty! which he had apparently thought of as something appropriate to the British Labour Party. If the gay aspect had been left out by Rex himself, the reason might have been to make Ray love him as a soul, if he thought Ray held that against him. Ray was tired. Nobody likes to say goodbye, he thought. His eyes were burning. *Tears rushed from my eyes*, Keletso had said in some connection. That's what he needed. There was a jingle going through his mind, ending mea culpa youa culpa din dan don, which was from "Frère Jacques," the din dan don, if he was right. People separated from their siblings in childhood moved heaven and earth to find them, these days, to get back in touch. He knew he had been singing a deformed "Frère Jacques" to himself as mental background music. What could he do? He was far from sleep. Now his brother was trying to kill him with love, with guilt, with proof he should have appreciated him. Too much is enough, he thought. He would be able to sleep nevertheless. The span of time he could sleep soundly in untoward positions was lengthening. But sleep had to come knocking. We can be wrong, he thought. We can be wrong about anybody, he thought. His eyes were tearing, a little. It was the Titles sections that hurt the most, stung hardest, because presumably they stood for ideas for potential books, articles a healthy person might have attempted. *The Importance of Being Important, The Future Assembles, All I Can Tell You Is This, The Urbane Guerrilla: Etiquette for Revolutionaries*, and another similar one, *Out to Luncheon: Notes Toward a More Elegant Mode of Disparagement . . . The Bungless Cask . . . Fumes from a Vial of Wrath . . . Flea Circus Rebellion*. Rex tried things. He wasn't afraid not to be great. I have to honor that, Ray thought. Pity was attacking him, threatening to fill him up. He was fatigued. There were animal eyes out in the darkness that flashed when he swept the flashlight beam around. They were low to the ground so were, presumably, attached to bush babies or some small and similarly unthreatening species. Ray pulled out a few narrative entries to read.

803. Friends

Two friends who worked in different departments of a Catholic orphanage met to talk. The kindergarten director had recently begun working additionally part-time in a different institution, a state mental health facility, one evening a week, teaching crafts to adolescent patients. She wondered if her friend might be interested in joining her.

Sylvia, the art therapist, said, "You know, I might. It would be easy for me. You know what we did today, for example? I brought in shoe polish . . ."

"What kind of a project can you do with shoe polish?"

"I brought in shoe polish and they played odds and evens and the winner got to polish my boots."

He thought he could go to sleep.
He slept.

26. *This Dead, Thin Person*

When the explosion occurred, it made Ray wonder if somehow the future was an already existing thing. Because he felt he'd known for twenty or thirty minutes before the blast that it or something like it was about to happen. Keletso was unhappy. They had to pull over and see what could be seen, and Keletso was showing his unhappiness at having to do that. But they had to.

Ray got out. He climbed onto the cab roof and stood up on it carefully, his feet placed precisely over the reinforcing rods whose locations he had early on ascertained by probing the fabric lining the cab ceiling with his forefinger. He was determined to return this particular piece of government property in unchanged condition. That was important to him. He didn't know why, unless it was because doing the small things right when the central thing he was supposed to be doing was so undefined, undefined but hazardous and probably stupid, seemed essential.

Using his binoculars, he studied the terrain to the north. It was high noon. The heat was insane, as usual. The horizon appeared to be writhing. He grimaced violently, to dislodge the little scabs in the corners of his mouth, which Keletso, who was watching him closely and with apprehension, mistook for an expression of fear. He shook his head to reassure Keletso, but clearly he was failing in that. He couldn't do everything.

There had been a significant explosion in the vicinity and it had produced a ball of inky smoke, which was now dissolving. The site was reachable, not distant, not more than three or four kilometers to the north. They were aimed east. Everything to the south and west was dead flat. To the north he could distinguish a succession of very modest ridges, three of them, bare along the crests, thick brush packing the intervals between them. There had to be a settlement or more likely a cattle post just beyond the horizon ridge. More smoke was rising, from several sources. The explosion had been unusual, manifesting more like a gigantic insuck of breath than like an outward push of air. He could make out a palm tree, just the top of it, in the smoky area, and as he studied it he thought he saw flames in the . . . not leaves and not spikes and not fangs, no, in the fronds, fronds, bright flame. The palm tree meant water. It would be a cattle post. He had to get over there, and now he was sorry he'd gotten rid of the mouth scabs, because now there were visible traces of blood where the scabs had been, no doubt making him look like a vampire just when he wanted to make a good impression. He knew what he needed, exactly what he needed, and didn't have. He needed a styptic pencil. He doubted they were even manufactured anymore. The ridges he would have to cross were reddish, gravelly-looking, with some glinting element here and there, probably mica. He had to get over there. He climbed down from the cab roof.

He readied himself to go alone cross-country. There would be a spur road into the post, a track at least, but he was hardly going to boldly drive up as big as life. He would have to go in subtly and alone, and that would mean leaving Keletso behind, with the vehicle, like it or not.

He had on a longsleeved denim shirt, which he buttoned to the neck. There was no time to enjoy the amazing colors this landscape displayed, the mustard-yellow southern reaches, flat as a lake . . . one of Rex's similes. He realized that he had two new central priorities in his activity here. One was to see that Keletso came to no harm. He had to get him out of this. And the other was to see that *Strange News* survived and got back into safe hands. He was going to do what he could for this what, concretion, of his brother, do it not because it was a great manifestation in itself. To his shame, he was relieved at how minor the sensibility gesturing in *Strange News* was. It was minor, but it was not nothing, and it was Rex and it was true that certain bits and pieces of Rex's collation were sticking like burrs in his consciousness, some because they were striking but obscure, *The Tree with Square Leaves*, some for no particular reason, like *The Bloom Too Ponderous for Its Stalk*, some of Rex's odd titles for unwritten works. Ray drove the cuffs of his jeans deep inside the tops of his boots. He applied sunblock lavishly to his face and neck. He put on a broad-brimmed canvas hunter's hat and fastened the chin strap tightly against his jaw. Keletso handed him a pair of work gloves. Ray had to be wary of ticks and any other upward-leaping insects that might be lying in wait.

There were thousands of species of uncataloged insects in the Kalahari, he'd heard. What some of them might be capable of was a matter of conjecture. He got out his darkest sunglasses. Keletso sprayed insecticide from a canister over Ray's pants legs. Then there was nothing to do but get going. He had already impressed on Keletso that *Strange News* was to be safekept, as Keletso had put it when they'd talked about it. Ray was ready. The drill for snakes he had down pretty well. It was time to go.

Keletso was fidgeting around unhappily. Ray knew what it was about, but he had decided definitely to go unarmed. Initially that had been because he hadn't wanted to alarm Keletso unduly about what he might be getting into. But then it had been a cloudier thing. It was that he had forfeited whatever authority or right he had ever had to kill anybody and that was because, because of killings the agency had superintended that he had looked aside from, or something like that. It wasn't exactly that in an abstract way he deserved to die. He didn't think he did, really. But that was all the time he could spare for this interesting question. And he was going unarmed. And he knew it was unnecessary to one more time tell Keletso to safeguard *Strange News*, but he wanted to, because of a notion that was getting too ponderous for its stalk to the effect that Rex had been so urgent about getting this olla podrida to him because Ray would be able to appreciate it, because he, Ray, was the one in the family who was supposed to be a writer, based on the stupid prizes he had won, his love of English, his power to memorize poetry, trivial shit like that.

Keletso wanted to have a conference. There was no time for it. Ray willed himself fully into an overruling demeanor he had never used with Keletso before. That was too bad.

There was a curt session. Ray made clear how it was going to be. Keletso would wait in that exact spot for not longer than three hours. If Ray hadn't returned within that period, Keletso would drive on to Nokaneng, four hours away, and find a way to report the situation to whatever authorities he could find. But Keletso had to understand that this was never going to be necessary. Ray tried to be light. But Keletso knew, Ray could tell, that there was improvising going on. It had been evident for a good while that Keletso had been living with the knowledge that Ray's site-inspection mission was a fiction, a pantomime, a cover for something else that was not necessarily Keletso's business.

Ray summed up. The vehicle had to be guarded because if anything happened to it they would both be in peril. Ray promised he would get no closer to what was happening over the ridge than he had to in order to ascertain the facts of the situation. He would be sly and he might not even show himself and he would be back to the vehicle like a shot. Keletso asked Ray if he wanted him to get his clipboard for him. It was not a serious question. But he was serious that Ray had to not forget the knobkerrie and to lash it around well in the grass as he proceeded. Ray knew the protocol for snake avoidance. He accepted the knobkerrie. They consulted their wristwatches to see that both were registering the same time. They were.

Ray set off, outwardly purposeful, inwardly the opposite. He was operating according to necessity. He had an act to complete, in this landscape seething with exotic and largely sinister life through which he would have to go on hands and knees finally, when he got to the last ridge. He had an act to complete and it was impossible to have an opinion about some better alternative now that he was launched. It was like being in the ranks during a war when it was time to get up out of the trench and charge the enemy lines, even though the strategy behind the order was obviously stupid or cockeyed. It was like that. He decided that proceeding inexorably on a ludicrous or unnecessarily dangerous excursion made the actor feel like he was made out of cork, would be one way to put it, not made out of the usual flinching prickling flesh stuff that reacted and recoiled and would make him give up, go back. He felt buoyant, which was logical if he was made out of cork. He would be able to walk fully upright at first, then he would have to walk crouching more and more, and then it would be time to crawl.

The brush was dense, and forging through it was work. There were no paths. A burnt smell was coming to him fitfully, along with another odor, acrid and chemical. It was conceivable he could be shot, he supposed, if there was shooting going on and his luck was foul. He didn't know why, but he was confident that that was not going to happen. He was going to approach the scene of the crime exquisitely, cringing forward, as his brother might put it. And secondly, he just knew it wasn't going to end that way for him. He was going to float through this business, like a cork. That was his assessment.

In the noise reaching him from his destination there were no identifiably human cries. That was favorable, probably, he thought. He did not want to find anyone screaming in pain. And he hadn't brought his first aid kit, except for the antivenom pouch that was part of it, selfishly. There seemed to be a gonglike, booming sound. Someone was banging on an empty tank. He would rather find dead bodies than living suffering bastards he would have no idea how to help, God help him. That was the truth. We are our limitations, he thought.

An elaborate beetle, big, a scarab, materialized on his wrist. Violently he struck and crushed it with his fist, leaving his arm throbbing. He knew that scarab beetles had something to do with death, according to the ancient Egyptians. One image he had to suppress was how his beloved, his Iris, would look when she got the news that some ultimate thing had happened to him, not that it imminently would. But no, if he concentrated on all the injustice she had created through her involvement with Morel, it could help his effort, it could, not much but some. Because he loved her like hell. Life is a scream, she had once said, his darling had.

Walking bent forward was a strain, to the degree that crawling would be a relief for however long.

He was at the base of the final ridge. He went to all fours. Burning makes noise, he thought. Things were actively burning, hissing, just ahead. Threads and flakes of soot were wafting down.

Flat down, he inched his way to the ridge crest, gouging up loose earth and pushing it ahead of him, building a hump he could use for partial cover when he emerged into visibility. Raising his head, he told himself to move *minutely*. In training in the dim past the importance of avoiding abrupt movements during surveillance exercises had been impressed on him. Take forever, he told himself.

The ruinous scene before him was frightening. He had to go down into it. He sank back out of sight while he gathered himself. He was close to the scene, right on top of it, really, fifty or sixty yards from it at most. This was a fresh scene. He looked again.

He could see four dead beasts. He was scanning for bodies, animal or human. Nothing had bitten him. There was nothing to prevent him from descending into the scene. Nothing had bitten him or struck him or injured him en route in a way that would have made it necessary for him to return to Keletso to save himself, nothing. He was fine. He was seeing something he had to check. He was seeing a naked human leg projecting from the doorway of a burning rondavel. There were two rondavels, both burning, by which he meant that their thatch roofs were burning, just the roofs, which had fallen in, burning, dropping like hells into the interiors of the pitiful, impossibly pitiful, huts. Dead cattle, beasts, he could deal with, but he wanted the leg to be an error, a roof pole, something that looked like a leg.

What he should do was approach circuitously, but he couldn't bear to do that. He had to walk straight in. Anyway, the scene seemed empty, fresh but empty. It was quiet and there were no actors that he could see. He got to his knees.

This was a small cattle post. Every structure had been touched with destruction, the rondavels, a dip tank gashed and gouting streams of greenish liquid, a tin pump shack now a mere shell around a violent oil fire. He had to get to the leg. He stood up. The dead beasts were in the kraal. Weak black smoke was rising from the borehole mouth, and the piping connecting it to the pump shack had been disrupted, half smashed. He had to get to the casualty.

He started down. He would go looking as innocent as he could. He would appear as a passerby.

"Hallo," he shouted, Britishly, not quite sure why he was choosing that mode. It was true that many Batswana seemed to like the racist British more than they did the what, the better Americans. The Brits got more loving care in the hospitals than Americans, as a rule, if he could believe a certain person who had the bad luck to get treatment in the Princess Marina Hospital in a ward where Brit patients were being fawned over whilst, as the Brits would put it, the Batswana nurses mocked the Americans behind their backs for their attempts at egalitarian camaraderie toward them.

"Hallo," he said again, striding as properly as he could down the rough far slope of the ridge.

Kerosene had been splashed liberally around everywhere in pursuance of arson, but the attempt had obviously been hurried and on some recalcitrant surfaces the kerosene had simply burned off, as it had on the kraal at the center of the cattle post. They had not gotten it to burn. It was an oval kraal made of gnarled sections of log meshed with smaller tree limbs all locked together with windings of different calibers of wire. It was not one of the classic traditional kraals, which were works of art, the logs set deep into the ground and artfully interlinked with the tree limbs into mighty fencing that could resist the worst lunges of irritated cattle, but interlinked without resort to any supplementary binding material. It was a dying art, like thatching. Thatching was being wretchedly done, according to the elderly.

God would help him now. There were two rondavels side by side. He ran to the leg and bent over and pulled on it. The victim was face down. A body followed the one leg. As he pulled, the other leg bent, and folded up under the abdomen. It was a man. It was a man, grown, not old. Something had crushed the left side of his head. He was wearing khaki shorts and a ragged tee shirt. He was shoeless. He was a small man. Ray turned him over. His eyes were open. Someone had to bury this man, to keep wild animals from getting at him, or the body had to be put under something or into something to keep it intact. He would figure it out.

Ray held his forearm across his mouth and nose and entered the rondavel, probing the burning thatch on the floor with his knobkerrie. The interior was full of burning or half-burned items of bedding, furnishings. Anything the size of a man he probed at. He retreated, satisfied that there were no further bodies there.

The second rondavel was a problem. The interior was pure fire. He got as close to it as he could manage and pointlessly shouted into the fire, saying in Setswana both "I am here" and "Are you in there?"

He tried to tell by the smell of the fire in the second rondavel if flesh was being consumed by it. It was all futile and he was taking in too much smoke. He didn't know how to proceed, except that it seemed to him urgent to pull the body of the dead man farther out, into the yard, and lay it out with the legs straight and together and the arms crossed, until he could think what to do to protect this shell of a human being. And it was even more urgent to find something to wrap around his wound so that he could look at this dead, thin person.

As soon as the conflagration in the second rondavel got less he would tackle it. Ray had a bandanna crammed into his back pocket. He had tied it across his lower face earlier during his transit through the beds of brush between the ridges but had decided against sporting it when he arrived at the site, on the theory that it might not be helpful to look at first glance like a bandit, to whomever he might encounter. He used the bandanna to cover the dead man's wound.

He guessed that the victim was a Mokgalagadi, basing that on the elaborate initiation scars on his cheeks and on a yellowish tendency in his complexion. He was somewhere in his thirties. He had a small face. His soles and palms were thickly callused. The whites of his eyes were charged with blood, but whether that was related to the way he had died or represented some prior condition was unknowable. He was thin but not emaciated. The man had been brained. He was a herder, probably the only one in a post of such modest size, he had lived a life of unremitting toil, he had all his front teeth, he had lived in unimaginable solitude, now he was dead. He appeared to be staring at something that displeased him, was how Ray would have to describe his expression. There was nothing to identify him in the pockets of his shorts. There was no time for communing. He wanted to apologize. There was no time. "I apologize," he said. He felt fairly safe, fairly sure that the malefactors were off and away, that this had been a hit-and-run affair, fairly sure of that but not certain. Someone might be aiming at him from anywhere. Let them, he thought. There were fresh treadmarks in the sandy track leading out of the compound and away ultimately to the same road he and Keletso were following. The good idea came to him of putting his knobkerrie down lest someone from a distance mistake it for a firearm. He had to finish, he had to look into the kraal, had to add things up and quickly, because he was tiring. His knees hurt. He hadn't been noticing, but they were painful.

It felt wrong to abandon the body, but he had to. Bitter truisms were tormenting him, all variants of the fact that this man would be leading his life if Ray had never come to Africa, never been born, never sent Pony to surveil Morel, never put Pony in a position to betray Kerekang. It was that the man's life had been so minor, such a crust of a life. No one had a right to interrupt so meager an existence. He had lived his days in a clearing a couple of hundred yards across, the ground baked into white iron, no softness, nothing to look at . . . although the terrain to the north was more rumpled and presumably more interesting than the sheer flatness commencing back where Keletso was waiting, waiting safely, God willing. God would keep him. And what had this man done with his spare time, if that was even an applicable concept? There was a shattered transistor radio on the rondavel stoop. He had listened to Radio Botswana and to the incessant sounds the animals made and what else. Animals never shut up, Ray thought.

He was ready to go. But he was seeing something wrong. He was picking up a shudder in the arras, the brown and acid-green tapestry the bush on the far side of the donga represented. Something was moving, possibly hiding, moving in fits and starts. Now it was not moving. Nothing was. Whatever was moving was light in color. He might be in danger. There was something to attend to. He knew what the possibilities were. There could be a wounded survivor in hiding, or a raider not wounded at all. Now he couldn't go. He was exhausted and he couldn't go. He was profoundly exhausted.

Black drifts of smoke were masking the part of the terrain he had to understand. When they weakened and he could see again he was ready. He knew he needed to continue looking as happenstantial as he could, given his butcherous appearance. He had to be unthreatening. He took off his sunglasses.

He proceeded to shout "Wapenduka" first, which was the Herero greet-

ing. There were Baherero herders, although very few if any of them
worked for Tswana cattle owners. But he happened to know the greeting.

He switched to Setswana, shouting "O tsogile," a request to know how
a respondent was doing, actually how a respondent was standing, oddly
enough.

He needed the Bushman greeting. He didn't know what it was. It was
normal to find Bushmen working at the most casual level of labor at the
cattle posts, coming and going, working for salt, sugar, and tobacco and
room and board, coming and going like phantoms. They had to be managed gently because they could waltz out and live comfortably in hell,
getting water out of tubers, dancing through hell.

He was waiting.

He definitely saw something white shuffling around in the brush. He
needed to sit down and concentrate, because standing, suddenly, was too
hard. He sat on the ground, closer to the donga.

He addressed the landscape, loudly, again in Setswana, "Ga ke na
sepe," which meant *I have nothing*, which he hoped would convey associa-
tively that he was saying he had no weapons. But then he wondered what
he had said, because he knew "Ga ke na madi" meant *I have no money*.
How many times had he said it to panhandlers? So it was possible that his
statement had been a double negative, a piece of nonsense. So he would
try something else.

"Ke sepe," he called out, which he was fairly sure meant *I am nothing*,
plain and simple, and which he hoped someone with any reason to be
dubious about him would take as an assertion that he was nothing to
be concerned about. He was having no effect.

He wanted everyone to speak English, everyone in the world, for
Christ's sake and for the greatest good of the greatest number. Someday
the world's business would get taken care of with such ease no one would
believe it, in English. Situations like the one he was in would dissolve, go
away, allowing people to go home. Disputes would still occur, of course,
but it would be different. He could hardly wait.

"Reveal yourself," he said rather than shouted. It was getting more difficult to shout.

He would promise to help anyone who needed it. "Ke thusa," he made
himself shout with reasonable force.

He continued to wait while nothing happened and warned himself not
to relax beyond a certain point, not to take a nap to refresh himself. He
wanted a nap. He would be joining the dead if he succumbed. He wondered what his audience was thinking about his performance. Nobody

could miss the fact that he was the one who needed help. That was all right. He was doing his best.

"I am ashamed," he announced. He didn't know what he meant but he could figure it out because he was intelligent. All he needed was a rest. In fact, as he got to his feet again, he figured out why he had said what he'd said. It was private. What he was ashamed of was that ever since he had come down into this burning place the bottom half of his mind had been converted into a prayer rug. He had been playing a constant Muzak of appeals to God, thanks to God for this and that. He visualized his brain sitting in a thick syrup like cough medicine. He began coughing just then and asked God to help him stop. He stopped. He thanked God. He couldn't not, it seemed.

He had a pretty clear notion of what he was going to find in the kraal. There were unlikely to be any surprises. But he realized that he had to look first into the donga, a deep donga, beyond the rondavels, at the edge of the clearing. It would be the refuse dump for this facility. It could hold horrors. He prayed to God not.

The crevasse was about twenty feet across and a hundred or so feet long, slightly curving, deepest at its east end. Ray walked around to the high end of the sloping burden of refuse the donga held. He knew how it worked, a pit like this. Everything would end up in it, cow bones, human waste, mealie cobs, ashes, slops, melon rinds, Fanta cans, chibuku cartons, broken tools, and when the stench got too evident paraffin would be pitched into it and set alight. Any horror would be down at the deep end. It had been a while, obviously, since the collation had been treated with fire. The stench was fierce.

There was nothing untoward there and he had to back away from it. The thing was not to die and end up in that particular flaw in the landscape, in the donga.

Next was the kraal. But first he had to take care of the body and it had come to him how he could do that. There was a zinc drinking trough he could drag over and upend over the corpse. He would be steadier if he could accomplish that.

It was easier than he'd expected. The trough was sizable, ten or twelve feet long. It was heavy, but he would be able to move it. It was kept in place by a low surround of stakes driven into the earth. It was near the kraal and not linked up by piping to the borehole unit. It had been filled by hand, Ray supposed. He heaved it free and slowly slid it over to the forecourt of the rondavel, in two long, sustained pushes. It would have been less work to move the body in the direction of the trough, but he hadn't been up for it.

There was no time for ceremony. He got the body under the over-turned trough. He was getting blood on himself. He wanted to say something from Milton but all he could think of was *To be weak is miserable*, which was true but not what he'd had in mind to say. He said it anyway. Next was the kraal.

There should be a dog around. Every cattle post had one, at least one. Some posts had many, multitudes. So there was something amiss. He didn't know what it meant, unless the dog or dogs had been killed, which would have been a feat if the dog happened to be a ridgeback, which was overwhelmingly the commonest breed over in the bush. Ridgebacks were smart, vicious, quick, paranoid creatures. You can't get near them quietly, he thought. So there was something to keep his mind on.

The kraal gate lay on the ground. It was a standard pipe-and-wire crossing gate. It had been wrenched from its hinges. The classic kraals relied on clever maze entries, whose construction was yet another dy-ing art.

There were four dead beasts, as he'd calculated from a distance, three heifers and a bull. They were distributed in a line against the kraal fence, the heifers closer together, the bull alone. The bull was a Charolais, although how he knew that escaped him. Like the heifers, the bull had been shot multiple times behind the ear. The bull had been running and had collapsed forward. His head was turned under, his neck undoubtedly broken. There was thick yellow foam in the nostrils of the bull. The bull was a black and white, the heifers were black and tan. The largest of the heifers had been shot in the haunch as well as the head. He had collected a sampling of cartridges. That was enough. He was not going to dig slugs out of cows.

Anyway, he didn't want to contribute to whatever prosecution of those who'd raided this cattle post might finally result. Unless that man's death had been intentional. That would make everything different. He ought to collect a slug or two. There was no way he could believe that Kerekang would approve the shape this raid had taken. It had to be that this was the handiwork of the movement he'd generated. Yes Kerekang wanted the absentee cattle owners punished, burned out, driven out of the northwest quadrant of the country. And he was willing to massacre cattle to arrive at that. But he had never killed the herders. There could be parasites on the movement, uncontrollable elements. That was the trouble with move-ments. And so far he hadn't found ISA written or scratched on anything. The movement had a name. To Make Happen was its name. ISA. ISA was a political signature and he hadn't found it anywhere, so this could be a piggyback situation, rough elements getting in on the action. He wanted to entertain that. It was hard, though.

He needed to wash. He needed a towel, at least. There was no water. There had been a relic of water, the only water he had come across in the compound, a couple of gallons of it in the drinking trough, and he had poured it out on the ground, stupidly. What was plentiful was fire, not water. The individual fires were flagging, thank God, and the gap between the burning structures and the dry thornveld beyond hadn't been crossed, that he could see. So thank God, he thought. But in fact he didn't care if it all burned away, burned to the horizon, leaving nothing.

His right hand and his right sleeve were red. He didn't like it. He had an idea. Someone had kicked a drum of powdered milk over and hacked at it and Ray went to the lean-to where he had seen it and rolled his arm and hand around in the whiteness of the spilled powder. It made no sense. There were two storage lean-tos and they had been dealt with in a cur-sory way. Sacks of World Food Organization rice had been slashed open. Someone was not thinking. These were supplies. They could have been taken and used. He patted more milk powder on his arm. It looked odd but better. It would look odd to Keletso when he got back to him, but not as frightening as the alternative.

One last task was to find heavy things he could heap on the drinking trough to keep it secure until the authorities could come. There were no heavy things. He needed the drinking trough to be in place over its con-tents, its contents . . . Because the Cape vultures would be coming soon, dropping down through the smoke. He had been creative. There was no time to do a burial. What he could do was cap one end of the trough with the tipped-over three-legged pot sitting in ashes next to the second ron-davel. It was a heavy item, very heavy, a cauldron. It was iron. It would do.

He rolled the pot into place and tipped it over and got the mouth solidly over one end of the drinking trough. But then for the foot of the trough he had nothing, unless he made a collection of less heavy items stand for something truly heavy like the three-legged pot. That was all he could do. He brought fire-blackened rocks from the ring around the cooking space the pot had been in the center of. And he found a sledge-hammer head, solitary, detached from its shaft, that would add something. And then he dragged the kraal gate over and laid it on top of the rocks. And that was as much as was possible. He began coughing again and again asked God to help him stop. He stopped. He thanked God.

Whatever was twitching in the landscape across the donga was not being aggressive. He could see more of the shape than before and it was low to the ground. He had to proceed around to that side and get close enough to what he was seeing to determine what it was and help it or kill it or run or do whatever God might suggest at that point. He was nowhere nearer believing in God than he had ever been in his adult life, and yet he doubted he could have gotten through this excursion without the God-talk. No doubt someone like Morel would sneer at him. He wouldn't mind discussing it with Morel someday. His wife liked to talk to Morel. She found him interesting. But the God-talk was like an addiction, like needing to chew gum. God-talk assuaged something and got people through extreme situations without turning them devout, so what was the problem? It was a puzzle for people like Morel.

He got around to the far side of the donga and advanced delicately toward the object of his attention, which was inert, not moving at all. It was a white low lump, a long white low lump half obscured in the wreckage of a rough trellis that had once supported granadilla vines. Now the trellis was destroyed, pulled down, the vines uprooted. Someone had taken the trouble to dump diesel oil into a pathetic melon patch in the same area. He could see now that the white bundle was only partly white. He was seeing white fabric, a bedspread, stained red in places, swaddled or caught around an unknown thing. He wanted to leave it alone but knew he couldn't. He was afraid. It was impossible not to think it might be a child, a small child, or an infant, swaddled up there, dead. Hello I must be going, he thought. God would keep it from being a child.

He pulled at the fabric. It was fixed to whatever it contained. A metal spindle or sharpened rod had been driven through it and into the body within, because it was going to be a body. Blood had welled up from the wound the rod had inflicted.

He unfurled the bedspread. He thanked God for his goodness, because the bedspread had been wrapped around a dog, a dead dog, newly dead. It was a ridgeback, gaunt, as they always seemed to be, wolflike, gray, with its coarse coat of hair tufting peculiarly along the spine. This must have been the camp watchdog. It was an old animal. And it was clear what had happened. The dog had a dart in its throat, a flimsy metal thing, a Bushman dart. So a Bushman had gotten close enough to blow a dart into it, to shut it up, and the dart would have had one of their paralyzing poisons on it, and then to completely neutralize the dog someone had muffled it up in a bedspread and jabbed a skewer into it for good measure. And what Ray had seen was the dog dragging his shroud feebly around, unable to bark, obviously, giving his last kicks and twitches. The dart proved that Bushmen were involved in this. He would have preferred not knowing that for a certainty.

A washtub caught his eye. He could use it. He pressed the dog bundle into it and overturned it and placed it next to the drinking trough tomb, under the kraal gate. It was pointless. Nothing could stop the legions of carrion eaters for long. Everything is a gesture, he thought.

Now it would be interesting to see if he had the strength to get back to the Land Cruiser. He was filling up with hollowness, if such a thing was possible. It was his right knee that was problematical. If he could go slowly enough he was sure he could manage, but if he went slowly he ran the risk of getting back to the road just in time to see Keletso driving off toward Nokaneng. He had twenty minutes, he calculated. He had to start off immediately. There was no time to do more than he had. He retrieved his knobkerrie. He could go.

A terrible cry alarmed him. There was more happening. Someone was screaming somewhere. He had to hide, but he had to go as well. It was too much. His knee was bad, hurting.

Another berserk cry came, as a figure appeared on the crest of the ridge he had to cross to get back to safety, a figure waving an ax. But then it was fine, a fine thing.

It was Keletso, disobedient man, angelic man, trying to terrify any antagonists there might be.

27. *Nokaneng*

They were in Nokaneng. They had made it by early dusk. They were in Nokaneng, eating.

Nothing is perfect, Ray thought. They were under pressure to finish eating with dispatch. There was a bathing shed attached to the Golden Wing Restaurant and General Dealer and he and Keletso had booked hot baths and the donkey boiler was heating up as they ate, but the proprietor, Rra Makoko, wanted them to eat and bathe and begone, so that he could close shop on time. Closing on the dot was a ritual in Botswana. Ray wanted to relax over his food and in fact *dine* for a change. His meal seemed delicious. It was rice with chicken gizzards in powerful peri-peri sauce, with bread rolls and Pine Nut soda. And tea was coming. Nothing was bothering him much, not even the outrageous five-pula charge for the load of cow chips and kindling that would be consumed in heating their bathwater. The help wanted him to finish. An elderly woman, barefoot, in a blue housecoat and white headscarf, was circling their table, at a distance, it was true, but still it was unnerving, as it was meant to be. Iris knew how to stop that when they did it. She would make a scene if she had to. She was bold. He loved her.

He sent Keletso off to bathe. Ray's exhaustion, which had abated during the drive from the cattle post, was back, toweringly back. He wanted to put his head down on the table for a few beats, but that would give the impression he was drunk. The proprietor was a severe sort. He watched his plate being taken away. He had almost been finished. He held tight to his half-full tumbler of soda.

He liked the dim light in this room. He liked the Golden Wing. He found it interesting. It consisted of an old colonial residence much repaired and added to and attended by huts and outbuildings and derelict vehicles and parts of vehicles. The residence was a low, rambling wooden structure whose exterior was covered with green-painted panels of metal stamped with geometric designs and whose corrugated iron roof was painted rouge red, in mimicry of terracotta roofing, Ray supposed. There were numerous windows, all heavily barred, and some of the window-panes clearly dated from the turn of the century or earlier, if that was what the thickness and irregularity in those panes meant. There was a broad veranda and there was a cactus garden flourishing, if that was the word, on three sides of the place. The store or dealership took up what had been the front parlor and dining room of the colonial house. It was aromatic because the wooden shelving, the wide plank floors, the wain-scoting were all kept in a state of high polish. The grounds of the place looked like a cyclone had tossed things around. There was no external upkeep. But indoors there were armadas of women constantly mopping and oiling and dusting. He knew the pattern. And probably it made sense to concentrate on the struggle for interior cleanliness and amenity against the ceaseless intrusions of dust and sand and whatnot the Kalahari could be counted on to deliver. Nothing could be done about the Kala-hari, the outdoors. This was a desolation, after all. Nokaneng had been founded in a particularly bleak part of the desolation. Trees of any kind were scarce thereabouts.

They had been served in the main room of the store, at a refectory table placed near the front. Three gas refrigerators, industrial-size units, took up most of one wall. The shelves were well stocked, but the selec-tion was, he would say, on the limited side, featuring the usual staples, sacks of mealie and sorghum and rice, tinned pilchards and beef tongue and beetroot, cooking oil, boxes of Joko tea, containers of paraffin, pack-ets of fruit salts. Four candles were burning on the counter near the baroque, gleaming, antique cash register. A woman, a different woman than the one waiting on them, emerged and pinched out two of the can-dles and retreated into the back, smartly. It was as though pinching out candles made up her particular work assignment. The other woman could have taken care of it, since she was mainly occupied in waiting for him to down his scalding tea, which yet *another* woman had just set before him. Ludicrous overstaffing was normal in rural outfits like this one because labor was so cheap and because nobody was checking. He would be willing to bet that most of the Golden Wing staff worked for rations. And the very casual meal service the Golden Wing provided was without question a derivative of the staff's morning, noon, and night preparation of food for itself, an overflow from that. There was no menu. He hoped the five-pula note he was leaving in payment was right. It would be. It was a lot.

He got up to go. Closing time was like a guillotine blade coming down, with doors slamming and bolts shoved home and lights doused and help dissolving away into whatever obscurity was available. He would join Keletso in the bath shed. He had to get his pulsing knee into hot water and he had to thank Keletso again. He had to thank him better.

The bathing shed was a sort of rude crib structure with oddments of canvas hung haphazardly over it. He announced himself. His torch was weak.

Lo! he thought as the main building of the Golden Wing complex went dark, or virtually so. There was a faint glow showing in the rearmost room, Makoko's quarters. And then even that was gone. And the garage, where they had gotten refueled, was silent and dark, too.

Keletso said, "Rra, you must come to this water whilst I leave."

"What do you mean, rra?"

"They say there is only one fire for two, rra."

Ray walked around to the donkey boiler. It was an oil drum sitting on a metal stand over what were now only embers, a remnant of fire, shreds, nothing, not embers, even. The pipe leading from the bottom of the oil drum into the bathing shed was slightly warm. He knocked on the drum. It appeared to be empty. It didn't matter.

So he would take whatever was in the tub. His knee was screaming.

Keletso said, "Rra, there is no soap. The woman has taken the soap, since I said to her yes I have used it and then it was gone and she was gone."

"It doesn't matter. Here I come."

Night wants me, Ray thought. He shook his torch. Its light was weaker yet. He shook it more, to no effect.

"There is no towel, rra. That woman left some mere rags, and not clean ones."

"It's no matata," Ray said.

Keletso was finishing up in darkness. Ray set his torch down on the ground, its weak beam pointed discreetly away into the yard. Staff from the Golden Wing were leaving en masse and with a celerity that made it seem they were fleeing something. Celerity was another one of those perfectly good words destined for the bone pile. It was ghostly, the women rushing through the dark, no torches no candles, muttering, a ghostly experience but over in a shot.

Ray undressed. Keletso wanted him to hurry. The water was cooling.

He got into the soiled bathwater, which wasn't exactly the term he wanted. He didn't care that he was second. If he had been offered the chance to precede Keletso he would have declined, out of respect, abject gratitude, everything. Keletso had held him up, hauled him along like a baby half of the way back from the cattle post to the Land Cruiser. And Keletso had cleaned him up, as best he could, before stuffing him into the Cruiser and driving like a banshee on fire away from there and back to the trunk road and the safety they expected to enjoy in Nokaneng, should they get there and not die in a crash en route. He submerged himself in the tepid water and rubbed his limbs. He would have to find something to tie around his knee for a day or so. And next time he came to the bush he would carry a pumice stone for eventualities like this. He would get Iris to find one, except that he wouldn't, couldn't. She was not going to be available. She was better at cutting his toenails than he was. There was a craft element to the way she did it. Half the time it needed to be done she would offer to do it, out of love. You can't step into the same river twice, he thought. He would be cutting his own toenails now, forever, if he was right about things. He was afraid he was. He knew he was.

And then they had arrived in supremely strange and negligible Nokaneng. It barely existed. You were on twisting, sandy roadway and then you were on a segment of graveled road and there was the Golden Wing complex on one side and, opposite it, a cinderblock cube supposedly housing a suboffice of the Northwest District Council, shuttered, showing every sign of being not in use, and then another cube, the health post, also locked up and visibly empty, nothing in it, no furniture, and then spreading away in the dusty haze to the west a scattered handful of widely separated household compounds, many of them in disrepair, unoccupied, and then near the road a long sloping dome of maize husks, small stock fodder, glimmering in the gloaming, and then the raw sand road began again, twisting north. A general furtiveness characterized the few inhabitants they had managed to interact with so far, it would be fair to say. People had seemed eager to avoid them or to deal as briefly with them as they could get away with, given that some of them wanted their business. The tall, sinister-looking Rra Makoko, who had claimed to be both the proprietor of the Golden Wing and then, later, not the proprietor at all but a factotum for a German named either Gaster or another name like it that he couldn't remember, the real proprietor, who lived far away in either Gobabis or Walvis Bay over in SouthWest. Makoko's eye patch had put him off. And initially Makoko had had no difficulty transacting with him in English, and then it had become more difficult, and then everything had had to go through Keletso, in Setswana.

Still, certain things had been accomplished, certain difficulties overcome. Tomorrow Keletso would be out of this and Ray would proceed on his own, alone. He had produced a letter for Keletso to present to his superiors at the Transport Office pronouncing that Keletso had performed superbly in all his assignments and that he was no longer needed by Ray, whose only remaining task was to find a restful place where he could collate the materials he had collected, prepare his final report, and then return to the capital via the main roads, which were so much less difficult to traverse. His chief trouble in writing the letter of reference had been to control the ragged beast his handwriting had become. The idea of sending along a letter for Iris, entrusting it to Keletso, was something he had considered. But he had dismissed it because . . . there were too many reasons not to. She would be alarmed at his penmanship. She would see through anything he wrote. She would grill Keletso without mercy and she would make the most alarmist interpretations of what she got out of him. He had no idea what to put down. Of course he wanted her reassured that he was physically all right. Keletso could call her. That would be the best. The idea of writing filled Ray with uncontrollable anxiety. Partly that came out of his furious sense of betrayal. And partly it came out of a sordid desire to punish her with his absence, with worry about what might have become of him. And then also there was the pathetic ingredient, id est, the shard of hope that his absence and the shadows of danger hanging around it would bring her back to her senses, back to loving him, violent scenes with Morel, showing him the door, scenes he could imagine. Keletso expected him to write something for Iris. He knew it and he knew Keletso would think ill of him, seriously ill of him, if he didn't write something for his own wife. There was no way to avoid it. He had toyed with the idea of sending a dummy letter, an envelope containing a couple of sheets of blank paper, sealed up tight. That would appease Keletso's feelings. But it would be an impossible event for Iris, opening it. He couldn't do that. As it stood, Keletso was to convey to Iris that all was well and that Ray would be back sometime soon. And there would be no mention of the cattle post raid. But Keletso was still expecting him to hand him a letter. There it was. He couldn't do it.

Keletso was dressed and waiting. Ray got out and, still damp, entered his clothes. This was his last pair of clean dungarees. The clothes bloodied at the cattle post were balled up and cached someplace under canvas

in the back of the Cruiser. He had worn the most presentable of his accumulated dirty clothes into Nokaneng. He might try to arrange to get
some laundry done tomorrow or he might not. He had to be on his way,
alone, there was no alternative.

At loose ends, they stood together by the roadside. Ray wanted to do
something, even if it was only taking a walk, before they retired. The
Cruiser was parked next to the district council office cube and they were
going to have to sleep in the damned vehicle again. They had been looking forward to getting some kind of normal accommodation that night.
But that hadn't gone right.

Other important things had gone right. They had gotten loaded up on
petrol and oil and other necessities, by the skin of their teeth, before the
Garage and Panelbeaters Golden Wing Proprietary had closed up, earlier than the restaurant, with a clangorous display worthy of grand opera,
slamming, locks snapping. Something strange had been going on long-
distance between the garage and Makoko on the veranda. He had been
giving hand signals and whistling in an eerie way when he wanted the
garage foreman's attention.

"I want to walk a little," Ray said.

"Rra, your knee is not strong."

"No, but walking will be good for it."

Ray liked to have destinations when he strolled.

He pointed out a substantial termite mound a little way into the bush
just beyond the graveled stretch of road. It would do for a destination. It
gleamed in the starlight. He had the idea he would like to sit on it or
climb on it. Termite mounds were amazing things. This one was the size
of a sedan, white, smooth. Thine alabaster cities gleam, would be an
appropriate comment to make to a termite.

He started off and Keletso came with him, reluctantly, hoveringly,
poised to catch him if he stumbled. One object of taking a short walk was
to convince Keletso that his knee was improving enough for him not to
be concerned. He put his mind to it.

Keletso's resistance to letting him continue alone tomorrow had been
prodigious. It had taken some heavy argument. The matter was closed.
Apparently the cattle post scene had shaken Keletso less than it had him.
Their argument had concluded with a certain amount of white lying, so
to speak, about what he was planning to do next, the final stage of his mission, that is, that he would be resting up and working over his notes and
sketches and maps. To start with, it was a lie that he had a mission. What
he had was a trajectory and a trajectory that it was his fate to feel he

absolutely had to complete. And that was true. It was remarkable how well he and Keletso had gotten on within the shell of deception the expedition had involved. They had lived companionably within the necessary lies. Keletso was a man.

Cooking fires wagged in some of the lolwapas. Some people in this extreme part of the world were at home, just then. They were kicking their sandals off and saying "Ah."

He had misused his time in Botswana in so many ways. He hadn't sunk into the particularity of the place, and there was plenty of that. He hadn't, for instance, concentrated really closely on what the Golden Wing represented, what it was . . . a weird relic of a fantasy time of white overlordship. He knew what the green-tinged irregular windowpanes of the Golden Wing reminded him of. It was a particular brook in Tilden Park, a particular run, perfect water flowing gently wrist-deep over beds of dark gold sand. And of course that was a line surviving from the part of his life he had wasted in the assault on poetry. It didn't matter.

The termite mound was more like an inflated seal than a sedan. It had a chimney or necklike projection at its high end, which registered the height it had reached in consuming utterly the tree it had claimed, or they had claimed, the termites.

"It seems you must be forever roaming, rra," Keletso said.

"No more tonight, though. We can turn in."

"Yah, but I will go again for a place in that house for us. I will make a fracas and see about it."

"You can try, I guess. But it won't work, rra. He doesn't like us."

They started back.

Keletso farted softly. He said, "Ke ditiro tsa Modimo."

He said it because it always made Ray laugh. As Keletso had explained it, he was saying God did this, or That was a deed of God's.

"Shame on him, then," Ray said.

Certain things had gone well. The Wildlife connection he had made had gone just right. He let himself relive it. Approaching Nokaneng, a government bakkie coming from the opposite direction had appeared and blasted right past them. But some instinct had prompted Keletso to swing perilously around and roar after it, pressing the hooter nonstop, shouting. And Ray, jolted awake, had contributed by rolling down his window and pounding on the door. And it had worked, the angelic Keletso driving like a devil from hell and the racket they had produced together had worked. The bakkie had pulled over.

Keletso had seized the moment. *Carpe diem* should be your personal motto because you carp about one thing or another every day, Iris had once said to him in a moment of joke pique. He should write down her *bons mots* and whatnot sometime but it would be too pathetic of him. Ideally it would be a thing they would undertake together. She would remember certain things and he would remember certain things and out of that would come his little anthology. The time to do it had passed him by. *Life is a scream* would be in it.

Keletso had explained that he had sprung into action on the hunch that this might be their only chance to make contact with some goromente employee, a chance they should not pass up, since goromente was so little in evidence around there, no police, no army, no veterinary trucks.

So then Ray had machinated smoothly with the Wildlife officers who had been going somewhere in the bakkie. He had quickly gotten out the news of the raid. They had been electrified. They knew the place. They had seemed capable. He had dealt mainly with the senior man, a tough, leathery character. Of course it had started out awkwardly with them, but he had overcome it. Striding over to greet them, he had been struggling to contain a fit of coughing caused by the volumes of dust he'd taken in during the chase. And he had tried to spit, preparatory to trying to machinate. But unfortunately his saliva was less than normal. He had tried to spit just casually and it had been an embarrassing moment because his saliva was viscous and the spittle hadn't detached normally via its own weight and he had had to pinch it off his lip, in front of people, to get it to drop. Diet was affecting his saliva. He needed vegetables. And he needed peaches, if he could get some. That was what he thought.

But then he had worked it all out. They would come back the next day for sure and pick up Keletso and carry him down to Maun. In Maun goromente was still functioning and Keletso would be fine. He would have no trouble organizing transport down to the capital. Ray had given them an enormous deposit of fifty pula and thrown in another twenty rands and he had promised Keletso would give them the same amount when they returned for him. It was settled. They were burning to get away to inspect the raided cattle post. They were fearless, apparently. They were competent men, or seemed to be. They had yards of maps to consult. He didn't doubt that their eagerness to get to the raid site had to do with salvage, the opportunity to field-dress the fresh carcasses, assuming the Cape vultures had been detained in arriving. But he was guessing about that. Cape vultures had come up in their exchanges and, as he understood what they were saying, the Cape vultures were becoming very scarce, along with other carrion birds.

They had thanked him profusely for the information. Clearly they were unafraid of the people who had been responsible for the raid, but then, of course, they had armloads of rifles, Enfields, on board, a regular arsenal. They had everything they needed that he could think of. They had roof-mounted spotlights, camping gear. There was a smell of drink coming from them, which was not something so far out of the ordinary that he had to draw any conclusions, negative ones, from it, necessarily. And then he had been relieved when it had become evident that it was the junior man who had been drinking. Ray felt he had handled the negotiations well, clinching the deal by making it clear that the payment he was making for Keletso's passage was not something that would need to be reported to anyone.

Keletso was determined to make *one* last appeal to Makoko. Ray trailed along as Keletso prowled noisily around to the back of the Golden Wing and began knocking on windows.

"You have to say who you are," Ray said. Keletso understood why. They wanted to avoid Makoko taking it into his head to start shooting at intruders. Keletso amended his campaign of harassment immediately.

The building was voluminous. There was obviously plenty of space, corners for two people to stretch out in. Makoko was the sole occupant. They knew that. There had been reference made earlier both to sleeping rooms and to a sleeping cabin, not by Makoko but by one of the serving women. Keletso had taken the matter up with Makoko while Ray was concerned elsewhere and had been told, as Keletso reported it, that the sleeping facilities were not "functual." And they had decided to drop it because Makoko was already acting generally so peculiarly toward them. Ray thought he knew some of the reasons why. He and Keletso might be anybody. The property Makoko was in charge of, whether it was his or belonged to someone else, deserved expanded protection while unrest was raging in the neighborhood, naturally. Ray had been unwilling to press for lodgings because the booking process could easily have required him to produce his passport. Even in remotenesses like this one, it might have been requested. And it would have made no sense to whine for lodgings while there were other things they sorely needed from Makoko outstanding. So the time to go for lodgings had passed. Essentially, Keletso was playing. It could go on for a while without doing any harm. Keletso hadn't been reconciled to sleeping in the vehicle one more time. This was ventilation. It could go on a little longer. Keletso would feel better.

Hissing and calling out "Koko," Keletso was being persistent. Koko was the Tswana announcement that you were present and ready to come in, which, it occurred to Ray, Makoko might take aslant since it happened to constitute two-thirds of his surname. It might be taken as mockery. He thought he would retreat from this exercise. He was staying on his feet too much. He would retreat to the other side of the road and sit and wait and that would encourage Keletso to give this up and come to the vehicle.

In fact, it was urgent for him to get off his feet. He wanted Keletso to stop. Suddenly what Keletso was doing was seeming foolhardy, foolhardier than it had originally. His judgment is shit, he said to himself.

"Itlhaganele," he called over his shoulder. And he knew another way of saying to hurry up, so he said that too, "Dira ka bonako."

He leaned against the Land Cruiser, but that was still too arduous. He found a wooden crate next to the district council building and he turned it over and sat on it, not a moment too soon, he was collapsing.

Yes, no question that he had been too cursory with Africa and had taken too instrumental an attitude toward it. He regretted it. Someone had said there was a Herero section in Nokaneng. And it hadn't occurred to him to bother to find five minutes of time to walk around in it. It was exotic. It was a unique what, venue, but not venue, something else, milieu. Iris would have found a way to get a sense of it, scope it out, and in a way nobody would have objected to. The Herero women were something, with their stuffed bicorn headdresses, their patchwork copies of nineteenth-century gowns, their two front teeth knocked out to enable proper, as they saw it, pronunciation. It was an art to go among unusual people and see what you could and give no offense. He remembered now that Iris was interested in the Baherero. She had bought books about them from the Botswana Book Centre. Baherero were not to be found in the capital, the south, at all. He could have reported what he saw to her. It was too bad. No, he had never gotten to the marrow of Africa, and the termite mound visit of a few minutes ago was exemplary of how to be superficial about amazing Africa. No, because if you thought about it there was a kinship of sorts between manunkind and the termite nation or race in that they were the only two species whose main defining activity was producing hard hollow permanent structures. It was something to think about. Of course there were the coral reefs. He forgot whether they were created by some individual species or by congeries of fungi and bacteria and so on. He was very tired. He had known more when he was young. There were things he should have read. He had been given, twice, by people he respected, copies of *The Soul of the White Ant*, one of them by beloved Marion Resnick, and he had been told it was the book he had to read if he wanted to know the essence of the amazing termites of southern Africa, and they, both copies, were sitting unread in his bookshelf at St. James's.

He put his head between his knees, preemptively, for a moment. Yes, he was lightheaded, but no it was not going to be a problem. He would get strength. He looked up at the stars. They were strong. They were strong things. He felt that. There was astrology, there was Kipling, his poem, the something the something the something dum dum While the Stars in their courses / Do fight on our side. The stars were better, brighter, in Africa.

Keletso would stop his agitating about now, if he had any sense. Everything was going to unfold. I am having a feeling, he thought. It was an intense thing he had had once or twice before, to the effect that everything that was happening had already happened but that the consciousness of beings like himself who were subject to living at a certain crawling rate were only discovering what had already happened, a minute at a time, something like that. That was the notion that we, man, were advancing through something that was already *over*, in some way, like his marriage. And what went with the feeling was an image. And the image was that everything was connected by invisible lines or pulsing lines something like the sequencing lights on the top and bottom edges of movie marquees and these connections were invisible except to the occasional seer, possibly, and they ran between every kind of object not excluding himself and his friend, good friend, Keletso. Ray went faint, but he recovered before he fell off the crate.

Keletso was back, laughing.

"Wa reng Moses?" Ray said. He had more Setswana in the midden of his mind than he gave himself credit for. Keletso liked it when he was addressed by Ray in Setswana. Wa reng Moses? was a faintly irreligious slang way of asking someone what was up. He could have picked up some additional Setswana from his friend if he'd thought of doing it.

Keletso said, "I am just laughing, rra. He sayed to me, 'Matlho me a bokaletsemy,' two times. So then I was knocking his house even more.

"But then whilst I am knocking the most, he says out, very loud, 'Ke otsela, Ke otsela.' Time and again! I am asleep, I am asleep.

"Rra, we can do nothing with this donkey."

"Yes, but what was the first thing he said to you? I didn't get it."

"He sayed, My eyes are heavy with sleep."

"Oh, right." He wanted to finish up with more Setswana, but he was fading and sinking.

Keletso held his hand down to him and he took it and rose out of himself, his weakness. Deep breaths would help. He considered the pinpricks of firelight strewn thinly through the dark. Some of them represented happy marriages, some fraction of them. How many, though, was a question only an anthropologist could answer. Some should be invited to take up the question, get out there and find the answer. He would like to know. It was germane to a feeling he was having, a sort of swelling desire to give some advice to Keletso. Tomorrow his opportunity to advise the man would be gone.

He was not entirely himself, which he knew. But if he could deliver some advice he would feel better and sleep better. It was a generic desire to give advice that he was suffering from, but he could narrow it down. And he had to be careful to be sure that what he said was all right, not unusual. It was some consolation if the mistakes that added up to a particular life could be crushed to yield a vial or two of advice.

He was going to concentrate on advice henceforth. That was an idea. He would find Kerekang and give him advice too, if he could find him. We should be kind. The world is a terrible machine, he thought.

Wait, he thought. Because he wanted to shout something before he began advising, to the effect that he was older. He had turned forty-nine. Two days ago he had turned forty-nine and not noticed. There had always been a strain with Iris over birthdays, which she loved and that was fine, but which he considered celebrations of what, sheer duration. She had always prevailed on the question of doing something, a little something, dinner with what, he couldn't remember what, something extra, some wine they had had at someone's house that he had said was delicious and that she had remembered and gotten for him, always something. And then always, no matter what he said, some sort of giftlet, always. Or a real gift, a book he wanted, something.

Ray said, "Rra, I want to give you some advice before you go, which is tomorrow."

"I am listening, rra."

"It's about a wife, when you come to find a wife, what you should do. One and number one, you should be true to her. Yes, be true, but that is not enough. Okay, *I* was true, and . . . But nevertheless it is number one."

Keletso groaned, Ray thought.

He said, "What is it?"

"*Nowhere* am I finding my wife, I . . ."

Ray interrupted. "But you will, my friend, and let me tell you what you must do, according to me, you see, when you do. Number one you must forget this testing of women by taking only one who can make a child. No, my friend. I know all about this."

"I am old, rra," Keletso said.

"No you're not, Keletso."

"Yah, I am forty years. So I must find a young woman for a wife. You can see."

"Well, I understand. You want children. I understand. But you have to think of other things, too, when you look at women . . . and you have time, in your life. Do you know how old I am?"

"Nyah, rra."

"I am forty-nine, just."

"*Is it?* As from what day, rra."

"Sunday, it was."

"*Ai*. You sayed nothing. Yah, cheers. Cheers, rra."

"Cheers. Thanks."

"So we are two monna mogolo."

"No, I am. You're not."

"You have a wife. I cannot catch you up."

"You can. And you can keep her.

"You will find someone and, Keletso, listen, when you touch her with love the first time, you must find words to say how you love to touch her, how much. Say, This is heaven, to touch you. If you see what I'm saying. You find some way to make her feel your love like a knife going in, so it is different from any touch before. You can say anything, Your flesh is God, strong words, anything you like. And every day hold her hard against you. And say the same thing or anything similar, but strong. Your breath is like water, and so on.

"Because, rra . . . women are very decent. They can drown us with sweetness and love, if we let them . . ."

"Ehe," Keletso said, uneasily, Ray sensed.

I'm saying too much but I have to, Ray thought.

"And you must be willing to seem a fool, when you tell your feelings. You must be extreme. You must be what they say in West Africa, fou. I don't know what the Setswana is . . . mad is what it is in English . . ."

"Setsenwa," Keletso said.

"Good. You want her to think this chap is setsenwa. And you want her to say to herself, No other man will feel like this toward me. He does not exist.

"And as to finding a wife and having children, it will happen."

He was finding it impossible to get out the image that was filling him, to release it and plant it. He wanted Keletso to have it. It was that women are what, that the right woman is a locket or not a locket a jewel box, a jewel box full of something so beautiful and rich and rare, and yet men fixate on opening the catch, the lock, the word wedlock was wrong, but opening the lid and leaving the lid just open, failing to throw back the lid, turning to something else, satisfied. It was poesy and it was true, wasn't it? But it was useless. It was too ornate. It was too ornate.

"You are right," Keletso said.

"About what?"

"I am too much with chasing up these young girls."

"Yes, if that's what you're doing. There are fine women, widows, women with children already. No, it's a question of finding that *one*, that one, the correct one."

"And rra, what do you say as to presents, because I am always too soon with presents, it seems. And I see I have just put my money to burn away to smoke. They are looking for presents, rra."

"Well, you have to be careful about that, I would say."

It was time to stop. He had gotten out as much of the essence of his great conclusion as he could. On the details of courting, he had nothing to offer, he was ignorant, a self-taught ignoramus as Iris had described herself in one of her modes, funnily self-deprecating modes. And he was an ignoramus on the subject because he had only seriously ever courted one woman in his entire life. Now she was turning to smoke.

Ray wanted to be useful. He would try.

"Keletso, I know you want to have children. But I can tell you something about it.

"I would not put it first. You see me. I can swear to you before God that I am the happiest husband in the world. I have no children with my wife. No man was ever happier with a woman."

It was all true, but he felt he should have gotten at least the shadow of the past tense into it.

He got to his feet. He was sorry for the unmarried. He was as sorry for the unmarried as he was for himself, in his situation.

Keletso said, "You are happy in your home, rra. So you must ask God for nothing more."

Ray's eyes were filling up. He doubted Keletso could see that they were, but he turned his face away.

"Keletso, do you know where the aspirin is?"

"Ehe, rra. But is it your knee?"

"A headache."

He needed to sleep. It was urgent.

28. He Was Not Going to Be Allowed to Remain in the Shade

He was driving cautiously and so far successfully. He was keeping himself hydrated. He had two water bottles. He had Weetabix crackers to munch. He was going to keep his blood sugar up and compensate for the fact that it had been Keletso who had reminded them it was time to snack, have a meal, not go too long without eating.

The sky was overcast, a burning white. The landscape was flat and blank and yellow tending to white on the left, also burning. And the landscape was the same but then dark green in the near distance to the right, where the delta was. The road had swung closer to the delta. The road was more sinuous. He wondered if he would ever see the delta, where it was exotic, exotic Africa. He was uninterested in tourism except as a form of shared fun. He had done too little of it during his wifetime. He had to smile. His accidents were amusing and that had been one.

He bit into a cracker. He had learned things from Keletso he needed to remember. Driving at night, if you felt sleepy, a good thing to do was to take an apple and make yourself eat the entire thing, chew it slowly, down to the bitter seeds. It would keep you awake. He might need to.

He estimated that he had covered twenty of the fifty kilometers between Nokaneng and the next even smaller and more negligible hamlet, Gumare, which he would transit hoping to reach Etsha by nightfall. The road surface was passable, a little grittier, the grit consisting of bits of ancient shells from the time when all this had been deep underwater. He knew about the shell bits from someone in Gaborone, a geologist.

He would overnight in Etsha and the next day creep along Route 14 and somehow find the spur road that led off to Toromole, the Jerusalem of ISA, the site of Ichokela Bokhutlon or what was left of it. He liked

Endure to the End as a motto or name for something. It was a good
motto for what he was doing. And when he got there he might find nothing or he might find a mound of ashes. He thought, The past is a bucket
of ashes but so is the near future sometimes. The past is a bucket of fishhooks, would be more like it. His mind was tending to aphorism because
he was dipping into *Strange News* from time to time, during stops to pee
or stretch, and he was extending his breaks for the purpose of meeting his
obligation to finish reading his brother's last will and testament. It was
important for him to get through *Strange News* and it had been right of
Rex to struggle to get it to him. He seemed to be saying to him something like I hope you like this better than you liked me. It was something
like that. He could endure that, liking his brother's best efforts. Rex was
supplying entertainment, in this solitude he was being propelled through,
or dragged through.

There was something wrong ahead. He had just come around a sharp
curve and there was something black in the straight stretch of road
directly ahead. The road was sinuous above Nokaneng because it moved
over to follow the irregular perimeter of the floodplain of the Okavango
River, snaking its way around salients of saw grass and reeds, beds of dry
reeds, patches of elephant grass. The road straightened out and then
curved east just beyond the black thing in the road. He wondered when
the last time was that floodwater had come this far inland. It had been
many years. These days the Okavango River was a shriveled thing. When
the wind went through the grasses and reeds it made a sound more like
clattering than something normal and sibilant.

There was a person in the road. And something was doing in the field
of elephant grass. The grass was very high. Something about the texture
of the scene was wrong. There could be tents or netting half showing. He
would know soon enough.

The figure in the road was a man, just one, a black man standing
blocking the way with his arms held out at his sides like Christ on the
cross. He was certain that that was what he was seeing, but of course in
Botswana you could see in the middle distance or on the skyline what was
clearly a bush twitch and strut away, becoming an ostrich. But the imita-
tion of Christ he was seeing was a man. He looked civilian enough. Ray
needed to get closer. This assignment had been hard on his eyesight, the
constant brightness had. His sunglasses were dark as night. He thought
his night vision was a little worse than it had been when he started out. It
had been helpful to have Keletso handle night driving. And now his distance vision was seeming a little lacking. Glasses were coming in the next

segment of his life. He had gotten Iris when his face had been naked and unencumbered. Even so, he had always been amazed that someone so much beyond his reach had wanted him. In the future any search to be made for a new companion would be undertaken by a bespectacled man, not that that should make a giant difference. But still it was interesting. The design of glasses had improved. Iris always said that when the subject of his possibly needing glasses came up. He would get the best glasses he could. But how would he know which ones were the best? He would figure it out. Morel was a little younger, of course, but as he remembered it, Morel needed reading glasses. We all need glasses, ultimately, he thought, feeling stupid. Because obviously what he was doing was trying to tally up ways, however trivial, in which he was the better man than Gunga Din. It was as though he was preparing for an event, a debate or argument that would decide who Iris would cleave to on the basis of one of them getting a higher score in enumerated qualities.

There was still time to stop, reverse, and turn back to Nokaneng, if he acted immediately. He had been driving with great circumspection and deliberation, out of consideration for his knee. Reversing and swinging around and getting the hell out of there would demand some vigorous moves. And it would conflict with what he thought of as his Trajectory. It would truncate everything. He would discover one of three things, up ahead, or of four things. One would be that this was lifti lifti, a random hitchhiker, innocent. One would be that the person blocking the road was goromente, legitimate. Another was that the man was one of the counterinsurgency specialists from koevoet over in SouthWest. They were killers. He knew that they were present and operating against his friend Kerekang and Kerekang's friends. And he knew in his bones that Boyle was involved with bringing these teams on board. It would be their job to do the cupping. Mercenaries were scum. They would be setting up cups where they were the only power. Of course the final discovery possible would be that this would be someone from ISA he could communicate with and who would get him to Kerekang. The odds on that were small. But that was what he wanted more than life because he had advice for Kerekang. He was full of important advice. It was keeping him awake at night. He drove forward, at a crawl. You are in the rapids, he thought.

The man in the road wasn't police, not in any kind of uniform, which might mean he was a hitchhiker. He did look civilian. He was wearing cargo pants, sandals and not boots, a workshirt whose sleeves had been torn off at the shoulder, revealing arms on the huge side, intimidatingly huge arms, in fact. Let me call you Nemesis, Ray thought.

Nemesis was trying to look amiable. He was smiling broadly. And he was doing something clever. He was wearing a baseball cap with the bill pulled sharply down. His big smile was in evidence but the rest of his face was innocently, supposedly, obscure. He was showing himself to be demonstrably unarmed, his hands empty. But he did have a bandanna loosely tied around his neck. If things got critical, it could be pulled up. Mercenaries hated to have their faces seen.

Ray came to a halt. The tone of the encounter was changing already. Ray was receiving peremptory beckoning signals from his nemesis. This was the cup, the edge of the cup.

There was definitely an encampment off in the saw grass. He could make out the tops of tents. There were vehicles under camouflage netting, olive drab bakkies and a jeep. They had selected a good spot to bivouac. The saw grass was thick and the elephant grass was very high. You had to be on top of them to know anyone was there.

The question was whether they would want to take him for questioning or send him back to Nokaneng, kick him out.

The smiling man approached. He was a young fellow. He was keeping his head down, making a show of studying something on the ground. He came to the driver's side and motioned to Ray that it should be cranked open. Ray hesitated, until he noted in the rearview mirror that a bakkie had come from nowhere and edged into the road behind him, closing it. Ray opened the window.

"Can you step down to me, rra?" the smiling man asked.

There had been no greetings, no dumelas, no entshwarele.

"Dumela, rra," Ray said. It would be an interesting datum if his nemesis knew English but not Setswana. He could be Ovambo, in that case.

"You must step down, rra."

"What is it about? You aren't BDF. I am going to Etsha, so what is this?" He sounded obstreperous to himself, more obstreperous than was exactly wise.

"The road is closed from here, rra, for safety."

"By whose order, rra?"

"It is goromente, rra. Can you please step to me."

Ray sat unmoving, seized by an anxiety he knew was irrelevant. He had a thick section of *Strange News* in a clipboard on the seat beside him. He had to guard it. He didn't know how much of the manuscript Iris had managed to photocopy before she'd thrust it on him. Maybe none of it. The whole process of getting it into his hands had been frenzied, here, and, as he understood it, back in the States. He needed to get it out of sight before he opened the doors of the cab. He had to do it deftly. He thought he could. It felt urgent. There were ink notations in his brother's own maddening minuscule hand on the pages. His brother was dying, or dead. That was news he was going to receive. He had to get the manuscript under the seat and he could do it now while the smiling was still going on and his nemesis was still bothering to deal coyly with him, his gaze off-center. The Land Cruiser cab sat high, meaning that sight lines were in his favor if he tried to bury the act of ditching the manuscript within the business of bending and reaching to unlock the passenger-side door. He would have to move like lightning.

He hesitated. He didn't know what he wanted to happen. He wanted to escape this in the easiest way he could, but he wanted to know what it was, too. He wanted that more. People experienced this who had never asked for it, never deserved it. At the far end of every avenue twisting off from each of his mundane exercises undertaken for the agency, at the extreme far end, was the possibility of something like this for someone who, unlike himself, had never volunteered for it, roadblocks and worse, roadblocks that were gateways to the unimaginable. But now he had to safeguard *Strange News*.

He said, "Gosiame, rra. I will come out."

He unlocked the door on his side and then proceeded to stretch over to accomplish his little trick. He got hold of the clipboard and was spiriting it under the seat when he was caught. He had miscalculated and the smiling man, no longer smiling, in fact with his lower face covered by the bandanna, was on him, having jerked the driver's-side door open without further ado. It was war, then. He felt like a fool. Nemesis pulled him out of the cab, swung him out of the way, and clambered up into the cab himself, emerging clutching *Strange News*.

Nemesis had associates and here they were, wearing balaclavas despite the impossible heat. There were four of them. They were in camouflage outfits. One was carrying an assault rifle, an Uzi.

The thing to do was to look indignant and baffled for as long as he could. He had to hold down his impulse to beg his nemesis to be careful with the manuscript. That would be idiotic. He wanted to. His knee was bad again. It had been improving. But he had nearly fallen when he'd been pulled out of the vehicle and he hadn't been able to protect his knee.

He was not going to be allowed to remain in the shade, narrow and minimal as it was, of the Land Cruiser. Nemesis beckoned him out into the road, into full sun. An associate ran forward with a camp stool, but it was for Nemesis. Ray would have to sit on the hot ground. The arrangement was that he would sit with his back to whatever was going on with the vehicle. He would be able to hear the rough interrogation his vehicle was undergoing at the hands of the associates, but not see it. Nemesis would be able to see it, direct it.

The questioning was about to begin. Nemesis tucked the hanging point of his bandanna up under the material binding his cheeks and nose, so that his mouth would be free to shout clearly, to imprecate, whatever his plan was. Ray was having a moment of strength. It was strange. Nemesis kept his cap on, but he raised the bill just enough to let him see Ray without impediment.

A sheaf of papers, Ray's documents, taken from the glove box, was handed to Nemesis, who went tediously through them.

Nemesis said, "Your passport, rra. I must see it."

"It should be there."

"Nyah. Where is it?"

"It should be there. You are alarming me. It must be there."

"Nyah, I have some things. I have your driver's license, your third-party certificate papers, and these Letters of Reference, one, two, three. That is all."

"Let me go and search. It was there."

"Nyah. Give me your hat, rra."

"Why?"

That was wrong. Nemesis reached over and plucked Ray's hat off, made a cursory examination of its interior and threw the hat aside. Ray knew he would now be asked to stand and turn his pockets out.

That happened. Afterward, he was allowed to sit again. His hat was not returned. There had been nothing of interest in his pockets. He should be pleased with himself, since the point of tearing his passport to bits and burning it had surely been to court something just like this, the scene he was in, or entering. Or at least not to be under its protection during it.

Nemesis was leafing through *Strange News*.

The man was superior in rank to his associates. Ray decided to rename him Uno. What he had seen of Uno's mouth and chin and his eyes would be enough to identify him whenever, if ever, he saw him unmasked. I have my skills, Ray thought.

And Uno's immense arms would help identify him, although overmusculature was not in short supply in this milieu, from what he could judge of Uno's associates. And the degree of physical development they displayed meant some formal training regimen, with weights, and that led back to koevoet and to the South African Defence Force's special units division. Lips were more individual than teeth, often. He would know Uno. And voices were absolutely individual, miraculously.

Uno shouted something and made a slashing gesture and Ray knew what was coming and he was right. The engine went silent. That was fateful. A corner had been turned. They were not going to send him on his way. He was ready.

The sun was beginning to hurt. He was drying up. His lips felt like balsa.

Perversely, it had been a relief when the engine was shut off. It made his path clearer. He was in the cup. For how long, he couldn't guess. He was feeling better, definitely. He had an image for his sense of improvement. It was that there was an outline around his body, invisible but real, and that now he was expanding, his self was, to fit it, snugly.

"You are not BDF," Ray said. He felt he needed to be more resistant. He needed to sow a few pips that would grow up to give pause, hints, hints of threats.

He went on. "I want you to understand something, rra. I am expected in Maun this week. If I am not back there soon there will be an alarm. I am performing a mission for the Ministry of Education . . ."

Uno cut him short. "Yah, I see your Letter of Remit. It is a lie. It is nothing. Why would you be carrying on with this mission whilst you are in the midst of bandits? Why shall you come out in the midst of burning and fighting? They are burning everything hereabout. They think it is SouthWest coming again."

That was interesting. Ray was seeing something in the shape of events that he had missed before. The Boers were finished in SouthWest. In fact, there was no SouthWest. It was Namibia. SWAPO had won. The Boer death squads that had been in action there, like koevoet, had been pushed out but had reconstituted themselves as mercenary veteran outfits operating out of floating camps in eastern Angola, where Savimbi was in charge, or up in Zaire. They had numerous sponsors. Some of the nicest governments in the world were sponsoring them, off the books of course. He could imagine Boyle imagining the possibility of a linkup between SWAPO and ISA. He could imagine Boyle selling his paranoia to goromente and/or vice versa. Things were going haywire in Zimbabwe, but Boyle was fixating strictly on Namibia and its discontents, on a country one-twelfth as significant as Zimbabwe. God save us from the geopolitical mind, he thought. Boyle understood nothing when it came to ISA. Ray had done what he could to make him understand. It had been pointless, useless. I *know* Kerekang, Ray thought. He had a moment of agony caused by the feeling that he himself could sort everything out, given a modicum of power, he could. But he had no power.

"Oh *God*," he said, unintentionally. He hated himself for it. It had been fervent.

Uno looked at him with interest. He wondered if Uno was religious and if some specious bond had been accidentally forged between them by his outcry. He wondered if something could be done with the impression, which he could amplify, that they were cobelievers, if one had been created. There was no conflict between being a murderous thug and being a believer, being a pious thug. They were everywhere. His intuition was that there was something here to work with. But he was tired. What he wanted was to get out of the sun.

A drumfire of unintelligible exclamations was coming from the associates as they rummaged through everything in the Land Cruiser. Uno seemed not to be attending much to them, though.

"Oh God," Ray said again inadvertently.

Uno regarded him oddly.

"Yah, God sees us." Uno's tone was interesting.

"He sure does," Ray said. It wasn't what he'd wanted to say. What he wanted to say on the subject of theology was something more like If God existed he would turn every scene of impending violence into electrifying tableau, he would drench every scene of impending murder with X rays that would show all parties that they were gesturing skeletons, brothers under the skin, pathetic. He could imagine it, imagine something like a phosphorus shell going off and making everything transparent and leaving all concerned too bemused to kill each other. He wanted to express something like that, but it would take more energy than he had to spare.

"Jesus must come," Uno said.

Ray couldn't think of how to play this intelligently. He wanted his hat back. His other nemeses, who were manhandling his goods in the Land Cruiser, had evidently found something exciting. They were Ovambo, definitely. They were unintelligible to him. He was missing some opening with Uno. His mind was everywhere. Far away to his right off in the haze he could see tiny white objects he believed were marabou storks, four of them. People traveled long distances to see marabou storks. The storks were moving around fitfully. They were carrying out their mission in life.

Ray said, "Yes, Jesus is coming soon, they say. And it will be judgment for all."

Uno was nodding vigorously. He seemed mournful. He stood up. He was being summoned to the Land Cruiser.

"Come right back," Ray said. He was reaching the point of being nonsensical. It was the sun doing it. It was torture, pure and simple. He could probably amble over to retrieve his hat and get away with it, but he wouldn't do it. Obedience was the ticket, for the moment anyway. And there was another consideration arising. He had to think of Iris. It would be impossible for her if anything really terrible happened to him. She didn't need that. He hadn't really thought clearly enough before about what it would do to her if anything genuinely terrible came to pass with him. His thinking was too volatile. He was leaving things out. One way you could tell if baldness was starting to pluck at you was if you noticed that for the first time when you happened to pat your head after you'd been out in the sun it was tender, or if your wife happened to pat your head affectionately then.

Uno trotted past, not looking his way, clutching to his chest the consolidated *Strange News* manuscript. They had the whole thing now.

Sol Invictus was the Roman name for the sun, which they'd worshiped. He could understand worshiping something powerful and inexorable that there was nothing you could do about, he supposed.

The storks were gone. He had been right, they were storks. It was important to be right.

Uno had disappeared around the curve of the road. Ray waited.

Finally Uno reappeared. Another figure, a stocky man in regular military kit but wearing a kepi, came out into the road. He was holding *Strange News*. He was Caucasian. His face was ruddy. He was too far away to make out clearly. You'll see him again, closer up, don't worry, Ray thought.

Uno returned, trotting again, carrying a blindfold and plastic handcuffs.

29. *Riding on Events*

He was a bundle in a bakkie. He was being conveyed somewhere. He was blindfolded, his hands were cuffed behind him, he was a bundle bouncing on the naked metal bed of a bakkie. He could sit up, just. The cap affixed over the bakkie bed was low-rise. It was work trying to keep himself braced into one corner so that the bouncing around would be less violent. It was difficult. He hated his trick knee. His captors were driving at speeds that made him love Keletso all over again, love his moderation.

But if he was right, this wouldn't go on for very long. He had a good idea of where they were taking him. Time would tell.

It should never be said that there's no progress, he thought. Clearly, restraint technology was marching on. The cuffs were of a design new to him. His hands were bound under notched plastic strips secured in a key-less ratchet locking mechanism. The cuffs were firmly but not painfully cinched.

And his blindfold was also a novelty to him. It was a standardized man-ufactured product, obviously, made out of a hybrid fabric more like neo-prene than cloth that had a propensity to cleave to human skin. Foam rubber pods were sewn into the eye-socket-covering segments of the blindfold. It was a successful design. He could see nothing down the sides of his nose. Someone had shaken the hand of the designer of the damned thing and said Well done!

What would it have taken for one of his captors to throw a blanket into the back, for cushioning? He was bruising up, with the jolting he was tak-ing. They were brutes and he wasn't. He thought, Though I've belted you and flayed you, by the living God that made you, I'm a better man than they are Gunga Din. What was it about Kipling? He had more Kipling than he did Milton. Kipling was in the pores of his mind.

And while he was on the subject, how in hell could belted you and *flayed* you, by the living God that made you, et cetera, but *flayed* you, get into a poem taught in junior high schools all over the world? *Flaying*, for God's sake, meant lifting strips of living skin off a living body. Was the narrator of the poem *flaying* somebody? Apparently so.

He had to remember that they were being gingerly with him so far, inflicting their indignities in a mannerly way. Someone had pitched his hat into the bakkie after him before locking him in. There was that. They had given him a little water to drink and they had invited him to urinate before cuffing him. And he had done that.

They had stowed him briefly in a hot tent, where he had devoted himself to listening heroically, or at least with heroic concentration, for leakages of information, anything. He hadn't extracted much. He had counted voices as well as he could. He estimated that there were seven malefactors active in his aural vicinity. There was one Boer, who was addressed as Kaptein by the rank and file but as Quartus, twice, by Uno, when the two of them were presumably alone together. Quartus could be a nom de guerre, maybe having some reference to ranking position. It sounded numerical. But he did know that Quartus was an actual Boer Christian name, like Fanie or Bastiaan. In any case, it was a nugget.

They had broken into the weapons compartment in the Cruiser and Uno had come into the tent shouting questions about licenses, where might they be? In Botswana it was a serious offense to be found in possession of unlicensed weapons. It could get you eighty-sixed in a flash, gone, out of the country. Uno made that point. Ray had protested his ignorance about guns and licenses, both. He was improvising.

And worse, and genuinely surprising to him, too, they had found smoke grenades in the compartment, two of them. He was too worn out to be enraged at Boyle or whoever the quartermaster had been who had equipped the vehicle. The smoke grenades had been somebody's idea of a useful extra. They hadn't bothered to mention them to him. Of course, he hadn't been as scrupulous about inventorying the gun compartment as he should have. He had been slipshod. He hated guns.

They had gotten him out of that tent not a moment too soon. The canvas was impregnated with insecticide and the fumes had been making him feel sick. Also, some solid creature in the soil under the tent floor had been trying to get into the tent, eat its way in. So it had been good to get out.

He had to compose himself as well as he could for the serious interrogation he knew was coming. Technically, all he was required to supply would be his name, rank, and serial number. This was a war zone, so the Geneva Convention applied, he would say. The difficulty was that he had no rank and no number other than his Social Security number, which they could have if they wanted it. Frame of mind was what was critical for interrogation. He had to be calm.

He was going to be calm. He should be able to be. He was fairly sure he knew where he was being taken. So there were unlikely to be surprises in that respect. It was the logical place, and if he had it right this little period of conveyal, which was not a word, conveyance was what he meant, would be over in less than an hour, at these speeds. He was all right. He was riding on events. Aside from the jolting he was taking, he didn't mind the feeling. It was the polar opposite of entrepreneurship. There were drivers and passengers in the world, more of the latter than the former. And in his obscure and secret way he had been among the drivers. Whether or not Iris or anyone had ever fully appreciated it, he had lived a consequential life of more or less permanent effort, exertion, listening and matching and watching and putting two and two together. So he didn't mind the feeling of reposing on events. It felt all right. Who was it, someone important in Africa, Livingstone, who had described relaxing into a sort of bliss when the jaws of a lion closed on his leg? And then the lion hadn't eaten him. And if he remembered correctly it was because when he went limp he appeared dead to the lion and lions abhor carrion. He didn't know if he was making that up. He forgot why the great man hadn't been eaten.

There was a vehicle closely following. He knew the sound of its engine by heart. It was the Cruiser. And that was favorable because it meant that it was still conceivable that they would dismiss him, tell him to drive off. With the Cruiser available, that could happen, that should calm him.

They were changing direction, which fit with his notion of their destination. He had three tasks, to sum up. First, to remain calm. Second, to retain what he could about anyone who laid a hand on him or anyone else so he could give evidence against them, not that it would ever happen. These bastards were finished in this part of Africa anyway. He wondered if they knew it. This was their last roundup. Mandela was coming. Mandela was going to rule and these bastards would have to get out. Nobody would have them except warlords and other scum farther north. But that was number two, to be ready to testify. And his third task was to get hold of *Strange News* again. He could do it. He would consider violence to get it. No he wouldn't. But he would get it.

It made sense that the koevoet command center would be set up at Ngami Bird Lodge. That was the way they were headed. There was a lurid tale connected to Ngami Bird Lodge. It had failed. It was bankrupt. The facility was shuttered and empty but not derelict. It was in litigation. But the infrastructure was intact, the generators, food stores, and so on. And, ah yes, it had a landing strip.

It was famously grandiose. Iris had wanted to see it, the mock-Moorish buildings, the rock gardens done by a famous landscape artist, date palms, chalets so-called, a zoo, if he remembered correctly. It had been built on the edge of a famous pan where flocks of birds came and the migrating wildebeests and the others. And then the drought had come. The pan had dried up. There was no birdwatching to be done. Pink marble facing had been trucked in from South Africa for the main building, he remembered.

There was more to the story. His knowledge of it was a cartoon, though. An English lord, the last of a noble lineage, had blown his patrimony on Ngami Bird Lodge and on a celebrity tart, a Coloured lounge singer supposedly then the toast of the Cape Town demimonde. He had brought her into the Kalahari to be the lodge's chatelaine. Then he had proceeded to drink himself into irrelevance as the project failed. There were remarkable things about the woman, the main one being that she had had devil horns strategically tattooed on her lower belly so that they appeared to be emerging from the top of her pubic escutcheon, had been the story. English eccentricity had come into it too. The earl had commissioned the creation of something called a sand fountain, a monumental device and the only one of its kind in the world. It had never been constructed. Aside from the drought, the lodge had been affected by the accelerating collapse of apartheid. The idea had been to create a mini-rival to Sun City that ethical tourists and gamblers and birdwatchers could visit in good conscience. But apartheid had faltered spectacularly. There had been a shooting, the earl was having a prolonged recovery somewhere in Dorset, and the woman had escaped justice and gone back to singing in bars in South Africa.

So, finally, he would get to visit Ngami Bird Lodge. Unfortunately he was going to be blindfolded during his visit. But that was life.

30. *Tomorrow It Would Be Combat*

He was where he had predicted to himself he would be, on the grounds of the Sand Castle, that being the original name for what became Ngami Bird Lodge. It had been abandoned when one of the backers of the project had pointed out the negative associations the name carried.

His home, for the time being, was a storage room twenty by twenty laterally by eight or so feet floor to ceiling. He was obligated to think about escape possibilities, even though he had just arrived, and he was sorry to have to say that the possibilities looked dim. The zinc panels forming the ceiling were laid over gum tree pole joists and securely fastened to the joists via wire lashings run through perforations in the metal. This was a solid structure. The walls were cement block. He had stamped on the softwood planking of the floor. It was chewed up and featured a display of standing splinters here and there, but it was in good shape. The planking had been pressed directly into the concrete footing. Clearly, heavy equipment had been stored in this space. There were oil and grease stains in the flooring.

It's roomy, at least, he thought.

The place was windowless but a pittance of light came in through nine vent slots irregularly distributed along the tops of the walls. It would be possible to push an arm through, assuming he could get up that high. He had managed to get a look into the one over the double doors to the shed by climbing up the cross braces on the inside of the doors while hanging on to a ringbolt set into the lintel. He had just gotten his eyes level with the opening, discovering that crushed wads of fine-mesh screening had been jammed into the slot to discourage ingress by animals and the heavier, more ungainly insects. So now he knew that much. There were hooks and other ringbolts screwed into the walls at shoulder level in no particular pattern.

His furnishings were basic, limited to a red plastic bucket lacking a lid or cover of any sort, and his pallet, a twin-size canvas sack filled with chopped maize husks. In fact there were three more pallets, so it was possible that he should be expecting company. He wouldn't mind company. No blanket had been provided, but the pallets were wide and could, he supposed, be doubled over if it got cold. He would see. He understood why it was that his captors didn't want him to have a blanket. They were afraid he might do something untoward with it.

They were still treating him acceptably, he would say. They had given him a plastic water bottle, half full, and a Cadbury chocolate bar, hazelnut, the jumbo.

He wanted to wash up. Tomorrow he would see if they'd allow it. He wanted his toothbrush. He would ask about that tomorrow, too. He'd try to present his requests all at the same time. It was a good idea to group his requests together, to avoid bothering them repeatedly.

He wanted his belt back, which they had taken. But that was delicate. There was a hyperthin carbon steel saw blade sewn into it. They were unlikely to discover it. But he didn't want them handling his belt unnecessarily. He truly needed his belt. His jeans were loose about the waist. He was losing weight. He would have to improvise something. He had known they would take his belt. It was standard procedure.

He was in his stocking feet. They had taken his boots. It was the laces, primarily, that they wanted him not to have. They could have unlaced his boots, or de-laced them, but it was easier for them to simply take them. Well, they were busy.

He had made one pleasing discovery. If he pressed hard enough against the closure line of the massive double doors to the shed he could create a slit of a view. There was a deadbolt lock on the doors, but there was enough play in the wood and the hinges and enough slippage along the bolt to allow him to see . . . another wall, the wall of another building a couple hundred feet away, a pinkish wall.

It was almost night. He hated it to be night so soon after he'd been liberated from his blindfold. He would be in pure and total darkness until morning came. But there was nothing he could do. And logic told him that the blindfold would be back.

Night had come. He was tired of listening for anything that might tell

him something. There were voices but they were too far away. Nothing
was happening. Vehicles were coming and going. A generator had been
started up and was chuffing along.

He had eaten half of his chocolate bar. He had a back tooth that was
sensitive to sweets. Rinsing his mouth out sparingly hadn't helped. He
had scrubbed his teeth with the tail of his shirt. That was the best
he could do. At last his sensitive tooth was quieting down.

He was facing a trial, tonight. It was minor, but it was real to him. He
was lying down, his arms folded on his chest, considering how he could
slide toward sleep with nothing to read. What he had for a pillow book
was *Strange News*, if he could get it back from these villains. It was somewhere here on the grounds of this madhouse. He almost felt like escaping
for the sole purpose of getting hold of it and a flashlight. And having
them, he would be willing to creep back into his cell and not complain for
a while. Of course if he asked outright, they would be more convinced
than ever that his brother's manuscript was sinister.

Tomorrow it would be combat. He had to sleep.

He had to conquer his thirst by not thinking about it. He was thirsty.
He wanted to save most of his water for the morning.

He was a husband. Every path he took swung around and led to her
and so to guilt and worry and wakefulness. *Every* path did.

It wasn't the agency, his life in the agency, that filled him with agitation.
He had conducted that life in a certain way that fell short of being shameful. Regret was one thing and shame was another. If everyone in the
agency had conducted himself as delicately, as carefully, as he had . . . then
the agency would have been an innocent ineffective waste of the taxpayers'
money. Unless he was overly flattering himself, that was true. He had lived
a Kantian life in the agency, for the most part, unless he was flattering
himself again. There were certain parish priests in the Roman church who
winked at everything and did palpable good while the mother church
rolled on telling poor devils never to use condoms on pain of hell.

That wasn't exactly the analogy he wanted. There were better ones.
But the fact remained that he could think about it without falling into
shame and despair, and he *would* think about it, later. There would probably be time.

No, it was Iris he had to keep his mind away from, his failure with her,
the great failure of his life.

He needed the right mental games. Earlier he had tried one game and
it had failed him.

He had played Backwardation for a while. Backwardation he owed to his brother, whose ability to pronounce words in reverse had shown up at an absurdly early age, during his prodigy phase. It had been pretty remarkable and Rex had flaunted it, with the help of their parents, of course. And of course Rex had been challenging about it to his older brother, and as his older brother, Ray had been unable to elude the challenge. There had been various ways to lose to Rex, having to do with the length of words as well as the rapidity with which they were successfully reversed.

They had been out walking in the neighborhood when Rex had begun reading street signs backward, just like that, in his piping little voice. At first it had only been street names and the names of landmarks and points of interest. Nedlit Krap, he remembered, Tilden Park, had been a very early success of Rex's. But then there had been Llihtoof Draveluob and on and on.

So he had played Backwardation briefly earlier, giving it up for a couple of reasons. He had seemed to be unable to keep the place names he was backwarding, African place names being the category he had chosen for himself, unable to keep them from getting closer and closer to home, to Gaborone, to his neighborhood, their street, their neighbors, and ultimately to Siri Hcnif herself, the evol of his efil. He would try something else.

One thing he could do was settle the question of what the best food, the best taste, was, the best-tasting food, in the world.

He thought about it and decided that the answer was bacon, crisp, hickory-smoked. That was if only one single food could be chosen. But if foods could be combined, then it would have to be ripe avocado slices on freshly baked whole wheat bread, with olive oil, with shreds of red onion, and with fresh-ground pepper and sea salt. Which would be very good with the crisp bacon on it. And this was a mistake. He was salivating. And it wasn't a game.

But there could be a game connected to food. One had just suggested itself. The game would be to convert great literary names into main dishes. Salmon Rushdie would be an example. And there was Rice Edgar Burroughs.

There could be Bacon Francis, of course.

Nothing was coming. Rex would be an ace at this. The problem was that this was not a game they would ever play. Rex was dead. He knew it. And if he was, it was too much.

There could be Oats Joyce Carol or it could be simply Joyce Carol Oats.

Some people, like Rex, were very good at games, and other people were not. He was not, himself, very good at games. He was very good at a game no one knew he was playing, or almost no one, only the people who paid him. So there was that.

Ermine Melville was a possible, if people ate that animal. Probably in the Middle Ages they had. In the Dark Ages they ate anything.

Lamb Charles and Dorothy was too easy.

Another possible would be Edgar Allan Po Boy, after the New Orleans sandwich made with oysters and something else and with hot sauce. They were supposedly delicious.

He had run out of anything presentable. He was going to reject Edgar Allan Poi and Sole Bellow and Spuds Terkel and Graham Greens.

He thought of what he should do next. It was an exercise and not a game, but it would work. It was something Iris had come up with. The point of the exercise was to recapture the feeling of utter fatigue and physical constriction that passengers suffered on endless nonstop transatlantic flights like the one from New York to Johannesburg, seventeen hours with one brief refueling moment at Ilha do Sal. They had taken that flight together how many times? And the trick was to remember the yearning and envy everyone felt toward the flight crew, whose members could take shifts napping full length on foam rubber pallets in a special compartment. And then the trick was to identify your own present ability to be lying flat in the bed you were tossing and turning in with what it would have felt like to be permitted to lie flat sometime during the last three or four hours of that flight. All paths led to his girlfriend.

He put himself in the plane again, with Iris beside him. Unconsciousness would sweep toward him now. It had begun to move. It would have him in no time.

31. *Beware Me*

His first formal interrogation was about to begin. He was in place. It was morning, still early.

Early rising was the order of the day. He was famishing for light, because the gap between coming awake and being blindfolded for the day's business had been disappointingly narrow, a blink. He was under the impression that they would dispense with the blindfold when he was on his own in the cell, as they had yesterday. So far, the drill being imposed on him was straightforward. When the banging on the door began, the prisoner was to rise and go to stand at the far side of the room, back to the door, hands high on the wall. Then came the blindfolding. And then came a little breakfast, cold maize porridge in a tin bowl which he had been expected to eat with his fingers, a cup of tepid bush tea. There had been two people in his cell, a male to handle the blindfolding and the cuffing, and a female server. Their voices, in the fragmentary exchanges between them, in her murmurs, had told the story. She had guided him to rinse his hands in a basin of water, after drizzling a substance like Phisohex on them. And then his hands had been cuffed behind him.

He had been expected to remain standing for eating and ablutions, such as they were. All he could say was that his captors seemed to be following some definite set of standards of treatment. This was not, as yet, chaos and the fiery pit. The woman had been in a state of fear, though.

They had led him across open ground to the main building. He had counted exactly two hundred and twelve paces between his cell and this venue, a room, probably a bedroom. What he had picked up in ambient noise on the way over was mundane. There was poultry somewhere around. There were a few dogs. Someone had blown a police whistle. Confused shouting had gone on elsewhere in the building he was in, but briefly. That was all he had.

They had placed him in a heavy armchair whose feet were nailed or bolted to a smooth wooden floor. Rare woods from the forest around Kazengula had been used in the Sand Castle's interiors. With his feet, he detected added metal bracing securing the chair legs to the floor. A leather belt had been passed around the chairback and over his chest and cinched tightly but not painfully. He could get his breath. His wrists had been cuffed to the chair arms, again tightly but not cruelly.

It was almost boring waiting for your tormentors to get to work. He was realizing something interesting, though, as he sat in idleness. They had made a mistake in not letting him at least rinse off his face even minimally before blindfolding him. His skin was greasy, especially the skin of his face. He could make the blindfold slip, he was fairly sure, even though it was on tight.

He decided to try something. By forcing his head over and down against his shoulder he was finding he could drag the blindfold down on one side. They had left him alone in the room and there was no one to stop him from doing what he was doing. He was elated. With luck, he should even be able to repeat the action in reverse, assuming no one caught him. He was going to do this. They were taking too long. He did it. His right eye was free.

He was in a disused bedroom. Along three walls mattresses and tall cylinders of rolled-up matting had been propped, imperfectly blocking the room's windows. Some light was coming in at the tops of the windows. He would have to be standing in order to see out at all. He wondered if the mattresses were intended for anything more than making looking in or out a difficult feat, intended for example as improvised sound-sops. He hoped not.

There was no housekeeping going on. There was sand on the fine broad-planked hardwood floors. The rug, a mock Persian or possibly the real thing, had been roughly rolled off to one side. There were dismantled bedsteads crowding one side of the room. There were oddments of debris strewn around, lager cans mostly. There was no air in the room, only heat. There was nothing he could do about the sweat drops burning his eyes. That was torture of a sort, but not something anyone would mention, because it was nothing, compared to what could be done, was done. It was nothing. No man would mention it. Sweat was eating his eyes alive, however.

Adequate light came in over the mattress barrier, but there was an array of candles in saucers, some fresh, some half burned, on the card table directly in front of him, the candles tending to suggest that interrogations were proceeding into the night and that there was no general power supply in the building. There were fixtures on the walls, sconces with pink torch-flame-simulating bulbs in them.

His interrogator would sit on the straight chair behind the card table, facing him, and begin by having a leisurely smoke. There were cigarettes on the table, a lighter, a carafe of water and two tumblers. There was no ashtray, which meant that very restricted time horizons were controlling this phase of whatever was going on. And there was no cassette recorder in evidence, which was a further support to the image that everything was very present tense. Ashes and refuse were going on the floor and nobody cared because this place was going to be vacated sooner rather than later. That was what he thought.

He saw nothing exotic in the way of abusive implements on the table. There was a vial of liquid that might be ammonia. And that would be to revive people who fainted during their torments. There was a giant flashlight on the table. But there was nothing like a thumbscrew, say, or pliers.

He knew what most of the props were for. His interrogator would sit down at the table and make him wait lengthily while a Santos Dumont was smoked. The conventional idea was that everybody was dying for a smoke and it went with the parallel game of pouring water into a glass noisily and sipping loudly from it at intervals. Ray was not particularly thirsty yet, which was good. He had had the tea and the leftover water to drink.

There were four open cartons on the floor near the table and in one of them he could identify items of his projecting out, his map case, his knobkerrie. This was a discovery. His documents would be in the carton and so would *Strange News*, he would bet. This was a victory and it was enough. He should reset the blindfold, if he could.

He took too long being pleased with himself. The door opened and his interrogator and his assistant strode in. The assistant was a new character, a young black African in sunglasses, another example of physical culture taken to an extreme, a man rather festively dressed in a cherry-red silk longsleeved shirt and plaid Bermuda shorts, his chest crossed by bandoliers. Ray was sure the wardrobe was expropriated. Maybe it had come from the closet of the Englishman who had built the Sand Castle. The bandoliers were for ornament only. There were no cartridges in the holders, so far as Ray could tell. But he couldn't be sure.

His interrogator was going to be Quartus, and he was in a rage seeing
the state of Ray's blindfold. *Hopping mad* would capture him. He was a
peculiar figure, a gaunt, bald man in his forties whose prominent,
knoblike cleft approached deformity. It was severe enough, in its resemblance to a pair of buttocks, that it might, Ray thought, have pushed
Quartus out of the main game where the most symmetrical and physically standard usually won and into the military realm where traits like
ferocity would carry you up the stairway to power no matter what you
looked like, if you didn't get killed along the way, and where rage at what
nature had done to you could be productively redirected at selected representatives of the more normal population. He was cursing in Afrikaans.
I have regular features, Ray thought. His appearance had never been an
obstacle to whatever he might have wanted to do, for which it made sense
to be thankful in the There but for the Grace of God Go I sense, a plati-
tude which in itself ought to be enough to destroy religion at the root the
moment anyone employing it fully grasped what it meant about God.

He was having a seizure of sympathy for Quartus, for his joke of a chin
and for the dire anxiety showing in his exhausted-looking face. Ray had
seen him plainly up close and he was not taking it well. Oppression is
hard work, Ray thought.

Quartus was a Boer, definitely. His eyes were cornflower blue. One
eyelid was burdened with a sty. From gums to mid-level, his teeth were
tobacco-stained. If he had a wife she would pity him, seeing him as Ray
was seeing him.

Both men lunged toward Ray, converged on him. All in the same
moment his blindfold was jerked back into place and he was slapped
across the mouth, twice, and then once, harder, on the side of the head.

These people knew how their blindfolds worked. And they had both
immediately concluded that the thing hadn't slipped down on its own, by
happenstance. They hadn't even given him the chance to claim that it was
all an accident. They knew. And then one of them hit him again on the
side of the head. The previous blow had left his ear ringing. Now it was
howling. People are fools, he thought. Hitting his ear was counterpro-
ductive. Why would they do it if they wanted him to answer their questions with any celerity? They would have to shout. He would tell them
why.

There was a lull. He heard the door close. And then they were back
and someone was behind him forcing a hood over his head and pushing
the blindfold down as he did. It was a black hood with a drawstring
mouth. It was totally opaque and the thick cloth it was made from was

saturated with a foul musk combining the odors of garlic, blood, and sweat. It was his own fault. He was breathing the perfume of his predecessors, the previous wearers of the hood. The thought gave him a perverse feeling of cold strength.

Another lull began. He had to keep in mind that all this hysteria about keeping him from getting a good look at the players was an indicator that they were expecting at some point to release him rather than kill him, or that at the very least they were interested in preserving the option. He held the thought. He wanted them to come back. He wanted this to start, so it could end.

It had started routinely, boringly, even. It had begun with Quartus smoking, blowing smoke Ray's way, taking his time. Ray had been asked to give the story of what he was doing in the area, slowly, with detail. And he had. And Quartus had informed him repeatedly but patiently that he knew he was lying. And then Quartus had given him the opportunity to deny that he knew anything at all about the incriminada, the guns, the packets of rands and pulas, the stupid smoke grenades. And then Quartus had gone down a list of names, African names, starting with Samuel Kerekang, twenty names exactly, and given him the chance to admit he knew these names and knew how the names were connected and knew what these people were doing to innocent people all through the northwest, the crimes they were committing. And Ray had denied any knowledge of any of the names. And Quartus, affecting sadness, had said that, after Ray had taken a little time to think more, it would be necessary to go over the list again, only the second time there would be measures taken to help his memory. And then, after a break, when the session resumed, Quartus's assistant had rewarded each denial of acquaintanceship or knowledge with blows to Ray's arms and shoulders, not open-handed blows during this round, no. Ray had been struck with what felt like an enormous knot tied at one end of a length of rope. The thing came whistling down. The knot was the size of an orange. Quartus's assistant swung the knot around in the air, making the whistling sound, more often than actually striking with it. That was for terror purposes. It was childish. He was a hitting-beast. It was to keep Ray off guard, never knowing when the next blow would land. And as to the implement itself, there was a reason it was being employed. The knot was yielding. You could hit more and bruise less. It was like the bar of Ivory soap in a kneesock that some bastards used for hurting people during interrogations. The theory was that when it was brought down full force the bar would break in two along the grooved line scored into its midsection, making bruises but not breaking bone, if he was remembering correctly, or was it that the soap broke precisely before causing unconsciousness, hurting and shocking the victim just up to that point? He couldn't remember. The knot was different but similar. It wasn't like being hit with a mallet. It could go on longer, obviously. So far they were hitting him mainly through his clothing. There was protection in that. Everything was subject to change. They were taking another break.

He devoted himself again to listening. He had a task, which was to remember, record, register *everything*, against the possibility that someday somebody would be interested in punishing these stupid villains, unlikely as that might be. He would be ready, he himself, by God above. We all need a task, he thought. Iris had been given a task, by him, her task being to be his beloved, his be-all, which she had gotten tired of or gotten to dislike. If that was the case he was sorry, but it was still true that we all needed tasks. He thought, I'm not a great . . . thing, thing to love forever . . . I am not great nor do I think continually of those who were truly great, which would be a waste of time, colossal waste of time. Only a fool would do that. He wanted the interrogation to proceed. The hard part was coming. Life is extreme, he thought.

He was getting an idea. He could do something on the order of who was it, Lee Marvin, in *The Dirty Dozen*, when he fouled up a word association test by taking every response from baseball, being completely unhelpful to the psychiatrist testing him, giving him nothing. In his own case he could answer every question with a gem, a quotation from English Literature, verse especially. He could try it. He could try it a little later, depending on how things went. And if he could pull out quotes that were somehow apposite to the question he was refusing to answer, that would be best of all.

The door opened and closed and his friends were back. There was some shuffling of papers. Someone was lighting a cigarette. No, they both were. Someone was standing over him, close, blowing smoke at him, probably the assistant. There could be something positive here. He would never want to be a smoker again, after this. The negative associations would be helpful. It was Iris who had gotten him to stop smoking even before the worst news about the health effects of smoking had come out. So the question was whether his vices would reassert themselves in the next stage of things, when he was alone, when she was somewhere else, not helping. The answer was no, he hoped. *Your charred breath* was a phrase of hers from the first days of their marriage.

Quartus began. "Meneer, now you are going to tell me the truth. I am finished with playing about. I am finished and that is all. So." Papers were being handled.

Quartus continued. "So, meneer, I will tell you why you have come to be with us. You have a friend, meneer, who was at one time to be found not so far away, at Toromole. You came to call on him, isn't it?"

Ray said, "No. Nothing you are saying means anything to me. I'm not going to Toromole. And what shall I call you? How shall I address you properly? I know I asked this before but I think you failed to answer."

"Call me nothing, meneer."

Quartus's English was decent, but the hardness of his b's and d's and his phrasing reflected the influence of his bedrock Afrikaans, a language whose standard delivery, in Ray's opinion, resembled biting more than it did normal talking.

The smoke was too much and Ray began coughing. It was bad. It was torture, in fact, coughing inside a hood. It was clever, too, as a form of torture, if you were concerned to leave no marks, half suffocating a victim with smoke while he had a hood on. He hadn't heard of it. He would have to be ready to hold his breath if this was going to continue. The varieties of torture here were pretty infinite. His chest hurt. His throat, too. He craved water. They wanted him to beg for it.

But someone else was coughing, having a coughing fit right along with him. Like diamonds, we are cut with our own dust, he thought. Whoever was coughing had a condition. He thought it must be Quartus. For a moment they were animals together in a similar affliction.

"Who do you think I am, then?" Quartus asked, when the fit had passed.

It might be time for my little program, Ray thought.

He said, *"Truly, My Satan, thou art but a Dunce, And dost not know the Garment from the Man."* That was Blake, a little blast of Blake for his tormentor, and not bad if he did say so himself. Not knowing the garment from the man was good. That was what he was going to get, Quartus, if he kept this up, English Literature. Now Quartus was going on again about telling the truth.

"The truth is bald, and cold," Ray said. It was from Emily Dickinson.

Quartus didn't like it. Ray could hear him getting out of his chair and coming forward in order to deliver a personal piece of punishment. It was possible Quartus had taken the mention of baldness in a personally irrational way, which meant that he needed to scrutinize his quotations a little better before using them. His punishment was a little more smoke sent his way and Quartus pouring water into a glass and sipping so he could hear.

Unasked, Ray summarized everything rapidly, who he was, his seconding from teaching to this mission for the ministry's search for new school sites, his marriage, his wife who would be frantic if this continued much longer, his absolute ignorance about who Quartus was and what was going on. And he added something new as to how very advisable it would be for him to be let go because the American embassy would shortly be involved, and that would be unpleasant for everybody detaining him. That was it. That was the fiction he was going to stick with no matter what. He was tiring and he needed to get it out and get it clear before fatigue weakened him and he began deviating, altering things. He had done it for his own benefit. That was it.

Quartus sighed hugely. He continued sipping voluptuously.

Ray was singing mentally *Let me call you Satan*, to the tune of "Let Me Call You Sweetheart." It was for amusement. Interrogation, with its calculated halts and longueurs, was so . . . boring. He wanted to say something funny to Quartus. He had an idea.

He said, solemnly, *"I know that I shall meet my fate . . . Somewhere among these clods below."* It was funny to him. It wouldn't be to Quartus, though. He wanted to make Quartus laugh, if he could.

His thinking was interrupted by a blow to the right side of his neck. He had been struck from behind, with the side of the hand this time, a medium-hard blow but essentially a nothing, a kiss, as these things went. But they were escalating.

Ray said, "Stop hitting me for a second and I'll tell you something you might want to know."

"What would that be? And you must speak louder, meneer, because of the hood. What will you be telling me?"

Ray said, "Okay, first uncover my mouth. Tie this thing above my mouth. I can't get enough air to speak properly. And you can't really hear me." He felt it was worth a try.

They surprised him. The drawstring tie was undone and the hem of the hood was brought up and the hood retied above his mouth. There was bunched fabric against his nostrils, but still it was better. He could get a decent volume of air through his mouth. He swilled air, getting ready. He wanted to bait Quartus. He wanted to blast Quartus with something classic. Speak, English! he thought. He wanted it to be Milton but it couldn't be because he was coming up dry. Something pithy was needed. He only had a minute and Milton wasn't pithy. But it came to him that "On the Late Massacre in Piedmont" might do.

He began, loud. *"Avenge, O Lord, thy slaughter'd Saints, whose bones . . ."* The blow he had been inviting came, stopping him. Again it was a side-of-the-hand blow. He felt like asking to be hit on the left side of his neck the next time around, for balance.

"He is saying poetry to us. He is a poefter." That was Quartus's assistant, obviously. He was exasperated. Poefter was Afrikaans for homosexual. Ray knew that much. Rex was a poefter, in fact.

Quartus hissed angrily at his assistant, who obviously had stepped out of his role.

The Milton had been mildly apposite to Quartus but he should have used Yeats's "Irish Airman" instead, again, just to get *Those that I fight I do not hate, Those that I guard I do not love* in, for his consideration. He might want to convey something about what, fate, about something like the feeling in the poem about the guy in the hammock hearing the cowbells as the cows came home to roost and thinking he has wasted his life, a poem he wished he knew but didn't. He felt like *teaching* Quartus something. It was in his nature. Why not try? He wanted to bait him and teach him at the same time. How productive was that? He was a fool.

Wearily and almost gently Quartus said something about teasing being pointless and about his not enjoying this situation no matter what anyone might think, and then he began screaming at Ray, from a distance of a few inches. It was one more redundant demonstration of florid unpredictability, niceness turning into hell without warning. Never think you know when you can relax, is what it said. He was putting his heart into it.

Briefly Ray lost the power to follow the thread. His lightheadedness was coming and going. It was cumulative, being hit. And he was hungry. The burden of the diatribe was that there would be no further discussion of who Ray was. There was no time for that. It was *Strange News* they were going to discuss because the truth of Ray's assignment was buried in those pages. Quartus seemed to have convinced himself that everything in *Strange News* was somehow coded, that it was a master document, a skeleton key to the uprising, something like a set of instructions. Together they were going to tear it apart, he was saying.

He was sorry for Quartus. How could he conceivably get what *Strange News* was, lacking any acquaintance with the genre, which, say, Coleridge's

Notebooks would be a reasonable example of, lines like *My Bowels shall sound as an Harp* interspersed with all sorts of oddments and sentiments like *Let us contend like the Olive and the Vine to see which can bring forth the best fruit* rather than contending like wild beasts or whatever the negative comparison had been. He couldn't remember. He couldn't be expected to remember everything. Also it would be a safe bet that Quartus had never bumped into, say, a reproduction of the Mayan Codex, which *Strange News* with its sequences of enigmatic bits and pieces reminded Ray of, sort of. And then there were the nosegays the French made, bêtisiers? compilations of everyday grotesqueries and stupidities. Intelligent people spent their entire academic careers staring fruitlessly at items like the Mayan Codex.

Iris adored Michael Ventris, or was it the type, the type being any academic lucky enough to decipher a dead language that had resisted the best efforts of generations of other scholars, to the eternal disappointment of their particular wives. He knew he was making assumptions about Quartus's educational history, the man at best graduating secondary school in some pathetic dorp before his descent into the maelstrom of military life . . . But he was sure he was right.

"My memory is not what it was, right now," Ray said, eliciting a sound of disgust from Quartus. I am not making complete sense, Ray thought.

"I'm a teacher," Ray said. He knew it was disconnected of him. But he was sincere. It felt urgent to keep saying it. Thin places were appearing in his what, his thought-flow, thin places or bleached places. Quartus needed to be careful with him. Quartus knew that. Unconscious he would be useless to Quartus. And they *were* being careful with him. All hands were aware of that, all hands on deck. They were observing limits. Being white was a significant protection. It was a fact. There was nothing he could do about it. This was a drôle d'interrogation, so far, and a good match to the drôle de reconnaissance he had been conducting in the bush himself, when he had been so rudely interrupted.

Quartus and his beast were consulting in murmurs. They could do their worst, even kill him if they wanted to. He was even curious to see how far they were going to go. It was a feature of the situation, was all. He was ready to fight them, and to fight them adequately he had to look ten steps ahead, at death, and not be afraid.

Out of nowhere came thoughts of his mother, overwhelming him. It was a deluge. He didn't often think about his mother. They kept in touch in a nominal way, with Iris doing most of that. It could be that all the death business was making him regress. But there was something else, an insight utterly new to him. It was that the secret key to his mother's whole mode with Rex had been her fear that Rex was a potential suicide. Iris had described his mother as stupid but not shallow, which was about right. So all his mother's favoritism might have come out of, had come out of, an apprehension about something that happened with gay adolescent boys at a rate far above the average. She had sensed something in Rex, an inclination. It would have been instinctual with her. She had sensed it in him when he was little. Dealing with Rex had been a campaign to keep him willing to carry on living, however annoyingly he needed to conduct his life in order to enjoy the process. And of course now, with the virus, it was conceivable that he would take his life, or had, probably had, fulfilling her fear, her intuition. He was dead, his brother was, his little brother.

Ray was struck from behind, on the top of the head. It was bad.

And then he was struck again, on the back of his neck, on the skin. He had been hit by a fist armed with rings. They had made him bleed. He had been struck with that intent. It didn't take much of a cut to produce enough blood to be alarming. Blood was sliding down his spine. Breaking his skin had been the point, to establish that they were willing to do that to him. They had multiplied his problems, too. Now he would have to worry about infection, take that worry back to his cell with him. They knew that. He had to try to keep his neck immobile or as close to immobile as he could, so that the clotting would start. This last blow had been a demonstration. He knew what it was about. It was to create intimacy. His wound had lips. He was supposed now to be really afraid. They would see. They would see.

He would take the initiative. If they wanted to talk about *Strange News* he would lead the way. Quartus had moved the card table closer, Ray had heard him doing it. There was a way to quell, to overcome, a feeling of impending faintness that he had learned in an agency workshop, if he remembered correctly. But he couldn't remember the particular move, the trick, no, only that he had been taught one. He could hear Quartus preparing, pulling pages out and talking to himself, reminding himself of questions he had. So far, only Quartus's assistant had physically abused him. They were preserving a distinction. It was fine to think of Quartus's assistant as his beast, his creature, his beast. But the true beast was Quartus, who was about to destroy something he needed to think about, his mother and his brother, his new thought, the light it shed. He couldn't do it there and then. He had to get the interrogation over with so he could think.

He said, "You think *Strange News* is something it isn't. Because, look, it isn't anything. It's literary, you could think of it as a codex . . ." Ray knew immediately that he had chosen the wrong word, the wrong word.

"A codex," Quartus said, weightily, and spat, on the floor, doubtlessly, a good sign confirming that keeping the room neat and clean for extended use was not a concern, which in turn meant that this would be over sooner rather than later, if he was correct and not grasping at straws. He was outsmarting himself. He had wanted to attack the question of what *Strange News* was without using the term postmodern, and he had chosen a bad alternate route. Obviously what Quartus had heard in codex was *code*.

Ray said, "No, look, a codex is just a certain kind of manuscript volume with certain materials in it in a disorganized state, materials we may not immediately understand, exactly . . . for example, there are a couple of them left by Leonardo da Vinci full of stuff that's still mysterious to us. That's all I meant. By codex." There is such a thing as too much education, Ray thought.

Ray continued, "I want you to understand what this is, meneer." It was dubious, calling Quartus by his own term of mock respect. He felt a little insane doing it. But he had to call him something.

"What this is is a work of art, by my brother . . ."

"And where is the name of the author, then . . ."

"It doesn't have a standard title page. It's just a manuscript. But his name is Rex Finch."

"I don't see it here. Very strange."

"Take my word for it. And it's a work of literary art and that's all it is . . ."

Quartus laughed nastily. "Em . . . so what does he mean by *patriotute*? What is that?"

"Well, someone who . . . well it could mean someone who sells himself to the nation, or it could be someone who sells the nation itself, I suppose. It isn't exactly clear. There are a number of coinages of his in there. *Pollutician* is another one. Mostly they're clear enough."

"And why is it given number four hundred, meneer, that number?"

"No idea."

"And here, this little story, what does it mean, about the chap who is a blood giver, blood donor as you term it, but then here he says he's through with it because he's afraid his blood might go to someone who voted for your President Reagan, since there is no way to prevent that? What sort of story is that, meneer? A man who hates your greatest president in this century, isn't it? I tell you I pray *God* will send South Africa such a man."

"Well, that story is about someone with strong feelings against our former president, obviously. My guess is it's probably a true story, something my brother heard somebody say."

How he could be having what resembled a regular conversation on a political topic with someone who was torturing him was a question of its own. Reagan, the amazing Reagan, had acquired a universal cult following. The left reviled him, but the great mass of everything to the right of the narrow left loved and adored him, why? Was it because he was a mirror figure unaccountably raised to power and getting away with it, an amiable man with about five simple beliefs . . . astrology, the Second Coming, America Columbia the Gem of the Ocean the Greatest Country in History, succeeding in business being proof positive of virtue and genius, what else? Oh, never changing his mind . . . And he was always optimistic. Nothing got him down. He had luck, geopolitically. The Russians had imploded, or started to, during his tenure. People worshiped good luck.

Quartus said, "So what is this, number twenty-five, *A specimen of surprise is to discover on your wife's buttocks handwriting in ballpoint pen in letters of a minute size?*" Ray had detected embarrassment in Quartus's reading of the entry.

Ray didn't know what to say, other than, "I don't know. It's an image, something that seemed funny to him . . ."

The blood drying on his back was making it itch. Stuck away somewhere among the things Iris had packed for him was an aluminum backscratcher with a collapsible handle, a Japanese novelty, something he could count on to be there as unfailingly as his nail clippers and his chloroquine. She loved him. She was wonderful with splinters. What would he do? His bleeding reminded him of something, Iris when she'd cut the palm of her hand slightly in the kitchen and had come to him holding her palm out and saying, *Hey I'm getting stigmata . . . It must be our relationship.* There had been a storm of clues about trouble coming and he had just stood there in it.

Quartus and his hitting-beast were consulting in murmurs. Ray interrupted them. He needed to speak rapidly. "I'll tell you something you're right about, if you let me.

"And it's this. You're right there's a puzzle in this manuscript. In a way it's a bigger puzzle to me than it is to you, and you can believe that or not. My brother . . . somewhere in these lines is his soul as he wanted me to see it. That's what I think. So very good, ask me questions. Maybe it will help. Because the truth is I treated my brother badly. I was unfair. I was ignorant."

"You are talking shit. I have no time for this."

"Do you have a brother?"

"What business is it of yours?"

"Why do I have the feeling you do? I think you come from a very large family. I just think that."

"It is no business of yours." The man was roaring.

"I hear you," Ray said.

"This is *shit* you are talking," Quartus said, but Ray thought he was detecting a hairline crack in the man's vehemence, a wavering, as though he might be considering letting Ray go on wandering in this area on the chance it would lead to something productive.

"I was not the friend my brother needed. That may be the message in these pages, I don't know. Maybe you can help me." Ray felt himself edging into a certain state. He was a little aside from himself. He was a companion to his speaking self, for the moment. He sounded unafraid to himself, strong, even.

"Also I believe he's dead. There it is. Here we are. Oh and by the way, yes he is what you would call a poefter, my brother. Yes indeed. But he's dead. Or so I believe. No, he is."

The beast was objecting to the turn things were being allowed to take. He was grumbling and hissing. "He must *shut* it," he was saying repeatedly.

Ray said, "And he was no fool, my brother Rex." He wanted them to know that. He wanted it said.

"I'll tell you how he made his living. Listen to this. He thought of things. He sold ideas. How many people can do that and live on it? He's a clever bugger. Or he was, rather. Why don't I just stay with the past tense, since he's dead?

"For example, did you ever see, in the early eighties, about, a comedy series *The Triumphs of Inspector Lestrade*, on television? Granada television, British, but it was shown all over the Commonwealth, like *Mr. Bean* was, which I know they had on in South Africa. *Lestrade* was my brother's idea. He sold it to the producers."

A snort of disgust from Quartus or the other was his only reply. Ray didn't care. Rex deserved credit. The concept, built on reversals, was clever. In the series the thickheaded Inspector Lestrade of the Doyle stories was instead a brilliant Scotland Yard detective perennially harassed by a bumbling, intruding, fantastical screwball Sherlock Holmes, a formerly celebrated consultant to Scotland Yard who had gone off the rails through cocaine abuse. That was the nut of it. *Lestrade* had provided a steady trickle of money to Rex, culminating in a really handsome lump-sum payment during the ultimately abortive run-up to a feature film version of the property. Ray had never wanted to know the details. He had avoided paying close attention to his brother's coups and deals, out of envy, pure and simple. And he had erected an unjust caricature of his brother as someone who scanned the world for literary cultural figures people got pleasure out of and turned them into figures of fun. He had seen him as a specialist in mockery, a mercenary specialist in mockery, but where had that come from? There was only *Lestrade*, as an exhibit. And Rex thought of things and gave them away, too, he should remember. For example he had given away gratis the idea for a short subject consisting of three or four minutes of banal family drama and twenty minutes of credits, a thing that had been a hit for somebody in art house cinemas during the period when movies of sleeping people, Warhol movies, had been in vogue. The film had won a prize, in those stupid days when prizes were awarded for flies crawling up walls. He wanted to tell his brother something. He was sorry for certain things. People had apparently found the movie with tedious credits hilarious. And *Lestrade* looked like becoming a permanent cult item. His brother's name was there forever in the credits, which was immortality of a sort, more than he himself would ever have. Rex had probably been looking for a reaction from him, anything, and he hadn't given one. He was sorry.

He said, "It's a parody of the Sherlock Holmes mysteries. It makes an idiot out of Sherlock Holmes. You can rent it."

It was oddly interesting to return to *Lestrade*, which, of course, had been a delayed attack on his own personal boyhood cult of Sherlock Holmes. He had wanted to *be* Sherlock Holmes.

Quartus said, "That's enough."

"This is interesting. You watch television. Of course you do. It's on videocassette. Maybe you've seen it.

"By the way, the whole thing was an attack on me. Because Holmes was a hero of mine. I was bookish. I read all the Holmes stories over and over and forward and backward, really. When I'd read them all I was very depressed that there weren't any more of them. Anyway, my brother made Holmes an idiot, in this series. And he made the true hero gay, by the way, a poefter, to you. Ah well . . ."

He was struck on the neck. It was pro forma.

He hadn't thought about his Sherlock Holmes phase in years. It had been important. He had saved money in his adolescence to buy a book of pastiches of the Holmes stories, a limited edition, by a man named

August Derleth. They had supposedly been the best of the pastiches produced by fans of Holmes who wanted more. But they had been inadequate. Reading them had made him feel worse.

"This is real," he said. They wouldn't get it.

Another hit to the neck came, more a swipe than a hit.

He was having insights, ridiculously. He understood something that
had been pestering him. He had made a deduction. Recently he had
developed a slight mania to have something in his right hand to grasp,
like a tube of Chap Stick or a pen cap. It was the recurrence of a mild
grasping mania that had surfaced earlier in his life during periods of
stress, although mania was too strong a term for it. Out in the Kalahari it
had resurfaced and it had only defined itself as a problem when he had to
take over the driving, because he needed the use of both hands, obviously.
He had never inquired into it, this tic. It had been transient enough that
he had never bothered to ponder where it came from. He was feeling the
need just then, even. It was present. But now he understood why.

"You know what," he heard himself saying, stupidly.

He ignored a shouted question about Toromole, another one. Because
what he was onto was much more interesting. It was as though lights on
the bottom of a swimming pool had been switched on, showing various
bodies in the depths, some moving, some not. It was as though the light
pouring up was hot and was showing or melting little frozen scenes from
his early life, his early boring life. He wanted to look at these things but
stay safely above them. Scenes starring himself were lighting up, saying
Hi. This was nothing Quartus could understand. He felt like calling him
Watson, but he wouldn't. It would be funny to address Quartus as My
Dear Fellow, except that it wouldn't, it would only mystify him more.

There was another slap. Quartus said something unclear. Ray's ears
were ringing. They were interrupting his thoughts.

Now the gripping-tic could go away. It might. He knew where it came
from. In his boyhood he had owned and loved a little lead toy, a rocket
ship, blue and white, with minute pulley wheels set between the top fins
so that Buck Rogers could be sped along a taut length of string to get him
to wherever he and Wilma and Doctor Huer had to be. He had loved
Buck Rogers. And he had loved the goddamned rocket ship, and somehow clutching it had gotten associated over time with falling easily
asleep. It had been an intermittent practice but it had persisted as he
what, adolesced, persisted longer than it should have because it was so
inconspicuous a thing to do. It was his version of a teddy bear. He had
pretty much forgotten about all this. He had hung on to the rocket ship

and how peculiar was that considering that millions of grown Greek men never leave home without their worry beads, which in his humble opinion was not so far out of the rocket ship bailiwick?

And he had kept his ship cached in a tobacco pouch nailed to the wall behind the headboard of his bed, cached along with kid contraband like the occasional cigarette that had come his way and his first condom, lonely thing sitting there endlessly. And then at some point his ship had disappeared. And he had known in his heart it was Rex. There had been no one else to suspect. And all his maneuvers to force him to confess had failed. And the option of bringing it up with their mother had been unthinkable. How old had he been when it had happened? He didn't know, but old enough for the issue to be a humiliation. And he had done a magnificent job repressing all this until now, if he did say so himself.

He was thinking of thanking Quartus for the insight when he was slapped smartly on the mouth. His face was going to swell. The level of pain was rising and was not as episodic as he would have liked. He wasn't cooperating. They were saying that.

What else was there about the rocket ship and why had all this disappeared until now? Well, in fact, the ship had been the size of a solid, erect penis, or a little under, but as a proxy penis it certainly made sense. Deep in his soul he had been terrified of masturbation. He had been so infrequent a masturbator as a boy he hardly qualified for the title. He had been afraid. From their mother had come the message that the practice was terrible and weak and it had somehow gotten firmly into his mind that losers masturbated and that winners in the life game didn't because they didn't need to. And then of course the fact was that his brother had been a precocious and florid masturbator, not that their mother had known anything about it, but Rex had gone out of his way to let Ray know what was going on with him. MASTURBATION IS SELF-RAPE was something he had seen written on a bathroom wall in junior high.

This must be therapy, he thought. He was going to change his opinion about therapy.

"This is therapy," he said, not that Quartus would understand. He didn't care, and said, "I don't care about much that much." He wasn't making sense.

Quartus was saying something about Cuba Ray couldn't follow. He had a headache, so his head was hurting from the inside out as well as from the outside in, from the hits and smacks it had taken.

Apparently Quartus had found something about Cuba in *Strange News*. Ray was tired, but it would be good if he could somehow point out to Quartus that he was being inconsistent in the way he handled the material in *Strange News*. Because on the one hand he was claiming everything was coded and on the other he was picking out statements like the statements about Reagan that he regarded as openly subversive, inflammatory. So how logical was it that his brother's book was both things at once? It was too subtle, though. Also how could he explain his brother's cold eye on certain anecdotes that were bound to strike Quartus as leftish, but that Rex was registering for purposes of mockery, like the one that was very deadpan about the young woman who had abandoned her master's thesis on Sartre after she realized he was a smoker, a chain-smoker, abandoned it halfway through. Nothing is simple, he thought, Rex's attitude toward Cuba was focused on Castro's antigay policies. But all Quartus was seeing was the word Cuba. One thing Ray knew was that Cuba was the only country in the world where married men were required by law to do one-half of the housework. That was just a fact. It didn't relate to what he wanted to say. He was too tired.

Quartus seemed far away. His voice was rubbery, going from close to far or from loud to soft. It was stretching away from him. Ray needed to steady himself. He thought of singing a slow song inside his mind, like "Old Man River." He made himself do it.

The oddness passed. He felt steadier. Although it would be good not to think about rivers, water, brooks, because he was thirsty. He had to steer his thoughts away from that.

Nothing was going on, suddenly. He was alone there.

It was boring, waiting. He wanted them to come back. He wanted to see what they would do next. In fact he wanted them to do their worst and get it over with. There was plenty they could do, even if they were trying hard to keep from marking him up too much.

They hadn't pushed his head back and poured water down his nostrils, for example. They were playing, petting him. The thought depressed him. He was violating his own rule about not thinking about water.

I need to concentrate on my distractions, he thought. He resumed listening conscientiously for anything interesting going on in the vicinity. He could make out music distantly issuing from a radio or cassette player and it was "Rivers of Babylon," a song he knew, sung by Boney M, a soft reggae piece that had gotten popular in southern Africa and been immortalized on the background-music tape loop that was never changed year after year at the President Hotel.

He had to conceal from them how thirsty he was, when they came back. He would think about water but try to extract something from the images if he could, instead of suffering from them. He could try it, anyway.

He would let himself relive going to Orcas Island with Iris, years ago, in August, on vacation. The San Juan Islands constituted a terrestrial paradise. They always would be, for him, a drenched, moist paradise, emerald-green humps sticking up from the gray waters of Puget Sound, silken, the waters, in some places and in other places herringbone. They had stayed at the Rosario Hotel, a rara avis of a hotel, a hybrid of mission style and art deco, built on the beach of an inlet, steep green hills making an amphitheater around the harbor, the jetties, the pleasure craft.

And at first, when there was no sun, they were unhappy. But then they had gotten more than used to the cloudiness, the fog, the periods of soft rain, the mist sticking in the tops of the firs until noon every day and then lifting. So it had been an apotheosis of succulence, moisture, and they had embraced it.

And they had walked everywhere on the one-lane roads of the hiking paths forking through jungles, evergreen jungles was what they were, the deadfall so thick you had to stick to the trails. And then coming on the little vestpocket farms with chive-green meadows and a few cows or sheep for decoration. Every shade of green was represented perfectly somewhere on Orcas Island. So then the one time they had ventured off the marked trail and gone wandering through the brush they had stumbled on an abandoned cottage, abandoned for some time obviously because the firewood in its crib had rotted away and there were furnishings going to pot visible through the windows, and then she had found a tricycle completely involved in vines, abandoned in the yard, invisible until she almost tripped over it. And that had been melancholy for her. And for him.

She was tender. When they had hiked to the top of Mount Constitution and then climbed to the top of the observation tower on its summit, the thing she took away from the experience was not the magnificence of the view but pity for the ranger on the top platform who obviously had to answer the question hundreds of times a day if a particular piece of the landscape was Vancouver Island or not, an unnecessary question because everything was explained by the very clear map under glass fixed to the platform railing. But still people asked. It was not Vancouver Island. It was obvious it wasn't.

He had never liked cod until then. True cod, it was called, they had eaten. And they had visited a kelp farm, something he had never known existed until then. Her lips had tasted of salt.

She understood what was wrong with repetition of experience, voca-
tionally. She understood why he had never wanted to be just the one
thing, a teacher, for that reason. She had understood about what the
agency work had meant to him. The agency had provided him a recepta-
cle, a chamber, a secret chamber where what was going on was not boring. Secret adultery would undoubtedly accomplish the same thing for
other people. He wanted to think about something else.

He thought, Everything ends . . . The ferry to Anacortes comes and
you have to get on it and go back.

His thirst was better, somehow.

They were back and doing names again. When he denied knowing a
name he could expect to be hit on the legs with the knot.

His legs were hurting. He thought he might acknowledge knowing one
or two names, just for the respite he might get. He had been asked about
Dwight Wemberg and he had denied knowing him. But that now seemed
dumb, because their paths could logically have crossed in Gaborone. He
would say that he'd been mistaken and that now he remembered.

Quartus was close to him, affecting weariness, pronouncing names
directly into his right ear.

"You are giving me aggro again," Quartus said.

"I'm sorry. I am doing my best."

"Is it? Then think again, meneer, if you know who it is, Rra Bloke
Molefi? He was very big at UBS, Student Representative Council, very
big. You teach at UBS."

"No, well, I did. I haven't for a while, and the way I knew him was just
hearing about him. There was a strike. It had to do with the tuckshop,
money missing. I paid no attention to it. I was only there once a week. I
am so thirsty." He hadn't intended to say that.

It was so boring, the protocols. In a minute Quartus would go and
have another of his voluptuous drinking experiences.

Ray had an idea. He said, "Why don't you hit me yourself, meneer,
when I don't know? Why make your African hit me?"

He heard Quartus asking for the knot and then a painful blow to his
knee came and that was the answer to that. He wanted Quartus to have to
do the hitting himself.

He would see to it.

"Who is Dwight Wemberg?" Quartus asked coming back, drinking
whatever he was drinking, tea, water, Ray wanted cold tea. I want cold
tea, he thought.

"I'll tell you who he is. I just realized who he is. He's agriculture. He's a sad case. His wife died while he was out of town and she was buried by the time he got back and now they won't let him exhume her and take her back to the States. I realized that's who you meant. I think I met him a few times at embassy parties. That's all."

Quartus said nothing. But then in a rush more names were asked and Ray began thinking about names, funny things about names in general. He was going to need a new name himself in the next phase of his life, he realized, if he survived into it, because he was going to have to cut sever and smash any connection to the specious present, what he had been, especially if he was going to write for a living, which he might have to, which he might have to attempt, with God's help. Names were funny things, like his own name, which was not Finch but Fish or Fisch, in truth, that name glimmering under his public name like a trout in a pool of milk, under a lily pad or something. In the thirties there had been a famous magazine editor with the perfect last name Crowninshield, a name that had struck him at first contact as pretty perfect, Crownin- shield. Of course his first name had been Frank, when it could have been what, Beowulf or Manfred. Ah well, he thought.

Yes, he would need a new name because he knew like thunder and lightning what he was going to do in his new life. Pym, from the Poe story of the guy who went down a maelstrom, might be good, because he was going to pitch himself into the ocean of words, stories. He was going to write Lives, like Aubrey's *Brief Lives*, not that all lives weren't brief, anyway. That was the answer to what he was going to do with the stub of his mortal life that was closer to the bone of everything. It was continu- ous, as a thing to do, with his work in the agency, his Profiles. He could feel and see himself doing it. Of course there was no market for the little perfect compactions, compactions was the word, the rendering of the life you spent so long in living, the deals, strivings, loves, all that, your shots at love.

There was a consultation going on. They were taking their time.

But there would be a market for what he could do. He could compress any life into a jewel. Rex would know where the market for this was, would have, he meant. Of course he knew what Iris would say. She would say, Oh obituaries. But obituaries were the opposite of analytic and the opposite of what he had in mind. And he was not going to limit himself to the dead. He would do anyone he felt like, if he wanted to. Beware me, he thought. He would do the poor as well as the eminent. He would do it. He could. He would find Wemberg and make him a jewel. Aubrey was wonderful but naive, and he, when he did his Lives, would be the opposite of naive. He would do evil subjects, too, which Aubrey as a courtier couldn't. Quartus would be a good subject. Of course he would need to support himself somehow while he wrote, but that could be arranged, he could always teach in Africa, in a second. He would be the freezing eye of the basilisk. He thought, My eye and hand will be sovereign, beware me.

"Thank you," he said. He had reached a conclusion about his life, the life to come that he was grateful for. He was grateful to Quartus and his minions. He was reminded of Iris saying to him, When I want your opinion I'll beat it out of you. It had nothing to do with his situation. But he was grateful to Quartus for the thoughts that had been what, knocked loose. I can be anything, he thought. James Joyce wanted to be a tenor. Joyce *was* a tenor, but he had wanted to be paid for it. He should have tried more. I might sing, he thought.

He was clutching the armrests and a hard hit came to his hands, one two left right, pretty hard. Up to that moment they hadn't hit his hands. We need our hands, he thought. He also didn't want to be hit on the head more than he had if he could help it. He was too dry to spit, spit at them. But also it was true he didn't want the consequences of spitting at anyone. It was like joining the army and saying okay, if I die, then okay, if I die doing the job, the job of being all I can be, killing people. People joining the army were prepared to imagine themselves vaporized, made nothing, and to accept that. But they weren't embracing the possibility of ending up permanently crippled in a ward someplace, which was of course likelier than getting blown to vapor. Someone should publicize the actual odds.

His thirst was getting dire. If they hurled water at him whatever little he might contrive to catch by having his mouth open would almost be worth it. They knew he was thirsty. There was more water-pouring and lip-smacking water-drinking going on.

He felt like singing something, but he was afraid to. But he might hum. He was achieving something, being obstreperous. He was using up their time. They couldn't stay in place forever. He was getting across, he hoped, the idea that he was crazy or being made crazy.

He wanted to sing, but first he would hum. It was too bad he didn't know how the Boer hymn went, "Die Stem." That would have been good. What he was humming had started out indeterminately but was, he realized, turning into "How Much Is That Doggie in the Window?"

"He is a moffie." That was the beast calling him a homosexual by another Boer term.

"*Shut that,*" Quartus said, but it wasn't clear to Ray whether it was directed at him or at the beast. He continued to hum.

Quartus was very close to him again, close enough that with a sharp lunge Ray would be able to bang Quartus hard in the face. It would hurt too much because his head was already caged in pain.

Quartus said, very deliberately, "Meneer, this is what you must understand . . .

"You can stop this humming. Now.

"And you must understand that you *will* tell us what we need to have you tell us. Ah yes. And if you prefer to tell us tomorrow, in the afternoon tomorrow, that will be fine. Or in the evening, fine as well . . ."

Ray was going to escalate into song. They would hate it. Some deep flow of pressure to really sing was rising, rising.

Ray said, "I am going to sing now."

That confused them. They were listening, wondering if he was saying something in American they were not up on that meant he was going to cooperate. He liked that.

"Yes, meneers, is that correct, the plural, but yes. I have decided to sing. Sing for you."

He cleared his throat. He had a faint hope they would offer him something to drink, as encouragement. He couldn't wait for that. Nothing was offered. He cleared his throat again.

The flow swelling up through him was fine, it was driving him to sing, but the song was important. It should be apposite, if it could, otherwise it would be a waste, like his life. What we call songs were originally what, cries, roars, screams. An apposite song would be one with the line *The guy behind you won't leave you alone.*

It was a good idea to make them wait for everything, as long as he could, because they were going to have to go and there would be less time for the next victim. Now he was making them wait because the song to rise up with was a problem. He would rise with the song, like a rocket ship, rise, slip upward. He had it. He had it.

Not only could he sing, he could be a singer, become one. There was the story about Chaplin launching into an aria for a lark at a party and doing it so excellently the crowd was stunned and Chaplin saying that he hadn't been singing, he had just been impersonating Caruso or whoever it was. Be all that you can be, he thought. He had his song, or the main part of it.

That was another thing his brother had driven him crazy with, but that now he had to be grateful for. His brother had listened to crap teen music while he had been trying to get the basic classical music repertoire into his head via Doug Pledger on KFO, really trying. And

there had been no way to control his brother and the noise coming from
his room. And anything he had objected to had made Rex play it more. So
he had stopped. But he remembered a perfect thing, "Town Without
Pity," a thing he had heard over and over and over and now it was perfect
for his needs. God moves in mysterious ways, when he moves at all, Ray
thought.

Like an egg opening in his mind and disclosing a jewel, he had the
whole thing end to end. He loved his brother. Rex, I love you, he thought,
commencing to sing, loud.

He threw himself into the whining, petulant, portentous tone the
thing needed, needed to be real, be what it was, then. His brother was
dead. His brother was dead.

The force to really sing was coming from somewhere, deep somewhere . . .

He sang,

> *"When you're young and so in love as we*
> *And bewildered by the world we see*
> *Why do people hurt us so*
> *Only those in love would know*
> *What a town without pity can do . . ."*

He hoped they wouldn't hit him because the denouement was coming.
He went into it.

> *"If we stop to gaze upon . . . a* star
> *People talk about how* baad *we are*
> *Ours is not an easy age*
> *We're like tigers in a cage*
> *What a town without pity can do . . ."*

He had sung it deeply whiningly, emphasizing but not mocking the
stupidity. How stupid had his brother been to love this crap, except that
of course, of course he understood why now, the gay implication, okay.
He went on. To a really stupid bridge part.

> *"The young have problems, many problems*
> *We need an understanding heart*
> *Why don't they help us, try and help us*
> *Before this clay and granite planet falls apart . . ."*

Poor bugger, he thought, Rex, poor bugger, I wish I had loved you.

There was a funny something going on. People, thugs, were being brought in to hear him sing. The room was fuller. He could feel that. He didn't care. Rise into it, he thought.

> *"Take these eager lips and hold me fast*
> *I'm afraid this kind of joy can't last*
> *How can anything survive*
> *When these little minds tear you in two*
> What a town without pity can do . . ."

He was thinking that if you were able to add up the amount of fun any-one had had in their lives, fun had, a quotient, it would tell you some-thing. This singing was fun. It was deep.

He sang hard,

> *"How can we keep love alive*
> *How can anything survive*
> *When these little minds tear you in two*
> *What a town without pity can do . . ."*

Then, really hard and wild,

> *"No it isn't very pretty what a town without pity*
> *Ca . . . aan do . . ."*

He had inhabited a song that had been a curse to him. Now he would sing like someone else, because he was not through singing, no.

"Come in," he said to no one.

Now he would sing as himself. He was lost in himself. He would sing "Carrickfergus" the way Joyce would have sung it, may have sung it, he had no idea. How he knew this song, he had no idea. He had heard it sung at a party and he had heard it on a record at another party and because of God he had it, most of it, the greatest song ever written expressing being totally drunk, it was being drunk at its best, stupid best, and he had remembered it and at another party he had volunteered to sing it and Iris had said No in the name of God, no, don't. Because it would embarrass her because he had been at the time very drunk. But then that part of their life had come to a close long ago and he had been fine since.

And he was starting to sing before he even intended it, and not as himself, as a drunken soul, the inspiration of this expression . . . He was full of song.

He wanted to startle them with his loud sound.

He did.

> *"I wish I was . . . in Carrickfergus,*
> *Only for nights . . . in Ballygrant*
> *I would swim over . . . the deepest ocean,*
> *Only for nights in Ballygrant.*
> *But the sea is wide and I cannot swim over*
> *Nor have I wings . . . so I could fly!*
> *I wish I could find . . . a handsome boatman*
> *To ferry me over . . . to my love and die . . ."*

He was certain there was an assemblage in the room. Someone began to applaud but the act was quashed. Ray seemed to have nonplussed his tormentors, for the moment. He felt a little triumphant. He even felt a little drunk. They could applaud if they wanted. He had sung piercingly, Irishly.

Someone was softly laughing. Ray wanted water badly. He thought he could sing the part about the handsome rover singing no more till he got a drink. His throat was dry. It was stinging.

> *"Ah in Kilkenny . . . it is reported*
> *There are marble stones there . . . as black as ink.*
> *With gold and silver . . . I would support her*
> *But I'll sing no more 'til I get a drink.*
> *For I'm drunk today, and I'm seldom sober,*
> *A handsome rover from town to town,*
> *Ah, but I'm sick now, my days are numbered,*
> *So come all you young men and lay me down."*

He relished the silence that his effort had produced.

"I'll take a drink, now," he said, retaining a touch of the character he had sung as.

There was laughter, and some murmuring, and then like a slash water was flung in his face. He caught some, enough to make a decent swallow. He had been ready. It was a triumph. He had bitten some water out of the air, was the way it felt.

"Tomorrow you'll give us another show, meneer. Yah, man, but with less music."

Ray was unstrapped from the chair without ceremony, roughly. His hood was jerked fully down and retied more tightly than was necessary. He was pulled to his feet and pushed forward. He almost fell, but saved himself by clutching onto Quartus's table and leaning on it until the whiteness behind his eyes receded.

Definitely they were rougher, hustling him along, two of them, than before. Everything is a signal, he thought.

Crossing the open ground back to his cell was hard, at the faster pace being forced on him. He wasn't being allowed to place his feet tentatively enough to knock rocks and pebbles and other impedimenta out of the way. He needed his shoes back. He was in stocking feet and the soles of his socks had turned planklike with sweat and filth, which was some help. But he wanted his shoes. And he wanted his wristwatch and he wanted to know how he looked, as a subject of abuse. He was curious. His beard was coming in. He wanted a mirror. He needed a haircut. He needed Iris, his barber. He was going to have to go to barbers, regular barbers, after she went away. She was going to. He knew everything that was going to happen.

"How do I look?" he asked stupidly, as he was thrown into his cell. He did the drill, stood with his back to the door while they took his hood off and then left, leaving him standing there locked in, with more to say.

"*Okay,*" he shouted after them.

He needed help. He collapsed onto his pallet and all his injuries began pulsing in unison. He felt like an ad, a display.

The whiteness in his head was back. He was yielding to it. He couldn't help it. But tomorrow would come and he was not through singing.

Night came and went. It was very cold. He was given food and water the next day, but that was the limit of the attention his captors paid to him, and then it was night again. He slept well in spite of the cold and spent the day following in a condition of anticipation that proved to be pointless. Again he was fed. But no one came for him. He wondered whether he was being deliberately ignored, whether that was part of the protocol, or if it was the press of other business that was the explanation. In any case he was weathering it. He was learning that he didn't need to attack each onset of dead time with games or exercises or purposive thinking. He could enter the absences and stay in them with everything shut down,

the associative thought-chains fading out. It was unusual to not be thinking and to be aware of it, thinking about it at the same time. If he was correct, this condition was a prize that mystics labored to grasp. There was
nothing blissful about it, at least not in the scraps and fragments of the
state he had attained to so far. He could do without it.

Night came again.

32. The Subject Matter

He came out of sleep raggedly, resisting coming out. The eruption of noise and light, whatever it had been, was already over. It had been brief. There had been flailing shafts of light, a crashing sound, unlocking and slamming and relocking of the shed doors. Now there was nothing evident. He had been dreaming and then his dream had been wrecked around him and he was out of it, in the black present.

He felt he should be afraid, but he had no energy for it. He should be afraid because there was a change. He was no longer alone in his prison room. Someone was breathing heavily and brokenly muttering and beginning to move around.

Ray waited to do something. He thought that probably he should get into a fighting crouch, but it was all he could do to sustain the sitting position he had achieved, his back to the rough wall. The darkness was seamless and absolute.

There were different possibilities. This could be part of the torture. A madman could have been dumped in on him. That kind of thing was done. It could be someone who would keep him awake. That was torture and more than torture in the shape he was in. It could be an animal. It wasn't an animal. It could be someone injured in some way he would be unable to do anything about, who would keep him awake.

He was going to say something as soon as he could penetrate what the new arrival was doing. He was doing something. He was apparently crawling around the edges of the room, feeling out the space. That was not an unintelligent thing to do. He had no idea how much the new arrival had been able to notice when he was hurled into the room. Not much, he would bet. It would be better for Ray to say something to this person before, in his explorations, the man stumbled across him.

He was going to say something first. That would be best. And instead of the plain Dumela greeting he would use the more honorific Dumela morena, Good day sir, why not? And then it would be O tswa kae, to find out where his new mate came from, was journeying from, and then finally O mang, Who are you? And he would watch his delivery, keeping it soft and nonbelligerent. His enunciation was going to be strange because his lips had swollen up and his mouth was so dry.

"Dumela morena," he said, partly for practice. He had tried to keep it pleasant.

His words produced a charged stillness.

And then he was leapt on crushingly. Large strong hands found his throat and gripped it.

He grappled with his attacker, struggling to get a purchase anywhere on his head, his nose, ears. By the feel of his hair he was an African and he had been eating onions, something that gave Ray a twinge of hunger, oddly.

A voice he knew growled, "O mang?" But with the pressure on his throat he couldn't reply, but he knew who it was. He did. He would be all right.

It was *Morel*. Somehow it was Morel.

Feelings of relief and hatred confused together swept hotly through him. He fought to get the breath to speak.

"It's me," he managed to say, trying to sound like himself.

Morel let him go.

"This is you, Finch. This is you. I found you," Morel said. It was Morel's strong voice but higher than usual, lifted into a higher register by fatigue and fear. Fear was there. Ray heard male elation and triumph in Morel's voice. He had done something.

"Is Iris all right?" Ray asked urgently.

"I can't believe this. Yes, Iris. No she's fine, except over you. No she got frantic about you. Nothing coming in, no news. You know. Ah God. That's why I came. No she was threatening to come up to look for you herself and I stopped her. She was going to come. So I stopped her, I came. It was the only way I could do it. She was raising hell at the embassy and getting nothing, getting the runaround worse than you can imagine. You don't know. She gets insane. You don't know.

"Ah man, this is you, but man, you *smell*. I smell blood. Have you got a torch, a match, any light so I can take a look? I don't have my bag. They took it."

Ray was amazed. Morel was not acknowledging the secret. That was interesting.

Ray laughed. "They've been hitting me. I've been hit. That's all. I think I'm okay. There's no light, nothing for light, sorry. My head hurts. I've got a scalp wound but it's scabbing up okay, I think. I clot fast."

"Sit still," Morel said. He was talking unusually rapidly, for him, skating over the one thing, the one thing. He lightly touched his palm to the back of Ray's head. He blew his breath out in a meaningful way.

"What?" Ray asked.

"I don't like it, man. Did you lose consciousness at any point? Think if you did. Shit, I need light to see this. We've got to get you cleaned up. You better get flat, stay flat until I can look at you. What the fuck is this place?

"I'll get a torch from these bastards. I'm a doctor."

"So how will you get them to give you a torch?"

"I'll yell, I'll kick the fucking doors . . ."

"Believe me, don't. They won't even come. Conserve your strength. It gets light in the morning, not bright clear but enough, you know. You can see. It's like twilight but you can see . . .

"Listen to me, the best thing is if you can rest. They get started early around here. I don't know what they have on the schedule for you, but they start early.

"There's another pallet you can sleep on. In fact there are three more, so you can take your choice. It's cold, so you have to fold a pallet in two and sleep in the fold. It's easier if you jam yourself into a corner.

"And let's see. Okay, you said Iris is okay, so when were you in touch with her last? Because now she'll be worrying about you too, won't she?" He let his words come out a little more darkly than he'd intended.

"No she's all right. I talked to her from Maun two three days ago." Ray could see that Morel wanted to rip through any matter relating to Iris at high speed. He understood why. He had a secret. He was nervous. Too bad for him.

Ray wanted the light to come for his own reasons. He wanted to see Morel with the eyes, the eyes of what, a cuckold. He wanted to see what she was seeing that he had missed. This was not a good subject matter for the moment at hand. Hell was another man's cock going into your beloved's cunt. That was the long and the short of it, so to speak. He had to have light so he could see guilt, the signs and traces. He was not going to accuse Morel of anything in the total dark and let him get away with anything. He was going to get him in the light of day and get the answer clear as hell and see it.

Morel was arranging his pallet. And he was giving a brief travelogue that was uninteresting to Ray, his difficulty in renting a vehicle, his cleverness in certain situations, all boring and all beside the point.

There was a silence when Morel was settled, but a short one.

Morel's voice was coming closer. He said, "You know who these people are, don't you? You do. You know what's going on up here. You know what this is."

"I have an idea," Ray said.

"You know what they want," Ray said.

"I have an idea."

Now he could hardly hear what Morel was saying. He had to ask him to speak up.

"Do you think it's safe for us to talk? I mean, I know we have to keep our voices down. But what do you think?"

"You mean have they got this place wired? Don't worry. They're not even taping the interrogations. You don't know how primitive this operation is. They've got their hands full. They have to get out of here fast. They know that.

"They want to get one man, Kerekang. That's all they want. They think I can help them with that, but they're afraid to go too far with me because I'm white and they figure people are going to be looking for me. Like you, for example.

"They're not going to go too hard on anybody white."

"Oh that makes me feel good," Morel said.

"Don't worry. You're white. You're included. You're American. To them you're white."

"*Listen . . .*"

"Doctor, don't bother."

Morel had moved his pallet closer yet. "We should keep our voices down, though, just out of prudence . . . right?"

"I don't think it matters. But let's do that."

"And I'm sorry you got into this. You were saying how you found me. I'm sorry if I wasn't listening. Say it again. So go ahead." He needed to be fair to Morel, who was just newly into this nightmare that he himself had had a chance to get used to. He had taken a risk to come looking for his lover's husband. Probably he'd expected to fail creditably but instead this had happened and he was in hell, for his trouble. Probably he had just wanted credit for a good try. That could be unfair. There is a kind of heroism that stupidity or ignorance allows to happen, Ray thought.

Morel wanted to keep on conversing, or if not conversing, just talking, describing his situation to himself, trying to do that over and over until he had something he could accommodate. Because not everything he was saying was being said for Ray's benefit. He was being repetitive. And he had again moved his pallet closer.

Ray was getting desperate about sleep. He didn't want to seem ungrateful or inhospitable, if that was the word.

Morel was expressing himself in fragments.

"I drove up to Maun. That was easy. Your assistant is still around there, waiting for you, I guess. He got through to Iris the one time. By the way the whole top of the country is out of commission . . . Emergency area. They keep saying it's temporary and being vague about bandits coming down from Caprivi, some bullshit story . . . You know this. So I found him, and it was a problem because he wanted to come along. He just gave me bare basics, where he'd seen you last and so on. I don't know if I should have brought him. I didn't want the responsibility. Also I had what he could tell me. Also I didn't think this would take long . . . I don't know why. So I came. I'd had to fight once already with your wife about coming along, big fight, so I was . . . I'd fought on the issue and I said no to him. You hear what I'm saying . . ."

"Doctor, I do but we've got to sleep, if we can. I do, anyway."

"I know, yeah. And they don't tell you anything. These people. They don't tell you anything.

"They tied me up. Blindfold. But I had to come up here."

Ray thought, Sure you did because you love her, you fucking miserable what, *cock*. He said, "So you came up Route 14 and they snagged you at Nokaneng. I don't know why they didn't just turn you around, though. Did you use my name, mention me? Bad if you did. Did you?"

"I did."

Morel didn't know it, but his voice was being studied by Ray, because there was going to be a discussion, an interrogation, about Iris that would let the truth escape, get it out. That was coming. He was getting a base reading of Morel and how he sounded when he was delivering true things, trivial things. Morel would try to lie. It wouldn't work.

"I shouldn't have," Morel said.

It was clear as a bell that the one thing Morel was never going to want to admit was the truth about his cock and Iris. But Ray would get the truth however he had to, keeping in mind that they needed each other, he and Morel, to survive this, survive koevoet, get out okay, if possible.

Morel would defend his innocence with his life. It didn't matter. The answer was there, burning. I have my ways, Ray thought.

"They took my boots," Morel said. He could barely say it.

Ray said, "They took mine too. They tend to do that." He was sorry for Morel. He was going to be hobbling around. One of his legs was shorter than the other and it was going to be humiliating and ugly. Ray wanted to say something that would help, but there was nothing to say. Pity was his enemy.

It was colder than it had been recently, unless he was wrong and it was just that his reserves were depleted. He had to fortify himself with sleep. Morel had to shut up.

"Listen," Morel said, being relentless.

"We've *got* to sleep. And I mean now. It takes work."

"Yeah, but listen. One thing I have to tell you tonight. I'll tell you why I have to. We don't know what's going to happen. They're in charge. They could separate us anytime, right? She sent me up to tell you this."

Ray was rigid. The secret was burning its way out into the open. He could smell the smoke. He was afraid. He wasn't ready. It was asking too much. He was thirsty. He was clenching up and it was making his wounds blaze. He would prefer to be up and around when the news came. That would be his preference. He had no strength.

"Listen, this is what I have to tell you. She wanted me to tell you personally, if she couldn't herself . . ."

"*What*, please," Ray said, his voice unnatural.

"Your brother died two weeks ago. I'm sorry."

"Ah," was all he could come out with. He was in agony at the news and at the interposition of this news over the secret yet to come, to be extracted. Life is pain, he thought. He had taken too long to do what he could, what he should have, for his brother. Iris had pushed him, but it had been too late.

He began to groan.

Morel said, "She said you had to know. It wasn't painful for him at the end. I'm really sorry."

Ray wanted to press his forehead hard against the wall. He thought it would help. He was sure it would.

He got on all fours and set his head against the wall. He groaned more. He released low, grinding groans.

Morel was distressed and came closer.

"When I get my bag back, I'll give you something," Morel said.

Ray slipped down and lay on his side.

"You must have been close," Morel said.

"*No*, no we were not. There's no point talking about it. I knew it was going to happen. In fact I think I knew it already had happened. I really did. There were signs."

"Your wife thought it was important for you to know."

"My wife. Of course she would. She probably would have liked me to go for the funeral. She could have gone herself. I don't care what she does. That isn't what I mean. Look, she was closer to Rex than I was. She liked him. He was a queer duck. He wrote some stuff I have to get back from these cocksuckers. It's too complicated to explain. How is my mother doing? Did Iris mention her?"

"Only that there was a ceremony, large thing, in San Francisco for him and that she wasn't there, your mother wasn't. That's all I know. Iris has material to show you about this event. It was big. He was apparently a local celebrity."

Ray folded the pallet over because the cold was strong and he was beginning to shake and he didn't want Morel to know, if he could help it. He was shaking. It was strange, he thought, that he had no impulse to weep. Of course, he was dehydrated, hugely. He wasn't sure if the system that made tears was the same one that made saliva, which he had next to nothing of. He was shaking embarrassingly.

He said, "Don't worry. I'm all right. Nobody worry. I'm going to write his Life and I'll be in it as shit, a villain, so don't worry. I'm tired. Right now I am. My role as a shit will be there.

"But watch out. Any Life I want to write I will. I spare no one. You don't understand. I spare no one."

Morel put his hand on him, then he was feeling his face, and then his wrist, trying to take his pulse, Ray supposed.

"You mean you're going to write his obituary."

"Nah nah *no*, you don't understand no. Watch out. I . . ."

Morel was at the shed door, kicking and shouting, butting the door with his fists and knees. It had to be with his knees, because they had taken his boots. He was going to fuck his knee up, with this.

He was keeping up the ruckus for what seemed a remarkably long time. It came to nothing.

Morel gave up finally and came back to him.

"You're still shaking," Morel said.

"I know."

"Look, it's freezing. So this is what we need to do. We've got to pile these extra things on us. We fold you into one and I get next to you. We have one under us and one over us, or two over us, and we use body heat, trap it."

"I think this is psychological," Ray said. He was ashamed of his trembling voice.

Morel said, "It doesn't matter if it is. It wears you out. We have to control it. I don't love this idea, but we are going to be buddies tonight. No, wait a minute and listen. I am getting in with you. If you stop shaking, I'm gone. I can't check you out in the dark. I should check you out. I don't know if this is malaria . . ."

"It's psychological," Ray said.

"Yeah but I would like to look at you for bites, lesions. I can't. You're taking your chloroquine?"

"Well, I was."

"When did you take your last tablet? Try to remember. It's very important."

"I don't know when it was. A while, is all I know."

"Well do you have any prominent bites on you, things that itch, anything like that?"

"You know, you get bitten constantly around here. But everything itches anyway. I've got cuts."

Morel was hauling things around. And then he was flat against him, his front against Ray's back, holding him still as he finished arranging things.

Ray was being pushed into a corner and held there. That was his life.

He thought he should bid goodbye to his brother. He whispered what he wanted to say until Morel asked him what he was saying.

He went silent. He thought, My dear Rex, silly fucking poefter goodbye you poefter: We missed the boat.

He meant everything. But he was shaking even more.

He continued, out loud, We missed the boat and you are going away, goodbye mon semblable mon frère goodbye: Something you wanted to hear is what I want to say, you were smarter . . . I hated that, but you were.

It was difficult. Morel was saying Hey, hey, calm down, hey, hey.

Ray whispered into the pallet, Goodbye, we are all turning into ghosts bit by bit anyway . . . you were smart, a smart person, and you could write, and that is the truth.

There was something he wanted to promise but couldn't, because of life, the way life is. What he wanted to say was *I will tell you this, your life will be famous*. He couldn't quite. He was in captivity. He didn't know what was going to happen. How could he?

I will help your ghost, he thought.

"I will make you live," he said aloud, alarming Morel.

They were in a corner. Folded over, the edges of the two pallets covering them barely made a closure that would keep the bitter cold out. And then there was a third pallet laid on top of the other two. And the point was to move around as little as possible so as not to disarrange all this delicate architecture Morel had organized because then the cold would come in like a knife and wake them up. It was the coldest night he remembered, by far. There had been a shift in the weather. The skies change, but not ourselves, was a quotation from somebody on the subject of not expecting too much out of sheer traveling to exotic places, like Africa, the Kalahari.

Ray was on the inside, toward the fold. It was Morel's job to keep the lips of the pallets together if he could.

They had evaded calling each other by their first names. That wouldn't do. That needed to be settled in the morning. The idea of having to call Morel *Davis* was intolerable. The vivid fact that Morel had so far never just spontaneously called him Ray was a further burning indicator of the guilt he was bearing inside himself like a nasty jewel. It was there, like the jewel between the eyes of the nasty monstrous frog idol in adventure stories. He was going to pry it out. He had to because it was all he could see when he looked at the man. He would do it.

If anybody had to get up to pee during the night the whole house of cards would fall apart and they would have to start over. He rarely needed to get up at night to pee. And of course just now he was so dehydrated there would be no question of who would be to blame for wrecking things, if anyone did. My prostate is fine, he thought. That was a plus about him he wondered if Iris appreciated. Would she miss it in him if she got with someone who had to pop up to go to the toilet two, three times a night? Would she think back, Ah, those were the nights? Nights she could sleep like God, who could presumably sleep at will. Benign prostate hyperplasia was what most men his age had, if he was correct, or possibly it wasn't most, but it was many. He could ask the doctor. He could ask Davis. In any case he didn't have it, thank God.

Definite warmth was slowly materializing.

There was a falling asleep trick he just remembered. He didn't know where he had picked it up. He hadn't thought of it for years. It was possible that it was something he knew from training, or from beloved Marion

Resnick. The idea was to take the sparks and lines and curlicues and all the other bright fragments in the eidetic display that shows up behind your eyelids every night, eidetic debris it had been described as, and catch the bits and pieces and through willpower force them into a solid coherent shape like a triangle or an oblong or a circle. He remembered doing it successfully. It was a strain to do it and it no doubt worked because the peculiar effort took your mind off the crimes and failings that rose up gnashing their teeth when it was time to rest so that you could continue your crimes when the sun came up the next day.

Morel would be interested. Davis, he meant. But Morel was asleep, judging by his breathing pattern.

It was a measure of the state Ray was in that he had to quell the impulse to wake Morel to tell him about this wonderful trick. He was insane. It was a thing Rex would appreciate. It could be in *Strange News*.

He used his trick and sleep came.

It was daylight. Bright gray was what he would say the light regime was.

Morel was up and active.

Ray pushed his way out of the pallet mound.

Morel was performing calisthenics of some kind. He halted when he saw Ray emerging and gave an almost joyful cry. He had reconstituted himself as a fighter and winner, Ray could tell. He was acting buoyant. Some of that was for Ray, including possibly all of it. It was pitiful when Morel came over, walking unevenly despite his best efforts to correct for his short right leg, trying to make his gait more normal by arching his right foot, walking on the ball of that foot. He couldn't help wondering if Iris had seen Morel hobbling around much. Ray's guess was that Morel would keep his built-up shoes on as much of the time as he could. That was what he would do, in his shoes, so to speak. Maybe she had seen him in his true state in the bathroom, the shower. Although it was possible he had special clogs to wear. All he knew was that in Morel's place he would be doing his utmost to reduce the moments of elision when he would have to appear as what he was, afflicted.

The roosters were up and screeching.

In any case, this was the man Iris wanted. She preferred him. No question he was the sturdier type, more sturdily built. He was very squarely made, straight-out shoulders for example, not sloping at all. He was athletic. In his safari shorts and shortsleeved shirt and khaki kneesocks he looked like a large Boy Scout or better yet a scoutmaster. He was thick through the chest. He had heavy calves, like bleach bottles. His arms and forearms were bulky, both, and about equally, by which he meant in good proportions. For guys who worked out it was so common to get the proportions wrong, and Morel clearly worked out. It wasn't unusual for people with a disability in one quarter to devote themselves to making the other three quarters superb. He understood it. There was more he could have done in his own case, just to contradict the weediness that time brings. And in fact he could still do it, take it up, except that it was a little late and if he did it would be a little obvious.

Morel was a good specimen, a goodlooking devil. He had good dense close-cropped hair, a little grayer maybe than Ray recalled, but not much grayer. It would be easier for him to remain within normal ranges of acceptable appearance, even in absurd conditions like this, because that kind of hair cut that way took care of itself. Morel seemed to have more and deeper lines in his brow than Ray remembered, but that only served to make him look consequential and serious. His underjaw was very tight. His throat was not swallowing his chin. He looked younger than forty-five. When it came to teeth, it was Morel hands down, for brightness, evenness, the works. Women would notice his eyes, too, and that would snag them, because the man was black, but his eyes were a light bluish gray. His eyes were counter to his usual type and in an aesthetically pleasing way, or so Ray supposed. I am completely within my type, Ray thought. That was it. I look Dutch, he thought.

What Ray had been looking for was anything unexpected and pleasantly negative that he might have missed before, some negative detail or other. But here was the man she preferred, surviving stress and fatigue and the humiliation of having to hop around and there were no new debits. He looked good.

Black was of course not entirely right for Morel, not in black Africa. He wondered if Iris was tired of whiteness, white men, like he was. He was both, he was one, and he was tired of them. He felt like laughing, but it was too early in the day. He was queasy.

Just for the sake of completeness he wouldn't mind if a glance at Morel's penis came his way. Living cheek by jewel, by which he meant jowl, it was probably in the cards.

"Let me look at you," Morel said.

He led Ray to a spot where a spray of light came down through one of the vents in the upper wall.

Morel began with an unbearable, to Ray, diagnostic stare. Morel moved him around gently in the available light. Morel's nails were clipped and clean. Ray's were filthy. There was no point in being ashamed of his grooming, but he was.

"One thing first," Ray said.

"What?"

"We're not using our first names. We're avoiding it. I think I know why."

Morel went past that, shot past it, saying, "*Right*, yeah, of course. Right. Ray . . ."

"Call me Ray."

"I just did. And you call me Davis."

"I will." He would try to have sympathy for Morel. It had to be an ordeal for the man to try to keep reasonably level, compensating for his disability. At the moment, he was bracing his right foot on the wall six inches up. It was acrobatic. And he was trying to make nothing of it, keep it invisible.

Morel said, "In fact call me Dave."

That enraged Ray, for some reason. He contained it. He said, "Who calls you Dave? I never heard anyone call you that."

"Oh some people have. But Davis is good."

"Well, does Iris call you Dave?" He was getting ahead of himself. It was a mistake.

"No."

"Then Davis."

"Put your tongue out," Morel said. Ray was sure it was a move to break this line of discussion. But he complied.

"Jesus," Morel said, and then said, "Sorry, but do you ever scrape your tongue, usually?"

"No, but my wife does."

"She scrapes your tongue?"

Ray knew an attempt at lightening the discourse when he heard one. It was a leaden attempt.

"No of course not. She scrapes *her* tongue, as you undoubted know. Brushes it, anyway, when she brushes her teeth. She is devout about it."

"Okay, well, it's an important thing to do and most people don't. Frankly . . ."

"Frankly what? My tongue looks bad, so what else?"

Morel turned him around. He fiddled with the scab on Ray's scalp, disengaging strands of hair that had become stuck in it. That seemed pointless to Ray and he wanted Morel to stop. Then Morel pressed the margins of the scab in three places.

"That hurts," Ray said, lying. He wanted the examination to end.

"When is breakfast?" Morel asked.

"Any moment now. But you realize that it's all the same, what we get to eat, breakfast, dinner, it's all the same. It's mush. And some powdered milk sometimes."

"No vegetables or any sort of fruit?"

"Please be serious. No."

"What about water?"

"They play with you about water. I had a water bottle and then I didn't. And then I did and it was half full. And then they took that and now I don't. I need water, though. I'll tell you. It's serious."

"We both do. I'll get us water."

"You will? And how will you do that?"

"I'll insist. It's medically necessary. Actually, you have no temperature. But I'll say you do. And I want my boots. And I want my bag, or at least I need them to let me get into my bag and get stuff, even if they stand there and then take it away when I'm through. I'll propose it."

"Good luck."

A thing Ray had been turning over in his mind off and on thinking about Morel in the last few weeks was the question of who would look better at sixty-five or thereabouts, which of them, and he had been thinking that it would be himself. He would be the better deal. Of course there was the consideration that he was going to get there first, alas. But he had been entertaining the idea that Morel might be doomed in the context because his monobrevipodia might conceivably put him in the wheelchair-user category, something Iris might not have faced up to. Of course, he had no way of knowing if there was anything progressive about Morel's leg situation. And he could tell that the man had done wonders in keeping the musculature on his short leg up to snuff, through some miracle of focused exercise. The calf on Morel's short leg was better than either of Ray's calves, not to put too fine a point on it. Ray felt that his own arms, because he had lost weight, looked old.

The examination was proceeding. Unless he was wrong, his friend Dave was being rougher than he needed to, pushing Ray's eyelids sharply back into his head while he made him roll his eyes clockwise and then counterclockwise not just once or twice but a few times. It was like no examination he'd ever had. And the outcome of that particular exercise seemed to be that Morel could see no signs of jaundice. He wanted to know why there was any reason to think he might have contracted jaundice.

And then his side was squeezed, hard. That was to do with his liver or spleen, he supposed.

And then Morel put his ear against his chest, which Ray doubted could tell him anything except that his heart was beating at present, otherwise the invention of the stethoscope was a superfluous event. He was being unfair to Morel. The examination was a physical feat being accomplished, with all the difficulty Morel was having in keeping himself from toppling over.

Morel said, "Your ears are extraordinarily clean."

"She does that with a thing, a bulb . . ."

"Syringe."

"Syringe, yes. I'm getting old."

"Really clean. I never see that."

"No she does it every couple of weeks. She's very faithful about it. Debrox is the name of the what is it, acid? She puts acid in the porches of my ears."

"I'm pleased."

"Well, good, because she started doing it at your suggestion, you might recall. It's part of your regimen, I believe."

Morel said nothing, but motioned for him to take his stinking shirt off. There was a punitive element to the proceeding, in Ray's opinion.

"We've got to clean you up. I have to get to my bag."

"Look at this. You have contact dermatitis all through here on your chest, under your chest hair. And it's showing on your neck. It must itch."

"It doesn't," Ray said, and that was true. But now that it had been brought to his attention he could feel the itching begin there. He hadn't noticed any itching because he had been, this was his theory, distracted by the rich selection of wounds and bruises he was otherwise sporting.

Morel said, "I can fix that with hydrogen peroxide if they give me my bag.

"You have slight *pectus excavatum*. You must know that . . ."

"I don't think I know that. Sunken chest, that is?"

"It's really slight."

"What does it do to you?"

"Nothing much. Yours is so slight."

"It's more like a natural feature than a condition or defect, right? Like a cleft chin."

"More or less."

"I had a heart murmur when I was eight. It went away."

Morel was going interminably over his back and shoulders, looking for bites or any sort of interesting defect he might mention.

"Just a second," Ray said. He had realized there was a task that had to be done, which was to redistribute the pallets to their separate original positions. He went about it. It was important. Morel seemed puzzled by his anxious eagerness to complete the task.

"What're you doing?" Morel asked. Then he said, "I can do that."

Ray said, "They'll be coming. You want everything to look the way it was before they left. Believe me. I can explain it more if you really need that."

"No. Hey."

Ray felt lightheaded and then felt his head beating with new pain, a supreme headache, a classic worse than anything from yesterday. He had to remember not to stoop, not to get his head down low.

"I have to lie down for a minute," he said.

Morel himself had sunk to a sitting position against the wall. He seemed to be doing breathing exercises.

"I'm not finished examining you," Morel said.

"Yes you are," Ray said.

"I am?"

"You are. You covered the waterfront. And if you found something, what, terrible, what can you do? You have nothing. They won't let you. That's *it*."

"Listen, I am going to get my bag, I promise you. But even without it there are certain things I can do."

"Like what?"

"Like various things."

Ray said, "Right now I have a headache that on a scale of one to ten is nine. Iris gives me that aspirin with codeine you can get in the Republic. You have no codeine. That's what this one is eligible for."

Morel hauled himself up and limped over, kneeling beside Ray on the pallet.

"Okay," Morel said, breathing complexly, theatrically, Ray thought, then saying commandingly, "Close your eyes . . . um . . . Blow all your breath out . . . Now."

I am not an idiot, Ray thought. But he did as he was told.

Ray felt thumb pressure being applied to the midline of his forehead, and then knuckle pressure being applied further up along the same axis but stopping short of his scab area. Morel was being careful. And then the knuckle pressure continued harder, rocking. It hurt. It was cruelly hard. And it was infuriating that he could feel his headache receding.

"Sit up slowly," Morel said.

Ray did, furious. His head pain was shrinking toward the manageable. And then toward the negligible.

And then it was a vestige.

That was a parlor trick, he thought. It was undoubtedly the trick of using one kind of pain to trump another kind of pain, a parlor trick.

"How is your head?"

"Getting better."

"Good, then." Morel withdrew.

Now Morel was over at the waste bucket.

"Can't we get a lid for this thing?" Morel asked over his shoulder.

"Of course not. It's part of the program."

Morel was studying the contents of the waste bucket. Ray assumed he was considering evacuating into it. But still the staring into it was an invasion of privacy, in a way. Not that it was important.

"When was your last bowel movement?" Morel asked. Ray wanted this line of attention over with. The question was a reaction to there being only urine in the bucket. So Morel was reaching a conclusion. But of course the bucket could have been emptied any number of times. Why did he have to answer this particular question, he wanted to know.

"I don't know," Ray said.

"Give a guess."

"I don't know."

"How long, though? A week?"

Ray had to think. He said, "Since I've been here. Almost a week."

"Not good," Morel said, continuing to contemplate, irritatingly, the contents of the bucket as though if he stared long enough some wisdom would leap up and strike him.

"Look, I have to go, Ray. I'm sorry," Morel said.

"What in the fuck are you apologizing for?" But he knew why Davis was apologizing. He was apologizing for being closer to normal, in better shape, in that way. Actually, he was being delicate, Ray decided. Maybe he was apologizing for having had plenty to eat and drink recently.

"Of course. Go ahead. I'm sorry. Of course, go ahead."

"Um, I see there's no paper. No paper."

"That's right. I don't know what to tell you. That's also part of the program. Part of the treatment."

"Bastards. I'll get some paper from them."

"No you won't. No. But I'll tell you what you do. This is what I would do. You sacrifice a piece of your shirttail. Tear off as little as you can get away with for the purpose. And when you use it be real careful, scientific. That's what I would do. If I had to shit. Which I don't. I mean, about the shirt, you don't know what else you might be going to need it for. I'm just trying to think ahead. Anyway."

Ray turned his back to Morel. He went to stand as close to the shed doors as possible. He heard cloth being torn.

Grumbling softly, and, Ray believed, still apologizing, Morel emptied his bowels, suppressing as well as he could any sounds of relief or satisfaction, natural reactions.

You have to appreciate him, Ray thought. He had qualities.

A standardly foul odor established itself.

"Don't apologize," Ray said, which led to some suppressed but still evident amusement on Morel's part.

Morel was through and he was brisker.

"I'll get that thing emptied, don't worry, or I'll get a lid for it out of them. I will. I will, man. Also, I'll get my bag. I'll get my boots. They can keep the laces if that's what they're worried about and I want my watch, but that's nothing, they can keep it. I want my toothbrush. They can watch me use it if they think I'd like to turn it into a weapon, a shiv or something. Fuck them. I've got to clean you up. And I want water available in here full-time, not only when they feel like it now and then. No no."

Morel was in a sort of dancing state, a punching state. It was unusual.

Ray said, "Dream on. You'll get nothing. Be prepared."

But against his will he was finding Morel slightly inspiring. All assholes respond to extreme self-confidence, he thought. Morel was like a coach. He was the type a white college under pressure to diversify would fall on their knees for, somebody smart about getting along with the white alumni but jive or tough enough to motivate the black and white team, the troops, into crushing the enemy of the moment, the team from another venue. There was a weak but distinct in-and-out pattern in his friend Davis, a modulation from a regular sort of down-home black up into the doctor, good schools persona. Iris probably loved that without knowing she did. One minute the man was tough, and the next it was would she like some Constant Comment tea and had the last issue of the *New York Review of Books* arrived and where had she put it? Because she had a habit of putting things in odd places. Davis would discover that. Ray did know that Morel had a subscription to the *New York Review of*

Books. Whether he read it or not was another question. He was thinking of himself and his own backlog of *Times Literary Supplement*s which this nightmare hell trip had at least allowed him to eat into. Not *one* of his unread *TLS*es had ever gone astray. She had just been being considerate, but saving them so strictly had constituted a reproach, not that she knew it. How could she? He had said they had to get the *TLS* because in Africa that was the way he could keep in touch with the other world of thought and writing, which he had meant, he had meant it, but it had been a lie. Because over the years it had gotten more and more painful to look into the world of the scholarly literary others busily producing, dancing. But she had continued saving these painful things, faithful to the end.

He heard something. "They're coming," he said.

"Breakfast, you mean?"

"Right, probably, but listen. I have to know what you told the people who captured you, took you. I have to know what you told them about me. We have to be on the same page. You understand. Jesus, we should have talked about this before. So, quick, please. They're coming."

Morel said, "No don't worry. No, this is what I told them. I'll tell you.

"I told them you were with Education and you were in the bush looking for school sites. That was what you were doing."

"And so what did you tell them about why in the name of God you were up here looking for me?"

"Okay, this is what I told them. And forgive me. I told them you were my patient and your wife was worried about you."

"You said I was your patient."

"Yeah. I came up with that and I thought it was clever. I was coming to look for my patient. Look, they knew I was a doctor. There was no question about that. And I didn't have anything ready to say and I came up with that. I don't know, I thought it was clever, kind of, at the time. I went into how upset your wife was, distraught . . ."

"You said I was your patient. I had escaped from you. I needed to be under control. So the implication was, is, was that I was a what, mental patient?"

"No a therapy patient. You were receiving therapy."

"Christ almighty. It's a little humiliating, isn't it? From my standpoint?"

"I did my best."

"Let me think about this. It's a shock. But maybe it isn't all bad. Let me think. I'm an escaped patient . . ."

"Look, all I said was *erratic*. You were behaving erratically and it was a concern to your wife and to me and so on. They seemed to buy it okay. Come on. You can work with it. Come on."

Be a realist, Ray said to himself. There was the singing outbreak of the day before that this idea comported not so badly with. There was his attachment to a peculiar and, as his captors saw it, incoherent manuscript.

"This is going to work out," Morel said, squaring his shoulders, projecting the impression that the matter was settled, radiating definiteness, resilience.

Of course that was what Iris needed and had a right to have, an optimist. I am a traveling grave, he thought. Billowing dark sorrow over his brother rose up, as though for emphasis. He pushed it away. No, what she needed was a congenital optimist, so to speak. Morel was a heroic optimist. Anyone who thought he could break the grip of the white hand on Africa by arguing the continent into rejecting the Lord Jesus Christ was an optimist at the extreme end of the spectrum, a caricature figure worthy of Molière. It was at the level of comedy. I am a traveling grave, he thought again. It occurred to him that Morel would make a very good choice for one of the Lives he was going to write. He would think about that more, later.

"Are they coming with breakfast?" Morel asked.

"Room service is coming. Don't worry."

He was realizing something. Iris could be loving something she hardly even knew she needed. She could be loving a clean heart, the lightness of being that a clean heart gives, gives the eyes, the voice. She had a right to love someone with nothing to declare versus someone . . . someone else. Because a certain amount of his mortal life had been given over to burying certain matters, misgivings, and to not disclosing things having to do with the agency, what blessed Marion Resnick in the grip of red joy had told him about Malawi, to name just one thing, killings, by Banda, by Banda and not the agency, but the agency allowing events to go on without acting.

He was starving but he had no appetite. He would have to ask his physician how that could be. And he was surprised at how little fear for his body he had felt so far.

We bury death, he thought.

Morel was talking to himself. Ray knew what he was doing. He was repeating the list of items he was going to get their captors to give him. He was making himself believe it was going to happen. Ray couldn't help admiring the exercise and even more the ability to think it was worth doing. Morel was moving around oddly, dancingly, clenching his hands softly behind his back. What a guy, Ray thought.

"They're coming. This is going to work out," Morel said.

Morel thought he was going to fix Africa. Ray wanted to tell him some things about Africa. Africa was broken, and broken everywhere and broken worst where the West had come in, intervened. He was thinking of Angola. How could it ever recover? Angola had happened during his time in the agency, not like Indonesia, say, which was earlier and far away. Angola was going to limp forever. Resnick had been against helping Savimbi and he hadn't been careful about letting it be known. And that hadn't helped him in the South Africa Region Office with his superiors. But he had been right about Angola, of course, Resnick had. By the time Angola got back to normal the undamaged white West would have vaulted further onward and upward, out of sight, the white gods, technologically speaking, would be unattainably ahead. Land mines kept going off in Angola, removing people's legs and arms. He was part of the system that had led to that. The mines would outlive him. He had to let all this come into him, everything he had struggled to keep out. He had never been interested in wrecking anything in Africa.

Something was going on at the door.

Morel was striding arduously forward, friendly and resolute, which was wrong. There was a routine to follow.

"Davis, we have to stay over there against the wall," he said.

There would be trouble. They were supposed to have their backs to the door, their hands over their heads. There would be trouble and it would be his fault. He knew the routine and they would assume he had communicated about it.

"Dumelang," Morel said, booming it out, full of morning cheer, as the doors were pulled open.

Ray didn't understand.

Two men in black balaclavas had delivered breakfast, a genuine breakfast, of sorts, not just a dish of samp or mealie-meal. No, they had provided a leathery brown omelette, an ostrich egg omelette, served on a square of kraft paper, cold. And with it had come two kinds of crackers, eight of them, four of each kind. The omelette had been huge, and there had been eight figs, pretty dried up but still edible, which Morel had insisted Ray eat all of. And there had been a plastic liter bottle of cold tea and another one of plain water. And Morel had done a song and dance and the guards had agreed to leave the water in the cell.

And then Morel had made as if to hand the waste bucket to them, to the guards, to take care of, and they had bridled, but they had allowed him to carry it out and empty it himself, a little away from the shed. And he had brought it back tolerably cleaned up. He had shaken sand around in it.

And there had been no repercussions over not following the standing-against-the-wall-with-back-turned protocol.

Ray didn't understand. It was showing.

"I know what this is," he said.

"What what is?"

"This . . . all this. This food."

Morel was secreting the paper the omelette had come on, folded up, in a crack in the wall.

"No, they're softening us up. This is the softening-up phase. They'll alternate. You'll see."

"Maybe they're through with us, Ray."

"That's what they want us to think. Don't. Don't relax."

"You're the coach," Morel said.

There was a knock at the door, a knock, not a barrage of banging and pounding. And the door was unchained again.

The guards were back. This time an old woman was with them. She was carrying a large basin of hot water. Steam was rising from the water. Ray wanted to sink his face into the water however hot it was. A sponge was produced, a couple of not too unclean-looking rags, and a bar of yellow soap, laundry soap but still soap.

Morel's Setswana was very good, surprisingly good. That had to be part of the explanation for the improvement in their situation. He could only follow what Morel was saying after the fact, by repeating to himself whichever line or fragment he could catch and remember. Lere ditlhako tsa me meant Bring me my shoes. It was in the imperative mode. Morel thought he was going to get his shoes returned. It was laughable. Morel spoke Setswana rapidly, too rapidly, like a native speaker. If he would slow down I could understand more, Ray thought.

For some reason, their captors were being less paranoid about allowing them to see something of the grounds, the surroundings. They still had to do their little tasks, like eating, inside, with the doors closed. But Morel had been allowed a few moments in the open. And incidental glimpses of the main building were not being forbidden.

Closed in again, Morel and Ray crouched down at the basin. There is no civilization without hot water, Ray thought. Washing up would be voluptuous. He wanted to at least touch the water while it was still hot. The question was whether or not he should go first, whether he should assume it would be fair for him to go first, because he was the filthier. Or would it make more sense for Morel to go first because he was cleaner and so would need less water? Inevitably meanwhile the water was cooling. He couldn't stand it.

"You go ahead," Ray said.

But Morel had his own protocol and that was the one that would be followed. Apparently, according to it, Ray would be allowed right off the bat to lavishly wash his face, his orbits, his eye-pits if that was the name for them. He was encouraged to do that. He did it.

And then began the painstaking, assisted part of the procedure, the scalp-cleaning, followed by all the secondary ablutions, the laving of his armpits and so on. It was all done expertly, stretching the water, as Morel put it, carefully lathering up a particular area before rinsing with the sponge. The wastewater fell to the floor.

Ray felt like a baby, once it was done, but he felt much better.

Morel used the remaining water on his own face and feet. He had dedicated the precious water almost entirely to Ray.

"Thank you," Ray said. It was awkward.

He felt restored. He was less his body and more himself, less his body pulsing and hurting and preoccupying everything, more his consciousness of Iris, he was sorry to say. But it was true. He was sorry because now it was time to take up the question of Iris, with Morel. He knew he should put it off but he couldn't put it off.

He was ready to go. He was gathering his breath to begin when there was an interruption, noise outside. And then the doors were unlocked and cracked open and Morel was summoned out, and then, and this was new, the doors were pushed shut but not locked.

He didn't know what to conclude. Something was new.

An evident altercation was taking place just outside and then Morel was back, pushed into the cell. Ray had gathered pretty well what the altercation had been about. It had transpired in English and Setswana and it had been about Morel's shoes. He had been demanding the return of his shoes as a precondition for whatever it was they wanted. And Ray was getting clearer about what that might be, what the explanation for the better treatment they were enjoying might be, that is.

There was something undeniably what, tough, about Morel, something tough or reckless and more reckless than tough. It was one thing to be tough if you fully appreciated what these evil cocksuckers were capable of doing to you and another thing if you didn't. These bastards came trailing clouds of murder and arson and beatings. Morel knew it, but he knew it in the way you know something you read about in the paper. That is, he knew it but didn't know it.

But Ray knew the truth, which raised the question of why he wasn't himself considering the question of throwing himself on one of the bastards and breaking his neck with a move he knew how to do. In the grand scheme of things that would be a worthy thing to do, removing one of these bastards from the phalanx they were in, making one fewer of them in the world, even if it got him killed and removed from life, which it would.

He really ought to think about it. Koevoet was an evil plague. It would be doing something. There was the question of his life, of course, and whether he could do something more useful than that with it. He would have to take the idea under advisement, killing one of them. He would have to take the idea under advisement. He had numerous ideas under advisement. This would be one more.

But it was all academic because of Iris, because he had to conclude with her and it had to be face to face. It had to be done in the flesh. It had to be open. It had to be a clear thing. He had to let her argue her side, argue, say, that they should stay together despite everything, not go, not go.

And she needed to hear what he had to say, not that there was that much on his side. And he needed to hear the dire truth or whatever lies she might want to try on him, showing how abject she could be, how much she wanted to take everything back. And he needed to see what that would do to him, if that was the way things went. So he had to live.

But that meant he had to get the whole truth out of Morel. That was his next task. And it was an urgent task, urgent to tackle right away because something might separate them anytime because they were in the hands of others.

Whatever strength he had now, he owed to Morel. That was beside the point.

Ray said, "We have to . . ."

Morel cut him off, with a sign. He didn't want to talk. He wanted to listen. He was concentrating on listening for cues from outside. There was a consultation going on just outside.

He hated Morel, then. The man was nothing if not self-confident to the point, judging by his expression, of smugness. He knew something. Or he expected something.

And then the doors were inched open and somebody placed two neatly folded blankets on the floor, withdrew, and then a hand reached in and deposited, on the stacked blankets, Morel's shoes, thick-soled high-quarter shoes, laceless but cleaned up, rudely polished, even.

The shoes were works of orthopedic art. They matched nicely. But clearly the right shoe contained a substantial orthotic. Staring, Ray could make out certain telltale differences in the right shoe, but not anything that would be noticeable when the shoe was being walked around in. And of course such shoes would have cost in the high hundreds, at least. He didn't know why that depressed him. It did.

Morel's eagerness to get his shoes on was understandable. He understood it. He was sorry for Morel being pitched into this morass and having to deal with everything from the standpoint of being lopsided.

"What is going on?" Ray asked.

"Guess."

"I don't know." But he did know.

"They want my services. They need me to look at some people."

"So you bargained."

"Right. I wanted more. I wanted my toothbrush. Yours too. I didn't leave you out. But I really wanted my shoes. They knew that."

"I understand. Of course. This is interesting." He was wondering if this leverage of Morel's meant that there would be an extended regime of better treatment and if he would be included in it.

There was another novelty. Someone knocked at the doors before unlocking them.

Two hooded men appeared, invited Morel to come along, and closed and locked the doors with the rough ceremony Ray had earlier gotten accustomed to.

Ray decided to pace around for a while, vigorously, the way Morel had said he should, for exercise. Morel seemed to be saving him, in various ways. That seemed to be the picture. In addition to proposing to their captors that Ray was a mental case, Morel was getting benefactions for him. They both had blankets, now.

It didn't matter. When Morel came back they would have to discuss Iris.

They had to. And in the meantime he needed to be able to refer to Iris and the Iris question without using her name. Inwardly he was going to refer to it, to her, as . . . the subject matter. That would make it easier.

Because it was odd about her name because when he said it to himself even in the most passing way he felt the impulse to say it to her, to feel himself addressing her. So this would make life easier.

It was harder being alone, now, waiting. Having company had somehow done that. He was losing the equilibrium he had developed.

There was nothing. For present company he had dust motes and flies, a few flies.

It was remarkable how rapidly it went from cold to hot in the Kalahari. Already the heat was beginning to press. His grasp on the passing of time was not what it should be. Morel had been gone too long, he knew, but how much was too long in minutes? He didn't know how long it had been.

He kept pacing around dutifully. He detached a splinter from the chewed-up wooden floor and used it to clean under his nails.

He wanted to know what was going to happen next.

Morel was back. He looked ashen, which was bad because there was the subject matter to deal with.

Again the locking up was noisy and emphatic. Everything is a sign, Ray thought.

Morel looked beige, true beige, a shade lighter than his usual tan coloring. He had been through something.

"What?" Ray asked.

"What kind of place is this?"

"You mean the Bird Lodge? Well, it was supposed to be a resort for birdwatching, game drives . . ."

"Because apparently they had a zoo here, too, a small zoo."

"That's right. I remember that. One of the attractions was a private zoo. I don't know that they ever got around to stocking it."

"It's stocked now."

"What do you mean?"

"They have people in cages. They're holding people in the zoo cages."

"What, they took you there to treat them? And how many people? And who is it?"

"I don't know who they are. They're local, mostly Bakgalagadi, I think. They understood my Setswana okay, but when they spoke it was not the Setswana I'm used to. I don't know any Sekgalagadi, unfortunately."

"How many were there, I mean how many are there?"

"Twenty. Four women and the rest men. All the people in the cages are black, of course . . ." Morel was agitated.

"Calm down," Ray said.

"There were only black people in the zoo. And I'm in *here*, with you."

"I can see how you feel, but look. It's an accident. The zoo was meant to attract white people, tourists. It was a facility, it was available, it got put to use."

"I saw three exposure cases. What am I supposed to do? I have nothing to work with."

"Who are they, though? Did they tell you anything? Are they from the Toromole area . . . ?"

"I couldn't talk about anything but their symptoms. And that's all they were allowed to talk about. That was the restriction. I followed orders. There were two of those goons with me. I feel like killing. I feel like killing."

"I know. I do too."

"I said they had to get those people indoors. Or at least they had to let them have fires at night, allow that."

"Will they do it?"

"They laughed at me. I'll get them, though, somehow I will, I'll testify against them. If I get the chance."

"We need to keep calm, come on."

Morel squeezed his eyes shut and began breathing measuredly. Ray waited.

"Now I'm all right," Morel said.

But he wasn't all right. He was in a state of agitation. He was in the corner gesturing violently that Ray should come over and boost him up so that he might examine the ceiling. Escaping was on his mind, clearly.

Ray went over to him. "This isn't a good idea. If they come in and see us doing this we're in trouble. Really. I've gone over this. We'd need tools to get out through the ceiling. There's chicken wire, layers of it, up there. And it doesn't make sense because even if we got out we'd just be here. They watch this place. There's nowhere to go except the bush and we don't even have water. They patrol around here at night. You can hear them. Listen to me. Believe me."

This was bad. He didn't want to have Morel obsessing on this. There was a subject matter they had to discuss. He needed Morel to be calm, in his right mind, because of the subject matter.

Now Morel was scrutinizing the floorboards, pointlessly.

Ray said, "Tell me anything you observed over in the hotel."

"What did I observe? I observed they have a problem. They don't have a functioning medic with this unit. And they have two guys with serious sepsis, infected wounds. I don't know what's wrong with the medic. He's comatose. I think it's an overdose of some kind, maybe Mandrax. There's plenty of dagga in the air, by the way, over there. That's what I observed, this is a messed-up group of people. This is a messed-up operation. It could go any direction you can think of. That's my sense of it. That's what I observed."

33. *The Truth Shall Set You Free, All That*

Morel was continuing the business of studying the inner surface of their place of confinement. It was compulsive activity, something that would make him feel better without necessarily leading to a course of action. It made sense for Ray not to interfere. He would watch.

Before long Morel reached the point of examining for the second time aspects of the place he had already gone over. He was in a loop. He would recognize it momentarily, Ray was sure. And he would stop when he recognized it.

Ray could wait. The subject matter was waiting.

No one was coming for them.

This was the time to take up the subject matter. He would regret it. He expected to regret it. He couldn't help it.

They were sitting on the floor, on opposite sides of the room, which seemed favorable to Ray, favorable to the project at hand. Getting a discussion going and sustaining it if they were closer, in closer proximity, would be harder. The distance was a good thing. The acoustics in their prison were good.

"My wife," Ray said.

Morel said nothing.

Ray had to be sure he was being heard. He would have to speak a little louder. He might have to move closer. He didn't want to startle Morel.

"My wife is okay, you said."

"Iris is fine, yes."

"You've examined her, of course."

"Yes and she's fine."

Ray wanted to know urgently and irrationally if Iris had had to undress for her examination, if she'd been naked for it. If it had been a full-scale examination, then of course she would have had to. Of course she would have been wearing one of those inadequate paper tunics. There were protocols. But of course he was being ridiculous because Morel had been with Iris naked under, how should he put it, under worse circumstances than an examination, worse from his standpoint, anyway. It was unlikely that they had gone to it without undressing. He needed to know everything, and he meant *everything*. And he wanted to know how it had started, what the actual trigger had been. And he wanted to know if the actual trigger was something, some act, some particular mistake, that he'd committed, so that he could direct the time machine he was going to get into in order to go back and redo everything to the right moment, the right date. He needed to know everything, but he had to recognize that there were limits to the detail he could expect to extract. He had to be rational.

He moved forward a little, away from the wall. He didn't like raising his voice, and somehow that fact reminded him of something funny Iris had said, once. She had said it apropos the communications officer at the embassy. She had observed him in a number of settings and she had said, You know there's something wrong with a guy's relationship with his wife when he lowers his voice whenever he refers to her despite the fact that she's in another country.

"So you examined her." He was back to that. He didn't want to be.

"I did. I said I did."

Ray wanted to get unstuck from the medical side of his subject matter because in fact Morel had been helpful with a few concrete things, like teaching Iris to hock mucus out of the back of her throat, and, irritatingly, with her cystitis, and with her regularity problems. She had been grateful. And one thing Ray didn't need was any reason to wallow in areas that implied he should be in a state of gratitude himself, toward Morel, not with what he had to do, what he had to get out of him.

There were too many sides to the subject matter. One minute he wanted revenge, if he could get it, and the next he was what, avuncular, wanting to know what Morel's intentions were. There was no avoiding that question, ultimately. It would make a difference if his intention was to marry her after taking her away, marry her and be good to her forever. That would be one thing. Somehow that had to be determined.

Be yourself, he thought. That was an all-purpose thing he had heard from his mother ten thousand times in completely disparate situations. It was a bromide. It was the answer to how to get through any conceivable situation. He should be more charitable toward his mother. She was suffering over Rex, her favorite.

"What do you think of Iris?" Ray asked. He'd wanted it to sound like a different question than the one he'd been asking so far. But it sounded like a repetition.

"I think she's doing fine. Medically she's excellent. But there are, or there were, rather, certain areas I helped her with that I don't feel I can go into. But as of right now, she's fine. I mean it."

Ray found this enraging. He controlled his rage.

He said, "You mean because of doctor-patient rules? That's why you can't say, exactly." He knew he was sounding hostile.

"That's right."

"But I'm her husband."

"Of course. But that's not relevant."

"Don't give me that, man."

"That's the way it is."

"Let me put it this way to you, in case you don't know. She tells me everything anyway. If there was something she neglected to tell me, it was by accident, something that got away because of circumstances. I guarantee you that. Anything she told you is something she would've told me, I guarantee you. We told, I mean we *tell*, each other everything."

"You're getting excited. Don't get excited."

"I'm not excited, I'm just trying to get you to understand something."

"Anything going on with Iris, physical things, anything, I knew all about. So, okay. That was our history. That's our history. Same with me telling her about my problems, my ailments.

"So okay.

"So okay the only thing I can think of, kind of thing I can think of, kind of thing there might be a case for keeping secret, would be sexual things.

"Sexual, and I don't even know what I mean, unless I mean something like a sexual disease she got someplace she didn't want me to know about. Or catch from her. I'm using my imagination here.

"What else, a miscarriage she didn't want me to know about. An abortion. I don't know how that would ever happen. She wanted children. She always did. But I'm using my imagination, and let's say the father was an insignificant other not myself. I am exhausting my creative powers."

Ray felt himself doing something stupid, and sensing it was bringing him close to panic. He was referring to Iris and their life together as past, over with, past tense. That was impossible. He was giving away the barn. It was destroying his strategy for getting the whole truth, not that he had a strategy worth the name. He had some ideas about how to proceed. But he was putting their relationship in the past tense too much, which was tipping his hand. There was a way to do successful interrogations.

He waited as long as he could for Morel to respond. He had no patience. He went ahead.

"So I can imagine situations it would be legitimate to keep confidential. Of course they're fantasy situations, if I know anything about my wife, and I know a great deal about my wife. But I can imagine them and I don't contest that it would be legitimate to be confidential about them. I'm repeating myself, I see.

"So you can do me a huge favor and just tell me yes or no, was it, is it, something like that, something she would legitimately need to keep private. I can imagine similar cases for myself, similar fantasies, which is what they would be. But . . . and I know I'm straining the limits of your professional oaths and all that, no doubt, but just tell me if what you're talking about that you can't elucidate was something in that category, that's all, just that. You can do that."

Now he was skirting another abyss he had to avoid.

Imploring was the abyss, or rather it was right next to it, the real abyss being begging, sheer begging. He could see himself falling into that as a last resort, if his interrogation strategy failed, which it couldn't. He was a professional. He had been trained in unusual subjects. He had to remember that. Be yourself, he thought.

Morel was being intolerably dignified. Ray felt he couldn't take much more of it.

He had to go on. "Look, can you do me the favor of saying yes or not, I mean no, no it wasn't anything sexual, some sexual thing, accident, misstep, what have you, or yes unfortunately it was, whichever is the truth."

He had kept himself from saying please, by a hair. He was glad. But he seemed to be in a maze, with every step, every turn, taking him back to the beast at the heart of the maze, the beast with two backs, in fact.

"Don't put me in this position," Morel said.

"I don't mean to. But look at it this way. This will be medication for me, sort of."

Ray had something he wanted to communicate about sex before he forgot it, lost his grip on it. The thought was important. But Morel was hardly the correct recipient. And Ray wanted to remember it, for later. And it was an insight he was having about the sex act with a beloved, and the insight was that the poets were wrong and that sex was not a metaphor for loving, a good metaphor for love, for entering a beloved, unifying with her, making a unity. It was difficult to put clearly. But sex was not a good metaphor for loving because there was a form of connection between real lovers that made sex look like an approximation of it. People like Lawrence were responsible for getting the less important thing moved up to the head of the line where it didn't belong. It was possible he was making this up so good sex between Iris and Morel wouldn't be so painful. Iris would understand what he meant, or she would have. And there was the rub, so to speak. Of course it was possible that his insights were commonplace and uninteresting. That was why he needed Iris. Because not only would she know if they were, no, the fact was that just framing a way to set something in front of her mind would cause him to think twice, see it for what it was, dump it or postpone it, or improve it enough to go with. That was then, he thought. It was something he had to get used to.

Morel said, "Okay look you can stop worrying about that kind of thing." He said it rapidly and Ray knew why. He was speeding through it because it made him feel false. He was affirming that there hadn't been some kind of precursory sexual situation with Iris, which he could do with a clear conscience. And at the same time he was skating past the fact that he was having an affair in the present, right at present, if affair was the right word for it. He was skating past a sex situation that was worse, more monumental.

"Thank you," Ray said.

"My pleasure," Morel answered. Ray resented Morel's choice of language.

"So then can you just go a little further for me, on what it is you feel you have to be confidential about? I mean, narrow it down in some way."

"Okay, let me see. Well, very generally, it was for therapy."

"As in psychotherapy."

"Yes."

"She was . . . what?"

"She was in need of therapy. Oh fuck it, man, she was depressed. That's it."

"And now she isn't."

"Right, she isn't."

"Now she's happy."

"I didn't say she's happy. What I am saying is that she isn't depressed."

"Clinically depressed, you're saying she was?"

"I don't know what that is. It's a label. She was unhappy enough to want to talk about it and do something about it."

Don't make me kill you, Ray thought. The fact was he had some respect for Morel's ethics so far. He was holding back information he knew would be painful to Ray, holding it back as well as he could. And he was couching everything he did say so that nothing would be a lie direct when they got to the heart of the labyrinth and met the beast, the one with two backs. Because they were going to get there. On the other hand the man was intolerable and it was intolerable that what he was saying without actually saying it was that Iris was much happier now that she was receiving the doctor's mighty affection, the doctor's love and care with the emphasis on love, the clouds lifting, landscapes of joy by Maxfield Parrish springing into view, paradise, *O paradise*. And she was a paradise . . . a portable one, apparently. No, Morel was smart and tough, but he was going to have to let everything out. It was coming. The man was intelligent. He had to know.

Ray was ready for Morel to be adamant in denial, but this was probably the best moment to go in for the truth. *The Adamant Penis* would be a good title for a porn thing. It could go with the titles of unwritten books in his brother's olla podrida. *The Butcher Elf* was one of those. He had to get *Strange News* back from the bastards who had it now. It was urgent. He had to try.

"You admire my wife," Ray said, which was wrong, which would remind Morel of her legal status. It would put his back up. He was going to stick strictly to Iris for the foreseeable future.

"Of course," Morel said.

Ray felt he needed to switch his angle of attack.

He said, "By the way, I don't know if this is the right question but what, um, school of therapy are you in, or from? That is, who do you follow? I'm curious."

Ray waited. There were a number of ludicrous or exploded names he could think of that might be mentioned, like Jung, like the Englishman whose name he couldn't remember who had encouraged people to go nuts as a form of liberation. And of course Freud himself was in a certain amount of bad odor. It was too much to hope for that Morel would mention somebody Ray knew was an established fool. We live in hope, Ray thought.

Morel said, "No particular school. I took the basic courses for qualifying in psychiatry but I never got a certificate. I read a lot and I rejected a lot and I came up with my own mix."

"Your own mix."

"Yes. Well, I like the work of Erich Fromm, *The Fear of Freedom*, do you know it?"

The name was a name he knew and that was all he knew. But he didn't necessarily like the title of the book Morel had mentioned. And he did realize he had made a mistake, opening up an avenue to a discussion of different schools of therapy instead of getting to the subject matter. He had to retreat so he could attack properly, reculer pour mieux sauter, was the phrase. We live out phrases we barely remember, he thought.

Suddenly something intrusive was going on outside, at a distance. There were cries. He and Morel tried to listen seriously together. The cries stopped. Ray realized that his injuries had come back to life, hurting, all at once. They had been fine when he had been concentrating on the subject matter. Something terrible was going on in what it was fair to call the outside world, but he wanted it to stop mainly so he could continue going where he had been going with Morel. He couldn't help it.

Morel wanted to keep on listening to the fracas or whatever it was. He wanted Ray to listen with him and that was unacceptable because the subject matter had to be gotten through. Nothing would be normal until that was accomplished.

Ray said, "You find Iris attractive."

Morel made a show of reluctance in turning his attention back to Ray, to the subject matter.

"When did I say that?" Morel asked.

"But do you or don't you?"

"She's an attractive woman. Yes."

"So you find her attractive?"

"What is this?"

"She's staying at your place, isn't she? Can we establish that?"

"She came to the intensive, yes."

"And she's still staying there now." It stands to reason, Ray thought. He was guessing, but he was sure it was the case.

Morel was hesitant. He was contemplating the possibility that word of the arrangement had somehow reached Ray in the depths of the Kalahari.

"You're right. She's at my place, looking after things. After we decided I should come up here it seemed to make sense. She's been helpful around the place, in the office, in the clinic."

"She's helpful to you."

"She is, really. In fact we talked about a position."

"A position there, with you." Words are cruel, Ray thought.

"Part-time."

"So you find her attractive and maybe she could have a job in your establishment."

"I don't get this."

"Sure you do. But let me ask you a different question. Which is this. Assume something happened to me, say. This is hypothetical. Something happened to take me away. A misadventure. You would help her. You'd see that she was fine."

"Don't you have insurance?"

"Sure. But say she's distraught. She needs help. She wants to stay in Africa. Her family in America, forget it. She's at her wit's end. You'd help her, take over and help her, orient her. This huge venue you live in, plenty of room. You take people in, you have. She told me about that. It's something you do. And this is a woman you've helped to get on her feet from something that was bothering her, whatever that was. How would I know? But you've gotten her out of depression, an episode. She depends on you."

"Well of course. But . . ."

"But nothing. You've formed an attachment. You'd see that she was all right. Her family is a zero, her mother. She has a sister, you may know about her, a basket case with a child, and we even thought, mainly Iris thought, we should consider taking her in . . ."

"Oh hey God *damn* me, man, I forgot. I have news about Ellen Iris wanted me to give you. The news about your brother drowned it out, I guess. Sorry.

"Anyway, Ellen met someone. I have to be sure I have this right. She teaches in a Montessori school and what was it, she ran the music program. And she ran a recorder consort, as part of that. And a parent of one of the students, a widower, young widower, joined the recorder consort. Well, young. He was fifty. But in any case they came together and he fell in love with her. He's an attorney, very, as she tells it, well fixed.

"There's more to the story. At some point after some stumbling attempt of his to participate correctly in the recital she went up to him and told him she loved him, like that, just announced it . . ."

"It runs in the family, being very direct. Iris was direct with me. She wasn't what I was used to," Ray said.

I have to escape this, he thought. Scenes from his courtship of Iris were the last things he needed to descend on his ass, her straight pure declarations, how little jockeying there had been, the shocks of straight truth, her pure face, her face so graphic.

"So you know all about her family."

"Oh yeah, pretty much." He had the decency to say it lightly, but still it stabbed, bit. Everything he says hurts, Ray thought.

Morel kept on. "The main thing is that they're married. He adores her and the child. So it looks fine. Just between us, I have to say keep your fingers crossed. But Iris is looking on the bright side. She's very relieved."

I am plunging into something, falling down, sinking, Ray thought. He wanted to know what it was, why it was, because it was terrible, worse than anything.

I know what it is, he thought. It was Iris needing no help being Atlas, and holding up the world the way it had taken two of them to do. She had only been able to do it with his help, up to now. On the one hand there had been her sister and on the other had been his brother and now there was nothing, the mist leaving the trees. What it reminded him of was the brilliant cover on the magazine *Impreccor* that the Communist International had distributed around the world in the thirties and forties, not to mention the twenties, with the graphic of the muscular worker raising his sledgehammer for yet another blow against the chained-up globe, the world, the chains breaking but also the underlying world fracturing, incidentally. It was all there. He had studied those pages like a madman in the days when communism was going to be a permanent half or three-quarters of the world, including China, and there was going to be destruction, machines of destruction, created in those dark precincts and then it had all turned into mist stuck in the trees on Orcas Island until the sun came out. His brother was gone and her sister was fine. All their thinking of what to do was over and he was unnecessary. Morel had money, like a thick soft cloud and pillow under anything he wanted to do, enough for two of them, enough for her to develop causes and projects of her own. The truth of the matter was that she could begin to think differently about what she wanted to do in the world now that money in larger magnitudes was heaving into view. He couldn't help but wonder if this hadn't occurred to her. It was a truth. He was giving her situation a Marxist analysis, which was to say a cui bono analysis. And there was nothing wrong with Marxist analysis, only with Marxist prescriptions. He was not saying she was mercenary, because she wasn't, as God was his witness. But she would have what, scope, more scope, scope was the word, with Morel. He had intimate knowledge of Morel's financial status. It was impressive. No, she could think up any number of causes she might want to throw herself into. Or she might want to join the good doctor in his great crusades against circumcision and Christianity, turning back the tide of Christian belief, like Canute. Be yourself, he wanted to tell her. He wanted her to do anything she wanted to. It was only fair. Wife is unfair, John F. Kennedy should have said. In Uruguay there had been a radical group he had read about in training, Grupo los Canuteros, and it was odd that it was only now he realized the deliberate irony in what they had called themselves. They had identified with King Canute and his broom and sweeping back the waves. They were long gone. Irony weakens, he thought. Morel lacked irony, which was why he was strong and attractive to her and up for a few more runs at the brick wall constituted by everything that was the case.

He said, "Well, that's good news. Genuinely, Ellen was pretty unstable. We didn't know what to do. We talked about it a lot."

Ray got up. It was time to go head-on with the subject matter. He had to be on his feet for that. He wanted his shoes, not that there was anything he could do about it. He wanted to be on the same footing as his rival his betrayer, so to speak. It was unfair that Morel had gotten his shoes back and that he had to proceed with his performance in stocking feet.

He said, "We both want the best for Iris." He put it as neutrally as he could, as much like an observation about the weather as he could.

Morel nodded. Ray could tell he was back into wariness.

"And also we both believe, you and I, believe in the truth. I mean, that's what your mission is, here in Africa, basically, I believe . . . to get the truth out . . . the truth shall set you free, all that, the truth till it hurts." He had botched the tone. He hated himself.

Morel was annoyed. He replied sharply, "Why would you say *you* believe in the truth? Maybe you do. But I wonder why you think we're in the same boat on this."

This was a gauntlet and Ray hadn't been expecting it and here it was, take *that*, bang.

Maybe it was all right. Maybe it was for the better, in a way, a contest framed that way. Morel would get war if that was what he wanted.

"You've reached a conclusion on me, I see. Based on what?"

"We don't need to go into it. I'm sorry I said anything."

"Oh yes we do. You think you have the truth, some kind of truth about me. Go ahead."

"I know what you are. What you do."

"Oh and what am I?"

"I don't need to tell you what you are. You know what you are."

"You think you know more than you do." Ray warned himself to slow down. He was talking too fast, agitated. He was on war footing. This was war.

"What do you think I am?"

"I know. Trust me."

"So Iris told you something."

"No, not a word. She didn't have to. What a laugh."

"What do you mean?"

"You think nobody knows who you work for. It's a laugh. I was hardly off the plane and I knew."

"She told you."

"You'd like to think that. Wake up. Everybody knows who Boyle is, the consular officer you can never get hold of. That woman who works for him does everything in the office."

This was bad. It was impossible for Ray, the idea of presenting the complete picture of what he was and what he was doing and what he had done, justifying himself. It was the wrong moment. He had to get out of this. He was on the wrong tack. And now he had to deal with the new question of whether, in addition to everything else that had to be settled, whether Iris had revealed what he did. They had an iron agreement about that. Whatever happened, it was supposed to be honored.

"Iris never said anything. That's what you're telling me."

"*There was nothing to tell me.* I told her what I knew. What was being said. It was common knowledge. She wouldn't even confirm it. She talked around it."

"But finally she did confirm it to you."

"All right, after I hounded her. But she only confirmed it after she was convinced I knew."

"I'll tell you what's wrong with this. She knows there are specially, specially approved doctors to go to if anybody connected to the agency needs to see somebody. There's one in Pretoria. She shouldn't have done it. She broke an oath."

"You seem unable to grasp that I *knew* already. She couldn't keep denying it without being in an unproductive position. I *knew* . . ."

"You didn't know. You couldn't prove it. You *thought* you knew."

"Have it your way. I thought I knew, okay, and I was *right*. I was right, wasn't I? And it was material to her situation."

"To her depression."

"Yes."

"To her unhappiness."

Ray thought, I have to get off this route, give it up. He was outsmarting himself. He could see this leading into the story of his life, the justification for each step he had taken, the justification for the whole edifice he had created, something he was hardly in the right position to undertake since he was leaving the whole thing, he was gone, he was out of it. And he knew what Morel's picture of the agency was going to be, the cartoon it was bound to be. And in a way he agreed with most of it, even though it was the sixties refusing to die that lay at the root of it, the sixties cartoons forever.

Maybe what Iris wanted was the sixties, which she would get redivivus in Morel. What could he do? He was inhabiting a stupid paradox. He was through with the agency, for his own reasons and for other reasons that owed something to certain ideas of the sixties, to be entirely fair about it, but he was on the exit ramp. La guerre est finie, with the Russians, was one of the reasons, a large reason and one he was not about to go into with Morel, agreeing yes this and that and the agency, Guatemala, Indonesia, terrible, mistaken, bad, but did Morel know why the Taiwanese happened not to have the atom bomb to play around with? It would be ignominious. He was not going to declare himself a turning worm as a basis for the next level of discussion here.

Under the right circumstances he would be happy to discuss the generic question of lives getting stuck and set in certain patterns. It was too large a subject right now. Somehow powerful personalities, hysterics among them, got to determine whole trains of events that innocent, less powerful personalities got caught up in. Who were these strong personalities and why were they so prevalent? Morel was a strong personality choosing to operate in a forceful way in narrower and narrower ponds, the United States, Cambridge, and now in the still, small pool Botswana constituted, the pond Ray had been happy enough in until this giant toad had flopped into it waving and croaking. We would all like to be great, if at all possible, Ray thought.

Morel was waiting for him to say the next thing. Time was passing.

If she wanted the sixties she was going to get the sixties in spades, so to speak, with Morel. The sixties annoyed him. The sixties said that if you knocked down certain well-meaning but imperfect institutions you would get something altogether more beautiful and wonderful flowering up to replace them. People never appreciated how touch and go it had been with the Russians at certain points, the ongoing possibility of a sociopath asshole getting into control of the magnificent death technologies science had created and that the Russians had brilliantly stolen.

"Well, let's leave what I do for a living out of this, if we can. Let's say you're right and let's set it aside. For the sake of the argument, let's do that."

"I loathe what you do," Morel said. Ray was taken aback. Morel had presented his feeling very evenly, as a statement, not a cry or shout.

"Okay, I understand. Maybe that can be on the record and we can get on with this. I . . . look. I agree with a lot of what I assume you think. You might be surprised at how much we agree on. But there is no way I can get this into the right perspective for you."

"I loathe that word."

"What word? Perspective? Then how about how about there's no way I can enter all the germane facts into the discussion. You loathe everything."

Why was Morel being so absolute on this? Ray thought he knew why. He was suddenly seeing more deeply into the surroundings of his downfall. He thought, How better than perfect could it be for a seducer if by seducing the fair maiden he was saving her from association with an enemy of the good? Of course that was assuming that Morel was the seducer, something he had no evidence on as yet. He had his ideas and that was all he had.

There was no time for a seminar on the proper attitude to take toward the triumph of the pretty good over the utterly abominable that was roughly a fair summary of the Cold War, roughly but of course incompletely. He granted that. And Morel couldn't help it that he hated imperial America. That was a truth about America that had to be lived with, but it wasn't the whole truth.

His cover had been a laugh, clearly. The idea that the suspicion might be out circulating was not something alien to him. But it had been comfortable keeping the possibility there in a pallid way, not in boldface.

He was making life difficult for himself by carrying on two dialogues at the same time, one with Morel and one with himself. He had to concentrate, to get away from the extraneous. There were certain words he needed Morel to say and he was going to extract them. He was close to getting them. When he got them he would be able to breathe normally.

Ray said, "Okay, you have your own opinion of me and of my relationship, such as it is, to the truth. I don't have the time to prove to you how misguided you are. But maybe someday.

"So. So, pushing the reset button, let's agree that you have a shall we say certain relationship to the truth that's superior to mine. Truth blows away the night and fog and makes you free. Everybody says so.

"In a way you might say you've devoted yourself to being against lying, institutional lying but not only that kind, that form of lying, untruth. You hate that."

Morel said, "Make your point. Stop the overture. End it."

"Very good."

Ray decided to skip some absurd introductory piety about how much he respected what Morel was doing. He was not in superb control of himself, his voice. It would show in his voice that he resented that Morel was able to do what he wanted to do because he had the money to allow it, support it. Even if it didn't show in his voice, there was the danger he would bring it up as a discrete item, just mention it glancingly, mention how nice it was to have inherited the money that would let you be a certain kind of moral paragon, how nice indeed. And he also knew that it wasn't Morel's fault that he was rich. That was another thing.

Ray said, "I want to know if you love my wife and also if you're fucking her."

Waiting for the answer was too hard. He went on. He said, "Yes, go ahead, here's your chance. Truth can speak to untruth, in the person of myself, yours untruly." He needed to stop being antic.

"This isn't funny," Morel said.

"No indeed." Being antic was stupid. It created byways for Morel to duck away into. But Ray was having to struggle with the temptation to be reckless. Because he felt reckless. He felt reckless because of the extremity of the scene he was in.

He shouldn't crowd Morel, but the man was taking too long. You have to have patience, Ray thought. Demonstrating the patience to wait for the truth to be spoken gave the sign that the truth was already there and that he knew Morel was going to have to yield it.

"Take your time," Ray said.

Sounds of a disturbance reached them. Morel held his hand up for silence. He wanted them to listen together. Ray held down a surge of grief and irritation. The disturbance had to go away. Morel would use it for a diversion. In Morel's place, Ray knew he would do the same thing, buy time. I am going to pray to God and Jesus if this doesn't stop, Ray thought.

And then it did stop. The shouting trailed off. The banging sounds ended.

He let Morel continue waiting.

Morel broke. He said, "I don't think this is the best time to have this discussion."

"On the contrary I beg to differ," Ray answered, stumblingly. He persisted. "In fact I can't think of a better time and I'll tell you why. And why is because the hammer of death could come down on us, either one of us, anytime.

"And I'm not saying it will. We have certain things going for us. But nothing is guaranteed. These bastards are high on Mandrax. You smelled the dagga out there. And we have a right, or not a right, precisely, but it would be, what should we call it, it would be morally preferable to go into death in full possession of the truth on this subject matter at least."

"The subject matter being . . ."

"Oh quite simply the truth about you and Iris, my wife. Which I already know, in any case."

Morel was thinking about it. The truth was coming. Ray tried to feel self-congratulatory. He was going to get what he wanted.

"Why are we going through this if you already know?"

He will do *anything* not to answer, not to have to lie, Ray thought.

"Believe me, I do know. But that doesn't change anything. Because you owe me the truth. As a man, you owe me the truth. You may as well tell me. Oh, and another consideration. We have to cooperate if we're going to get out of here and that means I need to trust you. We need to see into each other . . ."

"This is *wrong*, God damn you. It is."

Rail, Liar! Ray thought. That could be an addition to Rex's little collection of palindromes in *Strange News*, but of course that would make it a collaboration. Rex had been fascinated with palindromes from an absurdly young age. In all their early life together Ray hadn't come up with a decent one of his own, none that wasn't marginal. Rex had . . . I moan, Maori . . . I mean, Naomi . . . and they were in *Strange News*. Of course now computers would take over the whole process and this would never be an issue between two brothers again. Goodbye, he thought. Madam I'm Adam was something he could say to Iris, not that it qualified for anything in any way.

Ray said, "One other thing you need to consider. We're not *even*. You know everything about me, to your satisfaction, which I'm sure you think is fine. So an element of balance comes into it. You know what I mean."

Morel said, "I don't have to say anything to you."

"Of course you don't. But that would be a basis for a conclusion of some kind, wouldn't you say?"

Morel said, "You say you already know something. That's interesting. If there was something there, some secret, why would Iris send me up here after you, exposing me to all this, your suspicions? Would that make sense?"

"Hey, she had no choice, did she, Frank Buck? Do you know who that is? She had no choice, you were it. She has a conscience and so do you and so do I. She needs me to come back alive. And she needs me back in town so we can burn everything down we ever had, us, there, settle everything so you guys can go on sweetly. Oh well. You know, I am not a troglodyte like some people. I can give my blessing to this if I have to, but I can't give my blessing to a *liar* for my girl, for her next husband, because as you know she was married to a *liar* and it wasn't good, was it? What a *mistake* she made, not realizing that. Frank Buck went to Africa and brought back lions and tigers for zoos and circuses so delicately and always alive. Frank Buck never hurt Africa . . ."

"You're hyperventilating."

"I am fucking *not*."

"You need to stop this."

"I won't and I can't. Why should I?"

"Because it's too much. I'm hypertensive. I am. I can take a lot. But they have my medication. I need that." He was taking his own pulse.

"Does Iris know this? About you?"

"No."

"Well why the fuck not, my man. Here we go. I have *perfect* blood pressure."

But slow down, Ray thought. It would be one thing for Morel to come to a bloody end through the stupid actions of their captors and something else for him to end up having a stroke and lying there like a log for the rest of his life, grateful if he could blink once for yes and twice for no.

"Let's go slower," Ray said. The man is less than perfect, he thought.

"Slower is better," Morel said.

Ray nodded. "Fine. I don't want to give you a stroke. And in any case I consider the question answered already, and I'm not referring to what I know separately about this subject matter. But even leaving that aside, the question is answered by the sheer volume of resistance I'm getting from you.

"I'm sorry for you. You're condemned by your own what, scruples, ideology about lying. You could have lied outright, fast, in an absolute way, when the question first came out. It wouldn't have done any good, in the long run. But you didn't do that. You began circumambulating." I have him, Ray thought.

"Excuse me," Morel said. Now what? Ray thought. The man was an eel.

"What?"

"I have to use the bucket." So there would be another interruption so the man could defecate. It was going to be defecation. If he had just had to urinate he would do what both of them had done, he would have gone over and done it without missing a beat. No one could argue with defecation. And what a prodigy he was. Even in captivity his bowels functioned like a Swiss watch. Defecation demanded silence. Momentum would be lost.

Ray went to stand by the door, keeping his back to Morel and his business.

There was some significant flatus. Ray wondered if silence might not be less kind than doing some patter.

He said, "Your bowels shall sound as an harp. Coleridge."

Morel was not having his easiest evacuation, Ray couldn't help but gather. This was going to be a little embarrassing for a man whose religion was regularity. He had gotten that impression from Iris, who could be raffish and funny about the lower self and its discontents. "Must you *fart* so?" was something she had said to him in mock pique. It was hard to say exactly why that had seemed so funny. It still did.

He said, "I'll tell you something. This is in the category of trivia from my history with Iris, our life. I just mention it. Most of the places we lived in had the tub and the toilet in the same room, not like here in Botswana. So when it would happen that Iris needed to go and I happened to be in the tub, we developed a protocol. I would sing some nonsense to overwhelm any sounds that conflicted with her . . . her darlingness. And of course I would keep my eyes closed throughout."

"Do you want to sing something? Go right ahead."

Ray thought of doing "Carrickfergus," and then of doing the national anthem. He had to make a quick choice, if he was going to do something so antic. There was a feeling of sacrilege about the proposition of doing one of the songs he had actually sung when Iris was on the pot. "Greensleeves" was one of them. Singing it had been a jocular sort of choice, a sequel to conversations they'd had about whether that was the most beautiful song in the world or whether "Amazing Grace," Iris's choice, was, or whether "Down by the Salley Gardens," his candidate, was. All at once any impulse to sing was gone. There was nothing he could think of that would help, that would get him anything, in this situation, his wife's lover on the pot.

Morel was straining. Briefly Ray wondered if a flight-or-fight reaction had played some part in Morel's urgency, the urge to evacuate being one of the accompaniments of the physical mobilization for panic flight. I would like to think that, so it's probably wrong, Ray thought.

Humanly, he felt for Morel. Doctors hated to be sick. A holistic doctor would hate to be constipated. No, he couldn't sing. That was out. But he could recite something. Almost anything would do.

"I can't sing, but I'll recite something. I don't feel like singing."

Morel grunted something Ray chose to take as positive.

"I'm not going to sing. But you might be interested to know that her choice for the most beautiful song of all time is 'Amazing Grace.' We love that song. It might be the kind of thing you want to know, for the future. Anyway."

He cleared his throat and waited for the right piece to recite to suggest itself. It should be one of her favorites. In fact, it should be her all-time favorite, "Dover Beach." The poem could still move her toward tears. Or at least it had, the last time he had read it to her, which had been when? It had been pretty long ago, maybe as long ago as their vacation in the San Juans. "Dover Beach" was the perfect choice.

He began. " 'Dover Beach.'

> *"The sea is calm tonight,*
> *The tide is full, the moon lies fair*
> *Upon the straits . . . on the French coast the light*
> *Gleams, and is gone; the cliffs of England stand,*
> *Glimmering and vast, out in the tranquil bay.*
> *Come to the window, sweet is the night air!*
> *Only, from the long line of spray*
> *Where the ebb meets the moon-blanch'd sand,*
> *Listen! you hear the grating roar*
> *Of pebbles which the waves suck back, and fling,*
> *At their return, up the high strand,*
> *Begin, and cease, and then again begin,*
> *With tremulous cadence slow, and bring*
> *The eternal note of sadness in."*

He paused. He was shaky on the next segments. He plunged through them anyway, raising his voice even higher. There had been errors. He didn't care.

This last part he knew cold. He would make it as close to song as he could. He had tears in his eyes, he was interested to note. He wondered if this poem had ever been set to music. Take this, he thought.

> *"Ah, love, let us be true*
> *To one another! For the world, which seems*

To lie before us like a land of dreams,
So various, so beautiful, so new,
Hath really neither joy, nor love, nor light,
Nor certitude, nor peace, nor help for pain;
And we are here as on a darkling plain
Swept with confused alarms of struggle and flight,
Where ignorant armies clash by night."

That was it. That was it. That was her favorite poem and what had she *done* and what had *he*, the man at stool, to use a good English Literature archaism, done, and what was that man thinking right now, this minute? Ray thanked English Literature for what, for being or giving him a weapon.

Now, stupidly, he wanted something from Morel.

He said, "That was her favorite poem."

Morel said something indeterminate.

"Still *is*, I assume," Ray said.

There was an outburst, Morel saying, "*Oh shut the fuck up*. You're an idiot. Would you consider shutting up?"

Ray knew why it was happening. "Dover Beach" was about fidelity. So reciting it had been a form of rubbing it in. Still, it was what had come to him and in fact it *was* her favorite poem.

"Sorry. I was trying to be helpful."

"You never shut up, is the problem. You're an idiot."

This would pass. Morel was forgetting who was the injured party and who wasn't.

Ray waited while Morel finished up and reorganized himself.

"I only used half the paper," Morel said, pushing the unused paper into its previous crack in the wall.

"Thanks."

"You're not an idiot. I'm sorry."

"I am an idiot. I beg to differ."

"And by the way, My Bowels shall sound as an Harp isn't Coleridge."

"Yes it is. It's in the *Notebooks*."

"It may be, but it comes from the Bible. Isaiah. That's where he got it."

It was a small thing, but Ray hated it anyway. He felt shown-up at the professional level. He was an idiot.

"I won't argue with you."

"I'm right, believe me."

Sounds of glass breaking came from the direction of the main building. It was possible it meant nothing. There was no sequel.

Morel placed himself against the wall, leaning on it a little, his arms crossed on his chest. Ray sat against the opposite wall, on his pallet. He wanted to be in a standing position for what was coming, but the prospect of finally getting the truth had made his knees weak, as in the cliché. He would get up when he could.

"I'm sorry about that," Morel said, gesturing toward the bucket. There was no need. It was the way it was.

Morel said, "One way we could go with this would be for you to tell me just how you know about Iris and me. You say you already know. That would save a lot of time. And I'd be interested."

"I'm sorry, I can't."

"I see. And why would that be? Because it would reveal, what do you call it, 'sources and methods'?"

"No."

"Then why?"

"Because I was lying. I knew you'd think I had tapes or videos. That's why I said it. I sort of regret it. But when I said I knew, it wasn't that. It was signs and indicators I kept trying to put together to mean anything else and they didn't, I couldn't. It was partly a literary exercise, in a way. The only story that made sense was the painful one. I don't know what to say to you. I had a premonition about this and she agreed to an insane compact with me. She was going to tell me if she was going to cheat, or if she was tempted, warn me so I could do what, something. But the horse was halfway out of the barn by then and when she agreed to it she was already halfway into being in bed with you, dreaming in that direction anyway. But she thought she was in good faith, I don't doubt it for a minute. She was in the rapids and she didn't know it."

He had to stop. His eyes were filling with tears. It was unusual. It was philosophical. It was a generic sorrow for human beings caught in situations like theirs, the three of them, humans making declarations they meant at the time and that got undone and swept away by perverse events, the perversity of the future as it arrived so clumsily, giantly, smashing things. That was what it was. Except for the part that was about self-pity, that was what it was.

He said, "Say something."

"I can't." Morel was barely audible.

Ray said, "Look at it from my standpoint. I know the truth. You know I know. Do me the favor of letting me live in the world I have to face, once we get back, assuming we do. I am going to have to deal with this in detail. I need help to prepare. Because there is going to be an ending, a . . . what . . . an uprooting worse than anything I ever dreamed could happen to me. Arm me for that. Or if I die let me die in possession of the truth, in reality, as I go. Not to be too dramatic about it, but you see my point.

"And look, if you think I'm going to try to torture every minute particular out of you, don't think it. All I need from you is confirmation that I'm in my right mind, so I can proceed. We all need to be in our right minds, am I correct? That's your motto. People are drowning in false narratives, thus empire thus the papacy thus this and that, world wars, evil empires good empires, all the shit of history.

"Because I'll tell you, the details are unimportant in comparison to the general fact of the thing and what that means. The details can't make it worse.

"And also I'll tell you this, I know the situation you're in. I know what she told you. *Don't tell him*, in the name of God, don't. I can hear her. She said that whatever you do don't tell him, it will *kill* him. I know what she said. She said she had to be the one to handle it, it was her right to handle it. She was fierce. I know her. I know how she would put it.

"Of course her problem was that she was giving a lying task to the wrong person, tasking someone to lie who wouldn't lie. We both understand why she had no choice but to send you, but of course she was working from a bad model, myself, the person she formerly loved, a liar in several ways, a model that led her to expect something from you that shouldn't have been expected. Because I was involved in an established lie, occupationally, my work, part of my work, and of course from that flowed other lies, white lies, which is probably what we should call them, in Africa. But that's another story, another part of the forest . . .

"So, no *of course* she wanted to manage this with me herself. I would too. You would. And she'll be furious for a while when she finds out. But she'll get over it and forgive. She forgives people she loves. She forgave me for years. She forgave me as long as she could, which is all we should ask for, am I right?

"Don't make my life impossible."

Ray was thinking how impossible it would be, say, if he confronted Iris and she denied it and he had gotten nothing concrete out of Morel except his circumstantial silence. Where would he be then? Or, supposing for the sake of argument that she had done it with Morel and since then changed her mind and decided to creep back and reinstate with him because, because . . . for any reason, something unsatisfactory in the doctor, old acquaintance, fear of the less known, remorse, any old thing. And he would be in his normal position, weak, weak before her, unarmed, because of utter love, alas.

He had no regrets about his love for her up to now. She was on the verge of the change of life. So the idea that she was going for Morel so she could have a shot at motherhood was unlikely, taking a shot at his medical powers giving her motherhood. He was creating things in his mind that meant nothing. He had to stop. It was adieu.

He felt he had enough strength in his legs to stand up, even though his knee was still throbbing. He had to be upright for the finishing kick.

I will get my unholy grail, he thought.

He said, "Tell me now. Be me. Be me, asking." He was willing the truth to come out of Morel.

He could feel Morel composing himself.

Morel said, "Okay then. It's true, I love her. We are lovers, yes. So okay." It was clear he had spoken slowly to keep his tone under control.

"I can't believe it," Ray heard himself say. He would have to explain why he had said it. It had to sound bad to Davis. It sounded bad to him. It made him sound to himself as though he had made everything up and then used it to trick Morel. But it wasn't that way. It had been an expression about the point they had come to. He didn't want to be misunderstood.

There was a feeling of hollowness around him. His voice rang oddly. He had the fleeting conviction that elements of his surroundings, the walls, the floor, were hollow.

Morel said, "She'll hate me for this. She wanted to tell you herself. She insisted that that was the way it had to be. I agreed with her. She may never forgive me."

"Yes she will."

"I don't know."

"She forgives you if she loves you. Don't worry. I'll explain why it happened."

Morel was worried. It was ridiculous, but he didn't want him to worry.

"Don't worry about it. I said I'd explain it."

"You're lovers, that's all I have to know. I'm satisfied. I don't care who moved first or any of that. I told you.

"That's all. I guess my last question is about your intentions, going forward from here. Well, and her intentions, which she'll tell me. She's not here to speak, so . . .

"No, but your intentions. I mean, you want to have her, take her. That is, you're looking at this as serious, a permanent thing."

"That's what *I* want," Morel said.

It was difficult to keep talking. He made himself go on.

"You'd marry her, you'd like to. Once I'm on the other side of the horizon."

"You know, we haven't advanced to that. I don't want to flatter myself and say I know more about what she wants than I really do. But, yes, of course I would, of course."

"So you don't have philosophical objections to marriage."

"I thought I did. I thought I wouldn't ever marry again and I thought I'd, I don't know, reached conclusions about marriage, coming out of that. Let's put it this way. I'm prepared to be inconsistent. I want to marry her. I think she has more questions about marriage as a concept than I do, at this point, to tell you the absolute truth."

That hurts, Ray thought. He wanted the sickly lightness afflicting him to go away. Certain remarks of Morel's seemed to make it worse.

Morel said, "I do have to say to you that I absolutely love your wife. It's like nothing ever before, with me."

Ray said, "So, well, good. This is what it is, I guess."

Morel said, "I'm sorry."

Ray said, "I don't want to discuss this, the three of us sitting around a table, ever, please. It has to be between me and Iris, and then, if we need to, between you and me."

"That's fine," Morel said.

The feeling of lightness was prompting Ray to swallow repeatedly, as though through swallowing he would ingest something from the air that would restore his normal solidity or center of gravity, whichever it was that needed restoring.

"I'm sorry," Morel said again.

"Don't mention it," Ray answered.

"No. I am."

"Of course you are. Don't mention it." What Ray didn't like in Morel's apology was even the merest shadow of the notion that his regret extended to having gotten involved, which suggested the specter of impermanence, which could mean Iris ending up out on a limb. He didn't want that for her. And he wasn't going to be around to rescue anybody, like the rejected lovers in teenage songs, waiting around forever. He was not going to hang around Gaborone. He would be gone. And there was nothing he could do to predetermine the future she would have with Morel, her happiness.

The sound of breaking glass resumed. This time it was clear that they were hearing a deliberate, punctuated process.

Morel said, "Are you thinking what I'm thinking? In westerns when the Indians or outlaws are coming and you're holed up in a cabin . . ."

"You knock out the windows so you can shoot freely, right. I'm way ahead of you."

The glass-breaking came to an end. Others were acting. We're too passive, Ray thought. He had to refine his tasks, reduce them to the essential two or three. And then he had to find a way to complete them. One was his shoes, he had to get his shoes, or some shoes. Two was *Strange News*, which he had to get hold of and not let go of again. And the third task was to be sure, be *sure*, Morel survived the storm that was rolling in. It was obvious. If anything happened to Morel it would be Ray's fault. Iris would spend the rest of her life counting the ways her husband had been responsible directly and otherwise for the rising new love of her life's death, an impossibility that would lead to hell. There would always be the suspicion that he had eased Morel's way into death. His strength had to go into protecting his rival, the victor, like it or not.

Morel looked depressed.

Ray said, "If anything happens to me I want to be cremated. I just realized I don't think I ever discussed it with Iris. I think it was just assumed. But let me get on the record with you anyway."

"You may get your wish," Morel said. A strong odor of smoke was in the air, stronger than the occasional smoke from cooking fires they were used to, and with a chemical taint to it.

They both laughed.

The smell of burning passed. They had nothing to say to one another. Sounds of groups of men, heavily shod men, running, occupied them. But that too came to an end. There was more waiting to do.

34. *Escaping from the Enemy's Hand into the Enemy's Vast Domain*

A metallic crackling commenced. There were two episodes and then a continuing, spaced-out manifestation. It was the first gunfire. It was faint and sporadic but there was no question what it was. It was originating at a good distance, from the north, in the direction of the pan. It occurred to Ray that the ridge constituting the high side of the pan would provide a logical parapet for an attacking force to make use of. The elevation would be favorable and they would have superior fire zones.

Morel heard it and fell silent. He had been talking, lecturing really, mainly to himself. Ray resented having been told that he was the one who never seemed to shut up. Morel had been droning on about a writing project he had put off completing, which he now regretted, because, as Ray understood it, he had been planning to popularize a term for religious belief, immaterialism, that he had come up with and liked. Before that there had been a muttered discourse about how various false narratives, most of them religious in nature, had been to blame for the confluence of events, however he had put it, that had led to their being in the present fix. He's a bigger pedant than I am, Ray thought. Iris was going to be in for some surprises. Ray had pretended to be an interested hearer out of pity for the man. It was necessary for Morel to be doing something. He had a low tolerance for inaction, obviously. It had sent Morel into the monologue that was just mercifully coming to an end. They had to be quiet now. They had to concentrate, to follow, to scry out as much as they could of what was happening outside, because sooner or later it was going to come inside and get them. It was that simple.

Ray was thinking ahead. He said, "Do you know where they put my boots?"

"How would I know that?"

"Just asking in case you noticed anything about them when you were out."

"I have no idea where they put them. I didn't see them."

"I have to get them."

"I completely understand."

"I have another couple of pair in the Land Cruiser. Did you see where they parked my Land Cruiser, blue Land Cruiser?"

"I didn't. I was looking for my Land Rover and didn't see that anywhere. But I think they have all the vehicles on the far side of the main building. That's my guess. That's gunfire we hear."

"Small-arms fire, yes."

"You know what a gunshot sounds like to me? Like what a bar of metal *snapping* in two would sound like, if such a thing could happen."

"Well, that's suggestive. Of course different guns make different sounds."

"Can you tell things like the caliber of the weapons being fired, that kind of thing?"

"In a limited way. I'm not a weapons expert." A subtle shift was taking place. Morel was showing an unsolicited deference to Ray, based no doubt on his perception of him as an expert in peculiar matters like the present one, bloodshed. He wanted to tell him how misplaced his notion was. But he couldn't. What was the point in scaring him? Ray had gone out of his way to have nothing but the most minimal contact with weapons instruction. He had gotten the initial introduction and then he had evaded the subject, except for two mandated refresher courses there had been no way to avoid. The agency was organized guile, not organized gunplay, in his parsing of it, his own individual parsing of it. His practice in the agency had been founded on outsmarting, outthinking, on intellection. He had been so fastidious, so wonderfully fastidious. A bolt of ennui struck him. He was weary of himself.

"We have to get out there," Morel said.

Oh, just step out into bloody confusion and then get shot, Ray thought. He said, "We need to think about that. We have a couple of ways we can go. We can get poised to jump on whoever comes to the door and overpower him. We might want to attract attention by yelling when the fighting gets closer, if it does."

Morel was enthusiastic about that. "I like the idea of shouting. We could take turns. We could shout Kea tsala, I mean ditsala . . ."

Ray said, "No, that means we're each *other's* friends, I think. Correct me if I'm wrong."

"Oh, you're right. No it would be Kea lona ditsala."

"That's it. That might be good to shout. A good thing about it is that it wouldn't offend anybody, whichever side heard it." He had to come up with some semblance of a plan of action, even if it was for the sole purpose of calming Morel down while events unfolded into some more readable shape.

"But let's consider the opposite possibility. Stop walking around so much. We need to conserve our energy. And here's the opposite possibility.

"We have no idea who's going to win this thing. So the opposite strategy would be to keep our mouths absolutely shut. In other words, we sit tight and silent and then make a move when it's all over, when we think it is. For example, maybe we can go back to figuring out how we can rip our way through the roof up there, the thatch, once we think it's safe to appear in public. We could take turns being each other's footstools so we could get up high enough to claw away up there. You could be the footstool first."

What he was doing was wrong. He was yielding to the impulse to tease Morel, a little. But in fact he was just doing his best to suggest calming options, and the teasing was incidental. He did think that with some currently unimaginable exertions they might get through the chicken wire and the other impedimenta and then finally through the thatch, their fingers bloody shreds at the end of the procedure.

Ray said, "So there are different ways to go. It would help if we could get some room service. I'm starving."

"Let me give you some advice," Morel said, suddenly authoritative.

"Go on."

"Try not to think about food. Don't articulate what you're thinking, is what I mean. This sounds stupid but it isn't. Here is the thing. Don't name the thing you want or need to yourself."

"Funny, that's exactly what I was doing, not speaking of it. Then I lost it."

"Where do you think the fighting is?"

"You mean the firing. I don't know if there's any fighting going on yet."

"You mean you don't know who's firing or do you mean you can't tell if the guys down here are firing back?"

"Take it easy. I don't know anything for sure. What I think is that there's shooting coming from the west rim of the pan, the high rim. That's the only high ground in the vicinity. It overlooks everything. I'm sure it's the Kerekang people up there. I don't hear anything that sounds like local return fire, so far.

"I don't know what anybody's doing. But the pan rim is a good defensive position for Kerekang in case koevoet wants to go after them. Koevoet has some truck-mounted machine guns, heavy caliber, would be my guess. But they can't put vehicles into the pan, so they can't get close to him. I don't know. Maybe he's going to send Bushmen down to blow darts at these bastards. I'm just making that up. I'm doing my best here, with nothing to go on."

There was a crescendo in the firing.

"I hate war," Morel said.

"Who doesn't?" Ray said. Here we go, he thought.

The firing sank away.

Morel said, "War is unnecessary. All the monstrous stuff, weaponry, huge standing armies, all that . . . There's a way out of it and the way would be for all the countries of the world to decide to drop the load of competitive armaments by agreeing that there would be one body, the United Nations, and what it would do would be to operate a powerful force that would enforce agreed-on boundaries. That is, everyone's boundaries would be agreed, imperfect or not, frozen, accepted as final. So nations would go down to what they needed to police themselves inside secure boundaries . . . so if no country is threatened with any kind of incursion, then that means no need for overseas bases, no arms races, because the justification for those is defense of the realm. I'm not saying you could ever get to the point where this would suddenly blaze up as a good idea to all hands on deck. It's a thought experiment."

"Good idea," Ray said. He was truly astonished. It was hard to credit that he was hearing what he was hearing. What he was hearing was a proposition appropriate for a sophomore symposium somewhere, a colloquium. Morel was a type. He wanted to be fair to the man who was taking his wife away, far away, taking her in his arms and flying away with her and landing in some excellent place. Fear was precipitating him into little lectures, fervent ones. The pitch of his voice was higher. Ray would have to capture all this in words, in the cameo he would do of Morel, assuming they got out. It would be delicate, getting it right, but here was a man in fear of death urgent to register his bright ideas, in case he was going to die suddenly, register them with another potential corpse. The answer to the question *What is life?* is *Life is abnormal psychology*, he thought.

Ray was not going to spare himself, either. He was going to encapsulate himself but maybe not in the same book with the other Lives. Mine would be *My Life in a Nutshell*, which would be appropriate, he thought.

Morel seemed satisfied with having said what he had. No doubt he was rummaging something else up he wanted to be remembered as having thought of. I feel small, Ray thought. It was fairly horrible. This man was overflowing with items like plans for universal peace. There was a kind of idiotic nobility to it. I feel like flotsam, in comparison, Ray thought. And now he wished, for the sake of the sketch he was going to do, that he had paid better attention to a couple of other deliverances Morel had let fall in passing earlier. One had to do with a correct understanding of what the entire human race was basically up to, that understanding being that mankind was engaged not only in internecine conflicts unending but in a general collaborative war against the trees, as he remembered it, mankind as a kind of planetary mange. And the idea of these formulations was to make a light go off in the mind of man that would stop him or her in his or her tracks and lead to huge changes. The other deliverance was lost to him, for the moment. He had to get a pen, somehow, and a tablet, a notebook, anything.

"You think they're shooting down from the pan?"

"Yes."

A serious detonation shook the shed, jolting Morel into another presentation. Dust and grit sifted down over them from the ceiling.

Morel said, "I got a look at the pan. It's like a gigantic pockmark. I read about it before I came up here."

The detonation was significant and represented a change. Morel wasn't asking for his opinion. In fact he had no opinion. It was possible that it was a mortar hit. It was possible that through some accident some ammunition or explosives had gone up. It was serious.

Morel continued. "Do you know that there's some mystery about what causes pans? The geology is mysterious. One theory is that there were natural depressions in the terrain and that there used to be much heavier winds in the area that scooped them out and much heavier rains that filled them up, so that when they dried, these beds of clay and soda were left. But the problem with that theory is that there are no pans in other deserts, only around here."

Ray was fascinated. This was beyond wanting to deposit his aperçus before misadventure struck. This was sadder, a need to demonstrate that he knew certain things the average man might not.

Morel said, "The pan here isn't the biggest one in the Kalahari. This is a small one, less than half a kilometer I would say, measured longwise. It's an oval-shaped thing."

Morel was speaking more rapidly as he went on. Ray wanted to slow him up a little, not stop him.

Ray said, "The pan used to fill with water every rainy season and stay full most of the year. They say it was beautiful. It was shoulder-to-shoulder marabou storks and fish eagles, Cape vultures, rare birds. That's why they chose to build this monstrosity out here. Of course then the drought came."

In Morel's eagerness to proceed, he interrupted Ray. "Man, you should see it now. I saw it. Christ, it's an eyesore.

"You wouldn't go near it. It's a boneyard. You see cow skeletons stuck halfway in the mud. You see skulls sitting there. The floor of it is checkered and you can tell that what happens is that when you step on these individual slabs they tilt up and dump you into this white mire, muck.

"There are a couple of abandoned trucks in there, just the roofs showing. It's blinding to look at, it's so white, pure burning white, white as snow.

"I couldn't see much, though. That is, I couldn't look at the thing for very long without my sunglasses. That's another thing I want back. My bag I have to get first, first thing. People are going to be hurt."

Morel was neatening himself up, beating dust out of his hair and off his shoulders. Ray was doing the same.

"That last explosion, what was that?" Morel asked.

"That's what I'm thinking about," Ray answered. He didn't want to alarm Morel. And even if somebody was firing a mortar or mortars, they might not have many shells, maybe even only two, even only one.

"Is there anything we could make a white flag out of?" Morel asked.

"Your shorts, perhaps," Ray said, regretting saying it. Morel looked at him closely.

"That was an attempt at levity. And also a recognition of the fact that my shorts are khaki-colored and in fact the only white sort of thing around is your shorts. I'm not suggesting it's practical. My socks are white, or they were, it occurs to me. I don't see how I could give them up. They're all I've got to protect my feet. But none of this amounts to a flaglike item, if you know what I mean. I imagine if we started waving socks and shorts around, people would take it for an insult, and *bingo* . . . It was just a thought."

"I understand. But if we want to surrender, that is surrender even *more* than we have already surrendered . . . we just put our hands way up. I think that would do it."

"*Be quiet for a minute,*" Ray said fiercely to Morel. They had to be alert. Ray realized for the first time in his life that he sounded like his mother when he used the imperative mode, not his father. There was a whistling sound he didn't like.

"What is it?"

"Just *listen*."

Somebody had a mortar. Mortar shells whistled in flight and something was coming toward them and whistling. The whistling was getting stronger, so this was incoming. Now the possibility of getting pushed into death by one or the other of these ignorant armies was up a notch. Because mortars were not weapons that could be *aimed* in any real sense of the term. Or they could be aimed only in the sense that a shell would be fired and the people firing it would try to see where it had landed and then they would move their mortar around a little and try again. What that meant was that it was true they could be sitting ducks, by accident, and die. They could actually die. Either or both of them could turn into a terrible bloom, bloodmist, gobbets of flesh, shards of bone.

A violent detonation, close by, jarred them.

"Prosit," Ray said, for no reason. Morel had to be told what was happening.

Ray said, "They have mortars, at least one."

"That's dangerous," Morel said.

"Oh yes."

"We could die in here."

"We could."

"I never got a chance to talk to you about Milton."

"What's that? What are you talking about?"

"You're a partisan of Milton and I hate Milton and I've thought a lot about why you would like Milton so much. My father forced me to study Milton, memorize parts he liked. Well, forced is too strong a word, but . . ."

"Look, right now we need to figure out the safest place to stand in here, while this is going on. We want to be out of the middle area. I think we should stand in opposite corners. I'm not even sure it makes any difference. It would be better to be in the corner if the roof came down, those beams. And I think it makes sense to crouch down, contract the amount of flesh you're making available for injury. And let's each pull one of these pallets over us, which might help in case flaming fragments of shit come our way. It's all nonsense, but let's do it." Morel was agreeable.

When they were each huddled appropriately in their places, Ray said, "One last thing. Remember to keep as low as possible."

"What? You have to speak up. It's getting loud out there."

"Okay, just remember to keep as low as you can, because we could take automatic weapons ordnance through the door, or if they used heavier weapons, through the walls. It's only cinderblock and it shatters. I'm talking about the possibility of somebody feeling frisky and sweeping this structure with gunfire out of high spirits. So, obviously, we stay as much clear of the doors as we can. And since the level of fire would normally come in waist high and up, if we were unlucky enough to be standing at the time, that would be bad."

"So the idea is we should crawl, mostly?"

"Well, for the time being. Until it's quiet."

Morel was lying flat.

A little time passed.

Thin white smoke began to curl in through the vents near the tops of the north and west walls. They had smelled smoke before but now they were seeing it. The smoke was forming a stratum under the thatch and dissipating only very slowly upward through it. Morel was aghast.

Morel sat up. "I think we're on fire." He was frightened.

Ray said, "No. It's not us. It's not coming in that fast. It's from somewhere else. Also, white smoke you don't have to worry so much about. It's dark or black you need to watch out for. White smoke is from fast-burning stuff like paper and wood . . . It's not us. There's no extra heat in here."

"And thatch. Thatch would make white smoke, right?"

"Sure, but our thatch isn't burning." Ray was amused at his own performance of false expertise. He had to keep the man calm. What choice did he have? "And if you just watch you'll see the layer of smoke up there get thinner. Believe me. It's not us."

They studied the smoke religiously, exchanging impressions about whether the inflow was strengthening or abating. It did clearly begin abating.

"You see what I mean?"

"You were right."

A lull began. It was a waste of time, waiting to meet one's fate. There were things he absolutely had to take care of when, *if,* he meant *if,* he got back okay to Gaborone, things he absolutely had to do in preparation for getting free, getting out, excising himself. There were certain students he had to say goodbye to, for example. There were at least five students and two or three colleagues, and Curwen in particular, at St. James's that he absolutely had to say something to. And he had to collect various items, like his backup passports and some other papers, from various caches. He couldn't stand to think about his students. And he had to find Keletso and say goodbye. And he had to see Victor, his coconspirator at the airport, who was a decent fellow. Victor deserved a bonus. So did some of the other assets he was going to be abandoning. He would have to do something along those lines and it was going to have to be organized fast. It was a slight shock to realize how few people there were that he had to find and say something to or do a little something for valedictorily. It was true that there were enough of them to constitute a time problem. But there really weren't that many, given how long he and Iris had been in that part of the forest. But he had an answer for that. It was because certain people he loved had absorbed most of what he had to give. A certain subject matter had absorbed inordinate amounts of his love capacity, his leisure-time attention.

He could save Morel from the trouble of having to survive another near-death experience like the last mortar strike to propel him into his Milton lecture, which was something he had evidently devoted some time to perfecting, probably in show-off conversations with Iris, he could just invite him to get into it, since he'd mentioned it. The thought that Morel had been parading around in front of Iris delivering his show-off capsule stuff on Milton was infuriating. It was too infuriating. He had to find out about that. First he would get Morel to do his little act on Milton.

Confoundingly, it seemed that Morel had managed to doze. Ray couldn't believe it. Things outside were not improving. There was an intermittent filtering down of petty detritus from the ceiling thatch, the result of reverberations from intensifying shooting and shelling. Hunger is the best sauce for food and a clear conscience the best sleeping pill, Ray thought. How could Morel have a clear conscience? Is taking my wife away from me a virtuous act? Ray wanted to know. The shooting was at the level of static on the radio, for God's sake. It had risen to that! Ray's theory of the shooting he was hearing was that a jockeying exercise was in progress, one side trying to scare the other off with heavier and heavier barrages, followed by intervals of waiting to see if somebody was going to be pulling back, quitting. But then he knew so little about combat, war, serious war.

There was a cessation in the gunfire, and Ray said, loudly, "What was it you wanted to tell me about Milton?"

Morel sat up, blinking. Ray felt guilty. He should have been man enough to let him sleep through as much of the carnage and all its corollaries as he could manage. Sleeping like that in such circumstances was unusual. It was going to be up to Iris to figure out all these aspects and pockets in her new beloved.

Ray said, "You said you wanted to tell me about your theory of Milton and me, why the connection, I think you said."

He had really been asleep. Morel was struggling to get himself in hand. He began preambling about how Ray had to understand he had no opinions whatever about Milton's qualities as a poet, he had no opinions on the poetics. Some lines and passages were, he acknowledged, striking. But most of it he wasn't qualified to judge, other than to say that it seemed like a lot of the rest of classic English poetry, which he really found got interesting only in the late nineteenth century, because so much of it was crypto-Christian apology before that.

Ray thought, That's all I need, crouching here. All he needed was an attack on English Literature, which at that moment was giving him, Ray, two useless nothings, the phrase A Great Reckoning in a Little Room, which was by somebody about Marlowe's death, and then the other . . . bits of blurred recall of Beckett's plays, many of them taking place in settings like the one he and Morel were in. And Morel was saying again that the reason he had strong feelings about Milton came from having been forced by his father to read *Paradise Lost*. And then there were some disparaging remarks about Thomas Traherne and about Wordsworth and it was all too much.

"*Listen to me,*" Ray said, trying to be commanding.

"Okay."

"Know what, I want to jump ahead here. Just admit this. Milton came up, or her attitude to Milton did, Milton being important to me, and you realized you had an opinion and a theory and you went for it and she thought it was brilliant. It was negative. A negative take, shall we say. You had something negative in your backpack about Milton and you used it. It was part of courting. You went . . . *Hm*, Milton. You wanted her. You took a shot. Admit it."

"It was something like that."

"It was the equivalent of a cheap shot, but let's hear it. It might even be right. Just give me the *Reader's Digest* version of what you said. I guarantee you I can take it. And come on, do it. By the way, if you think you hear police whistles you're right. But it doesn't mean the police are here to save us. Guerrillas use them for signaling between units. Or it could be the villains. But it's not the police. So just give me a diagram of what you said."

"Okay, but I have to stand up." He was apologetic. He knew they had agreed that the huddled-down position was optimal in the situation they were in. But he was being asked to present something of significance. He had to be standing, to deliver his thing properly. Ray understood this from teaching.

Morel began walking around.

Ray got up. There was no way he could remain huddled like a pupil while Morel stood over him. So that was it, they would both have to risk being cut in half by heavy-weapons fire until the issue was ventilated. That was life.

Morel needed to get on with it.

"Just give me a diagram," Ray said.

"Okay, man. Yeah, here it is." But he continued thinking, preparing.

Unless Ray was wrong, Morel was reverting to a blacker, more ple-beian speech mode, the rhythm different. It was undoubtedly reflexive, a mode that offered some sort of protection. He had seen Morel do it before, but more subtly.

Morel said, "Okay, but, man, I can't hardly remember the whole thing, you know? Let's see . . ." Ray knew Morel was ashamed of the lurid *can't hardly* because he had half swallowed it to the point where it had been hard for Ray to pick up. Morel had to be embarrassed by the blunt black thing he was doing. But distress was behind it, it should be remembered. It did raise the question of who Morel was and the question of false pre-tenses . . . which, Ray realized, was a classic redundancy. And generations of linguistic professionals had looked at it and not seen it and it was exactly like rapid eye movements being discovered by a graduate student after generations of sleep experts and theorists had droned on and on, not seeing it. Typically of life he didn't know the name of the gradu-ate student who had finally seen it, discovered it. He should be famous. His name was Jewish, he knew that much. But that was all he knew, except that he Ray himself had used *false pretenses* all his life up to that moment.

A nearby blast shook them, and Morel resumed, finally.

Morel said, "No, what I said to her about Milton . . . in fact she proba-bly mentioned it to you . . ."

"She didn't."

"That's funny. She seemed to be struck by it. Well anyway I don't know if this is anything or not, but when I asked myself why in hell you liked a poet I especially didn't like and that I had been forced to read reams of . . ."

"You can stop mentioning that. It's been established." Ray sensed that Morel, now that he was having to present his thoughts on this subject, was feeling slightly in over his head. He had tossed something off and now he had to engage someone who had spent years confronting the Hydra of Milton interpretations, slashing at them in the privacy of his office.

Morel said, "Okay, so I asked my question and I saw a pattern. Here's what I'm saying. *Paradise Lost* the great Milton thing is a parable about how terrible disobedience is, using Satan's disobedience to God as a metaphor for disobedience generally, with Milton's disobedience to his king in the background.

"So now of course before he wrote *Paradise Lost*, hey, he had joined up against the great evil of his time, monarchism, the king. He goes for republicanism, joins up with Cromwell, who kills the king but then turns himself into Hitler. Milton works in the Ministry of Propaganda. Sad thing. And Milton is doing his job writing public relations stuff defending slaughtering the Irish and getting the English deeper into the slave trade. Then Cromwell loses, falls. Monarchy comes back and Milton has to live with it. So *Paradise Lost* is where he *takes it all back*, takes back his embrace of Cromwell, of republicanism, of political dissent. *Paradise Lost* is how he gets himself rehabilitated. The royals love it. I think that's about right."

"Well, it's too simple."

"But hey, let me finish, man."

"Proceed."

Morel was hyper. He said, "So here's where you come in. You're at the right age, pliable. There you stand. Communism is abroad in the world and it's a great evil and there just happens to be an instrument, like Cromwell was an instrument in his time, there happens to be this instrument that's working against the evil of our time and the instrument is the CIA. And the agency gets hold of you just when you're studying Milton and the sixties are happening.

"So you see an evil and you see an instrument against it and you join up . . ."

"If you could make it not sound so much like joining the Boy Scouts that would be better."

"Okay. So you're twenty-two, twenty-three, and you go with the instrument that you, well, you're in it. And the instrument you've joined up with is gradually becoming Satan. You signed up before Vietnam. And there you are, in revolt against your generation, your peers, their sentiments, their ideology, because the war in Vietnam they see as pure evil and they associate the agency with it. And it gets interesting because Satan is secretly the hero of *Paradise Lost*, despite Milton's intentions,

Satan is the secret hero. Milton couldn't help it. He set out to glorify obedience, but disobedience hogged all the glamour. No wonder it fascinated you, Ray. Okay, so you stay with the instrument. You have doubts
after a while, the impulse to draw back, maybe, but you're in it. Your generation is against the CIA in the most fuckingly absolute way. And they
focus on the exact things in the work of the agency you disagree with and
reject, yourself . . ."

"Just a minute, *Davis*, aren't we the same generation, the two of us?
How old are you?"

"Just forty-six."

"And I was just forty-nine."

"So you think I should have said *our* generation?"

"Don't you?"

"Okay. But Iris I put into the next generation down. She's thirty-six. At
thirty-six."

Ray had to bite his tongue. It was a shock because if she had given
thirty-six as her age it meant she had been willing to lie and the lie was a
sign that she had wanted Morel starting as far back as filling in the date of
birth on the medical history form, on her first visit. He couldn't believe
it. This was so far beyond unlike her that he couldn't believe it had happened. Could Morel be misremembering? That had to be the answer.

"Finish your thought," Ray said.

"That's about it. What I proposed is that *Paradise Lost* addresses
all your ambivalence about what you're doing with your life. And the
ambivalence gets more acute as your side wins. You feel it winning before
it finally happens. You have the victory, not like Milton, who had to see
the kings come roaring back into London. So I think *Paradise Lost* tells
you not to abandon an imperfect instrument, the agency, just because
most of your peers say you should, just the way *Paradise Lost* told Milton
not to abandon an imperfect institution like the monarchy just because
the people, a lot of them, said he should. And with your enemy down and
out you have the option of leaving the imperfect instrument . . . But it
looks like you can't."

Let this go, Ray thought. There might be some truth in it, but there
was a great deal that something so simple left out. Morel was stripping
away everything in Milton that didn't serve his thesis. For starters there
was the conflation of biography and art, a quagmire. He wasn't saying
there was nothing in Morel's construct. But showing Morel why it was
inadequate was something he had no strength for.

A loud explosion occurred, closer than the last one.

Ray said, "Well, that's interesting, isn't it? I'll have to think about it. I point out, though, that you generated this analysis of me not out of an interest in penetrating a fascinating truth, but out of an interest in penetrating my wife."

Morel looked stunned. "That's not the way it was," he said.

Ray said, "Some other time we can talk about it. I'll give it some thought." He was curt. There were numerous things wrong with Morel's thesis, not the least of which was taking a cartoon of *Paradise Lost* as representing the sum of Milton's huge labors and leaving everything else out, the *Areopagitica*, the pamphlets on divorce . . .

Coldness seized him. It was the word *divorce*. There would have to be one, of course. There would be procedures, papers. Only an idiot wouldn't have realized that. But it would have to be worked out even though it conflicted with his image of a quick vanishment into a new life, a quick and sharp exit. He was divorcing the agency too. It was over, all over. He was through. He wouldn't discuss it with Morel. He couldn't. Of course it would seem to him like a lunge or an adaptation late in the day to get Iris back by giving her what she had wanted for years, now, when it was too late. *Tsk tsk* goes the clock, he thought.

An explosion came, about as loud as the last one. A new flux of white smoke began feeding in.

Ray asked, "You know another thing white smoke tells you?"

"No, what?"

"It means we have a new pope."

It was nothing, but they both laughed, a peacemaking laugh.

Iris had been his pope, or something like it. He had believed in Iris, in her goodness, her patience. There had been an early time when he had believed in the agency. But that had gone. But he had always believed in Iris and her steadfastness, the way Irish drunks believed in their saintly wives. But that wasn't quite right. Now Morel was her pope, or she was Morel's pope. It could go either way, in life.

He thought he was understanding things better. A god that was not only gratifying but actual fun to obey was what everybody wanted, maybe. He didn't know. Or maybe he did know. Maybe she was looking for a god in Morel, the atheist. He had never been that for her, himself. Ah well, he thought.

Morel was disgruntled, Ray could tell. He had returned to his corner. He was muttering to himself. Ray picked up the phrase *Obedience is paradise*.

"We'll talk about this another time," Ray said.

Morel said nothing.

"It'll be something to look forward to," Ray said.

Ray returned to his corner and hunched down. Morel was going to be Ray's first vignette. He had decided that. But it was important to get him right.

Morel looked glum. Iris was good at cheering people up. She could be funny. He remembered her recounting a dead serious argument among her preteenage girlfriends over whether it would be more embarrassing when the time came to disclose one's breasts to a man or one's genitals. The position arrived at had been that it would be less embarrassing to unveil genitals because female genitals were all more or less alike, whereas breasts differed a lot and so were more personal, and also they were on a scale of judgment that genitals weren't, more might be expected. And it was funny when she talked about changing her raiment before they went out to eat. It was strange that he could think of so many amusing things she had said to him but virtually nothing amusing he had said to her unless you counted throwaways like his saying to her, You are like Power because you abhor a vacuum . . . cleaner and then he had used the phrase "multiplying like coat hangers," but he couldn't remember what it had been applied to. And she had laughed when he had taken to declaring horniness by saying, It's sex o'clock. But then after he had done it a couple or three times too many she had asked him to give it a rest.

The sounds of battle were closer and louder. Voices were part of the mixture. The notion of what it would be like if he managed to get himself killed saving Morel's life in some mayhem yet to unfold was something not to pursue. It would be an ironical gift for her. This was regression. It was ridiculous, wishing he could see her face when she found out what had happened. He was in a *sundering* process in his life and he had to embrace it and not end up like the British painter who kept writing letters to his first wife for nine years after her death, Stanley Spencer, an interesting painter, too. Ray had appreciated being shepherded by Iris to exhibitions in cities they'd visited. She had seen it as her responsibility. Now he would have to figure out on his own what to go and see when he was in venues where there were museums or galleries. He was going to be somewhere. He wasn't sure where that would be. He would be consumed doing something that consumed him. That was all he knew.

Ray thought he could hear the sounds of running feet. The sound died.

A deafening, confounding blast, the worst yet, jarred them. The air was full of white dust. Something nearby had been pulverized. Dust had puffed in through the vents.

Morel stood up, coughing, brushing at himself. His hair was white with dust. He had been caught directly beneath one of the vents. Ray thought, I'm getting to see how he'll look when they're old.

Morel was pointing, jabbing furiously with one hand and holding a finger to his lips with the other.

Ray saw what it was. The north wall was showing real damage. A ragged crack ran upward for a foot or so from the floor near one end of the wall and curved over and ran to the proximate corner and down the crease and back to the floor, which, in that area, was sunken, canting down. Plainly it had been partially undermined. The wedge of masonry outlined by the crack was roughly the size of a duffel bag.

Ray crouched down to get a closer look at the damage, his heart racing. He tried to insert his fingers into the crack. He couldn't, but it was close. Air was feeding in through the crack, whose bottom edge was inset a little. There was a definite separation between the base of the wedge and the plank flooring touching it. He pushed at the wedge. It wouldn't budge. If it could be driven out there would be an exit that a man, men, could fit through. He wanted to say to the wedge, You are yearning to be a door, so be one, swing open.

Morel was elated. But he was conducting himself ridiculously, in Ray's opinion. He was gesturing frantically to the effect that they shouldn't say anything, that they should be quiet, avoid attracting attention. Ray understood Morel's impulse, but he was going on too long with it. They had to get to work to see if this crack could be made, ultimately, to let them out. They had no tools.

They knelt together at the crack.

Morel was shaking. He tried, himself, to work his fingers into the crack, but with more force than Ray had used, which struck Ray as dangerous and premature. The wall might shift in the event of another blast and Morel's fingers could be crushed. Or the wall could shift on its own. There were other fractures in it, higher up.

"This is just cheap cement block," Morel whispered.

"Get your fingers *out* of there."

"Don't shout at me. We have to be quiet."

"I didn't shout. I just don't think it's going to be helpful if you get your hands stuck."

"This cement is cheap shit. It's crumbling."

Morel had thrust the fingers of both hands well into the crack. It was reckless. Ray thought he could see blood. He was considering pulling Morel forcibly away from the wall. He didn't think that what Morel was trying to do could be done. Unaided brute force had its limits. They needed to think together, think how to combine their strengths. He thought Morel should stop acting Herculean. Or probably he himself should join Morel in futility just to be friendly. He had to come to a conclusion. He had no role, just standing around observing.

Morel was being primal. Maybe it was good that somebody could get into that mode. And maybe it was something to do that felt better than wallowing in the impossibilities in a situation. For example there had been all that debate about what they should do as the battle got closer, whether they should keep mum and stay where they were, play dead, or whether they should move heaven and earth to find a way to break out and then run and hide in a donga until the battle was over, or whether they should barge out and get into the fight. It looked like Morel had resolved everything unilaterally. They were not going to stay in their dungeon if at all possible. He was going to create an exit barehanded singlehanded. There really wasn't time to discuss any of this again. Their deliberations had taken place when it hadn't been clear that the battle was ever going to reach them. Now it was not a question. There was such a thing as slipping out into a scene of confusion and finding a place to hide while everyone was distracted with killing. Maybe they could still do that, if they got loose.

Morel was determined. There was blood showing on the back of one hand. He was ignoring it.

"I don't recommend this," was all Ray could think of to say.

He knew what Morel was attempting. He was trying to get his fingers in as far as the void at the core of the cement block so that he could get a solid grip on the fragment and really wrench away at it, pull it hard. He was endangering his hands. Fortunately he wasn't a surgeon, but still, he had to touch people in his practice. His diagnostic procedure involved a lot of touching. That was what holistic medicine was, apparently.

"You're going to hurt yourself," Ray said. He couldn't see how Morel had gotten his fingers so far into the crack, but he had.

He had to try to help. Morel was being a machine. The fucking chunk of wall seemed to be actually moving, tilting. Morel's shirt back was dark with sweat.

"We need a crowbar," Ray said, provoking a hiss of exasperation from Morel.

Ray hastened to assist. The crack was tighter where he was, to Morel's right. But by brute force he was now getting his fingertips in up to the first joint. He had to do better. He had to get them in far enough to bend them down into a hollow space so he could grip and pull, like Morel.

Morel was extremely strong. Ray could feel the effect of his force in the definite rocking movement being produced in the fragment. Morel was pretending the abrasions on the backs of his hands weren't happening. I have to help, Ray thought. He drove his fingers in and found the void in his segment of the chunk and grasped hard.

Ray said, "I think we should push. We should stop rocking this thing. It hurts when it rocks back in. I think we need to just push out." There were ridges of scraped-off skin midway between his second and third knuckles, on every finger. Morel seemed not to be listening to him. Ray's hands were in agony and the kneeling position he was in was hell on his bad knee.

Morel was still insisting on whispering. He was saying that they were not coordinating. They paused. Morel put his ear to the wall. Ray couldn't imagine what the point of doing that was. Morel seemed satisfied, though, and resumed his efforts, pushing, only, now. The floor was drooping under them, but not alarmingly.

Ray scanned the fractures in the upper wall, thinking that they had, what was the word, ramified, since the last time he'd glanced at them, raising the possibility of a Samsonic, if that was a word, conclusion, as in the entire side of the edifice collapsing in on them, burying them. It was far-fetched but it added something to the moment. And there was still the possibility of one or even both of them getting caught like idiots with their hands stuck in the wall. He didn't know how it could be, but he seemed to be having fun, despite everything, the pain. He wanted to see if he and Morel could do this thing.

Morel was resting again. That was natural. His exertions had been greater. But they had to continue soon. Ray had the germ of a feeling, a spark of belief that they could do this, do it together if they kept the momentum up. And if he could exclude from his mind questions like whether, once they got the chunk detached from its what, its moorings, they should push it all the way out or just edge it out as far as they could without creating a glaring cavelike hole for all to see. The question was should they pause and wait once they were sure they had an exit, but without using it immediately. The thing to do was to proceed. There was no exit yet.

Morel was kneeling and resting, his forehead against the wall. He appeared to be talking softly to himself. What he was doing resembled praying, which couldn't be. Ray felt he had to know.

"You're not *praying* there, are you?"

Morel looked balefully at him. He said, "How could you ask me that?"

"I don't know. That's what it looked like."

"Well, it wasn't."

"Well, I'm relieved." That was true. The idea of Morel praying had been unsettling.

But Morel resumed murmuring to himself. This was obviously some personal ritual he was going through preparatory to their climactic next effort. Finally Morel seemed to be through.

Ray couldn't help himself. "What were you saying, if you don't mind my asking?" He was truly curious. If he were to write a vignette of Morel the answer to that question would be just the kind of thing that might turn out to be emblematic. And he had no idea what Morel might have been saying, unless it had been some idiosyncratic mantra to the first atheist or to Bertrand Russell, except that mantras weren't addressed to particular heroes, now that he thought about it.

"It was nothing," Morel said.

"It was."

"I don't feel like telling you, to tell you the truth."

"Okay don't."

Morel was not going to be able to not tell him. He wouldn't want Ray alienated at this point. Ray was exploiting that. Drop it, Ray told himself.

Morel said, "All right. I was thinking of someone. I was imagining someone. I was drawing strength from . . . from the image. It's something you can do, one can."

"Ah," Ray said. He knew that this was where he should stop interrogating. It was ridiculous. They both had their hands in the crack still. He should stop interrogating. Because, without being told, he knew who it was Morel had been holding in front of his mind. It was Iris. And Ray didn't want to hear that. He didn't want to know that. But he also felt he had to know, right or wrong, because it was possible he was wrong, as always. We can always be wrong, he thought. He felt a proprietary rage. Morel hadn't known Iris long enough to what, appropriate her this way. It was vicious.

"Do you mind telling me who it is?"

"Yes I do mind."

"Would it be someone I know?"

"God *damn* it! Could you possibly shut up until we get this done?"

He doesn't want to deny it, or to have to say it, Ray thought. He resented the situation and blamed Morel for creating it. He was hating him. His little murmuring act had been provocative. It had to have been deliberate. Maybe it was a genuine reaction to the extremis they were in. Or maybe it had been reflexive, like the matador pointing out the woman in the stands he was going to present the bull's ear to, or like a knight tucking his earl's wife's underpants into his armor, under his breastplate, before going off to some feat of arms.

Morel had a grim look. He had extracted his bloody fingers from the crack and was repositioning himself, getting on his back with both feet against the wedge. Ray withdrew his fingers too. Morel was tireless. Now he was working his chewed-up fingers around the lip of the flooring, getting purchase for his new approach to kicking the wedge over and out. He was still muttering to himself.

Ray thought, Call up your own image of Iris. It could be when she had been looking for him, with anxiety. It could be a moment from their great hours on Orcas Island. They had been following a trail in the woods and she had been ahead, eager to get to the view or whatever they were searching for. He had stepped into the underbrush to urinate, without alerting her. And then she had looked around and seen the trail empty and she had come back, calling his name. He had that moment, the note in her voice, if he wanted it.

It was time to finish. Ray duplicated Morel's position, with some difficulty. He was able to get only one hand around the edge of the flooring. It would have to do.

"Push," Morel said.

Ray felt serious movement occurring. They were winning. They both groaned. Light was coming in, and air. They could have stopped and left the wedge tilting, which would be less likely to attract the attention of passersby, but they couldn't. They had to completely dislodge it. And then they had done it. Their feet were in the open air. They drew them back.

Ray got on his knees and bent forward, his face in the gap, breathing in heavily. He could see that there was an impact crater just outside, by the wall.

He had to contain himself. He wanted to get out. He had to keep himself from acting stupidly. But the prospect of getting out was creating a fire in him to physically *do* that, get out, be out, dance around, be in the open. But there were decisions to be made, such as who should go first. It would have to be him. He didn't know why, but he would think of why. He was on fire to be outside.

It had been hard work. Bare feet hadn't made anything easier. Our feet are delicate, he thought.

Something was wrong with Morel. He was lying flat, his arms crossed over his eyes. Ray was afraid for him.

"I'm all right," Morel announced.

"Are you sure you are? You don't look great."

"I'm getting my breath. We got that thing out. Maybe we shouldn't have shoved it all the way out, but it's too late. It's out."

"You rest," Ray said. Morel had a right to rest. He had done more. And he was the one who had made them do it at all. Morel's short leg was trembling, only the short leg.

"I think I should go out first," Ray said.

"Why you?"

"Because, well, I'm limber . . ." What he meant was that he was a lot narrower, thinner. Either one of them could get through the hole, but it would be less work for Ray. Morel could see that. And there was the question of Morel's leg problem. His leg was trembling. Ray didn't want to be explicit.

Morel said, "First we just look out, get our heads out. You can do it first. Then you duck back and I'll look. Then we decide how it looks. We decide whether one of us should go or whether we should both go, one after the other, at the same time. You see what I'm trying to avoid, which is, one of us gets out there and God knows what happens, something happens, I'm still in here and have to scramble after you. I'm making this up as I go along, you may have noticed. And Jesus, look at our hands. I've got to get some hydrogen peroxide someplace."

Ray was calming down. They needed to act while the firing was in recess, which it seemed to be, unless, of course, it would be better to go out when there was more confusion, more firing, more distraction.

Morel sat up. "You go," he said.

"Go? You mean . . ."

"I mean put your head out."

Lying on his belly, Ray shrugged his way into the gap. It was tight, not more than eight or nine inches high and about four feet in length.

It was painfully bright out. He would adjust. It was sometime in the hot afternoon. What he could see wasn't telling him much. He was being careful. He was only visible to his enemies from the bridge of his nose on up, assuming they were interested.

What he had achieved was a prospect of the western end of the back wall of the main hotel building. It was unevenly pink and it was crenellated along the top. There were aprons of broken glass on the ground outside every window on the ground floor. The open ground that he could see between the shed and the hotel was cratered in three places, not counting the crater immediately to his right. His eyes were clearly not what they had once been, evidently, although possibly his nutrition lately was partly to blame, that and being kept hooded and in the dark so much. He certainly hoped so. Morel's eyesight was undoubtedly better than his. Morel was tugging at Ray's heel.

Ray had to digest everything he could see. Furniture and planking and sheets of metal had been pushed together variously to make barricades in the first-floor windows. There were lines of bullet holes, arabesques, in the upper wall.

The view to the west wasn't alarming. Black bursts of chemical-smelling smoke were washing through the scene. The fire generating the smoke was on the other side of the hotel, possibly in the courtyard, used as a parking area, that occupied the space between the west and east wings of the U-shaped building. Their shed faced the outside of the bottom of the U, the rear side of the hotel. Nothing he was seeing was immediately alarming. The smoke from the fire, which was at a safe distance from them, seemed to be lessening. There was shooting going on behind him. The loudest fire was proceeding from the west wing of the hotel, overlooking the zoo and, farther out, the pan, if his interpretation of the soundscape was correct. Somebody's labor had come to nothing. He was looking along the path at clotheslines bearing laundry very much the worse for war, would be one way to put it. The bed linen hung there was blackened and here and there listlessly burning. He was seeing no activity in any of the windows, no activity generally. This front was dormant.

Morel was pulling sharply at his legs. Ray edged his way back inside. Morel was going to be in favor of waiting until nightfall before they actually both got out and began to peregrinate. Ray didn't want to wait.

"Tell me what you see," Morel said. He was anxious.

"Well it's all quiet on the western front, from what I can see. Except for the shooting. And the smoke. There may be a fire over in the parking area. You said that koevoet had their military vehicles herded in there, in the courtyard, for security. You saw that out there, didn't you?"

"That's right, just their military stuff, trucks, and one personnel carrier, one of those funny-looking South African ones that you can feel safe in running over a mine. A Casspir. But I didn't see our vehicles. I don't know where they put those. Somewhere around, I guess."

"I'm guessing that that's where the fire is, where they've parked. I can tell you that if it was me attacking this place, I couldn't wait to put a mortar round into that spot. But would Quartus be stupid enough to not disperse his vehicles? The fire is on the way out. It's not a conflagration or anything out of control. But I'm going to edge farther out to see what else I can see."

Morel was agitated. "Wait a minute. Let's think. Say it turns out that we're in a sort of backwater in the fighting, for now. Let's think what it would be smart to do. I mean, this might be our moment, if their attention is elsewhere . . ."

"Let me take another look."

"Wait, we need to figure out in case it looks like we should jump into action. Right now we're at risk, with this hole in the wall, not to mention your sticking your face into it. I don't know. Maybe we should concentrate on breaking out enough more of the hole so I could get through too, in a pinch. So we'd be ready. It wouldn't take much."

Ray tried to be measured. Morel was unraveling. Ray said, "Look, it's possible I could get out and slip around to the front of the shed and see how they've got us locked in. All we know is that when we push on it we see two segments of chain across the opening. We don't know if there's a padlock. Why should there be? It's more likely they've just got a chain looped around and cinched up someway in a knot."

Morel was breathing rapidly. "No I think we need to both get out of here together, both of us at the same time. I don't think we should work it so that just one of us goes and leaves the other waiting to see what in the name of fuck is happening. You see my point. I think we should take our chances together, like a team."

"Maybe so. But let me take a good look in the other direction first."

It was clear Morel didn't want to be abandoned, which was interesting, as a development. Ray was feeling brave. Against his will, Morel was showing he was afraid. But of course Morel had something to lose that Ray no longer did.

Ray inched out again, this time as far as his knees. Morel was holding his ankles and producing muffled protests and instructions.

There was something frightening to the east. It was a body. It was a dead body. The body of a man was lying near the footpath fifty feet down. The dead body *was* the scene, with the rest of what he could see secondary to it, a frame for the dead man. He was assuming this man was dead. He concentrated on detecting any sign of life. There was nothing. Gunfire rattled from the far ridge of the pan and there seemed to be some action taking place on the floor of the pan to the west. He could make out part of one of the zoo cages. It appeared to be empty.

The body was face down. The back was bloody and seemed wrong, torn up and irregular, not smooth. The man was clad only in bush shorts. And he was wearing combat boots. Ray had to tell Morel.

He withdrew into the shed.

"What's wrong, man?" Morel asked.

"There's a body fifty feet down the path, lying there. A black guy. I don't know if he's one of Quartus's men or not. He could be a cook or one of these locals they're making do chores for them. I think I need to go look at him. I think he's dead but I don't know. There's blood all over, but he might not be dead."

"You're not going out there."

"I think I need to. The fact that nobody has bothered to collect him shows that nobody is paying attention to this side of the hotel right now. Or it means he's nobody. I just think I have to go see, ascertain if . . ."

"Don't be insane. What could you do? Say he's still alive, what could you do?"

"I don't know. I have to see."

"Listen. This is the deal. This is what we agreed. We don't do anything out there we don't both agree has to be done."

"We never agreed that."

"Well, de facto we did."

"We didn't. I'm going out there."

"Were you raised religious?"

"What the fuck does that have to do with anything? But okay, my family tried, with me, but not very hard. So what?"

"You're saying you're going out there in broad daylight. You could die. You'll be exposed. You don't think you're going to die, do you? That's one thing religion does for us, it plants the conviction that we're going to live forever. It explains a lot of irrational action."

"So does needing a pair of boots," Ray said.

Morel was silent.

Ray got down and prepared to exit fully. The ragged slot was tight against his shoulders. His shirt was ripping but he was making it through. He was full of urgency to get to the corpse, if it was a corpse. He was hoping it was a corpse because he was going to take the man's boots. Morel had boots. The dead man's boots represented power. He would be more than back to normal if he could get the boots and get them on his feet. It would change everything. It could save him, save Morel too.

Excelsior! he thought, aware that it wasn't quite the right word. He wanted something that signalized getting out of confinement in a more specific way, but all he could think of was *Voilà*, which was funny.

Excelsior! he thought again, emerging. He was about to be free. One arm was free. It would be helpful if Morel would grab his legs and push, help him, but he could manage without help.

He was locomoting, if that was the word, on his right side. Both arms were free and God was good because dark smoke was building up again in the space between the sheds and the hotel proper. He was feeling giddy. He was afraid, but, irrationally, he wanted to dance around, flail his arms around. He was afraid, but that was what he wanted to do.

He was out. He made himself lie still, lie against the wall like a slug. His heart was beating violently. He needed to think of something to calm himself down. The lines *Escaping from the enemy's hand . . . Into the enemy's vast domain* came to him. Perfect, he thought. But he wanted to know why it was always the twentieth century that provided him with what, literary comfort. What was wrong with Milton? He had to force himself to be calm, to keep his movements small and incremental. He looked back at the hole he had squeezed through, feeling a ridiculous pride and a sort of fascination with it, the smallness of the aperture. He was almost in control of himself.

There was a conflict between what he wanted to do first and what he ought to do first. He wanted to go for the boots like a shot and he was having a slight mania about them that was impelling him to do that, instead of what he ought to do first. He had his eyes on the boots. The mania he was having was in the genre of the wallet connected to a black thread and left on the sidewalk on April Fools' Day to be jerked away by a joker when some dupe reached for it. In this case it would be the dead body getting up and strolling off saying Gosiame, demonstrating that this had only been someone who happened to be taking a nap in a pool of blood. He knew he was being insane.

What he ought to do first was crawl around to the front of the shed to ascertain how they were being locked in. It was conceivable that he could undo it and be the one to throw the doors open for Morel, let him out, usher him out into the melee.

He would crawl around to the front of the shed, take a quick look at the situation, and decide what to do. That was enough of a plan. Crawling was painful, but he was discovering something interesting in the process. His knee was hurting, but only intermittently. Fear and pressure had given him the power to dissociate from his panoply of injuries, all of them, including the new abrasions on the backs of his hands, his head wound, to dissociate for decent intervals. Now everything was hurting. But he was adapting. A shattering barrage of firing began and ended.

He paused at the corner of their shed. He had a clearer view of the dead man and it was definite that he was dead. Ray turned the corner. He thanked God that he hadn't had to look into the man's face, so far. That would come.

He got to where he needed to be and he realized he had to stand up to see what the deal was on their door lock. He could see it was a padlock, but he had to get up and handle it to see that, say, it was locked, that the hasp was pushed in all the way. He got up. The padlock was massive. It took a key to open it. It was fully locked.

He was through with crawling. He was up for good. It didn't matter that he was being attacked by an irrational impulse to dance around. He was equal to it. Iris loved to dance. He had never been much of a dancer, because dancing had always made him feel false, in some way. Dancing went with inner cheerfulness, which came and went, with him. That was his view, anyway. Of course, why he wanted to dance around just then was a question for somebody. Morel probably liked to dance, despite his leg. He would ask him. Iris deserved more fun. She could even go to dinner dances now, if she wanted to. She liked to dress up. *Excelsior,* Iris! he thought.

He approached the dead man and bent over him. Ray rolled him over onto his back but he couldn't bear what that revealed so he rolled him back onto his front again, shaking. This kind of thing has to stop, he thought. Something had blown away half the man's face, the side of his neck, his shoulder. It was hideous. It was unnatural for the inner workings of the human machine to be on display in a shattered condition. Ray wondered if the mortar round that had compromised the wall of their shed had done in this poor bugger. He was wearing a belt with cartridge pouches strung on it. There might be a weapon somewhere in the vicinity, knocked away by the blast that had killed the man, it occurred to him. He didn't see anything nearby, but maybe he would do more of a search later, after he had the man's boots off.

He had to turn the corpse over again to get at the lacing of the boots. He crouched down. Definitely he did not want to be shot before he could get these seven-league boots on, which is what they would be for him. His feet were hurting almost as much as his knee, his scalp, just from the minimal walking around in stocking feet on the rocky ground, to tell the truth.

He got the combat boots off the corpse. He wanted to say something aloud in thanks, even though the boot donor, if that was the right term, was probably a death squad guy, a killer. But then indirectly he was a killer, himself, Ray Finch, indirect killer.

He got the boots on. They were too big but that was nothing. He wanted to kick things and in fact he still wanted to dance. Here I come, he thought.

It was wonderful, the way he felt.

He looked down at the corpse and said "Thank you."

He had laced and tied the boots very tightly, too tightly. He would adjust them when he got back inside.

He gave a little time to ranging around in search of a gun the dead man might have been carrying when he was killed. But there was nothing.

He returned to the hole he had to reenter and studied the wall around it. It was radically fractured. Now that he was shod, they could break more pieces out and enlarge the getaway gap. He knew they could. He felt full of strength.

He put himself into the hole again. Morel cried out, relieved, and then apologized for making noise. He pulled Ray back inside.

Ray got to his feet. He stamped his feet. "I got them," he said. He felt like kicking the wall, so he did. He kicked the wall in various places, concentrating finally on the margins of the hole they had made together. He kicked demonically. He couldn't stop. He would be able to stop when he succeeded in making it bigger, knocking a chunk off. That would prove something.

"You're going to hurt yourself. Stop that," Morel said.

Ray continued the assault.

Morel asked if he had seen anything useful lying around outside, a tool of any kind, a crowbar, anything.

"I didn't see anything. But then I didn't go very far afield, looking. I thought I should get back. We have to plan. Since we don't exactly have a plan."

"There could be something useful in one of the other sheds in this cluster. There are about six, that I saw, around here. Did you check to see if they were locked, by any chance?"

"No, I didn't. But we're locked in good here. No, when I was out there I stuck to the outside of this place like a leech. I thought I should keep it crisp out there. And did you notice something? Nobody killed me. Here I am. We're padlocked in. But I feel good. I'll tell you, you feel like dancing once you get out in the open."

"Lay off the kicking for a minute. Give it a rest."

"I will in a second," Ray said. But he didn't know when he could. The kicking was turning into a kind of dancing, in his mind. Dancing had hold of him, the idea did, the picture of it did. He thought, The whole thing is a dance, life is, from our first steps until all we can do is twitch in our wheelchairs.

Morel came up to him. He said, "You're getting a high out of this. I don't like it. Take a rest."

"Don't touch me." He didn't want to be touched and he didn't want to be interrupted.

The dance is already going when we have to step in, he thought. That's what society was, the dance. The agency was a dance he had stumbled into, a dance within a dance. He thought, We have to dance . . . we have to find a partner, we look and we look and then we find one and then in the dance we get tapped on the shoulder and it's Morel and the rules say it's his turn, because the dance has rules.

"My brother could dance," Ray said. It was true. Gay people were good dancers.

His right leg was hurting considerably. He wanted to kick the building down. He put all his concentration into the point of his right boot. He kicked desperately, willing the wall to come down, which it failed to do, but as he gave up, sat down, and watched his failure, a piece of concrete the size of a cauliflower fell away from the arch of the existing hole.

Morel gave a shout and bent down and pounded Ray on the back.

"Don't touch me," Ray said. Immediately he wanted to apologize.

"Right, I forgot. But this is good, man. Just a little more work and I'll be able to get through that thing."

"I think you could get through it now, really, but I'll work on it more if you give me a minute. Getting my breath."

"I'll work on it myself."

"Okay, go ahead. And here's what we have to decide. Okay when we get out either we stick together or we separate and find someplace to hide individually, you understand, individually, we discussed this, individually out there, which would be optimal for one of us surviving. Because this thing is going to come to an end at some point and the forces of law are going to drift in and we might be there, waving, Here I am, over here. So if we're both in the same place and the wrong guys find us. Well. You understand the odds."

"You mean we scramble out and split up and find a ditch or something out in the veld or something to get behind and wait, wait until this is over one way or another?"

"That would be one way to go." And it was the best way, from the standpoint of reason, Reason, as his brother would have put it, with his capitalizations, Reason, his poor fuck of a brother, his poor brother. The problem was that there was a slight misunderstanding on Morel's part about Ray's vocational qualifications for this kind of situation. He had hated his brother and failed his brother and now his brother was dead. But the truth was that he had no special operations training addressing anything like this hellfuckshit hell going on. But that was his own problem.

Morel began kicking at the wall as hard as he could, with his good foot. Ray got up, but before joining him in his effort, scrutinized the crack structure developing in the wall, the crackage, as it was undoubtedly referred to among professionals in what, walls.

He thought, We have to kick scientifically because we are wearing ourselves out.

"Stop," Ray said.

"Why?"

"We need to study the crackage so we bang at the right spot. Which would be right there."

"The crackage," Morel said, dryly.

"Right, the crack pattern."

"It's very important for you to have the right word for everything. Hey look, frankly I think you made that up."

"I may have. I may *have*. I like the right descriptor being applied to the correct object. Vocabulary is important. Iris is the same way, about words. You'll see. The working vocabulary of Americans is half what it was in 1950. That's horrifying. I have students in this country with better vocabularies than Americans their age, English vocabulary."

"I hear what you're saying," Morel said, which infuriated Ray.

"Of course you do, you're not deaf. And don't ever use that expression again. Iris will think you're an asshole. What I was saying is this, and I am being helpful, and it's that you are going to come under a lot of pressure to play Scrabble, if you haven't already. She loves it. I wasn't good about it. She stopped trying to get me to play, over time. You may wind up playing Scrabble a lot, if you know what's good for you. It's just a word to the wise. About Scrabble my excuse was that I was doing English morning to night at St. James's and that I wanted surcease from English. It was a mistake and we all make mistakes and sometimes a lot of small mistakes turn into a gigantic mistake." He felt okay. He hoped he had created for Morel a vista of postprandial board games being part of his utopia with Iris. He would bet that crackage was there in the Oxford English Dictionary.

Morel was going ahead without him, jerking and hauling with his hands at the wall in the wrong place, according to Ray's judgment, when an astonishingly large segment of the wall, a jagged huge rind, came away.

They were free to go.

Morel said, "Okay, we have to leave now, and I think we should stick together whatever, out there." It was an appeal, but it was unnecessary because Ray had already decided it would have to be that way. They would have to be brothers, temporarily. The man had a short leg.

Ray said, "It's a deal. That's the only way. Right."

"Okay, good."

Ray didn't want to say what he was going to say next. It was going to sound like an ultimatum. It wasn't. It was just a necessity. He said, "Okay, but look, first we need to get into the hotel to get my brother's manuscript, if we can. I hope you don't mind."

Morel was going to object. Ray didn't care.

"That makes no sense," Morel said unhappily.

"I know it. But I have to. Look, you don't have to go in with me. In fact, wait here if you want to, which is not exactly the protocol we agreed on. But that's where I'm going first, if it's physically possible, if it looks like I can get in. So wait here, I'll go, I'll come back, and then we jump out together. I have to try. Because I don't know where we're going to end up, how far from here we're going to end up, hiding or whatever we do. The whole place could burn down while we're watching it, burn from a distance, you see. Man, I have to."

"Okay then that's first thing. We'll do it together. I need to find my bag, anyway. I think I saw it in the torture chamber over there. I'd like to get my car keys, too. We'll try it together."

The wall made a noise, a brief grinding noise, and they both jumped back in unison, like a dance team, Ray thought. They were abashed about doing that.

They had to get going. The wall was rotten. There was new crackage showing. They were both thinking the same thing, that the wall was unstable and something could happen. The wall could come down, the roof with it, they could be sitting up to their necks in thatch attracting attention.

Morel was afraid. It had helped that they had agreed to stick together out in the maelstrom, but he was still breathing fast. It was not going to be possible to have a blueprint for every step.

Morel was gathering himself. He wanted to act well, outside. They both did. They both knew that the other might be the main surviving witness to how he had comported himself at the very end.

They had to go quickly. Ray had the urge to say, Shall we dance?

Morel wanted to lead. That was all right.

Morel was hesitating over whether to go out feet first or head first. He decided on head first. The clearance was just adequate. He proceeded very carefully, seeking to have as little contact with the wall as he could manage, put as little strain on it as possible, as he squeezed through. It was because the wall seemed delicate.

Ray prepared to follow. Morel was out. Before Ray could enter, Morel's hand appeared in the gap. He seemed to think Ray could use help, this time. Morel was all right. He was doing his best. Ray hissed at him, to move him back. Ray got through very neatly. They were free.

Morel wanted something. He wanted to shake hands. They did. Morel was vibrating, vibrating, not trembling. He was wound up. He was gesturing about something. He wanted to say something in Ray's ear, apparently.

"I think we should whisper," he whispered.

"What do you mean?"

"If we have to communicate, we should. But mostly we should use gestures, watch each other. Give signals."

Ray didn't want to laugh, but it was funny. Morel needed a manual, a new manual for each fifteen minutes. And it was funny to worry about being overheard in the pandemonium unfolding around them. He was adapting to the steady sound of firing. The most concentrated popping sounds were coming from the front side of the hotel, around the corner from them, to their right, and it was likeliest that the shooters would be in the second-story rooms, or on the roof. That was something to keep in mind. If there were shooters moving around on the roof the chances that they would be spotted were better, that had to be communicated to Morel.

The smoke was thick. He was grateful for it but they had to get away from it. His eyes were stinging. He rubbed them. When he opened his eyes, Morel was gone.

It was nothing. Morel had dashed off to look at the dead man. He was crouching over him.

Ray went after Morel full of irritation. They had an understanding.

But he knew what Morel was doing. He was being Hippocratic. He was a doctor. All I need to hear right now is that the guy is alive and wants his boots back, Ray thought. But he wasn't alive. Half his neck was gone. Ray should have mentioned that to Morel earlier. Morel was asserting himself, making the point that he was a doctor and so *this* was the first thing that had to be done.

Ray tapped Morel on the shoulder and signaled urgently that they had to proceed. Morel was shaking his head sadly. Ray mouthed the words *We must go*. Morel was being irritating.

What next? Ray thought. Because Morel was dodging around patently looking for something to cover the body with, which was a piety they had no time for. And there was nothing around they could use for the purpose except the smoldering laundry, which he was not going to mention. Everything Morel was doing was a piety and maddening when they had urgent things to do.

He took hold of Morel's arm and yanked on it, to stop him. They had to make use of these periods of intense fire, like the present one, for their riskier movements when they had to operate without cover. They had to exploit the distraction of their captors. That was the theory. Their task was to dash across the open ground between the sheds and the hotel and find their way into the hotel by getting lucky and opening one of the three doors or breaking one of them or by breaking in through a window and then finding the room they wanted . . . and getting what they needed and then splitting with it and getting back across the open ground and then up and away and out into the veld and into a ditch, that was all. He had to get this through to Morel. The deafening racket of the guns was going to be helpful if they had to smash anything noisily, too.

Morel broke away from him and ran in the wrong direction. The man was a nightmare.

Ray followed. Morel was up to something new. He was investigating the other sheds, planning to. He had gotten the doors open on the shed nearest theirs and was disappearing into it. Ray caught up with him.

The shed was empty. It was identical to the one they had been kept in.

"Good," Morel said, walking past Ray on his way to the next shed.

"What are we doing?" Ray asked.

"I just realized it, but we can't go over there until we see if there's anybody in these other sheds. We can't abandon them and then have something happen to us."

"Okay, but this wasn't the plan."

"But you see why we have to do this."

"I see why you want to, but the fact is if they're locked in the way we were it's not going to be possible to help them."

"No, but that would suggest we ought to look for keys over in the hotel, say, or tools, an ax, a hatchet, even. We could chop them out, chop the doors down. But we need to know. Also they might join us. Help us."

Morel was knocking at the doors of another shed. There were only three more to check, after this one.

The exercise was developing a French-farcelike feeling, with Morel bounding around but managing to look over his shoulder half the time, with doors being pulled open and slammed shut, Morel disappearing and reappearing. Ray stayed gamely with Morel until it was over. All the sheds were vacant and none contained anything useful to them. Ray wondered if Morel was coming up with these virtuous procrastinations because he feared going into the enemy's citadel and was at some level hoping it would blow up or burn down before they had to go there. He dismissed the suspicion. He didn't want to think ill of Morel, if he could help it. He was going to have dealings with Morel into eternity, it felt like. He would have to keep on top of how Morel was treating Iris, someway. He should be able to work something out with friends in Botswana. Morel was going to be in his life. He was losing a wife but he was gaining an ex-wife, was the way to look at it. And what was the correct term for his relationship to his former wife's new husband? There should be a term for that, there were so many of them in the culture.

They were back at their own shed, poised to sprint across the open ground to the hotel.

Morel led. Ray decided to stop halfway, in the lee of a monumental terracotta urn set on a high pedestal. The rim of the urn came to the level of his neck. There was refuse in the urn. Dead vines trailed out of it. There were mates to the urn dotted around the grounds, five or six of them. Something made him not want to leave the spot. He didn't know what it was.

He knew what it was about the urn. It was an erotic memory featuring an urn and his wife. It was long ago. They had been visiting someone or using a house that had been loaned to them and there had been an urn at the center of a patio and Iris had run out of their room in the middle of the night, naked, and had posed variously, leaning against it, to tease him. And then there had been magnificent sex. Something like that would never happen to him again. That was a fact. He wondered if when people, couples, got old they stopped fucking at some point sheerly because it seemed like such a frail copy of what they had once been able to do with joy and strength, if they stopped out of homage to their earlier fucking selves. Morel was shaking him.

He made himself run the rest of the way. He collapsed when he got to the hotel wall. He had breathed in too much smoke, in his exertions. He needed something like a bandanna, or better yet a gas mask. His feet were painful. Morel was sitting on the ground next to him. It was hopeless, but Ray wanted to convey to Iris that if they stayed together, or if they *had* stayed together, depending on which fork in the path he was at when he was expressing himself . . . he was losing the thread, but he wanted her to know that if it was up to him they would be *old* lovers, going on and doing it forever, however it looked, however disreputable anyone else might find them if they discovered what they were doing, the two old birds.

Morel was trying the door. Ray was certain that this was the exterior door he had been taken through to be abused. The door was locked.

It was a single door. Morel had his good leg up, his foot against the frame, and was jerking fiercely at the doorknob. He gave up.

"We need an ax," he said. He was winded. He was barely able to say anything.

"You keep saying that."

Ray got up to take a turn at pulling and hauling. He was positioning himself when he thought he heard something inside, through the door. He thought he heard someone coming.

He mouthed the words *Someone is coming*.

"We need a plan," Morel whispered.

"Like what kind of plan?"

"Like, you stand back when they open the door and I'll fucking jump them before they know it. Or I'll stand there and you jump them. Whatever you want."

"They could be armed."

"Doesn't matter. I'll be out of sight. They'll be looking at you. Try to get them to step out toward you. We can do this. Try to look sick or something so they come out."

They poised themselves to do something. They would be swift about it. But nothing happened. There was silence.

The door they wanted to open was painted with dark pink enamel which was scaling badly in places, revealing a bright red undercoat. It was reminiscent of afflicted flesh, to Ray. It reminded him of a plate in a medical text on skin conditions. That was where his mind was. And the wooden door was a massive, medieval piece of work, not a candidate for brute force.

Morel seemed to be in charge of getting them inside. He was alternately feeling exquisitely along the edges of the door and looking over his shoulder at Ray with expressions that seemed to be asking Ray not to be impatient, communicating that progress was being made. The door was a dilemma because trying to break it down, assuming they could find a way to do that, ran the risk of attracting the wrong attention from the interior, with the result that they would only have succeeded in escaping back into captivity. It was a possibility he was responsible for because of his insistence on making a good-faith effort to retrieve his brother's manuscript. He accepted that. He had to, was all. He could imagine bursting in and Quartus coming up to them saying, Hello, *entrez*, nice to see you again, take *that*. But the furor and action was on the roof, so far as they could tell. There was now some shouting mixing in with the rattle of gunfire.

Ray turned his attention to the barricaded windows on either side of the door. They would have to pluck the fangs of broken glass out of the window frames first, then dislodge and push through the mixed barriers of planking and plywood and furniture as quietly as they could. Clearly some of the planking had been nailed in place, and there was some random interweaving of barbed wire throughout the different assemblages. But the whole project looked extremely improvised to Ray. But there would be noise involved there, too. How they could manage to enter like thieves in the night was the question.

Morel was trying something new. He was knocking softly on the door, very softly, politely. It seemed ludicrous and probably it was going to lead to nothing because he was tapping so softly.

He was knocking and then pausing and putting his ear to the door and then knocking again.

Something was happening just behind them. Ray spun around. What he saw looked like buried clothesline being jerked up into the air. But what he was really seeing was automatic weapons fire ranging for the first time along the area between the hotel and the sheds. Dust hung in the air. Somebody was firing close to them. The way back was threatened now. Morel was not paying attention. He was still knocking politely on the door.

The door opened a crack, and then a little wider, and Morel, beckoning wildly to Ray to follow, slipped inside. Ray was right behind him.

It was dark. They were in a hallway and there in the semidarkness, crowded to one side, was a body of people, Africans. When his eyes adapted he would count them. Morel's eyes were better than his, obviously, because he was already having exchanges, murmured exchanges in Setswana. These people knew him. He had visited them in the zoo cages. Morel was taking care of business, seeing to things. He seemed to be making sure that the door was securely relocked, for one thing. There were no more than a dozen people in the hallway.

Abruptly he needed to sit down. His knee was torturing him and his boots were uncomfortable. It was odd how pain went away during periods of excitement and fear and came back when you felt safer. He had to rest while he refilled, was the way he was thinking of it, while he refilled with his solid self. Outside in the open with death in the air and no cover to speak of, he had felt light and empty, untethered, light on his feet but inwardly light too. Sitting against the wall, he felt better by the moment, heavier.

The air was foul. Ray thought he could smell blood. The word ngaka was going around, meaning Morel was being identified as a doctor. That would make him popular. Doctors are always useful, Ray thought.

Ray felt useless. It would be helpful if he could get the right metaphor to apply to the life he was going to lead post-Iris. That would strengthen him. So far the images he had come up with were feeble. One of them had been to see his life as the plates and glasses and cutlery that miraculously remained undisturbed when the magician jerked the tablecloth out from under everything. It was an image that had no force. He thought, This is what you'll do: You will think of your life in panels with one panel not necessarily having anything to do with the others. What he meant was that each panel in the triptych or whatever a four-framed or five-framed set of panels should be called, would be judged totally individually. If the first panel was beautiful and was by Maxfield Parrish the point would be to have the appropriate reaction to that and pay no attention to the next panel, which happened to be by Hieronymus Bosch depicting the same subjects as in the first panel except that in this panel they were in hell and it would be fine to be horrified. And then there would be the next panel.

He could see well enough to count the crowd. There were twelve people, men and women, no children, lined up pressed to the wall like caryatids. He thought, Hey that's how useful I am, able to supply the right term for these poor bastards at a single bound, caryatids.

An old woman came over to him. He said, "Dumela, mma," and she said nothing and he said "Dumela" again and she said nothing. And then he said, "I am useless," and again she said nothing.

This hallway, at least, was in the hands of the victims and not the villains, so Morel had been right. Or he had been right. One of them had been right. He didn't know which one. He should be doing more. He should get up immediately. He had the impulse to shake hands with the caryatids, do something to reassure them because they were obviously frightened. They were in terror. He could tell that much. He made himself get to his feet.

Hell is where you don't know anyone, he thought. Alarmingly, there was a white face floating toward him from the depths of the hallway. It was smiling. It was a face he should know.

He did know the face. It was Dwight Wemberg the long-lost coming toward him, the man driven mad by not being able to get his wife out of the ground, dead wife out of the ground. He looked dead himself. He was emaciated and oddly dressed. He was wearing a headband, unless it was a bandage, and he was in fatigues spotted with filth. He was carrying a rifle. He was smiling inordinately.

Ray didn't know what to do. There was the feeling that he should be reporting to someone that Wemberg was alive. But that was easy to dismiss because it was part of the past way of doing things. Boyle had been desperate to find Wemberg.

"Hello, man," he said to Wemberg.

"Nice to see you. Why are you here?" Wemberg seemed happy.

"Well I was doing stuff for the ministry and these bastards caught me. I was doing site studies."

"Our boys are the best," Wemberg said.

"What boys?"

"Don't worry. You'll be okay. We got these guys trapped on the roof. We came down and you know what we did? We came in and blew their fuel pump to hell before they knew anything. Two of our boys. Anyway."

"Dwight, you don't look well."

"Well you know what, I lost a lot of blood. But you know what, it's good to see you. But what you better do and better do it fast is put one of these on." He touched his headband.

"Okay," Ray said.

"And the doctor too. You know why, because that's how we know you're with us, so we don't shoot you."

Morel came over to them. He exchanged greetings with Wemberg, bemusedly.

Ray said, "So Dwight is saying we need to put some kind of headband on, to identify us."

Wemberg said, "Not headband, *witdoek*. That's the correct term. Witdoek."

Ray said, "Okay, fine."

"You can find something around here."

"You remember Dwight, don't you, Davis?"

"From Gaborone. Sure."

"Well I guess we can gather he's joined up with Kerekang's people, somehow. It's pretty amazing. This is a war."

Wemberg was nodding vigorously. He said, "Kerekang is here. He's leading us. This is koevoet's main base, you know. In this country."

"You need to sit down," Morel said to Wemberg.

"There's no chairs," Wemberg said.

"We'll find something for you," Morel said.

Wemberg said, to both of them, "You knew my wife. You know about that. What they did to me."

Ray said, "I met Alice. And I think my wife knew her."

"Your wife is Iris. I know her. I know you love your wife. You do. So you see how I feel. They wouldn't tell me where she was buried at first, you know. Not even that."

"I know," Ray said.

"She's asleep," Wemberg said.

Ray nodded. It was disturbing. It was grotesque, too, seeing Wemberg standing there armed, injured, involved in killing. Obviously losing his wife had dislodged Wemberg from his normal life and left him exposed to violent propositions and outcomes and urgings. Pay attention to this, Ray thought. He wondered what it meant for him, if it was cautionary. He wanted to say something comforting to Wemberg but nothing was coming to him. Ray felt a tortured moment of envy. Wemberg's love life was over, all his love-struggles, all the striving to get and keep one excellent person. *All life longs for the last day* was somebody's line. That was exhaustion speaking. He would be fine.

Cries, sounds of running feet, came from the roof.

"What should we do to help?" Morel asked.

Wemberg answered, "I don't know. They sent me down here to watch the stairs, I think they said."

Morel said, "Sir, I would like to examine you, if I can. Just quickly."

"Then you guard the stairs," Wemberg said to Ray, handing his rifle to him. It was an Enfield, single-barreled, a .458, very heavy. There was a bullet in the chamber. Ray didn't want the rifle, but he took it.

"Do you have any more bullets for it?"

"No."

Morel was busy. He was now looking into some of the rooms opening off the hall. He had gotten a torch somewhere. He was being decisive. His solidity had returned. He was giving orders. He wanted to examine some of the caryatids too, not only Wemberg. People were doing as they were told. Morel's solidity had returned faster than his had.

Morel had found the venue with the most light and was creating an examination room there out of nothing. He had chosen the rearmost room on the right and was overturning wooden crates and pushing them together to make a platform to sit on or lie on and he didn't care about the rubbish and crockery he was spilling out and kicking aside.

In a moment, he had Wemberg sitting down, taking his shirt off.

Morel was moving too fast for Ray to be helpful.

Ray stood watching. You have to be a weight lifter if you're going to use one of these .458s, he thought.

Morel said, "You know what you can do?"

"What would that be?"

"You could go look for my bag. I need it." Morel was shining the torch into Wemberg's mouth. Morel's face was bright with sweat.

"No, I can't," Ray said.

"What do you mean? Why can't you?"

"I have to guard the stairs. I saw a stairway at the back."

"Oh come on."

"Also how can I see anything? These rooms are dark."

"I need my bag. It's more urgent. There's not much light in the room but there's enough. If you need me I'll run in with the torch. Just shout."

Someone handed Ray a burning candle.

"Good," Morel said. "Find the interrogation room if you can. They went through my bag in front of me there."

Ray felt like an idiot. He had an urgent mission, finding *Strange News*, and that coincided with looking for Morel's bag, and he had been standing around witlessly objecting to things.

"I'm going," Ray said. Morel was picking at cumbersome bandaging fixed across Wemberg's upper chest. The strips were cut from towels. The inner strips were bloodsoaked. As he left the room, Ray heard Wemberg saying something about fainting, about Morel not worrying if that happened because it had happened before and he was all right. It was Ray who felt faint.

Ray decided that the first room on the left, as you entered the building, would be the interrogation chamber, based on his reckonings when he had been blindfolded, counting his steps. The door wasn't locked, but it would only open so far, a few inches. He butted against it first with his shoulder and then with his rump. Obviously he was accumulating bruises without even knowing it. Everything felt tender. His strength was going. Two caryatids were watching, not helping. He beckoned to them and they all pushed together and the way was clear. Gum tree poles and furled carpets inexpertly placed against the wall on the side of the door had been the culprits. They had fallen over. He was in.

And this was the place. There was the table, Quartus's chair, his own chair.

He felt proud of himself, being there again, looking around. He had to guard the candle and keep it from flickering out. He had to proceed slowly.

He was making out features of the chamber new to him, like the two iron hooks screwed into a ceiling beam directly above the chair he had been abused in. He approached the chair with the idea of sitting in it valedictorily. He couldn't see why he shouldn't. But the chair seat and the floor immediate to it reeked of urine. Someone had been beaten into incontinence there, someone else. He recoiled.

The floor was a debris field, a display of cigarette butts and empty soda cans and, here and there, roses. He was amazed, but only until he realized that the roses were wads of bloodstained tissue.

He felt like destroying something. He could at least kick Quartus's table over.

But first he had to dispose of the hunting knife lying on the table. He didn't want to touch it. He motioned for one of the two Africans who had entered the room with him to take it.

The old man came forward reluctantly. Ray pointed at the knife, more than once, but the old man remained hesitant, not taking it.

Ray introduced himself hurriedly. He didn't catch the man's name. He bowed and waved in the direction of the woman caryatid who was there, hanging back, but ready to help. He had been afraid when the old man had thrown himself against the door, imagining him shattering like a rickety character in a cartoon.

There was a correct way to touch hands, which was what the standard greetings gesture came down to. The most you ever got in greetings was a soft, the softest and briefest, handshake. You were supposed to hold the fingers of your left hand, slightly cupped, against the wrist of your right hand as you reached forward. He was overburdened. How could he give proper greetings? He had to drag the Enfield around with him and his right hand was out of action. It was being slowly entombed in melted wax.

He let go of the gun, for a start. He had to free his hands. He supposed that he could ask the old man to take charge of the gun for him, as well as the knife, although there was something odd about the idea. Now he knew why the great white hunters had always had gun bearers. Guns were encumbrances and they were heavy.

He didn't like the idea of asking the woman to be his candle bearer, either. It was an unpleasant job. The wax was hot and annoying. He needed to move around with the candle so he could look into corners and there was something uncomfortable about the prospect of directing the woman to do that for him.

The gun was on the floor. He was stuck. The few small things he had to do seemed mountainous.

The woman came to his rescue. Her name was Dirang. She pried the burning candle out of his hand and set it securely in the middle of the floor, pressing it down into its own bed of soft wax.

Ray scraped the wax from his fingers as well as he could. Dirang was not a young woman. She was wearing a headscarf and a faded wash dress and she was barefoot. The old man was her father, Ray gathered. The old man was barefoot too.

He had more respect for the ability to go barefoot without complaining continuously than he had had previously. Because he had tried it lately and it hadn't even been full-bore barefootedness because his feet had been protected by his socks. You stopped appreciating people being barefoot and what they were undergoing when you saw it so regularly every day, even in the towns, even in Gaborone. He remembered the first time he and Iris had seen barefoot white people, underclass white people, going barefoot like rural Africans, in some of the decayed areas of Johannesburg.

In any case, he was going to be more sensitive about it. Not that he had any idea what being sensitive about it would entail, unless he was going to pass out shoes and sandals, carry them around in a satchel. He would see. He had to remember that the naked sole of the foot would toughen up over time.

He was finding it hard to get moving, even though he had gotten away from his burdens for the moment at least. He wondered what it would be like in the world if enough people decided all at the same time to do nothing, not even be parasites, not even be mendicants. But then there was the question of why India didn't collapse under the weight of its nonachievers, its gurus and beggars. But then he was thinking of an even more complete withdrawal than that. He was thinking of "Bartleby the Scrivener" becoming some kind of creedal text, the story of somebody who refuses to do anything. But he did know what he was going to do next.

He was going to kick Quartus's table over.

He stood in front of the table and kicked as hard as he could, overturning it. He liked doing it. He was thinking of uprighting the table and kicking it over once again when he realized something.

Quartus's chair had been drawn up to the table. Visible on the chair seat was the thing he had come for, he was sure, *Strange News*, sitting there, a stack of pages, thick rubber bands around its middle.

He collapsed on the manuscript, clutching it to him.

He was seized with the need to protect the manuscript immediately, shield it, disguise it.

He needed fabric, sheets, curtains, a blanket, anything he could wrap the manuscript in, doubling and tripling the wrapping, folding it in. And in addition he wanted to strap it to his body if he could, but in a way that wouldn't be noticeable. He knew he was being insane.

He knelt down with the manuscript, next to the candle.

All of the manuscript seemed to be there. He bent the top half of the bundle back and riffled the pages slowly.

One enraging thing leapt out at him. Quartus or someone had made notes in Afrikaans here and there in the text. There were checkmarks and arrows connecting certain entries. He wanted to tell Morel.

He calmed himself. The markings were a sort of defilement, but if the original entries were still legible that would be okay, really, he would be able to accept that. He would have to.

He had to find something to wrap the manuscript in. He got up and wandered along the wall, poking around among the oddments collected there, until, occultly, his fingers found an edge of cloth jammed between pieces of furniture. It seemed promising.

He tugged it free. Something fell and shattered back in the tangle of furniture. He didn't care.

It was a bedspread, not especially savory, a tan chenille bedspread stiff in spots, and stained, but usable. It had been employed to sop up something unpleasant, but it would be fine.

Dirang and the old man helped him fold it into a square. He placed the manuscript in the center and delicately wrapped it up. He wondered what

Dirang and the old man were thinking, if they had some idea that this was an item of some value. They could see that he was excited. In fact he was more than excited. He was happy. He wondered what Rex would think if he could see what he was doing and feel how he was feeling. It was funny because he had been assuming that his happiest moments in this life were probably behind him. Now I need rope, he thought.

There was a row of open boxes and cartons in the space between Quartus's chair and the barricaded window. There should be something. Torturers needed rope.

Ray hauled two boxes over into the candlelight.

The first box he looked into held an unhelpful olla podrida of doorknobs, serving trays, jars of nails, screws, and glazier's points, and no cord or rope or twine. The doorknobs could be hurled at an enemy, in a pinch, during a fray, though they would miss the enemy and he would just hurl them back with greater accuracy. But rocks were scarce in the Kalahari, which was a reason to not forget the doorknobs. Anything can be a weapon, he thought. A sigh is a weapon, can be, a pause before answering a particular question can be, an averted glance can be, everything can be a weapon, your beloved angel of a child can grow up and kill you for nothing, for fun, he thought. It was something that happened from time to time. A handful of glazier's points flung into a ruffian's face when he least expected it might be effective for two seconds. He set a jar of them aside.

He thought, Rightly considered, the world is a congeries of weapons, an assemblage. He had seen a movie where a gangster visits a deadly enemy after being searched up and down and stabs his victim in the eye with a wing of his reading glasses, and kills him.

He had to move on, and more rapidly. His helpers were looking oddly at him and he knew why. They were concerned. He was hugging the bulky parcel containing his brother's soul, would be one way to put it, a sentimental way.

He couldn't keep sitting on the floor, either. He got up and sat in Quartus's chair while the process of looking into boxes continued. His legs were weak. It looked like he couldn't let go of the manuscript, which was true. He wanted another box brought to him by his bearers, which was not what he meant, he didn't mean they were bearers.

He had to stop using his main force to clutch *Strange News* to his chest. There was war in heaven, meaning what was going on on the roof. It was thunderous up there again. He wanted to explain about *Strange News* to his helpers, but how could he? It was not a great thing. *An airliner hauling its roar through the void* was a fragment that had stuck with him. It wasn't great. In riffling through the pages he had glimpsed Rex's odd little poem, he supposed it was a poem anyway, *A perfect Specimen of Surprise / would be to discover / on your wife's Buttocks / handwriting, in ballpoint pen, of a minute Size*. It was obvious why that would have embedded itself in his mind even if Quartus hadn't brought it up, but there was nothing great about it either. It was silly.

He was looking through another box. It was devoted to plumbing-related items. There were lengths of pipe, joints, tap handles, cans of joint compound, rolls of duct tape. The tape was giving him an idea. It was thick and metallic and extremely sticky, still.

Ray took his shirt off. He would summon the old man to help him. There was plenty of tape. There was roll after roll of it. He was going to tape *Strange News* to his person. Then he would put his shirt back on over it and continue participating in the affray. He would have the use of both hands. Affray was one of those words that was vanishing from the language. The makers of the English language would be appalled, whoever they had been. There was nothing to be done about it. He was capable of feeling sorry for the English language as an entity, at odd moments, if anyone wanted a perfect specimen of sentimental stupidity.

The tape was very tough, but they had the hunting knife and could use that to segment it up as they needed. He thanked God for the knife.

He decided to hold his arms straight up above his head, as a signal. He did, but saw he was producing confusion. What he wanted was for the old man and Dirang to stop what they were doing and address his new idea, help bind the manuscript to his body. He looked like he was surrendering to these two, in all probability. He knew what he needed them to do. He was going to tape the manuscript to his chest. He had reached that decision because if it was taped to his back the manuscript might slide down or fall off and it would be more awkward to reach around and catch it than if he had it right in front where he could grab it.

"Thusa," he said. Thusa meant help. It was so fucking annoying and unnecessary, the multiplicity of mutually uncomprehending cultures. He wanted to say in Setswana *Put this on me* or *Strap this on me* and he couldn't remember how. Stress was bleaching out his Setswana lexicon, such as it was. He would have to use signs, gestures.

They understood. He made the bundle as tight as he could, first, and then lapped tape endlessly around it until it looked like a block of armor. He held it to his chest. They understood what he wanted.

His helpers exhausted roll after roll of tape, looping the bindings creatively around his neck, his shoulders, his thorax. He had to keep his lungs inflated while his helpers worked because once the bundle was firmly affixed he didn't want it to be difficult to get his breath, because he would be participating in the denouement of this fray, whatever it might be. He stood up, to test his burden.

He nearly pitched forward onto his face, but he righted himself in time. The parcel with its wrappings and bindings was monstrously heavy. Now he had to try to find the box containing his effects. He wanted clean clothes, he wanted his watch, he wanted anything of his that he could find. And he had to do his best to find Morel's medical bag. That was urgent.

His helpers returned to the labor of dragging crates and cartons over to his post near the guttering candle. Time was short. It would be better to dump the boxes out in situ. He would help.

But there was a problem. He could button his shirt over the parcel but it made him look ridiculous. He would have to leave the parcel showing, his shirt open. He would have to explain a few times. They would get used to it.

A box of spoons was overturned, creating walking hazards. He kicked his way through to the action.

He saw his boots. They were desert boots and he loved them. The old man had found the correct box. He could see his knobkerrie in the box. The old man seemed to be considering Ray's boots for his own use. It wasn't true that people would choose to be barefoot over going about in normal shoes. Here was proof. But he had to explain the situation. Dithlako meant shoes. He shouted it a few times and pointed at his feet. Dirang smiled and said, "It's all right."

It was all right. The old man was backing away from the desert boots. Ray would give him the dead man's boots he was wearing. They would be too big, but they would do. Dirang spoke very good, easy English. Who was she?

The light was execrable. Ray needed help getting his boots off. The bundle was in the way. His fingers were weak. Dirang bent to the task. Finally it was done. The old man had the dead man's boots. He seemed grateful. He was putting them on.

Ray thanked Dirang and the old man in Setswana. Dirang replied, softly, again in English, "You're very welcome." Ray answered in English, "Thank you, mma." With his own boots on, he felt reborn. Going quickly through the few remaining crates and boxes, he satisfied himself that Morel's medical bag was nowhere around.

Ray resumed charge of the Enfield, heavy as it was. He could manage it. He was adapting to the millstone on his chest. Everything that could be taken care of had been taken care of.

He made his way back to Morel's venue. The man was remarkable, it had to be said. This was an organized scene and there had been improvements during the short time Ray had been elsewhere. There was more light, there were more candles, and the caryatids were directing torchbeams in a coordinated way, at Morel's instruction. Ray thought, You have to stop calling them caryatids. They were active. They were helping.

The simulacrum examination table formed by lining up overturned crates was now covered with padding, toweling. Pots of hot water had been procured from somewhere. There was an astringent odor in the air. A Basarwa woman was sitting on the examination table and Morel was attending to her neck. Ray remembered being fascinated by dead skin as a young boy. His brother had produced yards of it. His brother had gotten too much sun for his skin type, during summer vacations. I never wanted to be a doctor, Ray thought. He had been squeamish. His brother had chased him around while he was peeling off sheets of dead skin because he had figured out that Ray found it upsetting in some way.

What about these people's children? That was a question. It looked like he was not going to have children in this life. There were orphans in the world. He could teach orphans if he could find a way to do that.

Wemberg had been taken care of. He was lying on the floor wrapped up in drapes, still alive. He had to be alive because his head was showing. If he had died his face would be covered. Ray was relieved. A surge of heavy firing shook the building. Dust sifted down from the ceiling. Ray wondered how strongly the building was constructed. He had his doubts, but there were more pressing things to obsess on, like the expression on Morel's face.

Because Morel was staring at him. He could see that. Several torchbeams had swung in Ray's direction, lighting him up.

Ray said, "I couldn't find your bag."

Morel said nothing.

"I looked around," Ray said.

"That's all right. No, I found it. No someone found it for me." Morel's tone was odd.

Morel kept talking, still oddly. "All the drugs were gone but everything else was there, except for the drugs and my hypodermics, but okay. Oh also what about the first aid kit you had, any sign of it?"

"No, none."

Ray realized what it was with Morel.

"Oh, *this*," Ray said, touching the parcel bound to his chest. So far it was sitting solidly against him.

Morel said, "What *is* it, for Christ's sake? Because you know what it looks like, it looks like a bomb strapped to you. Really. Really you look like one of those people with bombs strapped to them. It looks like metal, like a bomb, like some fucking thing, man, an infernal device. All you need is a fuse sticking out of it or something that looks like a detonator in your hand and that's what you are. I know you, man, and you scared the shit out of *me*. Whatever that is, take it off."

Ray wanted to laugh. He said, "Man, *relax*. This is my brother's manuscript, I *found* it."

"Well take it *off*."

"Are you kidding? I won't. Never. This goes with me just like this until we get out of here. Or not."

Morel threw his hands up. He turned away.

Ray saw that Wemberg was beckoning to him. Ray was delighted. Definitely Wemberg was alive. He felt kinship because Wemberg was a widower and so was he, in a way. There was no noun, not in English, for the man who takes away another man's wife. There should be. It could be something like *plucker*. And there was no particular word for the man whose wife had been plucked away. The French undoubtedly had a word for it. There should be an Académie Anglaise. He wouldn't mind working for that kind of body. He was going to need a job. It would be a job that would let him elevate some of his brother's coinages like *to harbinge* into the dictionary, some dictionary. There were other coinages that weren't bad. He was carrying them around on his chest, next to his heart.

Wemberg was rolled up in floral drapery. One arm was free. He was rolled up like Elizabeth Taylor or Vivien Leigh in a carpet in *Caesar and Cleopatra* when she was hauled up into the fortress and let out of the carpet by the then handsomest man in the world, Stewart Granger. We have too many images for things, he thought. It was the media. It must have been better before the media.

He sat down next to Wemberg, whose eyes were closed now and who was no longer beckoning. He had certain things to say to Wemberg. He wanted to tell him that he appreciated, really appreciated, that Wemberg and his wife had done good in the world. He wanted to let Wemberg know that he was going to be doing good, himself, next, in his life. He wanted to tell him that he was going to be more like him and Alice.

"Dwight," he said, but that was all he said. Wemberg had a smile on his face but he seemed suddenly asleep. Ray thought he must be dead. Now look what you've done, he said to himself, in agony, involuntarily getting back to the question of why in the name of God his mother had found the Laurel and Hardy movies so funny.

He couldn't stand the idea but Wemberg was dead. He wanted to shout. He did shout. He shouted for Morel to come over.

"What?" Morel said, unable to contain his irritation.

"He's dead. Wemberg is dead."

"No he isn't," Morel said. He prodded Wemberg with his foot and Wemberg began to cough.

"Don't get him excited, he's weak," Morel said.

Wemberg was plucking at his headband and whispering something urgently.

"What does he want?" Ray asked. He wanted to do anything Wemberg wanted. He put his ear next to his mouth.

"Wear my witdoek and go to the stairs. You have to be at the stairs. Take the rifle and go to the stairs. I told you."

"Okay, don't worry, I understand."

He knew he had to leave Wemberg if he was going to be a combatant. But he was reluctant to leave the man. Morel was busy. Wemberg was odd, he was phasic. He would manage to get out a few words and then he would fade into silence. His face would go slack. And then in a few beats he would be back to himself and he would produce another set of words. And for some reason each time he commenced again he accompanied his effort with a forced smile. It made no sense to have priorities in a situation like the one he was in, but Ray had a couple of strong ones. He wanted Wemberg to live and settle the hideous problem of his wife, her disinterment. He wanted to be able to help Wemberg with that, as one of his last acts in this part of the forest. And he wanted to get hold of Kerekang and talk to him and see if he could extract him from what he had gotten caught in and get him away and into safety of some kind. He had confidence that he could do that if he got the chance. He had a set of unusual skills, thanks to his years in the agency. He knew how to get behind the arras, that kind of thing. He would expend his skills, burn them to the ground, to help Kerekang and Wemberg to undo things. He wanted other things, too. He wanted Morel to survive, of course. He deserved to.

Ray took Wemberg's hand, and that stimulated another smile and a string of words.

"Take my doek," Wemberg said. He repeated it.

Ray slipped the headband free. It had a rank smell. He didn't care.

Wemberg's head was larger than his, apparently. Ray had to retie the doek rather than slide it directly on, which, strangely, disappointed him.

He was ready, then. First he had to push away certain associations he didn't want to have, associations from Kurosawa movies mainly, of samurai getting ready to go out and do battle by, as a final preparatory act, tying on a headband. He wanted what he was going to do to be what it was and not what it resembled. He patted Wemberg's forehead very softly. He had to detach himself from the compulsion to keep seeing if the man was still alive.

He was ready. Unfortunately he was going to need help getting to his feet. It was his knee, not to mention the millstone around his chest.

"Thusa," he shouted. Two Batswana heard him and came to him and hauled him erect.

The Enfield was heavy. He picked it up and made sure that the single shell he had was correctly chambered so he could fire it into someone's body.

He hesitated. He wanted Morel to notice that he was on his way to war.

He posted himself at the foot of the stairs. He stood there until he felt that he should be doing more. He would go up, at least to the second floor.

The staircase was a beautiful thing, he realized. Money had gone into it, rare hardwoods. The railings were artworks. The handrail was carved in a serpentine shape. He didn't want this stairway to go up in smoke. There must be much more throughout the building that was worth preserving. Eccentric rich people had indulged their tastes here. The treads of the first flight were bare, but he could see, from the landing, that the carpeting that had once covered the treads of the second flight had been ripped free and pulled down into a hump, an obstacle. It was difficult employing his torch and keeping his rifle in any sort of threatening pose. Everything was too heavy, including the torch. The stairs were crowded with boxes and rubbish.

He decided that it would be best to set the rifle aside and take his torch and negotiate the stairs to the second floor. And when he got there, after surmounting the debris in his way, he would creep around and attempt to locate whatever stairs or ladder gave access to the roof. It was clear in his mind that he had to go up onto the roof, where hell was. But first he would come back for his rifle. But for reconnoitering he would need to be nimble.

He found a niche for his rifle between two wooden crates filled with metal shavings, the sort of waste that collects under lathes. He wondered why it had been saved, or if the answer was that plans to dispose of the waste had been interrupted by bankruptcy. You'll never know, he said to himself.

He was at large on the dark second floor. He was using the torch in short bursts. He thought that was best, even though someone hanging head down clinging like Dracula to the wall might see it as a code, if they were near a window. The battle was directly and loudly on top of him. Individual voices, taunting or imprecating or whatever it was they were conveying, were distinct. He had to keep reminding himself that when his breathing was laborious when he was exerting himself it was because of his medallion, *Strange News*, which was still cleaving reasonably tightly to his chest. He decided to discard his shirt. He took it off and rather than look for a place to cache it in he tossed it over his shoulder.

It felt better with his shirt off. He prowled swiftly through the second floor, looking into rooms, finding one bedroom mainly intact and ready for tourists once the dead insects were swept up and the dust had been beaten out of the various upholsteries and the bolsters. Every room had apparently been supplied with giant bolsters. He might have occupied this room with Iris if life had been different. Pausing to look at himself in the baroque mirror the room contained gave him an idea, the inspiration to do something with the fact that he looked like hell, skeletal, his ribs showing, his arms womanish and thin. He was minimal. If he was anything he was the object he was bearing more than he was anything else.

Back in the corridor, he was toying with the idea of going up, once he found the way, going up onto the roof naked, although not naked so far as his feet were concerned because he would cleave to his shoes forever or until Christ came again. He wanted to do something helpful with the impression he seemed to be capable of giving that he was carrying an infernal device around. Taking his shirt off had been smart. It made the bomb central. But dispensing with his jeans might help even more, because arriving in hell showing his sacred penis, showing he didn't care who saw his sacred penis, would mean that something serious was up and that they should be afraid. He felt suddenly that he could do it. Embarrassment would be nothing to him after he was dead. He removed his jeans, half disbelieving what he was doing. He would certainly be an alarming spectacle unless, of course, somebody just turned around and reflexively shot him the minute he popped up and they saw his white headband. And that thought suggested he should dispose of the headband, because, on balance, it created more potential problems than it solved. When it came to Kerekang's people he could just shout out who he was. A problem was that his head was going to be the first visible part of him when he emerged from a trapdoor or looked around a corner as he arrived on the roof. He pulled the headband off. *My Brief Career as a Human Bomb* could be the title for a chapter in someone's unfinished memoirs.

He went back to find his discarded shirt, folded it neatly, and carried it into the intact bedroom where he pushed it under the bed, out of sight. He wanted to be able to reclaim it. He didn't know how things were going to go. People might say you're dithering, but you aren't, he thought. He was planning. He was doing his best to plan.

He was listening hard to see if he could make out anything in the firing patterns that might tell him how the fighters were deployed. Unfortunately it was hopeless. Either the firing was lighter or he was losing his hearing.

Sweeping his torchbeam around the bedroom one last time, he noticed a possible accessory for his human bomb costume. A metal crank showed at the edge of the heavy purple drapes shrouding the windows. That was how the windows were opened and closed. He wanted the crank. He seized it and tugged at it and it slipped easily off the shank it was meant to turn. The shank was square and it fit into a square slot in the butt of the crank. There was no securing pin or screw. He had been worried that the crank mechanism might have been rusted. But in the Kalahari nothing rusted. That was worth keeping in mind. He wanted to laugh. He had the crank. It was going to look good. He forced the butt of the crank deeply into the overlapped tape bindings so that the handle projected at the foot of the bundle, where his right hand could quickly grasp it. Of course, it was a joke. But it was a joke that only had to remain unpenetrated for a relatively short period of time. He went to the mirror again and lit himself up, armed as he was for war. He realized that there was a sense in which to the intelligent eye the crank would seem to imply that the bomb he was carrying was primed by clockwork of some kind. He didn't care. It was the overall effect that counted and the overall effect was good.

He disheveled his hair. It was an afterthought. It seemed appropriate.

In the corridor again, he felt he was getting better oriented. This main building was in the shape of a laterally stretched-out block letter U, with the shorter elements, the uprights, constituted by the east and west wings, and the long base span between them constituting the central mass of the building. It was a considerable piece of construction. He was through with this wing of the building. The stairway connecting the first and second floors was located at the southwest elbow of the building. The endless-looking corridor to the east wing lay unexplored before him.

The place was eccentric. The baseboards were carved in the same serpentine pattern as the banisters. Armies of people had been charged with keeping the woodwork polished. There were heavy black beams in the ceilings. He didn't want this place to burn.

Exactly halfway down the corridor of the main section of the building he found what he was looking for. There was an alcove with a narrow tin-clad door set into one wall. There were nail-punch designs in the tin facing, fruit motifs, insofar as he could tell. This was not going to be a door leading to a closet or pantry. He didn't know how he knew, but he did.

The door was unlocked.

He inched the door open. There was light coming down from above. A wash of heat touched him. A steep, straight flight of iron stairs led to the open sky. The sky was streaked with smoke. There was a trapdoor at the top of the stairs and it seemed to be secured in the open position. He closed the door. There had been blood on the stair treads. He knew the smell.

He could go up immediately or he could go back and retrieve his gun. He was feeling strongly that he had cached the gun too far away. If he had the gun, he could drag it inconspicuously behind him as he proceeded with his original plan or he could stow it someplace closer to where he was going to be. It wasn't that he was giving up his plans, his plan, it was that he was trying to refine what he was going to do.

He ran to retrieve the rifle and returned with it to the alcove, where he let himself collapse, sinking down against the door, to get his breath. He was hungry.

He had to go up there now. He supposed his idea was to terrify people into doing something he ordered them to. He would decide how to act once he saw what he was going to be confronted with, that is, whether he should act like a fou, a nut, or like a coldblooded type, a zealot but cold.

He started up the stairs. He couldn't let go of the gun. He thought, Anyway, we are all fragile puddings, doomed slumping puddings trying to stay hard as long as we can. It was conceivable he was just about to expose himself to sudden death. He had to get himself in order, be clear, concentrate his mind. He couldn't set aside more time to do it because he'd already dithered enough. He had to be in order, though. He would give himself until he got to the top of the stairway to the roof. He would have to be succinct. But he had to mount the stairs very deliberately anyway, because he had to avoid slipping in the blood on the stairs and because he had to favor his knees, his right knee, spare it for whatever exertions were going to be called for.

He began the ascent. The angle was not quite vertical and there was no railing to grip. Dragging the rifle up with him, behind him, was difficult and made for slower going. He wanted to be clear, as clear about what he was doing as Yeats's Irish airman.

One, step one, was Iris, and there was nothing to say about Iris beyond love and the size of his loss and that was it. If he was going to be shot to death and Iris was the last thing on his mind he wouldn't mind.

Two was Africa. He had been happy in Africa and he was guilty about that and he would do something for Africa in the next act, because it looked bad for Africa, and not only Botswana. There was the virus, seropositivity as they called it, and Morel saying that it was going to be a holocaust. There was nothing he could do about it. Of course Morel no doubt thought the answer was to go and dynamite churches, and possibly Parliament as well. They were doing nothing, and Africa was slipping into the valley of the shadow of death. He didn't know whose fault it was. He wanted Morel to be wrong about this and for science to come up with something. He prayed for it.

Three was the agency. He had to have mixed feelings about the agency. After all it had come into existence only after the West realized that the communists had organized a huge espionage machine larger and more aggressive and successful than anything in the West or even than the whole West together, and after the West realized that legal communist parties everywhere were being used as spotters and resources for spies, and after it became obvious the communists were setting new standards in ruthlessness, as in throwing oppositionists into crematoria during the Spanish Civil War. And then there had been the likelihood that the people at the top of the communist machine were clinically insane, paranoid, as the Moscow Trials demonstrated. So, all that was true. But then the agency had gone wrong, in places, in many places, in the marches of the empire, in Indonesia for sure, in Central America the same, in Afghanistan, and in Africa, especially in Malawi and Zaire, but not only there. And he knew that the agency was going to survive the collapse of the Russians and continue using its power dubiously, which was why he had to be out if he escaped this alive. Being in the agency meant making impossible judgments, weighing justifiable or virtuous acts against inexcusable ones, mainly because so much on either side of the equation remained secret.

The rifle was proving useful as a crutch. Four was English Literature. He loved it. It was always with him. He thought, On the roof I will do such things as will be the terror of the earth, but what they will be exactly I have no idea, like Tamburlaine. He had been attracted to the Elizabethans, Webster especially, but had decided they were too bloody. Imagine that, he thought.

The stair treads were fixed in a metal casing. There were no risers. He had to grasp at the treads above, using one hand only, and drag himself up, hellward. Sweat was sliding into his eyes but the best he could do to get rid of it was to rub his eyes against his shoulders, which was ineffective. He needed a spare arm. The smell of blood was making him ill.

Five was Rex. He wondered how anyone was supposed to compete with a brother whose first word was brioche and whose last word, according to what had been reported to Iris and relayed to Morel and then to him, whose last word was Mama. My first word was car, he thought. Apparently his parents had given Rex a bite of brioche at some early point and he had loved it and wanted more and voilà. Ray had gotten tired of hearing about it and about Rex's magnificent and precocious vocabulary in general. Rex had been impossible, but still, on his own end, Ray knew he had mismanaged things. He would do what he could for his brother, who was one of the *aoroi*, the dead-too-early. He didn't know why he remembered that. In any case, if he lived, he was going to do a Life of his brother, a vignette, and maybe a chapbook of the best bits and pieces from *Strange News*.

Something was bothering him.

It was the crank. The crank would make him look like an organ grinder. That would be the first impression. He didn't know why it hadn't occurred to him.

He had to get rid of the crank. When he appeared he would just hold his fist in a significant way at the side of the bundle and that would do it. It would have to.

He brought the rifle up onto the step he was standing on and got it between his left leg and the casing, holding it there by pressing his weight against it. With his right hand free, he pulled at the crank. It was difficult. He had done an excellent job of jamming it in among the tapework.

A wavering shadow fell over him as he struggled. He looked up.

It was too literary, or did he mean Gothic? There seemed to be a bird of prey, a vulture, clutching the rim of the opening at the top of the staircase, looking down at him, raising and lowering its wings, shivering them. It was small. Vultures were bigger. It must be a buzzard.

He wasn't afraid. Everything was extreme. He was out of his element.

Because of the brightness he was staring up into he was getting more an impression of the beast than a clear image of it. A string of liquid dripped down from the bird, narrowly missing him. It was vile, whatever it was.

The crank he had been worrying and tugging at came free just then and he flung it underhand as hard as he could, blindly, in the direction of the bird. He hit the thing. It made a feminine-sounding utterance and jerked away and was gone.

Ray continued climbing. He felt urgency. He wanted Quartus. He wanted to bet someone that Quartus was there for him, on the roof.

He crawled out onto the roof. He had his rifle with him. He had dragged it up subtly behind him and now it was with him. The sky was very bright. The roof was a burning plain of white pebbles enclosed by a low ornamental parapet with regularly spaced embrasures, like the roofline of a medieval castle. The parapet was seamless along the edge of the roof.

He looked around as well as he could, keeping flat.

There were veins of smoke in the sky. Before, there had been streams of smoke, sheets of it.

He could see something of where he was and he was in luck. This sector of the roof, at the midpoint of the long transverse connecting the outward wings, was in the hands of the witdoeke. That much he could tell. He was in the midst of a group of witdoeke-wearing fighters, for which he thanked God. He was among them but to the rear of their main position. He counted about a dozen, exactly a dozen, fighters.

The pebbles were burning hot. He needed gloves. He needed water, also.

The fighters were disposed in an arc to his left, west-facing. They were utilizing everything available to them for cover while they fired. The shooting was sporadic but too loud when it came, too loud for him. These were his friends, shooting.

The core of the position was a complex of low-built galvanized iron utility sheds and a pair of absurdly large wooden water tanks set on a raised concrete foundation. No one was paying the least attention to him. The position they were defending was highly improvised. Men were dodging around, firing or just aiming, from beside the service sheds, from behind piled-up sacks of gypsum, if he was reading the lettering on one of the sacks correctly. One of the three sheds had been half kicked down and its siding appropriated and jammed in among the struts supporting the water tanks, augmenting the cover provided by the waist-high concrete base under the tanks. It was all very motley and ragged and people would have to be careful when they shot past their own forward positions.

He had to see more. He stood up. This was the obvious choice for a defensive position. The rooftop ran away blankly, featurelessly, on either hand all the way to the ends of the wings, so far as he could tell.

He wanted to see who was here. He wanted to shake people by the hand and tell them they were doing well, putting up a good fight, which seemed to be the case. He needed to introduce himself.

Standing, he could see where the villains were. They were around the elbow of the building and out at the end of the western wing, collected together there behind their own improvised barricade of ammunition lockers. He thought he saw Nemesis, but he couldn't be sure because of the distance, which had to be at least a hundred yards, and because of the heat-shimmer rising from the roof. He thought he could see some heavy weapons, tripod-mounted machine guns. They were more exposed than the witdoeke, but the range of their weapons was superior. He realized that having to fire at an angle toward the center disadvantaged the villains because they had to thread their fire through the crenellated parapet at two points.

Someone was yelling at him. He couldn't tell who.

He decided to kneel. That would be nonthreatening. The roof surface was littered with spent shells. The witdoeke were miscellaneously armed. Some had hunting rifles but most were using assault rifles, the ones with the curved magazines whose name escaped him. He wondered where the witdoeke had gotten them. He had paid poor attention during firearms training at the agency and now he regretted it, but not much. He didn't know if people were shouting at him, to him, he meant, or about him, to one another. There was a lot of shouting.

Someone was gesturing violently at him from beside one of the sheds. He raised his hands over his head. He hoped that was what they wanted.

He had a theory of what had happened with the villains. They were stuck. His theory was that originally they had gone up and installed themselves on that part of the roof in order to rain fire on attackers coming from the direction of the pan. And that would have been an ideal site for an emplacement. But then somehow Kerekang had gotten a team into the building and up onto the roof by stealth. And now the villains had their backs to the pan, from which some light gunfire was still proceeding. And something was keeping them from rappeling down the building, which surely they were equipped to do, although possibly not. But of course that would mean abandoning equipment they couldn't let fall into Ichokela's hands, Kerekang's people's hands. And then likeliest of all was that Kerekang had shooters on the ground close enough to make rappeling unthinkable. That was his theory of the situation.

He thought he should push his rifle farther away from him. He leaned toward it, reaching, which led to actual screaming from some of the witdoeke. He was being misunderstood. He had wanted to give a reassuring sign.

"Dumela," he shouted.

He pointed at his forehead. "Witdoek, ke witdoek," he shouted.

Someone came up behind him and pressed a gun barrel into his back.

Impulsively, he stood up and turned around.

A young man, a boy, really, was pointing a pump-action shotgun at him. He was in a state of alarm and confusion. He was retreating a few steps. Ray realized he knew the boy, from the university. He was wearing bush shorts, and a tee shirt from the main craft shop in the capital. It was a sky-blue tee shirt and bore the legend Keep Botswana Tidy. Iris had bought three of those shirts to give as presents. The young man was wearing his witdoek, like his comrades. I would like to have comrades, Ray thought.

Ray said, "Dumela, rra. I believe I know you from university. I am a teacher, rra. I am from St. James's. Ke mang St. James's."

The boy was thin. The combat boots he was wearing belonged on sturdier legs than his. It was wrong for this boy to be here. It was altogether wrong. He had to do something. The boy was moving further back. He slid the pump action forward and back. Obviously it was the bundle on Ray's chest. It had to be that.

Ray slapped the bundle, prompting the young man to drop to a crouch, a firing stance.

"No," Ray said, slapping the bundle even more heartily and forcing himself to smile.

Two other fighters, older and rougher and more rustic-looking men, approached, their rifles aimed at him. It was peculiar, because everyone in the encounter was hunched over, stooping to one degree or another, out of prudence. And that reminded him that he needed to get his head down too. He was taller than any of the three people he was dealing with. He doubted that the two new arrivals spoke English. He would tell them he was with them, that he was their friend.

"Ke tsala. Witdoek. Ke tsala."

The older men wanted him to do something about the bundle. He wasn't going to. The damned loops around his neck were cutting into his flesh and it would be his pleasure to get the whole thing off him just for ten minutes but there was no way he was going to relinquish it in the circumstances he was in.

He addressed the boy, the student, whose name was coming to him. It was Kevin. And his last name was coming to him and it was Tsele. He had been a member of the Student Representative Council. They had spoken. Kevin had been a firebrand of some kind.

Ray said, "Kevin, listen to me. I am Professor Finch. I am here to help you. Look, this is only a manuscript, here. You can feel it. I will hold my hands all the way up, like this. You feel it. I know what you think. But this is paper in here, a book."

Cautiously, Kevin approached, saying something to the two other men. He lightly punched the bundle. Then he pried at it.

Kevin said, "It is like a bomb, rra, to my eye. But so why are you carrying it about in this way? And rra, you are naked, I see."

"Because it is a precious thing of my brother's. It is a keepsake. It is a very long story, Kevin. He is just dead." Ray was using locutions from Botswana English. Normally he didn't. But he wanted to be completely comprehended. Because he wanted to find Quartus and get him and he wanted to shake Kerekang's hand and help him get out of this and begone, be somewhere else, if he would go, walking around with all his limbs working, somewhere else with snow and lakes.

"Ehe, then come away. You must have to explain why you have come amongst all this. But you may do that in time, rra. Because we are in a spot. But you are naked."

"I know it," Ray said forcefully.

Kevin led him away to crouch in the lee of the water-tank foundation. Kevin was uneasy with him, naturally. He reminded Ray to keep his head low. This was the safest area in the whole position, Ray realized. He appreciated being put there.

The two older men were returning to their places. They were taking his rifle along with them. They were staring at him. He wanted them to know that there was only one bullet, that it was chambered, and that he had no more ammunition. He thought the word for bullet was lerumo but he wasn't certain. He was tired. They could come back to him if they wanted more information.

Kevin sat down next to him. He said, "Rra, you know these men who are killing us, they are killers from Namibia, koevoet. We will send them back to that place. They have killed in Namibia from before. So we have to kill them. We are taking their weapons."

Ray explained about Wemberg's rifle and its solitary round.

Kevin said, "I want to know how is that old man. We said to him he must stay back, but he came following behind us and then we saw he was all blood. We sent him down, then. And when I went to look he was gone."

"Yes, that's a man I know from Gaborone, a very good man. No, I hope he's okay. He's being seen to. There is a doctor. We were held by koevoet, but we got free. The old man is my friend."

There was a violent fusillade. The tanks were hit. Bits of shattered wood showered on them. The tanks were dry.

"They are hitting high, you see," Kevin said.

"That's heavy ammunition."

"Ehe, and now we see they have their second gun back to use again. For a time they had only one big one to use. We have got to go and kill them. Come and I'll show you something."

Kevin crept over to the parapet. Ray crept behind him and joined him there.

"We have done this," he said. He directed Ray to put his head through one of the embrasures and look down.

Below was the vast courtyard filling the space between the arms of the U. Koevoet had made the mistake of turning the area into a car park and, obviously, not guarding it securely. Ray was looking into a well of destruction. There were ten vehicle carcasses, some still smoking, most of them trucks of different sizes. But at least one armored personnel carrier was among the wrecks. It was a brilliant example of what guerrillas could do with a box of matches, if they got a chance, if the wrong door was left open. It was astonishing that the building hadn't gone up too. Apparently there had been enough distance between the clustered vehicles and the building walls to keep it from happening before some form of firefighting had taken place. He could see places where the walls were blackened. He didn't want Ngami Bird Lodge to burn. And he was making a mental inventory of the damage he was observing. It was a reflex.

Kevin brought him back to the place under the tanks. Ray wanted to know where the water had come from to fight the courtyard fire if the rooftop tanks were empty. He asked Kevin about it and was told that there were two deep wells out near the pan that fed directly into another set of tanks under the kitchen.

"I am going to kill these evil things," Kevin said, aiming his shotgun skyward.

He meant the buzzards. Three of them were circling low over the roof.

He said, "You see what they do, these koevoet. We saw it. If one of their comrades dies they push him off onto the ground to lie there. So as to keep these birds down there."

"I saw one of them. I took his boots."

"You should have taken his trousers . . . I was shooting down these birds, but our chief said I must stop."

"To save on ammunition, you mean."

"Ehe."

"So who is in charge of this group?"

"Nyah, rra. We cannot discuss about it."

"What do you mean?"

"We are forced to be secret. We can take any name. We are not giving names to be reported. And when you return to Gaborone you must never say you saw Kevin Tsele."

"So what name are you using, then?"

"Myself, I am Lesheusheu, if you know that word."

"No idea."

"It is a scorpion. The big yellow one."

"Ah, those. So is Rra Kerekang with us here?"

"Rra, you see in ISA we cannot speak about who is leading us. Because that is what koevoet wants to know, where is Setime. They want to take him away."

"Setime is fire-thrower, am I right, means fire-thrower, or means incendiary, arsonist?"

"Ehe. We are laying fire everywhere. We will chase Domkrag away from here. We will burn this place."

"This building? You don't want to do that."

"We do."

Ray wanted to argue, but he was too tired for it. He had to husband himself for what he was going to do. He was going to make a contribution. He was going to perform an act. He needed water. He had to get clear about Quartus, where he was. He needed his binoculars. He shifted his position in order to keep himself squarely in the shade of the tanks.

Kevin wanted him to come away to another part of the position. Ray didn't want to leave the shade. Kevin wanted him to follow him into one of the service sheds. He was explaining why. Someone in the shed needed to see him, their chief. He needed to say what would be done as to him, Ray. He was being summoned.

It was true. Somebody was waving urgently from the shed doorway. Ray couldn't see him. It was dark in the shed. He wanted it to be Kerekang. He wanted to see Kerekang and convince him to get away from this before he was caught, get the hell out. He wanted to go to the shed but he didn't know if he could manage. If someone promised he could get iced tea in the shed he would be able to manage.

A new blast of gunfire shook the tank above him. He was shaking. He was looking at Kevin. A splinter had been driven into his neck. The tank had been struck at a lower level than before. The villains were improving their aim, getting it lower.

Kevin was cursing, which was a good sign, Ray hoped. Ray went to him. He wanted to be the one to pull the splinter out. He was afraid Kevin would be too abrupt about it and break it off or not get all of it out.

"Don't touch it," he said to Kevin. The boy was frightened. He could die, Ray thought.

Ray nipped the splinter with his thumb and all four fingers where it went into the boy's neck. He didn't know if it was more a shard or a splinter. It wasn't really a splinter because it was bigger, it was the size of a what, a thing much thinner than a pencil but still not a splinter. The question was how far it had gone into this child's neck.

"Close your eyes," Ray said. He was being an automaton. Kevin obeyed.

Ray repeated himself. "Close your eyes," he said even more forcefully as he pulled the splinter out, jerked it out, and pressed the wound closed.

"It's fine, really is," Ray said, feeling faint. It was a small wound, but it was bleeding a lot. An antiseptic was needed.

Kevin was being compliant.

Thank God it's regular bleeding, not a vein, not an artery, so thank you sweet God, thanks a lot.

He was afraid to let go of the wound, but did.

They crawled toward the service shed, Kevin wiping at his wound.

He had to do something. He was being overwhelmed by the wrongness of things. And there was something else. What he was going to do had to be done soon, because he was not a black person and the sun he was getting on the roof, amplified by its white pebbled surface, was going to fry him. It would be beyond sunburn. He needed a hat. He needed his pants. He needed his shirt. He was an idiot. His dead skin would slough off like his brother's, in the old days, in his youth.

It would be great if suddenly the sky were full of flying saucers, fleets of them, all the same size, metallic, confounding everyone, and then there would be a voice on the media the radio the television everything saying there was a person who was designated to say what should be done to fix up the wrongness of the world and it would be him. And maybe a beam would come down from one of them, the main one if there was a main one, and touch him and he would rise up, full of power.

He felt better than he had. He was going to be part of history. Somebody would be interested in this what, skirmish, these events, and he would be part of the story, some part of it. People found him terrifying, with his brother's manuscript on his chest. He wanted to look terrifying. He stood up and shook himself. He was still going to be part of it. He was going to. No one was stopping him. And when the beam touched him he would have the power to turn any weapon every weapon of every kind including the most secret, most mountainous weapon into shit.

He stood up and stretched. He needed to look as tall as possible for what he was going to do. He was tired of hunching over.

It felt like all the witdoeke were shouting at him at once from various points around the position. "Lower yourself," someone shouted. And they were giving shrieking whistling. It was a campaign to get him to get down and go into the shed. He had never mastered the art of sticking his fingers into his mouth in a certain way and producing a sound so piercing his mother would come and say to quit, immediately. His brother had. And his brother had refused to show him how it was done.

Kevin was in the shed. Ray wanted to follow, go in and say hello and shake hands. He wanted to say hello to the chief, assuming the chief was there and available. He thought, By now Kevin will have explained me, explained who I am, a bystander but on their side, a friend of Wemberg, a naked friend of Wemberg, all of that. The feeling of wanting to shake hands with everybody was something he had to stop. It made no sense.

He wanted to shake hands with the chief and he wanted the chief to be Kerekang, his friend Kerekang. He had to go in there.

The shed was a windowless crude squat structure built so low that it was impossible to stand up in it. There was light coming in from a long horizontal gap in the west wall, where the siding had been dislocated and wrenched downward to make a firing port. A witdoek was sighting his gun through it but not, Ray thanked God, firing. Because the sound of firing in the enclosed space of the shed would be enough to drive anyone insane, and he was already insane. He noticed something that made sense. Witdoeke in the shed had shredded cloth jammed into their ears, threads hanging down. That included the chief, with whom he wanted to have a chat.

I have to get out of here before they begin shooting, he thought. And that was because he wanted not to be deaf in his next life.

The chief was not Kerekang. He had a long face. He was about forty. He had one good eye and one half-shut, scarred eye. With his bare hand he was dabbing gasoline on Kevin's splinter wound.

Kevin said something, indicating the chief. Mokopa, was what it had sounded like, which would no doubt be the chief's nom de guerre. Kevin said it again. Ray didn't know what mokopa meant. One guess would be that it meant an animal, a ferocious one. Ferocious creatures were popular when you were renaming yourself and getting into violent undertakings.

"Mokopa is the black snake, the long one, rra."

"Dumela, rra," the chief said, reaching to feel the packet on Ray's chest. The man had terrible body odor. Someone in the shed did. Maybe everyone in the shed did. The chief was wearing a cowhide vest stained black under the arms and a pair of somebody else's khaki slacks. They were huge on him. He wanted to lock away in his mind a decent description of this man. He was good at description, but he was apprehending people generically or in outline, not individually, because now fear was not letting him concentrate and also because he wanted to get as far away from this man's effluvium as he could. These people were individuals, and when he arrived at writing about them someday he wanted to have distinct images. But he felt he had to get out of the shed immediately and get on with his plan, such as it was.

He could see that what they were doing was making gasoline bombs, Molotov cocktails. They were decanting gasoline into Castle lager bottles and then stuffing torn-up cloth wicks into the mouths. They had produced seven or so of them. The enterprise going on there constituted another good reason for him to exit and get on with his own plan, solo. It was dangerous, what they were doing. Some kind of spark and he could be an ingredient in a fireball. Also the shed was an oven.

Another witdoek came over and began investigating Ray's packet, but too roughly. These friends were not realizing something. They were jerking at his packet and laughing. But they were overlooking something. His packaging was weakening if not yet unraveling, exactly. But it had a limited life span, like everything except rocks and sand and death itself, which went on forever, so far as anyone could tell. He could imagine a situation where he would be presenting himself as the terror of the earth and his bundle would come apart and reveal that he was terrifying everyone with pages and pages and pages of this and that, text, pages fluttering, flying around him like doves, the stupidest bird in the animal kingdom, if he remembered correctly. Already he was having to hold it together more. And there would be laughter, hideous. But in the shed everyone was accepting, no doubt thanks to Kevin, and that was nice, but it had to be adieu pretty soon. They were seeing him as an eccentric but good person of some sort. They trusted him. That was fine but he had to get out of there. The witdoeke were looking at each other, patronizing him kindly, evidently, so far as he could tell in this pocket of hell he was in. No one was looking at his penis.

"I am going to try something," Ray said to Kevin, but including the chief in his zone of discourse, with his glances.

"What is it, rra?" Kevin asked.

"First, does Rra Mokopa understand English, or will you have to translate?" Ray felt foolish asking the question but he had decided it was a better choice than asking Mokopa directly and having him shake his head no, which was to say that as a choice it was less shaming, but only if he was right and the man's English was going to be rudimentary. The Batswana were preternaturally sensitive to things they thought were insults, he was sorry to say, but it was true.

Kevin said, "Rra, he can understand you, but he will not speak it except a little, at times."

"Gosiame. Okay here is my plan." Ray was glad to be talking about his plan because it would allow him to discover what it was, in fact. What he had was parts of a plan.

Ray said, "First do you have any pistols among you, handguns?"

Kevin said something to the chief, who said something to the others, and the answer that came back was no. So that was one part of the plan he could forget, using a pistol or two in his grand advance, his great act.

Kevin said, "Rra, you must be more quick and we must all of us be quick. Because they can be summoning help from Omega, helicopters. We think they have some radioing equipment with them there. So we must crush them in some way, and very soon. But if we go over there they will slaughter us, and if they come down this way we will kill them one by one. So they must stay with their heavy guns. We are both stuck. We have more witdoeke behind the pan and a few on the ground nearby, a few only. But our comrades behind the pan are held down by koevoet, by the heavy guns. There are twenty left, koevoet, after we killed some. And they have no escape. We have burned their transport . . ."

Mokopa was clearly following. In the country of the blind . . . Ray thought, not needing to complete the quotation. And he thought he was detecting a gleam from Mokopa's good eye suggesting interest, suggesting that this lakhoa might be able to do something insane but useful. He obviously wanted to know what it was Ray wanted to try. I am a fox, Ray thought. He needed help, for his plan, a more appropriate weapon than the Enfield, covering-fire, anything they could do.

A new blast of firing shook the shed. Ray noted the pinging sounds of bullets striking metal, not the shed but the piping and the understructure of the water tanks. Everything was telling him to hurry.

He pulled out the witdoek he had stuffed under his wrappings and tied it on, nonchalantly, he thought, like a nonchalant samurai. It was an association he couldn't resist and why should he? Iris loved Toshirô Mifune. She had loved him as a young actor and she loved him middle-aged, so she claimed, nothing had diminished in him, which was the way the eye of love should work.

It had been a good idea, putting on the witdoek. His comrades liked it. That was good. Although he was taking a chance wearing it, because there was a way in which if he had to approach the killers at the end of the roof with the witdoek as an identifier it might cut down the time he could get close enough to them to let them interpret his bomb costume and feel fear and trembling and the urge to surrender and throw down their arms. He had every reason so far to think he was a convincing simulacrum of a human bomb. I am a triumph, he thought.

He had to hurry. He said, "Here is my plan. There is a man among the koevoet, their chief, I want to capture and take away. His name is Quartus. He has a big chin. I believe he is there. It makes sense that he is there." There was a murmur among his friends. He thought it meant that they were affirming that Quartus was there. But they weren't being absolute about it. Because he kept saying he was going to give them his plan and he hadn't done it yet. All he could think of was catching Quartus and putting him in a sack and taking him back to Gaborone and opening the sack and letting him out and asking him politely how he had come to be in this fine country Botswana and what he had been doing in it and who had paid him and what else he had done in Namibia and elsewhere.

"Rra, we are going to kill them, to a man," Kevin said.

Ray said, "I don't think you should. I know you want to. I tell you, though, this man is important. He knows things that can make big trouble for Domkrag. If I can catch him, you can ask Kerekang, ask Setime. I am telling you he will agree with me. We can hold this man for Setime, if I can catch him. But here is my plan."

He was improvising furiously. He said, "This is what I need. I am going to creep on my hands to the corner of the roof and then you will fire at them to keep their heads down while I run close . . . And, I don't know, you could throw one of these fire bombs, maybe, just to distract them. You see I have to surprise them . . ."

He had a theatrical image of how it could be. There would be confusion. There would be obscurity, smoke, distraction, and he would step out of the obscurity and be fearsome, striding at them, possibly shouting something he hadn't yet decided on.

Kevin was translating. Mokopa was listening but seemed to be smiling, or controlling smiling, would be more accurate.

There was more to it. "Listen, you will have to lend me an AK." That was essential. He would need a respectable weapon to reinforce his command of things, if things went his way, at all. The Enfield was no threat. It was more trouble than it was worth, just for the one big shot it could deliver.

Kevin said, "You say you can frighten them."

"Oh I think I can. I'll tell them they can live, we will spare them."

There was a sharp, quick exchange in Setswana between Kevin and the chief. Something was being kept from him.

The thing was to do something great, a great act. Ray could feel himself entering the act, getting ready, believing he could do it and crushing away any thought of what it would be like if his act failed, which was easy because that would be endless night.

The chief signaled to one of his soldiers that he should turn over his assault rifle to Ray. Ray couldn't believe it. He had to remember the drill with the AK. He had fired them in the past. It was coming back to him. His hands were trembling. Everyone was looking at him. The AK was much lighter than the Enfield.

I am a bomb, he thought. He scuttled backward out of the shed, delighted to be in the terrible sunlight again.

If this was going to work, it was going to work like a dance. Once he got to the corner it would become a dance and he would have to stop thinking and dance it through. It would be a ballet, starring him, or a musical, starring him. He hated musicals. Iris liked them and probably so did Morel.

Ray could feel a vague rearrangement going on among the witdoeke.

There were more of them than he'd thought, tucked away in various niches. They were emerging to get a better look at him, it seemed. Mokopa had come out of the shed and was crawling here and there consulting with his men or telling them what to do, all with reference to Ray. He was feeling honored that they had so readily turned over one of their prime weapons, the AK-47, to him. But he was realizing something. They had a surplus of the weapon. He saw one fighter carrying three of them in his arms, cradling them, pushing himself along backward in a sitting position, taking the guns to the command shed.

Ray examined the AK-47. It was an intelligent machine. It went together intelligently. Everything was fine with it. The magazine was heavy. He hated it. He could spray death all over the place with it, killing idiotically. He wanted to avoid that if he could. The rifle was going to play a secondary role. He slipped the shoulder sling around his neck and shifted the rifle well back, along his left side. It would just be there, available, when he needed it. But it was more like a prop. That was what he hoped it would be.

He had worked his way over to the parapet on the north side of the roof. Kevin had come out of the shed and was crawling to join him. The boy had a strip of cloth tied around his neck, covering the wound. He didn't look well. He looked gray. All of this would be changed one way or another.

Kevin caught up with Ray. He had a Molotov cocktail with him. His pockets were stuffed with something, probably shotgun shells. Ray hadn't noted that before. But Kevin had come without his shotgun. He had only the one task of creating a bloom of fire Ray could dance around in his role as the angel of death. It would be best if he could actually appear out of it, emerge out of a cloud of flame, but that was not imaginable. He would burn up, for one thing.

Behind them a thunderous blast sounded. They looked around and could see a sheet of metal like a wing flying off and over the side of the building. One of the three sheds was now roofless, not the command shed. One of the heavy machine guns had done its work well. Everything was combining to tell Ray to go.

"I have to go now. When you see me at the corner and you see I am standing up, straight up, that is when you pitch that thing out as far in front of me as you can. Where are your matches?"

Kevin held up a lighter.

"Gosiame. Wish me luck, Kevin."

Kevin saluted, which surprised Ray. I like it, Ray thought.

"Wait, rra. This also. When you see it explode you must wait and count to five, Mokopa says, to let us fire on them before you advance, so they don't shoot you down from a distance. It will give you some seconds to go forward."

"Very good." He saluted Kevin. It seemed appropriate, although odd because Kevin was still with him as he crawled toward the elbow of the roof. He was at his heels. Saluting had been saying goodbye, but Kevin was right there. And of course it made sense for Kevin to be as close to the emplacement as he could get, so that he could plant the fire bomb well down the roof. Nothing mattered.

It would be a relief to stand up. But he was not standing up quite yet.

He put his head out around the turn of the roof, put it out more minutely and slowly than he would have believed possible. When he could see he made himself freeze. The headband was performing a function. It was helping keep sweat out of his eyes. He definitely could see the enemy.

He didn't know if the emplacement was as formidable as it looked or if it was mainly the comparison with the, he would have to say, rather free-form ad hoc picture the witdoeke position represented. Everyone he was seeing was in fatigues. The men operating the heavy guns were wearing helmets or some sort of protective headgear. There was a substantial barrier fronting the position, consisting of presumably empty ammunition lockers for the most part, which looked better than it could possibly be. It was a Potemkin barrier. Maybe sand had been poured into them. If the number of lockers piled up in front of the position meant anything, the villains had lots of ammunition to play with. They were also well equipped otherwise, to the extent that they had parasols they were using. The heavy-caliber guns looked extremely nasty. Two were aimed at him directly, it felt like. They could fire in a broad arc, and had been firing at the extreme north end of the arc, picking the witdoeke position to pieces, until just now, when they seemed to be trained specifically on the field in which he was about to dance. He could make out Quartus. He was seeing a man urinating over the side of the building and it was Quartus. That was all he needed. He would dance.

Goodbye, then, he thought. He stood up.

He could see Botswana all around him. It was a temptation, the vista was. To the west Botswana was yellow and brown and rumpled, in the south it was yellow and flat, to the north it was impossible to say because smoke was in the way, and to the east it was yellow and flat and then it turned gray-green at the horizon that was the delta. He liked this country. He filled his lungs and began to run.

He ran crouching, keeping close to the parapet.

He had to think of what he was going to say. He had been assuming it would be obvious to him. So far nothing was suggesting itself. He was going to announce himself as *what*? *Think*, he thought.

He saw the fire bomb, lit and smoking, curve through the air. It landed and exploded brilliantly to his left, ahead of him. The heat from the burst struck him. In fact he had been splashed with fire and was burning in one spot on his bundle. Frantically, he slapped the fire out, and reminded himself to run more slowly because there would be some helpful shooting in five or was it ten or was it twenty seconds. The blaze was a success. It was big. In fact it was not one fire but several separate ones. He was going to be able to run between the fires and appear out of their midst exactly as he had wanted. He slowed down.

You have to slow down, he thought. Definitely he was hearing shots coming steadily from behind, from his friends. That came to an end.

He stepped away from the parapet and stood up and shouted hello. He moved out to the center of the roof and entered the garden of flames, as he thought of it.

He was going to approach walking. That would flummox them, or some of them. I am a bomb, he thought. There was the song from a musical that went Be a tree be a sled be a purple spool of thread. Be a bomb, he thought. I am dead, he thought.

He held his arms out like Christ on the cross. He made a roaring sound, a nonsense sound, which was the best he could do. He had to be slower. He had to stride, even strut. He kept going.

The garden of fire was relaxing, shrinking, he was glad, because he had been afraid it might set the whole roof on fire and then the building would go and then he would fall through fire. He had almost come here with Iris, which might have been lovely and changed everything between them. Who knows? he thought.

And now he would be a gem for her, his beloved, a thing in a locket in her mind if anyone could be counted on to record or remember what he was doing, however it went. There was going to be a story in any case whether he won or he lost, and if he lost, it would be Morel downstairs, safe, fucking around, who would tell it. Because he wanted to be a brave thing on her cheating heart forever, the locket of her heart. They could fuck themselves.

He was close, he was close to the emplacement. This was it.

"Go back," he said.

And then he said something like *Ho*, fiercely.

And then he said, "*Go back go back*. I have a bomb, go back." And he said it, shrieked it, again. He hardly recognized his own voice. His voice was a separate thing, separate from him.

Smoke from the fire-bomb blaze came with him, helping him.

He wanted to be large, straight as a post, and full, full of obvious danger.

He stopped ten or so feet from the emplacement, amazed to be still alive, still standing.

A bullet kicked up pebbles from the roof near his feet, but it came from behind him, from his friends. He wished they would stop now. Everything was up to him. They could stop.

"Go back," he shouted again, unnecessarily, because they seemed to have already done that.

He hesitated about climbing up onto the barrier of ammunition lockers. His instinct was to surmount it gradually, but that was wrong and he knew it. He had to be the opposite of cautious because he was in possession of death. He pulled two of the lockers out of the stack, so he could enter this new district of hell. The lockers were empty. They were heavy things but they were empty. They were fakes.

He expected to be dead shortly. He climbed through the breach in the lockers.

"*Go back and put your guns down. Throw them down,*" he shouted, arriving among the enemy.

They were cowering back and there were fewer of them than he had calculated there would be.

"I will blow you to death," he shouted, embarrassed at the formulation.

They were believing him, the seven or eight villains, no only seven, that were there packed in around their cumbersome big artillery which was now useless to them, couldn't be aimed at him, because he was there and they were believing he was the angel of death.

"You don't want to die," he said. He said it to Quartus. Quartus was to the rear of the position, near the third heavy gun. He was wearing sun goggles. He was not smiling.

Ray had to stop telling them to put their guns down, he realized. Because they had only been employing their mounted guns, one at the back and two at the front, and relying on their superior force and range to keep the witdoeke back and bit by bit chop their position to pieces. Their automatic rifles were stacked to one side. They had been overconfident. Quartus did have a holstered pistol strapped on.

"You, you fuck, put your hands high. You hear me?" Quartus put his hands up. Ray couldn't believe it.

Ray knew he had to be swift. He was an illusionist and the illusion was not going to work for long.

He was creating unhappiness. He strode to the cache of automatic rifles and stood over it. If he ever got reinforcements he would toss the rifles off the roof. He wanted Quartus's pistol but he didn't want to approach him to get it. He didn't want scrutiny.

"Take off your belt," he said to Quartus.

Quartus was moving too slowly in complying. Ray knew what to do. It was time to bring his own rifle into play. It was delicate, switching to a different way of menacing these bastards, because they might all jump at him in a rage when they realized his bomb was not a bomb, as they would soon enough. And then he would be forced to spray death at them, real death.

They might think that since he couldn't kill all of them it would make sense for them to rush him. He had to get them on their bellies spread-eagled. It was going to be hard on them. There were the burning pebbles to contend with and there were glittering and equally burning hot spent shells everywhere, strewn everywhere. And he had to get Quartus disarmed and under control. Quartus was operating in slow motion. He was looking for an opening. But his rage was evident. He was nonplussed. I love it, Ray thought.

"I said to take your belt off. Let your pistol fall. Do what I tell you."

He had to get everyone in a single clump, down on their faces, all of them, the six underlings and Quartus the boss. The six were conveniently arrayed side by side sitting on a low bench. They had responded beautifully to the threatening motions he was making with his AK. They had been drinking, if the empty beer cans in evidence around the position meant anything. Also they had been eating canned pineapple. Ray began to salivate. These bastards had had it cozy, with their beer, water bottles, cigarettes, parasols. There was a tarpaulin stretched over a framework and in the shade it provided were two cots. They had been able to get out of the sun if they'd wanted to, in shifts.

There was a surprising amount of equipment and gear collected there, which meant there must be another route of access from below at this end of the roof. He could see where it was. It was a large trapdoor, much larger than the one covering the stair-ladder access he had come up, at the center of the roof. Awkward objects had been brought up. The machine gun stands were bolted to heavy wooden skids. The good thing was that the trapdoor lid was locked, or shut securely, rather, with the hasp of an open combination lock passed through the hoop closure at the rim. There would be no surprises coming from that source, at least.

Quartus had dropped his belt and the pistol had fallen to the roof, still in its holster.

"Kick it this way," Ray shouted.

Quartus complied, but feebly. Ray knew what Quartus would do next. He would kick the holster and belt as hard as he could in the direction of the other villains, on the chance that one of them could make a grab for it. That was not going to happen.

"Step back all the way," Ray said to Quartus. He wanted him in the right-hand angle of the parapet, away from the mounted gun pointed down into the pan, away from anything. And then he would bring him around to join his fellow villains on his belly on the roof.

Quartus had taken his sun goggles off, ripped them off. He was staring at Ray. He had wanted to see if what he was seeing could possibly be right, that a naked man with some kind of box on his chest was indeed in charge of events and that the box on his chest was not a bomb.

It was urgent that he get the six foot soldiers down, flat, out of the way.

"Lie down, all of you! All you six, you lie down, ribama." Ribama meant stomach in Setswana. Robala meant lie down, but it meant lie down and go to sleep.

They knew what to do, and they were spreading their arms without being told. And they were groaning.

"What are you playing at?" Quartus screamed. He was alarmingly red in the face. He was normally ruddy, but this was a new level of color.

"I'm not playing. I'll kill you if you don't listen to me," Ray shouted.

"You prick, look at you! Your prick is showing. Cover your prick. I see they have let you out . . ."

"Ah no, meneer, I broke out of your prison. Hahaha."

"You are going to die, I tell you that."

"You move into the corner where I'm pointing. Go. I'll kill you if you're slow about it, meneer. And you say nothing to me from now on, nothing. Put your hands higher than that. The catch is up on my rifle."

Quartus was beginning to obey, beginning to edge in the direction he had been ordered to take. Ray was feeling gratified. He had let his penis show, let it be there like nothing more exotic than a nose or an elbow, because that had been what was required. It was a personal victory, a thing he had done for the cause. The hair in Quartus's armpits was red.

Quartus shouted something in Afrikaans. Ray had an idea that what he was saying was that Ray was carrying a fake bomb around, not a real bomb. He couldn't be allowed to talk again.

"*I warned you, meneer,*" Ray shouted. And he pressed the trigger of his rifle, pressed it as tentatively and lightly as he could, intending to release a very short burst, not more than five bullets. The violence of the burst surprised him, and the volume of the fire he had released. He had used at least ten or a dozen bullets. He was trying furiously to remember how many shots there were, in the magazine. He had to be frugal. Quartus would be counting. He had only the one magazine with him.

Quartus was limping. Ray had directed his fire at the roof near Quartus's feet. He hadn't intended to hit him. He was sorry if he had.

The shooting had been salutary in its effect on the foot soldiers. Any restlessness among them was gone. They were unmoving. They were like carvings.

Quartus was where he should be, sitting on the parapet far to the right, his hands still raised. His legs looked all right. Ray didn't know why he had seemed to be limping. It might have been a trick. Anything could be a trick.

Ray thought, This interlude has to stop being an interlude. He needed help. He needed reinforcements. He needed his friends to come to his aid. Where were they? He needed to get out of the sun. In fact he needed to get his naked penis out of the sun, especially. Because the two items of the body most susceptible to sun damage were, if he remembered what Iris had said on the subject, the penis and, sort of oddly, the eyelids. It had come up during a discussion of nude beaches. In any case he wanted his penis to accompany him into the next stage of his life. He might need it.

His ears were ringing. It was astonishing to him that technology had failed to address the fucking deafening racket guns made.

He was noticing something important at the back of the shelter housing the two cots. His attention had been drawn there by Quartus, who had been glancing nervously in that direction. And the important something was a radio setup. There was an aerial mast sticking up. He had missed it. He felt stupid for having missed it.

I will blow it to hell, he thought. He crouched and aimed and fired and his bullets tore the thing to pieces. But he had used more ammunition than he'd intended, again. Quartus was screaming at him. That meant Ray had done a good thing.

It was too difficult keeping his menacing attention equally on Quartus where he was and the foot soldiers where they were.

"*Come over here, now*," he shouted at Quartus. Quartus stood up. He seemed to be smiling about something.

"*No, get down and crawl, meneer. Crawl to me.*"

Quartus was wearing a tank top and jodhpurs. He loved jodhpurs, apparently. He was moving slowly. He was continuing to smirk. Ray didn't like it.

Witdoeke should be on hand. He wanted to know why they hadn't shown up. Something was amiss.

Ray looked back along the roof and saw instantly what the problem was. He was appalled. He couldn't allow himself to look for more than a moment at the calamity developing behind him. It felt like a calamity, but possibly it was only going to develop into one.

There was a broken wall of fire stretching across the roof, the offspring of the Molotov cocktail blaze that had preceded his foray, a blaze that had seemed to be declining but that was now robust. He could see why Mokopa had probably been holding back on the Molotov cocktails. This was a tarred roof. There was tar under the pebbles. A fire had gotten going in the tar. It wasn't a conflagration, at least not yet. No it was at the stage where if everybody cooperated it could be beaten out, villains and rebels together. The problem was the quantity and blackness of the smoke being generated. Tar was something used in wars to produce smoke screens.

So the fact was that his friends were in the dark about his accomplishments, which now that he thought about it pretty much resembled his situation in life, not that he had ever had that many friends. But you digress, he thought. So his friends were unaware of what he had accomplished in the enemy camp. It wasn't right. It was too much. Too much is enough, he thought.

But at least Quartus was doing as he'd been told, crawling along the rooftop toward him like a dog. And he was a dog. Except that no man is a dog. And *No Isle Is a Mainland* was one of his dead brother's gems. He was afraid. He was in peril. He was weakening. He had to perform strength. He wanted to wrap a towel around his waist in behalf of his penis. He couldn't. He was fully occupied. There were no towels. This was not a locker room.

The witdoeke had no idea what he had accomplished. The dog Quartus crawling toward him knew. But everything was precarious because everything was precarious. All he had to offer, all he really had to offer, was his willingness to kill. They had to believe that, the villains did. He would do it. But he wanted to tell someone what he was going to have to do, to do soon. It was all over for his mock bomb, he knew that. He was sure all of the villains had figured that out. And here was the snake Quartus crawling toward his subordinates like a dog. And Quartus was saying something out of the side of his mouth. There was the word piel in what he was saying, whispering loudly, which Ray just happened to know meant penis, prick, in Afrikaans.

The witdoeke should be arriving, fast. They would like what they would find. There was plenty for them. There were at least two mortar tubes they could take and put to use and there were the shells with little fins on them like little fat goldfish, which had to be around somewhere, unless they had been used up. He didn't know about that. There was booty. Come quick, boys and girls, and help me, he thought.

He motioned Quartus to lie down with the foot soldiers, but not among them, at the outer part of the cluster, nearest him, so that Quartus would kindly reduce the number of targets Ray had to be prepared to aim at from two to just one.

Quartus was still talking subtly. It had to stop. Quartus was whispering. He could die for that, if he kept it up.

Someone had to come to help. There was a ding or a thing going on deep in his body like the tickle that tells you twenty minutes before it happens that you are going to vomit. But this was about fainting. And there was the rub, because if it got any worse before he got help he was going to have to commit murder, kill everyone. The sun was to blame. It was the sun and it was everything else.

He had to get control of the thing, the ting, like hearing the librarian's desk bell ting when he was deep in the stacks, far from her desk but hearing it, clear, and knowing it was time to go, it was closing time.

Piercing whistles sounded from behind him. That was good news. Of course they didn't know he couldn't respond, if that was what they were looking for.

He was thinking odd things. He remembered the faces of the librarians in his life, especially the ones from his youth, with peculiar definiteness and clarity, compared to, say, the faces of tradesmen, the postmen, or even the teachers whose hands he had passed through, whose faces he had stared directly at for hours on end. He was thinking odd things. Quartus had roan-red axillary hair and he was thinking that in his life he had never before seen truly red armpit hair. He couldn't believe his life experience had been so limited. But there it was. It had. So he was going to have to kill a unique specimen, unique as far as he was concerned.

The whistling was closer and more urgent. It meant that his comrades were on the move, coming. He wanted his brother to come back from the dead and whistle for him, whistle anything.

The people under his control didn't like the whistling. The group as a whole was responding as a single organism. It was stiff, stiffer. They probably had their own repertoire of whistles, signaling-whistles.

Little things were going on that he had no time for. The tarpaulin over the cots and the radio set was in flames, adding to the merriment.

His captives were all looking at him out of the sides of their eyes. There was more smoke coming in their direction. He began to cough.

The boy stood on the burning deck, he thought. He could smell mutiny among his captives.

They had to believe he would kill them.

He knew what he had to think, or rather not think but be, and he could do it. He had to be Satan, he had to be Satan saying *Evil, be thou my good,* Book Four. He tried to inhale this thought.

Abruptly, Quartus stood up and ran at Ray.

"I am going to kill you, you poefter," he screamed, astonishingly to Ray, ignoring the gun in his face and grasping at the packet on Ray's chest, this time, flinging himself fully against Ray and trying to do something clever. He was trying to twist the neck tapes into a noose, trying to detach the packet from its main bindings around the back, and strangle Ray in the neck bindings by twisting the packet around and around. But his fingers were slippery with blood and Ray saw what he was trying to do and got the gun barrel up into Quartus's stomach, which calmed the man.

Quartus fell away from him. He fell on his side and then sat up.

They glared at each other.

"Go back with them," Ray said. He wanted them all in one place again, his enemies, all compact. This time he would kill them if anyone forced his hand. He could do it. It had helped him, surviving Quartus's best efforts. Helped his resolve. He had reserved the power to kill them and he hoped they would see that that made him more formidable. He could take a minute to congratulate himself so far. He was a leaning tower but he was still in charge. One thing that had helped him defeat Quartus had

been his nakedness. His legs, his body, everything was slick with nervous
sweat. So there had been utility in his madness, if not method, exactly.
And Quartus had not helped himself in the struggle by being drunk. He
had been drunk. He had smelled of alcohol. And he had been erratic. But
it was true that groups like these drank just routinely.

"*You, you go back,*" he said again. Quartus was stirring but not really
moving.

Ray had the right to pause, to rest. That was the way he felt. There was
the view. He was seeing more death in the landscape than he had when
he'd looked before, dead bodies in different shapes, more of them against
the ground, here and there. From the sky, they would look like dots and
commas, like seeds.

I am going to have to summon my friends right away, he thought. And
fortunately he knew exactly what to say, which was Tla kwano, Come
here. But unfortunately he was hoarse. His friends needed a sign.

"Tla kwano," he said, testing his voice. It was feeble. He cleared his
throat and tried it again.

He was making mistakes. The incorrigible Quartus said, "*Oh I shall
come to you, my man . . .*"

"*I wasn't talking to you, meneer. Go back with your lackeys.*

"*None of you move,*" he screamed at the lackeys.

It had not been helpful being Satan, thinking *Evil, be thou my good,* he
didn't know why. He was not well. He was not doing well.

He realized that Mokopa had sent him off without a spare banana clip
for his rifle, which implied that Mokopa had assumed he was probably
going to be a burnt offering and that however it went it would be a spasm
event and not something involving extended firing. That is, they had
thought he would do what he could do and they would follow on and that
would be it. He didn't blame them. He had half a magazine left, enough.
So that was what Mokopa had thought and now there was the fire.

He didn't want the building to burn. He didn't want various things
to happen. And he had to shoot, because Quartus was doing something,
rolling over and over in his direction, rolling over and over like a log,
rolling across the ten feet separating them. It made no sense. Ray fired,
uselessly, striking the space that the demonic Quartus had already
traversed.

Quartus was at him, he had him by the legs and was trying to pull him
down, and even worse, Ray realized, the man was biting his right leg, in
fact. Rage and disgust transformed him.

It was too much. Ray had been unprepared because Quartus's rolling over and over like a log had not been a normal aggressive act. It had been something else, an invention.

Ray roared at Quartus. He *would not allow it*, what was going on, let alone just being touched by the animal Quartus. He unslung his rifle and, gripping it with both hands, raised it over his head and brought it down like a spear, driving the barrel into Quartus's bare shoulder, tearing the flesh. It was not enough. Quartus was keeping on, like an animal. He was trying to pull Ray down. Quartus was strong.

Again Ray raised the gun and brought it down with all his force but to the right of the previous wound he had inflicted. It was weak of him and he should have deepened the original wound but it was not something he could do. There was a fresh new wound, anyway. There was blood, plenty of it.

Ray was in danger of being capsized, dragged over, despite what he had done to Quartus, but then he wasn't and he could see why. He had hurt something in Quartus's left arm enough to make it weaken almost to the point of not participating. Quartus couldn't grip hard with it, claw at him with it. Ray was able to kick his right leg free. He was winning.

He was okay. There was something he wanted to say but he didn't know what it was, except that he wanted to say it to his wife. Ray brought the gun down again, but this time Quartus had gotten out of the way, like a snake, an eel. He was half lying down, injured.

Ray steadied himself and brought his attention back as he had to and as well as he could to the huddled masses of the enemy yearning to be free and kill him, dismember him. He got his gun around properly and put two rounds into the space between them. They were restless. A couple of them were on all fours instead of lying obediently flat. They are restless, the natives are restless, he thought, and these were not conscripts, which was important. All present and reporting were bona fide volunteers. Quartus was lying doubled over. He was touching his wounds. All was well.

He hoped his enemies had seen that he was learning to be more tender with the trigger of his murder machine. He was getting the hang of it. He was being less profligate with his ammunition. He would have enough for everything.

But Quartus was on his knees suddenly, looking like he wanted something from Ray. And almost immediately then Quartus was diving at him, at his legs, again.

It was the same but not the same. Quartus was crawling up him violently. Ray now had the weapon in aiming mode, for the benefit of the foot soldiers, so he had to maintain this and strike to the side without compromising his stance. He caught Quartus on the neck with the stock of the gun, ineffectively, and then struck a glancing blow that grazed Quartus's forehead, again ineffectively. He was going to have to kill the man, if this kept up. It was then that Quartus bit his bad knee, his swollen bad knee, giving Ray more pain than he had suffered from all Quartus's previous efforts.

He wanted to kick Quartus to death with his better leg, the free leg. He tried it. He tried to kick Quartus hard enough to break something. But he wasn't in the right posture to put his full force into it.

"*I am going to fucking kill you if you don't stop,*" he shouted, hearing the hollowness in his own voice, kicking him again.

But he meant it. He was willing to do it, kill a bleeding man.

Quartus had his arms around Ray's right ankle. Ray stepped back. He stabbed the muzzle of the rifle into Quartus's cheek. He wasn't sure what Quartus was doing or what he was understanding. Except of course that he had to not like what his men were seeing.

Ray said again, "*Understand me, I am going to kill you if you don't stop.*"

The two fires he needed to pay attention to were the one behind him and the little one in the lean-to over the cots and the radio set. Fire went badly with ammunition stocks. He had to keep his mind on too many things.

His legs were trembling. His enemies could see that, which was bad. And he could see that both his knees were bleeding, weakly but definitely. And he had to wonder about what foul germs the dog Quartus with his prominent canines had put into him.

Quartus plunged at Ray yet again, aiming for the knees, making a plaintive sound. Ray jumped back but not quickly enough.

Quartus had Ray's penis in his grasp. He had it with both hands. He was dragging at it and twisting. There was white pain all through Ray. It was unbearable and it was unfair. He was already fighting faintness.

I am killing you now, he thought.

He fired down, with the gun barrel touching Quartus on the hip. *This is what you get*, he thought.

Quartus screamed and let go. His jodhpurs were filling with blood, one leg of them was.

It seemed nothing could make Quartus lie still or be quiet. He was making animal sounds. His men were showing signs of doing something and they had to be stopped. Quartus had tried to damage him. He was still trying to swallow the pain.

He had put too many rounds into Quartus. He had wanted to cripple him, mainly, but he had been willing to kill him, and now he was bleeding to death.

Quartus was jerking around. It was pitiful. He had done it. He had shredded the man's hip. He was deluging blood. It was coming out and staining the pebbles and it was making Ray sick.

It was unnatural not to want to help the dying man, if he was dying, and he probably was. He wanted to get help for the fucking stupid man. There was nothing he could do. He wanted Morel to appear and help. He prayed to God Morel would appear. Because he had been damaged, he was afraid. He was afraid the fucker had hurt his penis beyond just hurting it, actually damaging it.

Quartus's men wanted to help him too. They were getting to their knees, up on their knees. He couldn't blame them.

"Get down," he said. They were moving around too freely, and he was in hell.

He gathered himself and shouted something to the effect that they should do something, sit down, it was glossolalia, really, just blurts of sound, pleading sound.

Quartus was writhing around, still. He was making small sounds.

An episode of black smoke began, obscuring everything. He got down on his knees. He didn't know which was worse, standing or kneeling.

He was through killing now, if he could help it.

Piercing whistling rose and twined together into something hard and terrible, and then his friends were there, thrusting through the smoke, Mokopa, Kevin, everyone.

They were firing everywhere.

He wanted to explain what he had done, but there was no time.

He wanted to tell them he needed to speak to someone because he had killed someone. But there was killing going on.

He wanted to explain that they had obeyed, Quartus's men, they had been okay.

He put his rifle down and relaxed onto his side.

He wanted his wife. He wanted to explain.

Confusion was expanding around him and in his weakness he wanted to wave it on like a traffic cop directing things. He wanted to wave it on to encourage it so it could go where it had to so that he could rest. He was already resting. He wanted to sleep more than anything he had ever wanted he could think of. But the confusion had his blessing, was the way he felt.

Shyness, for the first time, covered him, for his penis. He wanted to shield his shy penis with something if he could find anything. He was on his side, pressing his penis back in between his clasped legs. He could feel the pebbles burning a design of their own into the flesh of his side. It was his fate to be marked. Later he would see what the design of his life would be.

He was fading, and then Kevin, his friend, was there, crouching beside him and touching him. He felt better immediately. His friends were jumping through the smoke, howling.

This is it, he kept thinking.

There was the feeling that this was it, that this was the world, the world was what he was seeing. He was seeing his friends arriving shooting and the villains jumping up and scattering, disobedient villains.

Come, Satan, he thought, waving his arms.

And then he was seeing one of his friends tearing the burning tarpaulin free and winding it into a manageable burning mass and hurling that off the side of the building and then finding himself burning, his clothes, and then dropping down and rolling around in a way that reminded him of Quartus rolling around.

It was hard to participate, lying down, but thank God for his friend Kevin. But he was seeing something. And it was the world, it was one of his friends, his witdoeke friends, doing almost a circus act tearing out and crushing against his chest the flaming tarpaulin and then hurling it over the side and managing to crush the flaming thing into a mass he could fling high out into the air and over the side. And then he knew it was over for him, he was seeing things twice. He had seen the same thing twice. He was afraid.

"I am sick," he said to Kevin.

"Ehe, rra," Kevin said, touching Ray's head. Ray was understanding that Kevin had been assigned to him, to protect him like a wife. That had to be the explanation. Because Kevin had his gun with him, his popgun his shotgun and he was not using it against the foe.

He never wanted to see the same thing twice ever again in his life. He didn't want to experience anything twice just in general. He wanted everything new, if that could be arranged. He didn't know if it could.

There was carnage going on. He couldn't see all of it. He wanted to stop it.

The witdoeke had arrived shooting but it had failed to stop the villains from jumping up. They had done that. Ray thought, I have an idea how to end this.

He tried to get up but Kevin pushed him down.

"Thank you," he said to Kevin. But he still wanted to rise, to speak.

There was something he wanted Kevin to do for him, which was to go and check Quartus, who was lying still. Quartus was dead, Ray was thinking. He wanted someone to say so.

"Kevin, can you go look at him?" He pointed at Quartus, the dead Quartus.

But as Kevin crept toward Quartus, horribly the man got up on one knee and with his undamaged leg projected himself up and into a launch toward Ray, both arms extended, like a flying gargoyle, something, a horror from the media, the moron media, something like that.

Kevin pumped his gun to shoot, but before he could fire Quartus had arrived next to Ray, almost on top of him, his face in a grimace of fury, his fiery gums showing, his face very white. Ray had wanted to take him back alive like Frank Buck the animal catcher, the zoo supplier, whatever he had been Ray admired him, as a boy. He couldn't remember everything.

But now Kevin was over them and Kevin was killing him, Quartus, again. Everything was happening twice.

Quartus's shoulder and neck disintegrated. There would be mainly his head to take to his what, his friends his beloveds. Blood went everywhere.

"It is all right," Kevin said. He was shaking.

Ray wanted to say things were all right, but one of his friends was throwing a villain off the roof and no one had consulted him. The man might be just wounded and not dead. It made a difference.

There seemed to be a victory. Action was stopping.

He said to Kevin that he was through with everything, but Kevin was leaving him. There was a new problem, the fire behind them. Kevin left.

"I'm coming," Ray said, unable to move.

His friends were stamping in the flames, beating at them with nothing, with their own shirts. It was not going to work. It was too late. My knee is a bulb, he thought, a globe, making himself get up.

He had to tell his friends there was another way down, not to worry. Only he knew about the trapdoor. He had to tell them. But also he felt he had to vomit. It was bad, but he felt the need not to contribute more than he already had to the mess going on. He was fighting for control, and it was odd how something a purely physical impulse could be defeated by a scruple, something so imaginary. But in any case he was conquering. He was swallowing himself.

Kevin wouldn't leave him. Kevin was nice.

Quartus was no longer dying, he was dead. There seemed to be blood leaking out of his eyes as well as from his nostrils, his mouth.

It was difficult to tell what was going on, except that the buzzards were back and there seemed to be more of them, but he could be glad about one thing, the smoke, the smoke from the fire that was eating its way east west north south, the smoke was having the useful effect of keeping the carrion birds up high above, in their own layer, black above black.

He had to get up and help his friends, but not with what they were doing, still doing at the moment, which was throwing dead bodies off the building.

He had to get up and make them stop, and stop it before they got to Quartus, and he didn't know why. But he didn't want Quartus thrown over. And he had a right to not have that happen because he had killed Quartus before Kevin did, so Quartus was his, but it was making him sick to look at his handiwork again. So he didn't know what was for the best and maybe everything was for the best.

And then he noticed that he was whistling "The Mexican Hat Dance" through his teeth and it was almost enough to make him laugh, because deep in the heart of the rose of their relationship Iris had noticed that whenever he was nervous he would start whistling the damned thing through his teeth, and she had pointed it out to him. He had never realized he had been doing that, something that was such a dead giveaway, so he had stopped doing it, until now. And it had been the same with his drinking, being embarrassing to himself and not knowing it until he saw it in her eyes, the eyes the mirror of the soul, but not her soul, *his* soul, because what the mirror of the soul meant was that it was the asshole's soul that showed up glittering in the eyes of the trusting woman who had married the asshole, beloved thing, helpmeet, beautiful thing. And she had been like a spy because the way he had whistled it between his teeth was so softly as to be almost a subliminal thing, until she came, like light, like the morning, illuminating everything.

When that bout of smoke cleared away Quartus was gone. There was nothing he could do about anything except to get *something* to cover his nakedness, his groin, with. Because he had the strength to stand, probably, but not until he got dressed, or mostly dressed. Because as he was, he was an exhausted device, a joke, like a jester running around doing tricks when the castle is in flames, falling.

He needed pants, but it could be a diaper, a loincloth like Tarzan's, except that he would need Tarzan's secret jockstrap to go with it, the reason Tarzan's penis had never peeked out during his exertions with the various wild animals giving him no rest.

"Can you get me something?" he asked Kevin, gesturing at his groin.

Kevin wanted to help, Ray could tell. But he was baffled. He looked wildly around.

Kevin left him, strode off to find something for Ray. And Ray croaked at him to keep down. It had been a reflex. But at least for now it was safe to walk around normally so he had made a fool of himself.

Kevin was doing something. He was stripping a pair of bush shorts off one of the corpses.

Kevin presented the shorts to Ray, and turned his back, pointlessly but courteously, pointlessly because he had already seen everything there was to see. But it meant that things were going in the direction of normality. Courtesy was important during bloodshed. He thanked Kevin.

Ray got the shorts on. They weren't clean and they were loose on him, but they weren't bloody. It was surprising how much pants helped. He got up. He was a little unsteady. But he wanted to join in.

Kevin asked, "Are you fine?"

Ray said he was, but in fact he didn't know how he was.

Kevin was hovering around him too much and now he was off fetching one of the parasols Ray had observed in use by the koevoet earlier. They weren't parasols, they were umbrellas, heavy dark canvas umbrellas. He had had no idea that such a thing as a military umbrella even existed.

"No thank you, my man," he said to Kevin. And he wouldn't allow Kevin to hold it over him, either.

But he wanted help getting *Strange News* off his chest because the tape was burning where it was passed across his bare skin. There was some chemical reaction, something unpleasant, and the tape was cutting into his neck and sweat was biting badly where the flesh was raw.

"Can you help me take this off? I need to take it off now."

Kevin insisted Ray sit down again, out of the way, against the parapet on the south side of the roof. He began to disentangle the bindings but stopped when he saw that skin was coming away in places as he lifted the tape away.

"This is going to be bleeding, rra."

"I don't care. Just pull it off."

"Ehe, but I'll pull it fast, like that. Be ready."

"I am ready. Do it."

Kevin had a knife, a small thing. He sawed the bindings apart. The bundle fell into Ray's lap.

"Now I am pulling," Kevin said, and then he did and it was hot pain again but mainly unbearable around his neck. The tape came away more easily from his back. Certain spots were bad, little hells, on his back. He needed something, some Vaseline, some sort of balm. But at least the weight was gone.

He wanted to get up and join in the effort to scavenge the roof for anything useful for killing. That was what his friends were doing. They were furious because the mounted guns were bolted to wooden skids and there was no time to find tools, wherever they might be, to use in dismantling them, because the building was on fire behind them. Trying to stamp it out had been a gesticulation. They were letting the building go. But it was not something to argue about.

They had the hatch to the end set of stairs up and were pitching whatever they could lay their hands on that they wanted down the stairwell. They had discovered those stairs without him, which was fine, but he had wanted to be the one to lead them to it, or if not that point it out to them, at least.

Ray got up, the bundle under his arm.

He knew what he was going to say to Morel when he saw him. He was going to say You may draw my bath. That seemed very funny to him, but it was also what he wanted most from anyone who could provide it.

Mokopa wanted him to leave the roof, go down the hold, go downstairs. He was being urgent about it.

Ray went over to the stairs. He didn't want to go. Mokopa was praising him in Setswana and he understood enough to know he didn't want to go until Mokopa was through doing that. And then he was through. And then Mokopa's attention was elsewhere, off over toward the pan. He was yelling joyously. People were yelling back. People were coming down into the pan, a line of them, waving. Mokopa came and got him as he was about to descend the stairs and pulled him over to the parapet facing the pan and raised his arm and waved it for him. "Tau" was something Mokopa was saying in reference to him, which Ray knew meant lion, and then it was "Dilau" over and over, which Ray was going to have to ask someone about. It was just another thing on his list. He wondered who anyone thought he was, out there, what the people in the pan thought.

He hated leaving the roof, the scene. He wanted to delay if he could a little. He wanted Morel to appear and see what he had done, or the results of it, see him waving. He wanted to shout along with his friends. So he shouted "Dilau dilau dilau," picking that word out of Mokopa's

praise of him, and produced unexpected hilarity in the men around him.
That was fine. Everything would be revealed.

Someone was calling him from the direction of the fire. Ray couldn't
tell who it was. There were two kinds of darkness over the roof, the darkness of the smoke itself, coming in blurts, and then the darkness of the
shadow of the smoke. And there were the buzzards but not only the buzzards. There were smaller birds, some sort of carrion bird specializing in
the leftovers of the buzzards and vultures. He knew nothing about
birdlife. He had never been interested. And neither had Iris. She had
been invited to birdwatch with a birdwatcher and had said to the birdwatcher, What I say is let the birds watch *me*. The birdwatcher had taken
it the wrong way, missing the funniness.

It was Morel calling him, calling and coughing at the same time, bursting through the smoke barrier. He was carrying his medical bag. There
were two new witdoeke with him, new to Ray, not from the roof team.

Kevin had Ray by the elbow, which Ray didn't want, especially now.
He pulled himself free and drew himself up.

Morel looked battered and befouled. He had soot on his face and
his safari suit was chaotically stained. He was trying to maintain some
kind of presence. Ray was sorry for him. I don't care how I look, Ray
thought.

Morel came up to him. He was out of breath. He snorted.

"Christ, look at you," Morel said.

"I know."

"We need to clean you up."

"You may draw my bath now."

"Oh very funny. What's wrong with your voice?"

"I've been shouting at people."

"Let me look at your neck. And when did you get new pants?"

"It's a long story."

The new witdoeke had been mingling with members of the roof team
and now returned to stare at Ray. Morel was beginning to understand.
"Dilau," they said.

"They thought you had a bomb, you ran around like that with that
thing. That's it, isn't it?"

"Roughly."

"I can't hear you."

"Roughly."

"Well do I get any credit?"

"What are you talking about?"

"I gave you the idea."

"I don't get you."

"I gave you the idea when you scared the shit out of me when you walked in with that thing on your chest."

"Okay I give you credit. Are you happy?"

"You've got to tell me how you did it, man, everything. But how is everybody up here?"

"I think mostly okay. What is dilau, by the way? You're the linguist."

"I don't have a clue."

"Because they're saying I'm dilau, I think."

"Rra, I can tell you," Kevin said.

"What does it mean?"

"Rra, it is saying you have the lerete of the lion."

"What is that?"

"It is the genitals, rra. Dilau. The genitals of the lion."

"Thank you," Ray said to Kevin.

"Quite a compliment, man. But you need to sit down and we need to get out of here."

"Stop telling me to sit down. Everyone's doing it. I'm okay."

Ray could see, as the smoke shifted, the fire like a vast bright claw gripping the roof. They did have to go.

They had to go especially because the faintness was coming back. He didn't know if he would be able to quell it this time. He might lose consciousness, and it was impossible to tell how long a spell of unconsciousness might last, not excluding forever. There was something on his mind. At some point Iris would be notified about the outcome of all this, by someone, notified about who had survived. That moment would come. She would be waiting for it. Probably she would rather hear that Morel was alive. Or at best she might want to know equally. But in fact he knew her heart and if she had a button to press that controlled the news of their respective fates with one button telling his fate and the other button telling Morel's fate she would punch the Morel button first. It would be a reflex. She wouldn't be able to help it. He could see her doing it. She wouldn't want him to see. But that was what he would see.

He was on the stairs. He was descending carefully. He was holding his bundle against his chest. Kevin was descending backwards, holding lightly on to him, which he didn't approve of. Going backwards down the stairs was dangerous for his friend Kevin.

"Wemberg, the old man, is dead, Ray," Morel said. Morel was just behind him on the stairs.

So that was another entry on the list of things he could do nothing about. The world was turning white.

"*Catch him,*" was the last thing he heard as he sank into vibrating whiteness, all the way into it.

He came awake looking at something like the sun and realizing he was being conveyed roughly away from the brilliant thing he was interested in. He was in a blanket turned into a hammock or sling in which he was being dragged somewhere else. His behind was suffering, which was only fair since unlike other main parts of his body nothing had been done to it to make it hurt. Two people were moving him along.

His mind was on the thing it had been on just before this, it was on Dwight Wemberg. It was important. He wanted to get up and get out and do something. The man had a history that had to be honored and it was unthinkable that his body might be left in the terrible desert. It couldn't be allowed to happen, because it had been the agony over his wife's body, being unable to reclaim it, that had led him out into extremis and his own death. There was some kind of parity that had to be honored. Wemberg's body had to go back to Gaborone, *his* body at least had to go where Wemberg would have wanted it to go, undoubtedly to where Alice was buried, to Gaborone.

Two men were hauling him along. One of them was Kevin. He could communicate with Kevin. The other man was a stranger. He was wild-looking, a rustic, very thin, wearing seedpod armlets. He was straight out of the bush.

Kevin would understand about Wemberg. And if he didn't, there were others he could inform about the problem. Except that he was being dragged away from the center of things, because of the fire.

He didn't like to look at the fire, but he was facing it so he had to. He would never be able to come here with Iris, assuming that the world could have evolved in some inconceivable way, their world, and that Ngami Bird Lodge existed in that world . . . It was burning to the ground before his eyes, they could never come here. This would have been if she was through with Morel or he was through with her, if by some unimaginable turn of events either one of those things had happened and he had somehow heard about it.

The entire roof was in flames, it was a platform for spikes and leaping snakes of fire. It was crownlike. And smoke was beginning to leak and pour from the windows of the second floor, and that would be because burning stuff from the roof would be dropping down and setting the wainscoting, the carved wainscoting he had liked so much, and the other carved appurtenances, on fire. It would all burn. The furniture would burn, the beds, the bolsters, the rugs.

"Stop," he said to Kevin.

"We must go as far as that," Kevin answered, pointing. Ray couldn't see where that was.

"This is far enough, isn't it?"

"No, rra."

Explosions, five or six of them, very loud, caused Kevin and the other man to speed up. The explosions had come from the east end of the burning building.

"It is ammunition, now," Kevin said.

So it was prudent to get well away. Obviously there hadn't been time to extract all the munitions or other gear the witdoeke might have wanted.

"I can walk, Kevin, rra. I can."

At least he thought he could. He looked down at himself. He had been tended to, somewhat. There was oil on his skin. Someone had put a longsleeved shirt on him, not a clean shirt, a filthy one, but that was all right. It wasn't oil on his skin, it was Vaseline. He had his boots, still. His bad knee was crimson, but it was nothing but Mercurochrome, the redness, on Quartus's bite mark there. He felt his bad knee. He had to suppress a groan. Still, he knew he could get around. He had a knobkerrie. It was somewhere. Probably it was in the building and on fire itself. So he didn't have a knobkerrie to prop himself up with.

"Stop *here*," Ray said, jerking on the blanket.

They obeyed. Ray wanted to jump up. He couldn't, quite. He rolled out of the sling he was in and got on all fours and laboriously got erect.

"You see," he said, and immediately fell down.

They put him back in his hammock and dragged him along to the sound of even greater explosions. The entire building was going. He could see people running around like ants. Sobeit, he thought. And he went into darkness again.

. . .

He was awake. He was on a slight incline, he was beyond all the outbuildings. It was getting late.

He was by himself. He had been left there like a turd on a doily.

He stood up. He had the bundle under one arm and he was clutching the waist of his shorts tight. He thought he could manage his right leg.

And the conflagration was absolute, nothing would be saved. It was peach and black. He needed Kevin.

Things were going on near the conflagration he needed to be part of. He had to hobble toward the event.

It was hard, going there.

And his comrades the witdoeke were doing something that had to be stopped. They were throwing bodies into the flames and one of those might be Wemberg's. He didn't know. He needed to discuss Wemberg with them.

He needed to find Kevin, Morel too.

"Hey," he shouted, entering the heat from the conflagration.

He saw people he knew.

"Here I am," he said to Morel and Kevin and, there he was, Kerekang.

It was Kerekang, sitting on an overturned washtub, exhausted-looking, gray in the face, his hair grown long. He was wearing a witdoek, appropriately enough. He was wearing a fur vest and he had bandoliers crossed over his chest. He looked Mexican somehow. His arms were sinewy but too thin. He was wearing cargo pants whose pockets were loaded with things. He was wearing sandals. He was looking at the ground.

Ray went up to Kerekang. He cleared his throat. He had too many things he wanted to say.

"Dumela, rra," he said. Kerekang looked up.

"We have met," Ray said.

Kerekang stood up. He looked at Ray and then looked differently at him. He had heard about Ray's exploit, it was obvious.

Kerekang strode up to him and embraced him too hard. Ray was in danger of losing his balance, briefly.

The dead had been collected into a heap and a pair of men with bandannas over their faces were taking one body at a time and running with it through the zone of heat around the building and getting as close as they could to the flaming doorway Ray and Morel had entered after their escape from the shed and hurling the body into it. The bodies had been stripped. The work had just begun. There were fifteen bodies, at a first rough estimate, waiting to be incinerated.

Kevin was with him. Ray asked him how many bodies had gone into the flames and Kevin held up three fingers.

Kerekang was sitting again. He seemed to be in a kind of reverie. He looked caved-in, was the way Ray described it to himself.

Ray needed a belt. Kevin would help him.

"Kevin, can you get me a belt?"

"Ehe, rra." He seemed to have an idea. Ray saw what it was. Kevin was going to the litter of clothing taken from the dead. You'll have your choice of belts, Ray thought.

And it was so. Kevin brought him three belts to choose from. He took the shortest one and threaded it through the belt loops. But with the tongue in the last punch hole, the belt was still too slack, so he discarded that belt and took the longest one instead and secured it with a knot. He felt ready then.

He considered the tableau he was part of. They were in an open space beyond the outbuildings, one of which had been his prison. Which reminded him that Morel was not in evidence. He was full of anxiety. There was Kerekang, on the washtub, now bracketed by armed men. More fighters were filing in from the pan, their legs and shoes and lower pants legs covered with white dust like tooth powder. The pan was dry as bones. But where was Morel?

The staff people from Ngami Lodge were present. All the faces he had seen in his moments on the first floor were there. They had survived. That was good. He would talk to them later, if he could, say something, thank Dirang and the old man again.

Salvaged weapons and ammunition were being sorted in the area just in back of Kerekang, and certain items were being brought to Kerekang's attention from time to time and he was nodding in precisely the same manner to each item presented for his reaction. He was an automaton.

Ray went up to him. He bent down and touched Kerekang's shoulder, to get his attention. The armed men bristled and one of them put the barrel of his rifle in Ray's stomach. He had white legs. He was a new-comer, from the pan. He wouldn't necessarily know about dilau, that he was dilau. Kerekang said something rapidly and the rifle went away.

Ray said, "Rra, excuse me. Listen, this burning of bodies . . . Listen to me, you have to let me find Rra Wemberg. He is among the dead and I know you know the man you love him you loved his wife Alice, and Dwight needs to be buried with his wife, rra. I can take him, you can give him to me. I will do something. And do you know where my friend is, the doctor? He will agree with me. Do you know where he is?"

The men surrounding Kerekang, which Ray couldn't help thinking of as a chorus, were saying something, chanting something, and it was Setime. Ray thought he knew what was up, which was that he had to use the right term of address, which was Setime, bringer of fire, fire-thrower, whatever it was.

Ray began again, "Setime, man, please tell them to stop until I can find our friend."

Setime nodded, mechanically, not looking up.

Ray was at the pile of bodies.

The pile was smaller.

Anything can happen, he thought, and he was thinking a body he might find would be Morel's. The king on the throne was just nodding, Kerekang on his washtub.

He thrust his hands into the mass of dead bodies, pulling the topmost ones aside. He wanted to see if Quartus was there, but he didn't care what happened, now, to his body. He needed a better framework for what he was doing, because it was too terrible. The bodies had been piled midway between Kerekang and the building, and that had been a mistake. Because Ngami Bird Lodge was dying in a roar, the fire was a roaring thing, a beast. Every window was sprouting horns or prongs of fire. The conflagration was tending in one direction, to the east, coming to a furious point to the east. Another clutch of explosions went off. He was getting bloody again. Whoever had cleaned him up had wasted his time. He was sorry not to know more about the dead he was pushing out of the way, but he only wanted one thing, he was sorry to say. The original team of body-tossers had withdrawn because of the heat. That was sane of them. He saw a white foot, a white leg. It was Wemberg. He was on the bottom tier.

He needed help, but where was help? And where was Morel? That was next, after this.

"*What do you think you're doing?*" Morel said. Morel was there, had found him.

"Help me, man. This is Dwight. Help me."

They worked as one and got Wemberg's body free and together dragged it back out of the blasting heat. The side of the building came down. Bits of burning stuff fell on them. It was the body of an old man, someone not far from death in his original life, that they had rescued. It was the naked body of an old man. Ray's face was cooking. He was afraid for his eyes.

"Where have you been, by the way?" Ray asked.

"Man, I was looking for you. I lost track of you. Also I was being sick."

"So you were off puking somewhere."

"No I was looking for you."

"Well so you were doing both things."

"That's what I said."

"Then okay. And have you drawn my bath?"

"Not yet."

Ray took Wemberg's body by the ankles and dragged it as far as he could. He was weakening. He collapsed onto the ground. He made himself sit up. He had to get his bundle. It was exposed.

The men who had been feeding bodies to the fire had followed him. They were taking Wemberg's body by the arms and starting to drag it back toward the fire.

Ray attempted a howl as he threw himself on Wemberg's body. He had almost no voice. He was in despair.

These men were as strong as devils. He was being carried along. No notice was being taken of him. His right arm was scraping the ground, the arm that was under the body. He needed help.

Morel was helping. He was pushing his way between the devils and pushing one of them to the side.

Ray's progress toward the fire stopped. He could say that he was ready to go into the fire with Wemberg except that that would be a lie.

The fire was lunging out at them. Everyone needed to be away from where they were or they would all just constitute a disposal problem for some other group yet to appear on the horizon.

Morel had been knocked down. If what Ray had seen was correct, Morel had pushed at the devils and then swung at them with his doctor bag, which he had been keeping close by him, and it was funny, to Ray, Morel using it as a weapon, like that. It was like a woman striking a criminal with her purse. And he was so grateful. His wife's boyfriend was a physician and he was not supposed to injure anyone and there was all of that.

It was too hot for the devils. They were dropping the project. And they were not devils they were his friends.

He smelled a certain smell. It was meat roasting, and another smell that reminded him of hair burning. He touched his head. It was someone else's hair, not his, burning.

He got himself to his feet and began dragging Dwight Wemberg's body back to safety. His arm was dripping blood. Morel was not helping him, he was lying still. He was lying on the ground, back there.

He dropped Wemberg's body and ran to see about the good doctor.

He had a strange feeling as he ran, which was that he was running on a sheet of glass or on some thickness between himself and the ground, a thickness he could run on forever and that he would never tire of running on if he had to. He was probably using up vital forces from his what, his bone marrow or his coccyx or somewhere. It was connected with something, a line *I staggered banged with terror through a million billion trillion stars.* I can step on anything and not fall, he thought.

What was left of the building was heeling over in their direction. Morel was conscious, but he was stunned. Ray seized him by the belt. Morel felt weightless to Ray, a slight thing he could pull along after him on the glass, a thing that could slide like those things on ice, hockey things.

The building was singing as it came down, or something within it was.

Morel got to his feet.

They kept moving back. Morel was helping him with Wemberg's body yet again. He was strong.

With a harsh, giant sigh the building came all the way down, thrusting out billows of flame and burning debris.

He stopped. He had to get his bundle. His vision of things was showing perforations, black perforations.

He had his bundle.

The perforations were expanding.

Kerekang was approaching him. He had been sitting with maps open in his lap and he was standing now and the maps had fallen to the ground and he was coming over.

"I have to lie down," Ray said to Morel.

"Okay," Morel said.

"You have your bag?"

"I'm okay. Yes, I do."

We must look strange, Ray thought. He had hold of Wemberg's left wrist and he was clasping *Strange News* tightly under his other arm. And Morel had Wemberg by the right wrist and with his other hand had a death grip on his medical bag, which was not completely understandable because it had been rifled, as he recalled, emptied of anything useful except Vaseline and Mercurochrome and witch hazel. It was going to feel peculiar going back to a world where business was conducted by decently groomed and normally dressed people not at their wit's end every minute. He was confident he would be back in such a world. He didn't know why.

He sank to his knees, to rest. So did Morel. It was companionable of Morel to do that. He was worse off than Morel, closer to being unable to contribute, a drug on the market, someone to be attended to. He was sorry. And he was sorry that his knee was not allowing him to rest, his bad knee. He hauled it up. He was unsteady. Morel steadied him.

Kerekang was walking toward them and dropping things on the way without realizing it, like the maps and something else, a watch or a compass, more likely. It was fatigue. People were picking the dropped items up for him.

Kerekang said, "Rra, we have to clear out. We have little time. Look behind you, you'll see why. The fire is revealing where we are."

Ray made himself look fully at it. He hated the sight. It was undoubtedly all the exotic wood used in putting the place together that accounted for the fury of the blaze. There had been objections at the time to timbering operations near Kazengula, but by the time that had been stopped the people behind Ngami Bird Lodge had gotten all the wood they would need.

"I understand . . ."

"You see, once they have us marked, koevoet can come over by helicopter from SouthWest or from Caprivi where they still have a camp, Omega."

"I understand, but . . . we must cover that old man."

Ray saw that the dressing on Wemberg's chest and side had been lost in the last phase of dragging his body back and forth. There were his wounds. How he had been able to walk around wounded as he was Ray would never be able to understand. He had bled to death and there was no way, with those injuries, that anything could have been done. Your pubic hair is going to be white someday too, if you're lucky, he said to himself. It was going to happen. He hoped he would be with someone who wouldn't mind. He would never see his wife's thatch go white. Someone would.

A disordered negotiation ensued. Ray could barely contribute. Someone had given him a cup of water, but he wanted more. Morel's Land Rover had been destroyed. He wanted to reclaim Ray's Land Cruiser. He wanted to drive the Land Cruiser back to Gaborone, taking Ray, and Wemberg's body. But Kerekang wanted the use of the Land Cruiser. There were wounded to transport. He wanted to get away to a place of safety in the bush. Morel and Ray would have to accompany him, at least for a day or two. They could safely bury Wemberg in the bush and mark the place. Then they could separate from the group and depart for Gaborone, taking the Cruiser.

Morel wanted to know why his Rover had been destroyed, while the Land Cruiser had been spared.

Kevin had an explanation. "I don't know, but I'll tell you what I think is that Quartus wanted to keep the blue Cruiser to himself. You know how it is, we like these Toyotas."

Ray was feeling heavily proprietary toward his vehicle. It had served him well. It was still nicely provisioned, unless the villains had raped it. He could get into it. He could drive it. He could drive it in rough country. The idea that Quartus might have wanted to drive his Cruiser away forever into Namibia for his own use was enraging. There was also the question of who was going to be liable for the vehicle that had been assigned to him if he went home without it. But that was sordid, or was it. He was going to have to sign papers unless he could bring it back alive. He wasn't prepared for this. He had assumed his good vehicle had been destroyed in the general destruction. But it was there in front of him, the engine running.

The witdoeke were swarming over the Cruiser. They were delighted with it. The petrol drums were full. They had topped everything up in Gumare. There was plenty of water.

"How did you get it started? I have no idea what they did with the key," Ray said.

Kevin answered, "Rra, it was in the pocket of their captain, the ugly man. He had keys of all kinds. We had taken his vehicles and burned them, but he had put your vehicle aside, it was not with the others."

Morel was almost rebellious. Ray understood it. Before the appearance of the Cruiser there had been only the difficult choice of going deeper into the bush to some unknown fate or striking out down the road toward the main route, where there might be nothing happening once they got there. This part of the country had been sealed off. There were a thousand ways to die hoping for something that was no longer available. And the Cruiser was there, humming and promising a way out for the two of them.

Morel wanted to be with Iris at the earliest possible opportunity and to warn her, this was burning in Ray's mind, *warn her* that the cock was out of the bag, get to her so they could together figure something out because the cat was out of the bag and it was over, everything was, which she was going to feel was what, was something burning down and singeing her hair . . . It would be so much like this castle burning down behind them. However anything came out, it was going to be a race to get to Iris first and it was a race he was going to win.

His enemy Morel was very strong, and would try to get there first before Ray could look into the face of hell himself, first, his wife's beautiful woman's face, his wife's face saying it was true what she had done, admitting it. He had to be there for it, and without Morel. He had to be there before Morel could confuse things.

"We should go and get into the Cruiser, be on the Cruiser. We have a right to be there, through me," Ray said.

He was trying to convey something important. The Cruiser was going to be a luxury vehicle, compared to the two battered bakkies they might be trying to find a place in or to the two huge lumberous Bedfords that apparently constituted the rest of the witdoeke fleet. He was trying to convey that there was a tide in the affairs of men and that they had no choice but to swim along with it.

And there was the question of what would happen to Kerekang if koevoet caught him. He would be dead, and this fight was going to end in defeat for Kerekang and his cause. Because this . . . revolt, this effort to tear up the status quo, had been doomed from the start. But maybe Kerekang could be preserved to fight another day, and to achieve that would take special skills, extracting him, getting him out, getting him away from what he had been caught in, a subject his wife's boyfriend would know nothing about.

"Everybody is going to want to be on the Cruiser," he said to Morel.

"Come on," Ray said to Kerekang. He was trying to push, to create a moment, a feeling they should all get aboard.

"Kevin, my man, help me with Comrade Wemberg, please rra," Ray said.

Kevin looked to Kerekang for instruction. Kerekang nodded. That was good. He was approving what Ray wanted.

There was another thing. Ray wanted Kerekang to be on board, on the Cruiser. If he could arrange that he could relax. He could sleep. He could lie back someway and wait, asleep, for the next place they were going to, but he could sleep knowing that when they came to a halt Setime, his friend Kerekang, would be there. There would be a campfire and they would be able to sit down and talk.

Kevin had summoned help and Wemberg was being stowed less tenderly than Ray would have liked in the back of the Cruiser, along with three wounded men, walking wounded, they would have to be called, who were joining Wemberg there.

He was going to volunteer to ride in the back, out in the truck bed. He thought that they might not allow that because they would want him inside in comfort to show their appreciation. But either way would be all right, either in the cab in the rear seat or in the sun and jolting around. The sun was not at its worst in any case and there would be twilight soon, and then blackness and stars.

He was yawning too much, thinking of rest. And it was catching. Kerekang was yawning.

Ray said, "Rra, let's go together in my Cruiser. And the doctor, of course."

There was a frenzy going on. Canned goods were being tossed into the bed of the truck. The wounded men were shielding their heads with their arms. Labels on the canned goods were charred and falling off or absent altogether. People were being profligate with the water drum. They were crowding around to drink from the spigot projecting over the side and they were wasting water. It would be a lottery with the blank cans. Some would get pilchards and some would get lichee nuts.

"I want to talk to you," Morel said to Ray.

"We can't, man. We have to go," Ray said.

The cab was occupied or almost. There were two witdoeke in the back seat of the cab already, and there was the driver. Ray wanted Kerekang to be in the Cruiser. He said so to Kevin. He said it urgently. He knew what he himself was going to do. He was going to climb into the bed of the truck and wedge himself in, lying down as best he could among the wounded and his dead friend. And Morel had to come because he might be needed especially to help Kerekang, who was in frightening shape and who might be helped to recuperate by a medical doctor, the only one in this part of the wilderness.

He took Morel by the hand and pulled him toward the Cruiser.

"We're going with you," he said to Kevin.

Ray pulled hard on Morel's arm. He knew what he was doing. Morel wanted to go back to peace and also to getting ahead of him in speaking to Iris and warning her and letting a screen go up. It was a problem, and it was too much of one, but there he was.

Morel had jerked himself away from Ray. He was entertaining hopes of a different outcome, still, Ray thought. The man wanted to go to Iris, embrace her, warn her, embrace her and get together with her to figure

out how to deal with the man she was married to, the spy. It was a paranoid notion and he knew it, except that it might be true, and didn't the
agency act on ideas of things that might happen, that might come true, all
the time, and stop them from happening?

Ray led Kerekang to the Cruiser. No one objected. He helped him
into the front seat. Mokopa was the driver, which seemed wrong. It was
wrong to have a one-eyed driver if there was an alternative. Ray's legs
were shaking at the prospect of being able to lie down flat in whatever
conditions for long enough to sleep, with nothing being asked of him.

He got Kerekang seated.

He turned to Morel with the idea that he would ask him to volunteer
to drive. But Morel was looking disaffected and adamant in some way,
and he was marginal, gray in the face, strong as he was, and he was a
strong specimen, but he was drooping and fighting not to show it. It
would be better to have a one-eyed driver than someone who could fall
sleep at the wheel.

"Come get in the back with me," he said to Morel.

Morel was still trying to think of his own alternative, Ray could tell.
But there was none.

"This is the best idea, come on," Ray said.

The truck bed was filling up with fighters. Others would want to lie
down too. Ray got to the tailgate of the Cruiser but was too weak to pull
himself up into the madding crowd who had gotten there first. He didn't
want to reveal that. He tried to look pensive. A problem was that he had
his bundle to protect. He couldn't bear to let go of it.

Morel was helping him up. And he was mounting the tailgate himself,
so the decision had been made.

It was good Morel was there. He was clearing a space next to the wall
of the truck bed. He was being rough about it. He was pushing wounded
men over. No one was objecting. It was because he was a doctor.

There was shouting and ululating as the fighters packed up. Some
were filing off on foot, not many. Presumably there would be a rendezvous with the people in the vehicles, later. He hoped they would be
all right, the ones going on foot. The Basarwa at least would be all right.
They could live on nothing, they knew how.

They were a convoy of five vehicles, two big Bedford trucks, two pick-
ups, and the beautiful blue Cruiser. They were actually moving, all
of them. A whining sound came from the burning hotel. The fire was
stupendous.

He had a space to lie down in. He would be all right. Next to him was the dead body of Dwight Wemberg, wrapped in a blanket, his face not showing. Morel was not lying down. He was nearby, sitting on a crate. He was being watchful.

"Rest if you can," Morel said, taking his bundle from him and placing it under his head. It was not the greatest pillow in the world but it was better than having his head bouncing on the metal. Morel was doing everything he could.

Ray wanted food. It was ridiculous but he believed that if he asked Morel to get him some he would do it.

No one knew how hungry he was. Iris could look at him and tell if he was hungry whether he said anything or not. That was because she was attuned to him. He wanted a meat loaf sandwich, her meat loaf. She had once put raisins in a meat loaf, in the spirit of experiment, early in their marriage, when she had been cooking more than she did now, because now they had help in the kitchen. And the raisins had been a terrible idea, but he hadn't said anything, and then the next day she had caught him prising them out of the slab of meat loaf in his sandwich. And she had made him promise that he would always tell her the truth about food she prepared. And after that, he always had. He should tell Morel that story. He didn't know why, unless it was to remind Morel to tell her the truth. She enjoyed the truth.

I'm learning to sleep anywhere, he thought, and fell asleep.

35. *A Different Sea*

His first thought, when he awakened, was that he must be in a cave, which was not possible, or rather not compatible with the geography of that part of the Kalahari, as he understood it, which was poorly. Only the Tsodilo Hills, where the Bushman paintings were, were substantial enough to have caves in them, and they were too far away, impossible to reach in anything like the time he had been traveling asleep, which was the best way to travel, in a berth on a train or in first class on a plane where you had leg-room and seatbacks went further back than the seats in coach.

He was alone. He was looking up at a ceiling, a slanting-to-the-rear ceiling, or rock. It was low where he was and ascended higher toward the back, higher than, lying there, he could determine. His head was elevated. Whoever had placed him on the tarpaulin had stuck *Strange News* under his head, like a good person. A candle was burning back in the more open part of the definite cave he was in. It was Houdini who had slept with a special pillow full of his mother's letters every night. He had been interested in Houdini, as a boy. How Bess, Houdini's wife, had felt about the mother-pillow was a question. There were questions no one could answer. There were going to be permanent secrets. But in his case he would know soon why he was being taken care of in this cave. The cave had a sour, organic smell.

He sat up. He could touch the rock surface above him, so he did.

Sounds were coming to him from the narrow mouth of the cave. Whatever was going on was going on there.

He was hurting everywhere. He was delighted not to be dead. Waking up, he had thought for a second he might be dead, dead but also alive,

alive in the way you would be in all the religions, with their various hells and paradises and so on.

He turned himself around and began to crawl toward the opening of the cave, and he had the thought that in fact he might be existing in some kind of illusion, the illusion that everything was real around him, that this cave was real, but that in fact he was dead, and crawling toward the dim light at the mouth of the cave was an illusion that was a kindness to him.

And as he crawled the fifteen or so feet to the dim light and toward the discussion he could hear going on he hoped to God this was real because there were the stories of people dying and going down a tunnel toward a source of light and meeting their relatives and a neon version of Jesus at the end and then a voice saying your work is not done and then snapping back like a rubber band to the operating room.

Ray thought he would be willing to die if it was going to be pitch black, hello zero, diving through the zero like a clown through a burning hoop and then nothing. He hoped to God the atheists were right. Because if there was an afterlife it would be institutional because somebody would have to run it and he couldn't go through that again. And the only worse thing would be reincarnation and back to the ocean of human institutions again.

Ray crawled and rested and crawled on. His knees were in hell. He realized that he wouldn't mind meeting his brother, now, in the death place. They would have new things to say to one another.

He emerged.

"Here I am," he shouted. He wanted to see if that would have some effect. Because if he was in a death drama, a comic opera of crawling toward the light and toward relatives, nothing he could say would have any effect on it because it would be a script, an ordained thing, like Orientation Day in college.

His voice was better, he noted.

He wanted, by now urgently, to see people he knew were alive, still, as of the time before he went into sleep.

No one was answering. The opening into the cave was raised above the ground by six feet or so. It would have required effort to get him ensconced in that cave. The stars were thick, as usual, in the sky. But of course the managers of the afterlife could arrange whatever decorations they wanted.

"Stay where you are," Morel shouted to him. A torchbeam swung up to find him.

"Help me down. Please!" Ray said. He could have shouted, but he wanted to preserve his voice, for what purpose beyond talking to Kerekang, he was unsure, but he felt strongly that it was important to be able to shout if the need arose.

He cleared his throat. "Testing, testing," he said softly. He was better. He wondered how long he had slept. He hadn't been able to find his wristwatch before they'd left Ngami Bird Lodge. His guess was that it had gone from some koevoet to some witdoek. He didn't care where it was. Iris was in favor of cheap watches. His watch hadn't been cheap but it hadn't been expensive either. He was going to stay with even cheaper watches in the future.

The cave mouth was set back from a ledge. He sat on the ledge and rubbed his throbbing knee.

Morel was being very canny with the torch, using it for short intervals and then turning it off. They were being hypercautious about signs of their presence being picked up. But he didn't know if they were being extreme or not, really. They were afraid of helicopters. He didn't think they had to worry about helicopters being used for spotting. They might be used for extraction, getting whatever was left of koevoet out and away before too much attention got fixed on the exercise and especially on where the villains had come from and who had organized them to come and who might be paying them. They were mercenaries. They were supposed to disappear.

Morel was reaching up to help him down. Ray knew he was better because small things were bothering him again, as they normally would. It was bothering him that they were being so chary with the torches. He wanted to light up the black rocky bulk rising up behind him. He wanted to know where he was, physically. He needed the free use of a torch.

"I can make it okay," he said to Morel, and pushed himself off the ledge.

He landed and collapsed but got up right away and began dusting himself off. He could smell food, something frying or roasting. He was salivating so copiously it was an impediment to telling Morel he wanted the torch for a minute.

"Can you give me that?" he said.

"Why?"

"I just need it for a second."

"Here it is, man," Morel said, surprising him.

Ray was grateful. He would be brief in his investigation. He could see where they were immediately. This was a monadnock, a pile of boulders, some of them huge and all leaning against each other like a tumulus out in otherwise flat country. It wasn't part of a chain of hills it was just a solitary upthrust of reddish granite. *The red rock wilderness shall be my dwelling place* was something from the Bible and the only person in the vicinity he could ask about the Bible was his wife's boyfriend.

Morel was examining Ray's wrists and his neck. There were new bites, little ones, not so many of them, on his wrists and hands. Ray wanted to know how badly his face was bitten but didn't want to ask Morel.

There was a small fire burning out among the debris boulders on the monadnock. He wanted to go to it. The food smell was coming from there. He was ravenous.

There should be no light if that was the object, really no light at all. He wanted to tell them about his father, who had been an air raid warden during the Second World War for about three or four months, and how strict he had been, Rex and he had heard about how strict he had been, with an armband and a helmet and a torch, or flashlight, rather, going around, saying to put this or that light out. And there had been black blinds on their windows. His father had been handsome.

"Where is Wemberg?" he asked Morel.

"It's fine. We buried him here. I'll show you the grave. And this place is on a topo map, so it can be found again, his grave. I'll show you."

"And did you say anything, did you say a word, a farewell or anything?"

"I didn't. I didn't because I didn't know what to say. I know I should have. Kerekang said something. In Setswana. I couldn't hear it because he mumbled it, but he did. And another guy spoke."

"Show me the grave, then."

"And don't worry about finding this place. It has a name, something knob, it's a knob, it's very prominent. I'll show you. Come on."

There were three graves, three patches of darker earth with a small boulder sited at what would be the head end, Ray supposed, of each. The graves were laid out close to the base of the monadnock. They would fade into the landscape so rapidly it would be a genuine task to find them again. Ray was going to try to fix in his mind anything particular about the configuration of the monadnock that would mark the spot. The stones marking the graves could shift or be rolled away.

Morel followed along uneasily while Ray studied the monadnock. It was an abrupt feature, a roughly pyramidal jumble of stones, some of them huge, with thorn brush growing out of crevices, especially lower down. The monadnock was about a hundred feet high, Ray judged. It wouldn't take long to walk all the way around it.

Morel said, "Don't keep it on. Shut it off once you've seen what you need to."

The pressure was making it impossible for Ray to make out anything distinctive, anything he was likely to be able to remember. In order to do that he needed to be in a more composed state.

"I need a hatchet," Ray said.

"A hatchet for what?"

"Look I need to chop a mark, an X, into the rock above where his grave is, just to be sure. In case these boulders you put there happen to get moved." Boulders was hyperbole. The markers were stones the size of soccer balls. They were half buried. It looked good. But they could be exposed if there was a downpour, which sometimes happened, if not very often. He wanted to chop a mark onto something huge overlooking the graves that was not going to be affected by any freak weather event. The earth around the monadnock was soft, not hard. He didn't know why that was.

Morel said, "Nothing's going to happen to the markers."

"But it might. And by the way, which one is Wemberg's? It matters which one gets buried next to Alice."

Morel hesitated, it seemed to Ray, before indicating that the middle grave was Wemberg's. That was intolerable.

"Aren't you sure which one it is?"

"The middle one, right here. I told you."

"You hesitated like you didn't know."

"I fucking did *not*. You're being crazy. It's the middle one. Calm down."

Ray couldn't. Things were getting him excited more than they should. It didn't matter. He was feeling urgency and anyone who wanted to say it was undue was welcome to.

Morel said, "Kevin helped us. I'll get him and he'll confirm it. Just wait."

That seemed to tally wrong. Morel clearly intended to go and get Kevin, get him out of Ray's sight, get him and fix it so he would say whatever Morel told him to say because Rra Finch was going mad. And it would be like Morel getting to Iris first, to warn her to say this, say that, because he knows, her husband knows, and the two of them cooking up what to say. He knew what was going to happen, if Morel had his way, which was that somehow they would be traveling back together, somehow either in the Cruiser or some other way and at some point it would happen that Morel would say *Wait here a minute I have to pee* and he would disappear and there would be a call made and Iris would be forewarned and there would be an exculpating scenario devised that he would have to use his last ounce of strength to penetrate. What he wanted was the naked truth. He wanted to surprise her. He wanted to look her in the face and see if she would lie. He didn't want to know in advance she was going to lie. She had always been truthful with him.

"I'll go get Kevin. You stay here," Ray said.

"You can't get Kevin."

"What do you mean?"

"If you look over there, where the light is, Kevin is in there. We can't go in there. They told me. It's the cadres, talking. They said we had to stay away until we get a sign. That's what they said."

"I need a hatchet or a crowbar or something hard I can gouge with and I need Kevin. I mean it. I'll tell them."

"Then go ahead and ask. You want me to stay here, I'll stay here." Morel was dealing warily with him.

The blackness around them felt irregular, like a fabric being shaken. It was bats at work, swerving and fluttering their ugly wings.

Ray wandered toward the light and the food and the murmurs.

An armed man came out to stop him.

He saw where the cadres were. Tarpaulins had been thrown over the crests of two low thorn trees growing in the midst of an isolated group of tall boulders, making a false cave. There was a Coleman lantern burning and there was also a small bright fire and meat of some kind roasting over it. There were sleeping bags on the ground. It was cozy, in there. He could see Kerekang. He thought, They have no idea how hungry I am. There were others in the faux cave.

Ray said, "Kea batla Kevin."

The armed man said "Nyah."

Ray raised his voice. "Kea batla Kevin. Kevin can you come and help? *Kevin.*"

Kevin appeared.

Ray said, "I'll need a hatchet, rra. And can you come with me and point out Rra Wemberg's grave?"

Kevin was hesitant.

"Just tell me which one it is, of the three."

"He was put in the middle."

"Good. Thank you."

"I think it will be okay. I think it is deep enough. I think so, rra."

That meant he was doubtful if it was deep enough and that some beast

of the wild could come and dig the body up. The picture filled Ray with
horror and a renewed exhaustion. The task of exhuming Wemberg and
putting him in a deeper hole was beyond him and it was something he
couldn't ask for help with. People were doing their best. He had to think.

Kevin was chewing.

I need to eat immediately, Ray thought. The need was connected to
what he had to do next while there was time, which was to make a cairn
over Wemberg, collect stray stones and pack them over the grave to create a good-faith impediment to the beasts of the wild. He would do it
himself to the best of his ability, after he'd eaten. And whoever wanted to
join in could. And he would put stones on the plots of the men buried on
either side of Wemberg, too. He was ashamed that he was only thinking
of that now, that he hadn't inquired who they were, their names, paid
attention, any kind of attention, to them.

It was meat he needed. There was something ultimate about meat on
an open fire. Barbecuing was supposed to be bad, and it was possible Iris
was right and it was, but that didn't mean it wasn't ultimate. There was
the story by Jack London about a Mexican revolutionary who came to the
United States to raise money for the revolution by fighting for prizes,
prizefighting. And the Mexican had somehow been unable to get a steak
to eat before the fight. He hadn't been able to afford it. The title of the
story was blunt, "A Piece of Meat." And then the fight had taken place
and the Mexican had fought like a demon as hard as he could and had
almost won, then he had lost because he hadn't been able to get his piece
of meat. Rex had been a fan of Jack London's stories. And there was the
one about the guy struggling to build a fire to save his life someplace in
the Arctic and getting the fire going and the fire melting snow stuck in
the branches of a tree overhead and killing the fire, and him. Rex seemed
to love stories where you struggle with all your might and then at the end
you lose.

Ray said, "I am interrupting your supper."

"Nyah, gosiame." Kevin sent the armed man away. Kevin was using
more Setswana, becoming more Tswana, it seemed to Ray. That was called
acclimating. His comrades were bush Tswana, a lot of them. There had to
be other students, people of Kevin's type, somewhere in this madness. A
number of them had left the university to join up with Kerekang. He was
curious about them. He wanted to know where they were, but he couldn't
ask without looking like a spy. He was not a spy.

Kevin was chewing and pulling strings of tough, unchewable meat out of his mouth and throwing it away. Ray thought, When I say ultimate about meat and fire, I mean ultimate in the same way a woman's breasts are ultimate, an ultimate thing you want to see and touch, a fact that will never change. When he was old he would still want to touch her breasts, assuming he was in the position to do so, Iris's breasts, which was not likely, to say the least.

He wanted to go into the faux cave and eat with the others and he wanted to escape from the feeling that the blackness around them was shuddering because of the bats engaging in their activities.

"What are you eating?" Ray asked.

"Rra, you can come to have some. It is noga."

That was a word Ray knew. It meant snake.

Kevin said, "You see when we put you for sleeping in that place we first took some snakes. Now you can come and enjoy them."

Snakes had been in the place they had slipped him into to recuperate in. It had been a good idea, except for sand flea bites on his wrists and so on. They had gotten the snakes and were eating them for dinner.

The idea of eating a snake made him want to be able to be the one human being in history who could fly, a human bird, fly to Gaborone and land in his patio and see his wife and see what she would say, seeing him. Here I am, he would say, and what do you say?

His tasks were mounting up too rapidly. There was getting *Strange News*, his packet, for one. And then there were all the others. But to get *Strange News* he would need help, he would have to be boosted up. He didn't like asking for help. He had asked for help too much already. And in fact if his entire life picture could be put up on a screen he wondered if anyone here, around here, would say he deserved help.

Kevin was pulling him toward the fire, the faux cave.

"We are cooking tea," Kevin said.

"I would like some."

There was a small, hot, resinous fire, and on a grill over the fire, coils of white ribbons of meat, snake meat. Mokopa the one-eyed chief was tending the ribbons with a knife, tossing them.

Kerekang was looking better. He stood up and held his hand out to Ray.

"Gosiame," Ray said. He had a strong desire to apologize for his absence during the time it had taken to get to the point they had all reached, this faux cave, full of men. This was something he wanted to enter and not go away from until he had to. It was a feeling between men that he wanted to have, not that he ever could, not with these men, because he was white, and for other reasons. Everyone around the fire was serious. They didn't know that was remarkable.

Kerekang ushered Ray in, conducting him to a place near the fire. Ray squatted down. He had done it with bearable discomfort, which was an improvement. He began shivering. He had been holding his reaction to the cold in abeyance. Now he was letting himself be cold and at the same time letting his bites itch and sting to their heart's content.

Mokopa was skillful with his knife. He was able to maneuver the whole tangle of snake flesh with just the one blade, one or two thrusts, turning it. Mokopa was salting the ribbons of flesh. Three large snakes had been killed. There was a good bit of meat. Two Basarwa were there, to the back, eating. Mokopa put a pot, mouth down, over the snake meat. The meat would be smoky. He would eat it however it tasted. He was getting the impression that to Mokopa grilling snake meat was a commonplace, a skill he happened to have. An eye patch would make a nice gift for Mokopa.

He found a tin mug full of hot tea in his hands. Sugar was being poured into it, too much sugar. But the calories would be good for him. It was black tea, very strong.

He looked around. He didn't know who to thank.

He thanked Kerekang, who was reclining now and smoking a rude cigarette, hand-rolled cigarette, and not smoking tobacco. It was dagga. Ray knew the odor, and that was dagga, he was sorry to say. It was very upsetting. No doubt Kerekang had a right to take a drug to calm down, the way, when he himself had been a drinker, he had taken a belt of scotch. But the problem was that he had to talk privately and seriously to Kerekang, to a Kerekang in a clear state of mind. But first he had to eat some snake meat.

Mokopa, lifting the pot, furled a darkish ribbon of snake meat onto his knife and held it out to Ray before repositioning the pot.

Ray sought to accept the furled ribbon in an insouciant way corresponding to the manner in which it had been offered. He pinched it off the knife without cutting himself and crushed the coil into his mouth. It was salty and delicious but inedible, unfortunately. Or at first blush, it was inedible. He smiled in thanks. He chewed steadfastly. He continued to smile.

He had a new vocation, chewing. There were nutrients in this protein and he would get them. And he would go and get Morel so that he could have some of this feast. And at the same time he would retrieve his parcel and bring it into the faux cave with him. But first he would get Morel and praise the delicacy he was going to get.

He got up. He thanked God he had all his teeth. That was one more thing he owed to his fanatically flossing beloved. The spines that grew on the branches of thorn trees ought to make passable toothpicks. He would collect some.

He had to talk to Morel. He wanted him to eat, if he hadn't already. They had work to do together. They had to talk sense to Kerekang. Morel knew Kerekang better than he did. And he wanted Morel to say something about dagga. They had to get Kerekang aside and lean on him, save him from this war he had lost control of. And what about Kevin? The dagga was a bad sign that had to be addressed and Morel was a physician.

There was other food to eat. Mokopa was opening cans with his knife while the smoking of the snake meat continued. Mokopa could do anything with a knife, apparently. He was very deft.

The collation, laid out on the ground, on a sheet of newspaper, was still developing. There was a stack of irregular pieces of crispbread. There was a can of peach halves. There were four cans of Vienna sausage. He had to get Morel right away, so that he could have a decent choice of what was on offer. He ate some crispbread and was delighted when Kevin produced a clutch of massive chocolate bars, Cadbury, Hazelneute, and handed one of them to Ray, who began eating it immediately. He finished his tea and asked for more.

He went to find Morel, carrying his tea with him. Morel was sitting on Wemberg's headstone. He had a penlight and it was on and it was being used to illuminate a small notepad he had open on his knee and was writing in. Hearing Ray's approach, Morel snapped the penlight off.

Ray didn't like it. There was something secretive about it he didn't like. He needed to escape his fixation on warnings and notes and forewarnings from Morel preceding Ray to his meeting with Iris, contaminating that moment, but this wasn't helping.

"What're you writing?" he asked.

"Nothing."

"No, really, what?"

"My will."

"It's none of my business. But really, what were you writing?"

Morel was silent. This is all wrong, Ray thought. They had tasks to complete together. But he needed to know what Morel had been writing. They had to find more stones for Wemberg's resting place, for one thing. He couldn't help himself.

Morel pointed his penlight at Ray and turned it on for an instant. He saw something in Ray's expression that softened him.

"Okay, I'll let you read it. And you'll see it's nothing, it's about a piece I was writing before I came looking for you."

Ray was ashamed of himself.

Morel said, "And now I'll show you the page itself."

"You don't have to."

Of course what Ray really wanted was for Morel to hand the notepad over so that he could read everything in it.

Morel said, "What have you got in your mouth?" Ray kept doggedly chewing, but he was nearing the end of his ability to continue.

"This is snake," Ray said, spitting out the irreducible wad he had in his mouth.

"Jesus," Morel said.

"It's protein. But there's other stuff to eat."

"I had something earlier, those little sausages with the red insides and some tea and some applesauce."

"There's crispbread. And they have chocolate. And just to be polite you can try the snake."

"I'll eat anything they let me."

Kerekang was standing off by himself, outside the faux cave, like a fireman without a hose, which was Iris's phrase for people in hapless solitude, or appearing to be.

"We have to work on him, the two of us," Ray said.

"We also have to get ourselves out of this at the earliest."

"I know, but first we have to prevail on Kerekang."

"No, first we have to get our own asses out. I can't take too much more. I've got to get back to Gaborone. I mean it." Morel spoke with sudden fierceness, an unfamiliar fierceness.

"Well, but—"

"I'm telling you, *I have to get back.*"

Something was happening with Morel. He was vibrating.

"Let's go back and sit down. We can talk to Kerekang later," Ray said. They could go back to Wemberg's grave and the other graves and he could bring tea and food from the collation. They could eat with their fingers. He hadn't seen any silverware in the faux cave, any napkins, but they could still have a sort of picnic. He would make it a picnic.

He said to Morel, "Let's eat something before we do anything. Go back and sit down. I'll bring us more stuff to eat."

Morel nodded and moved off in the right direction. Ray was very worried. Morel had been fine. Possibly it was the effect of being out of the immediate zone of danger, in fact it had to be that, all the high-mobilization processes coming down suddenly, in a heap.

He looked over the collation. The Vienna sausages were gone. There was no sign of chocolate. There were peach halves, a couple of them. There was some crispbread left. There was an open can of something that looked like pigeon peas. They were untouched.

Ray drained the last syrup out of the peach can into his tea mug. That would be the main vessel. He lifted up a few strings of snake meat, as a courtesy to Mokopa, who was watching what he was doing. He dropped them onto the peaches. He was dubious about the pigeon peas, but he shook most of them into the peach can. You never know what another person loves, he thought. He had a vague notion that pigeon peas were like black-eyed peas, which were favorites of black people, but not the black people around the fire, it had to be said. And he refilled his cup with the last of the tea.

Morel had gone back to Wemberg's grave and was sitting where he had been sitting before. Ray shone the torch briefly on him. This time Morel was sitting on his hands. At first Ray was bemused by it, but then he realized Morel was trying to conceal the degree of shaking he was suffering. It was severe.

"What is it?" Ray asked.

"I have to get to Gaborone," Morel answered.

"Me, too, but what's going on? Are you cold?"

"No I have to get to Gaborone. That's it. I have to figure it out."

He pressed the tea on Morel, who accepted it, but set the cup down on the ground and returned his hand to its prior place under his buttock.

"Do you like pigeon peas?" he asked Morel.

"What are they?"

"Well then I guess you won't like them. They're a legume. They're like black-eyed peas. If you don't know what they are you won't like them. They have a strong odor." He felt it was important to make Morel talk more, keep talking, get off the subject of going back to Gaborone, which was something nothing could be done about.

"I can't do anything here," Morel said.

"Sure you can. What do you mean?"

"I have nothing to work with. I have zinc oxide, what can I do with that? I have petroleum jelly. I have a headache. I don't even have any aspirin."

"Look, eat something and you'll feel better. You have low blood sugar. Drink some tea."

"Don't tell me what's wrong with me."

"No, that's just, I don't know, it's what Iris says to me when I get ragged and crab at her and I eat something and I . . ."

"It isn't that. I have to get back to Gaborone."

"You keep saying that. Why do you have to get back more than I do? Why is it so urgent? We're in a mess, here."

Morel murmured an answer.

"I didn't hear what you said."

"I have to see Iris," Morel said loudly and brokenly. Ray felt a rage of emotion, outrage, fury mixed with injury and indignation at the breaking of rules between men. He could hardly breathe.

He trained the light on Morel's face. It was an aggression. Morel was about to cry. Tears were coming. He was distraught. Ray wished that the beam of the torch could be scorching, hot enough to burn Morel, make him cry out, apologize, apologize, apologize with a scream, a begging scream. He turned the torch off. He was reeling.

Who do you think you are? Ray wanted to say, except that it was so feeble. He wanted to attack Morel. Morel needed to see Iris so much he would do something insane. It was love. He wanted to say that he hated Morel, but he couldn't.

"I'm sorry," Morel said, reaching for the cup of tea.

Ray emptied the cup on the ground. My hand did it, he thought. It had happened without his intending to do it. He was surprised at himself. There was no more tea. More could be heated up, but there was no tea right now, nothing to put in Morel's trembling, reaching hand, here in the desert.

Ray didn't want to see Morel's reaction to his act. He was ashamed.

Both of them said something about being sorry at the same time.

But Ray was in a state of blood-red rage, still. He wanted to say things that were wrong, couldn't be said. He was wanting to go into the whole stupid whatever oath there was about doctors not screwing their women patients. There had to be something like that.

"I'll get some more tea," Ray said. He hoped there was more. There would be. It was possible Morel thought that the tea had been spilled accidentally.

"No, don't. I have to talk to you," Morel said.

"What?"

"I'm worried about her."

It isn't effrontery, it's worse, it's weakness, Ray thought. Effrontery would be better.

"Say what you mean," Ray said.

"This isn't the way she wanted it. She's going to blame herself. She's going to blame herself for sending me into this. She . . ."

That was effrontery. It was astounding effrontery. Morel was obsessed with the need to go back and comfort Iris and reassure her that *he* was fine, he the doctor was fine.

"*Get hold of yourself.* You don't even know what you're saying. I can't believe you. Didn't she send you off to find *me*, if you recall?"

"She's not so strong."

"You don't even *know* her."

"I do. She's not that strong."

"You don't know anything. She's strong as a horse. Look how long she put up with me." Get some levity into this, he thought. Because he was feeling violent.

"I want to tell you I'm sorry about it, with Iris, but I can't. I have to be truthful."

"You're not sorry because it's so wonderful, with my wife. You want her. You love her."

"I do."

"I'll see if there's more tea." There was nothing to do with his feelings of fury and betrayal and inadequacy. Ray had been preoccupied with confrontation, with inducing the truth by allowing her the chance to be shameful and lie to him. Morel was thinking about how she might be doing, thinking more about how she might be doing without her new lover than without her old lover, it had to be said, but still.

Kevin was keeping the fire going.

Ray asked, "Can we make some more tea?"

Kevin leapt up to attend to it. Ray thought, He would make a nice son. But of course he already was somebody's son, somebody else's. There was nothing he could do to protect Kevin from the hazards of war. He would die bloodily. What can I do? Ray thought. It was late in the day. He could hardly put himself in the position of trying to make special provisions, arrangements, for everybody he liked among the witdoeke and not for the others, the ones he barely knew. And there was the further fact that he was not in a position to do anything, alter anything, provide any kind of alternative. And when it came to alternatives, he wasn't clear what his comrades and friends were planning to do next, what he would be trying to think of an alternative *to*. He had to talk to Kerekang. Every food can in the faux cave was empty. Fighters were already asleep or preparing to sleep. Some had sleeping bags and some had scabrous, filthy blankets and quilts. No pillows were in evidence. Kerekang was still outside somewhere, off on his own.

Kevin had put too much water in the pot. It was going to take too long to boil, especially now that the fire was in decline. Water was precious in the desert. He couldn't tip water out of the pot and onto the earth. He knew he couldn't. He waited until Kevin's attention was elsewhere and poured the excess water into a can and drank it down. Shortly, the water boiled.

Ray went to Morel. "Here's tea," he said.

"I was out of line," Morel said.

"That's all right."

"I was. And there's another thing I want to say."

"Please don't."

"No, I want to say this, then that should do it. I didn't know you. I didn't like you. I knew you were in the agency. So there was that. It put you in a category I'm not proud about. I had my objections to the agency and what it represents, and you know what, I still do. And I don't want to make an excuse out of it, but it did go on the scale. It added to the feeling I had that you didn't deserve her. Everybody knows you're in the agency . . ."

"I think you told me that once before. I had the pleasure of hearing that when we were locked up."

"Well, I didn't know you. That's all I want to say."

"Now you love me. You think I'm great."

"I'll just say I'm sorry I didn't know you better. It's cold."

If what he was hearing was an apology, it was only making Ray feel worse. What was he supposed to do with this information? He couldn't think of a thing.

"If you're cold, come on. We have to figure out where to sleep. I'm not going back into that cave. I don't know what's in there, and I notice nobody is fighting to use the space. Come on, doctor."

"You're supposed to keep a fire going as a preventive against lions and jackals, aren't you?" Morel asked.

"Yes, and leopards."

Ray noticed something. There were five stones on Wemberg's grave. Morel had been active, doing that, waiting for his tea. Ray was grateful. It was a gesture. To make a serious cairn that would pose some kind of real barrier to carrion eaters, energy would be required that neither of them had.

They went back to the fire. Someone had gathered stacks of wood, for the night. Probably it had been the exemplary Kevin, who was now lying down, sharing a blanket with someone Ray had not been introduced to. There were so many of them. He counted ten sleepers by this fire.

Kerekang was away. Kevin was asleep. Ray didn't want to call the disorganized or unorganized state of things at the center of the band of fighters dysfunctional. He had to believe that there were organizing templates that were expressing themselves in this casual scene, people sleeping, smoking dagga, that made sense. Meetings must have taken place earlier, when he was out of it, and decisions reached that left everyone in a relaxed, recreational mood. But things looked askew, lax.

"Stay by the fire, doctor," Ray said.

Morel sat down and mechanically began to feed branches into the fire, bending them in the attempt to break them into shorter lengths but giving up when they didn't break because they were too green and setting them across the fire anyway.

"I'm going to get Setime," Ray said.

"Who?" Morel asked.

"Kerekang. Don't use too much wood. Don't use too much at once."

"I'm cold."

"I know you are. But still don't."

At first he couldn't find Kerekang anywhere. Ray went entirely around the monadnock without finding him. And then it occurred to him that Kerekang might be up on the monadnock itself. And, probing with the torch, he located him, at the summit, sitting and smoking.

Ray hailed him. Kerekang signaled vaguely back. Ray decided to take it as an invitation.

Everything is too much, he thought. He had to find a route through and over a mound of boulders ranging in size from medicine balls to very large refrigerators. And he had to do it with one hand, because he had to keep the torch in use, and one good leg. And he had to avoid various thorn-bearing types of vegetation. And he had to be alert for whatever animal menaces there might be, scorpions, snakes, although they had eaten whatever snakes the monadnock hosted that they could find, presumably. There was a way up, obviously, because Kerekang had found it.

He began his climb.

"I am coming, rra, with difficulty," he called out. He was hoping that Kerekang might be moved to come down and give him a hand up.

The monadnock was more bell-shaped than pyramidal, much less pyramidal than it looked from ground level. He was at the top, with Kerekang. The climb had been mildly difficult, but he had found what appeared to be a pathway, although who had pioneered it and who would ever use it constituted mysteries. The pathway had circumvented the large monoliths or gone behind them winding steadily upward to the top and the stars. The night was moonless.

Ray had to take a moment for the view. It was beautiful, he supposed, perfect in its emptiness, an endless flat surround dotted with small, isolate, gnarled trees. They must have come a good distance because there was no sign of burning or smoke from the direction of Ngami Bird Lodge, or from what he assumed was the direction it lay in, what was left of it. The smoke would be showing black against the stars unless it was all too far away, or unless the burning was over with.

Kerekang had brought a camp stool up the monadnock with him. He had been sitting, smoking, smoking dagga. Ray didn't like that. It was too continuous. Ray found a place to sit, on a patch of sand with a boulder to set his back against. He scratched at the sand before lowering himself onto it. The idea was to dislodge creatures like scorpions.

The stars were distracting they were so brilliant.

One thing in the landscape was bothersome to Ray. He could just make out another monadnock, of about the same caliber, in the distance, to the north. He was worried that he might not be able to find the right monadnock when he came back, or more likely when he sent someone out, someone hired, to retrieve Wemberg and, while they were at it, the other two bodies buried down below them.

"What is the name of this thing we're sitting on, this little mountain?"

"It is a knob, Pieter's Knob. I can mark it on a map and give it to you."

"And over there, then, what's that?"

"Oh, that one. That one is Pieter's Other Knob."

Ray was puzzled, until Kerekang said, "I'm joking. I can't tell you what it is. But I'll find it on the map, too. I have British army maps, the best there are."

"Don't let me forget to get that from you. And another thing, I would like to have the names of the two men who were buried on either side of Rra Wemberg."

"Gosiame, on the right it is Paphani Shagwa and on the left hand it is Mido Nthumo. I can write them down for you."

"I'll forget, otherwise."

Kerekang had a pocket-size book in his hand and opened it and wrote the names on a blank fly. Ray knew what the book was. It was Palgrave's *Golden Treasury*. He had seen it before. It had been visible among Kere-kang's other books on a surveillance tape Boyle had stupidly and pointlessly ordered him to make months ago, in the stupid past. Kerekang tore the fly out of the volume and handed it to Ray folded in half.

"These two men are from Shakawe. They were good friends, to one another and to me and to all of us. No one will know their names in Gaborone. But there you have them."

He proffered a hand-rolled dagga cigarette.

"No thanks, I don't like that stuff. And I wanted to talk to you about it, too, by the way."

"Please, it's okay. I know what you want to say. Don't say it. I use it very little. It helps me, like a drink. When this business is over I won't be using it. When this . . . all this . . ."

"I wanted to talk to you about that, too. Here's the thing. Listen to me. You have to think about how to get away, get out of this. You can't go on with it much longer."

"There was no killing at first."

"I know, but now there is. You can't control something like this once it gets into killing."

"There was no killing. Not even of cattle, not one beast, at first. We were trying to teach a lesson."

"What lesson?"

"The lesson was for the big men who were bringing their herds into the sandveld and pushing the people out, the Basarwa and the Bakgala-gadi and everyone, rra. We talked to the people. And then we began with the boreholes, to show we were serious. We blew them up."

Ray said, "And some of the large owners withdrew. That's where you should have stopped, stopped and reconsidered. You needed to bring your case to the capital . . ."

Kerekang laughed. He continued, "Then we opened some kraals. We let some beasts out. And we burned some kraals . . ."

"That's when you should have stopped, before anything could be traced to you. There could have been attention paid by Gaborone. You could have stood by, blinking your eyes, saying how terrible it was, but that it was symbolic and stood for injustices still going on that needed to be taken up by government . . ."

"By Domkrag, those people! Goromente!"

"There were people who could have helped you."

Kerekang was swilling dagga smoke, it seemed to Ray, holding it in, expelling it, taking in more. Ray wanted him to go on, say more.

Finally Kerekang said, "It's bad, rra, what this has come to. I know it better than you. We knew of two cattle posts where there were great abuses of the San people working there. Terrible treatment, terrible. We went there. Beasts were killed for the first time. The word of it spread. Attacks we had no part of began. We had no control.

"Then, when we went for the San people, that was when we were robbed. A man stayed behind, Ponatsego Mazumo. You must know him. He came to us in Toromole from St. James's. He was the devil. He took all we had, and what was it for, to buy cattle for his lands at Panda-matenga. The love of cattle came to destroy us through Pony."

This was the moment Ray had dreaded. He had known it would come.

Kerekang was lighting a new cigarette from the butt of the one he had smoked down. It was too much marijuana at once. Kerekang needed to be moderate if he was going to indulge. He wanted Kerekang to be able to understand what was being said to him.

The moment had come to say what he could bear to about his connection to the disastrous appearance in Toromole of his associate Ponatsego. He had never generated a plan regarding how to put anything. The subject was too painful. He was tired but he had to act. He had to not incur Kerekang's hatred forever or he would never be allowed to help him.

Kerekang was talking. He was continuing his narrative. Ray couldn't attend to it until he had the key to what he was going to say. He had the sense of his mind grinding away mechanically to produce an object. A small object would roll down a chute inside his head and onto the back of his tongue and he would utter it.

Kerekang was almost declamatory in the way he was speaking. It was the marijuana, no doubt. He was explaining how things had gotten out of hand after emissaries, or agents, rather, of the cattle owners, attacked and burned Toromole, and then he was explaining how easy it had been to acquire weapons, how surprised he had been, how easy to get them from brokers reselling stocks accumulated in the Caprivi Strip after the Boers abandoned everything there. Money had come to Ichokela from sources he was not identifying once the fighting and sabotage had begun. That was interesting. In his old incarnation Ray would have been extremely interested in that. There was always somebody delighted to fan the flames. It was always in somebody's interest. Now Kerekang was talking about an adventure. To escape pursuers they had been forced to cross Lake Lambedzi, Kerekang and his band, his original band, Lake Lambedzi being, as Ray recalled, a soda lake, a lake in name only, a depression in the earth covered with a crust of soda and with some acid hot smoking mixture underneath the crust. And the way they had crossed it was to follow *exactly* in the hoof- or footmarks of cattle that had made it across and avoid deviating and going near the carcasses of the drowned cattle who had gotten it wrong. The crust was uneven. And certain of their party had gotten off the track and fallen down up to their waists in smoking brine, although brine was just what he was calling it, it was acid. And they had pulled their comrades up and continued. And they had gotten across, all of them. Kerekang was repeating himself. There was some poetic thing there, in this account. Kerekang was getting into a mythic style. I have to stop him, Ray thought. He had to stop him before he lost his strength to go into the case of Pony. And he didn't want to stop Kerekang because there were threads or filaments between them only he was thinking about, Kerekang who loved Tennyson but was engaged in rough justice, call it, and he himself with Milton and now the hell he was in and had helped create, to be fair about it. So he wanted two things at the same time, as usual.

He didn't like doing it but he said, "Stop, I have to tell you something."

Kerekang was still talking about Lake Lambedzi. Ray touched him, shook him.

Ray said, "I have to tell you something." He hoped Kerekang would be ready to hear him, instead of floating in the great moments of his campaign, the top ten moments, which it looked like he was doing, thanks to the great weed, dagga. Iris had saved Ray from alcohol.

Ray went on. "I have to tell you this, I knew Pony at my school and I have to tell you this, rra, I was his friend . . ."

Kerekang was still declaiming.

Ray was proceeding still not knowing what he was going to say.

Ray said, "It was through me that Pony met you."

"I can't remember it," Kerekang said. He was puzzled.

"No, you wouldn't. Because you met him at the doctor's place when you were attending these sessions he gave, on God and so on."

"But I never saw you there."

"No I was never there. But I sent Ponatsego there to see what these sessions were about. I was curious. I suggested he go and then report if it was interesting."

He wondered if he had the gall to leave it there and not tell more, let his liability stop at that, just be a consequence of innocent personal curiosity on his part.

Kerekang flicked his cigarette, only half consumed, away, high into the air.

Ray tried to rush on, burying his connection with Pony under apologies. "I am so sorry I sent him. I was curious, you know. I couldn't go myself. All these seminars, whatever you call them, were restricted to Batswana, with no expatriates."

"So, rra, you sent Ponatsego to me."

"No, rra, I sent him to see what he could find out about the doctor's seminars, what was going on there. That was all. It was not about you."

Kerekang looked coldly at him, it seemed to Ray.

Kerekang said, "Why is it you would do that?"

"I wanted to know, rra. I had personal reasons. And curiosity."

"And what else?"

"What do you mean?"

"And what else? What would make you send this man, this colleague of yours? Did you tell him to do it as a favor to you, rra?"

"Not as a favor, no. Rra, you are understanding."

"There was a gratuity, then? Is that right?" Kerekang's voice was hard.

"There was." This is it, Ray thought.

"Was it just you yourself providing the gratuity?"

"No, of course not."

"What was the source of the gratuity then, rra?"

Ray thought, I have to. He said, "I have to explain what I was doing then. Please listen to me."

"Oh I am listening." Kerekang was suddenly very sharp.

"First about my interest in the doctor. Rra, he has stolen my wife, who was his patient, and it had just begun. We need not say more about this. What I need to tell you is that I was working for the American government, apart from my teaching job at St. James's, working for the American government."

"I am still listening. And I am sorry, rra, to hear the other."

"I was working for an American intelligence service." He had to lie about his connection because he couldn't bear to say he hadn't yet quit, that he was still a member of the agency. He couldn't. He had done something, some things that ought to show he was free of that, in Kerekang's eyes.

Kerekang was shaking his head.

Ray said, "I am through with them, Kerekang." He thought that was fair, and covered the situation, except for the papers he would have to sign.

Kerekang said, "Well it is good you say all this, because it is no secret to me that you were an agent, a spy, really. That was what was said."

Ray didn't know what to feel. Apparently knowledge about his status had been universal. He had been an actor in a different play than the one he had thought he was in. He wondered how much Iris had known about his nakedness. He had to believe she would have told him. He hadn't completely believed Morel, he had thought Morel probably just had suspicions, which he had made Iris confirm. Ray had known that Boyle was generally understood to be in the agency. But he had never truly thought that he himself had been picked out. It was odd to think he wouldn't have seen that in people's faces.

Kerekang was mentioning three other people he was also under the impression belonged to the agency. None of them were right. None of them had anything to do with the agency. Unless he was in the dark, in the wrong compartment. He was uncertain about everything. He wanted to say definitely that Kerekang was wrong, but he couldn't, not with any conviction.

"So you have left this organization," Kerekang said.

"I am out of it. But I have to be sure you understand. When I sent Pony to report on the doctor, it was for my own, my own personal information. This is complicated. The head of our office is Boyle, Kerekang, Chester Boyle. He wanted me to pursue *you* and I was opposed and I told him so. I said to him you were a patriot and an intellectual and a reformer and a good man. Of course now you are burning the countryside to ashes and I am helping you, so life is very strange. I am sorry to say that I believe the agency was behind some of your troubles in getting employment with the government. I had nothing to do with that. No, and the fact is that when Boyle said I should look more into you, more than I had, because I had done some looking, my idea was to tell him that the best way to find out more about you was through these seminars, where you would participate, at our friend Doctor Morel's house. And you know why I wanted to know more about the doctor. I hated him then. So I thought I could appease my boss by sending Pony to bring reports on these seminars where you were a participant. But Kerekang, nothing he brought to me was ever turned over, never. I swear to this."

In a way he didn't care what Kerekang said next. He was full of lightness. He would sleep well, he knew. Of course he was on the ragged edge physically, which would help. He was looking forward to sleep. Sleep would be different now. He was full of lightness.

Kerekang interrupted. "We know him. Nyah, rra, he is well known. And the one before him, the Jew."

Ray recoiled. He was shocked. He wanted to protest, say something, affirm his friend Marion, use his name to show he esteemed him. He was distressed that Marion had been as readily identified as the egregious, the cack-handed, as the Brits would put it, Chester Boyle. It was unfair. Resnick had been subtle in everything. And it was unfair, calling him the Jew, identifying him that way. Ray had determined that he was going to help, or to put it another way, save Kerekang, and he needed to like him as much as he could. Kerekang was his new friend, his new friend. The man didn't know it yet, but it was the truth. Iris had been his friend, but now she was dissolving, and Marion was gone. He had not lived a life where he could normally acquire friends.

"You don't have anything against Jews, do you, you're just saying the guy who came before Boyle was Jewish." He hadn't put it quite right, but it was the best he could do.

Kerekang was saying something, vigorously. "Ah, no. Even Jesus was one of them. I am not an anti-Semite, rra."

That was a relief. He moved on. He said, "Look I want you to consider getting out of this, how to get out of this."

"What do you mean? But speak quietly."

"Right. Because we can both of us see where this is going. You know what a jacquerie is, where everybody in the countryside goes on a rampage and tears up the pea patch but not in favor of any sort of program, just to destroy the old order and then the old order or its friends come back like thunder and make it worse than before . . ."

Kerekang said, "Do you know this, that some of us are *taking* cattle, robbing them from the Baherero, which was not what we set about. When we killed the beasts, it was to deprive the big men who had come out into the sandveld. Even so, I wanted the slaughtering part to stop once we had shown we have the power up here. Of course you can say it ran on too long and I will agree, and I have tried to stop it. But the killing was to shock the letleke, the ones with too much. And when the killing stopped, still it would hang over them, and they could see it would be useful to help Ichokela in future."

Ray was surprised. Because what this looked like was a sort of extortion scheme to get money or other resources from the cattle-owning elite to be put to use in Kerekang's social program, his homestead socialism, whatever it should be called. He could see how it had happened. Kerekang had fallen into it, allowed things to happen and then taken steps based on what he had allowed to happen, trying to turn mistakes made, or accidents, to the advantage of his group, his great project. This was a confession. Kerekang was very agitated.

Apparently Kerekang had a bottomless supply of dagga cigarettes. He was lighting up yet another one, murmuring that they were useful, the smoke was useful against dimonang, which meant mosquitoes. And the mosquitoes just at that moment were annoyingly active. It was better when there was any sort of breeze and worse when the air was still. Ray was tired of brushing at the mosquitoes, waving his hands around maniacally when the surges came. The clouds of dagga smoke did seem to discourage the mosquitoes. Ray felt a rush of temptation. Kerekang was in a state of elevation. He was speaking freely. If Ray joined him in this indulgence it might be helpful in reaching him on a certain level and convincing him it was time to save himself, to leave the scene and leave Botswana and save himself for a new life elsewhere, like someone else he could name. He was getting a more than ample sample, so to speak, of the perfume from the garden of delights Kerekang was inside. In a minute Kerekang would start mentioning pleasant things that were not relevant to the present completely fucked and unraveling situation. He would say that something was beautiful, something that really wasn't beautiful or that if it was didn't matter. You are psychic, Ray said to himself, because Kerekang was just then saying something about the earth being beautiful.

I would love to see beauty everywhere, too, Ray thought. He would like it even briefly but it was not what he needed.

Iris, her image in his heart or wherever it was, his mind, was helping him. Because it was Iris who had saved him from the deadly synergy of getting people to drink, in his official capacity, so that they would let relevant things out, and he had used the occasions to get drunk himself, which was a thing that had led to the downfall of more than one agency character, agents and officers and top dogs and not excluding Marion Resnick. But she had rescued him and had convinced him that he could do the sordid, not to mince words, the sordid socializing he had to do without being in bondage to alcohol, and he had succeeded, despite temptations that had come up. And because of that he would live longer than he would have, and in addition to giving up drinking there was the contribution to a longer and lonelier old age he had to thank her for via his giving up tobacco.

Ray had himself in hand. It was the image of his wife, his beloved, reminding him that it was important for him to be able to say truthfully that he hadn't used drugs if the question appeared on an application for a job in the new life that was en route to him in an age when you could be asked to take a lie detector test as routinely as you could be asked to urinate in a Dixie cup for whatever anyone wanted to know. How long the image of his beloved would burn usefully bright was something he would have to wait to find out, in the years to come. Because the truth was that it was going to fade, he could expect it to fade, because everything fades. It wasn't her fault.

Ray said, "You know what I think, rra, I think you have to get away to South Africa. Here in this country you are always going to be Setime, the fire-thrower, and you'll be hunted down by Domkrag. They know who you are. Listen to me. This will not be forgiven. Mandela is coming to power soon in South Africa and it is going to be a new day. It's coming, and you could be safe there . . ."

"They'll kill him first."

"No. His time has come. They won't."

"They say it was you Americans who whispered to the Boers where to find him."

"Yes, it was my agency, I know that . . . rra, I'm changing my life. I think I may be going to South Africa. It's going to be a new time, and rra, I have contacts there. I mean education people, not agency contacts. I have an idea for a school. But I do have agency contacts that could help you, people who know me from the life I'm leaving. Like I'm leaving my wife." Ray's voice buckled. He fabricated a coughing fit. He thought, I'm expressing myself poorly.

He had to be able to say it evenly because it was going to come up and come up. He said, "Yes, I'll be leaving my wife. That's part of it."

"I am sorry, rra. Truly."

"Nothing can be done."

What he wanted to express to Kerekang was that they could join together, he and Kerekang, leaving everything behind and doing their lives differently forever at the same time. It was notional, no doubt about it. And it was the movies. It had the feeling of the movies about it, which ought to be a warning to him about how seriously he should be taking this idea. But he was in the grip of it. He liked, in fact loved, the idea of taking his tradecraft and using it contrarily, using it to get papers or passports or whatever was needed to get Kerekang launched and circumstanced away from the mayhem and murder he was drowning in. Of course he was thinking ten or twelve steps ahead of where they were now, silent upon a peak in not Darien but Pieter's Knob and gazing out not at the Pacific Ocean but at the inscrutable sea of life they were going to put their canoes into, a different sea.

And then there was the question of whether Kerekang was going to feel he had any reason to believe Ray was genuine in his declaration of independence from the agency and the life he'd led, the entire life. Because it could so obviously be a maneuver, a ruse, a charade designed to conceal some underlying purpose of the agency, like sticking to Kerekang like a leech and finding out everything that would turn up about him and his associates everywhere. His warrant with Kerekang was what had been done to him at Ngami Bird Lodge and then what he had done on the roof of the building, insanely. Of course once you began asking questions there was no end in sight. For example how could he form a trusting partnership with anyone who believed him so easily when he said he was transforming himself so absolutely yet so abruptly? Your questions are non sequiturs, one non sequitur following another, he thought. He was paralyzing himself with questions.

On impulse Ray reached out and seized Kerekang's wrist, and then his hand.

He said, "This is serious, what I'm saying. I want you to think. Stop smoking dagga, why don't you. You've had plenty."

Kerekang seemed surprised but not annoyed.

He said, "That's right." He spat out the burning cigarette. There was something almost jaunty or jocular about the way he did it. That's the marijuana showing. It made people compliant with whatever was going on. Ray didn't want Kerekang to come around to this view because he was being helped there by the dagga. No, what he wanted was for Kerekang to come around because he had spoken to him from his heart, there was no other phrase for it, spoken from his heart to the man Kerekang, and had been understood, had been received man to man, Ray speaking from his situation, dying animal to dying animal, he couldn't express it exactly.

Kerekang was being agreeable. He was standing up and stretching.

"I had a wife, as well," Kerekang said.

"Ah. You did?" Ray was surprised. This was a lacuna. There had been nothing in Kerekang's dossier to suggest it.

"You were married?"

"Nyah, she was waiting for me, to marry. She was my betrothed."

"And what happened?"

"Well, perhaps you can tell me, because she surprised me after six years when I was abroad, studying, as we agreed I should do, while she worked in Gaborone."

"What do you mean?"

"Rra, I had one more year to be in Scotland. We were writing, we were telephoning. I had home visits, and they were just what you would hope. All the time I was abroad I was sending her poetry, this and that."

"So you had no sign?"

"Nyah, not one, rra."

Ray was amused that the agency had missed this information. It was an example of how defective the apparatus he was leaving was, how incompetent in so many ways.

"I'm sorry to hear about this." But he was and he wasn't, because if he was understanding correctly there was a bond glimmering between them that he hadn't known would be there.

Kerekang was walking around the narrow summit. He was holding his fists against the top of his head. He came back to Ray.

He said, "Do you know Thomas Lodge?"

Ray felt incompetent. He knew it was English Literature, but that was all he knew. It was not his period.

"I know the name." English Literature was the Pacific Ocean.

Kerekang said, "I know every word of his ode,

> *"Of thine eyes I made my mirror,*
> *From thy beauty came mine error;*
> *All thy words I counted witty,*
> *All thy smiles I deemèd pity;*
> *Thy false tears that me aggrieved*
> *First of all my trust deceived.*

> *"Siren pleasant, foe to reason,*
> *Cupid plague thee for this treason!"*

It was a consummate performance. Kerekang could take dead text into his chest and mind and heart and make it live, just as he had done with

Tennyson at the ambassador's residence. Kerekang was putting his sorrow away in poetry. He was standing up stanced in an artificial way as he declaimed. He was meant to be a performer. It was obvious. He was speaking blindly and brilliantly to the stars the air and to his one-man audience the English professor. "Bravo," Ray said.

"Thank you. I sent that to Eunice when she broke it off with me. And do you know she was married in two weeks afterward?"

"Eunice . . . not Eunice Kamphodza?"

"Yes it is. You know her?"

"Well her husband I know, Kamphodza, at the Ministry of Education. He is an obstacle to progress, mainly. He's number four, or three, maybe three, by now. He should retire. And I see her. I think she works at Tourism and comes out to get food at King's Takeaway in the mall for her office mates. At least I assume the food is for others. She's quite a heavy woman, if I'm thinking of the right person."

"Yah, it is. She is very fat now. She is an elephant. Tlou, we say. She wasn't so fat when she was younger."

It was probably the wrong thing to say but Ray felt impelled to say it. "So then do you . . . well, do you feel you escaped something, in a way? I mean, does it make you feel a little better about what happened?"

"I don't know," Kerekang answered.

Ray wished he hadn't said what he said. He knew what was behind it. He was feeling envy that Kerekang's missed prize had so quickly tarnished itself in the eyes of the world. That wouldn't happen with Iris. It was not something he could wish for, not something he should wish for. She was more of a prize as time went on and she held steady and rose in the eyes of the world and he became a drier and lesser version of himself, withering into the unpleasant truth of what he was, or not the unpleasant truth but the unimpressive truth. There were ten years between them. He was a dry person. He would long precede her into dryness, terminal dryness. But she was flourishing. In every period of her life she had been the ideal representative of what a woman could be in that span, her pretty youth, her beautiful young womanhood. She was still not a matron. She was flourishing, with her glossy hair, sweet dark eyes, good flesh, her lean face. Her breath was always sweet. She had perfect breasts, lower than when she had been young but appropriately lower and still full, perfect handfuls for the lucky man who could get into her bower. She knew everything there was to know about nutrition, what was good for the skin. She had avoided the sun, managed to do that in Africa, and without calling attention to it, being subtle about it. She had been in advance of the news that the sun was our enemy. She was a disciplined eater. God had given her teeth as white as cotton. His own hair was hanging on but it was less thick than it had been and across the crown there was a glow rather than a solid presence of hair. He might find someone if he could keep Iris's admonitions in mind, like remembering to sit up straight at the table because alphas always sit up straight. And there were her silky nipples, so delicate. Her voice had gotten a little huskier with age, but men liked that. He did himself.

Ray said, "Well then do you see her, do you encounter one another?"

"We did for a time."

"And what was that like?"

"Ah, rra. The truth is that she is rude to me. She moves away if she sees me, very fast, slick."

"That's too bad."

"Well it is because she knows what I feel about Kamphodza. He is powerful in Domkrag, do you know that? You must. In Ghanzi he is a tautona, with the lands he owns. She will inherit a lot when he goes. It was the dream of getting beasts that pushed her into his old-man arms, I am sure. Because the law is changing so that women can inherit lands. And he has no sons, or any children at all."

"Well okay, but what are your feelings toward her? I have no right to ask you, I know, but what are they?" He couldn't stop himself. He was taking everything as a rehearsal for what was coming with him. He wanted information.

"You see, rra. I still love her. Even today, I do."

"I understand it."

"Yah, but she is too fat now."

"We still love them," Ray said.

"Yah, we still love them." Kerekang seemed to be laughing.

"What can we do?" Ray said. The woman was obese and this good man still loved her, loved her soul or her previous envelope, younger envelope.

It was amazing how much light the stars gave. He could see everything he needed to see in the face of this tough, small, wiry man. He liked him. He liked him more all the time.

Kerekang was seeming sympathetic to the project of departure together that Ray was proposing. Of course what choices did he have?

Ray said, "What about the students, like Kevin, who came north with you to Toromole, what about them, where are they?"

Ray was uneasy with his own question and he knew why. It implied he felt a special obligation to do something to save the educated, bypassing the question of everybody else caught up in the insurgency, the rural people, the proles, all those who had swung in behind Kerekang just as solidly as the jeunesse dorée had. What was wrong with him? On the other hand, what was wrong with everything?

He couldn't help pursuing it. He said, "I see Kevin with you, but what about the others from the university?"

Kerekang said, "Ah, you see, he is very disobedient. He wouldn't listen. He is disobedient. The others, I sent them back. I sent them back one by one as they came in from hunting Pony, and not finding him anywhere. I said to them that they could come back at some later time. Kevin said no. It was a fight. Well. So he is with us."

He was going to help Kerekang, if he could, but there was going to be an absence of justice in the way it worked out, because it was a fantasy that Kerekang could gather up all his forces and make a speech to them saying they had done as much as they could and then urging them to follow him like Moses across the border into Namibia, assuming there was a way to do that, an army wending its way through the desert into another part of the desert, a safer part, without being destroyed on the way.

He had to narrow it down. He had to save himself and he had to save Kerekang and he had to save Morel and he had to save Kevin. And he had to save his brother's manuscript, which had been out of his sight and care for too long.

Someone was whistling, someone close by, someone approaching.

It was Kevin, and Ray was annoyed. He had been getting somewhere with Kerekang.

Kevin appeared.

"You must come and sleep, Setime," he said.

Now Morel was climbing up to join them. There were going to be too many cooks.

Morel was carrying Ray's *Strange News* bundle. "Here, take it," he said to Ray, arriving at the summit.

"Thanks, but what made you think of it?" Ray asked.

"I don't know. Some of the guys were looking around for paper. You can imagine why. They wanted to know if I had any tissues, papiri. I don't know if any of them understood clearly that what you were carrying around was a treasure of toilet paper, but I thought I would just preemptively get it. So thank me again." Everyone was feeling better, slightly better, slightly stronger. That was evident.

"We are having a summit meeting," Morel said. No one said otherwise. There was silence.

"It is," Kerekang said. His mind was still in a floating state, thanks to dagga, still half there, still showing a tendency toward compliance with the world as it was developing, the real world.

Kevin said, "I . . . I . . . rra, I want to be home. If I can. I have written a letter to you." He handed a folded sheet of paper to Kerekang, who stuck it to his waistband, nonchalantly, not receiving it in the correct manner, Ray felt.

They were becoming a conspiracy, it felt like, a *sauve qui peut* thing, and his hat was off to the French for their beautiful precisions, especially when it came to treachery.

Kevin was speaking. He was reporting that there was fear being expressed among comrades about staying too long there. It wasn't fear of being tracked to the spot by koevoet foot soldiers, it was fear of helicopters seeking them out from bases in Caprivi, once the news was out about what had been accomplished at Ngami Bird Lodge.

Kevin was saying, "We shall paint you with fire, is what koevoet says, when they threaten you. This is what they did in SouthWest."

Kevin was hugging himself. It was cold.

"You must come and talk to Mokopa, Setime," Kevin said.

"Why must I?"

"Because he is afraid about the vehicles. He says they can track them and find us. That koevoet will come seeking us because we've struck them in their pride."

Ray said, "I thought everyone was falling asleep down below."

"Nyah, they are awake. They are having a meeting. You can see they have built the fire high again."

Morel said, "It's too high. I thought we were supposed to keep the fire to a minimum."

Kerekang sighed heavily. He got up to descend the monadnock. Morel stopped him.

Morel said, "Wait a minute. Let me understand . . ."

Kevin said, "They say they are freezing and the fire will be for only until they can get warm. And they are saying they want to hide I don't know where. Hide for some days."

Morel, speaking quickly, said to Kevin, "So they want to abandon the trucks . . ."

Kevin said, "Mokopa says koevoet has strong forces in Caprivi and he knows they have helicopters. And this makes them look bad, so it will be necessary for them to come after us. He says we should do as Joshua Nkomo did when he was fighting Ian Smith in Zimbabwe and the war came to an end, with the Shonas and Mugabe coming out the top men, and Nkomo sent forth the message to his fighters to bury their weapons and come walking home, but to mark where they were, the caches."

Kerekang said, "Mokopa is from ZAPU. He fought alongside Joshua Nkomo."

Light breaks where no sun shines, Ray thought. A question was being answered. It would make sense for Kerekang's weapons to have come from ZAPU caches. And it was a fact that ZAPU had buried huge quantities of arms when independence came in Zimbabwe. This was the kind of information Boyle had sent him into the bush to come up with, and Boyle would never know. Ray felt like laughing.

Ray was thinking furiously. So were the others. He observed that everyone on the summit was visibly shivering in the cold breezes strengthening around them. No one was paying attention to the cold. They were too busy thinking. Individuals were clutching for handholds on slippery events, rapidly changing slippery events, trying to twist them to their own benefit. Morel wanted to secure a vehicle and speed home to Iris. Kevin appeared to want to be out of the fighting. And as for himself, Ray wanted to save Kerekang's life and his own. And Ray knew that he wanted to preserve Kerekang for himself, for a friend. What Kerekang himself wanted was in flux, partly because the man had gotten high. But Ray was glimpsing the outline of an argument he could pursue with Kerekang, urging that he follow Mokopa's advice about caching all their munitions and fading away with the idea that he might live to fight another day but in the meantime putting his talents to work in friendlier and more promising terrain, Mandelaland.

One last thing he wanted to know was where Kerekang had gotten the motley collection of vehicles they were bucketing around the countryside in.

He thought he knew how it had been done. It wasn't complicated.

"Kevin, these trucks and the bakkies, where did you get them?"

"We took them."

"You mean you stopped them on the road and forced the drivers out and then just drove off in them."

"Ehe, it was like that. No one was hurt and we saw that they were left with water and provisions enough to keep them to the next ride. We took so many vehicles, rra, in different places. It was fun, in fact. And we used them and left them. But the word is in the air now, for sure, so we have come to the end of replenishing our transport so easily that way. No, the people will shoot us if we approach. Yah."

Kerekang was seeming lost. He was saying softly that he wanted to write something. And with his hand he was making a motion like the one diners use when they want the check.

Ray understood. It was education speaking. He thought, We get into crisis and we need to write down where we are in our lives, write letters or manifestos or farewell to the troops, convert our confusion to text so we can read it and see if we can do what our words tell us we should. Kevin had felt the necessity to write a letter to Kerekang. I'm suffering from the same need myself, Ray thought. He wanted to write a master-piece letter to Iris, but there was no time and no desk to write on. He needed a desk. He thought, When we read poetry we like, tiny muscles in our throat clench and relax, showing we're speaking it, the lines, uncon-sciously. He wondered where he had read that. And then there was Dante writing letters to Beatrice Portinari he never sent, writing them for years, writing to a woman married by her parents to someone else, a woman he had been in love with since both of them were nine years old, saving up his letters and then learning that she had died. But he had written to her for years, never sending a letter, not one. And he had married, himself, but even after his own marriage he had kept writing. And then he had found out she was dead. And so on into the night. Where was Dante? Where was he, Ray Finch, right now?

Kerekang said, "If I go to SouthWest . . . Jesus, I don't know. I will have to explain. I will have to write something. Ah Jesus, I will. And I will have to send it out into the hands of people who can read it to the others. They burned our press at Toromole. How can it be done?"

Ray said, "It can. I can work it out. I promise you it can."

Kerekang made a sound of disgust, self-disgust.

Morel said, "Look, it's good. You'll be like who is it, plenty of people, Arthur, King Arthur, Robin Hood, they expected them to come back. Am I right?" He looked at Ray. "*King Arthur is nat dede*. King Arthur is not dead. It was a belief among the common people. Supposedly."

Ray was hating Morel at that moment, for his crude transparency. He was not helping. I want to handle this, he thought.

Kerekang said, "Ah but they are still waiting for those heroes. They're not coming, are they?" He was annoyed. He seemed to be getting a little clearer.

Ray said, "Well but you know what he means. And there's the slight difference that *you wouldn't be dead*. You'd be alive and in the neighborhood. Things are going to change in Botswana, out in the countryside, rra. If you go now, you'll still be alive when the time comes. This was not your moment, Kerekang. But you'll see your moment."

Kevin was nodding. Ray thought, You may have to enlarge your plan to include him. That was daunting, but since he had no real plan as yet, or only the vaguest glimmer of one, maybe it didn't matter much. He needed to have images, stronger ones, of what the future might look like. It would be in a school. Education in the Republic was going to be open to all kinds of new visionary things. Patrick van Rensburg was already sending down tentacles from his education-with-work system, the Brigades. And that was only one example. And Kerekang would be in a school where he could promote his homestead plans, backyard food self-sufficiency and part-time paid labor. It was the idea of progress he was holding out, that battered thing. And Kerekang would have a new identity. Ray knew how to manage that. And Kerekang could get his ideas into circulation through the mails and through the press. There would have to be some dissembling and subtlety about who this was who happened to be advocating ideas associated with the late lamented vanished Kerekang the Incendiary. He could pretend to be a disciple of his own dead self, or his brother. Stranger impostures had been tried and had worked. And Kerekang had the advantage of being Xhosa, from a Xhosa community that had overlapped into Botswana generations back. So he could speak Xhosa. That would be perfect for camouflage. Mandela was Xhosa. The school could be bilingual. That would be fine, just so that one of the languages was English. There was going to be money available for good works in the Republic, tons of it, foundation money, once Mandela was in power, tons of it especially for education, which foundations of every type and kind loved to fund. He was developing more and more enthusiasm for his idea as he what, fondled it.

Kerekang said, "That fire is too bright. If they want a fire, they should make it in that cave."

"You mean that cave you left me in?"

"Yes, they can make a fire there, not in the open."

Kevin said, "They won't go there because of snakes."

Ray said, "I thought they cleaned them out. I thought we ate them for dinner." He was feeling odd, just then.

"Yah, but more can come."

"Wonderful," Ray said.

Kerekang said, "I have to go down. I know what this is. They want us to have indaba. Okay, we can."

Ray was uncomfortably cold but he didn't want to lose the moment, go down to the fire, because he was getting ideas, here, upon a peak, et cetera. He liked the idea of an ideal school in a new country, which the Republic would be. He could burn bright to that. He hoped there was nothing pitiful in the idea he was nurturing for Kerekang and Kevin and himself.

They were all going to go down to the fire, it seemed. A general movement had begun. And now he couldn't wait to get to the fire and embrace it. Everything was hurting. They had put him in a cave with snakes. He wanted to lie down next to the fire and stop thinking.

He stumbled twice, descending. He would like to be able to contemplate going to a spa and recovering there, except that he could only do that with a female companion. Men never attended spas without their wives, their girlfriends, at least that was his impression.

He was too tired to think clearly, but he had a germ of an idea about a way out with Kerekang, which was that together he and Kerekang would concoct a false death story. Kerekang would go off to his contacts in Namibia and get to the Republic, but the story would be that he had died in the battle for Ngami Bird Lodge. Morel would sign on if it could be made absolutely clear why he had to, although there was the man's principle against lying. And if there was time Kerekang could compose a farewell to his troops. He would do it perfectly. And it could constitute the legend that Kerekang was going to be known by. Kerekang would need a legend.

All the comrades around the fire got to their feet as Kerekang approached. They exchanged a word, a greeting, but not one of the standard greetings, some private thing, as Kerekang entered the zone of firelight. Ray hadn't been able to make it out. There were twenty men there, close to the fire, and ten or so more back in the shadows. He couldn't be sure, but most of those in the background seemed to be Basarwa. There was a mystery about Bushman metabolism. Most of the Basarwa were shirtless. They were wearing shorts, regular bush shorts and not loincloths. They seemed not to be suffering from the chill of the night. The Tswana men near the fire were wearing shirts, shirts on top of shirts in some cases, and jerseys.

The faces of the witdoeke were still not individual to Ray, except for Mokopa and three or four others. That was explainable. He had only recently met any of them and that meeting had taken place under conditions of violent action, when the time for any kind of reasonable scrutiny was nonexistent. And then he had been conveyed along in a sleeping state broken into two periods, part one in the trunk and part two in the cave. And then when he had returned to normal it was the middle of the night. So he could be forgiven.

Kerekang was unified with the suffering that had brought these men to his cause. It was more than a matter of pity, which was the limit of the usual feeling evoked by poverty and injustice. It was sympathy, but a different order of sympathy, it was embodied.

Ray could aspire to it, was what he could do.

Ray knew himself. He saw his own limits clearly. It was true he believed in fairness, social fairness. But it was probably truer to say that he believed in *fairnessness*, which would translate as a belief in a certain quantum of fairness existing in any society, enough fairness so that the issue wouldn't be tormenting to people trying to get on with other things like art and scholarship and the rest of it. He was being hard on himself. He didn't care. He couldn't keep standing, though.

Without ceremony, and while some sort of intense preliminaries were still in progress, all in Setswana, Ray made his way around to the far side of the fire and wedged his way in among the Tswana comrades and sat down, embracing his knees. He was the only one sitting. The fire was wonderful. He didn't care if he was the only one sitting.

Morel had slipped around to stand in back of him. He was showing solidarity. I am not leaving this fire, period, Ray thought. He didn't understand concerns about the fire, the brightness and so on. Because as he understood it there had to be a fire all night, as a preventive against lions, and the bigger the fire the better. And the idea that koevoet would send helicopters, the idea that they would risk them on a night mission when all they would see would be one fire among others, normal cooking fires here and there in the desert, was not worth worrying about, in his humble opinion.

Kerekang was directing everyone to sit down. Kevin opened Kerekang's camp stool and got Kerekang seated and then he himself came around to sit cross-legged beside Morel, behind Ray. The three of them were becoming a team, a sort of team.

It was hard to attend to what was going on. Now that Ray was out of the maelstrom of danger, his injuries were hurting more insistently. He wanted a bath. He wanted to be ushered into a well-appointed large bathroom and left there with the hot water running. He wanted to get into a deep tub of hot water. When his brother had been a small boy he had liked to lather his hair and twist it up into devil horns to make everybody laugh, and they had laughed, and now his brother was dead. He wanted his brother to not be dead. He wanted to get into a tub and have his back washed by Iris, with a loofah. He wanted to be able to look forward to that.

There was a protocol to the present event. Each of the comrades was making a preliminary statement, in turn. Everything was in very rapid Setswana, but oddly accented Setswana. The language was spoken differently in the various regions of the country. The exchanges were more than usually opaque to Ray, but his fatigue was hurting his ability to concentrate.

He turned to look at Morel. His brows were knitted. He was struggling to follow. He was having his own difficulties with the Setswana, with this rapid and dialectal Setswana with, Ray was now realizing, inclusions of a second language, Sekgalagadi, laced in.

He was out of his element but he didn't mind. He was in the presence of a harmonious organism, the band of fighters, operating by cues and understandings he was not part of. That was fine with him. And this organism was operating in darkness, among boulders and thorn trees and odd cries, animal cries, coming out of the darkness. He would never see it again. What he needed to do was to concentrate less on trying to understand what was being said and more on keeping himself from falling over into another bout of exhausted sleep.

He was trying and then there was a blank moment and then he was being hauled to his feet by someone behind him, by two people, Kevin and another comrade, a Mosarwa. Clearly he had missed something.

Morel also was standing. They were being led off into the night by Kevin, who seemed sullen. Ray resented leaving the campfire. The night was bitter.

Ray felt better when he realized that their destination was another fire, a smaller one but still a fire, burning in the lee of a massive, slightly concave hump of a rock.

"What is it, Kevin? Why are we . . . where are we going?" Ray asked.

"Just there." He pointed at the fire by the rock.

Morel said, "They asked the makhoa to leave while they finished talking. They think we understand more than we do. They have a right, though, to their privacy. But I couldn't catch a quarter of what they were saying."

Ray said, "But Kevin, what about you? You and this man? Go ahead, you can go back."

Kevin said, "Nyah, rra. I was told to stay with you."

Morel was annoyed. He said, "Hey, what are we going to do, creep around to spy on you? This is silly."

"My orders are to stay, rra."

Ray felt as though he were being dragged to the new fire like a dummy. The small fire was better than nothing, but he wanted to go back to the main fire, where the sleeping bags were, and go to sleep there.

Morel said to Ray, "Stop talking. Kevin has something to tell us."

"By all means," Ray said. He wasn't aware that he had been talking. Who was it who had said, Don't interrupt me when I'm talking to myself. It had been Iris or it had been something Iris had reported her sister as saying. It was too bad that Morel couldn't have managed to cross paths with Ellen during his peregrinations and fallen in love with her instead of Iris. That would have solved a multitude of problems. The man would have made an excellent brother-in-law.

Kevin said, "Setime will come to tell you this himself, but we have reached a decision as to what should be.

"First they are saying you might take the Land Cruiser and drive it south as far as you can, straight south from here . . ."

Morel said, "You are saying drive overland, not go back to Route 14? I don't see why."

"You have to give your word to do it just as we say. You must go straight down as far as you can, down to Mabuasehube . . ."

Morel said, "The idea being to distract anybody who would be interested in finding the group."

Kevin said, "Yes, and then at Mabuasehube you will be below the line of control and you can find game scouts and others in the park to see you on to Gaborone. You will be tired, rra."

Ray said, "If you're still worrying about helicopters coming down from Caprivi, I can tell you the odds are so"—Morel subtly nudged him—"hard to elucidate," Ray said.

"Nyah, but we are listening to Mokopa on this one. And we will send two Bedfords that way, but not so far as Mabuasehube, but just to point toward that way."

Ray said, "So you figure all of the drivers would be taking the chance of helicopters coming after them."

"They would," Kevin said.

Morel said, "But don't forget that the farther south anybody gets the less the chance that koevoet would risk showing up and risking their most precious equipment. I mean, this country does have an air force and it

would be obligatory for them to take notice of an incursion coming anywhere near the population centers, places like Kanye or Jwaneng. Even if
the BDF is turning its face away from what's happening in the north, that
would be too much. I think."

"What will you do, Kevin?" Ray asked.

"I am deciding about it, rra."

Ray went on. "So one possibility would be that you would go with
Kerekang to . . . ?" He had to be careful with his questions, not to seem
like his former self.

Kevin hesitated before saying, "We have friends in Namibia. From
Gobabis we can go where we like." He was uncomfortable saying so
much, Ray could tell.

It was a shame. Ray's old self would have been elated to get any
shreds and pieces of information that linked Ichokela with SWAPO in
Namibia, which was essentially what Kevin was saying existed. I could
have gotten one of those invisible medals the agency gives, based on a
report I am never going to write, about the ZAPU caches and about this
new connection, he thought. He had done his greatest work, alas, in
this outing.

The cadres were going to disappear into the landscape, which would
be child's play for the Basarwa and less easy but possible for the other
rural types, where they would hibernate. Setime would cross over into
Namibia, to Gobabis, and then go down through Windhoek or Walvis
Bay to the Republic. There were hundreds of points of entry where
Kerekang would be able to get in without showing a passport.

Ray understood part of what was going on, but he wanted it confirmed. His notion was that the shock of unexpected success, at Ngami
Bird Lodge, was behind everything. They had done too well. They had
bloodied the nose of a supposedly invincible enemy force. They had to
let what they had done turn into a myth, a social myth. And they needed
not to be caught and punished, to make the myth work. And then there
would be another day.

There were a couple of things he had to know about. He said to Kevin,
"Tell me about the staff at Ngami Bird Lodge, what happened to them?"
He needed to know. Because they hadn't come out into the bush with the
witdoeke.

"They are fine. We sent them back to Route 14. We took them there.
They were slaves, rra, in that place. We saw that they were picked up. We
waited to see that they had transport. Phalatse was in hiding, watching,
and so he tells us it went."

"That's good," Ray said. He forgot what the other thing he wanted to know about was.

Morel, full of eagerness but trying to be delicate, measured, said, "And the idea is definitely that Ray and I would be the ones to take the Land Cruiser down to the south, to Mabuasehube?"

"He will tell you when he comes to talk to you, Setime will."

"When would we leave?" Ray asked.

Ray repeated his question. "When would we have to leave? Because I want to tell you something. If they say we have to drive by night, go now, drive tonight, I'm sorry. I'm too tired. I can't."

"Sure we can. I can," Morel said. He stood up and strode around a little, showing his readiness, Ray supposed. It was a little amusing.

Ray said, "We can't do it in the dark, I don't think. You have to find these tracks that barely exist. I know. I've been out in the bush more than you. It takes two people, one to navigate and one to drive, even during the daylight. I am telling you. Even then you barely creep along, unless you hit a well-defined stretch. I mean, we are going to be on rough terrain. You have to go around things. You have to keep getting out to set the front hubs for four-wheel drive. When I had a driver, one of us was always doing that. You can't stay in four-wheel drive all the time because it uses up gas too fast. Listen to me, man. You never got off government roads when you came up here, so you don't know."

Morel wanted him to be quiet. Ray understood why. Morel wanted to seize the moment because the situation could change in a second, for any reason. Ray could imagine a dozen things that could happen to kill this particular plan. Morel wanted to go while he could. He wanted to get to Iris. He was blocking out any possibility that the comrades who were certain that helicopters would come for them were right. Morel was looking past that. That was fine. Ray considered it as unlikely as Morel did. But if a helicopter did show up in the air above them and started firing at them it would be over in the blink of an eye, they would inhabit a fireball and turn into smoke and bits of bone and that would be the end of the affair.

"Do you think he wants us to go tonight?" Ray asked Kevin.

"He will tell you himself."

What Ray wanted was an impossibility, to stay in the desert, to stay indefinitely there. He liked the people he was with, the comrades, and now he was having to prepare himself to go back to Gaborone to be with people he didn't like or with people, a person, he loved but who didn't like him, or, to be fair, liked somebody else a lot more. He had crafted a life in which something was always happening somewhere, in one department or another of his life, the academic, the agency, or the personal part. It was quiet in the desert.

Morel was pushing too hard, saying to Kevin, "Can't you get Kerekang, or let us go over there? The night isn't going to last all day." Morel was tired. He looked at Ray to see if Ray had noticed his misspeaking. Ray gave no sign.

Ray had thought it was okay for the domestic panel of his life to be placid, the placid panel. It was the realm in which he had been attentive toward Iris, supporting her in her interests, but it was hardly a realm in which he had tried separately to make himself admirable to her, if that was what he meant. Anyway, he thought. It was too late. It was an irony, but now he was on the verge of doing something she would genuinely admire, if she knew anything about it. There was no way she could be kept up to date on his new life that he could think of. Unless he decided to send out one of those yearly-chronicle-type Christmas cards.

No, he had used the domestic realm as an asylum from the franticness of the work panels, a haven. That hadn't been right. It was what everyone did, but in his case, what he had been using her as a haven from was something she hated.

He was liking the quiet, the stillness of the desert. He had never particularly understood about early Christian ascetics choosing to go out into the desert because, after all, you could be an ascetic anywhere. But now he felt he had a taste or hint of why. The desert was humbling and calming. He felt calm.

It didn't matter that he didn't want to leave the desert, because he was going to have to. He turned his attention to tightening up his manuscript bundle as well as he could. He had seen a tough-looking creeping vine in the vicinity. He went off with his torch to see if he could find it and tear off a few lengths of it and tie them around *Strange News*.

Morel called after him to come back. One of the things Morel didn't understand was that Ray needed to get someplace where he could let go of his bundle, put it in a secure place and forget about its existence, for a change.

He found the vine. It was as tough as anyone could hope for. The Mosarwa turned up beside him carrying an alarming knife. They worked together, pulling and jerking and then shaving off the sharp little spines the vine bore. He thanked the man, who seemed to know everything there was to know about this piece of flora. It was clear that Ray was not the first man to figure out some of the uses this plant might be put to. He had two six-foot lengths of the vine.

Everything was irritating Morel, who was trying to discourage Kevin from adding any more wood to the remnant of the fire. And when Ray began artfully binding his parcel up, even devising a handle of sorts for ease of carrying, Morel showed growing impatience.

"We have to get this settled," Morel said.

"I think it is settled. Act normal or they'll change their mind about this."

Something was under way in the darkness, something having to do with the vehicles. Loads were being shifted around. He couldn't believe that people who had been through violent battle could still manage to carry out heavy physical tasks in the middle of the night. We should all be ordered to lie down and sleep, he thought.

Kerekang whistled. They were being summoned.

Morel said, "We're going to be on our way." He was having difficulty containing his anxiety. He was full of adrenaline. Probably that was good. It would keep him awake at the wheel. I know what my mission is going to be in the Cruiser, Ray thought. It was going to be to keep himself awake to be sure that Morel kept awake at the wheel. And he was going to insist that they pull over and park and go no farther and sleep, both of them, if he saw the slightest sign of fatigue making Morel nod off. Ray had no intention of having this experience come to an end due to poor driving.

Kerekang was whistling and so was someone else. There was a sort of harmony between the two different streams of sound. He had to go.

Kerekang was coming toward them, clasping maps under one arm, beckoning them to the fire, the main fire. Everyone at the fire was standing. It was going to be ceremonial, Ray could tell. That was not what he wanted. What he wanted was to talk separately and concretely to Kerekang about linking up in the Republic, assuming each of them managed their escapes decently. He was assuming they would. He didn't know why.

What was going to happen was that he and Morel would be said goodbye to and instructed to get directly into the Cruiser and get out of there. And that was going to be too bad, in a couple of ways, for him. Because it was going to be a tense thing, a race to get to Iris first, between the two of them. And he would have to never sleep or seriously rest in any situation where Morel could jump out and duck out of sight and get to a phone to warn Iris about the storm to come. Ray was determined not to let that happen. He was wondering whether a handshake agreement would mean anything, a promise from Morel to say nothing to Iris for a couple of days when they got back to Gaborone, staying off the scene. He doubted that an agreement would mean anything. It was the kind of situation in which the temptation would be to agree, make the deal, and then yield to a second temptation to break it. If he put himself in Morel's place he could see himself breaking that kind of agreement, out of weakness. Morel would want to protect her from the shock of learning that he had let the truth out, which had never been the plan.

Morel was holding up much better than he was. He had taken less punishment, of course. And was three years younger and of course got exercise and had never smoked, he claimed. Iris had always been more enamored of exercise than Ray had. So it was fine, she could join Morel forever after doing heel-and-toe walking or whatever was on the menu of the day.

Morel was hurrying ahead, with Kevin, Morel the human dynamo.

And Iris had always wanted to argue for the fun of arguing more than he had, except in the earliest days of their love. But then certain areas of argument had gotten tender, because one way or another they connected with the agency, even if only by implication. And then she had stopped initiating recreational argument. Their last memorable recreational argument had been over one of the Pinter plays, *Homecoming*, which they'd seen in an amateur production.

It was a little awkward, taking leave of the comrades. There was a round of handshaking, but the handshake was a particular kind of handshake, involving a mutual grasping of wrists after the initial standard handshake. And then with each handshake an exchange of words was in order. Some of the comrades said a good deal more than Tsamaya sentle, which was the only thing it was occurring to him to say, and which, he realized, was incorrect for him to say, because that was the leave-taking formulation for the speaker who was remaining, to be said to the one going away. It was Sala sentle he was supposed to be saying. He knew that perfectly well. It was just that he was tired. He got it right for the last five or six handshakes and hesitated over the idea that he should start over again, doing it correctly this time for everyone. He couldn't. It was hearing Morel do it correctly that had clued him in. The protocol had been to bid goodbye to each comrade. Many of them had wished Ray good luck, that much he knew. Morel had made a better job of it.

It was time to go. Ray was asking himself, in the routine normal for setting off on a trip, if he had everything when he realized that he had nothing, no personal effects, no papers, nothing but the clothes on his body and his bundle of *Strange News*. And there was no money. Koevoet had found the money cached in the Cruiser and done whatever they had done with it. And he had destroyed his own passport. And where his driver's license was he had no idea. Morel had his medical satchel with nothing but odds and ends in it. He didn't think Morel had been able to retrieve his wallet. He would ask him.

It was a miracle that the keys to the Cruiser had been located, although it could have been hot-wired. He knew how to do that. He half wished he'd had the opportunity to show it. But this was all right.

Kerekang and Kevin came with them to the Cruiser. Ray had an irresistible impulse to get into the Cruiser, to be sitting in it, to be asleep in it. He was tired of squatting and sitting on the ground and leaning against things. He got into the Cruiser.

There was a consultation over routes. Kerekang was directing a torch-beam onto a map spread open on the front driver's-side fender. Ray felt he needed to be more participatory. He slid along the seat and opened the driver's-side door. Why had it been assumed by all and sundry, Ray wondered, that Morel would be the driver and the maestro of the trip back? Ray felt his face. His appearance was probably against him, his beard. Morel had a very light growth of beard. Ray's knee was swollen. It looked uninspiring.

Now there was discussion about provisions and fuel. And then that was over and Ray had to move back to his side of the cab as Morel climbed in and got behind the wheel.

Kerekang came around to his side and stood looking at Ray.

Kerekang said, "Don't get too old before I see you again."

"I won't. When you get to the Republic, how will I find you? Wait, I don't know where I'll be. Wait, where will you try to stay?" Ray was full of anxiety. He wasn't thinking creatively about setting up a contact point. He could have Kerekang call his house in Gaborone, but how long he was going to be living there was the question. That was a problem. He couldn't think.

He said to Kerekang, "Call me or have someone call me at my house. We're in the directory. But I don't know how long that will work. But try that. And I guess I can leave a forwarding number for you or anyone else, if I, if I have to, which I am going to have to do for after I leave."

Kerekang said, "I can go to a friend in Hillbrow."

Ray said, "That's good. That's good. I'll see you. I'm serious about a school . . ."

Kerekang said directly to Ray, "I will use the directory to reach your house."

Morel said to Ray, "What school?"

Ray ignored the question.

"I will see you, rra," Kerekang said to Ray.

Ray made himself believe it.

III

This Is the Day

36. They're All Dust in the Wind

Ray was rehearsing as he drove. Morel had turned the driving over to him when they'd reached Lobatse, after a tense wrangle. But Ray had been insistent. He had his own reasons for wanting to be at the wheel when the moment of arrival came. Lobatse was only forty kilometers from Gaborone, so there was some imposture involved in his insistence on arriving in the driver's seat. Morel had driven every inch of the way to Lobatse, all the hard driving, three days of it in the bush, which could have been more if they hadn't diverged from their objective, Mabuasehube, when it seemed a total formality, and come straight over to Route 14. There had never been any sign of helicopters. They had ceased to believe that those represented any danger after the first day.

It was a question of appearances. It was his vehicle, or at least it had been assigned to him. And he had been adamant about being the one to drive it into his own driveway.

It was early evening. They would arrive while it was still light. What he meant was that *he* would arrive while it was still light, unless he could do something about it. Try it, he said to himself.

Ray said, "I can drop you off first, at your place."

"No, I want to see that you get there safely. You're a wreck."

Ray tried not to laugh.

"I'm fine," Ray said, which was a lie because his knee, heavily bandaged as it was, was hurting fiercely and there was some question as to how long he could keep using that leg, using the brake. The brake was working stiffly.

He was sick of negotiating with Morel. It was almost over. And they had arrived at some decent compromises about the homecoming, the main one being that all Iris knew was that they were all right and that they were both on the way to Gaborone. And that information had come to her in the form of a radiophone message from the district council office in Kanye. And it had been the only information that she would receive until they arrived in the flesh, and the pretext that justified that was that the regular telephone service was out, in the whole north and south of the country, out, which it had been, intermittently. So the cruelty of not knowing that both of them were alive had been put to death.

Ray hated Wagner, but he loved some of his music, like the homecoming music from *Tannhäuser.* He sang it, *"Once more, dear home, I with rapture behold thee . . . And greet the fields that so softly enfold thee . . ."* That was all he had. He couldn't remember what the story was, where Tannhäuser had been and how long he had been there that made coming home so sweet. He sang it again. The next line, something about Tannhäuser's native staff, escaped him. But that was all right.

"Please don't sing anymore," Morel said.

"Okay," Ray said.

This stretch of the road, approaching Ramotswa, the three-quarters mark to Gaborone, was pleasant. There were some rather abrupt hills on the left, green, scrub-covered. In fact the verdure on the hills had the tight, dense look of the hair of Africans, except that it was green, of course. That was not an observation he could do anything with. The traffic was light. He had to be careful to avoid the slow-moving donkey-pulled wood carts, not carts but the back-ends of derelict trucks cut away and used as wagons. They passed a eucalyptus plantation. He forgot what Kerekang's objection to eucalyptus was, but it was severe, it was a bad importation, it didn't belong in Botswana.

He wanted Morel to be out of the scene when he got home. And now that he was driving he had it in his power to just drive to Morel's place and tell him to get out, give him an ultimatum despite the fact that it wasn't what they had agreed on. It could be done but it couldn't be done. Morel would resist. And she would be expecting both of them, naturally enough, since she was the one who had dispatched Morel off into the red rock wilderness to find him, which meant that it might be logical for Morel to deliver him home. It was the completion of a commission.

Ray supposed it could be managed. He would make the scene brief. It would be difficult and complicated because he would have to keep his eye on the doctor to see that no hand signals or special glances were sent in Iris's direction. He would keep it brief and then he would send Morel away. He would let him take the Cruiser to his place. He would give a reason why that would make sense. He didn't know what it was. But he would make the homecoming scene just the last act in the sequence of scenes in which he had been keeping his eye clapped to Morel all the way back and especially since they had gotten onto the tarred roads, passing through real towns. He had followed him everywhere to see that he didn't get hold of a phone or find some other way to send his own separate message of warning to Iris, some way Ray couldn't even imagine. He had stood there in the washroom at the district council office while Morel shat and brushed his teeth and cleaned himself up, taking his own sweet time about it. He had shadowed him at every stop they made. The homecoming would just be a variant and he thought he could manage and get Morel out of there and away and then the fun could begin.

"Why don't you let me drop you off first?" Ray asked.

"Because . . ." Morel answered, straining to think of an acceptable reason. Ray knew what the true reason was. He wanted to lay his eyes on Iris. It was understandable. That was love. Something was necessary about seeing her. Because Morel knew that an ugly drama was going to commence and he doubtless wanted to see her, perceive her as she was before the struggle began. It was possible he thought that the outcome might go against him and that he might never see her again, which was not going to happen, but it was the kind of thing it was impossible not to fear. He felt like reassuring him on that one, oddly enough.

But then Ray felt cold. He was being an idiot. If he dropped Morel off first there could be the thing happening that he had turned himself inside out to avoid, a quick phone call and the deed would be done. He had to withdraw the offer to drop Morel off. He had to do it immediately, before Morel saw what his advantage would be if he was given the time.

Ray said, "No it's okay. We'll go with the original plan. You drop me off and you say hello and then you take the Cruiser and go to your place. I have the Beetle to get around in, so you can use the Cruiser to get home. That was your own vehicle that was lost at Ngami Bird Lodge. Then you'll have the Cruiser to get around in."

"It's fine. I have another car." Morel did. An expensive one, a BMW.

Ray felt frantic. "No, but really just come in, not in, but just say hello, just wave, be there and wave hello, then go."

"Okay that's good," Morel said barely audibly. He was slumped down. He looked like a bear or some other powerful animal sunk down and resting. It was guilt that was turning him into a jelly, a soft thing. He was agreeing to things.

Ray decided to drive fast and let slip the dogs of war. He didn't care. It was so rare to get stopped for speeding in Botswana that it was a joke. He sped. Morel sat up more.

They were in the outskirts of Gaborone, crossing an iron bridge over nothing, a former brook or river, a former obstacle no longer there.

They went through two roundabouts. It was getting dark. They were passing through the modest suburbs just adjacent to Extension 16, where Morel and he both lived, and which was suburban but at a higher level, larger houses on larger plots and more lavish landscaping, home, itself adjacent to the yet more excellent suburbs where the diplomatic residences were. Fikile, their security guard, would be where he should be, if he was on time, walking around in the yard. Their housemaid would be on hand today.

They were almost at Kgari Close. Morel was sitting up straight. Morel wanted to look good when he arrived and Ray wanted to look as ruinous as he could.

"You can drop me if you want to," Morel said.

"No, this is what we're doing." There was no fight in Morel.

They were there. Fikile was there. He was opening the gate. Ray could hardly breathe. They were there. The estate lights around the perimeter of the house were already on.

"There she is," he said to Morel. Iris had come out onto the stoop.

She was wearing a mock-leopardskin hair band, one he liked and one he associated with sex, incidentally. She was wearing a pale blue linen longsleeved shirt he liked, and jeans and sandals. She was thinner. She had washed her hair, which was gleaming. Her face was thinner. And she had made herself up to a degree, the way she would if they were going out to something on the gala side. She was made up in a sharp, painted way. Ray felt sorry for her, seeing that.

Ray got out of the Cruiser and as he descended he tugged at Morel to get him to slide over into the driver's place, to make it an automatic thing for him to drive off, be gone.

There was alarm in her eyes. He knew he looked alarming. He'd lost a lot of weight. His face was bruised. One side of his mouth was swollen. He had a heavy growth of a beard. He was wearing his beloved boots, stained shorts, a torn shirt half buttoned which he had acquired somewhere, and a baseball cap he had been given by someone at the district council office in Kanye, and he was carrying *Strange News* over his shoulder, in a sling bundle. And he had a few other things in a sakkie, a yellow sakkie. His knee was a spectacle.

It was too sad. She was carrying a present for him, something wrapped up, with a ribbon on it, a book probably, a birthday present because he had turned forty-nine while he was away. And under her arm she had a stack of papers, *Times Literary Supplement*s probably, and copies of the *International Herald Tribune*, also tied up festively in a ribbon. It was nice, but it was too late. On impulse he reached in and turned the headlights back on. He felt petty doing it. He knew why he had done it. It was to blind her, make it difficult for her to see Morel in the cab, see anything he might be trying to get away with in gestures, facial expressions. She flinched as she came forward. He regretted turning the headlights on and he reached in and turned them off, murmuring something that meant it had been an error.

Fikile came between them. Ray saluted him. Fikile wanted to welcome him back and he wanted to be acknowledged himself, in a more definite way. They shook hands and Fikile slid away. He liked Fikile.

Iris, trembling, embraced him, awkwardly because she was still holding his birthday presents. The papers she had set down on the stoop. Ray didn't want Morel to be observing this, but there was nothing that could be done about it. He would go in a minute and the fun would begin.

Iris released Ray and stepped back.

"You're all right, you're fine. You look terrible. But you're all right. He found you . . ." Her voice was artificial except for the genuine stress showing in it.

"I'm okay."

"You found him," she said to the Land Cruiser. She was afraid to go up to it and touch Morel, which was what she wanted to do, Ray knew in his heart.

She said, imploringly, again in the direction of the Land Cruiser, "Come in and eat something. Come in. Please. You have to tell me everything . . ."

There was silence from the Land Cruiser.

"He has a cook," Ray said.

"Of course. But I could make you both an omelette. We could talk. I know you both need to rest, but you could give me just the outline. And you could have a drink."

Dimakatso appeared. Ray had to be decent to her. She was a decent person. They exchanged greetings.

She said, "There is chicken all cooked up. There is plenty to eat. There is mince, for sandwiches. I have some buns . . ."

Ray said, "No, mma. I just want to lie down."

"Gosiame," she said, and then she too vanished, around the side of the house.

Morel was backing out of the drive, slowly. The man was being scrupulous, so far. Ray had no complaint against him.

"You'll call us tomorrow," Iris shouted after him, trying not to shout. She called out a second time, more softly, saying the same thing.

They went into the house, which struck him as very clean inside. The floors were brilliant. He hadn't been in a really clean place in weeks.

She led him into the living room and then, studying him, obviously decided that he should lie down, so she led him to the bedroom. He would do whatever she wanted. He sat on the bed and rolled over onto his side. She picked his feet up and took off his boots, grimacing. The room was dim. Everything was clean. Waves of weakness were sweeping over him. He wanted to surrender to them, but it was too soon.

He wondered if she would volunteer something on her own. He had the option of saying nothing, like a psychoanalyst, just nodding and waiting for the great confession to work its way up and out of her beautiful mouth, except that he lacked the strength for it. What he would appreciate most would be something voluntary. That would be the only event he could think of that would lead to his forgiving her, that moment arriving, his forgiving her in a fundamental way. His face felt metallic, especially around his mouth. His smile would be unnatural, if he had to smile. His eyelids felt metallic or stiff, like the eyelids in a ventriloquist's dummy.

He would love to forgive her, not that forgiving her would mean they could go on together, it wouldn't. But it would make the next phase of ending everything easier for him to bear, or so he thought. He could just sink his silence in a demonstration of utter fatigue and keep waiting, waiting for her to go first. And then if she did she could be forgiven in a flash, or not exactly in a flash but rapidly, pretty rapidly.

She said, "Do you want to open your present? I'll open it for you. It isn't anything. I got it at a jumble sale. Do you want me to open it?"

"No," he said.

"Because you're tired. You're just too tired right now?"

"Right." He laid his arm across his eyes.

"Do you want me to let you sleep?"

"*No,*" he said more violently than he'd intended. He wanted her to be in his presence. The phone could ring. If it did it would be Morel. Or she could make a call and whisper.

"You have to tell me everything, how you are, what happened to you.

I'm so glad to have you safe, Ray. I'll do anything you want. I'll do anything you need."

He said, "I want you to tell me everything too."

"What do you mean? You mean since you left, what I've been doing? It's nothing. It's not interesting."

"To me it is."

She said, "I know you've been through something terrible. You have to tell me about it." She was being careful. She wanted to know everything, but she wanted to be dutiful, too, and not ask about anything having to do with the agency that he wouldn't be comfortable telling her about. She was still trying to be his good wife. She had some feeling for him still. He couldn't stand it much longer.

"Tell me *something*," she said.

He sat up. He had to be at least sitting up for what was coming next. He should be on his feet for it but right then it was too much to ask.

He said, "I'll tell you something. You have a lover."

She had been sitting near him on the bed, but she jumped to her feet, looking indignant, but feebly.

"Are you insane?" she said.

"No, not yet. Just admit it."

"This is wrong," she said.

"Yes, it is. Yes, it is. But you have a lover."

"I don't. I don't. I don't know who told you that."

She was suffering. He didn't want that.

She was pacing up and down, manically. He had never seen her in such a state and he was in pain seeing it.

Now her tears were coming.

"I don't want this," she said.

"I don't either, but you have a lover and that's what we have to work with." Tears were coming to his eyes too.

"It isn't true."

He got to his feet and caught her to him. She had to hold him up. They sat down on the bed, side by side, in misery.

"It's Morel. Come on."

She was silent.

"Look, tell me the truth. I've already done most of my suffering over it. You were lucky not to be around for that. Just admit it and then I'll let you make me an omelette. I'm ravenous, suddenly. So just admit it. We've known each other a long time. Just say it."

"Okay, then. It's true."

"Life is unbearable," he said.

Each day since his return had been worse than the one before it, and there had been eight of them. Today it was the prospect of sitting down with Chester Boyle that was weighing on him as the moment approached. Otherwise he would say the day had been about equal in sadness and what, leadenness, to the seven preceding. But now the day was worse. He was sitting and waiting and reading in the American Library. The librarian knew him. When she felt the coast was clear she would admit him to the workroom and buzz him on through to Boyle's ridiculous tiny secret chamber.

Nothing was good. He was reading the *Weekly Mail* of January 18 to 21, 1993, the current issue. He was back in the present. The lead front-page story had to do with far-right groups in South Africa making secret deals with Frelimo to set up all-white colonies in Mozambique. It would never happen. Clinton, the new president of the United States, was apparently allowing the dictator Saddam Hussein to use helicopters against the Marsh Arabs, who had been encouraged by the United States to rise against Saddam. If there was good news in this issue of the *Weekly Mail* he wasn't finding it.

At home, with Iris, it was bad. Things were static. They weren't speaking much and she was coming and going again. For the first couple of days she had shadowed him anxiously, staying around him. But she had given that up and was coming and going again and not necessarily letting him know where she was going. At times he felt dead, but most of the time he felt himself dying, in the process, dying of sadness. Feeling dead was a respite, strangely enough. They were sleeping in the same bed but still not speaking except on mundane matters. She was still making some effort to talk to him. She was in distress. He wasn't trying not to talk to her, he couldn't talk to her. And he was being tormented by lust. It made it worse that she had stopped reaching out to touch him during the night. Their bed was too vast. It had been a luxury to them, in the past. Now he wanted the bed to be narrower. He was being tormented by lust and sexual memory, sexual memories. He remembered her saying, at some point not too long in the past, Celibacy I find very sexy in the person engaging in it. It wasn't doing anything for her lately.

He had managed to take care of a lot of housekeeping matters in the last few days, mostly housekeeping connected with St. James's. He hadn't told them he was leaving, yet. No one had seemed unduly interested in what he was doing there, why he was carrying his stuff out.

Now the librarian was crooking her finger at him and now she was jerking her thumb in the direction of the workroom.

Boyle was in place when Ray entered the secret chamber. Ray liked to keep thinking of it as that. It was claustral in there. He supposed Boyle liked that because some people would say anything to get out of an environment like that, agree to anything. There was a new banker's green-shaded lamp on Boyle's table with the shell of the shade tilted a little away from Boyle, toward himself. It would have been friendly of Boyle to adjust the shade so the light fell straight down. Of course it was intentional.

Boyle looked rather haggard. He was still obese, and he looked bad, haggard and blotchy. He was wearing a dress shirt and tie, a black tie. Somehow he looked like a mourner. Boyle was slow to reach for Ray's hand. The handshake was not warm. Boyle was studying him.

Boyle said, "Good to see you, Ray. I'm just back. I gather you're okay. You're all right? You've been to the embassy nurse. You're taking care of your knee. You're okay." It was a statement. There was no inquiry in any of it.

"I'm all right," Ray said. Boyle had gone to some trouble to check on his condition. That was interesting.

Boyle said, "You turned the Cruiser in. I saw the vouchers."

"It's all right too, the Cruiser."

"Good. I don't have a report from you. Unless I missed it. I've been in the field. You know. I have a ton of paper on my desk."

Ray said, "Yeah well here we are. You instructed me not to *write* my reports . . ."

"This is a debrief, not one of your essays."

"It's all the same. And there's no report."

Boyle stiffened. He looked narrowly at Ray. He wasn't stupid. He knew he was seeing mutiny.

Ray was uncertain about what he was doing. He was going to have to discover what he was doing as he went. His tethers to the world he had gotten used to living in were being cut, or breaking on their own. He would see what he was when the last tether broke.

Boyle was still studying him. Boyle's breathing was heavy. Ray wondered if Boyle had emphysema.

Boyle said, "I think you need to take leave, go away. You look like you need it. The both of you go, you and Iris."

"I'm not taking leave."

Boyle wasn't listening. He said, "You should do it. There's a regional conference on education in Mombasa. REDSO is running it. You should go. Beautiful beaches on the coast, Bamburi Beach Hotel. You could go after the conference. That could be worked out. It wouldn't hurt your wife to get away from Gaborone for a while."

Ray said, "Iris . . ." He didn't want her brought into this in any way.

"It would be good for the both of you," Boyle said.

"I'm not going, Boyle," Ray said, slowly. He thought, He's afraid of me.

"You should. You don't look good. I don't want you around looking like this. Your hands are shaking." That was true. Ray was fidgeting with a letter opener and wondering what Kant would say if he stabbed Boyle in the neck with it. Boyle had to be thinking about his next post . . . or more likely his retirement. The outbreak in the north had occurred and it had gotten serious and Boyle had been oblivious and that was the kind of thing Boyle was supposed to be on top of. But he had been oblivious. He hadn't warned the agency, hadn't done anything, known anything.

Boyle cleared this throat. He said, "You know I don't even want to talk to you about your trip. I don't need to. The fact is, I don't need a report. It's all over up there."

Ray said, "*You* fucked with Kerekang. You drove him into the bush, you. And I'm not going to the beach."

"You will if I tell you to," Boyle said very slowly.

"I don't think so."

"I'll fix it at the school."

Boyle was studiously not listening to him. It was close in the cubicle. Boyle's cologne or aftershave or whatever male fragrance he used was asserting itself. Ventilating the cubicle had never been properly worked out. He didn't know how Boyle could stand to do business there. He suspected that because he had insisted on having the damned thing built first thing when he arrived he felt obligated to make use of it.

Ray asked, "And what would you claim the leave was for? Medical leave? What?" He was speaking too loudly for the space and he knew it.

"Take it easy. Family situation."

Ray was understanding everything. Boyle was afraid of him, which meant he knew that Ray had seen koevoet in all its glory, sent to crush peasants, Bushmen, university students, Kevin, the son of the Permanent Secretary of the Ministry of Local Government and Lands . . . So far nothing about koevoet had turned up in the press, not a whisper. Vandals had burned down the abandoned resort, Ngami Bird Lodge. Any nexus between the agency and koevoet would be something that if it got bruited about would have to be shot down. Boyle wanted Ray over the horizon. Life was going to be interesting for Morel, too, down the road. But the irony was that Ray was going to be out of Boyle's hair and over the fields and far away because he needed to leave the neighborhood for his own personal reasons.

Abruptly Ray said, "I don't want to hear the word family or my wife or my wife's name out of your mouth again." He felt better.

But Boyle wasn't listening. He said, "Or you can do some courses. In the U.K. maybe. You need to get some kind of grip on ADP, just for example. You don't know anything about ADP, do you? You need to. That's where the world is going, ADP, ASAP." He smiled and then prolonged his smile in an attempt to get Ray to show a little lightness.

"What's ADP?" Ray asked, realizing that he knew what it meant as soon as he'd asked. He cursed himself.

"You see, Ray. It's automatic data processing. You make my point."

"I did know that."

Boyle was silent. And then he said, "It's all over up there. You do understand that."

"What do you mean, it's over? How do you define that?"

"Look. I don't want to talk about it too much. Just let's say the radicals stopped burning things down up there. Your friend the fire-thrower, he's gone . . ."

Boyle paused, then continued. "The radicals are all gone. They're all dust in the wind. And to just go once over lightly, everybody's happy down here. We had some college kids mixed up with radicals until they saw the light. They're back in school, all of them. They're accounted for. It's burned itself out, the whole thing, at last. The government is willing to forget a lot, and there's going to be some community aid. I gave them some ideas, Ray. They're going to put in some public boreholes, I guess you could call them, out in the bush. I could show you on a map." It's something, Ray thought. It wouldn't have happened without Kerekang going crazy. It wasn't much, but water was something, up there.

Everything was moving toward erasure, the way the Mexican government with a little help from its northern friends had erased the rebellions in Guerrero in the seventies, the Party of the Poor, those rebellions. And there had been another case in Nigeria, more recently. And there were other cases.

Boyle was still talking, saying, ". . . and what else can I tell you? I think that's all. Everybody's gone home." His last sentence had been spoken with emphasis.

Ray said, "Nobody's being punished, in other words?"

"Not to my knowledge," Boyle said.

Ray didn't like that response. It was a way of not lying, but that was all it was, a way of not lying directly. Ray waited.

Boyle said, "No punitive expeditions, if that's what you're asking. This isn't Zimbabwe . . . And I think anybody the government might be really interested in is off the scene, one way or another. Kerekang's gone. Some of them crossed over into Namibia. We know that. Nujoma can have them. But by the way we don't have any problems with him. He doesn't hate us. Not at all."

Boyle was letting himself brag a little. He was proud of having made a connection with SWAPO in their early days of power. Ray had only heard whispers about it. He didn't doubt it. And he didn't like hearing it. He didn't like the implication that the SWAPO government might well cooperate with the agency if an interest was expressed in the whereabouts of Kerekang's Ichokela group that had taken refuge in Namibia. He hoped to God that Kerekang had gotten through to the Republic as easily as he'd thought he could. South Africa would be safer for him than Namibia, if only because it was bigger and more diverse and more disorganized as black rule came rolling on, and also because there were so many more entities that would have to be bribed and traduced by the agency to secure lines of information.

Ray was hungry. He was almost weak from hunger. He wasn't eating normally. He couldn't bear sitting down to eat with Iris because it reminded him of sitting down to eat with Iris.

Boyle was shifting into a reflective pose. That was all it was. He was pretending to proceed from an agreement that hadn't in fact been reached, an agreement that Ray was going to go on leave.

Boyle said, "We might want you to make a report on your experiences later. You know, for historical purposes. For our files here. And we might want you to put that in writing. Who knows? When you get back. There's no urgency about it. We talked to your driver, very nice guy. He said not much happened. We have all we need to know right now."

Be careful, Ray said to himself. He was full of anger but it was difficult because he was angry at himself, too, himself, historically. There was Angola. It was looking better now in Angola, but he had been in Botswana when it had been hideous in Angola, with the agency supporting Savimbi and holding hands with the Chinese and the fucking Boers but with the whole thing being run, thank God, out of Kinshasa, so he had been able to look at it as something happening in a different compartment. His role had been tightly held to keeping Botswana clean and tidy, as the tee shirt said, the decent rational country Botswana. There was no defense for what the agency had done in Guatemala, Boyle's longest posting. That had to be said, sometime.

He wanted to hurt Boyle, but he wanted to protect himself when he did.

Ray said, "Well if I write a report, for myself, I might put it aside, just put it aside in case anything happened to me. Safeguard it." He was afraid he had been stupid, saying that. He wanted to rush past it, leave it as a seed, a germ, but rush past it.

Boyle seemed astonished. He leaned forward menacingly.

Ray rushed on, saying, "You brought koevoet in . . ."

"What's that? What's koevoet?"

"Don't do that. You know what it is."

"I know what it *was*. It doesn't exist anymore. SWAPO kicked them out. So I understand."

It was infuriating. Ray was seeing what had happened more and more clearly. He had been sent out under conditions of panic on a reconnaissance that became supernumerary thanks to his brilliant foot-dragging through the Kalahari with Keletso. And in the meantime other sources of information had opened up to Boyle and the services of koevoet had been arranged for without reference to anything Ray had been doing.

Ray's face was hot. He said, "Have you got anything to drink?"

Boyle said, "You're not supposed to drink, are you?" That was unkind. Boyle knew that that was an ancient problem. It meant he had been reading his file all the way back to the beginning, in preparation for this.

Boyle reached down and brought up a liter bottle of club soda. He pushed it across the table. And he produced a paper cup. Ray filled the cup and drank, using the interval to get himself under better control.

Ray said, "Listen to me. You know what you did and I know what you did. You fucking panicked. You didn't want anybody to figure out that you had Kerekang here in Gaborone looking all over the government for any kind of job and you screwed that up for him and he took off for the bush and then he turns into Kerekang the Incendiary. That's one thing.

And then when the trouble started up north you panicked again. It should have been a police matter. You had *crimes against property* going on. If you had left the man alone he would have been running boys' clubs, for Christ's sake. You wouldn't listen."

Boyle was tense. "They were killing cattle. You can call it property if you want but that's not how the culture feels about it. It's like religion, the cattle. It's not my religion but it's their religion."

Ray went on. "It could have been handled by the police, by the police, although maybe not as fast as you might've wanted. And then when you found out some of the sons and daughters of the top men in Domkrag were involved you panicked again. And look, I'm stupid too. Somebody I thought I could use to get the stuff on Kerekang you wanted turned out to be a hustler and a thief and that didn't help. It made everything impossible. I know that. Everything would have been placid if *nobody had done anything*, for a change. But anyway. So it didn't look good, the unrest up north, and you overreached like crazy. You got money on the side for koevoet. I know you. You got a lot of people killed. Including Kerekang. It didn't have to be."

Boyle was going to suffer. Ray would see to it. Stories would appear in the local press, and that would do it . . . and if that wasn't enough, Morel would work on it, too.

"Keep your voice down," Boyle said.

"Why? I thought this place was soundproof . . ."

"*Keep it down*," Boyle shouted.

"Go ahead, shout. You're incompetent. You think this is Guatemala and it isn't. You could do anything you wanted in Guatemala. Man, you're in danger. If it comes out about koevoet you'll look like a monkey in Washington. It's all over for your white pals in South Africa, too, and I can tell you it's going to be new times when the Bureau of State Security is run by black guys. And think how they would just love to hear about you and koevoet, how they'd like that, you fuck."

Ray got to his feet, breathing furiously. He picked up the soda water bottle and the paper cup and poured himself another drink. He swallowed the drink, then threw the bottle and cup on the floor. He wanted to do more. He swept the letter opener and the banker's lamp off the table. They were in darkness. He laughed.

He said, "You think you can hide this? Go ahead. But I tell you . . . you leave me alone. I'm through here. I'm getting out of this business and I'm getting out of this country and I won't think about you. But you're fucked, Boyle. Do you think they'll keep you in the field, you fuckup?"

Boyle began coughing. Ray found the door and pounded on it.

The librarian, alarmed, let him out. He gave her a particularly friendly smile. There were many people he would be unlikely to see again, and she was one of them. He would have to see Boyle again, of course, to finish everything up legally, but it would be upstairs, never again in the secret chamber, which was nice.

37. *I Want to Go Up There*

This is the day, Ray thought. He had been allowing himself to cooperate, without acknowledging it, with Iris's various stratagems of delay. But that was over. It had gone on for days and it was making him feel like a fool. It was making her look like a fool, or pathetic, but she apparently didn't care. She didn't want him to go. He assumed it was because she wanted to prolong his presence until she could determine what it was that she *really* wanted, and what she could get to happen following from that. But it could be anything. It could be that she was trying to stall his departure in the hope that when he left he would take with him a more positive picture of her in his mind than he currently had. Aside from the delays she was contriving, she was being lovely to him. Or it could be that what was acting on her was her sheer unreadiness for the gulf, the dangling problems, that coming apart as abruptly as they were doing would generate. He was doing his level best to clear up problems in advance. But there would be more to come. That couldn't be helped. And there were problems that they would have to dispose of together by long distance, by phone and letters. They would have to be in touch.

He was mastering his sadness. He had stopped describing his sadness to himself, stopped saying This is killing me. And that had been a help. His sadness was going to be a permanent possession, but he had to reduce it, compress it, so that other less sad items could fit in around it. And he had gone through a few days of routine depressed nihilism and come out of it. That was taken care of. *What is humanity for? . . . except more of Itself,* had been a pseudo-aphorism that had come to him. And that had been accompanied by images of himself, a childless man, using up his life in the service of the increase in numbers of all the others. And then there had been grim ruminations about literature, ruminations questioning why, if he had truly lost interest in humanity, he was concerning himself with understanding the pathetic signs and scratchings, which was what literature amounted to, the signs and scratchings of the uninteresting entity mankind, and teaching was handing the signs and the scratches on. And then he had indulged in fantasies of some essential monastic existence separated from books in every way. *Every city is a necropolis* was another dark observation from his lapse into nihilism. A more pointless truism would be hard to think up. Its only function was to inspire gloom. But he had come through.

They were working together, ostensibly, to get through the last of the papers he might want to take with him. She was the family archivist. He was considerately and as usual not demanding access to her aerie, her room of her own, so that he could get the job done with dispatch. He was describing what he wanted to look at and she would go in to find it and it would take her forever but she would finally come out with what he had asked for. She was always apologetic about how long it was taking. And she was keeping him supplied, in his place on the sofa, at the vast glass coffee table he would shortly never see again, with tea and delectables, like the sandwich, teewurst on a sesame seed bun, he was just finishing. Some things that had taken her too long to find had been genuinely misplaced, like his brother's death certificate. It was possible that her filing system was less of a marvel than he had been led to believe it was. But still it was taking too long. Today she was doing something more than just finding sets of papers for him. She was completing some other task. That was what he was picking up. According to the death certificate, his brother had died of cryptococcal meningitis. He wanted to have the death certificate, take it with him. He knew she wanted it too, but she had made no objection when he claimed it.

Sorting out which books to take, which to leave for her to forward to him when he got settled and which to discard, had been an odd experience. He was taking a handful of books, all poetry. He was taking his Milton, his Blake, his Yeats. He was abandoning Gerard Manley Hopkins, which before he had always had with him, for a funny reason. He had been riffling through the *Collected Poems*, stopping at *I remember a house where all were good / To me* and then looking through the late poems and finding one in which Jesus cried out that he wanted to return to earth incarnated as a British soldier, which he hadn't read before and which had struck him as the ultimate incarnation of Christianity in Empire. That had been enough. He had put Hopkins first into discard and then into save for forwarding and then back into discard. He wondered if Morel's ideas were having an effect on him, because he loved Hopkins but he had dumped him. He was surprised, but it felt all right. And the job was done. He could hold all the books he was taking under one arm.

She was taking too long. He was at the end of his list of what he wanted to see. He wanted to look at some limericks she had written. He had collaborated with her on some of them. He had only remembered them at the last minute. It was a reminder of better times, the limericks were.

She was being dilatory. His taste for language was coming back. Not that it had gone away entirely during the last hellish period of his life, but coming out of hell, he had seen his words and speech suffer. They had been instruments to get from one moment to the next as safely as possible. He was getting it back piecemeal. How many times had he wanted to say to her *Hello I must be going*, with his heart cracking? Trying to be light, that would have been, with his heart cracking, trying to be Irish in a pub, all the Irish manqué people letting it out in pubs.

He got up and went into the bedroom to look at himself in her mirror, the full-length mirror on the closet door. Because he was going to be himself elsewhere. She couldn't have missed that he was dressed for travel. He had decided to look more professorial. He had purchased some low-magnification glasses at the Notwane Pharmacy. He put them on and took them off, checking both images. He was wearing his black safari suit still sharply radiating the chemicals they used, not carbon monoxide but the other one, fresh from the cleaners. It was looser on him. His arms were thin. It was practically impossible to get safari suits with longsleeved jackets in Gaborone, but in South Africa it would be easier. Or he could work on his arms. He did so then a little, standing there, tensing them. Iris was looking for him. His bags were packed.

She had his folder, the limericks. He wanted to say, Hello I must be going. She would appreciate it, normally. But this was the wrong moment. He sat down and opened the file folder.

"I don't know why you want to look at these," she said.

"I don't know either," he said.

They were hers. When it had come to letters, she had been willing to give up only a few of his letters to her, and none of hers to him, saying she simply couldn't. So, after a lot of pointless agonizing rereading of the past, he had let her keep everything. He hadn't wanted his letters to her.

The whole thing had been a mistake. There would have to be a photo-copying session sometime. The imbroglio had taken too much time.

He read one of hers.

> *A man with no sense of direction*
> *Once, seized with an urgent erection*
> *Attempted to screw*
> *A Young Lady he knew*
> *Contusing her neck and midsection.*

Then there was one she had written on a visit to Dublin.

> *A man from the States had a query*
> *To put to his Gaelic League dearie:*
> *Er, Maeve is it fair*
> *To write down Dun Loghaire*
> *Then insist I pronounce it Dun Leary?*

That was about street signs in Dublin, place names. It was very personal and parochial. He wanted it.

And then there was

> *A difficult woman from Charlotte*
> *Though married became quite a harlot*
> *But she had an excuse*
> *For being so loose*
> *Her husband, she claimed, was a varlet.*

The past is a forest of signs, he thought. The problem was that you could only read them when you turned around and looked back, unfortunately.

"Do you want these?" he asked her.

"No," she said.

"Then I'll take them all."

There was something else he wanted but that he couldn't ask for or wait for her to find. They had played a game. It had been her game. She had been seized with the conviction that she had ideas for cartoons that were as good as those that were showing up embodied in *The New Yorker* cartoons. And she knew there was a market for cartoon ideas. And she had gotten the name of the person at *The New Yorker* who, as she understood it, received cartoon ideas and presumably farmed them out to different artists, hired hands, so to speak. Undoubtedly hundreds of underemployed smart married women the world over had had the same conviction. But she had set out to prove to him that she was right. So she had sequestered copies of *The New Yorker* and transcribed actual cartoons into idea form and then shuffled them in among her own cartoon ideas, her own captions, and he had been asked to say which ones he thought were cleverer. And the truth was that he had more often rejected the *New Yorker* actual cartoons as silly than he had hers. Hers had, on the whole, been as good or better, just as ideas. But then somehow it hadn't gone further. She had made her point and had let it rest there. Probably it could have been carried to the next level. She might have sold a few ideas. Somebody was selling ideas, here and there, to the art director at *The New Yorker*. But she had let it rest. She hadn't pushed on it. One of her ideas that he remembered involved a centaur standing confused in front of two doors, one for an internist and one for a veterinarian. There was the court jester saying to the king, Thanks, you've been great. There was the wife saying, Fred, is there someone else? to the husband behind the open *New York Times* with a lady obviously sitting on his lap. There was the angry punk saying, Get a lifestyle. He decided not to ask for the four-by-six cards on which she had collected cartoon ideas. It was too pathetic. And it was getting late. He had to make the Tlokweng Gate crossing with time to spare. There might be a line of vehicles waiting to get through. The line moved quickly enough on the South African side, through the corresponding gate, Nietverdienst, but on the Botswana side it could be slow or fast. His bags were on the stoop. The rental car, a Beetle, was gassed and ready to go. His heart was beating raggedly. He worked on his breathing and that helped.

He wanted to ask her if he looked okay, meaning okay for the world he was plunging into, the new world. He was used to being told he looked good and he was used to being warned when he needed to trim his nose hair and so on. He would have to adapt. She was acute about appearance. She had pointed out recently that the PolEcon officer at the embassy had gotten his hair cut inexpertly the last time, revealing for the first time to anyone with an eye to see that one of his ears stood off farther from his head than the other. Previously his barbering had been careful to leave more hair on one side than the other, the affected side. She had laughed over Boyle's bothering to dye the few strands of hair he had left yellow.

Iris asked, from the kitchen, "Have you seen my sunglasses?"

"No," he said. Why did she want her sunglasses, though?

She was hurrying around. He listened.

She said, "Never mind. I found them. I put them in my purse, unbeknownst to me."

She had been keeping the house nice, with displays of fresh-cut flowers in rooms where normally they wouldn't have been, like the bathroom. But it had been partly a facade. Certain things were sliding. There were thrips in the kitchen, little clouds of them over the bowls of fruit.

She came out and took a position in the archway of the living room that he read as declaratory. She was dressed sexily, he thought. She was jaunty, standing there. She had an overnight bag stuffed full next to her. She was wearing a tight short black skirt he had never seen before. She was wearing a denim jacket over a red satin blouse. She had washed her hair. She was wearing a plain black bandeau. She was made up, freshly made up. They were both losing weight.

He knew what he was going to hear.

"I'm coming with you on this trip," she said.

"No you are not."

"I am. I want to. I'm packed. It's just for the trip. Then I'll turn around and come back. I'll return the car."

"I can turn the car in down there, in Joburg."

"I know you can. But they like it better at the car rental place if the car is returned there. They said so. There's an extra charge if you turn it in across a national boundary, border I mean."

He was in turmoil. He was not going to consider her proposition. Or he was going to consider it for a couple of minutes. It was possible that it was a dodge, that she wanted an imbroglio that would drag on until it would be too late to make the Tlokweng Gate, which would give her another day with him to continue the exercise she was engaged in, whatever that was. He knew what it was. It was about pathos and love and fear. And it was about guilt. She didn't comprehend that he had to get going, get out of Botswana. In the course of saying goodbye to his contacts, he had learned that Kerekang was indeed in Johannesburg. Boyle might have that news too, in time, days probably. You have to get going, Ray thought. Plainclothes members of the Gaborone Police Unit, the Criminal Investigation Division, were occasionally driving up and sitting around in their cars outside the house. You're a person of interest now yourself, he thought.

"I can share the driving," Iris said.

"Look it's only four or five hours, depending on roadblocks. I can manage it alone." He expected her to look crestfallen, but she surprised him. She was defiant. But driving together was a cruel idea. They had had only good times doing that in the past. She knew that.

He said, "But you couldn't just turn around. You'd have to stay in Joburg and come back tomorrow."

"That's okay. Don't worry, I won't bother you. I can sleep on a couch, a chair, it's okay."

"Don't be silly. We've been sleeping in the same bed since I got back."

"Anyway, I'm coming with you."

He had to consider it, he supposed. There were things she wanted to say. Their exchanges had been difficult and some subjects had been aborted and others had been covered superficially. They had been going a little better in the last couple of days. It had been difficult on both sides. And probably she had a right to more from him than he'd been able to give on the really hard subjects, like what had gone wrong in the past. And it would make the time pass quickly. And then there was the matter of saying goodbye in some adequate way, something that matched what they had been to each other, for years. They had said only formal good-byes, half-goodbyes, so far, feeble ones.

He stood up. She came over to him and reached under his jacket and seized his belt. He pushed at her but she held her grasp.

"What're you doing?" he asked. She was trembling. It was cool in the house but she was flushed and warm. She had some kind of scent on. She rarely wore perfume, cologne, any of that, almost never. He wondered if Morel liked his women scented.

"You'll have to hit me," she said. He loved her breath. He had always thought of it as delectable.

"All right then. I don't think this is a great idea, but I guess it'll be all right."

"It will be," she said. She went to get her overnight case.

"Bring a jersey, it's getting cold," he said after her.

So far they were traveling together in what the Batswana would call *boiling silence*. He forgot what the Setswana phrase was. It was evening and it was cool, but they had the front windows cranked down. He felt he had to have cold air flowing over him, blasting over him, and so did she, although pretty soon it would be too uncomfortable and they would have to live together with the windows closed. But that was ahead of them. The car was a metal shell full of boiling feeling. He was driving faster than was normal for him. She wasn't objecting. The gale they were in undid the possibility of conversation, which was what he wanted until he was calmer. He had gotten angrier, without provocation, since crossing the border, where things had gone smoothly, which had been a relief. He had felt there was a faint chance that his name might have turned up on a watch list on the Botswana side, in which case the game would have been over before it began and he would have been going back to Kgari Close with Iris.

The light was fading over the low, repetitive, stony hills they were passing through. This region, the Groot Marico, was thinly settled. Most of the farmsteads were set far back from the road. Somehow farming went on in this dry terrain, on the flatland between the hills. From a distance the occasional isolated settlements of the black farmworkers looked like dice. You could only get a glimpse of them from an elevation, because the cement cubes provided for them to live in were packed together behind sheet-metal fencing which was always maintained on the side of the settlement fronting the road, randomly maintained around to the back. It was undoubtedly a cosmetic thing. There were no shade trees in the locations, as they were called. The Boer farm homes were uniformly bracketed with plantings of silver oak and eucalyptus.

The roads were broad and hard and smooth. The bridges spanning the dry creeks and gullies were unusually monumental. The agency theory was that they had all been reinforced to a standard that would support the weight of tanks. There were intermittent stretches where the road broadened to four lanes for no apparent reason, the true reason being that these were intended to function as landing places for light aircraft in an emergency. Certainly segments of roadway were densely lined with sturdy metal light poles. The road system had been militarized. Electric lines were buried safely away. Brush had been scoured back to deny cover to anyone out to injure the roads or the traffic they carried. It had all been futile, a preparation for the civil war that was not now going to be fought.

A petrol plaza appeared ahead of them. Everything within the double ring of security fencing was brilliant and clean. He could see shops, the petrol pumps, a restaurant. All the buildings were new-looking, constructed of brightly colored glazed brick. Stadium lights blazed down. Iris put her sunglasses on.

She said, "I saw a shooting star back there. This is a funny thing. My father was interested in comets. Something about comets interested him, but he had no interest whatever in astronomy, the surrounding discipline. It was just comets."

"Some people are like that," Ray said.

They had picked up Simba chips, bananas, and Appletiser at the service plaza. Iris was preparing to hand-feed him, as they would normally do on the road, but he couldn't bear it. He didn't want to hurt her, but the fact was that he couldn't bear it.

"I can't eat," he said.

"But you need to. You said you were hungry."

"I am, but I can't eat. Later on, maybe. But you eat, take care of yourself. Next time we stop I'll have something. But right now I can't."

She opened a packet of Simba chips and began to eat them, but softly, in small mouthfuls, moistening each chip in her mouth before she started chewing, following some impulse, as he saw it, to shrink and mute her presence. She was full of guilt. This maneuver was somehow appropriate to that, for her. She loved Simba chips and would only let herself eat them infrequently because they were so fattening. He was sorry for her but there was nothing he could do.

He said, "Did you let your boyfriend know you were leaving town for this?" He was being too hard. He was too angry.

"He's not my boyfriend."

"Sure he is. What is he, then?"

"Not my boyfriend."

"Your lover, then. Your lover."

"I haven't been with him since you both got back."

"Well I hope you dropped him a line. He might wonder. Okay, so, okay. It hasn't resumed yet. But you are in fact lovers and as far as that goes you still love him. Is that unfair?"

She was breathing rapidly. She said, "I don't know. I don't know how I feel, exactly . . ."

He sighed heavily at her. "Well let's figure it out, if we can."

"Right," she said.

"Look, I need to get everything straight. It's like this. You weren't supposed to do what you did. You weren't supposed to fuck anyone else, and if you were going to, if it felt like you were moving that way, you were supposed to tell me, warn me. You were supposed to give me a chance. That was the understanding. And it was the same for me. It was the understanding between us."

She was anguished. She said, "I know I know. But try to understand.

The thing is that our deal, our understanding, wasn't exactly what it seemed. What it was was a guarantee that it could never happen. It made it unreal. Because it would have led to a talk opera and you making declarations and promising changes here and there and I would have had to believe you and be the decent kind of person I'm supposed to be. And then time would pass and lo and behold the whole thing would become moot because I was too old, imagine that. And time would have passed and then I would be old, and possibly nothing would have changed, truly, between us. Reality. You always talk about being in reality . . ."

"That last road sign was Willowpark, did you see it?"

"It was. It's Swartruggens where you have to be careful. We're fine."

"Go ahead."

"Also, you were away when this was developing. I mean when it got serious, got this serious. That's no excuse, I know. But the truth is I wanted to do it. I wanted that. I was attracted to Davis. I was in a state of temptation that turned intense sooner than I was prepared for, and you were away. It turned intense. What I thought was that I could do it and then see, see how I felt . . . and I think, I *think* maybe I was assuming that the chances were okay that it wasn't going to be the greatest thing in the world and that I would conclude that, finally, but in the meantime I would have gotten something out of my system. I know this is crude, me being crude. I think it's the kind of thing men do and . . ."

"You have to stop for a minute. This is hard for me, my girl, my girl. Ah *Jesus.*"

"And I don't know if maybe I thought once I had been through it, through something forbidden, that it would be over and *we* could be back together."

That enraged him. He had plunged from a place where she had been creating a little sympathy in him, down into this. She was a fool.

"*Don't patronize me, Iris.* I'm not a *fool.* You say *that*? You destroy everything and you say *that*? So it was just about forbidden fruit? We have to speak the truth, here. What you're saying is cheap. My throat is dry. Jesus Christ."

She handed him the bottle of Appletiser she had been drinking from.

"*Don't make me stop*, Ray, even if I say something you despise me saying. I don't know how many times I can go over this, so I have to do my best. You're not going to like any of it. Of course you aren't. Anyway, a part of it was that I was tired of being good. At that moment, I was. It was weakness and self-pity all mixed together. There. But I was tired of being good. Being good had gotten me a life that had so much wrong with it. In a way I wanted to stop being good almost out of curiosity. And this is a confession, I'm well aware. I look hideous to myself when I say it, but it's true. I wanted to see what I was like on the other side of a certain line. Nothing I'm telling you is about getting sympathy out of you."

"Of course."

"Also he didn't want to do it, at first, at all. This may surprise you."

"It does and it doesn't." He couldn't swallow.

She went on. "Well it surprised me. I made it clear enough to him. I was the initiator and I had certain expectations about the target, about men. So I was pretty surprised when he resisted. When he turned me down. Like that. If he had yielded right away, I don't know . . ."

"I'm not following this."

"No it roused *me*. It galvanized something. I felt worse when he turned me down than I had before. I didn't like that. It was the worst outcome. You think I'm shallow."

He didn't know what he believed or thought. He remembered vividly one of her post-coitum triste moments when she'd answered his question about what was troubling her, because she had an odd look, and she'd answered with the strange assertion that she was sad that sex was about the greatest thing she could give him and that sex wasn't enough because she loved him so much. It was hard to credit, but it had really happened. He had felt what, ennobled.

"And there's this, Ray. There had been some incidents with you, not recent, but still . . . I was dwelling on them. You wanted certain women. You did. Oh yes you did. I'm not saying you represented an extreme of the way married men are, or men generically. I'm not a child. But I . . ."

"This is too much, really Iris. It's insane. I mean in the present circumstance, really. I have been utterly one hundred percent faithful to you and you know it. I *do* represent an extreme, a good one. This is too fucking much."

"Ray, I told you you wouldn't like this. I know you've been faithful. I utterly do know it. I believe it. I believe you never *acted*. That's what I believe. But I also believe that you wanted to act, because you've humiliated me more than once."

"*Humiliated* you?"

"Yes, exactly. Staring at that woman on the train, Rhodesian Railways, at that particular young woman in the dining car, even after I asked you to stop it. Turning around in your chair to stare at her like all the other men, doing it all through dinner, it was absolutely humiliating."

"That one again. I have apologized for that, I believe. Let me count the times."

"And there were other lovely moments. But I do believe you never acted. But I believe you wanted to."

"Never, not once . . . No."

"Oh *sure* you did. Don't tell me otherwise. But you're missing my point. And by the way, I believe you imagined yourself betraying me with the embassy nurse. Your juices run. You're not dead there. I benefited from that. You're a live cock. But this isn't my point. I don't know if I'm being too subtle for you. You were my model. I don't doubt that your history of rectitude would have been different if any of the ladies you enjoyed staring at so much had gone aggressive toward you. Do you doubt it?"

"Of course! I don't know what you wanted from me . . ."

"You're not getting the point I'm making. There was a certain imbalance that felt worse to me than maybe it should have when Davis showed up. The fact is that I have truly been a virgin when it came to feeling or showing anything toward other men. So when I decided to move toward Davis I had a certain model in my mind and a certain amount of historical aggravation to go with it. That I had never felt free to address because I didn't know how to address it and didn't know I had a right to address it other than asking you to cut it out in public, in the rare cases when that happened."

"Cases? Don't you mean case, singular?"

"No, cases. But this is a byway and not an excuse for what I did and I don't want to have it taken for an excuse because it's not an excuse. So let's stop talking about it. Let's pause."

They stopped at the side of the road near Swartruggens. He ate a banana.

He said, "So is this right? two things happened. First, it got, in your words, more intense than you'd expected it would, leaving *intense* undefined for the moment. And second, it came to my attention. I found out about it and I wasn't supposed to find out about it. Because you were preserving, or reserving, better, the right to have this thing evolve to its full stature and glory and intensity, at which point I would have been clued in, or not. And possibly you harbored expectations that you would gain knowledge out of this and decide to return to the mixture as before with yours truly in the dark forever? In other words, this was your variant of a very commonplace . . . *with other people* . . . situation. So is that about right?"

"I don't know."

"You do know."

"You're cold. You're being cold."

"No I'm not. Wait until I start on myself. But before I do that, I have to know everything I don't know about you and Morel."

"You mean the details."

"The details, yes. And I have to know about the question of love, who loves who. Because I love *you*. In all this, that's absolutely clear, crystal clear, as they say. I can't be with you, anymore. I know I can't. And that's because I love you, paradoxically. This is what I think and this is what makes everything impossible, and that is that even if you told me you loved me *again*, interesting concept, reloved me, I wouldn't be able to believe it. Believe it again. I'd be afraid you were being pragmatic or something like that. I mean, I could try to think of your adventure with Morel as an experiment that got out of control and that I was partly to blame for it in the first place. But I don't see how it could work.

"And I don't even know if you would be interested in convincing me that it could. That would be presumptuous of me, now that I bring it up. So, no. Yes, the details."

"You assume I stopped loving you, Ray."

"You must have. Of course you did."

"I can't stand discussing love. Ray, I can't."

"Ah."

"It's too simple. I have . . . feelings . . ."

"Love-feelings? Love-feelings. See, I understand what's going on here. The reason you don't want to talk about how you feel about Morel is because it would be disloyal to do that, to give the details to somebody else, such as your husband. You may not have thought of this. You develop a primary loyalty to the person you love and a secondary loyalty to the person you used to love and primary trumps secondary."

"You're making it too simple, the way you always do."

"Well, describe it in your own words, how you feel about him. By the way, I like Morel. He's sterling, my dear, in many ways. He has gone out of his way to have an interesting mind to present, interesting views. He was a friend to me in captivity. This is just by the way. But you owe me a description of how you feel. You can make it concise. But don't leave anything out."

"This is impossible."●

"Ah," he said.

"I mean, it's hard enough talking about this, but talking about it cooped up where you can't move is impossible. Could we just get out and walk around?"

He agreed to do it. He didn't like it. He didn't know how dangerous it was in this area. There was some SADF presence. They had been stuck behind a convoy of six army trucks for a few kilometers. He supposed it was all right. He had good, long vantages in every direction. There was plenty of starlight. They would stay close to the vehicle. He understood how she felt. They were discussing enormous subjects under conditions of restrictions that were unfair. He wanted to pace around and break things. But they couldn't. Wringing each other's necks would also be appropriate to their discourse. They got out.

She was sensitive to their need to abbreviate as much as they could, if they were going to make it into Joburg not later than nine-thirty or ten. He would have to find a hotel, find a safe place to deposit the Volkswagen, get organized so he could start out early in his search for Kerekang.

"We're having a sighing contest," she said. They were leaning against the car.

"We have to go soon, Iris."

"I know. But I want to get this part over with. You have a right to know certain things. This is so impossible. But you're going to quiz me about the sex with him, with Davis, and the part that played in everything. And in a way I'm eager to tell you, as much as I hate it, because it reflects well on you."

"This is a little too abbreviated for me. Say what you mean."

"Well. First is that you have nothing to be concerned about . . . about you, sexually. You're fine. You're unusually fine, I guess you could say I'm concluding, not that my experience has been so exhaustive."

This is how much I love her, he thought. He was alarmed at the idea that she was implying inadequacies, sexual ones, that she was preparing to live with. You are a prince, aren't you, he thought.

He had to ask. "Does he have some sort of problem? Something I should, I mean, I mean you should, be concerned about?" He was thinking of impotence. There were phobias about touching some people had. It wasn't size. What was it?

"Oh it's not a problem. Look I'm giving you a compliment, is all I'm doing. This is awkward to say. You're very skilled, Ray. What I'm saying is that I wasn't overwhelmed by things he could do that you can't or haven't. He's kind of prudish."

"I'm skilled? How can I be skilled? I'm what you made me, what we are together."

She couldn't look at him. He wanted to know how many times they had done it, and where, and how. She would tell him if he made her do it. He wouldn't. He wanted to apologize.

He said, "How many times have you done it?"

"*Please* don't make me go into detail, *please.*"

"I have a right to know."

"I don't agree with that."

"Okay, so you're saying I should be satisfied with what, the overview, let's call it. That you just gave."

"If you love me you won't make me describe everything."

"I wonder how many times that line has been used."

She was in misery. He could restrain himself on this, at least for now, he could. But there was another sex question he had to have answered. It was legitimate.

"I have to ask you this. You've been absolutely careful, haven't you? You know what I mean. About infection."

"Ray, he's a doctor."

"I know he is and that's good and I'm sure it gives him the fear of God he needs to have. But . . . you don't know everything about him. You can't, yet. And you know how it is in Botswana. Half the population may be seropositive. That's what the embassy thinks. A gigantic nightmare is coming. You know about this. You haven't been tempted to take any kind of chances, have you?"

"No."

"It's always with a condom. I'm sorry, but is it always with a condom?"

She nodded. She couldn't say it out.

So Morel had never been flesh to flesh with her, fucking. That was something. That experience was his private treasure, so far. Of course at some point, that would be taken away from him, as soon as she decided she could completely trust him.

"I know you trust him, Iris. But be careful. I think he's honorable, of course, but you have to be careful."

"If you're asking me if I trust him not to expose me to disease by cheating with other people, I do."

That formulation was painful. But it was all painful.

She said, "And he's completely terrified about HIV. He's made a nuisance of himself over it with people in the Ministry of Health. He's going to get them to be serious about it."

Good for him, Ray thought. This was hell, this part. He could feel himself releasing her. He had accomplished the intellectual act of release, but there was more, a visceral part, a corporeal part, that felt like physical injury, tearing. One had to be kept severed from the other. The intellectual act consisted of halfway imagining himself walking and talking normally and conducting business in the future, business of some kind, without her anywhere near the scene. Of course he would be doing business in hell, because his life post-Iris would be hell. He seemed to be attracted to hell, hell via Milton and hell via the agency, which specialized in making little hells for the enemy here and there, individuals and groups. True hell is your wife being in love with another man, he thought. He had known a couple of men in his time who were obsessed with pursuing other men's wives, mavens of married female flesh, and he had considered it a fetish and the men freakish, with their fascination with getting into colleagues' wives, with all the risks and betrayals that entailed. He had regarded them as unpleasant types and so had Iris. He should have paid more attention, understood them better. In *The Decameron* the seducer priest got his way with young women by convincing them that putting his penis into them was a pious act called putting the Devil in hell, back in hell, supposedly. Of course Iris might say he had been slightly complaisant at the beginning concerning her signs and gestures toward Morel, in that he hadn't opposed her going to the man. He didn't think he had been. If he had he was sorry and he would have to put it down to looking for a great refusal, a gran rifiuto, on her part, maybe. He thought, If you love hell so much you should have done Dante instead of pitiful Milton. He was surprised at the thought. It was too late to do Dante.

Joburg was one hundred and sixty miles from Gaborone, as the crow flies, and they were only halfway there.

Normally on road trips Iris was the navigator. He didn't need her help on this trip, which was straightforward. They both knew it by heart. But still she had gotten out the roadmap and was keeping it on her lap, refolding it as they progressed, keeping up. She was beautiful in profile.

"I want to go up there," she said, almost peremptorily.

He knew where they were. They were passing along a valley with one high wall. A curving side road ran up it to a picnic area, tables and benches strung along a railed escarpment, and there was a concrete observation platform. You could see Pretoria in the distance. At night you could see the amber haze that hung over it. They had been up there in the past. He couldn't imagine anyone would frequent it at night, using it as a lovers' lane, for example, because of the general fear over security that permeated the Groot Marico. There were toilet facilities on the site, as he recalled. She was willing to stop and urinate by the road, normally, but getting to the bush was more of a trek now that there had been so much clearing-back.

"Do you need to pee?" he asked.

"I wouldn't mind, but that isn't it." That meant it was nostalgia. He couldn't oppose that. He looked at her. He realized that she was tearing up, not weeping yet. His heart hurt. The thing was that he loved her, every inch of her, which it was pointless to keep saying. So they would go up and have a gaze. She wanted to and they were making good time.

He took the side road and drove slowly upward. Without prologue Iris reached in his crotch and pressed on his penis.

He had no words. He was unsurprised, but this was dangerous, an egg full of suffering for somebody, maybe everybody. He coughed. Out of pleasure, suffering, would be something in Latin. On the other hand, there was something fated about the prospect, and correct, because it acknowledged something about their personal carnal history to do it one more time, saluted something. She rested the backs of her fingers against his penis, moving them slightly.

She said, "Hm, I see you're at least bi. I thought you might be gay, but I see you're bi. Well, thank goodness." This was an old game between them. Gay meant he was soft, bi meant he was semihard. She would give the mock characterization that he was gay or bi if, when she was teasing him on the way to sex, he was not in his usual quite prompt hard state, his hetero state. It was a painful attempt to relive old stuff. He forgave her. He was sorry for her. He didn't know what she thought she was going to get out of the coming event. There was going to be one. He was hard, as they rose.

"Oh my," she said. That was another thing she did, acting prim as an ingredient in the course of lewd conduct. Lewd was her own word for herself.

"Don't do that," he said.

"Now you're hetero," she said.

"I know, I know. This is silly," he said. She was delicately unbuttoning her blouse.

They were near the top. In Dante there was something about *l'arte de tornar*. Turning back was an art he didn't have, had never had. He wasn't going to turn back. She was leading the way. He didn't know if he was being insane to follow. It was possible. Her eyes were wet. He had to watch the road, but she was unbuttoning her blouse, his wife. She was.

It didn't look like there was going to be any discussion. The parking area was of course marked *parkering*. It was empty. The whole site was theirs. He had no idea what she had in mind for a location for what she had in mind, which was probably not the car. It would be complicated in the car. But doing anything outside the car could be dangerous. It was getting cooler. And they would be exposed.

He parked. Her blouse was completely undone. He groaned. He couldn't help it. She knew what she was doing. He could see the inner side of one breast but not the nipple. That was meant to tease. She had perfect, sleek darkish nipples. There was a sense in which a woman wasn't naked if she had something obscuring her nipples even if everything else was there.

"It's getting chilly," he said.

"No it isn't," she answered. She was in a sexually driven state. He had seen it in their life together. He wondered if Morel had seen it. He was inflamed. Fluid leaked from his penis.

They would be in danger outside the car, in a generic way, white people naked, one a woman, in the dark, in South Africa, making themselves vulnerable in the most absolute way. The danger could come from Boer farm guard groups, from Boer police or from the army, even, or from ordinary criminals or from black guerrillas. He could propose that they wait until they got to Joburg and into a hotel but that felt like a bad idea. She was in the grip of doing it now and here. It would be extraordinary to do it now and here and not extraordinary to do it in the comfort of a hotel. There was a certain subcategory of the human race consisting of people who sought out and enjoyed public intercourse and the dangers that went with it, but he was not in it. She was going to have to let him reconnoiter the site thoroughly to make sure that nobody was hiding behind a bush. She was undressing all the way.

He said, "I have to take a look around." He found a torch in the glove box and let himself out. He made a circuit of the site. The toilets were locked, which was annoying. She always wanted to pee before sex and then after. He only needed to pee after. The good news was that she had been right about the temperature. It wasn't too cold. It was cool. It was all right. He was radiating heat.

Iris was naked, waiting in the car. It looked like there was not going to be any discussion. He got into the driver's seat.

"You don't want to be inside, in the car, do you?" he said.

She shook her head.

He said, "What's your plan?"

She pointed into the back. There was a thick pink acrylic afghan on the seat, along with a canister of towelettes. She had planned this. He knew the afghan. He had knocked a can of ginger beer over on it once. It was faintly redolent of that, still, and of motor oil. Usually it was kept in the boot of their own Beetle. He was not going to go out into the bush with her. They would have to stay next to the car, with the doors open so that they could jump back in should some kind of danger appear. They were not going to go off in search of a setting with a view. He would prefer it if he could leave the engine running, even, but that would be distracting. He was fully aroused.

He got out of everything except his loafers. He wanted to kiss her. He put his hand behind her head. She turned her face away. She was weeping softly and helplessly, not making anything of it. He wanted it to stop. Everything is impossible, he thought. She was beautiful, naked. Her breasts were like what, some perfect imaginary kind of fruit, like that platonic idea behind some paradisiacal fruit not known on earth, something like that. He was full of lust, which was hardly surprising, he was in a deprived state. She looked silvery. They had moonlight. Widely scattered strings and points of light burned in the landscape below them and the blur over Pretoria was visible.

He said, "We're going to stay right next to the car, and I mean right up against it."

She nodded. He would dispense with his socks and loafers and put them in the car where they would be safe if they had to leave in a rush. His experience of enforced barefootedness had left its mark on him.

He reparked, changing the heading of the car so that it was angled toward the mouth of the access road. He would see that the afghan was placed within the lee of the open doors on the driver's side. They would be shielded from the vantage of any approaching vehicle, but headlight beams would alert them before any intruder actually arrived.

They were out of the car. With the side of one shoe Ray knocked away the largest pieces of gravel on the ground immediate to the car. He

opened the car doors. Iris spread the afghan out. He could see that her
nipples were hard.

"We don't have to do this," he said. It seemed odd, saying it, considering his erection, the state he was in. It was not going to seem sincere to
her, but it was. Her weeping was less, at least.

She shook her head vehemently. The silence protocol was still in
effect.

"And you're not cold?" Her response was as before.

He said, "I'll go with you if you want to pee." He had the torch ready.
He escorted her to a spot behind the toilets. He couldn't believe that they
were taking care of business naked in South Africa, but they were. He lit
her up, as she squatted, but just long enough to see that there was nothing threatening in the vicinity. He stood guard. He couldn't remember
what the name of the odd duckbill bone at the base of the spine that
showed when anyone squatted was. Delay was only making him more
adamant, his penis more adamant. Iris made Ray turn around while she
used some towelettes. She was so fastidious.

They returned to the afghan. She knelt and she motioned to him to
do the same, facing her a foot apart. He did. She had some inner plan
for this.

They touched palms and then interlocked fingers and gripped hard.
She had touched her what, her introitus, briefly. He didn't want to think
pussy at that moment, he didn't know why. It was only an opening in a
human body but it was, in her case, so nice. Her pubic escutcheon grew
in a neat compact bar over her introitus, with almost no growth to the
sides. It was like art. He was not going to be pushed, once they began.
She was going to wait. He needed to be superb, if he could.

Without warning she pulled him over and down, to the right, to get
him on his back. Her touch was like fire, as she guided him. Why did he
have to lose her, he wanted to know. She was unusual. He remembered
her observing at an embassy event when the subject under discussion was
the food choices available at Kopano's Market that certain avocados here
smelled like semen when you cut them, which was true, but not the thing
to say. Other people had mentioned lame things like the teardrop-shaped
potatoes and fluted tomatoes.

She straddled him. Her hair was loose. It was cut straight across at the
level of her shoulders. It was hanging forward, hiding her face, except
for her eyes, which she was holding shut tight. She was being careful
about his cock, leaving it alone so far. On his back meant fun for him, Iris
taking her time.

He had to push his anxiety away. It would be easier for him to get up and take care of an emergency if she weren't on top of him. He had to forget about that. Some of their best sex had been with her on top, using him as a dildo, taking her sweet time.

One thing he loved that she sometimes did was to align their nipples and rub. Hers would be hard and his would be too. He didn't know if she would do that. In an ideal world she would do everything she had ever done with him, in farewell, a variety show, had they but world enough and time, which they didn't. There was too much.

She was dragging her hair across his eyes. Kiss me, he thought, anguished, because she wasn't going to, he knew. She lightly bit his shoulder. She was lowering herself more. She was brushing her breasts across his face. He wanted to take one of her breasts into his mouth, *either one*. He was frantic. He wanted to get as much of one of her breasts into his mouth as he could. Her breasts were killing him, her blunt instruments. He had called them that and she had laughed, long ago.

She was kissing his eyebrows, licking them and kissing them. He didn't want her to do anything tonight that they hadn't done before, anything she had learned elsewhere. He couldn't tell her that. But he could will her to stay within those lines. He felt pathetic. He was sure she had kissed his eyebrows before, maybe not as dedicatedly, though. When they got to it, she would come first. In a second or minute she would be using the head of his cock to open the lips of her pussy and that would be perilous. He would imagine a knot in the base of his cock. He would make it tighten as she tried to draw it loose, undo it and make him drown in her, which he would not do.

He wanted to turn the torch on her, to look at her. He couldn't do that.

She was pressing her pubis against his right hipbone. In a minute she would use his knee against her labia, hard. She was sweating lightly, despite the temperature. Her parts were perfect. In time of course they would go the way of all flesh, and he felt tender toward the body he would never see. He wondered if Morel would still appreciate her. Months back when she had described herself as perimenopausal he hadn't paid attention, hadn't linked it up with all the other medical jargon creeping into her conversation since she'd gotten in with Morel. She would be good for the long haul. It was genetic and it was never smoking and drinking and just by instinct keeping out of the sun. She was a genetically advantaged person. And she had been his. The world is a desperate place, he thought.

Overhead the stars were like salt in the wound that he was, as the band played on, she played on, teasing her cunt with the head of his cock, like old times. She was very wet. He tried to touch her there and she slapped his hand away. It was going to be no kissing and no hands sex. He would take it. She had an idea about this encounter and whatever it was would be okay.

He was going to remember every second of going into her, this last time. He had told her more than once in the past that he wished she could be him long enough to know the unspeakable pleasure of going in, hot, going in, being let in, rather, being allowed.

She wasn't ready for him to go in. She had his penis where she wanted it. She was sliding hard against the underside of the shaft, sliding her labia hard along it. His heels were in the gravel. He wanted a pillow. He would do better if he had a pillow. There was no pillow.

She was sweeping the wings of her hair across his mouth, her hair dark as death. In junior high school the words *Eat hair* had been a dire male-to-male insult. That was when oral sex was considered a perversion. She was sitting up higher again and he wanted her not to stop bending closer to him. He caught her hands and pulled. She resisted. He pulled again and she resisted again, harder. For a moment it felt like rowing.

He thought, We are all rowing toward death, keeping it behind us but rowing toward it and not looking at it while we study our pitiful accomplishments receding. In sex you might forget death. He could feel drops of something on his chest, tears or it could be sweat. She was being rough. He didn't think she was trying to make him come, really, before she did, to make some kind of point about his stamina, a mean point. No, she was doing the cooperative thing they did. He hoped that was right. But she was being rough. She knew his limits, or thought she did. Tonight was different.

She had raised herself up and was touching herself again. That was almost too much for him. When she masturbated she always wanted him to hold her free hand, which made it love and not sex, only, not only sex. She wasn't masturbating now, she was teasing herself, for him, he knew. She stopped. He wished she would say something.

This was not going to be dawdling sex or karezza or any halfway sex fun practices they had fooled around with. Here is my body and the things we can do together with it, was what she was also going to be saying to somebody else.

One thing she knew was that his cock could take pretty substantial provocation outside the snug sanctum it was aiming for. She was using that. But going in, the first minutes after that, were delicate, but if she helped they would pass and the band would begin to play and that would be fine, it could play on.

She was letting him in, just, and stopping there, and then bending over again and dragging her hair all over his face, which was cruel, if it was cruel, if it was anything but an impulse she was having but not meant to be cruel the way kissing would be. He wondered if what she was saying was You will never get a fuck like this again in your whole mortal life unless . . . unless something he couldn't imagine, something other than stay with me and see what happens. He knew it wasn't that, nothing as crude as that. It was something else. He had his own idea, by God, which was to ask for help from not God but Rhonda, help me Rhonda, help me keep her out of my heart, something cheap to make him slightly hate her, help me Beach Boys, anyone, help me, help me keep the knot tied in the heart the base of my cock, tied tight. She was letting him in.

He felt strong. He inhaled as hard as he could. That was usually helpful. He needed help. He needed everything *to be different*. He needed a time machine, of course, like anyone else. He was strong.

The knot keeping him from coming was threaded on his will, his willpower, his will, out of the night. Out of the night that covers me, out of the nineteenth century, the will, yes sir.

He was in and he was going to fuck her until she said to stop in the name of God.

And he needed to think of his semen bolt as a pearl of great price, a pearl, a containable thing.

He was in a little more. He grasped her waist. In Eden sex had been like a handshake according to Augustine, before there was hot sex, after the Fall. This was not going to be a handshake, except that a handshake could be goodbye as well as hello, as well as Hello I must be going.

He was in even more. She was being so careful. When she got close she wouldn't be able to maintain herself on top. She would clutch him and fall on him and drop and roll over onto one side and pull him over on top. Now she was grasping his shoulders.

He was in deep, she was letting him in, she was sinking down to seal it, that was it, it was perfect. She was pausing, holding him there. He didn't know what she was doing, whether she was trying to leave him with a fuck he would use the rest of his life to search for, to search for one like it, or was she trying to do something else, by this act, to change everything between them, everything in his mind having to do with what he should be doing, with what they should be doing. He had no idea.

She was starting and stopping. She was coming down hard and then she was drawing back a little way and then coming back down slowly and then waiting. There was sweat shining in the little hollows on either side of the base of her neck. She was moving her pelvis in a slow circle.

She was moving now. He grasped her breasts. *I'll just hold on to your breasts so's they don't get away* he had said to her once.

She was moving less carefully. It was going on. He tried to get outside himself. He tried to see the stars and the glints of light in her hair and on her teeth when she opened her mouth and looked up as one combined field. She was oblivious to the strength of her movements. She was edging them off the afghan. She was making small sounds in the back of her throat. She was a noisy lover, normally, but she was trying to be mindful of prudence, because of their situation, he understood.

There was a tear of sweat on each of her nipples. She shook them off, onto his chest. She was going to stay on top until she came. That was now. It was all right. He wanted to see her face when she came. She was getting close. Her legs were shaking. He wanted her to go first. He wanted to hold back and let her go and then fuck her just after she came until she came again, and until she said no, it was too much.

He thought of Guatemala, the agency, Boyle, to cool himself. He thought about Malawi and Banda and one or two things he knew about the agency there, things Marion Resnick had told him, a man who never lied. But he thought about these dark things in a new way for him, not by acknowledging them as things at a distance but as sites of horror, bodies, dead bodies, fields of them, like the bodies at Ngami Bird Lodge, spread on the ground, pitched into the flames of the burning lodge.

He held his breath. He held himself in. There were things he wanted to say to her. He wanted to say I want to say goodbye. And he wanted to say Remember me.

It was good. She came. She fell against him. He managed to stay in her as she fell and he maneuvered her over and under him. It was done with art and it reminded him of something they had talked about, which was how amazing it was that the configurations two people could get involved in when they slept in the same bed never seemed to be exhausted.

He wanted her to tell him to fuck her, but it didn't matter if she didn't. He moved in her. She was in one of the afterwaves of coming when

he began. That was what he had wanted. His heart was killing him. He
loved her.

He drove himself harder into her. She was whining with pleasure and
that was good. She would climax again right away.

He kept on, slowing himself. He pushed her knees up higher. He was
almost there and so was she, again.

And then the knot at the root of his cock dissolved in fire, melting. He
shouted when he came. Then she was snorting, trying to say something.
She was telling him to stop. She had come a second time and she wanted
him to stop. They disengaged, shaking.

He felt heavy. He accompanied her while she urinated and cleaned up.
She was very quick about it. She took care of herself not far from the car
this time. He went off by himself, further off, to urinate.

They pulled their clothes out of the car and dressed hurriedly. Before
he buttoned his shirt she stopped him and reached in to touch his chest,
his sides, tenderly.

He felt leaden. Because he didn't know what the message was, the message of what they had just done together. Or he felt leaden because there
was no message. She looked ravaged, tired, not the way he wanted her to
look after what they had done.

When he bent down to gather up the afghan she said, "Leave it."

They were in Johannesburg and almost downtown. They were passing
through the Observatory District, an odd, middle-class residential area
laid out on abrupt hills that had formerly been vast heaps of gold mine
tailings. The streets were empty.

Iris said, "What are we going to do?"

He said, "I'll tell you exactly. You're going with Morel and I'm going
to be down here, alone. I'm going to find Kerekang. And then I'm still
going to be here. But that's not what you mean. What you mean is what
are we going to do once we've done what we're going to do and it isn't
working out so magnificently, when we have regrets, if we do. That's
what you mean."

There was more, but he wasn't going to go into it. There was going to
be a school connection. He would be joining the new South Africa.
There was a certain heroic vagueness to his plans that he liked.

She said, "There's a certain heroic vagueness about your plans." He
was startled. It was a cruel reminder of the way their minds followed,
tracked together, unless it was telepathy, which was nonsense. He must

have used the phrase in some historical situation and it must have stuck in her mind.

"We have telepathy," he said.

"Ray, I always wanted us to be in a school, set up a school together, you know. Or open a bookshop together. I've had that idea."

"Right, an idea for going bankrupt."

"Maybe not."

"Believe me."

"I'm so glad you're out of the agency. It's what I wanted. I hated it."

"I'm glad too."

"We'll be friends," she said.

"I know. Of course. Forever."

"We're having a sighing contest. We should stop it."

"Okay, my dear girl. One last sigh."

"We're saying goodbye."

"Not yet. In the morning."

38. At the Beginning

He was sleeping well, better than well. It was one of the things about his life that he couldn't help wanting Iris to know. It wasn't the kind of information that would be of interest to anyone else he could think of. His bed was a cot with a foam rubber pad on it. His blankets were rough. His bedroom, in fact his entire domicile, was a caravan, a small one, an aluminum antique held together by ingenious repairs and wholly unlikely to survive any effort to tow it to some other site. But it was clean. It was overclean. He couldn't stop women, mothers and sisters of students in the school that was being organized, from coming in, whenever they liked, to clean up. The tiny galley was spotless. His shelflike table was polished every day. His water containers were always kept full. It was often cold in the caravan and he had been chided by the women for not making use of his paraffin heater. He would use it when he needed to. The cold wasn't keeping him from sleeping and he enjoyed being as frugal as he could in the circumstances. His life was like his circumstances, it occurred to him. It was poor and cold and clean. He got out of bed.

He lit his Coleman stove and put the kettle on to heat his tea and wash water. He felt like writing. In the morning he felt like writing. So, when there wasn't too much pressure to get over to the school, that was what he did. He liked writing by candlelight, in the dark mornings, but the mornings were getting brighter day by day and he was up a little later than usual and the light admitted by the peculiar lozenge-shaped windows in the sides of the caravan was adequate for writing. He was kept supplied with candles, too, by the women.

Outside it was bright and windy. A solitary slablike cloud was sliding away. Bleak fields of stubble ran northward toward a line of stony hills.

Thorn trees grew in clutches at the far edge of the field. His caravan was beached adjacent to the derelict farmhouse now under reconstruction as a schoolhouse. A toilet block had been his suggestion for one of the first improvements. It was done. He was glad. He could use it and it was a step up from the pit latrine he had had to make do with at first. To the south, across a red dirt road that carried almost no traffic, were more fields sloping down to a depression where the shanties the farmworkers occupied were laid out near a chive-green pond. Something was going to be done to cleanse or rectify in some way the pond. He wasn't sure what.

Back at his table, cleaned up and with a mug of tea at hand, he decided not to write anything else for the time being about his brother. He had already written too much. He was going to impose an arbitrary limit on each Life, maybe even a fixed number of words for each one that no one would notice or think of counting until later, when they were looking at the Lives for a second time. He liked the idea of some analogue of haiku being imposed on these lapidary biographies he was doing, going to do.

No, he was going to write to Iris. He got out his notepad. And he would write in pen, not pencil, proving to himself that this was not going to be a draft. Drafts were his enemy. He loved them. He had to write to Iris. He had gotten one letter from her during his time in Hillbrow. And then he had had to leave Johannesburg. And now he was where no one was likely to find him and he had to write her. There wasn't a telephone within five kilometers.

He wrote,

My Dear Woman,
This letter will be handed to you when you don't expect it. I have worked this out. I will use a courier. I don't want to use the regular post for a while.
And when you get this letter I want you to destroy it, silly as that may sound.

He stopped writing. He had someone picked out to be a courier. And he had yet another prospect. He would have to make a trip back to Joburg to set it up. But it would work. One of the two would be fine.

How interested in me anyone connected with the agency may be I have no idea. But I have learned to be circumspect and I am being circumspect.

Where I am. I am in a safe place. I am in the bush. It's rural.
When I can let you know exactly where I am, believe me I will. I
have my ways.

I can say this much about what I am doing. You know that the
farmworker children got little or no education, depending on
whether or not the owners wanted to put anything into some
minimal teaching scheme. Now that whole arrangement is falling
apart. The Boers are cutting their costs because they think they are
going to have to sell up, once Mandela comes, which will be soon.
So out in the countryside, education for farmworker kids is
collapsing. So ex machina there is a unit in the ANC that is thinking
ahead and wants to do something preemptively and which also has
some money, from the Swedes. So by devious and clever means I
got in touch and found people at St. James's to vouch for me and
here I am.

Now as to my life in Joburg, Hillbrow. I only stayed in the
Johannesburger Hotel for two nights, after which I descended into
hell. I decided I would try to live rough for a while, find a way to
live in one of the squats. Every other building in Hillbrow is being
squatted. I thought it would be economical, and that it would
extend the time I could devote to looking for our friend. It was easy
to get into a squat if you gave any sign that you had pocket money. I
got into one squat with white down-and-outers and I was taken
advantage of, shall we say. And then I left Hillbrow and went to
Yeoville, which was as I understood it a sort of bohemian area and
got into a squat and was taken advantage of. And then I returned to
Hillbrow and got into a mixed squat. I was presenting myself as an
alcoholic. I was believable. The whole time I was trying to find my
way into the realm of people with something to sell, information to
sell that might help in my search. I got nothing. It was a
mistake.

And then in the *Daily Mail* I saw something. There has been an
explosion of street performance activity of all kinds in Joburg,
singers, self-taught acrobats, fortune tellers. And I noticed in the
chronicle of crime stories they publish every day, in the *Mail*, one
story. Three Brits had been given fines for harassing a poetry reader
in the central train station. They had been tourists waiting to board
the Blue Train to Cape Town. They had been drunk. And they had
been attempting to bully the poetry performer into reciting Kipling
instead of his own repertoire of Tennyson. And there had been a

dustup and the police came and they were fined fifty rands apiece. That was all.

So I knew where to look. And I did go and did look and I found what I was searching for. I presented an aspect a little more frightening and off-putting than I realized I had achieved, but I made myself known. Our friend was living rough, not in squats but in the train tunnels. He should have called you. I wish he had, he was in poor shape.

So I have been able to help greatly. We are together here. Our students are Pedi, Xhosa, and Tswana, so we have our work cut out for us. We are at the beginning.

Anyway, I'm well. I'm sleeping well.

He knew what he was going to conclude with.

Going back to your last call, my last call, rather, from Hillbrow, before my disappearment. You were being cryptic, but I gathered from it that for a while at least you would be staying at Kgari Close, by yourself. You seemed to be saying that you wanted to come down and stay with me in the Republic at least for a while. But I was squatting so there was no way, in that phase, I could even think of inviting you.

Something you said on the drive down has stayed with me. I don't care if it was something you got from Morel. It was about the Incas and how people were living out their lives thinking they were living normally, getting and spending and mating, but in fact they were trapped in an insane system governed by a prophecy declaring that if a certain constellation they had been observing for centuries sank below the night horizon, then the Inca nation would be cast into hell. But its station in the sky was doomed. It was the precession of the equinoxes and the Incas were witlessly trying to mobilize their whole illuded nation to reverse it, primarily by selecting the most beautiful children in every district and sacrificing them. And that was what the society was about, more and more sacrifice, until the whole thing fell apart.

Well. I am living a new life here. I want you to come and see it. What I am doing and what these children will get out of it is very direct. I am teaching and doing curriculum and helping out as well as I can with construction for the school. You can give your own judgment on what I'm doing.

I am writing *Lives*, just my brother's so far, and it's not finished. There will be more.

I am full of love for you, but you can come however you feel about me. I have a way to let you know where I am and I will use it in a short time.

Love,
Your husband,
Ray

He folded the letter and sealed it an envelope, rapidly, before he could change his mind.

Ray tried to recall what was on his docket for the day. Kerekang wanted to plant some exotic species of fast-growing poplar around the school, for shade, which would be expensive. The seedlings had to be ordered from Cape Town. There would have to be a negotiation. And then there were two locals, potential teachers, to be interviewed.

He went outside to wait for the students. It was a moment he liked. The elements of the world were distinct. Kerekang, who was lodging in the farmworker location to the south, would appear at the head of the procession of children coming from that quarter. And there he was, striding, jocularly orchestrating his charges into a semblance of orderly marching. In twos and threes children were popping up, coming from other directions, on their own, unled.

Seeing Kerekang, antic man, the children from the east and the west and the north began to run.

Glossary

S: Setswana   A: Afrikaans

ANC: African National Congress
Baherero: members of the Herero tribal group
bakkie: pick-up truck (A)
Basarwa: members of the San, or Bushman tribal group
Batswana: inhabitants of Botswana. A single inhabitant of Botswana:
    Motswana (S)
BDF: Botswana Defence Force
bogwadi: the belief that widows are a main source of sexual disease, in
    particular AIDS
BoSo: familiar abbreviation for the left-leaning Botswana Social Front
braii: barbecue (A)
chibuku: maize beer (S)
CODESA: Convention for a Democratic South Africa—Constitution-
    writing exercise undertaken by opposition groups and the South African
    government, 1990–92
CTO: Central Transport Organization
CUSO: Canadian University Services Overseas
Dikgang: daily newspaper of the government of Botswana
ditlhamane: fairy tales, tall tales (S)
Domkrag: lifting-jack, meaning "the ruling power" (A)
donga: ravine (S)
ehe: okay (S)
expat: expatriate worker
goromente: government
gosiame: all-purpose term meaning variously: I agree; okay; everything's fine (S)

halal: Islamic kosher

Ichokela Bokhutlon: Endure to the End, the name of Kerekang's shortlived commune (S)

ISA: to make happen. The name of Kerekang's social movement (S)

"Ke Bona": Botswana's national anthem (S)

koevoet: crowbar. Boer-controlled paramilitary force in former South West Africa (A)

koko: Knock, knock. Said to announce oneself on arrival (S)

koppie: island mountain. Isolated stony hill

kraal: corral (A)

lakhoa: European (any foreigner). Plural: makhoa (S)

lobola: bride-price (S)

mealie: cornmeal

meneer: mister (A)

mma: mother, woman. Form of address (S)

Mmegi: local newsweekly, published in Gaborone

mobashi: street child (S)

moruti: preacher (S)

Ovambo: majority tribal group in Namibia

pan: craterlike depression (in the Kalahari Desert)

paraffin: kerosene

permsec: Permanent Secretary

POI: person of interest. Intelligence term

pula: the national unit of currency, meaning rain (S)

REDSO: Regional Economic Development Services Office. A department of the Agency for International Development

rondavel: traditional round thatched hut (squaredavel, ovaldavel— contemporary variants) (A)

rra: sir, father (S)

SADF: South African Defence Force

sakkie: plastic sack (A)

sangoma: traditional medical practitioner

Setswana: the national language of Botswana

SWAPO: South West African People's Organization

Tsamaya sentle, Sala sentle: Go well, Stay well (S)

Waygard: commercial security guard service

Wits: University of the Witwatersrand

ZANU: Zimbabwe African National Union; Shona-based nationalist movement led by Robert Mugabe

ZAPU: Zimbabwe African People's Union; Ndebele-based nationalist movement led by Joshua Nkomo

Zed CC: Zionist Christian Church

Place Names

Bontleng: a poor neighborhood in Gaborone

Caprivi Strip: a tonguelike extension of Namibia projecting halfway across the top of Botswana

Gobabis: a town in Namibia

Lobatse: a town in southern Botswana

Old Naledi: squatter settlement on the outskirts of Gaborone

SouthWest: regional term for former South West Africa, before and even sometime after it became Namibia

Toromole, Etsha, Sepopa, Nokaneng: villages and hamlets in settlements of upper northwest Botswana

Tsodilo Hills: isolated group of stony hills in northwest Botswana, the site of Bushman rock paintings

Tuli Block: area of southeastern Botswana along the Limpopo River

Walvis Bay: seaport in Namibia

Acknowledgments

I'm deeply grateful to my editor, Ann Close, and to my agent, Andrew Wylie.

And I acknowledge the great good luck I have in my family . . . Henry, Ding, Robert, Chris, Nick, Sheila, Lynda, Laura, Bruce, Renée, Peter, Josh, Luke, John, Max, Maia, Chloë, Mason, Jameson, Miranda, Gillian, and Sylvie.

I also want to acknowledge the encouragement given, when it was needed, by my sister-in-law, Ruth Gonze, and by our second family, the Roths.

MATING

In the National Book Award–winning *Mating*, an American anthropologist is at loose ends in the south African republic of Botswana. She has a noble and exacting mind, a good waist, and a busted thesis project. She also has a yen for Nelson Denoon, a charismatic intellectual who is rumored to have founded a secretive and unorthodox utopian society in a remote corner of the Kalahari—in which he is the only male member. What ensues is both a quest and exuberant comedy of manners, a book that explores the deepest canyons of eros even as it asks large questions about the good society, the geopolitics of poverty, and the baffling mystery of what men and women really want.

Fiction/Literature/0-679-73709-X

WHITES

Whether they are Americans, Brits, or a stubborn and suicidally moral Dutchman, Norman Rush's whites are not sure why they are in Botswana. And their uncertainty compels them to do odd things. Driven half-mad by the barking of his neighbor's dogs, Carl dips timidly into the native witchcraft—only to jump back out at the worst possible moment. Ione briskly pursues a career as a "seducer," while her dentist husband fends off the generous advances of an African cook. Funny, sad, and deeply knowing, polished throughout to a diamond glitter, *Whites* is a magnificent collection of stories.

Fiction/Literature/0-679-73816-9

VINTAGE INTERNATIONAL
Available at your local bookstore, or call toll-free to order:
1-800-793-2665 (credit cards only).